BOOKS BY HARLAN ELLISON

NOVELS: WEB OF THE CITY [1958] THE SOUND OF A SCYTHE [1960] SPIDER KISS [1961]

SHORT NOVELS: DOOMSMAN [1967] ALL THE LIES THAT ARE MY LIFE [1980]
RUN FOR THE STARS [1991]

GRAPHIC NOVELS: DEMON WITH A GLASS HAND (Graphic Adaptation with Marshall Rogers) [1986]
NIGHT AND THE ENEMY (Graphic Adaptation with Ken Steacy) [1987]
VIC AND BLOOD: The Chronicles of a Boy and His Dog (Adaptation with Richard Corben) [1989]

SHORT STORY COLLECTIONS: THE DEADLY STREETS [1958]
SEX GANG (as Paul Merchant) [1959] A TOUCH OF INFINITY [1960] CHILDREN OF THE STREETS [1961]
GENTLEMAN JUNKIE and other stories of the hung-up generation [1961] ELLISON WONDERLAND [1962]
PAINGOD and other delusions [1965] I HAVE NO MOUTH & I MUST SCREAM [1967]
FROM THE LAND OF FEAR [1967] LOVE AIN'T NOTHING BUT SEX MISSPELLED [1968]
THE BEAST THAT SHOUTED LOVE AT THE HEART OF THE WORLD [1969] OVER THE EDGE [1970]
DE HELDEN VAN DE HIGHWAY (Dutch publication only) [1973]
ALL THE SOUNDS OF FEAR (British publication only) [1973]
THE TIME OF THE EYE (British publication only) [1974] APPROACHING OBLIVION [1974]
DEATHBIRD STORIES [1975] NO DOORS, NO WINDOWS [1975]
OE KAN IK SCHREEUWEN ZONDER MOND (Dutch publication only) [1977] STRANGE WINE [1978]
SHATTERDAY [1980] STALKING THE NIGHTMARE [1982] ANGRY CANDY [1988]
ENSAMVÄRK (Swedish publication only) [1992]

COLLABORATIONS: PARTNERS IN WONDER sf collaborations with 14 other wild talents [1971]
THE STARLOST #1: Phoenix Without Ashes (with Edward Bryant) [1975]

OMNIBUS VOLUMES: THE FANTASIES OF HARLAN ELLISON [1979]
DREAMS WITH SHARP TEETH [1991]

NON-FICTION & ESSAYS: MEMOS FROM PURGATORY [1961]
THE GLASS TEAT essays of opinion on television [1970]
THE OTHER GLASS TEAT further essays of opinion on television [1975]
THE BOOK OF ELLISON (Edited by Andrew Porter) [1978]
SLEEPLESS NIGHTS IN THE PROCRUSTEAN BED essays (Edited by Marty Clark) [1984]
AN EDGE IN MY VOICE [1985] HARLAN ELLISON'S WATCHING [1989]
THE HARLAN ELLISON HORNBOOK [1990]

ODDMENTS: THE ILLUSTRATED HARLAN ELLISON (Edited by Byron Preiss) [1978]
HARLAN ELLISON'S MOVIE [1990]

RETROSPECTIVES: ALONE AGAINST TOMORROW A 10-Year Survey [1971]
THE ESSENTIAL ELLISON A 35-Year Retrospective (Ed. by Terry Dowling with Richard Delap & Gil Lamont) [1987]

AS EDITOR: DANGEROUS VISIONS (Editor) [1967] MEDEA: HARLAN'S WORLD (Editor) [1985]
NIGHTSHADE & DAMNATIONS: the finest stories of Gerald Kersh (Editor) [1968]
AGAIN, DANGEROUS VISIONS (Editor) [1972]
The Harlan Ellison Discovery Series: STORMTRACK by James Sutherland [1975]; AUTUMN ANGELS by
Arthur Byron Cover [1975]; THE LIGHT AT THE END OF THE UNIVERSE by Terry Carr [1976];
INVOLUTION OCEAN by Bruce Sterling [1978]

HARLAN ELLISON'S
WATCHING

HARLAN ELLISON'S
WATCHING

UNDERWOOD–MILLER
Novato, California
Lancaster, Pennsylvania

Harlan Ellison's Watching

Trade softcover edition: ISBN 0-88733-147-5

Library of Congress Cataloging-in-Publication Data

Ellison, Harlan.
   [Watching]
   Harlan Ellison's watching.
      p.   cm.
   Includes index.

    1. Motion pictures. I. Title II. Title: Watching.
   PN1995.E58   1989   89-5134
   791.43—dc20   CIP

TABLE OF CONTENTS

⟶

⟶

———————→

ACKNOWLEDGMENTS

So many years. Memory has mislaid the moments of help and wisdom in which those who ought to be thanked here contributed to the doing of the work. A studio publicist who went out of her way to sneak me into a screening intended only for exhibitors. A scenarist who supplied me with privileged background information on why a film went wrong. A copyeditor who caught a serious error and stalled the magazine till I could write revised pages and get them airfreighted overnight to beat the deadline. The friends who understood why I had to cancel out of dinner at the last minute so I could catch a screening and write the review before morning. The editors who caught the flak when I savaged one of the studios that advertised in the magazine. My staff, who put up with the unshaven maniac in a bathrobe who waits for their arrival five days a week. So many of them through so many years. The moments are gone, and only the work remains. I hope they know who they are, and that somewhichway they see this note. They deserve more, but all I've got at the moment is *thank you*.

And even among that special group, there are some who have been of special importance in the preparation of this book. Edward and Audrey Ferman of *The Magazine of Fantasy & Science Fiction*. Curtis Lee Hanson, now a successful film director, who was my editor at *Cinema*. Art Kunkin of the *Freep*. And Brian Kirby, who stood in the editorial wind at a couple of newspapers whose names only a few of us remember. Bill Warren. Tim and Chuck. Norman Goldfind. The writers and staff of the Writers Guild of America, west... who make it supportable to work in an industry systemically incapable of respecting the written word or those who slave to produce it. Kathy and Sarah and Sharon, and Michael & Nikki. Gil Lamont, who does more than I can thank him for. And my wife, Susan, the beloved Electric Baby. Did I remember to say *thank you*?

With friendship, for
BETTE FAST and HOWARD FAST
because one simply
must have heroes &
icons, mustn't one

"The great enemy of clear language
is insincerity."

George Orwell

FOREWORD
by George Kirgo

It takes but the reading of a single review in this collection to be aware that this is not your normal critic at work—nor, for that matter, your normal person.

Listen to Mr. Ellison as he writes of seeing *Joe*: "At the end of the film, it took my director friend, Max Katz, and his lady, Karen, to help me up the aisle. I could not focus. I was trembling like a man with malaria. There was a large potted tree on the sidewalk outside the theater. I managed to get to it, and sat there, unable to communicate, for twenty minutes. I was no good for two days thereafter."

But did he like the movie?

What sets Harlan Ellison apart from nearly all other reviewers is that he unblushingly exposes his psyche and personal prejudices with every film he views. He watches viscerally, reacts viscerally, writes viscerally. If you have the stomach for it, you will be rewarded. This book is, of course, just one man's opinion. But the man has a uniquely individual voice, a voice that never minces its words.

"*Spaceballs*," he writes, "rivals *L'Avventura* as the single most obstinately boring film of all time. An invincibly tasteless farrago of lame jokes, obvious parodies, telegraphed punchlines, wretched acting, and idiot plot."

He didn't like the movie.

Having made enemies, he cements the enmity in print.   i

Steven Spielberg and Gene Roddenberry are thrashed, and trashed, by Ellison's lash. More than occasionally, he is guilty of overkill; for example, the venom wasted on *Gremlins*. But, again, this is Ellison's Way. Passion governs his every thought and word. He's been like that at least since April 1964, when we first met, on the Paramount lot, both of us writing features. Twenty-five years (at least) at high pitch! I would be exhausted. Harlan isn't. As of April 1989, he remains one of those "who (wear) at their hearts the fire's center."

"Oh, God, the movies," he writes. "For four hours every Saturday afternoon," the movies transported him "away from that miserable lonely charnel house of childhood." The picture show continues to provide joy to Ellison the adult. "... the basic tenets of the Ellison Moviegoing Philosophy: (the movie) kept me rapt and happy all the while it danced before me. What the hell more can one ask from a mere shadow-play?"

And the keynote of the Ellison Movie Reviewing Philosophy: "I will, first and always, try to entertain."

He meets his own high standards. Never does he fail to beguile us. To pique us—even when one finds one's self in disagreement with his judgments.

It never occurred to me that *Mickey One* was "the finest American film of the year, and possibly of many years." Is the "compelling" *Lolly-Madonna XXX* the same one I saw and found to be the opposite of compelling? *Brazil* "... one of the greatest motion pictures ever made...in the top ten..."? (Is criticizing the critic permitted? I've never been a Foreword person before.)

Yet when he and I share a judgment (which I find, to my astonishment and alarm, is almost always), Harlan approaches bull's-eye perspicacity. "*2001* is a visually exciting, self-indulgent exercise...no story...no plot." And besides that, it's "seriously flawed."

Because of the times, I must get political. When Harlan and I wrote our first movies at Paramount (the titles will remain shameless; Fifth Amendment), the studio was a quiet little village; only a couple of pictures were being made. The lot was a summer playground for two kids, Gregg Hawks and Nick Kirgo, who wandered through dark and empty soundstages while their fathers, Howard and George, labored on a film.

Almost twenty-six years later, Paramount is doing record-making business. But some things, as Harlan points out, remain the same. The writer is still given the shortest shrift available, and since that era of benevolent paternalism, writers have had to strike four times (most recently six long months in 1988) to achieve any semblance of financial or creative progress. As president of the Writers Guild of America, west, I can testify to Harlan's unionist ardor (he's served two terms on the Board of Directors) and his devotion to the cause of his colleagues.

Ellison boldly fights the writer's war. He reminds the reader that every film he reviews began with a blank page (is the truth a cliché?). His essays are celebrations of films and celebrations of screenwriters. When a picture fails, he does not (always) pin the rap on the director, the producer, the actors, the agents, the cinematographers, the studios, the best boy, the gaffer or the gofer. Every film is the writer's responsibility, his blame—and his triumph.

The likes of Harlan Ellison rarely pass this way. Sometimes it is with great relief that I contemplate that fact. Yet, finally I understand that I, like all writers, must respond to his challenge, which is to do the best work we can. That is what these reviews are all about: people doing their best, trying to do their best, not doing their best. You're a hard man, Ellison. Don't ever change.

George Kirgo is: President, Writers Guild of America, west
CBS-TV film critic

Scenarist of *Redline 7000, Spinout, Don't Make Waves, Voices* and television scripts ranging from "The Mary Tyler Moore Show" to "Kraft Suspense Theater"

INTRODUCTION
Crying "Water!" In A Crowded Theater
PART ONE: *In Which The Critic Blames It All On A Warped Childhood*

Of me, the question is often asked.

Humphrey Bogart to John Derek in 1949's *Knock on any Door*: "Where did you go wrong, kid?"

Pat O'Brien to Billy Halop, Leo Gorcey, Bobby Jordan, Gabe Dell, Bernard Punsley and Huntz Hall in 1938's *Angels with Dirty Faces*: "Where did you kids go wrong?"

Patricia Neal to Paul Newman in 1963's *Hud*: "Where did you go wrong?"

Gazing on the imperfect handiwork, gibbering assistant Dwight Frye to Herr Doktor Victor F. in 1931's *Frankenstein*: "I don't want to second-guess you, Doc, but do you think it was smart to sew the left hand onto his forehead?"

Having reached middle age and having made the journey having accrued a modest degree of fame, some might say celebrity, others might say noteworthiness or renown (not to mention the guy over there with the placard that says *infamy*), of me, the question is often asked: "Where did you go wrong, kid?"

I take this opportunity to put the matter to rest. It cannot be blamed on my late mom and dad, Serita and Louis Laverne Ellison. As nice a pair of midwestern parents as one could hope to have had cleaning up after one's adolescence; they did the best they could, having birthed something that might better have starred in a Larry Cohen film. Opprobrium should not be visited on the many bigots, anti-Semites, dunderheads and random whelps who made my youth in Painesville, Ohio seem like the

v

lost chapters of Kierkegaard's FEAR AND TREMBLING or THE SICKNESS UNTO DEATH. I survived their tender mercies with nothing more debilitating to show for it than a lifelong blood-drenched obsession for revenge. Responsibility should not be laid at the door of evil companions, drug addiction, rampant alcoholism or tertiary syphilis; nor that of mind-polluting pornography, prolonged exposure to strict religious training, the evils of the Big City or snug Jockey shorts. Where I went wrong, how I first flouted the rules, when I turned from the path of righteousness and became the case study before you today, redounds solely to the legendary animators Dave and Max Fleischer, and an obscure feature-length cartoon they made in 1941 titled *Mr. Bug Goes to Town*.

Oh, yes, to be sure, there will be those among you on the jury who will scoff, sneer, and flick fish scales in demonstration of your rejection of this plea. Walk a mile in *my* snowshoes, I say, before you deal thus harshly with a poor, unfortunate symphoric nyctalopian, come at the dwindling twilight of his life to a state of repentance and hiatus hernia. Ah, you nullifidians, you!

I tell you truly: it was *Mr. Bug Goes to Town* (seen once in a while in the Sunday morning kiddie tv ghetto as *Hoppity Goes to Town,* the British title), an animated entomological extravaganza recounting the angst-ridden travels and travails of a grasshopper and other anthropomorphized insects, that first warped a sweet, theretofore-angelic child. It happened, exactly and precisely, as burned forever in memory, on Tuesday, May 27th, 1941. My seventh birthday. Stop building that gibbet for a minute, and I'll tell you.

My grandparents on my mother's side—a pair of kindly sexagenarians only slightly less lovable than Burke & Hare—lived in that then-charming section of Cleveland Heights known as Coventry-Mayfield. (It was called thus, because it was the area where Coventry Road intersected with Mayfield. I mention this, a seemingly obvious dollop of minutiae, only for those of you who have grown to maturity in a time rife with such portmanteau words as Sea-Tac for an airport serving Seattle and Tacoma; Wiltern, a theater at the confluence of Western Avenue and Wilshire Boulevard; and FloJo, an apartment house owned by Florence and Joseph Ellenbogen; and other blendwords of this sort that form a part of the *lingua non franca* committed in America today.)

Until the age of three or four or five, something like that, I had resided in a state of baby, right there, Coventry-Mayfield. But we had moved thirty miles northeast to the squalid hamlet of Painesville before I hit six, and every week or so visited Gramma Adele and Grampa Harry (who never, as best I recall, ever smiled at me save when they were doling out chicken beaks and feet onto my plate at the Passover *seders* I was compelled under pain of dismemberment to attend) who still lived on Hampshire Road in Cleveland. I looked on these visits with all the childlike joy one experiences at the prospect of a sigmoidoscopy. As I recall, I adopted a standard response, when alerted to an upcoming he-gira to the Grandfolks Rosenthal, that involved threatening to slash my wrists with the rusty pin that backed my Official Lone Ranger pedometer.

Nonetheless, with the sensitivity all parents demonstrate when their kids threaten to eat worms or hold their breath till they turn blue, I was schlepped to Cleveland regularly from Painesville and, when my parents went out for the evening, I was put to bed at the residence of The Ancient Jews from Hell, feigning sleep but lying alert for a sudden dive through a window at the first scent of beaks and feet.

In that neighborhood a mere forty-eight years ago, just seven months before Pearl Harbor, there existed now-lost and barely-recalled establishments whose names alone send a thrill through me even today: Coventry Drugs (where I bought my first issue of Street & Smith's *Shadow* magazine), Uberstine's Drug Store (where one could get three scoops of sherbet, all different flavors, in a cup cone, for 11¢), Benkowitz's Deli (in the days when the corn rye they used to make a combination corned beef and pastrami was so festooned with caraway seeds that one picked at one's teeth for six weeks thereafter) and . . .

The Heights Theater.

It was one of those small neighborhood cinemas built during the moviegoing explosion of the late Twenties/early Thirties. In retrospect, I know it was a modest house of movies, but it was glorious and gigantic to me at age seven. Out front the display windows held not only one-sheets and lobby cards in full color, but at least four scene cards in black and white from each and every film showing or coming. The ticket booth resembled a private stateroom on Cleopatra's barge, tenanted (as I recall) by a young woman so gorgeous and platinum blonde that merely laying down a dime for a ducat became an act of sexual congress intense enough to send the Rev. Jimmy Swaggart to the eighth and innermost circle of Dante's inferno. The candy counter traded in ambrosia and nectar, Chuckles and Forever Yours, popcorn freshly erupted every half hour and slathered with real butter. The scent of it could have distracted warring armies.

And the seats...and the usherettes...and the screen...and the ceiling mural...oh, how I loved that movie house, as I loved the Lyric and the Utopia and the RKO Palace...

Going to the movies was all the books in the library at once. It was an event. Even having to go in the company of one's parents was something Halliburton would chronicle. And going *alone*...! To be permitted to venture forth toward that mystic shrine all alone, pocket jingling with dime for ticket and three nickels for candy and popcorn; to know one could go into the Men's Room and not have to accompany one's mother into the Women's (oh god the humiliation); to select a seat way down front that produced a headache and neck-strain guaranteed to keep the Mayo Clinic solvent for three generations, a seat so far down front that one's parents would threaten you with having to cut the grass for a month if one didn't sit back in the middle "where any normal person can see."

Going to the movies alone was exciting; it was dangerous; it was, aw hell, it was Grown Up! And that was only for the Saturday matinee. But to go to a movie alone *at night*...!

Herman Kahn tagged it. *Thinking about the Unthinkable.*

Thus it came to pass, on Tuesday, May 27th, 1941, that my parents hied me to Cleveland. On my birthday! On my bloody canyoubelieveit goddam *birth*day! Of all days to have to go to Cleveland. But wait! Can it be? Could the universe have taken a nanoinstant from its rigorous schedule of creating galaxies and hedgehogs, pulsars and pips in oranges, to say, "Aw, what the hell," and to proffer a respite in the pissrain that is s.o.p. for little kids? Could it be that I would find myself only three blocks away from the mysterious and glamorous Heights Theater on the exact specific day of my birthday?

For this was the jewel, my friends:

It was the policy of the beloved Heights Theater to provide free admission (let me rephrase that: FREE!!!ADMISSION!!!) for any child previously signed up on that date as his natal designation.

It had never happened before. I'd always been in Painesville on May 27th. I'd often thought wistfully of being in Cleveland on my birthday, of sauntering up to the Heights Theater and saying, "Ellison's the name, birthday's m'game." And they would lift up the big register wherein were listed all the fortunate kiddies who lived within a reasonable distance of the Heights, whose birthdays entitled them to a free movie, and they would smile and say, "Harlan Ellison. Yes, here you are. Do, please enter, as our guest; and would you like a complimentary bag of our finest popcorn, it's the fragrant 5:30 pressing, from the sunny side of the machine." And the assistant manager in his impeccable tux, and a coltish gamin of an usherette in her livery, would march me down to the seat right up under the screen, and bid me enjoy myself *in extremis*.

I could not believe my good fortune.

So when we hit that Slough of Despond called Gramma's House (formerly tenanted by the Ushers), I rummaged about till I found a newspaper, and checked what was playing at the Heights.

Be still my heart!

It might have been a grownup's movie. It might have been *A Woman's Face*, with a script by Donald Ogden Stewart, directed by George Cukor, starring Joan Crawford, Melvyn Douglas and Conrad Veidt; it might have been *Tobacco Road*, written by Nunnally Johnson from Erskine Caldwell's novel, directed by John Ford, and starring Gene Tierney, Marjorie Rambeau, Charley Grapewin and Dana Andrews; it might have been *Ziegfeld Girl* with that great Busby Berkeley "You Stepped Out of a Dream" dance number, and Lana Turner and Hedy Lamarr and Judy Garland and Jimmy Stewart; it might have been *Citizen Kane* or Shaw's *Major Barbara* with Wendy Hiller and Rex Harrison; or Mary Astor and Bette Davis in *The Great Lie*; or *Meet John Doe* or *Singapore Woman* or *The Lady Eve*. And I wouldn't have been doing too badly with any of those—expect maybe *Singapore Woman* which, though it featured Heather Angel, starred Brenda Marshall, whom I never could stand—because they are all films I came to love in later years. But they were grownup's movies. I was seven. Sitting through the antics of Edward Arnold or Henry Daniell or Eve Arden or Barbara Stanwyck at age seven would've been something I'd do—because it was a movie, because it was my birthday, because I'd be seeing a movie at night—but the worm would certainly have gnawed my apple. It might have been a forgettable night. But...

Be still my heart!

The film that was showing at the Heights Theater on my seventh birthday, on Tuesday, May 27th, 1941, was a full-length animated feature, *Mr. Bug Goes to Town*, produced by Max Fleischer, who had earlier dazzled me with *Gulliver's Travels* and three double-length Popeye cartoons in which that greatest of all salts had met Sindbad, Aladdin and Ali Baba, directed by his brother, Dave Fleischer who would, within the year, knock my socks off with *Superman* cartoons that are spectacular even today, close on half a century later. The perfect movie for a birthday boy who, in that time of greater innocence, had seen the three Disney feature-lengths, *Snow White and the Seven Dwarfs*, *Fantasia*, and *Pinocchio*, and the Fleischer Bros.'s *Gulliver's Travels*, who was yet five months away from seeing *Dumbo*, who was living through the Golden Age of Animation, first-run, but didn't know it. The universe had selected the absolutely best choice for a movie to be seen at that special moment in my life. A nexus, a linch pin, a watershed; a turbid moment through which the dim future could be seen only vaguely; a branching of the path.

We're talking here about an *important* moment, y'know?

So I asked my parents, since they were going off to have dinner with friends, if they would drive me the few blocks to the Heights Theater, onaccounta it was my birthday and the Heights would let me in free onaccounta it was my birthday and they had this extra-special thing for kids who were having a birthday and once a year on their birthday they could see a movie for free and it was a *cartoon* movie, a special birthday coincidence treat that would mean a lot onaccounta it's my birth . . .

It was dark outside already. It was evening. Which preceded night. I was seven years old. Go out at *night*, all alone, to sit in a movie theater by your*self*, and how do you manage to come home those three deadly blocks, who'll come to get you, and what happens if you're kidnapped?

I would have received a more kindly reception had I asked permission to go join the British forces defending the Suez Canal from Lieut. General Erwin Rommel's *panzer* Afrika Corps.

It was decided on the spot, among my parents, grandparents and assorted relatives including Uncle Morrie, Aunt Babe, Aunt Alice and whoever Aunt Alice was dating at the time, that I would spend my birthday not in the animated embrace of the Fleischers and their gavotting grasshopper, but 'neath the sheets of the spare bedroom, trembling in expectation of the Lovecraftian horrors of beaks and feet.

And so it came to pass that I was stripped to my underwear and placed in the bed, kissed goodnight at the fucking ridiculous hour of 6:00 (showtime was 7:00 at the Heights, the newspaper had advised), and urged to sleep tight with the usual admonition not to let the bedbugs bite. Bedbugs, hell, I thought: beaks and feet, beaks and feet! The door was closed, I was left in darkness in a house whose only other inhabitants were a pair of Russian immigrants whose grandparently bodies had been taken over by Aliens from the Kid-Hating Planet.

It was then, in that half hour between being relegated to my bed of pain and the leavetaking of my parents, that I Went Wrong.

Previously I had been the very model of an Horatio Alger child. Goodhearted, free-spirited, clean and neat, the only kid of my acquaintance who did not step on anthills or tie tin cans to puppy dog tails. But at that instant, lying there musing on the nature of the child-adult liaison, considering the state of the universe, and only dimly beginning to understand the concept *injustice*...I was driven to a burgeoning sense of Self, and was stripped of my innocence, flensed of my trust in the omnipotence of adults. I Went Wrong.

In the dark I slipped out of bed, found my clothes, got dressed, opened the bedroom window, climbed out and hung by my fingertips from the sill, dropped to the ground, and ran off into the night. It was my *birthday*, goddammit, and I was *entitled* to the free movie I'd been promised. It would be wasteful *not* to take advantage of the prize. *Mr. Harlan Goes to Town!**

I was enthralled by the animated efforts of the insectile tenants in that weedy patch of earth "just 45 inches from Broadway" as they struggled to escape the skyscraper-erecting encroachments of Man, when the flashlight beam hit me in the face.

At first it was only an annoyance, a faint distraction to my

---

*The aphorist Olin Miller has written: "Of all liars, the smoothest and most convincing is memory." In the course of writing this bit of memoir, reference to the noted film critic and historian Leonard Maltin, and to a book on the Fleischers by Leslie Cabarga, made it clear that since *Mr. Bug Goes to Town* was not released till December 4th 1941, I could not possibly have seen it one hundred and ninety-two days earlier on May 27th. Nonetheless, memories of this pivotal incident in my otherwise stale, dull, and flatly uneventful life are blazingly clear. This happened *before* we went to war with Japan following the bombing of Pearl Harbor on December 7th. Don't tell me I'm getting senile, I don't want to hear it. The simple explanation that I saw the movie in May of 1942, on my *eighth* birthday, rather than my seventh, is ridiculous, Maltin! A first-run feature being shown five months after initial release in a time when they were making five hundred films a year and they had to change the bill at least three times a week?!? Not to mention, Leonard, that it's highly unlikely they'd be showing a *cartoon* feature, no matter how "adult," at an   xi right. But it persisted, and I glanced toward the aisle and got the flash right in the face. "That's him," I heard my Grandmother say; and then a younger female voice, an authentic Ajax Usherette Training School voice, whispery so as not to disturb the other patrons, yet husky and compelling, said, "Come out here, little boy."

Blinded by the light, paralyzed by the voice of authority, and not yet completely the scofflaw I was to become through this escapade, I began to tremble. "Come out here this *instant*, little boy!" The usherette was not to be trifled with. This young woman would no doubt grow up to be the head nurse in a maximum security nuthouse dedicated to straightening out guys like Jack Nicholson. "Harlan," my Grandmother said helpfully. "His name is Harlan Ellison."

(*Yes, Officer*, my dear old sweet Granny would say to the Secret Police when they came for me, *he's the one you want. And the evidence is buried under all his dirty socks and underwear at the back of the clothes closet.* Swell old lady.)

"Herman; you come out here, Herman Nelson."

Gramma: "Harlan."

Usherette: "What?"

Gramma: "Harlan, not Herman. Harlan Ellison, not Herman Nelson."

Patron: "Shhhh!"

---

evening performance on a *Wednesday* night five months later! No, I think not. Rather, it falls to me—however reluctantly and with apologies to all those whose historical writings must now be cast into question—to reveal a hitherto-undiscovered conspiracy on the part of Maltin, Cabarga, *Time* magazine, *The New York Times*, Walt Lee, Paramount Pictures, *Photoplay*, and your mother and father to wipe out an entire year in the early Forties, for what nefarious reason I cannot even guess. I find this all terribly disturbing, of course, but if it comes to a point of doubting What I Know To Be True, from the source of flawless recollection, as opposed to the alleged "evidence" of recorded history, well, my example is set by all those Fundamentalist and Charismatic Christians who know damned well that the time and date of The Creation by God was 4004 B.C., on the 26th of October, at exactly 9:00 A.M., as calculated by Archbishop Ussher in 1654, despite all the bogus "evidence" of geology, astronomy, paleontology, zoology, DNA-tracing, archaeology, radiocarbon dating, uranium and thorium soil-decay calculations, and X-ray microscopy in 3-D that attest to the age of the Earth as 4.55 billion years. Not to mention the thousands of rational men and women who come forward each week to attest to having been kidnapped by aliens who sucked out their brains and replaced the gray matter with crunchy peanut butter. In the face of all that, you think I'm going to believe I've made a mistake? Not on your tintype. Besides, I slept late on the 26th and didn't start the job till almost ten o'clock.

Usherette: "Harmon, I don't want to have to come in there to get you!"

Gramma: "It's not Harmon, it's Harlan."

Usherette: "What*ever*! Get *out* here, little boy!"

I got out there...before my darling Grandmother began handing out *Wanted* leaflets to the audience.

By the ear, like something from an *Our Gang* comedy, I was dragged up the aisle. What an ignominious reverse-path from my entrance to the Heights Theater.

I had run like a mad thing through the streets of Coventry-Mayfield, reaching the theater ten minutes before *Mr. Bug* was to begin. I'd given my name to the ethereal vision in the ticket booth, and she had looked it up and, smiling wonderfully, had told me to go right in, as she handed me a "birthday pass" that entitled me to free popcorn.

The young woman at the door had waved me in with another of those smiles that made the spine deliquescent, I'd bought a Tootsie Roll and accepted my free popcorn, and had allowed the charming usherette to show me to my seat, right in the middle of the third row. The theater had been pretty well filled, but even under such exacting circumstances the theater's staff had treated me properly as visiting royalty. It *was*, after all, as I told each person in my row as I shoved my way to my seat, my *birthday*!

And now, to be usherhandled up the aisle, my ear pincered excruciatingly, my dear sweet Granny kvetching along behind, intoning half-Yiddish gardyloos about my certain future as either a demented hunchbacked bell-ringer, or a Cossack love-slave...how ignominious!

I was, of course, dragged the three blocks back to the House of Pain, my wrist caught in a lobster-grip so maliciously tight that it would have drawn clucks of admiration from SWAT teams and Argentinian death squads. I was thrust through the front door into the presence of Grampa Harry, who was reading the *Jewish Daily Forward*, probably "A Bintel Brief", as he reminisced about the happy-go-lucky past in Russia filled with *kasha* and the grinding of the faces of the poor under the boots of the Tsar's kulaks. He looked up only long enough to spit the word *oysvorf!* And went back to the newspaper.

Brandishing a Swingline Stapler with which she threatened to attach me permanently to the mattress, I was once again divested of my clothing, and condemned to a state of supine anguish with threats of a "k-nok in the *kopf*" if I so much as hyperventilated too loudly.

I waited all of three minutes. Then I crept to the bedroom door, cracked it a sliver and listened. They were in the living room, and had just tuned in to *Fibber McGee and Molly.* I could hear Harlow Wilcox extolling the virtues of Johnson's Wax.

I located the contraband skeleton key where I'd hidden it a year or more earlier, under the rug beneath the bed, and unlocked the closet where my Grandmother (on whom Dickens had modeled his character Madame Defarge) had thrown my clothes in a heap on the floor. I dressed quickly, made it out through the window again, and raced back to the Heights Theater.

How I explained to the woman at the door that I was supposed to be there, I cannot remember. But I was adapting swiftly, metamorphosing in just one evening into a creature as sly and tricksy as a television network executive; and I conned my way inside. I got past the usherette somehow, hid out in a different area of the seats than the one previously discovered by the posse, and settled down with my thumb in my mouth to see how the evil C. Bagley Beetle and his two thugs, Smack the Mosquito and Swat the Fly, conspired to mulct Mr. Bumble, the proprietor of the Honey Shop (and the father of Honey Bee, Hoppity's girlfriend), out of his property.

This time I got to watch about twenty-five minutes of the film before I saw the flashlight beam bobbing down the aisle. I ducked. They went down the right-hand aisle, across the front of the audience, and up the left-hand aisle. I was on the floor. They missed me. I stuck my head up and watched the movie from the floor. Other patrons began hissing at me. I sat in my seat. I watched, mesmerized, despite the breaks in continuity occasioned by my frequent absences and nosedives.

They snuck up on me from behind, and snatched me out of my seat. This time it was my mother, in the company of the Assistant Manager. Gramma had called her to come back from the restaurant. She was not all that free with approbation for my ingenuity and tenacity. She held me aloft by my hair like a small beast chivvied from its lair by runny-nosed hound dogs. At the entrance to the Heights, the Assistant Manager waggled a finger at my mother and enunciated the evils of Interdicting Honest Merchants in Their Attempts to Recover from the Great Depression, culminating with remarks best summed as, "Keep your loathsome brat to home, lady!"

I was jammed into the glove compartment of the family Plymouth, was freighted back to durance vile, was stripped to the skin, was dressed for bed in a monstrously oversized pair of Grampa Harry's pajamas, and was stapled by Swingline into the bed.

My mother never hit me, but the voodoo curses and vivid word-pictures of my imminent demise should I budge from the bed served to cow me. My mother left, I heard the front door slam as she rushed away back to the restaurant, and I lay there for a full five minutes before I crept to the bedroom door, cracked it and heard Bob Hope introducing Frances Langford on the radio. And in pajamas fitted by Omar the Tentmaker, I made good my Great Escape for the third time. Barefoot. Crazed with determination. Now completely a creature who would ever-after have a helluva time dealing with rules and authority.

Knowing they'd be watching for me at the front door, I circled the theater in my pajamas until I found the exit doors. One of them was ajar. I slipped inside, and went to ground in the very first row, my head tilted up at a ninety-degree angle in hopes of making some vague sense of the plight of Hoppity and the inhabitants of the bug village, now displaced by the high-steel construction, in constant danger and seeking a place to draw a safe breath. As you might well imagine, there was a shitload of identification with the bugs.

Of course, they nabbed me again.

My memory at this point becomes blurred, possibly with the recalled pain of thumbscrews and vats of boiling pitch. The night passed with all the charm of Tom Brown's School Days, and I cannot tell you how many times more I broke out, or if I did get away a fourth time. When I dream of this incident, it does seem to go on for eternities.

I never did get to see the complete *Mr. Bug Goes to Town* until something like the mid-Sixties when it became available on videocassette. Today I have it in my private collection, and every once in a while, far more often than the quality of the film commends, I take it down and watch it. My wife has emerged from sleep in the wee hours to find me sitting cross-legged on the living room floor, watching insects.

But had it not been for the Fleischer Brothers, I might easily have remained a sweet, obedient human being who never uttered a cross word, never saw the flaws in the commands and dicta of Authority Figures, never became so obsessed with animated cartoons and other cinematic marvels that he became a film critic . . . and might today be a registered Republican.

Had it not been for Hoppity, I might well have remained untwisted, uncorrupted, placid and pliant. I would not have been arrested as many times as I have; I would not have had as difficult a time in the Army as I had; I would not punch out television and film producers when they mess up my screenplays; and the world would have been a quieter place.

I was a helpless pawn, caught in the grip of animation evil.

You can call me Hoppity.

PART TWO: *In Which The Critic Turns His Forepaw To Semiotic NeoMarxist Post-Feminist Post-Structuralist Lacanian Kristévan Uninvested Postmodern Deconstructionist Cine-Fabulist Scholarship Thingee Stuff*

You go to a movie. You turn on the set and watch a tv show. You don't think about it. You just *see* it. When you rise, leave the theater or punch the remote to kill the set, if you are thinking at all, your thought is usually something no more complex than *I liked that* or *I didn't like that.* (Actually, the latter impression is more likely to be *What a waste of time.* I call that the Geraldo-Rivera-Opens-Al-Capone's-Vault response.)

For an appreciably smaller number of exposures to film or television, the gray matter has not been stunned, and you very likely *think* about what you've seen. Then *I liked* and *I didn't like* become *What a terrific movie!* or *Gawd, I hated that, I'd like to slug the Producer, knock him down, go through his pockets, and get back the ticket money, the parking lot fee, the cost of the babysitter, and a few bucks for punitive damages!*

Filmgoers and television-viewers (and their mind-sets, which are completely different) justifiably judge a work in these visual mediums by what it *is*, not by the intentions of those who created it. They assume that what comes to them across the screen large or small is exactly what its makers wanted it to be. They have no idea—however knowledgeable they may be in the abstract—of the disruptions, the compromises, the disappointments and artistic roadblocks that come with the territory. Nor do they care. (I'm not sure anyone *should* care, on one everyday level. It is surely enough that the audience has trusted the creators sufficiently, in advance, to give over their time and their money.)

But, in truth, the average member of the viewing audience would rather cobble up his/her uninformed opinion that goes beyond merely *I liked* or *I didn't like*, and visit it on anyone who'll listen, with the force of an Obiter Dictum, rather than learn what really transpired in that minefield between initial conception and final presentation, why some movie succeeded or failed, sans conspiracy paranoia or, worse, the naive rural-hayseed folderol of Those Who Never Get the Message.

Because what is being indulged is a desire to comment, to voice an opinion, in short . . . to criticize.

Considering the question from both sides of the plow—as both scenarist and critic—insider and just-like-you moviegoer—I discover, to my surprise and pleasure, that the single most important problem of film criticism, whether scholarly or casual, is easy to pin. It is the same problem from either side.

Because movies (and by extension, television) are so damned accessible—they are the "common denominator" art forms of the masses, as pulp magazines and radio dramas were before them —they lie naked to the attentions of both the wise and the foolish. Where criticism of work in the print mediums requires *having to read* and (one hopes) a heightened degree of insight, if not good old simple common sense, as well as (again, one can only hope) some background in the form being discussed, anyone who plonks down the price of a ticket feels equipped to pontificate on a film.

That's just fine, absolutely peachykeen, if one is making judgments about a movie while standing in the waiting line, or tossing it around at dinner or *après*-cinema; we all enjoy putting in our 2¢ on any topic we feel even remotely within our purview. But—and having voiced these opinions in print more than a fistful of times I'm aware of the inevitable charge of Elitism, to which charge I plead guilty, on grounds of common sense driven by pragmatism—it is a lot less salutary than "just fine, absolutely peachykeen" when those uninformed opinions are concretized as Film Criticism.

For decades it was *de rigueur* on most small town (and many big city) newspapers to fob off the book reviews on anyone who would do the filthy job. A stringer who handled mostly box scores of the local high school baseball teams, would pick through a stack of review copies that had found their way to a newspaper, and select something that looked like it might be worth reading.   xvii

They usually weren't even paid for the "review." That became the process for film reviewing, too. A local lady who assembled the village bulletin board listings, or who held Great Books sessions at her home, would be assigned to report on whatever the town's lone moviehouse was playing this week. Or canned material, usually based on studio handouts, would be picked up from the AP, UP or INS wires. Larger papers had a "Hollywood Correspondent" who filed interviews with stars and dealt regularly in gossip.

Over time, serious film criticism began to emerge. Slowly, haltingly, and often to the bewilderment of city editors who used the material as fillers. Eventually, when a certain kind of academic began to perceive that there was Thesis Material in film criticism, a frequently-infelicitous attention came to be focused on Hollywood's product. I refer here not to the serious, thoughtful, informed writings of such as James Agee, Graham Greene, Louis Delluc or Roland Barthes, but to the opportunistic scratchings of backwater Educationists (as R. Mitchell calls them) whose passion was not for the film individually or the form *in toto*, but merely to jump on what they cynically considered a popular culture publish-or-perish target of availability.

And they passed along their parvenu perceptions to students who, because they had plonked down the price of a ticket, also felt entitled to pontificate, unfortunately employing the arcane jingoisms and semiotically-convoluted rationales they'd picked up from bloodless instructors unconsciously determined to leach every last morsel of pleasure from the act of filmgoing.

Thus, justification for dumb remarks was institutionalized in American society. Not for the first time. Religion, politics, morality, literature... each in its turn has vibrated to the disturbances of air justified by the expression "I'm entitled to my opinion." As I point out in one of my essays, the important word *informed* is always missing from that bleat. In my ugly, Elitist opinion we are *not* all entitled to voice our opinions; we are entitled to pass along our *informed* opinions. As Anatole France once wrote, "If fifty million people say a foolish thing, it is still a foolish thing."

People who wouldn't have the *chutzpah* to venture a Solomonic medical diagnosis, or even proffer an opinion about why your car's engine is missing, have no compunctions or modesty when it comes to raving about, or trashing, a motion picture.

Without having read all the drafts of the screenplay before it ever got into the hands of the production personnel, the line producer, or the director, without having been present on the set to experience the million contretemps that lobby for or against the written word's transmogrification, without understanding the skills and problems that go into the sound portrait, the color corrections, the editing, the looping and dubbing, or any of the other hundred-plus elements that meld to make a *movie*, self-appointed *mavens*—judging only what they receive as they sit in the theater—do the Critical Judgment Thing. They decide this actor was lame, that director can't handle action sequences, this noble scenarist's brilliant vision has been martyred, that producer is a venal swine who has sold out Art for Commerce.

And all of it is spinach.

With a universal constituency for film, *everyone* feels arrogantly competent...no, not even competent...*divinely inspired*...to pass judgments down to the most minute facets of the film. At a kaffee klatsch, that's just fine. Just peachykeen. In scholarly journals, and in allegedly critical reviews, it is unacceptable.

So the problem, as I see it, that most presses us when we talk about "film scholarship," is setting minimal standards of cinematic knowledge. And I don't mean those used to hand out such horseshit awards as Golden Globes or Oscars every year.

I'm *not* suggesting that before someone can speak with wisdom about movies that s/he must be able to quote verbatim from Siegfried Kracauer, Paul Rotha or Terry Ramsaye (though it wouldn't hurt to have such a rich background). What I *am* suggesting is that the least we must demand of anyone who sets him/herself up as a critic of film, is that said Oracle strive to operate on the level of, say, Agee, Arthur Knight (of THE LIVELIEST ART), Stanley Kauffmann, Molly Haskell, or just Pauline Kael.

This means, also, that the scholar should *love* film. Should *adore* just going to the movies, the way a kid *adores* going to the movies. Bearing with, a large measure of innocence; a large measure of *I'll sit here, you just* do it *to me*. Just purely love it, to the degree that s/he is willing to savage that which is inept, dishonest, historically-corrupt, pretentious or simply meanspirited. That which demeans the art form. That which lies to the trusting audience. That which rusts our innocence for no greater purpose than to con us out of our ticket money and get us ready to be manipulated into laying-out for the mendacious sequels.

By this standard, I discount such critics as John Simon. As brilliant and as uncompromising as Simon's dance and legitimate stage reviews are, as correct as I think he is most of the time, as deeply as I admire his erudition and his insights and his vivid writing, to the same degree do I find his film reviews unacceptable. He clearly thinks of film as a second-class art form, and it shows in every line he writes about cinema.

(He is not alone in this dichotomous, ambivalent attitude; and more on that in a moment.)

He does not love film as he loves the theater or ballet, and *his* Elitism seems thus, to me, corrupt. It does not escape my sense of the self-serving or ridiculous that as an Elitist I'm saying *my* brand of nobler-than-thou is more peachykeen than thine or Simon's. I got that. Nonetheless, I speak of these matters and make comparisons not to contemn John Simon—whose work I find constantly thought-provoking, which is precisely what a critic is supposed to do, in my view—but to make sure the reader knows I have no secret agendas. I think it is above-all-else urgent that the reader of film criticism be able to trust that the critic is right out there, holding nothing back, being absolutely candid.

It means, also, that the kind of overintellectualized barbarism of critics-*manqué* who see deep, redemptive significance in *Night of the Living Dead* films, though they "have problems" with *Brazil* or *Apocalypse Now*, cannot be considered apropos. We must remember that Philistinism makes lucid copy for dolts, and we must resist crediting that kind of thing, lest *all* standards be downgraded and eventually become flummery.

I would add that most temporal concerns when judging film are also suspect. Deconstruction, a trendy way of examining films these days, coupled with Marxist Feminist Dystopic Reified Orthodontist criticism (or whatever the goony-birds are currently using to feather their *vitae*) is ultimately hateful and false.

So the problem, in my view, is bringing into being a cadre of film critics and film scholars whose pronouncements are based not on academic need, cynical disrespect for the art form, or hayseed arrogant ignorance, but on background, knowledge, sophistication and—most of all—affection.

It is in such spirit that Hoppity has written what you find in this book.

PART THREE: *In Which The Critic Attempts To Escape The Gas Chamber By Explaining His Motives, Not Raising His Voice In Anger Though Insulting Everyone In Sight, And By Explaining How He Came To This Occupation*

The inescapable, core problem with writing critical comment about films is that the commentator is really given no option.

If the review is positive, if the film is something special that one wishes to inveigle the reader into actually going to see, literally conning the potential filmgoer into spending money through the seduction of words, one is limited. The word-pictures can only do so much. The restrictions are many and truly fearsome. The critic dare not give away the great scenes, dare not reveal the punch of the surprise ending or expose the killer; the critic may not hint at, or paraphrase, the memorable lines that everyone talks about interminably, at risk of robbing the movie-lover of the *frisson* of joyful discovery. It's as mean an act as telling the reader of a murder mystery who the culprit is, ten pages before s/he finishes the book.

The critic can only go huzzah and huzzah so many times before it becomes white noise. The critic is limited in vocabulary, because beyond a certain point it becomes dangerous and boring, and then dangerously counterproductive. Dangerous, because *nothing* can live up to such panegyrics; boring, because what can one say after one says *don't miss it*?

So the options are removed. And what one is left with is the negative, or killer, review. One can be infinitely more entertaining when savaging the unworthy, the cupidic, the inept, the dishonest. Like *Spaceballs.*

One can unleash the stream of liquid fire and chew a path of invective through the failed art with a candycane marker of didactic dirge at every gravesite. Make the stake of licorice, and one can drive it into an endless number of vampire hearts with relative impunity.

But even that choice is no choice; for very soon, the short memory of the reader comes to expect savagery and fulmination. Forgotten are all the palliating equivocations, all the positive comments, all the rave reviews. Only the violence retains the color of passion in a reader's memory. And no matter how deserved the evisceration of the unworthy movie, it becomes suspect. The critic is perceived as just meanspirited; bitterness for the sake of cleverness.

It's not that it's *easier* to write bad reviews, it's simply that there is so much more bad stuff than good with which the commentator must deal. That wearying truth notwithstanding, the critic is perforce manacled by the rigors of the game, as well as by the insatiable appetites of the readership.

Most people only read film reviews to see if they agree with the commentator, anyhow. And how does one win *that* pot?

There are smart critics and dopey critics. Pauline Kael and Molly Haskell and most of the time David Denby, in my view, are the models one tries to approach for quality and common sense, for important insights and the placing of a film in its historical context. I suppose Siskel and Ebert are the best of the populist reviewers, though I think the ceaseless demands of cobbling up artificial rancor between them for the delectation of a tv viewership that can be roused from torpor only by brouhaha, has made their duologues cranky and tiring. George Kirgo on CBS was dedicated and wise, but he rapidly grew so disenchanted with what he had to pass judgment on, that when contract renewal time presented itself, he opted out.

Intelligence is not necessarily a condition of employment for being hired as a movie reviewer on the tube. On-camera charisma seems the greater imperative. And what the bosses will accept as "charisma" is often bewildering. Case in point: Carol Buckland, the movie maven on CNN.

So the field is abandoned to fools or hypesters who, if they aren't in the secret pay of studios, sure as hell ought to be. Even hookers resent amateurs giving away the goods without recompense. The *Entertainment Tonight* mentality is omnipresent: David Sheehan, Gary Franklin, Rex Reed, Michael Medved, Jeffrey Lyons*, Bill Harris (several of whom I know personally and can attest are *mensches*) proffer a kind of comment on films

*Jeffrey Lyons—who is not only the talented son of the legendary Broadway columnist Leonard Lyons, but is one of the few guys I know privy to the knowledge that, contrary to popular belief, Heinie Manush and Goose Goslin never played ball together, not to mention that he has a better collection of baseball bubble gum cards than I (I lust for his Carl Yastrzemski rookie year card)—is the perfect amalgam of treasures and torments that comprise a television personality film reviewer. On the plus side is the inescapable thorn in the paw of reviewers in print mediums: Jeffrey reaches more millions with every review on the tube than does the most widely-read, most widely-syndicated newspaper or magazine critic. (And did you know, as a nasty attempt to alleviate the pain in the paw, that the New York Film Critics

that frequently ranges from uselessly bitchy to flat-out wrong. At best, it seems to me, it's plebeian and parataxic. One of the above-named, in fact, sat beside me at a studio sneak preview a couple of years ago, fell snoringly asleep two-thirds of the way through the film—a smarter way to go than those of us who kept slapping ourselves awake for its duration—and appeared on the 11:00 News an hour later...and reviewed what he had not seen!

But even if every film critic hired to do the job knew, with encyclopedic accuracy, all of the commentary of Agee, Kevin Brownlow, Rotha and Kracauer, we would nonetheless be left with the conundrum of dealing with ignorance on the part of the audience, as well as the almost insurmountable problem of trying to get past the general audience's bastardized taste for the tasteless and bastardized. Neither a small problem.

I mean no offense here. But one deals pragmatically with what one is given. And any concern that this is again a manifestation of my meretriciously Elitist attitude can be evaporated simply by considering the sorts of films doing huge box-office business: *Someone to Watch Over Me, Predator, Beverly Hills Cop 2, Soul Man, Like Father Like Son.* Like the lilies of the field, they toil not, neither do they spin. Or, as Benjamin Franklin said, "An empty bag cannot stand upright."

How, then, does the critic who loves movies convince a readership/viewership sated with *Robocop, The Living Daylights* and *Spaceballs* that worthier recipients of its adoration, if given the chance, might be *In the Mood* and *The Princess Bride*?

Certainly not by pushing bloated, self-important and phoney "art films" like *A Room with a View,* no matter how cunningly manipulated commercially to win an Oscar for its scenarist. Such films only give Art a bad name, and further distance the general audience from movies of serious intent that are, for all their struggles to uplift and inform, cracking good stories.

Simple reviews, therefore, seem to me to serve no worthwhile purpose. Without the essay in depth that illuminates the special treasures a specific film proffers, it becomes a niggardly busi-

---

Circle denies membership to tv critics?) On the minus side are the parameters of the tv format that truly honk off guys like Lyons: everything must be boiled down to three-minute jingoism and sound-bites; and very little of it can refer to the in-depth erudition or historicity that the good critic needs to buttress an opinion.

Jeffrey Lyons is a man of intelligence, wit, originality of opinion and meticulous honesty. This soundness of credential manages to reveal itself, despite the rigors of the medium in which he presents his views. I envy him his baseball card collection, but not the arena in which he plies his trade.

ness of popularity contests and hucksterism, intended at its noblest to demonstrate the critic's skill at being coy and arch, while separating the gullible from their hard-earned shekels.

As with most endeavors, those who assay the job at the least demanding level, are the ones who draw down the least calumny, the ones who make the smallest waves, and who go on year after year exacerbating the problem by refusing to challenge their audience. They subscribe to the cheapest rationale given by schlockmeisters for the perpetuation of worn-out templates, the callous disregard for historical or scientific accuracy, the purely mercenary proliferation of haggard sequels, and a widespread anti-intellectual subtext: "We're only giving the audience what it wants."

Well, since this is transparently bullshit—because how can an audience know it wants something not yet created?—even if it were truth as deep and solid as Gene Hackman's talent, as a critic I've tried to say in my essays that just because an audience *wants* something, it may not necessarily be good for them, and one is not impelled to give it to them if it ain't good for them.

(Don't start that crap of asking, "Well, who the hell are you to judge what's good for people?" We're dealing with common sense here, not the kind of obfuscation the Administration uses to keep Ollie North out of prison. That sort of *ad hominem* arguing is what keeps us paralyzed. Guns are bad things and ought to be eliminated entirely. Rock cocaine will fuck you up and to hell with how seriously we interfere with the economy of Latin American countries whose ability to repay American bank loans is dependent on the drug crop. Abortion is a matter of individual conscience and piss on those who deflect the arguments with ancient and creaking religious obsession.)

These are reviewers and critics who suck along recommending and tolerating films that are illegible, destructive artistically, transient, manipulative, ubiquitous, and praised by people of confused or no criteria.

Is it not endlessly fascinating how often in this life that plain, unadorned cowardice is deified by the words "prudent behavior"?

Let me give you (in the words of David Denby in *New York* magazine, 5 October 1987) "an all-too-explicit example of the way giving in to the audience can make a movie worthless."

ALEX FORREST (GLENN CLOSE), THE neurotic New York single woman in *Fatal Attraction* dresses entirely in white, like Lana Turner's murderous Cora in *The Postman Always Rings Twice*. Alex works in publishing, and when she meets

Dan Gallagher (Michael Douglas), a vaguely bored married man who's doing some legal work for her company, she goes after him. They have a drink together, and she's so attentive, she seems to be devouring him whole.

The movie takes her measure cruelly. She has a recognizable kind of New York willfulness, fueled by lonely blues. Her loft, in the meat-packing district, is too bare and white; she pushes too hard, exercises too much. Her initial sweetness—all attention and sympathy—dissolves when Dan returns to his wife at the end of the weekend. The rage she feels has an edge of emotional blackmail to it. She tries to shame him into remaining her lover.

British director Adrian Lyne and screenwriter James Dearden, who spend a fair amount of time setting up Alex as a credible, three-dimensional person, should have continued to take her seriously—they've made her worth it. Her isolated situation is painfully familiar (everyone in professional, upper-middle-class New York knows a stranded Alex). She has a characteristic way of pressing on what Dan says to her, violently holding him to what he's only mentioned in passing. She can't relax, and Glenn Close, who in the past has shown a tendency to darlingness, is scarily effective—sympathetic and dislikable at the same time.

Why does Gallagher get involved with Alex? There's nothing wrong with his marriage. The filmmakers seem to be saying that any married man, given the opportunity, will fool around if he thinks he can get away with it. When Dan tries to disappear after the weekend, Dearden gives Alex something of a case against him. She may have done the pursuing, but, as she says, their power positions aren't the same. She's single, getting older, and what's a weekend diversion for him is a major event for her. Dearden uses feminist perceptions and arguments as a way of creating Alex—and then he gives way to male paranoia and betrays her altogether. She tries to kill herself, and then becomes a vicious, knife-wielding gorgon, stalking Gallagher's wife and daughter. The movie falls to pieces. The last third is despicable—ghoulish horror with blood thrills for the jaded.

I can see the difficulty of working with a character who's never more than partly sympathetic. Where can the story go? The filmmakers' way out is to withdraw all sympathy from the character, which means trashing their own work. The awful thing is that in box-office terms, they aren't wrong. When I saw the picture (on opening day at the Loews Paramount), the audience, cheering on any sign of crazed possessiveness, was obviously longing for Alex to go nuts.

Coming up with a real dramatic resolution might have required more imaginative sympathy, art, and courage than anyone connected with this movie has.

Using that much of another writer's work analyzing just one film, as opposed to a pithy sound-bite of my own, all flash and no insight, is excusable only in the context of John Simon's remark, "There is no point in saying less than your predecessors have said."

Denby's example is *so* perfect, and the observations so smart and so simply stated, that though I thought long and hard of a better exemplar, again and again I returned to what Denby had said. Finally, I decided to hell with it; there are certainly critics sharper than I; and Denby is very likely one of those.

And what he's saying, apart from the obvious that just because an audience *wants* something doesn't mean you have to give it to them if it corrupts the work and panders to human weakness, cheapness of spirit, and, well, brutishness...what he's saying, is that if filmmakers who bask in the glory of the Seriousness of the Cinematic Art wish to continue enjoying the good press they get from the dubs and semiotic simpletons who see grandeur and subcutaneous significance in even the groundling-slanted swill they fob off on us every season, they're going to have to demonstrate a greater sense of responsibility. They can't keep on having it both ways, no matter how glitzily they mount each year's Oscar telecast. What Denby points out so sharply, is one of the main themes of this collection of essays, stated a hundred different ways: the accountants and attorneys and fast-shuffle merchants of the film industry have had a free ride for more than half a century. But in putting the buck before the honesty of telling a story truthfully, they have created an illiterate audience whose taste has been systematically corrupted. And at last, as we've seen over the decade of the Eighties, it is a venality that has come back to suck the blood of Hollywood like an AIDS-carrying vampire bat.

The audience is larger than ever, but it's also dumber than ever. Attendance at movie theaters continues to grow by lemming-horde increments: up 7% in 1987 over 1986; according to the U.S. Bureau of Census, as of 1 January 1989, we are more than 250 million strong, and there's a VCR in more than 55% of American homes; theatrical business accounted for 42% of the movie industry's total revenues in 1987, but with 40,000 titles available on videocassette, with more than five hundred new and vintage titles issued monthly, the 39% of the industry's total revenues that is represented by six *billion* dollars in total video stores' volume tells us the teeter-totter is about to tip, if it hasn't already. And the obvious conclusion we can draw from these statistics plus the evidence of our own experiences?

The audience is getting more illiterate.

(What's that? How does he come to figure such a thing?)

The focus groups and demographic studies all seem to agree: the audience for more difficult films, for subtler and more specialized films, is still extant. But it isn't going to theaters to satisfy its movie hungers. It's staying home, renting the films for enjoyment in convenience, safety and retention of pocket money.

The older filmgoer, the aficionado of foreign and experimental productions, is getting a full menu of movies on cable and through the good offices of the household VCRs. If one wishes to see either the original 1973 French charmer *La Bonne Année*, starring Lino Ventura and directed by Claude Lelouch, or its equally charming 1987 American remake *Happy New Year* (with Peter Falk in his finest performance since his 1960 role as Abe "Kid Twist" Reles in *Murder, Inc.* and the 1962 *Dick Powell Theater* presentation of Richard Alan Simmons's "The Price of Tomatoes", for which Falk won his first Emmy), one need only visit a well-stocked video outlet or wait a few days for both to appear on HBO. One does not go to the nearest multiplex.

A "little" film like *Happy New Year*, starring an actor best known to the immature film audience as Columbo—five-finger thespic exercises ever-available in tv syndication or in current blah *ABC Mystery Movies*—never had a chance in theaters. It sat on the shelf for a year before release, played the big screens for less than a week, and went straight to cable and cassette.

Movie lovers looking for that kind of pleasant, but not box-office-busting, experience stay at home.

So what part of our 250 million made up that 7% increase in theater attendance?

Teenagers, tv zombies brainwashed by thunderbolt commercials saturating primetime, MTV drones who can't get enough Madonna or Prince on the small screen, knife-kill flick devotees, and baby-boom yuppies who have such a total ignorance of even recent history that they do not see how corrupt *Mississippi Burning* is.

An audience that is, in large measure, cinematically ignorant. That does not resent bad and unnecessary remakes of *D.O.A., The Razor's Edge, The Big Clock* or *Mr. Blandings Builds His Dream House* because for a constituency that renews its cultural amnesia upon awakening every morning, nothing existed *before* this morning. An audience that, more and more, reads less and less; and thus is insensitive to plot development, the logics of story, complex characterization, or thematic subtext; an audience that judges a film's worth on how spectacular were the special effects.

We don't need stats to bolster the above-stated ugly and Elitist position. Common sense and the evidence of our own observations when we venture out bravely to see a movie more than suffice. (In this collection of essays you will come across more than one recounting of Journeys Among the Trogs and

Gargoyles. Compare them to your own experiences, and the case is made, no matter how egalitarian one wishes to be.)

With an audience that has been chivvied and prodded and dulled to a point where the product need never rise above the level of merely competent, however ethically debased, there is no need to overachieve. If you can make millions, fer shur, with another Rambo or Rocky installment, if you can do the dance of the rolling gross by throwing away comedic talents like Whoopi Goldberg, John Candy, Steve Martin or Eddie Murphy in fluff that is as forgettable as a zit, if you can cobble up some clinker based on the current teen rage... why bother to risk those millions with a film like *Happy New Year* or *Brazil*?

With handmaidens of hype like *Entertainment Tonight* or *People* magazine, abetted by Oprah, Geraldo, Letterman, Carson, Arsenio Hall and all the other "talk show" venues that push the devalued product, why buy into the delusions of Art and Creative Responsibility that are based on chance and danger and the likelihood of smearing the bottom line?

Or, to quote another knowledgeable source: "It is not difficult to win the approval of a wide audience when one laughs at the same things, when one is sensitive to the same aspects of life, and moved by the same dramas. This complicity between certain creators and their audience has resulted in successful careers." Francois Truffaut, in the 1984 revised edition of his excellent study, HITCHCOCK.

When I found that I had drifted into film criticism, almost without knowing it was happening, as purely a sidebar to my other writing, it became clear to me that my impossible mission, if I chose to accept it, was best summed in the words of Samuel Johnson when he wrote:

> "...illiterate writers will at one time or other, by publick infatuation, rise into renown, who, not knowing the original import of words, will use them with colloquial licentiousness, confound distinction, and forget propriety.
>
> "But if the changes that we fear be thus irresistable...it remains that we retard what we cannot repel, that we palliate what we cannot cure."

Now you know how I first went wrong and came to be one who cannot help but go against the flow, how that twisted view of the universe formed the philosophy of film criticism I've detailed here, and all that remains is to recount how I slid into writing about the art of cinema because of the basest motives in the history of movie reviewers. Complete with another long footnote.

I'll try to make this fast.

It was 1963. I'd arrived in Los Angeles on New Year's Day the year before, limping into the city in a battered Ford, with a number of encumbrances about which I've written elsewhere (see the introduction to my 1962 collection ELLISON WONDER-LAND if you cannot contain your morbid curiosity).

This is the truth, no hyperbole: I had exactly ten cents in my pocket.

The first year trying to break into filmwriting, even with substantial credits as a published author, was murder. I was always broke, had to write constantly, had to write some stuff that burst into flame and was reduced to ash eleven minutes after it was published, even found myself writing for *Confidential*, just to pay the $135 a month rent for the little treehouse on Bushrod Lane.

In those halcyon days of television, five months before the September "new season" would premiere, each show would have a "cattle call" for freelance writers.

Most series these days are written by a group of writers who are "on staff." They have such crazed titles as Story Consultant or Executive Creative Associate or simply Story Editor, but for the most part they just write the segments using the m.o. of a staff brainstorming session that cobbles up the storyline by committee, and then the individual episodes are parceled out. The producers insist they get a greater uniformity in the work by this method . . . and I wouldn't doubt it.

But there is very little freelance work left for the more than seven thousand members of the Writers Guild who, in former times, could get an entire year's worth of work in just three months of hustling. The shows used a wide variety of writers, not just the favorites they knew could meet their demands. And they found these other writers through use of the then-hated "cattle call."

Today, the staff personnel spend as much of their time in the pits, rewriting the scripts of the few freelancers who—because of terms in the Writers Guild contract, the Minimum Basic Agreement—*must* be assigned a certain number of the available script assignments.

As with *any* labor arrangement, there are positive and negative aspects to the current system, as there were with the routine   xxix in use in the '60s. More writers worked in those days, but the quality of the writing was frequently entry-level, because each writer would overcommit—the rest of the year was always catch-what-you-can—so they wrote as fast as they could, dashing from one cattle call to another. The word would go out to agents all over town, and special screenings of the pilot episode would be shown at one of the studio's little viewing rooms where producers looked at the previous days' shooting, what used to be called "the rushes," what were known in 1963 as "the dailies." These cattle calls ran in shifts, sometimes for as long as a week, with anywhere from ten to thirty writers at a time. Then would begin the feeding frenzy. Every writer would scramble from cattle call to cattle call, dreaming up ideas as quickly as possible, getting as many assignments of the available slots committed by the network as possible.

In the '60s, the networks gave orders for a lot more segments than these days. If you get a firm thirteen these days, you're considered a favorite of the Gods in the Tower. But in the '60s it was matter-of-course for, say, NBC to give every show an order for 28, 30, 32, 35 segments (which meant that each show put into work between forty and fifty scripts, knowing some would fall out or prove otherwise unshootable).

I got a call from Marty Shapiro in the early spring (or possibly Stu Robinson in those days, before Marty opened his own shop with Mark Lichtman, and was still with General Artists Corporation, now long defunct). Cattle call for a new show over at Four Star, being produced by Aaron Spelling. Spinoff from a popular segment of *The Dick Powell Theater*, starring Gene Barry as a millionaire police detective named Amos Burke. Go over and see the pilot on Thursday. I asked how many writers had been invited. Marty said it was an open call. So how many do you think? Maybe two or three hundred. How many slots open? They've already assigned a few to people who've worked for Spelling on other shows. So how many still open?

Maybe ten.

Great, I thought.

So I went to the cattle call, and saw the pilot. Cute show. I knew I could write it. But, in truth, I'd arrived the year before and had only done two shows—an adaptation of my book MEMOS FROM PURGATORY for the *Alfred Hitchcock Hour* and a half-hour syndicated script for *Ripcord*. I'd bombed out on everything else, and was really hustling. My credits were nominal, and my name was unknown. So I had to use cunning and duplicity.

The *modus operandi* for these cattle calls, the Proper Way to Come On, was to wait till the screening ended, make all the pattycake remarks about how great it is and how it'll run for six years, and then have your agent call the next day for an appointment with the story editor, to whom you'd "pitch" an idea.

As the lights came up, I spotted the guy who was doing the line producing for Spelling, a tall and distinguished, actually kindly-looking man, named Richard Newton. He had been a friend of Spelling's for years, all the way back to Texas, when Aaron and the late Carolyn Jones (who became Spelling's first wife) were all in college together. As everyone was shuffling in the seats, adjusting their eyes, Newton stepped to the front of the screening room and made a brief explanation about how the show would work: each segment would be titled "Who Killed—" followed by the name of the victim, as in "Who Killed Beau Sparrow?" or "Who Killed Avery Lord?" Each show would have half a dozen or more big name stars in cameo roles, to be shot all in one day. Each show would be sprightly, smart, urbane and filled with as many beautiful women as the scenarist could even semi-logically work into the plot. Oh, yeah, this was my kinda show.

Richard Newton concluded his remarks and asked, in a way intended to be polite but not actually to encourage any real time-waste at that preliminary stage, "Are there any questions?"

To which query I raised my hand.

Newton warily nodded at me, and I said, "How about I kill Hugh Hefner for you? Did the cartoonist do it because his career had been stymied? Did the centerfold of the month do it because she'd had his illegitimate child? Or was it the swami, the blind hunchback they find sleeping in the press room, or the venal publisher's own mother?"

Newton grinned at me and said, "Come on over to the office for a talk."

I'd beaten out three hundred other writers, and went to work on *Burke's Law*. It was my breakthrough, and Richard Newton (who can be seen these days as the judge in the *Matlock* series) took me under his wing. We remain friends to this day and he was one of the few producers for whom I would work for nothing; writing for Richard was always fun and artistically rewarding.

And that was because he was aware, right from the start, that he was dealing with a loonie.

My first script, "Who Killed Alex Debbs?"—the murder of a publisher of men's magazines—was written almost in secret, kept from Aaron Spelling by Richard till it was finished. Richard and I worked together, writer and producer, like the Corsican Brothers, telepathic twins who understood each other and trusted each other implicitly, without having to talk about it. But Spelling, who found my way of working peculiar from that of the other writers whom he'd hired, kept asking Richard, "What's with this new kid, this Ellison? What's he up to?" And Richard would fend him off, saying, "Don't worry about it. I'm taking care of it. He's a terrific writer, just be patient, you'll see."

And, because working with Richard Newton was a situation of trust and freedom, Aaron *did* see. "Who Killed Alex Debbs?" knocked his socks off to the extent that when it aired, Aaron threw one of those legendary Hollywood parties for its premiere. His enormous home in Beverly Hills was fitted out with a big tv set in every downstairs room, and he invited three hundred celebrities to see this first script by the kid he had "discovered."

At that party Sandy Koufax and Sammy Davis, Jr. and Ann-Margret and Vincent Price and John Huston treated me as if I were one of their inner circle. I wasn't, of course; it was just a moment in my life when my path crossed theirs; but to one who was still incredibly naive about Hollywood Life, despite having run away from home at thirteen and having grown up on the road, despite having been married and divorced twice, despite having served two years in the Army... it was heart-stopping and dazzling.

"Who Killed Alex Debbs?" featured cameo performances by John Ireland, Suzy Parker, Burgess Meredith, Arlene Dahl, Diana Dors, Jan Sterling and Sammy Davis, Jr. and it aired on a Friday night over ABC, October 25th, 1963. I watched in amazement as my work went out to all of America, and as the Great and the Near-Great and Those Who Hoped They Would Become Great praised me and shook my hand and told me I had a bright future in show biz. The following Sunday, the *New York Times*, reviewing the show, called it "a blissful melding of Noel Coward drawing-room drollery with Agatha Christie suspense." (Or words very similar. It's been twenty-six years, and though the clipping is in a scrapbook somewhere around here, I'll be damned if I'll spend a week hunting it down. But if I've misquoted, it's only a little, from dimmed memory. That's what the *Times* said, more of more than less. You can either trust me on this one, or go microfiche.)

And Aaron Spelling decided I was to be the fair-haired boy. I descended, intensely but thankgoodness only briefly, into what I now refer to mordantly as my days of "going Hollywood." During that period I wrote for, and got to spend time with, genuine legends: Gloria Swanson, Charlie Ruggles, Buster Keaton, Wally Cox, Joan Blondell, Aldo Ray, Mickey Rooney, Rod Steiger, and even Nina Foch. I went to Hollywood parties, I dined with celebrities and multimillionaires, I became involved with starlets, I went more than a little crazy. Even wound up married and divorced a third time, all in forty-five days. But that's another story.

Yet it was during that period that I began writing film criticism, and (even as evil can come from good, good can come from evil) it was as a direct result of falling under Spelling's enchantment for the better part of a year.*

This wasn't as fast to tell as I'd thought.

Anyway, what happened was this:

One day I was in the *Burke's Law* office, it's now 1965, and Aaron came in as we were trying to cast Betty Hutton for my script "Who Killed ½ of Glory Lee?" He was bubbling with excitement about the fabulous night he had spent the day before, at a "very exclusive new club" called The Daisy. He went on rapturously, explaining at length that this club was *so* exclusive that even if you had the Big Bucks for membership, you couldn't get in unless you Were Somebody. Well, I listened raptly (Richard listened with weariness and the boredom of familiarity). And

---

*Strictly speaking, the assertion that I wrote no film comment prior to 1965 is untrue. Like everyone else, I had opinions on movies from the moment I left the Utopia Theater in Painesville, Ohio on that Saturday afternoon when I first saw *Snow White and the Seven Dwarfs* in re-release in 1940. (That same afternoon, I saw Victor Jory in the first chapter of *The Shadow* serial.) And so, as it was with many of you, I wrote "movie reviews" for my high school newspaper and, not much later, "reviews of things seen and heard" for my fanzine *Dimensions*. Upon completion of the introduction to this book, it was pointed out to me by the indefatigable Gil Lamont, as editorial and copyediting amanuensis (and one strangely more familiar with my more obscure writings than even I), that I was leading astray the readers by suggesting that I had sprung full-blown as a film critic. That I was dissembling when I ignored the first sophomoric cinema scrawlings. Mr. Lamont reminded me that the demon bibliographer Leslie Kay Swigart had actually gone to Cleveland a number of years ago and, somehow, had managed to exhume copies of the East High *Blue and Gold.* He suggested that a sample of my pre-professional film comment ought to be included here, if for no other reason than to let a little air out of my sails. If you turn to *Appendix A* (page 469) you will find republished for the first time, a brief insight by the then-seventeen-year-old Ellison dated 26 September 1951. In the spirit of mental health and a determination to hold onto whatever vestiges of credential are left to me after bowing to Mr. Lamont's chivvying, I have *not* included any other examples of post-zit journalism.

after Aaron had strutted and fulminated about this den of grandeur whose portals were verboten to all but the denizens of the mountaintop, I said, "Hell, I could get in."

Aaron looked at me with a condescending smile. "Forget it, Harlan. They *only* take in members who are famous."

"I can get a membership."

"No chance."

"Wanna bet?"

"Bet what?"

I smiled that self-assured smartass smile that goes before a long fall from a great height, and I said, "I'll bet you a grand against a thousand dollars off my next script assignment, that I can not only become a member of The Daisy, but I can get in within twenty-four hours from right now."

Aaron searched around in his briefcase for his wallet, pulled out a plastic card and held it up. It was a membership card for the Daisy. "For a thousand, you'll have one of these, with your name on it, and actually be a member of The Daisy by..." he consulted his wristwatch, "...eleven o'clock tomorrow?"

I nodded, suddenly getting a little frightened. A thousand in 1963 was a *lot* of money. It may only be a loaf of bread and a jar of Vlasic pickles these days, but as a one-hour story and teleplay brought a writer top-of-the-show remuneration at $4500, that thousand dollars suddenly loomed very large.

"You're on," Aaron said, smugly. He made like a Great White and everyone else in the office (except Richard Newton) grinned back, prepared to see the smartass get his comeuppance.

When the meeting broke up, and I was on my way back to the tiny office where they kept me soldered to the typewriter, Richard overtook me and laid a big-brotherly hand on my shoulder. "At times," he said, with affection and concern, "I see you as a very foolish man who doesn't know when he's dancing at the lip of the abyss." I don't think I'll ever forget that moment: it may have been for me—at age 31—that I began belatedly to reach puberty. I might have tried to explain to him that I couldn't help myself, that I had been warped by Hoppity, but it wouldn't have made any more sense in 1965 than it does now.

Nonetheless, I was determined to pull it off.

In just such a foolhardy state of arrogance and braggadocio did Marie Antoinette say, "Let them eat cake!" and did Gary Hart challenge the newshounds to follow him and watch his every move.

Once back in my office, I began attacking the problem in just the way Sherlock Holmes would have gone at it. Logically. Quietly. Rationally.

Hysterically.

I started calling friends who were "in the know." I asked them to tell me everything they knew about The Daisy, and who ran it. The name that came up was Jack Martin Hanson, who owned the posh and trendy clothing shop in Beverly Hills known as Jax.

Nothing there.

I kept probing, and one of my contacts said he'd heard that Hanson had just taken over *Cinema* magazine from a guy named James Silke, that the magazine was intended as something of a high-profile purchase for Hanson, a way to gain greater access to the film community and the people who had enough money to buy the clothes his shop sold, not to mention the kind of money needed to afford membership in his restricted Daisy.

Bingo.

I tracked down the number of *Cinema*'s offices, and managed late that afternoon to speak to a young man named Curtis Lee Hanson. It did not escape my notice that Curtis Lee and Jack Martin had the same last name, Hanson. It turned out that Curtis Lee (now a successful and very talented writer/director, whose most recent feature was the thriller *The Bedroom Window*) was Jack's nephew, and he had just taken over as editor, Silke having departed to commence what eventually became an undistinguished filmwriting career.

Hanson was vaguely aware of my name, had read something of mine somewhere, so he was friendly and receptive to my writing for his magazine. It was a snazzy slick journal, filled with photos, and with a somewhat loftier view of film than most of the gossipy, ephemeral magazines of the period. I said my fee for such writing was high, but that I'd make an exception in the case of *Cinema*, on one condition. (Curtis Lee heaved a sigh of relief; the magazine was paying almost nothing; it was a matter of prestige and like that.) He asked the condition, and I said, "I want a full, free membership in The Daisy. And I have to have the card in my hand no later than nine A.M. tomorrow morning."

He said he didn't know if that could be done, that his connection with The Daisy was almost non-existent, that his uncle tried to keep the operations separate. I said it was non-negotiable, that it was *the* deal-breaker. Curtis Lee asked if I had something written already that he could show to Jack Hanson, to convince him that a magazine already publishing Bogdanovich, Dalton Trumbo and Terry Southern *needed* a Harlan Ellison.

I said, "Well, I've just written a review-critique of *The Train*, the Frankenheimer film that'll be opening in about three weeks. Would that do?"

He said yes, I said I'd have it messengered over to him, he said great, said he'd read it, said if it seemed up to their standards and needs he'd run it over to Jack and have *him* read it, said if Jack went for it he'd push for a Daisy card for me. I said thanks, hung up, and turned to my typewriter.

I wrote that review-critique in about forty minutes.

You will find it in this book.

At eight o'clock that night, having sent the review to Curtis Lee by messenger from Four Star around one-thirty that afternoon, I got a phone call at my tiny treehouse home. It was Curtis Lee. "You want me to bring your membership card around, or do you want to pick it up?"

I drove out, met Hanson for the first time in Beverly Hills, and took possession of Daisy membership card number 49. I also accepted an assignment to do a short piece on Edward G. Robinson as he neared his seventy-second birthday.

Both pieces, and two more, appeared in the July-August 1965 issue of *Cinema*. I was a film critic.

The next day, sitting in Aaron's office with Richard and casting director Betty Martin and three or four others, Aaron came rushing in, tossed the stack of scripts he'd read the night before on his desk and, without preamble, turned to me.

"Well?"

I looked innocent. I can do that. "Well what?"

"You owe me a thousand dollars," he said, Great Whitelike.

Everyone in the room looked nervous. It had been a good gag the day before, but they knew I couldn't possibly have pulled it off, and they now knew that Aaron would certainly call the business people and tell them that Ellison's next assignment was for a thousand less. Richard Newton didn't look happy with me.

"Well, uh, no," I said slowly, forking two fingers into my shirt pocket. "You owe *me* a thousand." I brought out the Daisy membership card. *High Noon. The Guns of Navarone.*

Go ahead, picture the scene in your mind. This is a book about movies, so run it through your head. It's good exercise.

I've written elsewhere, and at length, about my brief crazy

time of having Gone Hollywood. Much of that lunacy centered around the Daisy.*

But if it had not been for the cattle call, for Richard Newton, for my awakening awareness that I did not want to grow up to be Aaron Spelling and needed to one-up the Great Man; had it not been for having been twisted and bent by Hoppity and the need to assert the know-it-all in me who now writes pontificating film criticism; had it not been for Curtis Lee Hanson, my friend and one-time editor, and *Cinema* magazine, now long-gone but fondly remembered; had it not been for that odd congeries of circumstances, this book of more than twenty-five years' worth of film comment would not exist.

Having thus explained how I was corrupted, warped, driven to this unseemly stretch of writing, I know that those among you who paused in hammering together the gibbet to listen to this interminable screed, will now understand that I am innocent, that never has a cruel thought passed through my head, and that if justice is to be visited on anyone, it should properly fall on the ghosts of Max and Dave Fleischer and my Grandmother, on Aaron Spelling and Richard Newton, and certainly on Curtis Lee Hanson, all of whom ruined that sweet little Ellison kid.

For myself, I've never cried, "Fire!" in a crowded theater.

---

*In the September 1966 issue of *Los Angeles* magazine, appeared a 5200 word article titled "Nightmare Nights at the Daisy." I wrote that article. Apart from a minor reprinting in a men's magazine exactly one year later, that piece has never been collected in one of my books of essays. It forms an interesting Hollywood footnote to this introduction. If you turn to Appendix B (page 471) you will find it as it was written at that moment in my life when I came to my senses and foreswore involvement with the social scene in the movie colony. Upon rereading, I find it verbose, purple, overstated and wincingly melodramatic. But in its way, I guess, it is historical document at its silliest. Like the view of a former Flat-Earther after having taken his first space-ride.

HARLAN ELLISON'S
WATCHING

DARKNESS IN MAGIC CAVERNS
A nostalgic appreciation of moviegoing

Chill beneath a cadaverously-gray autumn sky, the tiny New Mexico town. That slate moment in the seasons when everything begins to grow dark. The epileptic scratching of fallen leaves hurled along sidewalks. Mad sounds from the hills. Cold. And something else:

A leopard, escaped, is loose in the town.

Chill beneath a crawling terror of spotted death in the night, the tiny New Mexico town. That thick red moment in the fears of small people when everything explodes in the black flow of blood. A deep-throated growl from a filthy alley. Cold.

A mother, preoccupied with her cooking, tells her small daughter to go down the street to the market, get a sack of flour to make bread for the father, coming home from work soon. The child shows a moment of fear...the animal they haven't found yet...

The mother insists, it's only a few blocks and across the bridge to the market. Put on a shawl and go get that flour, your father will be home soon. The child goes. Hurrying back up the street, the small sack held close to her, the street empty and filling with darkness, ink presses down the sky, the child looks around, and hurries. A cough in the blackness behind her. A cough, deep in a throat that never formed human sounds.

1

The child's eyes widen in panic. She begins to hurry. Her footsteps quicken. The sound of padding behind her. Feet begin to run. Focus on darkness and the sound of rapid movement. The child. The rushing.

To the wooden door of the house. The door is locked. The child pinned against the night, with the furred sound of agony rushing toward her on the wind.

Inside, the mother, still kitchened, waiting. The sound of the child outside, panic and bubbles of hysteria in the voice, Mommy open the door the leopard is after me!

The mother's face assumes the ages-old expression of harassed parenthood. Hands on hips, she turns to the door, you're always lying, telling fibs, making up stories, how many times have I told you lying will—

Mommy! Open the door!

You'll stay out there till you learn to stop lying!

Mommy! Mom—

Something gigantic hits the door with a crash. The door bows inward, and a fine spray of flour sifts between the cracks into the room. The mother's eyes grow huge, she stares at the door. A thick black stream, moving very slowly, seeps under the door.

Let me tell you something straight: when I draw my last breath, and finally buy it, and should Cecil B. DeMille have been dealing me straight all those years and there *is* The Big Hiring Hall In The Sky (though I tend to distrust a man who would have Moses marry Yvonne De Carlo), I'm going to pass up meeting Hemingway and Shakespeare and W. C. Fields and Bogart and Marta Toren first thing on my arrival, and ask to be directed to the alabaster palace in which Val Lewton is spending a happy eternity.

Oh, yeah. He'll be in a palace. Got to be.

Nobody who produced films like *The Leopard Man*, from which came that scene I described at the outset, could be treated less respectfully by a benevolent God. And I'll walk up there to the palace and find Lewton on the back veranda, telling half a dozen lesser talents how to put together some celestial cinema. And one of the archangels in charge of casting will come up with the old one about, "Yeah, sure, Val, but God's got this chick, see..."

And I'll interrupt them and say, "Mr. Lewton, sir, excuse me, but my name is Harlan Ellison and I've got you to thank for me not wasting my life, and for writing all kinds of stories people dug when I was alive, and for making my childhood bearable and...well, uh, er..."

And I'll lapse into an awkward silence, because he'll smile, knowing all the shadows and mirages behind those inadequate words. *He* knew what he was all about when he was making those B shudderflicks in the Forties.

But he could not have known, like pebbles tossed into a pool to produce ever-widening circles of impact, how important he was to me. But I know, and I'll tell you; and when you've been told, you'll know why all those martinet pedants of the New York Literary Establishment who *still* put down moviegoing live zombie lives of half-light. And you'll even understand why *auteurs* like Bogdanovich can't smell the flowers because they're too busy dissecting them.

You see, I was the only Jewish kid in Painesville, Ohio, about thirty miles east of Cleveland, and you wouldn't think that in Ohio—the Buckeye state, the center of the Great Amurrican Heartland—one would encounter much bigotry. You'd be wrong. They used to beat the shit out of me. Regularly. I was a little loudmouth of a kid, quick as a whippet and ten times smarter than anybody else in town, but that humble greatness wasn't what made them hate me, naturally. It was this Jewish business. They actually believed Jews ground up Seventh Day Adventist babies to make *matzohs* at Channukah. They called me a kike. I didn't know what it was, but I didn't care for the tone of voice. So I was the green monkey, the pariah. And I had no friends. Not just a few friends, or one good friend, or grudging acceptance by other misfits and outcasts. I was alone. All stinking alone, without even an imaginary playmate.

So I made my own worlds.

Worlds comprised of the dreams and visions to be found in comic books with Plastic Man and Airboy and the Heap and Hawkman and the Boy Commandos and the Spirit; worlds found in the radio programs I devoured so avidly my ears grew mouths: *I Love a Mystery, The Shadow,* Lux...presents Hollywood, *Quiet, Please, The Land of the Lost, Grand Central Station, Let's Pretend.* Worlds in the pulp magazines: *Startling Stories, Doc Savage, G-8 and his Battle Aces, The Spider, Black Mask.*

But most of all...the movies.

Oh, God, the movies. For four hours every Saturday afternoon I was taken away from that miserable lonely charnel house of childhood and was permitted to ride beside Don "Red" Barry, swashbuckle beside Jon Hall, sleuth beside Sidney Toler, drool

3

over Ann Rutherford and June Preisser, know fear as Kent Smith knew it and shudder helplessly as Rondo Hatton stalked the streets as The Creeper.

I was a child of the Forties. In a time before the word "alienation" slipped from everyone's lips as easily as a rolling stone gathers no moss, I was a thoroughly, hopelessly, totally alienated kid who could not exist in the real world. And though the studio money-grubbers who churned out those wonderfully awful pot-boilers could never have known what succor they were bringing to my parched soul, they provided me the only world to which I cared to belong. The world of dreams, of celluloid escapes, of glorious moviegoing.

(You know one reason I hate my sister, Beverly? She is eight years older than I am, see. And when my Mom and Dad would be at the store, downtown, working on Saturday, I was entrusted to her care. She had to get me downtown on the bus, to see the movie. Then she could go off and do whatever dull dumb things girls did in Painesville on Saturday afternoons. Had to be dumb, didn't it? She wasn't at the *movie*, fer chrissakes! But she used to torment me. She'd dawdle, and chivvy me, and tell me she wasn't going to take me, and then she'd put her dress up in back so her slip showed, and say, come on, let's go. And I'd say, we can't go with you like that, and she'd torment me with, sure we can, come on. And I'd sit down on my bed and start to cry, because I knew damned *well* we couldn't walk up Harmon Drive to Mentor Avenue and get on that bus and go downtown with her dress up in back so her slip showed. And she'd do that to me for an hour before we left. We always did, of course, but by the time we got downtown I was a nervous wreck. That's one of the reasons I hate Beverly. But that's another story.)

The Lake Theater on State Street in Painesville was the Taj Mahal to me. It was dark and filled with endless magics. Sounds no mortal ever heard: the choking gurgle of a *thuggee* victim being strangled for the love of Kali; the special whimpering bark as Lassie told some halfwit nit of a child actor that the baby was in a burning building; the insidious laugh of Victor Jory as The Shadow; the thunk of crossbow arrows plonking into the drawbridge of evil King John. Sights no mortal ever beheld: Sabu changed into a dog by Conrad Veidt; Wild Bill Elliott as Red Ryder, beating the shit out of a gang of bullies somehow vaguely reminiscent of the thugs that played in the schoolyard of Lathrop Grade School; Kirk Alyn leaping off a building shouting, "Up,

4

up, and awayyyy!" There was no end to the magic to be found in that dark cavern.

For four hours—with Bingo and two features and three cartoons and a TravelTalk and a singalong—I was in Heaven. A special dark Heaven even more private than the bathroom, which is the only place a little kid can go to, to be alone.

And I knew some day I would have adventures like that. Some day I would walk streets paved with gold, and all the bullies would step off into the gutter when I passed, and my Mother and Father would say, "The kid really knows how to live," because I'd be in business for myself, and even if my partner Miles Archer had been murdered and I *didn't* know whether the fat man or Joel Cairo had the black bird, even so...I'd be competent and tough, and I'd win out.

That was how it was when I was a kid.

Is there nobility in the moviegoing experience? Don't ask me, friend. I don't know from nobility; all I know from is survival and dreams.

And thank *you*, Val Lewton.

CINEMA
[1965–68]

THE TRAIN

Melville once ventured, "No great and enduring volume can ever be written on the flea, though many there be who have tried it." Even when the flea is photographed in Technicolor and Cine-maScope, its volume is a flashy but transitory offering. Melville dealt with whales, consequently.

Unlike most of the flea-marketeers of Hollywood, director John Frankenheimer is a man who would deal with whales, had he his choice. It is the choice of the louse as opposed to the air-breather. And in so doing, his sphere of attention becomes more cerebral, the purview of his cinematic documents ceases to be merely entertainment (which is that matter lightly dropped on the viewer, like tapioca pudding, e.g., Doris Day flicks) and becomes "art" (which entails active participation and, like a steak, mastication).

THE TRAIN is art, and as a result, many things can be said of it, not the least of which is that it is a *good* picture. In fact, it may be *too* good for the people who will eventually decide whether or not it is successful, at the box office. This is, I feel, a sin not of the producer, but of the culture, of the motion picture–goer. In the main, he has been surfeited with such an endless glut of pap films—usually because these were the ones he patronized most in the past, thus by his attentions demanding more of the same, and getting no better than he deserved—that a film of some depth and contrast leaves him confused and disgruntled; and rather than acknowledging that his imaginative faculties have atrophied, as with *Lord Jim, Dr. Strangelove* and half a hundred other superlative films, he will condemn the work set before him. It is a hideous conceit.

And I fear *The Train* will be another victim.

Behind and beside me in the theater, during the special screening, safe in the dark to express remarks of denseness and silliness that a lighted room would either force them to rationalize as "opinions" or keep unspoken, I heard typical moviegoers ask each other what the hell was going on up there, at points in the film any relatively cogent and informed person should have found self-explanatory. Again, I assert, this is not the fault of Frankenheimer & Co. but of The Great Unwashed (a term of surpassing arrogance and disdain I have hesitated to use before, but which seems frighteningly applicable here). And the answer to the problem is beyond me: the filmmaker can either pander to this Howdy Doody mentality, and bring forth an endless stream of Fanny Hurst/Gidget/Tammy/Ross Hunter charades, or go his way as has Frankenheimer or Kubrick or Richardson and woo his own Muse, letting the stock options fall where they may.

The latter course is one of courage, for it entails risk, loss of financing, and the roar of corporation executives. It is to Frankenheimer's eternal credit that he did not take the easy way out for, to repeat, *The Train* is a work of brilliance, perceptivity, depth and meaning. It approaches questions of morality and conscience that demand grappling. In short, this film, unlike much of what makes money these seasons, does not pass through the viewer like beets through a baby's backside.

Set in Paris, 1944, with the Allies always just "a few days away from liberation" of the open city, a small group of French Resistance operatives set themselves the task of rescuing a trainload of art treasures, masterpieces, "the heritage of France," from being shipped to Germany by the Nazi Colonel who has, for four years, pathologically kept the paintings from being damaged, ostensibly because they are convertible to gold needed for the war effort, but in reality because he is a man possessed of taste and discrimination, a man awed by the genius unleashed on those canvases by Matisse, Braque, Van Gogh, Gauguin, Monet, Manet, Picasso. His one single driving thought is to get those irreplaceable treasures away. He is a dedicated man, a man

10

with lofty motives, serving a beast master, and himself part-beast.

He is a man doing the wrong thing—for the right reason.

His opposite number is a man of controlled brutishness, a Parisian railroadman named Labiche, who counts the cost of sabotage in human lives. X number of lives to stop this train, X number for that train. Only the most valuable trains—munitions, troops, etc.—are worth expending the lives of his fellow saboteurs. He rejects the plea of the drab little Frenchwoman (sensitively played by Suzanne Flon, who will be best remembered, perhaps, as Lautrec's mannequin love in *Moulin Rouge*) who has been Colonel Von Waldheim's assistant, to stop the Colonel from ferreting away with the golden heart of French culture. Paintings mean nothing to him; there's a war on; what has art to do with it? Not until Von Waldheim executes old Papa Boule, the engineer Labiche has assigned to the train, for trying to sabotage the locomotive pulling that fabulous cargo, does Labiche swear to stop the train. But still, the paintings mean nothing to him. Crated in their boxcars—7 Van Gogh, they are stenciled, or 4 Roualt, like herring, like machine parts, like piece goods—they are merely a symbol of frenzy to Labiche.

He will stop the train, he will defeat the Nazi, Von Waldheim. And therein lies the beautiful dichotomy of the story.

Because he is doing the right thing—for the wrong reason!

In essence, this 133-minute film is a titanic duel between the personalities of Von Waldheim: dedicated, brutal, ascetic, implacable yet sensitive, determined...and Labiche: physical, vengeful, cunning, artless yet graceful, equally determined. And while the paintings mean nothing to Labiche, they mean everything to Von Waldheim, they are his obsession.

In the final moments of the film, after a staggering loss of life over the inanimate cargo, when the battle has been won, Von Waldheim, even then, is able to tell Labiche that the paintings are his, will always be his, will always belong to him or a man *like* him, to men with the eyes to see beauty. He tells Labiche that he has won, but without even knowing why, or what he was doing, that the paintings mean as much to Labiche as a string of pearls to an ape.

And Labiche looks at the jumbled jackstraw tumble of French hostages Von Waldheim has had machine-gunned off the train, and kills the Nazi. The camera spastically intercuts between the jumbled crates of great paintings half-unloaded from the derailed train, and the dead Frenchmen. Cut and intercut, and

11

only a dolt could fail to see the unspoken question: Were these paintings worth all these wasted lives?

It is a breathless visual posture of Frankenheimer as master of his craft, as symbolist, as preacher, as capturer of art for the masses, that does not demean the intellectual's praise. It sums up one of the basic questions of man in conflict with himself to preserve culture and civilization:

Is the life of a man greater or lesser than the art he produces in his most noble moments? Is it possible to equate the continued value of history and cultural heritage his finest work represents, weighed against common flesh, mortal clay? It is a question to which philosophers have only imperfect answers, and in restating the question in modern, cinematic, bold terms, Frankenheimer (and I would presume scenarists Franklin Coen and Frank Davis) has rendered a service. For more than entertainment has been provided, for those who would care to exercise their wit and intelligence.

Even serendipitously, this film provides marginal treasures, unexpected, and easy to love: a visual paean to the "high iron" of steam locomotion, a reverence for the filth and sweat and bravery of men who pushed the steam horses; a sensation of grandeur the diesel engineers of today cannot possibly feel about their semisilent zip-machines. It is a final hurrah voiced in closeups of sooty engines, long shots down on marshaling yards, pans and zooms to and away from specific bits of iron that speak of the majesty of the whistle-screeching, thunder-making days of railroading, now almost entirely passed into history.

And more: England's incomparable Paul Scofield as the many-faceted Nazi Colonel, rendering a portrayal of complexity and even—impossibly—compassion, with a minimum of arm-waving, with a reserve of style that bespeaks great talent. His every moment on the screen is a gesture of possession; he strides across this film as palpably impressive as the train itself, and in time, the train dwindles in import, and the man trying to rule it becomes the central figure of the drama, despite the plotting of script which offers us Burt Lancaster as Labiche. Correction. It offers us

Burt Lancaster as Captain Marvel.

When I was a child, and read the Capt. Marvel comics, I never *really* thought any harm would come to that great red cheese. He could always pull off *some*thing, after all, he was superhuman, wasn't he? My feeling was paralleled with Lancaster as I watched this film. He can act, certainly, but on what level above that of swashbuckling, I cannot conceive. The usual Lancasterite mannerisms—the clenched teeth, the balled fist swung across the body, the spread-legged stance and the furiously shaken arm, the tossed curls, all so damnably typical and cliché, so useless and needless here, in a setting of purest gold—the same mannerisms of Elmer Gantry, once again, for the millionth time restated.

The intrusive personality of Lancaster the acrobat, doing his special parlor tricks down ladders, over garden walls, superbly muscled and annoying as hell when they tell us over and over, "I'm not really Labiche, I'm Lancaster."

It is to Frankenheimer's credit that he has been able to direct around this more-than-minuscule handicap. His direction (blessedly done in black and white, precisely what the production demanded) is massive, great blocks of shadow and light, a study in chiaroscuro; dark, jagged, dense, swung with great authority, like the railroad crane needed to lift the wrecked locomotive off the tracks. Purposely ponderous at times, quicksilver hereand-gone at other times. He has filmed it with what might be termed "affectionate realism," a sense of proportion and piety that transcends mere naturalism, that lingers on the proper things for the proper amount of time.

Scofield, Jeanne Moreau, the Falstaffian Michel Simon as Papa Boule, Wolfgang Preiss adding another memorable characterization to his already-illustrious career with his portrayal of the Nazi railroad specialist Major Herren, muffin-shaped Albert Remy as the fellow-saboteur of Labiche, striking to the heart of the film's meaning with his gentle, skillful rendering of a simple peasant patriot . . . all of them lend tone and dignity and artistry to a film of notable proportions.

The Train is a success. It succeeds not only on its own terms, but on the greater, more stringent, terms of strictest art criticism. It is film of purity, it is even a loftier breed of "entertainment," and it deserves all the praise and attention we can give it.

Simply, it is a film not to be missed.

It is the whale, and not the flea.

VON RYAN'S EXPRESS

There is a grand tradition of the adventure film. In many ways it is a dichotomy: some of the worst films of all time have been the most memorable adventures; conversely, some of the best-made adventure films die hideous box-office deaths, and live even shorter lives in memory. *King Kong*, Korda's *Four Feathers* and *The Thief of Bagdad* leap instantly to mind, and in more recent times *The Magnificent Seven, Lawrence of Arabia* and even as flawed an epic as *The Vikings*—all prove the latter point, while we may take as example of the former almost anything Samuel Bronston has released in the past ten years.

Because of this body of history to the larger-than-life film of derring-do, comparison intrudes itself. And in the case of 20th's VON RYAN'S EXPRESS the comparison must inevitably be with *The Great Escape*, an adventure film of undeniable stature. The comparison is not altogether unwarranted, nor unrewarding. For if *Von Ryan's Express* comes out short in some areas, it makes the points up in others.

Late 1943, an Italian prison camp, run about as slipshodly as the entire Italian war. A camp filled with almost a thousand English troops, into whose midst comes a downed American Air Force Colonel, Ryan. The English officer-in-command has died the night before, so Ryan automatically becomes the ranking officer in the compound. He immediately raises the ire of the limeys by exposing their tunnels and escape procedures in exchange for medicine, clothing, showers, razors, all the basics kept from them by the Commandant as retaliation for their continued escape attempts. Inevitably, Italy surrenders, the prisoners take to the land before the Nazis move in, and are recaptured due to a humanitarian blunder on the part of Ryan. To make amends, he promptly steals the entire prison train, and runs it through Pauline peril after Pauline peril till they make it free to Switzerland. Ryan is killed in the process. But he does die a hero.

For the first third of the film, tedium is the keynote. About midway, the pace accelerates, due largely to the splendid performances of Edward Mulhare as the vicar impersonating a German officer, and Sergio Fantoni as the one-eyed Italian captain who helps the Ryan Express. As the denouement fast approaches, conjurings of *The Bridge on the River Kwai* and *The Guns of Navarone* swell, and never seem to be quite washed away, no matter *how* long the triggers of those German machine-pistols are held.

If the film is not a total success, blame lies, it seems to me, with director Mark Robson, who has once again demonstrated a pedestrian pace most clearly seen in his *Nine Hours to Rama*. The direction seems uninspired, matter-of-fact, strictly pronunciatory, without verve or dash or any of the bravura techniques such bravura plotting would seem to demand. It is, in many ways, a tale of danger and excitement, told by a man with the soul of a ribbon clerk. It has the same teeth-gnashing effect of a good joke, badly told.

And yet, the film manages to hold the attention, at least during the last two-thirds. It is to be hoped that the producers will see fit to trim the opening to embolden the pace.

The values of *Von Ryan's Express*, however, are serendipitous. The first is a conclusion about current war films, the second about the nature of the "star" system.

There seems to be a heartening—and totally inexplicable—trend toward films that point a shaft of rationality at the concept of "heroism" during wartime. Heartening, if one is to read the daily papers, and inexplicable in a time of Birching, pocket wars, and the concept of cleaning out Vietnamese foliage with low-yield atomics. We had *Dr. Strangelove* with its outright denunciation of the madness of overkill, *The Americanization of Emily* that boldly stated there is no nobility in combat, only loftiness in

16

cowardice, and, in recent memory, *Paths of Glory*, which showed the base drives of those who make our wars. Now, here, we have another, somewhat more enigmatic view of the problem. Trevor Howard's (occasionally overplayed) Major Fincham would rather sacrifice his wounded men to the grim reaper than sacrifice the medicine secreted as "escape rations" by his breakout-happy POWs. Sinatra, as the downed Yankee airman, sees this as madness. "Even if one escapes, it's a victory," Fincham tells him, but Ryan proclaims it lunacy. Break them *all* out, he maintains, all eight hundred of them.

For in his acceptance of another way to skin the Nazi cat, Sinatra/Ryan says, in effect: "War must be made, under any circumstances, with sanity." Even when he dies, and Fincham's words echo back to his fading spirit, we see the morality of what Ryan believed:

There is no nobility in war. While he does not quite go so far as to suggest that the most ignominious life is better than the best kind of death, still, he does not veer too far from this ethic.

As for point two, one of the more serious and blatant drawbacks of the "star" system asserts itself here, as regards Sinatra. So typed has he become, so much a caricature of himself with the snapbrim tilted over one eye, the trench coat slung over the shoulder, the fingers popping, Mr. Ring-a-ding alla way down the pike, that the character of Ryan, boldly assertive in David Westheimer's novel, from which the motion picture has been adapted, never really seems to take hold. At any moment we expect Frankie to wink and pop a pinkie at us. We are constantly intruded upon by the *Doppelgänger*, the Shade of Sinatra Past, and it is a shame: he acts, for the first time in many films, possibly for the first time since Angelo Maggio. He acts, and with elegant clarity of movement, conservation of style; he underplays, he strives for highs and lows, and in one well-turned moment—when he is compelled to shoot the Italian paramour of the train commandant—he captures us completely. It is too bad we must constantly be reminded this "star" is playing the part. To hell with "star" images, let the bankers and backers give us acting; acting is the seldom fire that lights up the CinemaScope screen.

MASQUERADE

Make no mistake, this is a praise review. But if you detect a piercing note of bewilderment, a sense of the reviewer spinning about gyroscopically demanding to know which way they went, it all lies in the nature and thrust of a delightful, current trend in adventure films.

That Man from Rio and the Ian Fleming–James Bond operas typify the movement, with *Topkapi* and *Charade* as minor entries in the sweepstakes. Lineally descended from Huston's *Beat the Devil* and several of the Hitchcockian posturings (notably *The 39 Steps* and *North By Northwest*), the keynote is handsomely-mounted spy or suspense thrillers, with just a touch of Professor Dodgson's Alice and the sort of flair style the French call *panache*.

You start with an intricate "threat" (no mere Maltese Falcon will suffice in these times of seeded bubonic plague and Doomsday Machines that will turn us all into a smelly specie of cosmic pizza) and you select the right sort of secret agent to thwart it. Be he suave and cool à la James Bond or rugged and realistic like Donald Hamilton's Matt Helm (as he is in the novels, not—I'm sure—as Dean Martin will portray him in the upcoming series from Columbia), he has to be ready to go anywhere, perform any task, and lay his life on the line from Beirut to Baton Rouge. He also has to be a little out of his gourd to sign up for cockamamie work like that.

The villain has to be larger than life, snarl a whole lot (if possible, in one of the lesser dialects of Bantu) and have a seemingly inexhaustible supply of super-weapons and super-schemes. He has to, the poor debbil, he's gonna lose in the last three minutes, anyhow.

It is a phylum of cinema nonsense we heartily endorse. After years of Odets–style social outrage, more years of Hollywood twin-bed unreality, and most recently a miasma of depravity films that set the adenoids to jangling and the teeth to scrape, a wave of movie madness is most welcome.

Add to the huzzahs an item called MASQUERADE, with Cliff Robertson as the world's biggest patsy, standing around with a Mickey Mouse expression on his matinee idol's face, as a conglomerate circus of super-and-lesser spies uses him for everything but the village basketball.

Is there a plot? Who the hell knows! Very possible, but don't expect any certainties. There's a kidnapped thirteen-year-old who will shortly become the ruling rajah of a mythical Oil Monarchy, a wily Grand Vizier, some foofaraw about leased oil rights, a retired but hardly recalcitrant English Colonel (*brilliantly* pavane'd by Jack Hawkins, who only improves with each year and wrinkle), a group of smugglers who aren't smugglers, a beautiful girl who keeps sucking on a bottle of Coke as though she were determined to stay out of The Pepsi Generation...a midget, a knife-thrower, a private detective, a ramrod-stiff British major-domo, and a cast of lesser estimables who pop in and out like the figurines on a cuckoo clock. The similarity does not end there.

Robertson is a delight, Hawkins runs close to amuck, the photography ranges from sharp and perceptive to pedestrian and drab, the script bears the unmistakable stamp of William (THE TEMPLE OF GOLD) Goldman's special demented Muse, and director Basil Dearden should be awarded the W. C. Fields Annual Juggling Award for keeping all those cigar boxes and top hats and brass balls skimming through the air. If we detect the crash of an implement or two in the b.g., there really isn't time to worry about it because Robertson still has to get that bamboo pole away from the white-crested vulture, so he can escape from the animal cage with that guy's wife, whom he has been balling throughout the picture, and catch up with the guy who records the Flamenco singers for BBC before he tries to steal the kid back from the double-crossing Home Office official with the donkey, attempting to cross that uncompleted dam in Spain... uh...try it: painless.

It might help if *Cinema* had a type font called Shrill Gothic.

MICKEY ONE

It takes a peculiarly slantwise mind to understand Kafka the first time out. It will take a similarly oriented mind to understand MICKEY ONE the first time it is seen. For the similarities between Kafka's writing and Arthur Penn's personal vision of what film should be, and do, are greater than the dichotomies between the two forms.

It is this reviewer's contention that *Mickey One* is the finest American film of the year, and possibly of many years. Despite the impending tragedy.

For the very obtuseness and existential disorientation of Penn's approach, the very qualities that hoist this film onto a plateau of brilliance and directorial bravura, are the qualities that will most alienate unqualified audiences, and condemn *Mickey One* to box-office shakiness. Already the tragedy is taking form: the night I saw it, in preview, at the Writers Guild screening, ninety percent of the audience—men intimately knowledgeable with the film form, allegedly—wandered out of the theater as if they had been stunned by the hammer. When they could not fathom what was going on, they turned to ridicule. In New York, the film has already opened, and as a telephone conversation with a friend in Manhattan informs me, "The reviews are bombing it." The name of the game is tragedy.

The same specie of tragedy that bombed Kubrick's *Paths of Glory* when it first was released; and again, the similarities are greater than the divergent themes of the two films might lead one to suspect. Only now are we coming to realize what a small masterpiece *Paths of Glory* has become; and I contend that while *Mickey One* will die an inglorious box-office death, years hence it will serve as a way-marker for avant-garde filmmakers, and be looked at with ever-growing respect.

(Which brings up the subject of the unworthiness of most American film audiences, a topic that desperately needs to be talked about. For without a concerted effort toward education of "the great unwashed," we will continue *ad infinitum* to be deluged with bad, sordid and inept films directed toward the slob mind; and experimental, daring films of this nature will continue to go unmade, because the economic loss will be built in. But that is a topic for another time.)

The story of *Mickey One* is a simple, contemporary entertainment, on its primary level. Mickey, a stand-up comic, has gotten into the Mob for a substantial amount of money, through gambling. To work off the debt, they buy up his contract and he is forced to work in Mob-owned clubs. But the constant fear, the constant surveillance, finally weigh on him to a crushing point where he flees, knowing if they catch him, they will kill him for welshing.

He runs interminably, becomes paranoid in the process, for everywhere he turns the invisible eyes of the Mob seek him out. He can trust no one. He becomes an alley man, a derelict. Then he meets a girl, and for the first time in too long, he is able to relate to someone. He gets himself a booking in a small club, and inevitably, through the innocent machinations of his agent, he gets a crack at a posh room. But he is terrified. If he gets seen, *they* will find him. He tries to turn the job down, but the manager of the club recognizes him and lets the Mob know who he is, that he has found the comic they have been looking for. The booker of the club—initially—is only interested in furthering the career of this "talented youngster," and so becomes a dupe of the manager and the Mob to put Mickey before the spotlight, where they can get at him. Mickey panics, manages to escape again, and is on the verge of resuming his blind flight, when he develops backbone, stands, and finds—in that Kafkaesque logic of human unpredictability—that they are done with him, he is off the hook, free.

24   That is the story; on the face of it, not particularly deep or

meaningful in terms of psychology or social influences, but then MOBY-DICK is only the story of a vengeful man after a big fish, if you want to make it a *reductio ad absurdum*.

It is the *telling* of the story that lends the colors and intricacies, the purport (as if pure entertainment were not sufficient). Penn uses symbolism in a manner that most brings to mind Kafka—hence the comparison. The Mob becomes the fear and death symbol. Mickey becomes the pawn symbol, the man manipulated by his Times and the pressures of a System he cannot even comprehend, much less fit into. (The parallel to K., the hapless protagonist of THE TRIAL, is inescapable.) The girl becomes the symbol of rationality. The club manager, Fryer (played with some confusion in a shrieking key by the usually memorable Jeff Corey), becomes the element of consciencelessness in modern man, the attitude that it is not the individual's responsibility what horrors are perpetrated on his fellow man.

But even here, in the area of symbolism, an area usually so mystic and clouded by variant definitions, Penn supersedes the trite, and parallels the Kafka implementation of *double-level* representation. For instance:

At oddly disjointed and seemingly irrelevant junctures of the fast-moving plot, a tiny Japanese junk-artist appears, motioning to Mickey One. The comic sees him everywhere: in an alley, beckoning with terrifying immediacy; riding on a junk wagon pulled by a blind white horse (the classic death symbol as typified in Andrzej Wajda's *Ashes and Diamonds*); on a lakefront staging-area in front of Chicago's Marina Towers, displaying a whirling madcap construction of spare junk parts and fireworks; and finally, when Mickey is contemplating suicide, in an automobile destruction yard where cars are squashed into cubes à la *Goldfinger*.

Every time Mickey sees the little Oriental, he flees in panic, and throughout the picture we come to believe the Japanese is Penn's handy pocket symbol of death and pursuing evil. Yet the construction is called YES! and in the end it is the little Japanese man, beckoning to Mickey, standing on the edge of that car-cubing destroyer, who saves Mickey from suicide. And in the final moments of the film we come to the realization that Penn has had us, that we have smoothly swallowed his red herring, that the Japanese artist is literally the manifestation of *Yes!* Yes to life, yes to courage, yes to continuing the fight, yes to fighting conformity and the System, *all* Systems that threaten to deaden and punch-file the individual in an era where the individual is   25 subjected to the rigors of keeping the machinery functioning smoothly.

An example of consummate directorial artistry.

Further indicated in the use of camera and editing. Penn has employed many of the Richard Lester/Sidney Furie/John Schlesinger techniques, but has studiously—and laudably—avoided their excess, their silliness or their bizarre aspects. There are no shots through keyholes, no slantwise camera postures that force one to tilt in the theater seat, no camera obtrusiveness for the sheer sake of *brio*. In point of fact, the dissolve (a sadly-neglected technique) has been utilized much more than the smash-cut or the upside-down camerawork.

(In one shot, Mickey, large in the foreground, stares into a destruction tunnel at the car-squash yard, where a vehicle suddenly erupts in a bouquet of flame. As this shot fades, and the car, tunnel and flames vanish, leaving only Mickey corporeal in the foreground, the incoming shot superimposes, and we see Mickey in the background, walking toward himself, up a dark alley. It is a very poignant and subtle way of showing a man literally looking at himself, studying his past, contemplating his future.)

Kafka's habit of sketching-out the denouement of a story, resolving the problems through the use of absence of resolution, is employed here by Penn, and inherent in this tactic is the seed of the tragedy mentioned above, for it will only serve to confuse the filmgoer who expects everything spelled out for him like a Giant Golden Book. Mickey is on the verge of being murdered by the Mob, and then, suddenly, without warning, he is free, and we see him playing the piano on Chicago's lakefront, the world stretching out all around him, open and free.

But for those who wish to seek beneath the surface, the point is fulsomely made: a man may win his freedom, even through endless flight, if he never turns his back on living, if he insists on saying Yes!

The players are all uniformly well-cast, with Warren Beatty's Mickey possibly the best work he has done to date. Even the labored pseudo-Method *shticks* do not rankle, this time. There is a pathetic quality, a feisty helplessness that Beatty brings to the role that fits glovelike.

Hurd Hatfield plays the club booker with a dash that forces us to wonder why we have seen so little of this brilliant performer. There is just the right nuance of homosexual attraction for Mickey on the part of Hatfield's Castle.

26

Franchot Tone is wasted, both in appearance and in this role, yet his professionalism and dignity manage to illuminate the few minutes onscreen in which his Ruby Lapp mysteriously assumes the mien of a Delphic Oracle.

If there are carps with the film, they are two, and minor. The sound recording is less than good, and with Beatty mumbling and murmuring, many of his pertinent lines (and even the comedic throwaway lines) are lost on the wind. The ending: while I cannot dispute Penn's option to go for artistic integrity, he might have saved this film for the slob mind, had he made Mickey's ultimate release more largely-written, more easily palatable. But this is a strictly commercial objection, product of this reviewer's having worked in the arena and having come to accept much of the totem and taboo as realistic thinking about what an audience will swallow. It has nothing whatever to do with the heart, soul or intent of the creator, and as such, here in these pages, is suspect and invalid.

There is an infinitude of other things to say about *Mickey One*...that it is a peculiarly *American* film, that it could not have been done in any other country with this sort of fidelity and verve, impact and message. That Penn has incredibly become something of an American Fellini, dealing with purely subjective subject matter in a totally objective posture. That the screenwriting is consistently impressive, sometimes almost blindingly so. That the word "pretentious" will be predictably used by every reviewer who cannot summon up enough freedom of horizon to plunge full up to the cerebrum in what the film tries to do. That...

Suffice it to say that *Mickey One* is more than an entertainment, more than a happening. It is a very personal experience, created out of honesty and a sense of purpose. Even were Arthur Penn to proclaim publicly that he hadn't the faintest idea what he was doing, that the entire company merely winged it, the film would still stand unscathed, for I suspect this picture came as much from the dark and mysterious *terra incognita* of the subconscious as from a Hollywood soundstage.

THE WAR LORD

When I was twelve years old, I walked out on a movie. It was *Wuthering Heights*, in its second reissue, at the Park Theater in Painesville, Ohio. I didn't understand it. I am considerably older now, and last night I walked out on my second motion picture. It was Franklin Schaffner's THE WAR LORD. I understood it too well.

There are films that enlighten, that point a moral, that enrich and beguile. There are films that make one think, that tell one something new about the world, that explore a viewpoint fresh and different. There are films that merely entertain. Nothing more is expected of them. But when a film bores, that is the cardinal sin. *The War Lord*, categorically, is the single most boring film I have ever almost seen.

Almost. This review is being written on half a film. I could not endure sitting through any more of it. As it will be my intention here to convince any reader to avoid this abomination, I will not go into great length, save to explain that the plot concerns an 11th century feudal baron (Charlton Heston) who is awarded a dank and ugly little duchy of swamps and fens on the Normandy coast. He spends half his time fending off the barbarian raiders from across the sea, and the other half trying to roll a local pig-girl in the hay.

It is the most obstinately endless film ever made. It has all the appeal of attendance at a snails' convention. Heston looks ten thousand years old in the roast-beef-red color Universal has filmed him. (One gets the distinct impression Heston makes a film a week; last week I saw him in *The Agony and the Ecstasy* and he was brilliant.) Here, he is carved from granite, and about as expressive. Circling Heston's Mt. Everest of impassive taciturnity is a sun about to go nova called Richard Boone. The ex-Paladin stalks about muttering tomfoolery in a very Robert Ruark hairy-chested tone of voice, and never cracks a smile. He is so loud and unappealing, in a role of no merit whatsoever, that one wonders why he took the part. The pig-girl is played in truly underwhelming fashion by Miss Rosemary Forsyth, a creature of pale blue eyes and very little visible talent. Even when she is naked.

Maurice Evans is a shock, Guy Stockwell barely manages to survive, the plot is guaranteed to induce tunnelvision and highway fatigue, the camerawork is uninspired, the sets (built on the back lot at Universal for a staggering sum) are ludicrous, and in all it is a classic example of bringing Universal's TV techniques to the big screen. (How long has it been since you saw that faint flickering purple line around an actor, when he stands in front of a process screen?) They attempt to give the impression of a big budget film, with nine horsemen, seven peasants and a horde of pigs. By moving them around and spacing them out, they have cleverly managed to give the impression of a struck set just before the stragglers sign their chits and go home for the day.

It is possible the film gathered steam in the second half and roared on to be one of the great cinematic presentations of our time, but I will never know. When I found myself yawning, spilling popcorn just to have something to do, and praying for the next scene, *any* scene, I asked myself a question all filmgoers should ask themselves: "Why should I subject myself to this?"

Consistent with the film, I got back an empty answer.

THE BATTLE OF THE BULGE

In sunny Burbank, California, where Pass Avenue intersects Warner Boulevard and Olive Avenue, there is a grass-covered traffic island on which stands a large billboard.

The legend on the billboard reads as follows:

THE HOME OF WARNER BROS. PICTURES
"Combining Good Citizenship With Good Picture Making."
—*N.Y. Times*

A screenwriter of my acquaintance, who had worked at Warners early in the Forties, when that sign was already long a landmark, several years ago (on a return to the lot) happened to mention to Jack L. Warner that the slogan really no longer applied, in that Warners was making "safe" films. Warner's reported reply was, "Let the young ones take the risks; we've got the quote."

The sign is a paint-peeling relic, twenty and more years outdated, a bit of memorabilia that suggests Jack L. Warner has a tendency to live in the past; to let the times pass him by. But for those out there in The Great American Heartland who may never get to that intersection of Burbank thoroughfares, Mr. Warner has seen fit to release an all-talking, all-singing, all dancing epic of modern filmmaking so tuned to the whispers of the dead years, that any who wish may draw their own conclusions as to his harkening-back to the good old days.

So hear ye! Hear ye! Gather 'round and listen to the drum rolls, the rah-ta-tah, the tintinnabulation of patriotism, the gospel of war, according to Jack L.

And at a massed cost of $6,000,000, one might even vouchsafe that World War Two was Mr. Warner's own private imbroglio. For surely no one man has made more bucks off our third most recent firefight than the vociferously-vocal patriot who has caused THE BATTLE OF THE BULGE to be made.

As the credits brochure handed out at the screening informs us, "Mr. Warner viewed the making of *Battle of the Bulge* as an exceptional opportunity to reconstruct one of World War II's most terrifying battlefield engagements, and at the same time he looked upon the picture as a vivid adventure for film audiences, as well as a resounding tribute to the Allied Forces which participated in those fiery days and nights combating the German invaders in the Ardennes."

What the brochure does not bother to tell us is that this is yet another example of Warner's view of Men At War, through glasses which may not be rose-colored, but certainly use a prescription that is thirty years outdated.

There is no need our dwelling at length in these columns on the dishonesty of the picture in terms of historical verisimilitude. The Department of the Army has already made its feelings public, and the shriek of the eagle may be heard abroad in the land. Nor any need to belabor the point that the film was obviously made not because it was "an exceptional opportunity to reconstruct one of World War II's blah blah blah," but because it filled a large hole in the Cinerama production schedule. Make one fantasy, they said, so *The Wonderful World of the Brothers Grimm* was made. Make one comedy, they said, so *It's a Mad, Mad, Mad, Mad World* was made. Make one western, they said, so *How the West Was Won* was made. Make one war picture, they said, so *The Battle of the Bulge* was made.

It is unfortunate no one has said, "Make a good film; forget the Cinerama tricks; forget the roller coasters and the onrushing tanks and the plunging trains and the flung spears; just make a helluva good picture, about people."

There is no need to hammer these points, for they are self-evident in the production. *The Battle of the Bulge* is no more than a 1940s-style soap-opera shoot-'em-up of the type Warners released during the war years. It is bigger, brassier, louder, more colorful, but in the final analysis, it is easily dismissed because it proffers a brand of thinking that is only rational these days for Birchers and dogfaces who look back on WWII as a pleasant experience.

This is not the face of war. The unifying facet of humanity is missing. There are great clots of armored Furies rolling across Belgian terrain, there are the usual stock cliché characters mouthing the usual stock cliché lines (not to be believed: General Grey to Lt. Col. Kiley as Hessler's panzers overrun them, "Looks like he's succeeded this time." Kiley: "He made one mistake." Grey: "What was that?" Kiley, with steely glare: "He got me mad."), and the attempt to convey a sense of order to an engagement that stretched down 85 miles of front and was fought in such a riot of disorder and counterthrust that even today Army historians are still finding missing pieces of the combat picture that explain why we won.

But worse than the Philip Yordan–Milton Sperling–John Melson screenplay that gives us a ludicrous answer to why we were not ground beneath the treads of those elite tanks, is the ancient and creaking philosophy of "propaganda" that suffuses the film, the swindle of hackneyed ideas wrenched whole and corrupt from films made to engender a fighting spirit in a nation at war.

It is a script filled with sound and fury, and like most of its ilk before it, this too is a tale told by an idiot. For Warners has eliminated the *people* in the war, and concentrated on the dubious joys of the spectacle of combat. It is the glorification of madness, without even the saving grace of being able to relate to the motivations of the men involved. Robert Shaw, as the German panzer leader, is wasted in a faceless color-me-rabid portrayal essentially as deep as a dish of tapioca pudding. Fonda, Ryan, Dana Andrews, the incredible Telly Savalas...all! Stick men! You drew them with wide, vapid smiles or beetled brows in your high school notebook. Comic book representations of flesh-and-blood men who lived and feared and came out the other side of the war with character in their faces. Character: something this film lacks in its totality.

A totality that mirrors the Warner slant on war and its fascination for the common man. Every film that spurred us to more and better bombsights, flying forts, M-1 rifles and the firm belief that God was on our side...all the films that said Democracy, Mom's Apple Pie and The American Way Of Life were the 33 answer. The films that lied to us, but served (I suppose) a necessary purpose in their time. But their time is past. Like the aging gunslinger in a settled frontier town, the citizenry does not want to hear how noble it is to die in combat. Or if they don't *want* to hear, they should be *forced* to hear. To hear the messages of *Paths of Glory*—that men are cannon fodder—to hear the shriek of *Dr. Strangelove*—that total war is total insanity—to hear that if we must make war, let us make it quickly and as humanely as possible...perhaps the arteriosclerotic leaders of the major powers out there in the arena, equipped with arbalest and mace, banging each other into senseless surrender. They must be told that we are a poor, puny race not one-millionth as old as the great lizards who died out with each other's fangs in their throats.

They must be told the truth, not the candy-whip fantasies of the Jack Warners, who served their countries in good faith, but must now learn that the time of the gunslingers is past.

Or, to sum it up emblematically: in a cutaway scene in *The Battle of the Bulge*, we are told that Bastogne was an important facet of the battle, and we see a bomb-blasted wall with a sign on it. The sign says THE BATTERED BASHERS OF BASTOGNE. No, Jack L. Warner, with your happy thoughts of bold strong men in combat, they were not called the battered bashers. They were called THE BLOODY BASTARDS OF BASTOGNE and that, *that* is where it's at.

Truth is the only weapon that will save us. This film is a lie, and, as such, is a disgrace to the men who died, and the men who made their story.

JULIET OF THE SPIRITS

Fellini's JULIET OF THE SPIRITS is a hysterical act of confusion.

Having so stated, I will address myself to comments of other critics, who have been in this elevator before me; and having done so, I can go on to some personal specifics I have not seen elsewhere in print.

Ray Bradbury, who reviewed this film for a California newspaper, and conveyed his opinions in conversation to me, made the valid point that, in previous Fellini films, the maestro dealt with hurricanes at the eyes of which were human beings. Cabiria, Zampano, Marcello—each was a fixed centerpost around which all the madnesses danced. But the reactions were those of the principals, and what happened to them mattered a great deal. In *Juliet*, as Bradbury phrases it, "The gargoyles have taken over." The horned gods have deserted Notre Dame to caper and cavort, while the priests are outside in the rain, staring in. Giulietta Masina as Juliet wanders semivacuously through a Hieronymous Bosch landscape, grinning gamely and praying for sudden sunshine. What happens, happens; not to her as much as to the film itself.

Another critic (whose name, I'm sorry, escapes me) made the comment that an overuse of technique does not represent expertise and boldness, but an escape into flummery and flapdoodle.

That the best art, the most carefully-constructed art, is that which does not look like art at all, which looks effortless (e.g., Fred Astaire dancing, Walt Kelly drawing, Vonnegut or Sturgeon writing) until you try it. The technique should not be apparent to the eye. The bones of method and construction should not show through. Another valid point, in the light of *Juliet*, for there the technique is constantly omnipresent—Fellini somewhere in the projection booth reminding us this is his first color film, and look at the coy uses of same.

While I *almost* entirely accept this point of criticism as bravely and succinctly tendered, in its aspects of truth, I reserve a caprice or two of dissenting opinion on grounds of past love. Fellini has delighted and moved me too often to suspect him of total bravura, and nothing else.

But having only recently seen *Modesty Blaise*, with its surfeit of Losey technique...*The Ipcress File* and *Darling* and *Help!* and *The Knack* with theirs...I am compelled to accept the truth of the comment. Trick technique is on the rise; and while there may be those who contend *A Thousand Clowns* was flawed because it was a stage play filmed as a stage play with occasional returns to "the filmed portion of our show," I agree that crotch shots through keyholes as in *The Ipcress File* cannot hold a klieg to straight-on filming of Robards and Barbara Harris discussing the ethical structure of the universe.

To be precise, I am not really sure *what* I think of *Juliet*, which is not really the way to come away from a film. The fault may well be mine, even though it isn't confusion, merely indecision. But this I *do* know:

Fellini has come too far away from the writer as a necessary tool of the film medium. All well and good to say one is setting his innermost psyche down on film, very nice: but where is the story? It is still—and always will be—the job of the storyteller to communicate a pattern of events, a progression of character development, a sense of order and ethic. No matter what medium, the storyteller is the minstrel. He must tell his tale, not merely dazzle with pyrotechnics. Fellini seems to have fallen into the trap (though there are four credits listed for screenplay) of plot-by-committee. He shoots as he goes along, and as a consequence what he has told here is a traditional soap opera: the cheating husband, the wife on the verge of psychosis, the search for meaning, and the eventual realization that life alive is better than life half-dead, living in delusions and dreams. Stella Dallas did it regularly on the radio, and the chief difference between

Stella and Juliet is that Miss Masina had the benefits of a charming Nino Rota soundtrack behind her.

To address myself to the acting, for a moment, much of it seems to me of the "momentary impetus" school. People couple and grin for apparently whimsical reasons, having very little to do with the continuity of the skimpy plot. And this is unquestionably not Miss Masina's kind of picture. In earlier films she was the compleat gamine, a street urchin with a wry and winning smile. Here, she is a weary middle-aged woman, and the revelation is not a charming one. I do not care to see her standing there empty as assorted noxious fluids and vapors are emptied into her.

In a way, she represents in this film what Mia Farrow represents on *Peyton Place*: a necessary vacuum whose removal would impel the instant implosion of all the other hysterical elements spinning around her.

One can never dismiss Fellini. His work is too important. Even when failing, he does so brilliantly. But I would like to offer the suggestion to Fellini, with all due respect, that the time for self-indulgence has passed. He has plumbed his own libido, and sucked out his own id. We have seen his secret dreams and fantasies. We have seen his wife's secret world. I pray to God he has no children, for if he does, then we may look forward to *their* adolescent fantasies. Or, lacking offspring, perhaps we will see the dream life of Fellini's housekeeper, his agent, his barber.

There is too little pure genius doled out in an eon to allow its waste on essentially unworthy projects. Yes, Fellini uses color brilliantly; yes, he knows film as few other directors ever have; yes, he is still the maestro and one cataclysm is not sufficient to sink Atlantis. But there is a cautionary note sounded by the direction and attitude of a film like *Juliet*. It is a discordancy, apparently tuned to the Lesters, the Schlesingers, the Furies, and Fellini.

It is a back-turning on the past, on the validity of already proved methods. It is a losing-touch with the roots of the medium, with the lessons learned by men who were neither afraid nor untalented. And to scoff, as this film seems to do, is to play the clown.

Fellini is too good for that. And to quote Lautrec: "A man may play the fool once, and be excused the rôle; but if he play it more than once, it must be assumed he enjoys the part."

YOU'RE A BIG BOY NOW!

Ten thousand times I have said if it looks like a duck, waddles like a duck, quacks like a duck and goes steady with ducks, chances are it's a duck. Recently, I was wrong. I saw something that looked like a duck, but it's really a turkey.

Fully aware that I am a hostile minority in the country of the blind, I refer to YOU'RE A BIG BOY NOW! which will undoubtedly make twenty-two billion grupniks at the box office and garner

Written 1966, previously unpublished

AUTHOR'S FOOTNOTE, 1988:

The motorist who has been driving erratically and at excessive speeds for years, flouting the law and endangering others, who finally gets pulled over by the Highway Patrol and is ticketed, complains at the injustice because *this* time s/he really *didn't* do anything wrong. There is, however, a kind of cosmic justice at work. The insensate universe struggling toward some kind of balance. It is, how shall we view it...fair. In a cockeyed way. Publication, at last, of this piece I wrote in 1966 is similarly...fair. It is a genuinely dopey review. Apart from the sterling ineptitude I demonstrated here, by managing not to review the film at all—can *you* figure out what the movie is about?—I was dense enough not to perceive any value whatever in the early efforts of Coppola. Somewhere in the latter section of this book, I go off my chump completely and say something like, "I have loved every foot of film Coppola has ever shot." Never having had this earlier piece published, I was able to get away with the panegyric. Unlike politicians running for office, whose sophomoric plagiarisms in college are dredged up to throw mud on their character twenty years later, I got away with it. I can no longer live with the guilt! I was shortsighted and seven kinds of a dolt. Which is not to say that *You're a Big Boy Now!* is much better a film

→

for writer-director Francis Ford Coppola all manner of future assignments. I believe the operable phrase is "bright young man." Wrong. A genuine no-no.

Mr. Coppola's comedy of awakening sexuality and the loss of innocence in Big City U.S.A. is straight CATCHER IN THE RYE derivative, by way of a castrated Tom Sawyer. The words precious, artsy-craftsy, overblown and juicy come to mind. The color is overwhelming.

There is little fresh or innervating in either the screenplay or the attack of this film. It covers ground so heavily-tilled the best that can be harvested is corn. Yet audiences leap and bubble for it. I think the phenomenon is a sad one. Films such as *10:30 PM Summer* and *Mickey One* and even in an alarming number of instances *Blow-Up* are regarded by an American cinemagoing audience with suspicion, hostility and outright confusion, while such films as this, *The Russians Are Coming! The Russians Are Coming!* and *The Fortune Cookie* touch the proper nerve-endings and are rewarded with accolades. They are the common denominator films. They are the idiot comedies, in which no one demonstrates a modicum of intelligence, perspicacity or style. They demand nothing of the viewer. They are merely palatable.

That *You're a Big Boy Now!* is so popular is strident testimony to the accusation that we have become a movie-viewing nation of systematically corrupted taste.

To this echoing tune, Coppola has added his own personal

---

than I said it was (time has not been kind to it, as verified by a recent Late Show tv viewing). I blow the whistle on myself (the slaphappy tone of all this being merely a surface candy-coating) as part of an ongoing need to keep my "credentials" credible. I've written elsewhere about the imperatives of an essayist having no guilty secrets. No matter how small. The urgency of confessional writing. It is the pathological dedication to being non-blackmailable. Especially by oneself. The parallel most applicable, in my experience, is this: once upon a time not that long ago, I was a guest on a national tv talk show. The host is a man whose name is common coin in households where Kafka, Conrad, Paul Muni and Sojourner Truth are unknown. In the course of his oncamera "conversation" with me, I became aware of an animus toward me and what I was saying that perplexed me and seemed unmotivated by what we were actually talking about. I won't be more specific than that, but when next you and I get together, I'll play the videocassette of the show, and you'll see what I mean. It was easily the most awful of the hundreds of such talk show encounters I've had in the last twenty years. And it perplexed me, the more intensely each time I re-ran that tape to attempt some penetration of the mystery. It was not until a friend of the host—whom I met some time later, and with whom I discussed this matter—let me in on the Secret Agenda. Which was that the host is both a seriously practicing Catholic and a practicing homosexual intent on staying in the closet. Understand: neither of these aspects of the man's life, in my view, is a contrapuntal variation. I will not belabor the point nor enumerate the tedious twirls of the plot that compel me to this conclusion, save in remarking that any film that casts Julie Harris as a character named "Miss Thing" is so obviously slanted for the cute and cuddly that it cannot be considered seriously.

Since the film is entirely the work of Coppola, all blame must be laid at his talent. I have heard Mr. Coppola speak on several occasions, stating his thesis of filmwriting, and he makes no secret of the fact that he will write hack in an effort to produce "quality" films of his own design. Mr. Coppola "hacked" on such monumental atrocities as *Is Paris Burning?* and *This Property Is Condemned* and so by action/reaction we should expect a "quality" film of his own vision to be as spectacularly good as the hacks were bad. But we get more of the same, except on a slightly smaller scale.

Rip Torn and Geraldine Page are hideously miscast, and their posturings in parts of little more than imbecile caricature are painful to witness. Elizabeth Hartman doesn't really have the kind of legs needed to wear miniskirts. Michael Dunn is wearing awfully thin indeed, not to mention grating. And poor Peter Kastner, who has some stuff going for him, is weltered down in a quagmire of nonsense and random murmurings that make him appear to be little more than a bifocaled epileptic. Tony Bill . . . well, the less said the better.

And all of that pseudo-Resnais walking through the streets of Manhattan, culminating in a 1930s off-into-the-sunset being

topic for discussion or the judgment of others. Neither as an Atheist nor as a heterosexual do I think being Catholic or gay is something to hide. But in the public spotlight, it is obvious why he feels the need to protect his privacy. And as a result of the ongoing cultural prejudices against either or both of these life-choices, can you imagine the hell in which he dwells every day? He has to pretend to be straight, lest he suffer the hellfire of his religion; and he has to conceal both from a viewing audience that might well become less enamoured of him. And because of this need to keep his secrets, his oncamera attitudes toward many guests and many philosophical positions become tortured, even warped in their logic. He is, sadly, innocently and tormentedly, a man who self-censors because he is blackmailable. In protecting his "guilty secrets," which in a sane world would produce neither guilt nor opprobrium, he produces "work," i.e., conversation, that is dishonest. For a writer, such guilty secrets can be crippling. The more one has to conceal about oneself, the more often one shies away from writing the burning truth about those dangerous areas, either consciously or unconsciously. The only way to insure that the writer goes as close to the fire as s/he can, is to hold nothing back, to tell it all, to reveal one's pimply ass to the world. This is considered suspect in many literary circles, and at least an act of gauche tastelessness. In England, for instance, when

———————⟶

dragged by a slobbering nitwit of a dog, was more treacle than my doctors will allow me to consume.

The only saving grace of the film is the brilliant and youthful score by John Sebastian of The Lovin' Spoonful. The songs are memorable, they capture the mood that Coppola may have intended but thoroughly failed to inject into his film, and they are well worth going to hear. But as I said in a recent record review of the soundtrack album, the Spoonful's music is so good it shucks one into believing the film has merit, when in truth it is roughly akin to having a Rolls Royce grill braised onto the front of an Edsel.

---

my short story collections are published, the U.K. editors insist that the introductions and sometimes the foreword be dropped. On the well-founded belief that such revelations of personal involvement with the fiction will offend critics and even readers. I've ceased arguing with them, having indeed suffered scathing negative reviews from English critics who spent the bulk of their copy on what an impertinent self-server I am, without spending much copy actually addressing the quality of the stories. Nonetheless, I believe to my shoe-tops that it is imperative for my "credentials" that I try to conceal nothing that will compel me to slide past a difficult subject. I am as weak and as strong in this respect as you, and I know how easily our species twists reality to make ourselves look good. As Olin Miller has written: "Of all liars, the smoothest and most convincing is memory." (Miller also said, "Writing is the hardest way of earning a living, with the possible exception of wrestling alligators," but that's quite another matter.) So I try not to give myself the opportunity of concealing even the few personal flaws that are not enormous enough for the most casual reader to perceive without a road map. This rambling footnote—size 20 triple-E by this time—thus goes directly to that auctorial policy. You might never remember, by the time you get to my praise of Coppola later in these pages, that at age thirty-two, more than twenty-two years ago, I wrote such a dippy analysis of one of the great film directors. But you might; and if you didn't, I would.

This is why murderers who've gotten away with it for a lifetime suddenly rush into a police station to confess.

BEAU GESTE

Universal's re-remake of BEAU GESTE, the venerable P. C. Wren tale of derring-do and swashbucklery at Fort Zinderneuf, will no doubt be summarily dismissed by the "serious" critics of cinema, both here and abroad. Such dismissal is not entirely unjustified. It is a well that has long-since run dry. But in the interests of fair play and offbeat comments guaranteed to startle, this reviewer would like to dwell on four points. Perhaps someone will take note.

First. This started out as a well-done version of the hoary old story of the brothers who wind up in the command of a sadistic Foreign Legion sergeant. It was a gratuitously emasculated version of the original story, done brilliantly not once, but twice before. One entire brother was omitted, the theft of the jewel was omitted, plot twists were omitted *en masse*. But nonetheless, it held the interest. It was nicely mounted. Until Doug McClure walked on the screen. Everyone in the theater laughed. Now before there is instant assumption that I am going to pan McClure, let me assure the readership that he performed more than adequately. He did all that could be done with the part doled out to him, a role whose dimensions were as vast as the horizon line in Bosnia. But McClure was laughed at. People smiled as he tended the sick brother lying in his bunk. They snickered and found the corners of their mouths turning up. It ruined the mood of the story. The reason for this unrestrained mirth contains a key to the senseless casting currently being done at Universal, and it contains a dire warning to either Mr. McClure or his agent, since his studio obviously cannot see what is right in front of them.

McClure is the most natural, most certain, most exquisite comedic talent to come along since Cary Grant grew gray in the service. He is what Rod Taylor has tried to be, what James Garner has failed miserably at being, what Tony Randall grows too raucous really ever to be, what Jack Lemmon does very well indeed. He is a *funny* man. A handsome, athletic, all-around leading man with a built-in laughmaker. When McClure walks onscreen, people sit up and *want* to laugh. To cast him in deadly serious roles where his grimacing and Superman good looks are incongruous is in the nature of a capital crime.

Had Universal one whit the intelligence they pretend to possess, they would launch McClure instantly in a series of big-budget sophisticated comedies, sit back and rake in the dividends. A word to the wise...

Second. The film inevitably falls before the derision of the audience, because it is fifty years out-of-date. It devolves on points of "old school tie" honor, of stiff-necked patriotism to hollow causes, of the sort of "into the valley of death" horse manure no audience of 1966 is going to accept. Not when they are faced full daily with a dirty, and some say immoral, war on the front pages of their newspapers. No one is going to accept the nobility of dying in the saddle (a scene Leslie Nielsen, who is far better than that, should have refused to play) when they can see newsphotos of bombed-out schools and churches with innocent civilians napalmed and disemboweled. No one *really* believes, any longer, that war is noble, that the *esprit de corps* is excuse for atrocity and stupidity and following atrocious, stupid rules of combat. Which brings us inescapably to the most important point about this film, which is

Third. The practice—often lamented in these pages—of remaking films that were made as classics originally. *Stagecoach*, *She*, *Room for One More*, *Mutiny on the Bounty*, *Rashomon*, and now *Beau Geste*: each of these was made the first time out as well as it could ever be made. Each has had a new edition released in the last few years and each one, without exception, has been an artistic disaster. The strangling stench of venality behind these remakes is so gagging that only the horse-blindered producers

44

who have fostered them could hope to accept the hypocrisy of their being brought into being. And only these same men could hope to swallow the rationalizations used to ballyhoo weak excuses for their latest incarnations.

If the film industry does not stop this ceaseless, senseless cannibalization of its own body, it will disenchant the filmgoing audience beyond hope of recall. How much longer can audiences be expected to swallow the patent lies of four-color lithography and slanted *Coming Attractions*? How much longer can people be expected to invest their trust, their ticket money, their time and their sense of wonder in shabby redone warhorses butchered by second-rate visionaries? What dreadful ghouls imagine they can match the marvels wrought for us first time out by Kurosawa, Ford, Laughton, Gable, John Wayne or Thomas Mitchell? What front-office callousness can be deemed even remotely acceptable for the production of inferior versions of treasured classics held dear in memory by movie lovers; films whose discovery by younger generations has been irrevocably lost or mutilated by the release of witless surrogates, merely for the money to be gained from a shameful resort to the reputation of the former version?

It is a disgrace the industry continues to flaunt in the faces of cinemaphiles who have deplored it for many years.

And fourth. Sympathy is herewith extended to Nielsen, McClure, Guy Stockwell, Telly Savalas and a fine supporting cast, who have been made to play a microcephalically written screenplay of sheerest ineptitude. The clichés roll off the typewriter of this film's Phantom Author like squares of toilet paper.

There are few excuses suitable for a scenarist who has turned out a script of this caliber. If he is a wise man he will spread the rumor that he was hammerstunned drunk throughout the entire period of scripting. In which case someone ought to offer him a better grade of panther sweat.

UP THE DOWN STAIRCASE

It certainly didn't begin with Mr. Luce and his bogus posed photograph of "beatniks in their natural habitat"—nor even with Harriet Beecher Stowe's fraudulent UNCLE TOM'S CABIN, purporting to be the gospel on how it was for de darkie way down South—but it was that particular Lucely manifestation of yellow journalism that surely brought it to its fullest flowering. (And he's still at it; a recent issue of *Time* features a ghastly slanted takeout on the hippies, once again ornamented by posed photographs purporting to be accurate representations of the hippie life and ethic, and are no more representative than Mamie Van Doren is representative of the Average American Housewife.)

What I'm plodding toward, of course, is the strange and frightening tendency adrift in the land, lo these last eighteen years, for nature to imitate art. *Life* ran the phony beatnik photo, and within months, every one of Kerouac's proselytizers—people who had not lived that way prior to the publication of the photograph though they might have subscribed to the "beat philosophy"—were existing in squalor that could have been a *Doppelgänger* for the *Life* environment. (And though the author of UNCLE TOM'S CABIN had never been any farther South than Ohio, Americans everywhere accepted her view of conditions and acted upon it, thereby precipitating, in part, the Civil War.)

Nature imitating art, rather than the reverse. An artificial reality accepted as an existing condition, rather than truth based upon observation. Nature imitating art, a flagrant warping of a natural state traditional since man first observed the wild dog and scratched its likeness on a limestone wall. (And spare me analogies of primitive man exercising his imagination on those same walls. He may have envisioned a seven-headed Cerberus, but that didn't *poof!* call one into existence.)

Now we subsist in a world molded by show biz; predicated on the huckster's image of us; preshrunk and plastic packaged. Everything that does not conform to this insanity seems bogus to us. It seems sometimes that believability is inversely proportional to the amount of bullshit suffusing it. The boundaries of shadow and reality have blurred, thereby causing us to wander terrified through a truly schizoid culture. Shadow, reality, they are now one and the same.

So who is to say: is the reality UP THE DOWN STAIRCASE or is it *The Blackboard Jungle*?

Who are the real kids in the schools? Bel Kaufman's tragic and somehow strangely winsome Alice Blake, her feral Joe Ferone, her demeaned yet noble Jose Rodriguez? Or Evan Hunter's stereotyped Negro, Greg Miller, his clichéd psychopath, Artie West (who could have been written for the young Vic Morrow, so pat was the image of a teenaged giggling killer; a post-puberty Johnny Udo as seen by Widmark)? Which image is more relevant of teachers today? Richard Brooks and Glenn Ford's Mr. Dadier, or Robert Mulligan and Sandy Dennis's Miss Barrett?

In the answer to these questions—and they're all the same question, obviously—we strike to the heart of the nature of responsibility of our cinematic creators. In the answer we can judge whether our universal prurience is being jellied or our spirits uplifted. The answer tells us whether we have become a filmgoing nation addicted to the cheap, the sensational, the fraudulent... or if we are capable of recognizing truth when it is presented to us.

It also indicates a safe path down which we can pass to discover which films are "good" and which are "bad."

That Evan Hunter's novel, on which *Blackboard Jungle* was based, was entirely a product of the author's imagination (as was his North Trades Manual High School, a creation that resembles not at all the New York technical high where Hunter put in a scant few weeks as a summer replacement) is not terribly relevant. The authors of the film could have opted for realism, rather than accepting the whole cloth presented to them. There *was* an option at the time. Now there is none. So the relevancy of the basic source's verisimilitude is academic, even as the authenticity of *Staircase*'s Calvin Coolidge High School is irrelevant. Pakula and Mulligan chose to go where it was happening. They employed authoress Bel Kaufman—seventeen years in metropolitan school systems as opposed to Hunter's brief and unhappy stint—as technical advisor. They did not cast Vic Morrow and Sidney Poitier and a host of overage Hollywood character types in T-shirts and jeans more suitable to lounging around Schwab's than slouching schoolroom desks. They interviewed school kids in New York, and hired them. They did not shoot on soundstages outside which the California popcornland lay drowsing dreamily; they did not shatter their illusion when lunch break was called and the finger-poppers dashed to phone their agents. They shot among the scrawled walls and rotting stairways of New York schools.

Some things are relevant. Others are not.

The inevitable product, of course, is what must finally furnish the answer we desperately need. By now, with late late movies doing the saturation for us, we have all seen *The Blackboard Jungle*. We remember the shapely teacher straightening the seam of her nylon beside the staircase, and then the attempted rape. We remember Glenn Ford's fight with Vic Morrow at knifepoint in the classroom. And we remember a somehow incongruously overage Sidney Poitier doing the best he could to look heroic and noble with Ford as sort of a Black Man's Burden. We remember violence, a touch of sex, some phony pittypat dialogue, a school filled with psychos, junkies, prostitutes, Machiavellian teenaged blackmailers, vandals, imbeciles and assorted rejects.

What story does *Up the Down Staircase* tell, by comparison? There is blessed little violence. Nothing a healthy peruser of *Playboy* could call sex. The talk is everyday, even as you or I, so that don't get it. And the kids who pass through this story seem like individuals, not archetypes. So what is there to remember about this film? And in the memory, do we find our answer?

The most repetitious memory, the one to which the mind turns without volition, is the feeling of helplessness for the children. They are boxed in. They attend school but learn only by chance, almost—it seems—despite the System. They come to the world wide open, and find it closed to them. The teachers they encounter range from inept and outright criminally untalented to devoted, dedicated and brilliant. But the film denies us the flight of fancy offered by most artless creations in this genre: there can never truly be a happy ending. If they learn by wild chance, by happenstance encounter, then the conclusion is inevitable: most of them will never learn. They will come away from the school encounter perhaps even less equipped than when they began.

This is something concrete the film tells us. That our educational system is unconscionably inadequate and outdated and gross. *The Blackboard Jungle* never had that to say. The most important statement of all, and it chose to tell, rather, of gangbangs in the wood shop.

Following closely on the initial memory is the recollection of the kids themselves, who they are, their inability to communicate, their hostility, their suspicion. Another strong statement that strikes directly to the heart of the problem of silence between the generations. Buried within the attitudes manifested by the kids in *Staircase* are the seeds of the hippie movement, the concepts of flower power and the love generation. All the lies and obfuscations the kids are forced to submit to, in the name of "getting an education," have poisoned them; the withdrawal symptoms are called hippies, protests, credulity gaps, getting high, dropping out. By studying the characters portrayed in *Staircase*, any forward-looking educator (and every square momma and daddy who just doesn't understand what all this long hair and hippie nonsense is all about) can make the linkages with the realities through which they move daily. One can get none of this from *Blackboard Jungle*.

Then there is the acting. Oddly, one tends to remember the amateurs in *Staircase*, rather than the professionals. Eileen Heckart, Sandy Dennis, Sorrell Booke, all do fine jobs (though I wish to God someone would tell Sandy Dennis that a persistent stammer, a waving of arms and invariably moist eyes does not necessarily connote deep intense feelings, but merely a studied inarticulateness that wearies as time passes). But it is the helpless character played by Ellen O'Mara that thrusts up from all the wonders of *Staircase* with a fragile strength that will remain with the viewer long after the subtleties of plot have faded.

Miss O'Mara's background and biography were sadly neglected in the Warner Bros. handouts on the film, so I have no idea if she is a student actress, a novice hired out of a Manhattan schoolroom, or possibly Dame Edith Evans in disguise. All I can say is that for me, her portrayal of the lovesick high school girl,

50

doomed to a life trapped in a body shaped like a pound of mud, hopelessly infatuated with an English teacher who is a coward and in many ways a rotter, was the high point of the film. It captured for all time the plight of an unlovely child in a world that is geared for the Pretty Plastic People. Her performance is worthy of much more than merely a nomination for the debased Oscar, but as that is the only yardstick we have at present, certainly that, at least, is due her.

The other younger actors—Jeff Howard, Jose Rodriguez, John Fantauzzi—and the ones who played Harry A. Kagan, Rusty, Lou Martin, Linda Rosen—all sparkle and glimmer as they perform the most difficult task an actor can undertake: to instill individual character into the personality of an unformed entity. Children have no real style, no real pattern. They cannot be tagged on sight the way adults can. They have no real touches with the master world. To indicate this, and yet separate each one as a human being with a face and a name and a way to go, is an enormously difficult chore. It has been done not once or twice in *Staircase*, but almost a dozen times. What do we remember of *Blackboard Jungle*? Poitier? Morrow? Rafael Compos? Certainly not Ford.

Which brings us full circle to nature imitating art. After *Blackboard Jungle*, all depictions of schools where the underprivileged were concerned modeled themselves after the inaccurate Richard Brooks high school. And soon, the reality came into being. The kids acted that way, the teachers accepted it as truth, the parents shuddered at all the knifeplay in the halls of academe, and it became a *fait accompli*. *Staircase* mirrors reality. It shows us what our schools have become. It does not belabor us with plot, therefore I have not bothered explicating the minimal twists and turns of same, but forces us by holding us roughly by the neck, to watch the kind of nightmare world in which the kids of today must function for eight hours, five days a week.

I submit *Up the Down Staircase* is a film that approaches perfection. It entertains, certainly, but it fulfills even more of the criteria for perfection: it stimulates, it touches, it understands, it deals with truth on several levels. It is my understanding that *Staircase* has not done smash b.o. business. It has done reasonably well in its first runs, but it is by no means one of the big smasheroo hit successes of the year. It does not approach *Blackboard Jungle* for public acclaim.

And therein lies the answer to the questions posed earlier anent the debasement of taste of the American filmgoing public.

ROSEMARY'S BABY

As a writer of fantasy, I cannot conceive of any way in which
ROSEMARY'S BABY could be improved. It is, for this reviewer, one
of the very finest fantasy films ever made. The promise of Roman
Polanski remains undimmed. The talent he displayed with *Re-
pulsion* is more controlled, more adroit, certainly more impressive here. The acting is beyond reproach: not only Mia Farrow
and John Cassavetes, who are so right they ring like finest
crystal, but a cast of the most exemplary character actors working at the top of their form; to be treated to the likes of Ruth
Gordon, Sidney Blackmer (oh, that glorious professional!), Ralph
Bellamy, Maurice Evans, Patsy Kelly and (unparalleled joy!)
Elisha Cook, all in one film, all *working*, is to know up front that
the vehicle rolls on the safest treads.

I will not deal with the plot. For those who read Ira Levin's
masterful novel (the best contemporary fantasy since Fritz
Leiber's CONJURE WIFE), be apprised it is followed faithfully.
Polanski, who both scripted and directed, is a friend to the
often-ignored novelist whose work is sold to films and then
masticated so thoroughly that even Shakespeare had "additional
dialogue." For this alone Polanski deserves hosannahs.

For those who have not read the book, and have not had the
film's puzzle explained to them by blathering reviewers who

should know better (lop off their hands!), best you go to it fresh and unsullied. For those who have heard descriptions of what it's all about, merely this: the film is about a girl named Rosemary who gives birth to a child, and is not happy about it, for reasons no one could consider anything less than horrendous.

It is difficult for me not to rush into the streets to sing the praises of this remarkable and compelling film, a darkling vision of unforgettable tension. It is the sort of film Hitchcock would be making today, had he not grown old along about *The Man Who Knew Too Much*. Polanski has not taken on the Old Master's mantle, he has created his own, with the warp and woof of black magic, danger, the essence of fear and a sinister simplicity that is like all great Art—so deceptively simple-looking, until one tries to take it apart and find out why it functions as well as it does, without any moving parts.

It would have been incredibly easy for a director as brash as Polanski—who would have had to be infinitely less talented—to muck this film up. All the elements for cheap sensationalism are there. But with the lean, hard scripting (idiomatically so American one wonders how Polanski managed such a flawless translation...until one considers Nabokov) and the fiercely underplayed acting, Polanski has spun out his tale dualistically—both as story of growing suspense and as study of young girl going psychopathically paranoid. It can be enjoyed thoroughly from the first moment, with none of the fantasy elements yet making their appearance, simply as an interesting mainstream story of a young married couple; evocative testament to the excellence of Miss Farrow's and Mr. Cassavetes's sturdy, craftsmanlike, entirely engrossing performances. A word more about Miss Farrow later.

Polanski. Jesus, the man is good! Let me tell you a thing: in all the canon of fantasy writing, the very hardest job of all is the creation of a contemporary fantasy, using the elements of ancient myth or folklore—gnomes, witches, demonology, dragons, dryads, mermaids—in such a way that the old horrors have relevance for our times. The new demons are with us, yet they are merely manifestations of the old deities. Today we tremble before the wrath of the gods of Neon, Smog, Freeway, Street Violence; the God of Machines and the Paingod, the God in the slot machine and that most jealous of Gods who needs to be worshipped daily, The All-Seeing Eye of the Teevee. These gods and demons can frighten us out of our minds where vampires and werewolves cannot. Polanski knows this. He has been constructing with his last three films a modern grimoire utilizing these ancient, dust-and-hoar-covered legends in their modern settings. And he has become a master at it. This is a task of great rigor, but Polanski has somewhichway tapped into the bubbling lava of fear down in the gut of all of us.

Additionally, the film is filled with a thousand goodies: the dichotomous artificiality of the apartment settings in which Miss Farrow and Mr. Cassavetes play out their nightmare. The rooms seem to be setups for *House Beautiful*; nothing could be more apple pie American in this day and age of materialism. Decorator furniture, mentions of Vidal Sassoon, Lipton Tea, the *Reader's Digest*: against which a crawling horror takes hideous shape. Even the usually-detrimental use of a publicized pretty (in this case the 1967 *Playboy* Playmate of the Year, the staggeringly attractive Angela Dorian) works to full advantage. Miss Dorian underplays and *acts*, seeming at once winsome and touching. Her exit from the film has genuine impact, extraordinary for the brief space of time she is actually onscreen.

But it is Mia Farrow who carries the production. No mean feat working chockablock with such inveterate and splendidly adept scene-stealers as Ruth Gordon, Blackmer and Bellamy. She is the exhibitor of a kind of tensile strength that I have seldom seen in recent years. Her characterization is fleshed-out completely. There will be no man in the audience who could doubt her selection by the father of the baby as his mate. What she never seemed to possess on television, even at her best, *presence*, she exhibits here with controlled passion. There can be no doubt after this film: Mia Farrow is an *actress*.

For those who need specific statements, who have not yet been able to grasp that this reviewer was knocked out by *Rosemary's Baby*, let me conclude by saying quite boldly: this film will be looked back upon with growing recognition as the years pass. It is in every way and by every standard of critical judgment, a classic of that most intriguing of genres, the film of fear.

LES CARABINIERS

Jean-Luc Godard's 1963 film is an exercise in audacity. It is also, like Kubrick's *2001: A Space Odyssey*, an exercise in directorial self-indulgence. It is, in many ways, an exercise in idiocy.

Life is too short. To be bored for even 79 minutes is too long. I await the *thunk* of poison-tipped arrows. The critics have acclaimed LES CARABINIERS a small masterpiece; friends whose cinematic opinions I respect, have labeled me a lout; followers of my reviews have accused me of carrying a grudge against Godard since I proclaimed I'd felt shucked at *Breathless*. I stand naked before mine enemies. Perhaps the nictating membranes that slip down over my eyes when I am being stoned into sleepiness by an "art film" have obscured my appreciation of a stunning experience. Perhaps. I suggest those who find this deprecating review of M. Godard's pud-pulling unacceptable, cross check with less-Philistinic reviewers and then go or not go accordingly. I can only report what I can report: and what I report is that this is an elaborate fraud, the practice of which by an American filmmaker would bring forth howls of outrage by the selfsame dilettantes who foam and fawn over Godard's silliness, merely because it is in French.

Disjointed, spastic, directorially on a level with the famous Candy Barr epic, *Smart Aleck*, self-consciously acted, it makes a point that was dulled along about the time William March wrote "Company K"; the point being that war is absurd. Oh, really! Don't tell that to Aristophanes, M. Godard, he thought *he* pointed that out with skill in "Lysistrata." War is absurd? Never been said before so powerfully (according to the critics)? What about *Dr. Strangelove*? What about *Paths of Glory*? What about *King and Country, How I Won the War, The Brave Italian People*? No, I'm afraid not. Which is not to say that Godard, or anyone else, shouldn't try. Saying what has been said already is an accepted attack; only the final product need be judged. By that standard, Godard fails dismally.

We open with two military police, *carabiniers*, visiting a rural hovel to deliver conscription letters from "the King." How do they do it? They charge in, Sten guns at the ready, and chivvy the women. With a certain pardonable crankiness, the husband of the house attacks one of the soldiers. They struggle and wrestle about on the ground (save for an instant when M. Godard's camera picks up the actors relinquishing their holds on one another to smirk awkwardly, as though "Cut!" had been called...then they go back at it again, once the husband has jammed his cigar in his mouth). The other soldier comes to his buddy's rescue. The four people on the farm are then held at gunpoint while one of the *carabiniers* lifts the women's skirts with the muzzle of his Sten. (And I can understand why these particular soldiers lose the war, for they don't even know how high to lift a girl's skirt to ascertain the worthiness of the goods. Calf-high just don't get it, fellahs.)

Then, with total lack of sanity, the husband invites the marauders into the house. They begin flirting with his wife. They laugh at him, whisper at his stupidity, and tell him if he becomes a soldier and goes to war he can steal, kill, maim and in every other way indulge his adolescent dreams of rape and pillage with impunity. This is more than enough provocation for the husband and his *lumpen* son (brother? friend? farmhand?) to rush off to the Holy Crusade. For the balance of the film we see these two basest evocations of the mud-condemned nature of Man shoot unarmed women, harass civilians, steal and kill and rut about like the foremost clots in the bloodstream of humanity.

Upon their return to the farm, the husband brings a satchel filled with all the treasures he has been promised by the recruiters. Cars, hydroelectric plants, pyramids, naked women, seaplanes, Tiffany's department store...all on picture postcards. This is to indicate to us that all of these treasures will be conferred on the brave warriors when they get in touch with the King. Sort of title deed by photo. But the war isn't over, and finally they are shot to death by the very *carabinierie* who recruited them.

Moral: If you believe all the shit the military feeds you in order to get you to re-up, you deserve anything you get. Or maybe it's: Those who live by the absurd, will die by the absurd.

In all fairness, I must confess to having been enthralled by a scene in which Wilfred *Lumpen* goes to his first movie. He sees the attractive strumpet in her bath. She goes offscreen to the right, and he moves far to the left, crawling over other patrons, in order to see around the corner of her bathroom. She comes back and goes offscreen left, he moves right. When she settles into her tub, he stands on the seat, so he can see down in. When that isn't elevated enough, he climbs up on the stage, begins pawing at her image, and finally crashes through the screen. There is a mad, Jacques Tati feeling to this sequence, and it is superbly done.

Again, in all fairness, I must confess to a recurring nibble at the back of my mind by the subdued Kafkaesque after-impression the film has given me. There is no doubt that Godard has tried to capture in 79 minutes the total insanity of men who think there is either nobility or personal aggrandizement in war. There are scenes that almost succeed in this vein: the shooting of the partisan girl who recites a poem to the grinning faces of the execution squad...the husband's attempt to buy a Maserati with his conscription letter...an unrelated shot of the two swine soldiers speeding toward us down a road in a motorcycle and sidecar...

But the surrealism of the conception clashes with the inter-cutting of stock combat footage, with the asinine overplaying of the actors, with the unbelievably moronic subtitling (*merde* does not translate as "darn it"), by the wandering microcephalic eye of the camera which focuses on empty sky or fields for no apparent reason.

On one end of the stick we have this film, and on the other we have *The Green Berets*. Which is worse? Is there a coherent answer? History has not provided one. Contemporary events certainly don't. It is, perhaps, inescapable to observe that war is such a crippling, imbecilic endeavor that even those who wish to put an end to it, who wish to point up its essential inhumanness, become as ridiculous, as ineffectual as those who prosecute the wars. Is it, possibly, that we have all had our fill of war? To such an extent that films like *Les Carabiniers*, *Dark of the Sun*, *The*

59

Green Berets, The Longest Day and all the way back to Robert Taylor manning his last machine gun on *Bataan* all become one; extended scenes in a film of no consequence whatsoever save to illuminate the fact that Man, unlike the lowest forms of animal life, never seems to learn from his mistakes?

DIVERS PUBLICATIONS

HARD CONTRACT

Fontenalle, French man of letters and aphorist, once proffered the definition of the creator as genius if he could "interpret abstract theory in a manner to wring the emotions." If we can credit this definition with any validity, then S. Lee Pogostin, the creator of a new film titled HARD CONTRACT, is indeed not only a genuine genius, but a cinematic emotion-wringer of the first order.

For *Hard Contract* is the interpretation of the McLuhan theory that megadeath and overkill, mass media and the "cool" values of residents in the Global Village, have made murder not quite moral... but at least not quite so immoral. *Hard Contract* is that incredible rarity, a film of entertainment that comes to grips with second- and third-level philosophical concepts. A film of meaning. In short, something for the mind to masticate, as different from everything that has gone before in film as Poe was different from everything that had gone before in the short story.

But there will be a fight across the body of this film. Not only among those who find the mere concept of murder-as-an-irrelevancy odious, but among the locust horde of film reviewers who will find little trickery but overmuch honesty in this, a film for *people*, but certainly not for professional commentators.

For the film breaks almost every ironclad rule of not only

traditional moviemaking, but of the *cinema verité* hornbook as well. Pogostin has, in point of fact, struck directly to the heart of the visual media by excluding, exorcising, denying and ignoring every hoary time-bleached cliché of scripting. His characters never say what is expected of them; as Pogostin phrases it: "When we see a scene in which a man and a woman are taking leave of a second man, and the men exchange the amenities, the banalities—'I'll see you tomorrow.' 'Yes, I'll see you at 3:00.' 'Take care of yourself.'—the audience has been conditioned by decades of films to *ignore* the words, and to *see* the way the second man looks at the first man's woman. In that look we know we are seeing the essence of the scene. All else is background noise. It is nonverbal communication, the essence of the visual expression."

And so, in *Hard Contract*, the characters seem to speak and act in a lean, sparse manner, moving along a plotline which is at best lightly sketched. And because of the innovative manner in which the characters seem to float in a kind of thespic "free fall," the audience is held much more tightly, straining forward to *hear* every word that is said. The best analogy would be the old saw about the only way to keep a bird from flying off is to hold it loosely in one's hand.

The plot, such as it is, concerns John Cunningham, a professional assassin. The compleat professional. A man so empathically tuned to his victims that—as we see in the opening sequence—he is able to stalk his victim by *preceding* him from a lunch counter to a skin flick theater, *knowing* the hit will go to the theater.

Cunningham—played no better or worse by James Coburn than any other role in which Coburn plays Coburn as himself (and, in fact, playing him precisely as he did the knife-wielding cowboy in *The Magnificent Seven*)—is assigned to murder three men in Europe. One in Spain, one in Brussels, and one as yet unlocated. In the process of stalking his Spanish hit, Cunningham becomes inextricably involved with a twice-divorced and highly-neurotic jet set beauty, played by Lee Remick. Till this girl, Cunningham's relations with women were as coldly professional as the novocained nerve he brought to the art of killing. But though he has always kept his emotions compartmentalized away from the whores who serviced him, and though she has never had an orgasm with a man, despite two marriages, something special happens between them, and Cunningham is suddenly stripped like a high tension wire and the bare copper exposed to caring.

From that point on, Cunningham's *modus operandi* deteriorates. He becomes steadily less a killing machine, an automaton of massacre, and more a human being. Until he is confronted, in the culminating scenes (played with bravura by Sterling Hayden, surely one of the finest and most underrated actors this country has ever produced) with *another* concept—this time one of behavioral psychology: it doesn't really matter what dark motives cause you to do wrong, to *stop* doing it, one first *stops*, then finds out why. In the abstract, the concept is fascinating, but set in the narrative arena of the numero uno killer facing the man who was numero uno twenty years before, it becomes compelling drama.

The strengths of Pogostin's personal vision are not merely in the complexities and innovations of the script. His direction—with the exception of one rather awkward scene in the bar of a hotel in Spain—is masterful, often daring, always clean and direct. Even audacious:

In Madrid's Prado, Pogostin must impart the core heartmeat of the "cool" overkill philosophy. It is an inordinately long vocalization of the basic theory, spoken by Cunningham's superior, Burgess Meredith (who is, as usual, merely excruciatingly excellent). Another director, surfeited with the Richard Lester trickytoe technique, would have whipped here and there, intruding camera and self. But Pogostin fills his screen with Goya's "Firing Squad," a curiously affecting manifestation of death as a repellant. Then, holding his camera absolutely still, in noble defiance of all the tenets of directing, moves his players in and out, back and forward, offscreen and on, in front of the huge painting. Even during the screening I attended—with an audience noted for its bad manners—I heard not a sound throughout the scene. A very long scene of pure information.

Irrefutable evidence of Pogostin's singular talent as a director is offered by the performance he pulls from Lee Remick, an actress who, in the past, has risen to excellence but rarely. Due either to the unexpected nature of reactions in Pogostin's script, or his charisma as a mover of players, Miss Remick's performance here is a *rara avis*, as flowing as silk, as mercurial as quicksilver, as delicious as strawberry soup.

It is rare as the auk to encounter the first major film of a director as scintillant, as compelling, as memorable as this. Surely the same critical reviewers and audience who overlooked or bum-rapped *Mickey One, Paths of Glory* and *Pretty Poison*, but who leaped with cries of joy on *The Graduate* and *Guess Who's*   65

Coming to Dinner? (two of the classic cop-outs of our time), will find *Hard Contract* the sort of picture they can neither dismiss out-of-hand nor champion with honest passion. It is the sort of picture that will force the fence-sitters to sit silently, the splinters paining them, as they inquire of one another, "Did I like that film?"

And they are to be pitied. For this is a film intended as a banner for a new generation of thinking, yet passionate, men. It comes before the filmgoer with all the verve and honesty of commitment, all the style and technique of an original mind, with pain and expertise and experience, and hope for a clearer understanding of ourselves in the Global Village. It offers not merely questions, but some solid answers. And it is entertainment of a rare high order.

In short, despite arguments to the contrary, this is a film not to be missed. The word through the underground, and the lines outside the Bruin Theater every night, indicate this to be so. For not to have seen *Hard Contract* this year is to be something less than *au courant*.

And in this long-fanged jungle world, not to be *au courant* is to be defenseless prey. You have been warned.

HARLAN ELLISON'S HANDY GUIDE TO *2001: A SPACE ODYSSEY*

Open to a portrait of the reviewer as a name-dropper:

So I'm sitting in Canter's at three in the morning, with Sal Mineo, and we're having matzoh ball soup and some conversation, when over walks Rob Reiner, and the first thing out of Rob's mouth is, "Did you see *2001*, and wasn't it a groove?" I sit quietly, spooning in bits of kreplach and hoping he won't ask again.

Mineo chimes in, "FanTASTic flick!"

I chew my matzoh ball.

They then launch into a highly-colorful conversation about the psychic energy of the film, how it obviously applies to the ethical structure of the universe as expressed in the philosophy of the Vedantist movement, and the incredibly brilliant *tour de force* of Nietzsche-esque subplotting Kubrick pulled off. My gorge becomes buoyant. I can no longer deal with the realities of good Yiddish cooking in the presence of such rampant hypocritical hyperbole.

"Listen, you two loons," I begin politely, "you haven't the faintest idea what you're talking about. *2001* is a visually-exciting self-indulgent directorial exercise by a man who has spent anywhere from ten to twenty-five million dollars—depending on whom you're talking to—pulling ciphers out of a cocked hat because he lost his rabbits somewhere."

They stare at me.

It is maybe because in the telling, I have confounded my syntax to the point where even *I* don't know what I just said. "Well, uh, what did it, uh, mean...to...you...?" Rob Reiner asks, a bit timorously.

So I explain the picture to them.

And then I realize it is the nineteenth time I've explained it to people in the week and a half since I saw the damned film, and once again I'm explaining it to people who came on like gangbusters with their total understanding and involvement with what Kubrick was "saying." I realize I am sick to tears of having to point out to phony and pretentious avant-garde types that all the significance they've dumped on this film simply ain't nohow, nowhichway, in no manner, present.

Now I will tell *you*. So you can tell your friends; and I can eat my matzoh ball soup in peace.

For openers, there is no plot. That simple. No story. I know this because I got it on the best authority—from one of the men listed in the credits as having *devised* the bloody story. He has said that after Kubrick had that staggeringly boring paean to the monkey wrench in the can (that first half that sent people stumbling from the theater half-asleep on the pre-premiere night I saw the film), he and some of the head honchos at Metro screened it, went ashen, and said to one another, "We ain't got a picture here." So they went out to the Kalahari Desert and shot the apes, and then they shot that Antonioni white-on-white bedroom, and they taped the second-thought sections on either side of the Man Against Space nonsense, and they called it the birth of the blues. So with that knowledge cemented into the forefront of your cerebrum, you can now see that any spiderweb superstructure of superimposed story you devised after you left the theater confused and didn't want to look like a *schmuck* to your friends, is just rationalization.

But let's pretend Kubrick *didn't* do that. Let's just say the story runs sequentially from the Dawn of Man and the apes through the discovery of that black formica tabletop on the Moon, and Keir Dullea chasing Gary Lockwood around 'n' around the centrifuge, to the surrealism of the ending and *Thus Spake Zarathustra* running as Muzak for the journey back to Earth by that homunculus in the bubble. Let's pretend such was the case. (For those of you who haven't yet seen the film, naturally this will make very little sense, but don't let it bother you; if you are one-half of the crowd-followers I think you are, you will be dashing to queue up for the film soon anyhow, and you can clip this guide, put it in your wallet, and read it during the half-time intermission so when you emerge, your girlfriend or husband will think you are the most intellectual item since Nabokov, a rare combination of beauty and brains.)

Now. Had you read the short story, "The Sentinel," written by Arthur C. Clarke (well-known science fact/science fiction writer and co-author of the screenplay of *2001*), upon which the film was loosely based, you would know that the black formica tabletop was a kind of radio signal left on Earth by aliens; left behind on their passage through our galaxy to somewhere else.

So. The first monolith, the one the apes find, is the one that gives the slope-brows the gift of reason (we know this because when one of them touches it, we hear *Thus Spake Zarathustra* and we are uplifted). And if you still had any doubts, the scene that follows shows the ape discovering the first utensil. The linkage is inescapable. *Res ipsa loquitur.*

So now we go from the ape hurling the bone-weapon into the air, to the space-shuttle spinning down through the void to dock (at unbearable length) at the space station.

Now we mulch on forward. They take half the two hours and x-minutes (it was 40 when I saw it, but I understand they've cut 17 minutes of boredom since then) of the film to let you in on the big deal surprise of another monolith being discovered on the Lunar surface...or strictly speaking, just below the surface, which is where the plot lies, as well. In Clarke's original story, the aliens had left the signal device—the monolith in the film, a pyramid in the story—on the Moon, because they wanted to get in touch with whatever life form developed on Earth only at a point when it was advanced enough to *get* to the Moon. (You knew, of course, that the ape-stuff took place on Earth, didn't you? Rob Reiner didn't.)

So they discover the monolith is sending out signals, and the receiver is somewhere out near Jupiter.

So they send out the astronauts to dig what is shaking out there. The computer that runs the ship—aside from being faintly high-camp gay in its mannerisms—does a bang-up job keeping them on course, until one day, for no apparent reason it goes completely out of its gourd and kills everyone on board with the exception of Keir Dullea, who is just too smart to be put down by a mass of printed circuits and mumbly memory banks. But, the question asks itself, unbidden, why did the computer run

69

amuck? The only answer that works within the framework of the film and logic, is that the aliens have somehow, by long distance, telekinesis or somesuchthing, sabotaged the thing. Reason: to capture the finest specimen of Terran life, the astronaut they know will be sent out to check that monolith near Jupiter. And they do. When he gets just abaft Jupiter, the formica tabletop comes for him, and then begins the section that will make this film a success...the astounding visual interpretation of a trip through hyperspace as the aliens cart Dullea back to wherever it is they actually live.

(This section, by the way, has already gotten a deserved reputation in the underground, and when they can scrounge-up the hard-ticket prices to see it, the waiting lines at *2001* are mini-deep in heads waiting to get their minds blown a tot more than usual. It will be this underground rep that will spread out into the Establishment, and thereby assure the film of big box-office.)

Now we come to the confusion.

Oh really? Where've we been already? But...onward!

Dullea wakes up (comes to? regains his senses? something.) in a Louis XVI bedroom, segues into a shot of himself a little older, segues again and he's wizened, segues again and he's lying in bed dying of old age. What is happening? Well, I see it this way (and being a science fiction writer naturally I am privy to all the secrets of the Universe, not to mention the mind of a director and the subtleties of a befuddled script):

The aliens are trying to decide whether to go and join Man in his march through space to fulfill his destiny, or to let him destroy himself. They are pumping Dullea's mind.

The periods of clarity for Dullea are those moments when the brain-draining ceases for a moment or two. Knowing that their environment is so alien to the mind of a human that he would crack, and be worthless for their purposes, the aliens have created a self-contained continuum for him to exist in, a dream if you will. It takes the familiar form of a white-on-white bedroom. It probably isn't *really* that. He may be in stasis in a gelatin tank, or hooked into a dream machine, or just floating free-ego in a never-never land of the aliens' design, depending on how alien and impossible-to-understand you care to make them.

Finally, they get all they want out of Dullea, make up their minds to help Man on his way to Destiny, and utilizing the Time-Is-Circular theory, they send another formica tabletop to him, which changes him—devolves him? retrogresses him?—

70

back to a baby with tarsier-huge eyes, and they send him back to Earth, ostensibly to make that second touch in the brain of Man that will give him an equivalent leap in intelligence that the first ape got from the monolith. Homo superior, the next evolutionary step, aided and abetted in the von Däniken idiom.

That's one way to look at it.

But then, is that really Dullea as a baby? It looked like an alien baby to me. It might even be an *adult* alien. Who says they all have to look like Raymond Massey with a fright-wig and a long beard? But even so, the storyline holds.

Unfortunately, this is not necessarily the story Kubrick and Clarke wrote. It may be a better one, who knows?

In any case, there are still innumerable unanswered questions in the film, such as:

If they found the monolith on the Moon, why didn't they find the one on Earth?

Is it the same monolith, and it moves around?

Why didn't the computer know Dullea would use the emergency exit to gain reentry into the ship?

Why did Kubrick take endless time for the discovery of the monolith on the Moon, a sequence that would have been handled better in the teaser of the worst TV space opera?

I could go on indefinitely.

Which is not to say I didn't like the film. As I said to Norman Spinrad, the science fiction writer who was seated next to me at the screening, "the first half is boring...but not uninteresting." He stared at me. How can anything be boring and engrossing at one and the same time? Well, visit Kubrick's Folly and find out.

The psychedelic segments are visually some of the most exciting stuff ever put on celluloid; in a way it's what cinema is all about, really. The ape sequences are brilliant, the special effects staggering, and my review brilliant. But I am compelled, once and finally, to say that this is a seriously flawed film. It fails in the first order of storytelling: to tell a story.

So go get stoned on acid, pack your pockets with hash, go sit in the Cinerama cocoon, and let Kubrick fly you to the Moon. It ain't gossamer wings, but what the hell do you expect for $X.XX per ticket?

71

JOE

JOE is not merely an extraordinary film, it is a small artistic miracle. Only rarely in the turmoil of human events does a work of fiction speak so clearly, with such brutal directness to the core truths of the condition of life that no matter what one's beliefs, there is no denying its validity. Zola's "J'Accuse" was such a work, Harriet Beecher Stowe's UNCLE TOM'S CABIN was another. In film, in recent memory, *Joe* is approached for sheer impact and importance only by *Z*, *Paths of Glory* and the final scenes of *Easy Rider*. No one conceiving this film, a year ago, could have known how loudly it would speak today. It is a one-in-a-million success, a story so simple and so terrifyingly on-target for our times, that the luckiest Vegas bookies, with all the *vigerish* in the universe, would lose their shorts trying to predict odds on its happening again.

Already the film is a legend. I saw it in New York (for the first time) early in July, the day after it opened at the Murray Hill on 3rd Avenue. By that time Judith Crist had come out strongly for it. Still, it was an unknown quantity to me, and though I was urged into seeing it by a film director friend of mine, I was reluctant: you can only see so many *Strawberry Statements*, so many *Getting Straights*, so many *Revolutionarys* without getting fed to the teeth by the exploitation of the dissent movement by the fat and cynical. But I allowed myself to be dragooned. (It is interesting to note that I had just come off a lecture tour through Middle America, two days prior to my trip to the Murray Hill. I had *been* through hardhat country.)

I was not disposed to be impressed.

I had had my guts twisted by *Z* and *Easy Rider* and I did not think they could do it to me again.

At the end of the film, it took my director friend, Max Katz, and his lady, Karen, to help me up the aisle. I could not focus. I was trembling like a man with malaria. There was a large potted tree on the sidewalk outside the theater. I managed to get to it, and sat there, unable to communicate, for twenty minutes. I was no good for two days thereafter.

Phone calls to the Cannon Group, the releasing corporation responsible for getting the film into circulation, brought me photo stills, production information and background on the story. I knew, even then, I would want to write some words about *Joe*.

Seeing it again last night, here in Los Angeles, I was afraid my first impressions would be blunted by all the foofaraw the film has generated, by reevaluations, by seeing it in company with a less-hip crowd than the Manhattan audience.

Though it became *my* turn to help someone up the aisle—my lady Cindy, who was (politely put) stunned—the film held as much significance and torment the second time around.

The film buff inclined toward *Cahiers du Cinéma* analyses of motion pictures may find this review somewhat wanting in phrases like mobility, color-sense, directorial thrust, cinematographic purity, characterization . . . the full sack of technical terminology that proves the critic knows whereof he speaks. The filmgoer whose exposure to cinema criticism rests on the high school book report level of getting a line-by-line retelling of the plot, may also be frustrated.

I choose not to tell the story of *Joe*. Too many clowns have already spoiled the experience (on television and in newspapers) by categorizing it as a story about a hardhat who kills hippies, as a study of the generation gap, as a modern terror tale, as any number of other literary flummeries. And it is all of these, and none of these. What it is, fellow travelers, is a visceral experience on a par with going black-belting with Bruce Lee. *Joe* will kick the shit out of you. It will set the blood slamming against your cranial walls. It will make you as cold as Ultima Thule.

So those who want informed and esoteric *précis* can look

elsewhere. The sole and blatant purpose of *this* review is not only to get *you* to go see the film, but to buy a ticket for a needy hardhat.

Because *that* is who should see this movie.

I drove down Ventura Boulevard this morning. Just a few blocks past Sepulveda, they're building another of those filing cabinets for people—a massive office building. The thing rises eight or ten storeys already. They have one of those giant center-post cranes on top, literally pulling the structure up by its bootstraps. And on the rigger's platform of the crane is a flagstaff, and flying proudly from that staff is Old Glory.

Across the street from the construction is a men's shop I occasionally patronize. When I park in front of the construction and walk across to the men's shop, the hardhats come out on the railings up there and they start doing Joe. I'm thinking of buying a hundred tickets and passing them out to the fellahs. Let them go and see Joe Curran, the prototypical hardhat, the middle-class homeowner, the guy with the knotty pine rec room and the "well-balanced gun collection." Joe, the guy who refers to Bud as the King of Beers, the guy who hates welfare deadbeats and niggers and kids who've fucked up the music and shit on the flag. Let them go and see Joe, and then let them try and reconcile it in their baboon brains. If they can.

Assaulted as you are, moment by moment, with urgings to read this and see that, to touch this and taste that, how do I summon the words that will impel you to the Four Star Theater, to *see* this film, now? How do I get you to do it, so you can get your parents and your friends and total strangers with short hair and a psychotic glaze over their eyes, to see it also? How do I do it . . . ?

Perhaps I do it by analyzing the film in terms of the great cinematic moments. Perhaps by telling you the chilling and wholly logical story so you'll want to see how it all comes out. And perhaps I just do what I've done—advise you that the only person who could walk away from *Joe* without a new awareness of the treadmill to tragedy on which America is running is the kind of person who *is* Joe Curran.

And maybe I just suggest, in a soft whisper, that the beast who is Joe lives in all of us, longhair or hardhat. And then, friends, we drop to our knees and pray.

SILENT RUNNING

Cogito ergo comparare. As a thinking animal, the species homo sap has this positively lemminglike urge toward myth and archetype. Every little kid lost on the grounds of Disneyland is a parallel to the Wandering Jew; every poor sonofabitch hoist on his own petard harkens back to Christ; every septuagenarian who slips out of Sun City for a stroll in the countryside is a *Doppelgänger* for Nietzsche's Old Man in the Woods; Henry Ford opened Pandora's box, Wilbur and Orville were Daedalus and Icarus, Howard Hughes is Croesus; every writer who writes lean and tough is obviously emulating Hemingway. Well, *sheet!*

And every sf film released post–*2001: A Space Odyssey* will have to suffer with comparisons to Kubrick's jellyroll; most of the time, the contender's going to come away bloodied. Apparently, in the massmind, it isn't enough for the creator of whatever film comes into question to have had the *dream* and the skill to solidify that dream on film. It isn't enough, because homo sap seemingly can't handle all that fresh input each time, consequently has to gauge the new film by the old one, even when they bear only the most superficial similarities to each other.

Well, hell, leave us cease beating around it. I'm talking about SILENT RUNNING, an outstanding film, albeit seriously flawed conceptually, and how much nonsensical balderdash it's going to have to put up with because it is the illegitimate son of *2001*.

Perhaps not all comparisons between the two are invidious, however. Special effects on *2001* were conceived and effected by a team of four, most prominent of whom was Douglas Trumbull: *Silent Running* was directed by Douglas Trumbull. *2001* depended heavily for its ambience of wonder on the hardware of space travel: *Silent Running* takes place entirely aboard the American Airlines space freighter *Valley Forge.* Heads dropped their tabs and went to freak behind the *2001* visual psychedelics of a jaunt through hyperspace: the most potent filmic technique surfacing in *Silent Running* is a violent, shuddering, kaleidoscopic ride through the maelstrom rapids of the rings of Saturn, using the same Trumbull-conceived cinematic vocabulary. Both are morality plays. Both anthropomorphize machines. Both deal with astronauts *manqué.* Both flaunt the minutiae of space travel and life aboardship inspace.

Yet these are merely surface similarities. The two films are as dissimilar as *Lolita* and *Rebecca of Sunnybrook Farm*, though both possess dirndl youth and femininity.

The dissimilarities of *2001* and *Silent Running* are infinitely more striking than their lookalikes:

2001 had no human characters with whom one could identify; *Silent Running* pivots on the character of Freeman Lowell, the last ecologist Earth ever produced. *2001* was heavily mystical; *Silent Running* is a myth anchored in materialism and realism, despite its fantascience trappings. *2001* was optimistic in the final analysis; *Silent Running* is a cautionary tale with a downbeat ending. *2001* was scientifically accurate (with only *very* minor errors) down to the last grommet and spanner; *Silent Running* makes no attempt to disguise its mythic qualities and the flaws in its physical sciences are numerous, consequently. *Silent Running* is essentially a romance, *2001* was not. There are more.

But the most important difference between the two films, from the standpoint of criticism, is that *2001* so stunned with its metaphysical and cinematic overkill that virtually nothing but "Oh wow!" is available to its audience after they have seen it (a common denominator for Kubrick films, from *Paths of Glory* through *Spartacus* to *Dr. Strangelove* and up to *A Clockwork Orange*); Kubrick is clearly a genius, well ahead of the game; while the makers of *Silent Running* are merely extraordinarily talented men, and the film can be commented upon rationally because it *isn't* that *rara avis*, the fever-dream of a Polanski, a Fellini or a Kubrick. It is susceptible to comment and criticism, it is flawed, it is—at core—more *human* than *2001*. And for that reason is more valuable to students of speculative fiction in films than *2001* because it bears the marks of human hands, it speaks to trends, it casts illumination on the directions sf can take in films: *2001* does not. It is a special vision and cannot be duplicated; it can tell us little beyond the rare qualities of a Kubrick.

So, at last, fighting off the lemming-urge to comparison, we come to *Silent Running* which, like the little girl with the little curl right in the middle of her forehead, is very very good when it's good, and when it's bad ought to go and sit on a cucumber.

Blatantly—and to its disadvantage—it is a message film. It says: Don't kill off the forests. It says: We have to be more ecologically humane. It says: If we keep going the way we're going, we'll fulfill Joni Mitchell's warning, "They paved Paradise and put up a parking lot." And the film says these now-all-too-familiar-yet-nonetheless-inescapably-true clichés *just that* nakedly. Making for some very difficult, pretentious speeches by the protagonist, played by Bruce Dern. It is a mark of Dern's acting expertise, and the exquisitely special quality he displays in the role of Lowell, that the speeches just manage to slide by without rasping the nerve-ends. But it's bad scripting.

More on Dern, and more on the script, later.

Shunting aside for the moment the plot-holes in which one could lose a cab rig and trailer, the story is an uncomplicated one. The last botanical specimens from an Earth devoid of vegetation (and I won't even comment on *that* wonky concept at this point) have been enclosed in enormous domes, have been attached to space freighters, and have been orbited out near Saturn. Lowell and his three shipmates have been on the *Valley Forge*—one freighter in a large flotilla—for eight years, tending the forests and desert areas in each of the five geodesic domes. One day they receive the long-awaited message from the flagship that tells them the final dispensation of the botanical specimens. Not the recall Lowell was hoping for, the recall to return the vegetation to Earth where it would flower anew, but a message that delights the three jaded and bored shipmates: uncouple the domes, blow them out into space and vaporize them with atomic charges. Lowell's buddies love the message because it means they're going home. Lowell is appalled. He has come to love the forest, its denizens, its foods he grows with his own hands and eats (to the amusement of his shipmates living off dried and fortified synthetics from the robochef onboard).

The others blow three of the domes, but when one of them

comes to Lowell's forest to plant the charge, Lowell—carried away in a violent fit of survival in the name of the land—kills him. Lowell then blows the fourth dome with the other two caretakers trapped inside. It explodes and Lowell has committed triple murder to preserve the forest.

He then plays a game of duplicity with the flagship, advising those in charge that malfunctions aboard the *Valley Forge* make it impossible to jettison the final dome, and he thinks his companions were in one of the blown domes. Then he pirates the freighter and, kidnapping the forest dome, he plunges into the rings of Saturn to escape.

With the aid of a pair of memorable drone robots—one other was lost during the wild ride through Saturn's rings—Lowell "runs silent" through uncharted space beyond Saturn, tending the forest, programming the drones to repair his injured leg, teaching them to play poker, and finally coming to grips with his horror at the murders he's done in the name of goodness.

Finally, Lowell is confronted with the situation of the forest dying. For moments a moviegoer dwells on the fascinating allegorical possibility that the corpse of the man Lowell killed, buried in the forest, has somehow poisoned Paradise. But it is merely that the freighter has sailed too far from the Sun, and the plants are unable to sustain the photosynthetic process needed to keep them healthy. At that point a search party from the flotilla, having been sent around Saturn in search of the *Valley Forge*, locates Lowell and advises him they're coming alongside to dock. Lowell rigs high-intensity lamps in the forest, tells the remaining drone robot that the responsibility for caring for the forest is now his, blows the dome into deep space where, ostensibly, it will continue on its trajectory to infinity, and alone save for a crippled drone that has become his friend, he assuages his guilt over the death of his companions by atomizing the freighter, thereby committing a kind of noble suicide.

Patently, the base story is ludicrous. Its errors in logic and science are horrendous. (When I approached director Trumbull, after the first time of the three on which I've seen the film, and asked him why in the world the simplest rules of physical science, rules known to every junior high Physics 101 student, were not observed—like, for instance, when the domes are jettisoned and exploded we *hear* the sounds in space, when *everyone* knows space is a vacuum and sound cannot be transmitted through a vacuum—he responded that they were telling a kind of "fable" and though they had dubbed the film originally *with-*

out the misconceived soundtrack explosions, they felt an audience would prefer to have the sounds, it would make the whole thing seem more identifiable. I conceive of this as a dodge on Mr. Trumbull's part, a weak response intended to fend off a criticism that cannot be overlooked. But further, it is a pandering to early-1950s horror film misconceptions of the ways in which sf should be treated. It may have worked to hear rockets blasting in deep space, to hear the sound of wind as meteors whizz by out there in the dead place between the stars, back in the moron days when Zsa Zsa Gabor was always a member of the first crew to the Moon, but *2001, Marooned, Forbidden Planet, Planet of the Apes, THX-1138, Charly, A Clockwork Orange, Colossus: The Forbin Project* and a host of others have clearly taken us past such redneck errors in filmed sf.)

The script is rife with such errors and skip-logic in basic construction:

If *all* plant life had vanished on Earth, as the film advises us, the ecological chain would have been broken before *anything* could be saved; Man would have vanished early on, the rains would have ceased to fall, the oceans would have died, and the story would never have taken place.

Why orbit the freighters out by Saturn? The cost of shipping even the most essential items into space would make the shipping of whole *forests* unfeasible by their incredible cost; and even if they *could* do it, orbiting around the Moon is far more logical than sending a whole flotilla out to Saturn. To what end? Why not Mars or Venus, closer in?

Our best astronomical information tells us that the rings of Saturn are only perhaps a dozen miles thick, flattened in their rotation around the planet by the enormous gravitational fields; further, the rings seem to be made up of ice particles. A spacegoing vessel like the *Valley Forge* would have had to be going at least four or five miles per *second*, and would have passed through the rings in a blink of the eye, rather than the minutes-long rapids-run *Silent Running* offers, though I freely grant the filmic twisting of astronomical realities made for good visuals.

Or, even granting the ship its journey, and taking the acceleration rate at a *very* conservative two miles per second, if it hit even a tiny particle, the impact would have torn the ship to flinders.

And how did the astronauts manage to keep walking around on the decks when the freighter was not spinning to induce artificial gravity? Why didn't everything float in free fall?   81

And how can we accept a science of Man advanced enough to accomplish the unbelievable feat of sending whole forests into space that would also build a drone robot that would catch its "foot" in a strut and get ripped off the gantrywork of the freighter?

The holes are many and gigantic.

Yet the film succeeds. Somehow, despite all the idiot errors that could have been so easily avoided had Trumbull and producer Michael Gruskoff merely sought out the technical assistance of, say, Dr. Robert S. Richardson of the Palomar and Griffith Observatories, the film makes it. (Jesus, they needn't have even sprung for an expensive authority like Richardson. Any moderately competent sf writer could have saved them this embarrassment. Even a hip sf fan could have poked holes easily filled during the scripting. But the scenarists, Deric Washburn & Mike Cimino and Steve Bochco were clearly inept choices, and on their heads rests most of the denigration of this film.)

(The casual reader, knowing this reviewer writes sf, might think I am taking a stance based on special knowledge. Even were this the case, which it ain't because I assure you I am a scientific illiterate who could no more program the correct technical data than perform a prefrontal lobotomy, the position would not be invalid. On speaking to students from Centenary College in Shreveport, Louisiana—where the film premiered simultaneously with its Los Angeles opening—I was given precisely the same complaints. Many of them rejected the film outright because of these errors, which put the believability of the entire story in doubt.)

But, again, the film succeeds. It is affecting. It is one of those hybrid fish-&-fowl creations that should fall under its own weight. But it doesn't. It is compelling, inevitably gripping, touching and somehow very true and dead to the heart of the Human Condition.

I attribute much of this to the stunning performance of Bruce Dern. For with the exception of excellent cameo performances by Cliff Potts, Ron Rifkin and Jesse Vint as the murdered shipmates (parts they honor with the thoroughness of their talents), and the amputees who rode inside the three drone robots, this is Dern's show all the way.

His Freeman Lowell is a full characterization, hot and cool and trembling. He emerges as the solitary focus of a drama that could so easily have become just another nuts-and-bolts space opera. When Lowell directs the drones to bury the man he has killed, and with his throat tightening with grief says a few words over the grave—via TV intercom—no one can be unmoved. When Lowell, out of the desperation of loneliness and guilt, anthropomorphizes the drones and plays poker with them, there is such a sureness, such a suspension of disbelief *on the part of Dern*, that it becomes a tragicomic scene filmgoers will always remember. In scenes where the dialogue written for Dern is as cumbersome as a hippo trying to insert a pessary, the actor lifts and flutes and dwells on note after note of the script with the precision of a master soloist. This is a case, one of the rare few, when the actor brings to an intrinsically awful script a genius that *must* be commended. With this film Bruce Dern steps softly but surely into the front ranks of American actors.

To comment further on the film would be to confuse myself and you, gentle readers, more than I have already. For it becomes clear that the more one picks at *Silent Running*, the more it falls apart. Taken in totality, it is a memorable and convincing film. I don't know why. Critical judgments evaporate. It is at once fable and warning and visual experience, and on those levels it was eminently worth doing. All concerned with the project—save those hack scriptwriters—can feel proud and pleased with what they've brought forth.

This is a step, however faltering, in the right direction for filmed sf; it deals with human problems in human terms, aided and abetted by the trappings of the superscience society. But more, it holds somewhere in its twisted skein, the magic elements that make a film unforgettable.

And if the review is illogical, chalk it up to future shock, or brain damage or the eyes of childhood that it seems to me are indispensable for looking at special dreams like *Silent Running*. And Bruce Dern can play on my team, *any* day.

HARLAN ELLISON: SCREENING ROOM
[1973]

1st INSTALLMENT

Most blessed of all novelists is certainly Graham Greene. Unlike the shat-upon Faulkner, Hemingway, Cozzens, Roth and Updike who—with very rare exceptions—have had their novels turned to mulch by filmmakers, Greene's books have been widely and handsomely adapted. *This Gun for Hire, The Heart of the Matter, The End of the Affair, Orient Express*, Hitchcock's version of *The Confidential Agent, The Fallen Idol* . . . all were superlative films, though not necessarily big box-office. One is forced to the conclusion that the man's work is purely translatable, and even flubs like *The Comedians, The Quiet American* and *Our Man in Havana* have elements to recommend them that clearly emerge from the original material. As a writer who has seen how wrong his material can go in the hands of the inept and artistically corrupt in what is essentially a collaborative art-form, I envy the blessings that continue to be showered on Greene, not the least but at the moment the latest being MGM's transmogrification of TRAVELS WITH MY AUNT from the printed page to celluloid.

Working from a lean and utterly delicious screenplay by Jay Presson Allen and Hugh Wheeler, director George Cukor demonstrates that even at age seventy-four his talent is as firm and juicy as a pippin apple. Greene's "entertainment" about Henry, a mildewy English gentleman more concerned with his garden than with the joys of living, whose world is turned cockeyed by his swashbuckling Aunt Agatha, does not rush, neither does it stroll. In Cukor's hands it is permitted to slide, to slither, to slip like finest silk from opening sequence to O. Henry ending. It is a bravura performance by all concerned, not the least of whom are the exquisite Maggie Smith (whose makeup leaves something to be desired) and Alec McCowen as Aunt Agatha and Henry. It is a film of pure pleasure, a simple and uncomplicated joy shot with grace and wit and intelligence, and I do not think you will pillory me for urging you to see it at your earliest convenience.

On the other foot, however, we have MAN OF LA MANCHA from United Artists, a debacle in virtually every particular. More, it is a thoroughgoing disgrace. The days of substituting Mitzi Gaynors for Mary Martins in *South Pacifics* were gone, we thought, and bad cess to them. But with unerring stupidity and an eye for venality unparalleled since 20th remade *Stagecoach* and took the box-office drubbing it deserved, producer-director Arthur Hiller has cast Peter O'Toole as Quixote in the role made famous by Richard Kiley off-Broadway, and replaced Joan Diener with Sophia Loren as Aldonza.

It is embarrassing. O'Toole's musical capabilities, light and frivolous and utterly beguiling in *The Ruling Class*, are here strained far beyond the point of tolerance by those who know and admire Dale Wasserman's musical play. Neither is it to scenarist Wasserman's credit that the interior tension and enveloping humanity of the stage production have been leached out for the big screen. The less said about Ms. Loren, beyond her undeniable and frankly sexist-appealing beauty, the better. Her singing is the pathetic burbling of a titmouse drowning in a milk pitcher.

Virtually without moment, this is a film that does no one involved with it credit. And the lunacy of shooting scenes that look like backlot setups, in Spain, at enormous cost, is only matched in derangement by the cacophony of O'Toole's British accent, Loren's Italian accent and James Coco's Bronx accent all going down for the third time under the weight of the Impossible Dream. Better the windmill should have won.

I'm probably the only critic in the country who'll say this, but I *enjoyed* National General's Barbra Streisand starrer, UP THE SANDBOX. The third release I've seen from the company of stars who call themselves "First Artists" (about the other two, *The Getaway* and *The Life and Times of Judge Roy Bean*, more later),

88

it is a mixed bag of fantasy and reality with Ms. Streisand as an upper-class Manhattan housewife trying to raise her consciousness with considerable difficulty. While I am not the world's foremost Streisand fanatic, I would be less than truthful if I didn't admit I *kvelled* at Ms. Streisand's performance. (If *kvell* is beyond you, ask your nearest Jew, of which some of your best friends are.) Irvin Kershner has directed Paul Zindel's script with a madcap berserkness that produces an ambience of fluidity and startlement. The film jumps back and forth between Streisand's dream-visions of what her life *might* be like and the no-less-intriguing realities of what it *is* like. Perhaps there are films that appeal to my less intellectual predilections, but *Up the Sandbox* jibed with the basic tenets of the Ellison Moviegoing Philosophy: it kept me rapt and happy all the while it danced before me. What the hell more can one ask from a mere shadow-play?

First Artists, however, will have to answer for THE GETAWAY, as nasty a piece of business as I've encountered lately—with the exception of American–International's THE UNHOLY ROLLERS, a film of pure depravity whose only saving grace is an incredible-looking female named Claudia Jennings who has every reason in the world to be proud of what she looks like with her clothes off. But not even the unnatural lust I feel for Ms. Jennings can keep me from returning to *The Getaway* with pickaxe in hand.

Understand: I am a *big* admirer of Sam Peckinpah's films; *no* one can express a greater admiration for Steve McQueen; the novel from which the screenplay was taken was written by Jim Thompson, one of the best goddamed hardboiled writers this country ever produced, in some ways better even than James M. Cain, and a man whose work I *tremendously* admire; but *all* of them, perhaps at the hands of scenarist Walter Hill or the dictates of producers Foster & Brower, have been served hideously here.

It isn't the violence that bothers me; in point of fact the violence is rather tame and predictable, hardly as innovative and eye-catching as that exposed in Peckinpah's brilliant *Straw Dogs* or *The Wild Bunch*; it is everything *around* the violence that sucks. McQueen is sloppy in his acting, Peckinpah is *laocoönian* in his direction, Quincy Jones's music is banal, Al Lettieri overacts, Sally Struthers underacts, and Ali MacGraw can't act worth shit. Perhaps that's where the major flaw lies. With Ms. MacGraw. And I would be a cad to pick up on the obvious straight line   89 about lying with Ms. MacGraw. There's been enough of that crap in the movie magazines; but even so, McQueen will have to take the rap for carrying his girlfriend in this film. It was a sad artistic judgment to put a no-talent lightweight like Ali Mac-Graw in a role that demanded a young Claire Trevor. Because, *Love Story* considered, Ms. MacGraw is the sort of actress of whom it can be said, when she comes onscreen it is as though she just went offscreen.

The Getaway is an utter bore. A failure as drama, as film, as entertainment. It is morally corrupt, artistically arid, conceptually outdated and in sum as thoroughly unredeemable a piece of shit as has been released this year, and the horror and wonder of it, is that it came from such massive talents.

Universal has added another black film to the current torrential downpour with TRICK BABY (from the novel by Iceberg Slim), and it is to their credit that the film is some kinda nother *thang!* It is a *mean* film. Tracing the fading moments in the lives and capers of two Philadelphia con artists, *Trick Baby* manages to escape the already-concretized clichés of black films (after the first seventeen minutes, which are embarrassing and badly-acted) to pound its story home like a good club fighter working a Friday night prelim. Mel Stewart, who plays Blue Howard, the senior partner of the flummoxing partnership, is for my money the hottest black actor in the country. I remember seeing him work in "The Connection" at the old Living Theater in New York, and being impressed with his ease and individuality on a stage. That was almost fifteen years ago. Now he has stepped forward, his time is *now*, to steal the film from director Larry Yust, from all his fellow actors, from the sensational Philly locations used to limn that special enclave of the black underworld, and he *is* Blue! The most engaging, outrageous, multifarious grifter who ever worked the pigeon drop! And when he tells a poker opponent trying to bluff him, "Don't con me, man, I'm bullshit-proof," the theater goes up for grabs. It is Stewart, and the growing beat of desperation in his rotting lifestyle that carries this film over and across the backs of the lesser black exploitation films currently glutting the market with a wash of honky blood and brains blown out to verify black *machismo*.

Trick Baby isn't *Sounder* or *Black Girl* or even *Lady Sings the Blues*, but it is just mean and tough enough to rip at the real world for 89 minutes and send you away knowing your time was well-spent.

90

SLEUTH is also fine. It isn't knockedout terrific the way *The Life and Times of Judge Roy Bean* is knockedout terrific, but it is so solidly put together one equates it with the English country manor house in which the action of the film takes place: sunk to its knees in the earth. Michael Caine and Laurence Olivier take turns outacting one another, with the former the Italo–English hairdresser having the affair with the wife and the latter the mystery novelist married to the wife, who has lured the former to his house to kill him. And if that sounds convoluted, it is only indicative of the Anthony Shaffer script, based on his hit stage play, which has more wrinkles than a Jack La Lanne reject. Set up in the form of the traditional Agatha Christie conundrum thriller, I would be a swine were I to unveil any of the plot. But director Joseph Mankiewicz has laid in one little goodie that *must* be brought to your attention. The name of the actress who plays the part of Marguerite is "Margo Channing." Toy with that in your skull for a while, and then you'll understand why you never heard of the actor who portrays Inspector Doppler. Beyond those clues, deponent sayeth not.

Those who know my work and my nature will attest to the fact that I am hardly a flag-waving VFW style Amurrrican. But I confess to misty eyes and a swelling of the chest as I emerged from 1776, the Columbia Pictures version of Sherman Edwards's Broadway musical, as scripted by Peter Stone and directed by Peter Hunt. In this stylized and too-frequently cartoony interpretation of how the fathers of our country got around to signing the Declaration, there is a kernel of grandeur that not even Hollywood flashslam can wither. Friends who've seen the film look at me as though I fell off the Moon when I tell them I adored it. They cite to me the staginess, the fustian, the pomposity, the flaws without number. I don't care. In fact, if the truth be known, I don't give a damn, Scarlett. It is a family picture with several moments—the young Union soldier's lament for the dead, John Cullum's slavery song—that stop the breath. It is the kind of film even revolutionary cynics like myself need to be drug to every once in a while, to remind us that as fucked-up as we are today, once we were the *first* true democratic republic. It's something we need to be told from time to time, and this elegant film does it nicely, thank you. And no, dammit, I don't need a Kleenex, so get the hell away from me.

JEREMIAH JOHNSON is too long, PETE 'N' TILLIE is absolutely great, I missed HIT MAN and John Wayne's new one for Warners, THE TRAIN ROBBERS, is like listening to a long, bad joke for a mildly amusing punchline. It creaks with all of that 1942 "you're a man now, son, and you'll know it by not getting on your hoss like a sensible lad and hightailing it out of here when those twenty kill-crazed badmen come ridin' over the dune to blow your brains out" garbage. Ann-Margret is exquisite and does the best she can being really miscast; Rod Taylor is wasted; Ben Johnson is starting to get on my nerves with his grittiness; and Duke Wayne is . . . Duke Wayne. If you dig that sort of bullshit, go see it; as for me, with the exception of *True Grit*, Wayne's last nine hundred films have gone through me like beets through a baby's backside.

Which brings me to the National General/First Artists flick, THE LIFE AND TIMES OF JUDGE ROY BEAN, starring Tab Hunter, Stacy Keach, Anthony Zerbe, Tony Perkins, Ava Gardner, a buncha others, and them sensational *bulue* eyes of Paul Newman, what get upstaged by a bear in the most hilarious faceoff ever recorded for posterity. *Bean* is one of those flagellant flicks where they sit you down and keep beating you and you keeping saying don't stop. It goes on and on, and you wouldn't cut a minute of it. One of the *damnedest* films you'll ever see. Keach, as Bad Bob, is the very last word to be said on mean gunfighters; Hunter is brief and brilliant as a hangee with a reluctance to be hanged; but that *bear*! He is a star; a furry, crotchety, lumbering, bloody star. I cannot urge you strongly enough to go delight yourself with Newman as Judge Roy Bean. It whips past at hurricane speed, spurred by John Milius's script and John Huston's superlative direction and, though one cannot detect the passage of a thought in its semimindless madness, it is for all that a treat. A two-popcorn-box treat. It opens with a shootout, it ends with a shootout, and everything in between is pure fool's gold. What I mean, a treasure for the childlike in heart.

2nd INSTALLMENT

In 1970 I read Wally Ferris's novel, ACROSS 110TH. It was a tough and uncompromising naturalistic novel of underworld life in Harlem, not as good as Chester Himes's Coffin Ed Johnson–Grave Digger Jones books, but a direct lineal descendant of James M. Cain and Jim Thompson in terms of honesty and dealing with the pragmatic realities of omnipresent violence. It was an upfront piece of street fiction, and I enjoyed it thoroughly. Consequently, I waited with some breath bating for the film version, having heard Anthony Quinn would be cast in the role of Detective Frank Sullivan (*Mattelli* in the film version), a role that promised to be his meatiest since Barabbas, Zorba and Conchis in *The Magus* in 1968. Trepidation assailed me when I learned Barry Shear was to be the film's director—I once worked on a film with Barry and I've followed his credits pretty closely since that time with, I must confess, a steadily increasing dismay with his film technique—and that Luther Davis would script from the novel. Mr. Davis's last film before this assignment was the seriously flawed *Lady in a Cage*, ten years earlier; and nothing between except television, a vineyard guaranteed to dull the originality and vigor of even the most splendiferous of toilers. But I waited. Somehow, the prerelease screenings were denied me, God and the Motion Picture Producers Association only know why. Then I read with joy Judith Crist's review in the 18 December issue of *New York* magazine wherein she lauded the film as a "ruthless, hard film that presents just the facts, ma'am —and does so with a slamming realism that makes this film something more than a Saturday night entertainment special." Heartened, I sojourned to my Van Nuys nabe last night to catch ACROSS 110TH STREET, top half of a bill that included one of my personal favorites, the undersold and much-denigrated *The Wrath of God*.

Thank goodness *The Wrath of God* was on that bill, because *Across 110th Street* was a total washout. A deceitful, dishonest, utterly unpaced and inept piece of violence for violence's sake, flensed of all logic and purpose, deaf to its own idiom, caked with cliché and devoid of any of the values to be found in the Ferris novel; a film that once again panders to the basest needs of the black audience, at the same time offering masochistic release for our white liberal guilt.

The film tells the story of three down-at-the-heels Harlem blacks who rip off a co-op Mafia/Black policy bank and are thereafter stalked to death by their brothers, the Family and the fuzz. The accent, however, is placed upon the machinations of the *mafiosi* as they ham-handedly exploit the black underworld in ferreting out the heistmen; and while the two films bear little resemblance I could not help comparing *Across 110th Street* to Fritz Lang's *M* (recently seen again, for the *n*th time). Both films concern, in part, the efforts of an underworld *apparat* to locate criminals who are endangering their own security. In the case of *M*, a child killer, located by the safecrackers, robbers and beggars in Berlin's Threepenny Opera underground of the early Thirties. In *110th*, the black Mafia hired hands of the policy/ pills/prostitution trinity. But where *M* paints an arresting portrait of the life and times of the era, however sordid and ominous, *110th* skims across not only the streets but the sense of life in the Manhattan ghetto. The devilish pull of intensity and individuality in Harlem is subjugated to the fripperies of technicolor bloodletting even Peckinpah has eschewed lately out of sheer familiarity, boredom and, yes, overkill. Black films like *Sounder*, *Trick Baby* and *Top of the Heap* have shown us ways in which the special world of the black experience can be viewed through anycolor eyes with the impartment of veracity and empathy. *110th* takes the cop-out route into insensate cliché and the vile charnel houses that lie at the core of all our souls. It is the route of anti-art and anti-truth.

I don't know how much of this ugliness is attributable to Davis's script, but I do know that Shear has tried to steal the film by upstaging plot, characterization, good taste and artistic reserve with a camera the like of whose cockeyed vision has not been seen since the earliest moments of Richard Lester–Sidney Furie keyhole-peeping.

(An example, the better to illustrate to those of you who wonder how film critics make their assessments of good or evil: in one scene the policy hoods have located the wife of the man whose car was used in the heist. They have her in an office in Harlem, sitting in a chair, and Tony Franciosa [brutal son-in-law of a *Capo Mafioso*] enters to question her. He walks to the desk, sits on it and leans far across in an unnatural posture, one hand on the telephone—which he never uses—forming a triangular hole through which the camera moves down and in to shoot through, framing the woman. It was clearly a staged motion, out of sync with the action in the room, ordered by the director to enable him to get an artsy-craftsy shot. Bad, because it was an unnecessary move by the actor, misleading because it directed the audience's attention to the phone which was never used, intrusive because it detracted from the tension intended to be built in the scene. It was Shear, saying, "Looka meeee!")

As for the actors, no one was permitted freedom and consequently all seemed hamstrung. Quinn could have phoned in his part, so mannered and flaccid was he in his portrayal of the aging racist cop. Yaphet Kotto as his black opposite number on the force was wasted. And as for Anthony Franciosa, the best that can be said for his grimacing, strictured antics is that his brief marital liaison with Shelley Winters failed to rub off on him any of her talent . . . but all of her hysterical mannerisms.

United Artists' *Across 110th Street* is a deceitful, shallow, crazed production that will look, in retrospect, like precisely what it is: a venal attempt to rip off the cinematic needs of both blacks and whites in a transition period of film where honesty is desperately needed, but in which we are being fed unpalatable helpings of gore and other vittles that can by no stretch of the appetite be considered soul food.

STEELYARD BLUES is an outrageously adroit high-wire act performed without a net over a terrain of orchestrated lunacy. Forget the direction by Alan Myerson, which is slovenly, fractious and framed with all the *élan* and artistry of a Super Bowl half-time choreographer. Ignore the screenplay by David S.

Ward—and as a scenarist who contends the *auteur* theory *and* Bogdanovich suck just rewards from the screenplay, you will not often catch me saying ignore the screenplay—but ignore it this time: unless you're one of those freaks who enjoys unraveling the "world's most challenging crossword" from the *Sunday Times* of London. Ignore, in fact, everything but the performances of the principal cavorters in this buxom brouhaha. It is an actors' film, pure frolic from opening sequence of *Trick Baby*'s Mel Stewart in a jail cell, spitting on Donald Sutherland... to final moments as Peter Boyle in gunslinger gear, sided by Jane Fonda, Sutherland, Garry Goodrow and John Savage, ride thataway over the horizon to the pocketa-pocketa sound of a chopper warming up for The Great Escape.

What plot there is consists of tracking Sutherland—as the slammer-prone, destruction-derby-loving brother of a politically upward-mobile district attorney—across an urban landscape of junkyards, rooftops, hooker-festooned doorways, lion shit–laden zoo cages and highways from which Goodrow tries to taxi a rattletrap PBY amphibian. Sutherland, as Jesse Veldini, is superlative; he mugs and dimples and beams with all the ingenuousness of Puck from the *Comic Weekly*, caught in the act of going down on Tinker Bell. His Veldini as societal outlaw plays vividly against the manic counterpoint of Howard Hesseman, absolutely perfect as the toothy D.A. brother, Frank... and it is a moth's wing contrast that writes the very last word on ugly sibling rivalries... or didn't you catch the name-play of "Frank" and "Jesse"?

Ms. Fonda melds the tastiest elements of her roles in *They Shoot Horses, Don't They?* and *Klute* to bring forth the character of Iris, happy hooker and ex-paramour of the erratic Veldini with a subtlety as strong as the best jazz bass line, and a graciousness that says watch Boyle and Sutherland, I'll be here when you get back.

One marvelous exchange between Sutherland and Fonda goes like this:

Fonda: "When are you going to stop thinking being a criminal is glamorous, Veldini?"

Sutherland: "I'm not a criminal, I'm an outlaw."

Fonda: "What's the difference?"

Sutherland (realistically): "I dunno."

But it's Peter Boyle (see accompanying interview) who pulls off the caper. His creation of Eagle, escapee from a lunatic asylum, ex–human fly, man of many schizoid incarnations, is a breathtaker. If he gets overlooked for an Oscar nomination as Best Supporting, may God strike the Academy members with bolts of lightning in their hardening arteries. He has to be watched every moment, like an IRT dip, as he becomes the hooded human fly, a carpenter, a mad dog, the 1950s pinball greaser, the platinum-wigged airline captain, and even (with one lightning line) a Bogart surrogate. He is simply remarkable. *Joe* was memorable, *The Candidate* was masterful, but as Eagle he emerges as one of the best all-around actors this country has produced since Robert Blake. In all the subcutaneous ways that keep a movie fresh in the mind years after it's faded from the screen . . . it is his film.

Clearly, the actors had a romp. They whirl and spin and do a dervish number that those weary of Burton/Brando deep breathing and boundaryless bloodbaths will applaud. In short, in *Steelyard Blues* Warner Bros. has a rare joy, *sui generis*, and one of the happiest ways to spend an evening in many months.

It was a lean two weeks for screenings, otherwise I wouldn't inflict this one on you; however, a word to the wise might save you a couple of wasted hours of TV watching on 21 February when ABC-TV's *Wednesday Movie of the Week* presents Lee Remick starring in AND NO ONE COULD SAVE HER.

What hag-demon possesses networks like ABC, or production companies like England's Robert Stigwood Organization, compelling them to proffer such pallid floral bouquets as this, their first cooperative venture into filmed-for-TV movies?

Surely no one connected with this dreary little "thriller" could have held any illusions about the freshness of the plot as concocted by Anthony Skene (a gentleman who ought to have his wits, as well as his pencils, sharpened):

Fern, heiress, has been married six months to Sam, a devilishly handsome broth of an Irish lad, who works for the Boston branch of the London Bank. One day he receives a cable, your father is dying. He splits for Ireland. Fern, who has a history of emotional breakdowns, starts to get twitchy when he doesn't call. Finally she flies to Eire (for no logical reason save the show would have ended after five minutes had she not) to track him down. No records of Sam. He isn't who he said he was. Plot complications ensue—devoid of logic or inevitability but simply programmed out of coincidence at the whim of the plot-manipulators—and finally we discover Sam is some species of Blarney-enriched gigolo, thrown out of prep school for "getting a girl in   97 trouble," womanizing through young manhood, making ends meet by making ends meet with wealthy ladies on tour boats, married already.

That's right, you've got it: marrying Fern, the cable, running off... it was all a plot so Sam could get Fern's money when she killed herself out of hysteria and grief at his loss. But when she doesn't (as chancy a piece of plotting as one could wince at witnessing in an adult drama), he decides to do her in himself. Fern is saved. Sam falls to his death. Fadeout.

The definitive statement of this arthritic plot was *Gaslight*, and that was 1944. A hundred thousand potboiler "gothics" and "women's novels" have celebrated it *ad nauseum*. Every hack writer and hack producer who didn't want to spend the location budget for a hack western or hack war epic has redone this story till only the most culturally deprived and cinematically naïve viewer fails to spot it within moments of the opening credits. It is a fool's game, and one even ABC should be above playing... at least publicly.

Lee Remick, as Fern, is her usual somnambulistic self, wandering through yet another eminently forgettable nonperformance; Milo O'Shea plays a Dublin attorney named (of course) Dooley with such overblown affectation it becomes more parody than portrayal—a hysterical mismatching of unequal parts Brendan Behan and drunken leprechaun; Jennie Linden, she of *Women in Love*, flashes onscreen too briefly, and has been dealt too mundane a role, to remain long in the memory; everyone else serves as shadows.

There is the stench of corrupted Abbey Players technique throughout, and only the camera lingering lovingly on sites and vistas of Dublin prevents this reviewer from suggesting the lynch rope for all concerned. Yet even the pleasures of watching a travelogue behind Ms. Remick's ghostlike peregrinations is not enough to succor us against the idiot script. It is a waste of time, an utter waste of time.

And to return to the original question, *why* does ABC cast all the way to England for a production company whose ineptitude and banality of product can easily be matched by our own, home-grown *schlock* outfits?

Leave it to the traditionally last-running network to avoid all the talented filmmakers overseas and grasp with both hands the overseas equivalents of the Quinn Martin/Aaron Spelling *dreck*-makers. ABC takes the lead at last... in the importation of offscourings.

A SORT OF AN INTERVIEW
WITH PETER BOYLE

What comes to mind first is: Why should anyone grant an interview?

The answer is a simple one, most of the time: To promote a property. If it's an author, the current book on the stalls. If it's a public figure, it's the career, the image, the upcoming trial, the political position. If it's an actor, the soon-to-be-released film he or she is contractually-obligated to hype. If it's a fanatic, clearly it's the need to be seen, to be heard, to be noticed.

But in the case of any of the above who can be termed "together," what is the impetus?

Letting an interview, if it's done properly, can only serve to unveil the inner soul of the celebrity. (Done at the usual level of interviews it remains little more than movie fanmagazine frippery, gossip, press release PR puff bullshit.) And who, among all thinking, feeling celebrities, wishes the soul unveiled? Masochism notwithstanding, it becomes an exercise in futility for interviewer and interviewee.

To do an interview properly, the writer must hang out with the subject for a period of time, to get the feel of lifestyle, to see the subject when he or she exists in unguarded moments, to find a thematic hook on which to hang a piece that will burn with veracity and insight. At least that is the method I've found workable; the *only* method.

For in each interview I've done (and because of the time and outlays of personal energy involved I've purposely done only a few in my seventeen years as a professional) there has come a moment, an instant in time, in which I've been able to see directly to the core of the subject. At least, in my arrogance and pride in craft, I *believe* I've seen that burning core. It came in the high desert beyond Thousand Palms, in 120° heat with Steve McQueen; it came in a noisy nightclub in Texas watching Jackie Wilson perform as I got the key to my piece on Three Dog Night; it was in the death cell at San Quentin when I perceived the parameters of the insane equation called Ronald Fouquet.

But short of such commitments, it seems to me virtually impossible to come back from a subject's world and ambience with anything but superficialities. All one gets is an encounter with the subject's public face. One asks questions one hopes are no more banal and familiar than those asked by a thousand other interviewers on the publicity circuit; one tries to establish a reality with the subject in hopes he or she will identify and reveal something fresh and meaningful; one prays for the moment of unconscious revelation.

In a one-hour luncheon conversation, with a studio publicity man in attendance, nothing can be gained. There is enrichment neither for celebrity nor for interviewer, and hence, no enrichment for readers of the interview.

So the second question is: Why did you go to interview Peter Boyle?

The answer is twofold. First, and quite honestly foremost, I wanted to meet and possibly make friends with Boyle. There are a few people whom one sees from afar, who seem to have a reality, a substance to them that demands acquaintanceship. It's a presumption, of course, on a moral par with calling a studio casting director to introduce you to a beautiful girl you've seen in a film. It's intrusion. But acceptable, within limits, because the studio and the celebrity are seeking promotion. There is a semisquamous give-and-take, a bargaining, an exchange of services.

I, the undersigned, wanted to meet Peter Boyle, for my own selfish needs of friendship.

But the second reason is how I justified it. Boyle—as my review of *Steelyard Blues* accompanying this article reveals—is, in my estimation, one of the finest actors this country has produced in the last twenty years. And so, give-and-take again, I would trade my need to meet Boyle for a (I hoped) informative and revealing piece on a talent worthy of attention.

That is why I went to meet Boyle and Warner Bros. press representative Vernon White for lunch at the Aware Inn, in the Valley.

What came out of that hour is very little.

I hasten to confess the fault was mine, neither Boyle's nor White's. Knowing what I've said above to be true about quick interviews, I should have either advised them I was not going to write a piece on Boyle, or committed the time to following along behind the actor for a day or so, circumstances permitting. But I did neither, and so herewith offer what few perceptions I *did* come up with, hence terming them a "sort of" an interview.

(And being painfully conscious of how me-oriented such half-assed nonwriting can be, I'm reminded of the terrible and dishonest piece Rex Reed once wrote for *Esquire*—a terrible and dishonest magazine—on Warren Beatty. Reed could not get his interview, was put off, was shunted from PR man to PR man and finally did a hatchet-job on Beatty to the tune of how put-upon he, Reed, had been in H★O★L★L★Y★W★O★O★D. I swear to you I will try to avoid such calumny in this article, but be compassionate.)

The studio limousine was parked at the curb on Ventura Boulevard, the chauffeur pacing up and down, all the signs that this was but one more quickstop on the flurrying radio and TV interview circuit, to be dispensed with as quickly as possible so the star could be whisked off to his next nameless stop. I was already late for the lunch and I felt no more secure on arrival than a sinner at the Big Gate.

Boyle and White were seated at a table near the window and the introductions were about par: White effusive out of some familiarity with my work and the needs of his job, Boyle pleasant but reserved, waiting to see what *this* encounter held.

We began circling each other.

Boyle doesn't *look* like a bird—he's round and balding and somatotypically Everyman-ish—but his *movements* are birdlike: bright-eyed, beaky, sharp and quick. That was my first impression: that he was avian, hanging miles above the world, tracking the passage of his dinner far below. Subsequent conversation proved it to be a not inaccurate observation on my part; the part of Eagle in *Steelyard Blues* could not have gone to a more perfect player.

Boyle is much more Eagle than ever he was Joe.

I handed each of them a copy of the review of the film. They read it quickly. "You're wrong about the script," Boyle said.   101

"Ninety percent of what you saw on the screen was in that script." That stopped me. I'd gone out on a limb in the review, for the first time suggesting the actors had had more to do with a film's success than the usually unsung writer.

"Even the changes of costume, the human fly business, that Marlon Brando takeoff? That was in the script?" I couldn't be *that* wrong.

"All in the script."

At moments like that I regretted I wasn't a drinker.

"Even the scene where I was dressed as a carpenter, that was in the script." He needn't have rubbed it in. "The walking through the window, even the glass-chewing, that was all written." The man had no mercy. "I did the mugging behind the window and the barking like a dog, but just about everything else you saw the writer gave us." I had visions of rewriting the review to avoid looking like a *schmuck*, at least to myself. Then I looked up from my note pad at Boyle. He was smiling.

Under that scruffy mustache was a gentle smile; and only for a moment did I see where the altered angle of that smile might become the expression of a psychotic racist named Joe or a noble lunatic named Eagle. Boyle meant nothing by the smile, probably didn't even know he was wearing it. He was merely passing time, talking a little small talk, fulfilling his obligation to the company store.

We rambled on together, passing each other in conversation, touching briefly at points where informational-load was transshipped: though the cameras didn't linger on them, the posters in Eagle's room in the nuthouse were Boyle's idea, tokens of the human fly's attitude toward life... Meher Baba, a smiling Don't Worry face, the Amazing Spider-Man; the order in which he'd made films since *Joe...T. R. Baskin*, *The Candidate*, *Steelyard Blues*, and the unreleased *Slither*, *Dime Box* and *The Friends of Eddie Coyle*; one of his heroes, someone *he* wanted to meet... Myron Nelson of Boise, Idaho, a man who rescues wounded birds and befriends them, everything from blind eagles to clawless hawks. I listened hard; time was running away from our hour, and I had the feeling we might never pass this way again.

I asked him about acting. About being Joe and what had followed. He sketched at stories of encounters, of casual horrors with those who had seen him as Joe and admired him, of those who had seen him as Joe and despised him. Of the few who had realized he was simply an actor playing a role. Of the night he had appeared on the Johnny Carson show and come to the realization that he wasn't there to be interviewed as Peter Boyle, the actor, but to perform as Joe, as some kind of primitive entertainment. "It was a shock. For a long time after *Joe* I couldn't play any violent roles. I was offered scripts, some of them excellent, but I couldn't do it. That was a bad time for me. Joe was the pure pre-Fascist man, straight out of Reich's THE MASS PSYCHOLOGY OF FASCISM. Did you ever read it?"

I looked back at him, pen poised over note pad. "Is that Wilhelm or Theodor?" He made a little birdlike move with his head and looked at me differently. I think he knew.

"No, I never read it," I said.

For an instant we were playing with each other, the way two men who secretly fancy themselves intellectuals play with each other. One, two, riposte and retreat. Then I had his public face again.

Thoughts on acting: "I act the way Mies van der Rohe talked about 'less is more.' An actor has to let himself be watched. I sit here and let the walls watch me, the chair watch me, the table watch me." I stared at *him* like a bird. I have never understood what actors were talking about when they got into all that "space" and "less is more" talk. It seems to make them feel good, though. I just report it.

There wasn't much more. We parted, and he took a couple of my books with him. I hope they don't wind up with the Gideon Bible in a dresser drawer in some Midwestern city on his next PR stop for the film. I didn't get my hook or my burning insight. At one point I thought I did, but when I got back to the typewriter I couldn't make it hang together. It had something to do with public faces, with masks, and about how much tougher it must be for Boyle to project those masks. They keep casting him as loonies of one sort or another, but he's apparently a simple and direct man, a good actor, and neither a Joe nor an Eagle at heart. But then again, all I had lunch with was a polite public face, a gentle and intelligent mask, so I have no way of knowing.

And lacking that knowledge, I can form no opinions.

Perhaps that's as it should be. Perhaps Boyle is having it just the way he wants it. Lautrec once ventured, "One should never confuse the artist with the art." Perhaps Boyle understands that to remain a private person he must present the pleasant, public face and by the magician's misdirection of a talented actor force those who would go beyond the performances to the performer, to settle for the better part of Boyle: his onscreen portrayals. Perhaps interviewers ought to mind their own goddam business and leave audiences to simmer in their own morbid curiosity. Perhaps all there ever was and all there will be of Peter Boyle is what he offers us in darkened theaters.

But never again, a fake lunch under false pretenses.

3rd INSTALLMENT

Cinematically, the most stunning thing happening currently is the cycle of *New Hungarian Cinema* on view at the Los Angeles County Museum of Art. Circumstances conspired to prevent an earlier broadside for this exceptional series of films, thus killing your chances to see the first three programs, but tonight (Friday 23 February) and tomorrow you can catch the fourth, fifth and sixth bills; the seventh and eighth next weekend. If you never listen to me again, do yourself a favor and cancel whatever else you have going, and don't miss this rich and bewilderingly varied testament to the health and muscularity of the Hungarian film industry.

To whet your imagination let me tell you about the first two films in the cycle, one a fourteen-minute short of almost heart-breaking insight and Kafkaesque surrealism, the other a dream feature that reminds one of the first bold uses of color by Fellini and Ophuls.

STUDENT LOVE is the short film. The story is deceptively simple . . . one of those ideas that seems so obvious upon viewing, one wonders why it has never been done before: a rural movie house, the audience sparse, a film of saccharine, adolescent romance. Suddenly the film breaks. The lights go up. The audience waits patiently a few minutes, then begins clapping, jeering, demanding satisfaction. From the shadows emerge first a silent woman who stares back at them: the assistant manager. Then the manager. Nothing can be done. The film cannot be repaired. They will be given passes to come back the next night. We want our money. We will give you passes. But the film tomorrow night will be a different film . . . we want our money . . . or we want to see the end of the film!

A semi-obese woman of middle years suddenly appears and says, "I will tell you how the movie ends." The audience is intrigued. They put a chair up on the stage in front of the blind screen. And the old woman begins telling how the film ends. But it is not the idyllic love story the audience wanted. It slowly turns into a nightmare of loss and shame and degradation. The woman's face is a special wonder, gentle readers. It cannot be described here with even the remotest accuracy. Pressed to explain the face and the expressions that consume it as she tells her heartbreaking story, I would use metaphor, and make references to the patina of sorrow left in the character lines of the face of one who has lost youth, lost expectations, but not lost dreams. Could the story the woman is telling not be the unseen film but a paradigm for her *own* life? One is not told. The audience rejects the ending, tries to retell it for itself . . . the short ends enigmatically, the old woman still sitting on the stage, the audience unsettled, having undergone a disturbing experience.

And by extension *we*, the *other* audience, have undergone a *doubly* disturbing experience. In fourteen short minutes director Gyorgy Szomjas and the film's scenarist (whose name, sadly, sadly, is unknown to me) have compelled us to reexamine the act of moviegoing. We have not been permitted—as the audience in the film has not been permitted—to go merely for escapism. We have been drawn into the vortex of life and its pain, its unutterable anguish. Moviegoing is traditionally a fleeing from the real world into fantasy realms. Go to the movie and forget your cares for two hours. But not this time. In fourteen minutes the condition of sorrow and loss has been laid open and it is our own viscera we see.

If by the above you perceive that this short film made its mark on your reviewer, more than even the longer and more technically adroit feature with which it was shown . . . you perceive correctly.

I have no idea if this film will be released commercially in Los Angeles, but if it isn't, stalk it across the world. Find it. See it. You will not soon forget it.

By comparison, the full-length feature SINBAD that accompanied *Student Love* fares well—for it is a visual and sensual cinematic revel, a celebration of diffused colors—but only because it is such an evocative piece of film art.

A lesser effort would have been washed from the memory instantly before the potency of that little black-and-white, fourteen-minute wonder.

But *Sinbad* is a stream-of-consciousness journey through the last moments of a dying roué's memories...a gallery of a thousand brilliantly-pigmented paintings. The women he loved, the places he moved through, the meals he ate, the emotional crises he survived, the billions of false sentiments he used to put his victims on their backs. Each one lovingly examined with an incredible visual eye that glances quickly but misses no detail, each one turned in the imagination like a faceted jewel, seen from many angles, returned to in the mind's view again and again...without genuine understanding but rich in the detritus of memory. Like the marrow bone Sinbad eats in one exquisite series of scenes, the memories of this Don Juan's affairs never seem to be wholly emptied of their aftertaste. There is always a bit of succulence to be savored.

Director/writer Zoltan Husarik, forty-one years old and offering this as his first motion picture effort, reveals himself to be a man with the talent to expand the film form: his use of color is breathtaking, startling, variegated and unforgettable; his story seems jumbled, erratic, non-cohesive, but when the film ends one realizes there was coherency in totality. One leaves the theater having seen into the smoldering, remorseless core of a certain sort of human being.

And if one accepts Faulkner's statement "...the problems of the human heart in conflict with itself which alone make good writing because only that is worth writing about, worth the agony and the sweat" as the truth, then the gift of Husarik is a precious and invaluable one.

Again, this reviewer has no idea whether after its museum tour this film (and the others) will be released commercially, but if the opportunity ever presents itself to see *Sinbad*, you miss it at your own risk of loss.

Michael Webb and Ronald Haver of the LA County Museum of Art's film program department are to be commended for their courage and foresight in bringing this outstanding cultural and entertainment cycle to our city. They've already been rewarded with three weeks of sellout audiences (making your efforts to gain admittance that much more difficult), but for the film buff seeking enrichment beyond escapism, there is no reward great enough.

Go, at once! Get tickets for the remaining programs. You will thank me for chivvying you.

Along with our sense of societal self-loathing, concomitant with our shame at racism, inhumanity, warmongering and profligacy, we the American people have recently been lusting after films about amoral anti-heroes. As if we were seeking, in visual explications of the utterly amoral and despicable, some catharsis: a release from the awfulness of our own corrupt natures by examinations of fictional counterparts incredibly more debased than ourselves through the logistics of fantasy manipulation. Some of these films have become classics: *Hud*, *A Clockwork Orange*, *Little Mother*, *The Godfather*: because they were made with Art and Understanding. Others, as *The Unholy Rollers*, *The Getaway* and *The King of Marvin Gardens*, have failed—however interestingly—because they chose to deal with the superficial, sensational aspects of that exhibited amorality.

The latest in the genre of loathsome flicks—and I don't want to overlook *McCabe and Mrs. Miller* or *Hammersmith Is Out*, which former I hated and latter I adored—is a *very* interesting nightmare from Cinerama Releasing under the title PAYDAY.

Starring the too-seldom-seen Rip Torn as country&western semistar Maury Dann, the film was written by Don Carpenter, whose 1966 novel, HARD RAIN FALLING, should be familiar to you. It was directed with a firm hand by Daryl Duke and marks the producing debut of jazz critic Ralph J. Gleason. In arresting supporting roles Ahna Capri, Cliff Emmich, Jeff Morris and Frazier Moss—most of which are names you may not know but ought to remember—add tone and expertise as solid background to Torn's bravura performance.

When I call this a "loathsome" film, I want you to understand I'm not talking about the quality or entertainment levels of the production, which are high; I'm talking about the philosophy presented as the viewpoint of the central character. He is a swine. An utterly amoral, mean and despicable swine whose sycophantic fans long for nothing more than to be fucked and/or fucked-over by him. I mean, when you're watching a film about a segment of show biz, and the most likeable dude in sight is a *road manager*, for Christ's sake, you *know* you're observing a barnyard full of genuine slop-swillers!

The plot is a rambling one, moving through two days in the road tour life of Maury Dann and culminating with "payday." During those two days the filmgoer is treated to an intimate evisceration of the squamous lifestyle of a contemporary god, one of the uncrowned American nobility—the musical idol. (And having traveled with The Rolling Stones and Three Dog Night, I can assure those naïve few of you who've never been to a rock concert, that the brutal meat-into-meat couplings, the ravenous groupies, the sudden maniac-flashes of anger and violence, the constant stench of *machismo* exhibited in this nice nice script are *far* from exaggeration.) The power of utter adoration with which popular musicians are gifted by their vampiric followers forces even the most gentle and ethical into attitudes of callousness and brutality. For those who are already twisted...it is a blank check to demean other human beings and develop a messianic view of the entire human race.

God knows it isn't a new story; we've seen it to telling effect in *Citizen Kane, A Face in the Crowd, The Great Man* and other fables, but it is a story that needs to be told again and again, a lesson that needs to be relearned (apparently) with every change in cultural mores.

This latest incarnation is a healthy one, and Rip Torn as Maury Dann will chill you to the spine. Ahna Capri as his toothsome little trollop-of-the-moment gives the best performance of her spotty career and is only less horrifying because she has less power in Dann's ego-world. There are special scenes that leap from the screen with telling impact: a moral blackmail encounter with a rural dj, a fight scene culminating in a kind of murder, and a scene following the slaughter in which Torn purifies himself by creating a country tune so sickly-sweet it could give you diabetes.

But it is the overriding miasma of loathsomeness that makes *Payday* a memorable film. It is a despicable film, in the most positive senses of the word. Positive, in that it holds up the mirror of life and wrenches us around by the hair, and demands, "*Look* at yourself!"

It is a vision only the most honest will admit has veracity. For the others...merely purgative.

Bud Yorkin has produced and directed a swell film going under the title THE THIEF WHO CAME TO DINNER. It is swell. It is dandy. It will make you smile. It will produce wonders before your very eyes such as Ryan O'Neal actually acting, Jacqueline

Bisset actually becoming invisible, Warren Oates actually getting a chance to show his stuff and—oh oh what an *and*—the remarkable, sensational, bewildering, blindingly talented Austin Pendleton stealing an entire motion picture away from the heavymoney stars.

Walter Hill's screenplay of the Warner Bros. caperflick has O'Neal as a former Establishment computer*schlepp* who decides as long as everyone is stealing from everyone else under the mantle of Big Business, he will become an independent operator. And to the strains of Henry Mancini music that is ultimately interchangeable with the score he wrote for *Charade*, O'Neal becomes "the chess burglar," a second-storey cat who leaves a chess piece and a note describing his next gambit at the scene of his high society ripoffs.

Oates is his Inspector Javert, an insurance dick with a stiff neck and an unbendable ethic. And for the first time in more films than I care to consider, someone has turned Oates loose. To telling effect. He is a pillar of strength throughout the film. But it is the character actors who enrich this pudding: Jill Clayburgh as O'Neal's former wife, so true and right in one touching scene that you can hear the ganglia of your familiarity mechanism twanging; pudgy Ned Beatty as the fence, Deams, locked in partnership with Gregory Sierra as his Chicano side-boy, Dynamite...each of them rising above the briefness of their parts to carve themselves forever in the cliff-face of your memory; and Austin Pendleton as the chess editor of the Dallas newspaper...

Oh my. Austin Pendleton ought to be on exhibit in the Smithsonian. He is a national treasure. People ought to come pouring out of the studios and bury him in money to make film after film, starring Pendleton as whatever he wants to be. He is *so* good, it's like the first time you saw Falk act, or the best evening you ever spent with George C. Scott, or the moment when you realized Lee Grant could act any other cinematic lady she chose under the table. Austin Pendleton is a winged wild wonder, and Bud Yorkin has had the good sense and good taste to let him gambol freely.

It is a helluvan evening's entertainment, and if you don't find yourself applauding and cheering the ending, have yourself fitted for daisy-space at Forest Lawn...you're neck-upward dead.

And I know you're going to think I've been bought off with nothing but rave reviews in this column, but what the hell can I do? Last time two out of three were shit, this time all four are sensational. It runs that way. So just shrug and accept the rolls of the dice as I launch into my final rave, in celebration of MGM, director Richard Sarafian, scenarists Rodney Carr-Smith & Sue Grafton, and a group of memorable players headed by Rod Steiger, Robert Ryan, Kiel Martin, Katherine Squire, Scott Wilson, Ed Lauter, Jeff Bridges and a sparrow named Season Hubley, all of whom have formed an unparalleled artistic gestalt to bring forth LOLLY-MADONNA XXX. (You can read that: Lolly-Madonna kiss kiss kiss.)

I don't want to tip the plot too much, save to advise you it is a terrifying story of mounting violence between two present-day Tennessee hill families, a feud film, if you will, but one that far outstrips the usual Hatfield–McCoy nonsense cityfolk conceive of as representing rustic animosities.

Steiger and Ryan play the heads of inimical households, and Wilson, Timothy Scott, Lauter, Bridges, Martin, Gary Busey, and Paul Koslo play the various siblings. Randy Quaid also plays one of the sons, and Joan Goodfellow plays the lone daughter. Their performances require special note, of which more later.

There is so much to say about this film, it is *sui generis*, I hesitate to say much more than don't miss it. But thoroughness compels me to note that the sole jarring note in the film is Steiger, toward the end of the story, whose thespian mannerisms rankle and attack the carefully-woven skein of everyone else's non-Hollywood performances. Scott Wilson is by turns brutally effective and soul-wrenchingly pathetic; Ed Lauter is simply superlative as Hawk and he brings off a death scene that a lesser actor would have found beyond him; Ryan is understated, totally in control of his characterization, and continues to be one of the masters of his craft, as worthy a player as has ever been ignored by the vagaries of a fickle industry; Season Hubley, in her virgin outing feature-wise, functions with charm and individuality as the catalyst of the feud, the girl who is taken for the mythical Lolly-Madonna—and after the many skin-exposures of esthetically disastrous bodies such as that of Glenda Jackson's, it is a pleasure to gaze upon Ms. Hubley in the buff; but now we come to Joan Goodfellow (Robert Ryan's 16-year-old daughter) and Randy Quaid.

Ms. Goodfellow plays Sister E., a breast-heavy country girl of simple desires and thwarted dreams. She is the only character in the film whom we know for certain escapes the debacle of the Feather–Gutshall Families' charnel house. Her performance is 111 skillful and highly promising of a long and honorable career. The rape scene in which Lauter and Wilson taunt and finally toss her is a directorial and acting masterpiece; Ms. Goodfellow manages to convey all the terror and bravery of a bird stalked by ruthless hunters. I commend her to your attention.

And Mr. Quaid, as the retarded Finch, is so awfully good you will find yourself clenching your fists, rocking back and forth with empathy, marveling at how one so young could know so much about the torment of the human condition.

I will say no more about Mr. Quaid, save to add that if there were nothing else in this film to recommend it, his performance alone would be worth the price of admission.

Lolly-Madonna XXX is neither a happy film, nor an easy one to forget. It *is* one of the most obstinately compelling films I've ever seen, and a credit to all involved.

This is your week to go to the movies: the treasures are littered everywhere, from the mansions of Dallas to the hills of Tennessee. If you have a dull week, it's your own fault; I *told* you where to go.

4th INSTALLMENT

So this *schlepp* wakes up in a hospital bed and the doctor leans over him and grins and says, "Mr. Traupman, I have some bad news for you... and some good news for you."

And Traupman, wincing, says, "Give me the bad news first, Doc."

And the doctor says, "Well, we had to amputate both your feet..." and Traupman breaks down and starts to cry piteously.

And when he gets hold of himself, snuffling tragically, he says, "Wh-what's the good news?"

And the doctor says, "The gentleman in the next room wants to buy your slippers."

Ugh.

Which brings me to the film reviews. I have some bad news for you, and I have some good news for you.

The bad news is *Lady Caroline Lamb*. The good news is *Slither* and *The Long Goodbye*. And just plain news is *I Love You Rosa*, which is neither good nor bad, but just is.

(The *really* bad news, like an incurable case of the pox, is Clint Eastwood's new flick, *High Plains Drifter*, which I saw but ain't allowed to talk about till release date April 6th; but two weeks from now, when I emerge from the primordial slime once again, I'll devote an entire column to *that* little bundle of charm. Watch for it; I don't get killing angry very often, but when I do it makes for juicy nibbling.)

Anyhow. LADY CAROLINE LAMB. Out of United Artists by way of *The Edge of Night*. Midwife at the Caesarean, Robert Bolt—he of *A Man for All Seasons*, *Lawrence of Arabia* and *Doctor Zhivago* —who wrote and directed. And a bloody birth it is, indeed indeed. Disastrous. Better a two-headed calf.

Where to begin, oh Lord, where to begin? Jon Finch—he of Polanski's wretched *Macbeth*—as William Lamb, M.P. (That's Member of Parliament, not Military Police: this is a costume drawmuh of Regency England.) No. Begin with (giggle snicker) Richard Chamberlain as Lord Byron (tee hee titter), his eyes dripping with kohl. No. Sarah Miles, her gnome's mouth wrenching and contorting more hideously than even Jennifer Jones's mouth at its most histrionic . . . Miles of mouth as Lady Caroline Bird, Chicken, Thing, whatever . . . ! No!

Not to begin at all. To ignore. To pretend that Bolt was denied access to his wife's bed—Ms. Miles is wife to Mr. Bolt, you see—until he cobbled up this historically wayward and artistically hebephrenic *lacrimulae amphora*. To forget that even the most talented, most heroic among us occasionally go bananas with a Fulton's Folly. To warn the unwary that this is what used to be called—in pre-lib days—a "woman's movie." To catalogue words like tearjerker, childish, simplistic, dishonest, tedious, portentous, laughable, ludicrous, silly spectacular and bathetic, with hopes that no one will be unwise enough to defy the endless bum reviews this overblown satin-bag of trash has garnered for itself. To end with a weary shake of the head. To move on to the good news. At a dead run.

Or, more appropriately, to move on with a SLITHER.

Which has got to be the world's longest, funniest Polack joke.

The characters are named Kopetzky, Fenaka, Kanipsia . . . and what they are engaged in here is a kind of orchestrated berserkoid behavior that must have caused the bank that put up the money for its filming many a sleepless night. MGM didn't release this film, as the saying goes, it *escaped*. Directed by Howard Zieff, written by W. D. Richter, photographed by the brilliant Laszlo Kovacs (*another Polanie*), *Slither* is what Cornell Woolrich would have written had he been reborn as Donald Westlake. It's one of those "no one ever found the embezzled money" yarns, but beyond that point of departure the landscape ceases to be *terra familiaris* and instantly becomes Cloud-Coo-coo-Land.

Dick Kanipsia—James Caan—gets out of the slammer after doing a stretch for car boosting, takes pause for a beer at the home of a con sprung along with him, and seven minutes into the film his ex-cellmate gets machine-gunned to death before Caan's eyes. Then Caan hides in the cellar of the house as his riddled buddy tells him there's this boodle of loot and "no one ever found the embezzled money," so he should go to such and such a town and look up Barry Fenaka and tell him "the name is Vincent Palmer." Down cellar slithers Caan, and his buddy pulls a bouquet of TNT out of an old trunk and blows the house to flinders. Next day Caan comes up out of the root cellar and starts thumbing his way to Barry Fenaka. Except he's being followed by this huge motorvan all flat-black and ominous (whose appearance onscreen is invariably accompanied by the kind of Saturday morning serial music you knew meant the bad guys were coming). And Caan gets picked up by this dingdong post–Flower Power freakette played by Sally Kellerman in her most manic phase, a freakette who, when they stop for lunch, for no particular reason, decides to armed rob the lunch counter. And then...

Oh, hell, why spoil it for you. There's the incomparable Peter Boyle as Barry Fenaka, resplendent as a Polish emcee with cornucopial lore about rec-V's, and his entire terrific collection of Big Band sides transferred to tape. There's Allen Garfield as Vincent J. Palmer, adding another chunky characterization to the store of memorables that are rapidly causing him to be recognized as a character player in the grand tradition. There's crazy Sally Kellerman in cutoffs, batty as a hundred battlefields, stealing every scene Caan doesn't use a big stick to beat her away from.

There's wildness and weirdness and some of the funniest sight gags since Chaplin's *Modern Times*; there's dialogue that you'll miss because you'll be convulsed with laughter from the one that just whizzed past; there's a lunatic celebration of systematized madness; and the emblematic line is delivered by Caan when he tells Sally Kellerman she'll like living in these here parts because, "Everybody's crazy."

Slither is not to be missed. It's not often you get to see what certifiable nuts can do when they're turned loose with cameras.

And if *Slither* sounds too wild for you to tackle cold turkey, you can go at it slantwise by catching Elliott Gould as Philip Marlowe in Leigh Brackett's sensational adaptation of the Raymond Chandler novel, THE LONG GOODBYE; call it a feeder dose of insanity that'll sustain you into the big time.

There's so much to be said about *The Long Goodbye* that aficionados of both cinema and the Raymond Chandler mystique will be kicking this around for years.

For those of you who aren't familiar with Chandler or his private eye hero Philip Marlowe, be advised this is the sixth of the seven extant Chandler novels to be filmed. *Farewell, My Lovely* was made in 1944 with Dick Powell as Marlowe; in 1946 Bogart assayed the Marlowe role in *The Big Sleep*; 1947 saw THE HIGH WINDOW filmed as *The Brasher Doubloon*; 1948's *The Lady in the Lake* with Robert Montgomery as the private eye was the most stylistically interesting of the Chandler translations onto film (till *The Long Goodbye*, that is) using the camera as point of view, the audience seeing Marlowe/Montgomery only when he looked in a mirror; in 1969 THE LITTLE SISTER was made, badly, and titled *Marlowe*, with James Garner looking ill at ease in the characterization. (There was also a short-lived Philip Marlowe TV series in 1959 with Granny Goose Phil Carey in the title role, but it was abortive at best.) Still unfilmed: a sad little thing titled PLAYBACK that Chandler published in 1958, just one year before his death.

(There are also assorted short stories that have been collected in volumes variously titled KILLER IN THE RAIN, TROUBLE IS MY BUSINESS, PICK-UP ON NOON STREET, though most of them were originally published in the marvelous volume called THE SIMPLE ART OF MURDER, containing Chandler's brilliant essay on mystery writing under the latter title.)

Of the three giants of the detective story genre—Dashiell Hammett, Cornell Woolrich and Chandler—Marlowe's creator has always seemed to me to be the best. (Though since the Fifties, Ross Macdonald and John D. MacDonald have inherited the crowns, not merely by default and the death of the three masters from whom they learned their trade, but also on the basis of their impressive writings.) Chandler was smooth, dealt with the undercurrents of venality and weakness that riptide through society's seamier depths, and in Marlowe eschewed the larger-than-life image of the detective as cultural hero, choosing rather to make Marlowe an average man with an above-average fascination for low-life. Because of the clarity of delineation of Marlowe, even the worst of the films made from Chandler's novels has had a *je ne sais quoi*, a vitality, a verve that detective films made from lesser sources could never touch.

And when Marlowe films have been right—as in *The Big Sleep* and *The Lady in the Lake*—they have become small masterpieces of Americana, for they've captured within the idiom of suspense a cross-section of the tone of life in our country at that time. And *The Long Goodbye* abides by the tradition. It is right. Very right indeed. And the responsible parties are director Robert Altman, actors Gould, Rydell, Van Pallandt, Hayden and Arkin, but most of all scenarist Leigh Brackett... about whom a few words and an open love letter.

Leigh Brackett once wrote a story with Ray Bradbury titled "Lorelei of the Red Mist." She also wrote science fiction adventure stories through the Forties and Fifties with smashing titles like "The Beast-Jewel of Mars," "The Citadel of Lost Ages," "The Dragon-Queen of Jupiter" and "Lord of the Earthquake" to name only the tamest. She also wrote a clutch of hardboiled detective novels such as An Eye for an Eye, The Tiger Among Us and, most recently, Silent Partner. She is also married to sf writer Edmond Hamilton with whom she lives in a tiny Ohio town, far from the Hollywood charnel house, which has not stopped her from writing the screenplays for such films as *13 West Street, Rio Bravo* and—surprise!—*The Big Sleep*.

I have known Leigh and Ed since I was seventeen years old, and I must tell you that being able to praise unrestrainedly her latest screenplay is a singular pleasure. For a while there—back in the Sixties when Leigh and I were on the Paramount lot together, she writing bummers for Howard Hawks, me writing bummers for Joseph E. Levine—it seemed the enormously talented Ms. Brackett might have fallen under the thrall of *schlock* filmmakers. But *The Long Goodbye* is tough, tight, tense and structured so intricately I *still* haven't unraveled some of the puzzle twists. The dialogue is as sharp and *au courant* as anything Leigh's ever written, the small script touches that light up the background are all there, and wondrously, there is none of that self-conscious hipness so many of our younger scenarists seem hellbent on cramming into current scripts.

And as all but assholes like Bogdanovich will admit, without a strong script from which to build, any given film's chances of succeeding artistically are reduced geometrically in relation to the arrogance and ineptitude of the director. But Robert Altman had the crafty and cunning Brackett script from which to begin, and on its solid base he has created a film in the mode of *McCabe and Mrs. Miller*, which he also directed, but which was far less successful than *The Long Goodbye*. In the former film, Altman and cinematographer Vilmos Zsigmond employed the "flashing" method of film processing to achieve a Brueghel-like muted

117

pastel look, smokey and fuzzy, and very unnerving to this reviewer. In that film there was also unrestrained use of mumbled dialogue that kept one straining and uncomfortable throughout. Altman and Zsigmond repeat the technique here, but somehow the mood and pace of a contemporary suspense thriller allow the fuzzy look and semi-audible jabber to play like a baby doll.

And in casting Elliott Gould as Marlowe (a choice I would have thought lunacy before the fact) Altman has struck a bold masterstroke. Gould is perfect. It is hardly the Bogart Marlowe, clipped, self-assured, dangerous... or the Montgomery Marlowe, urbane, witty, charming... or the Garner Marlowe, ill-cast and embarrassing... but it is a contemporaneous Marlowe that strikes the perfect balance between cynical optimism and tarnished knight errant. A little comical, a little self-deriding, a little out-of-touch and off-the-wall... but so splendid in totality that one can only hope Altman and Gould do it again, next time with a remake of THE HIGH WINDOW.

Supporting Gould—and it's his show all the way, make no mistake—Sterling Hayden is bold and more than welcome back on the big screen, Nina Van Pallandt makes a promising and well-realized debut performance, David Arkin is properly pixilated as a retard pistolero and Mark Rydell (himself a director of some talent) is outstanding as the utterly Reform Jewish thug, Marty Augustine. So impressive is Rydell that in one of the three scenes of violence in the film, a scene of sudden movement and madness, Rydell sets it up so well, plays it so consummately, that one feels one's heart go lub-dub as the Coke bottle smashes.

I have heard filmgoers who've seen this movie put it down as incomprehensible, oddball, and simply bad. They are wrong. *The Long Goodbye* is a brilliant film, cast and written and directed with brio and courage. I venture to guess that in years to come it will assume the proportions of a cult film, and twenty years from now people will be quoting from it the way they quote from *Casablanca*. This is a must-see film.

And finally, I LOVE YOU ROSA, this year's Israeli entry for the Best Foreign Film Academy Award, a motion picture I understand was "acclaimed at the Cannes Film Festival," whatever that means.

Written and directed by Moshe Mizrahi, the film tells of a time in Israel when the Hebraic laws decreed that a widow had to marry her dead husband's brother, if he was unwed, in order that his family line would not die out. In the case of *I Love You Rosa* the brother is eleven years old and the widow is a strongly individualistic woman who wants to choose her own husband. Similar to *Lady Caroline Lamb* only in both films' examination of the minutiae of cultural mores, this character drama succeeds where the other fell flat on its aristocracy. Ably acted by Ms. Michal Bat-Adam as Rosa and 14-year-old Gabi Otterman as the young Nissim, *I Love You Rosa* is a frequently-painful, occasionally-tendentious, ultimately-arresting study of emerging character in a time and a place most of us will find fresh and different.

It is a good film, but it is not one I can get terribly excited about. Perhaps it's because I'm Jewish and many of the supporting characters remind me of my relatives, memories of whom are better left buried.

Call this a reserved review.

Or call me Ishmael.

Either way, I have some good news for you...and some bad news for you, Traupman.

So Traupman says, "Okay, Doc, give me the bad news first."

And the doctor says, "Well, while I was operating, I sneezed and cut off your penis."

So Traupman breaks down, and when they revive him he says, "What's the good news?"

And the doctor says, "I ran a biopsy on it, and it isn't malignant."

See you in two weeks.

HARLAN ELLISON'S
WATCHING
[First Series, 1977–78]

1st INSTALLMENT

They have asked for a regular column dealing with fantasy and science fiction in the visual media: theatrical features, television movies, continuing TV series, stage productions, live performances other than plays and/or musicals. In short, everything but recordings and comic books. Okay, I can do that.

What I *cannot* do is another hype column such as the nonsense-festooned handouts one encounters in fan magazines, which are nothing better than culls from the trade papers of the motion picture industry, *Daily Variety* and *The Hollywood Reporter*. These are Rona Barrett–style ephemera that promulgate the wish-fulfillment stories planted by dynamiting publicists and every half-assed turkey who has taken an eighteen-month, two-grand option on a Zelazny or Dick novel, in hopes he or she can blue-sky a development deal with a network or studio.

Nor can I pretend to be a righteous, card-carrying *cinéaste* proffering reams of erudite and punctilious copy espousing the *auteur* theory à la Bogdanovich. I am unalterably opposed to the theory that the director is the "author" of the film, perhaps because I'm a writer and I *know*, from firsthand experience, that most directors cannot direct their way to the toilet on the set. But I'll talk about that another time. Right now I merely wish to set down a few ground-rules about what this column *won't* be. (True *Cahiers du Cinéma* mavens would be on to me in a hot second, even if I pretended to be a deeply serious student of film, when I copped to having fallen asleep repeatedly in *L'Avventura*, while having seen the 1939 Korda version of *The Thief of Bagdad* more than fifty times, clearly making it my favorite movie of all time, beating out *Vanishing Point* by only six viewings.)

With rare exceptions, I will not review specific films or series. There are too many self-styled authorities overrunning the scene already. (You must understand: any *schmuck* who goes to a movie and whose ego gets in the way of good sense, who runs one of those "cinematic insight" raps—as shown in example in Woody Allen's new one, *Annie Hall*—and then has the good fortune to con some editor into accepting such drivel, can be a film critic or reviewer. They do it not out of any deep and abiding love for motion pictures, nor even because of an understanding of what it takes to create a film...they do it because they can get free screening passes to the studio press showings. They are scavengers. Cinematic illiterates who pontificate without a scintilla of talent for moviemaking of their own. I put them in the same social phylum with kiddie-porn producers, horse-dopers and assholes who use the phrase "sci-fi."

(Scaphism would be too light a fate for them.)

What this column *will* attempt to do, and I'll make a small start at it in just a bit—patience is a virtue—is explain the way the film and television industries work. To describe what it is like to work *in* the media, the psychological attitudes that prevail, the trends and endless imitative ripoffs therefrom, and—not to put too fine a point on it—service your seemingly-endless morbid curiosity about how The Industry functions, how films are made, why such crap gets on the tube, who make the decisions, and in general inform instead of insult your intelligence.

In answer to the initial questions...

Q: If you despise television so much, Ellison, why do you continue to work in the form?

Q: How do you write a script for movies or television?

Q: What's it like working in H★O★L★L★Y★W★O★O★D?

Q: What is Robert Blake *really* like?

...I refer you (not out of venality or a desire to make even a farthing off you) to a 20,000 word essay titled "With the Eyes of Demon: Seeing the Fantastic as a Video Image" in THE CRAFT OF

SCIENCE FICTION (edited by Reginald Bretnor; Harper & Row;

1976). Questions answered in that exhaustive essay will not be answered in this column.

Now. Having labored through all the preliminary bushwah one feels required to lay down, here is a sample of the service aspects of this column.

One of the most rigidly remembered templates for a series format in the minuscule minds of television network programmers and production company executives is *The Fugitive*. Devised by Roy Huggins in 1963, it reduced to the lowest possible common denominator all the elements that stunned TV watchers have come to demand from continuing series: a strong, harried protagonist with a "mission" (find the one-armed man who killed your wife, Dr. Richard Kimble), a "deadline" or "running clock" that puts urgency into the situation (clear your name of the murder before you are recaptured and get sent to the electric chair), a not-too-closely-examined reason to get from story to story each segment (you are running from the police), and something behind him that "pushes him forward" while the "mission" exerts its pull (Lt. Gerard is obsessively on your trail).

In its limited horizon thinking, each network has attempted to repeat the success of *The Fugitive* with dozens of cliché imitations of this format. *Run for Your Life, The Invaders, The Immortal, Quest, Then Came Bronson, Route 66, The Guns of Will Sonnett*, I'm sure you can think of fifty others on your own. With the tunnelvision that lies at the core of what is wrong with television programming, the networks and packagers who sell their wares *to* the networks are clearly much less interested in serving the commonweal, of uplifting the taste of viewers, and of being responsible to the people (who own the airwaves) than they are to getting David Janssen or an identifiable somatotype of Janssen back on the road.

The most recent manifestation of this obsession, and one that concerns sf readers, relates to the success (or *apparent* success in the myth-misted minds of network honchos) of the film *The Man Who Fell to Earth*.

Within ninety days of the opening of the theatrical feature, and its seeming popularity among that demographically-desirable audience of youngfolk perceived by the networks and the advertising agencies as being best-adjusted to the Consumer Society, I received three phone calls: two from production companies, one from a major network. All three said, in either these exact words or in close approximations thereof, "We want to do something just like *The Man Who Fell to Earth*."

125

"So go buy the TV rights to the book or the film and do it," I responded.

"Well, uh, er, we can't exactly buy the rights, they're tied up," they said. "But we want you to think up an idea *like* that."

"In other words," I said innocently, "you want me to rip off the original concept of the book and/or the movie, and change it just enough so you won't get sued."

Much huffing and puffing. Much pfumph'ing and clearing of throats. Much backing and filling. "Not ezzackly," they said, wishing they had called someone a lot less troublesome. "We want to do an alien that falls to Earth, but not the movie."

"But the movie is about an alien who falls to Earth," I said. I was having a terrific little time for myself, listening to them squirm.

"We'll talk to you later about this," two of the three said. "We'll noodle it around here and get back to you."

Is there anyone who would care to guess how many centuries will pass before they call back?

The third call, from a production outfit that supplies many dozens of hours of prime-time product each season, did not end at that point. I was told that an industry-weary writer, with whom I'd worked when he was producer of a short-lived fantasy series at Screen Gems several years before, had written a ten-page *précis* of such an idea, and though the network they'd hustled with it liked the basic concept (an alien who falls to Earth), they wanted me to write the show's pilot. So the production company *had* to talk to me.

They wanted me to read the ten pages. I said I would. They sent them over. I hated them. I called the packaging producer, and advised him I thought the material sucked. I called it "sophomoric, derivative, predictable, idiotic adolescent twaddle." He asked me to spell "twaddle." I spelled it.

Then I explained it.

And explained why the ten pages were dumb. He liked my enthusiasm.

But the network wanted me, so he continued hustling, and got me to agree to come in for a network meeting. I told him I'd only badrap the material. He said that was okay, that it would "open up everyone's thinking." I suggested napalm would have the same beneficial effect. He laughed.

Well, to make a short story as tedious as possible, I took the meeting with the production company and the network, I told them how stupid I thought the original material was, and suggested a completely different approach. Not all that fresh and original, because they can't handle fresh and original. Remember David Janssen? But fresh and original enough that I wouldn't be ripping-off Walter Tevis, who wrote the original novel of THE MAN WHO FELL TO EARTH, and sufficiently fresh and original that I could develop it without suffering constant upset stomach.

So the upshot was that they went for it, put us into "development," which meant I had to write a treatment of what I wanted to do with the series and its pilot, I spent weeks arguing with the guy who had written the ten odoriferous pages and the producer, and finally came up with a *précis*, a treatment, an outline, what they call in The Industry "a bible" for the pilot and series...

And I called it *Two from Nowhere*...

And they started trying to turn it into *The Fugitive*...

And I made myself scarce...

And the network started bugging them for it...

And I'm hiding out from CBS and William P. D'Angelo and Joel Rogosin; and anyone tells them where I am, I'll punch your fucking heart out, as George Segal put it.

But what is this all in aid of? It answers your question, What sf can we look forward to next season? And the answer is *Lucan, The Man with the Power, The Man from Atlantis, Logan's Run* and several other "sci-fi" or related series.

All of which are surrogates of David Janssen running from Inspector Javert, trying to clear his name and escape the minions of the Law'n'Order till he can find the one-arm man... or the parents who deserted him in the forest where he became a feral child... or Sanctuary... or his father from another planet ...or his lost continent... or...

Which is to say, you can expect more of the same dreadfulness you didn't watch *this* season. And as for that *Star Trek* movie, gentle friends, before you find *that* one, you'll find your parents who deserted you in the forest where you became a feral child... or Sanctuary... or...

2nd INSTALLMENT:
Luke Skywalker Is A Nerd And Darth Vader Sucks Runny Eggs

Badmouthing STAR WARS these days is considered a felony; on a level with spitting on the American flag, denigrating Motherhood, admitting you hate Apple Pie, or trying to dope Seattle Slew.

In the hysterical wake of all-stops-out media hype, uncritically slavish reviews, effulgent word-of-mouth praise and the chance of being trampled to death by ex–*Star Trek* groupies, who've had their epiphany-conversion, as they queue up to see the film for the sixth or eighth time... anyone daring to suggest that *Star Wars* is less monumental than the discovery of the fulcrum and lever, runs the risk of being disemboweled by terminal acne cases.

This lemminglike hegira to worship at the shrine of director George Lucas and "the return of entertainment!" has been so carefully orchestrated that otherwise sane and rational filmgoers whose desiccated sophistication has led them to find flaws in even such damn-near-perfect movies as *The Conversation, Taxi Driver, Oh, God!* and *Nashville*, roll their eyes and clap their hands in childish delight. And I think *childish* is the operative word in this lunatic situation.

And though I find the role of Specter at the Banquet somewhat less than salutary for my social life, as a practicing writer of fantasy (into which genre science fiction and space opera of the *Star Wars* variety plonk comfortably) I'm afraid I must reluctantly piss on the parade.

Hollywood has *never* understood the difference between making science fiction films and making westerns, spy thrillers, Dr. Kildare flicks, historical adventures and contemporary dramas.

In an industry where nothing succeeds as consistently as repeated failure, the ex-CPAs, ex–mail room boys, ex-hairdressers and ex-agents who become Producers conceive of imaginative fiction as just another shoot-'em-up with laser rifles. They have a plethora of hype but a dearth of inventiveness. And they think of films in terms of making the deal, not of presenting the logical story. For most of these yahoos, a "film" is something, *anything*, they can get Streisand and McQueen and Pacino to star in. The script can come later. What the hell does it matter if it's good, bad or imbecilic . . . just as long as the names of the stars can be featured above the title.

But science fiction is a very special genre. It is the game of "what if." *What if*: we were forced to abandon the land and adapt physically to life in the seas? *What if*: everyone was telepathic and could read everyone else's mind, how could you commit a murder and not be discovered when your thoughts gave you away? *What if*: the male contraceptive pill became as common as the one women use? *What if.*

And playing that game is the core of the story. But it must be internally consistent. It must have a much more rigorous logic than an ordinary, mimetic story, because you are asking the audience to suspend its disbelief, to go with you into a completely new, never-before-existed landscape. If what goes on in the story is irrational and diffuse, then it all comes up looking like spinach.

But Hollywood doesn't understand that. They make films—like *Star Wars*—that are nothing but *The Prisoner of Zenda* or some halfwit wild west adventure in outer space.

Good science fiction films have been few and far between. I suggest as a quality level toward which to strive, the following films:

Charly
1984
The Shape of Things to Come
Wild in the Streets
The Conversation
A Boy and His Dog

And there are a few others. But they grow harder and harder to name. Because all the films that we *thought* were great, like *2001*, become, in retrospect, merely exercises in special effects. There are damned few "people" stories that deal with what science fiction at its best and most valuable handles better than any other kind of story: the effects on human beings of technology, unusual happenings and the future. Discount films that make us tingle, like *The Thing* or *Dr. Cyclops*, because they are really only horror stories told with a pseudo-scientific flair. I'm talking here about stories where we care about the people, films that cast some new light on the human condition.

Also notice, the films I select as the best are films you probably never even considered sf. *Charly* and *The Conversation* are classic examples. They weren't marketed or reviewed as sf, because they were free of overpowering special effects. They didn't *look* like orgies of bizarre technique, and they did very well at the box office, even with people who hate science fiction. Because they were "people" stories. They couldn't have happened without the scientific bases, but they took those technological advances —raising the I.Q. of an idiot by chemical means in one case, and electronic surveillance in the other—and dealt with them in terms of human *angst*.

This important measure of worth is missing entirely from *Star Wars*.

But before I enumerate the dangers of this classic simple-minded shootout movie, let me give you a few horror stories.

Incident:
During the third weekend in June, for three thousand dollars —the only thing short of bamboo shoots under the fingernails that could get me to do it—I spoke at something called *Space-Con IV*, held at the Los Angeles Convention Center. In the neighborhood of ten thousand people attended this combined *Star Trek*/ space science/tv addict media melange: a hyperventilated whacko-freako-devo two-day blast that served as cheap thrill fix for a tidal wave of incipient jelly-brains who would rather sit in front of the tube having their minds turned to purée-of-bat-guano than have to deal with the Real World in any lovely way.

Traditionally, the dealers' rooms, wherein one can buy (at usurious rates) Spock ears, Federation starship gold braid and frogging, German versions of *Star Trek* comics and hairballs called tribbles, has been a place where *Star Trek* reigned su-

131

preme. A wad of Kleenex, authenticated as being the very item William Shatner honked into during the legendary phlegm epidemic of the second year of the series, could bring a price that would permit the dealer to return to his native island a rich grandee.

In June, however, *Star Wars* had been open for nearly three weeks; and those who formerly festooned themselves with buttons that said LIVE LONG AND PROSPER or TAKE A KLINGON TO LUNCH now paraded around wearing buttons that proclaimed LET THE WOOKIEE WIN and JEDI KNIGHT and the catch-phrase that has replaced the splay-fingered Vulcan greeting of *Star Trek*, MAY THE FORCE BE WITH YOU.

Dealers loaded down with *Star Trek* memorabilia had their annuities flash before their eyes in a brief two-day nightmare as *Star Wars* posters, light sabers, Darth Vader masks and Ballantine Books paperback novelizations vanished as if they'd been warped into hyperspace.

Even panels of erudite writers and NASA space shuttle engineers were overwhelmed with trivial badinage about *Star Wars* and the effects it would have on the course of Western Civilization.

And the only adverse criticism *of any kind* I heard, from *anyone*, was a comment from the science fiction writer Alan Dean Foster, who had just handed in the manuscript of the novelized sequel to Ballantine; a comment that removed, finally, any vestige of ambivalence I'd had about badrapping *Star Wars*. That comment, in a moment, but first, another:

Incident:

I called Tony, to ask him if he and Gail wanted to go to dinner. Gail sounded terrible. "What's the matter?" I asked, thinking maybe Tony had gone back to the bottle. "I haven't seen him in a week," she wailed, actually crying over the phone. "Where the hell is he?" I asked, thinking maybe I'd have to go pry him out of an X-rated motel down on Ventura Boulevard. "He's seeing *Star Wars*," she said, sobbing. "I think he's seen it fifteen or sixteen, maybe more, times. He won't come out of the theater, except to come home and shower and then go find another place where it's playing. What am I gonna do!?!"

Incident:

I stopped off at A-1 Record Finders, to pick up the new Jaco Pastorius side, and the dude behind the counter asked me if I'd seen *it*. No name, just *IT*, like the Second or Third Coming. So I ran a few negatives, and then I noticed these two teenaged kids lounging against one of the record bins, giving me sidelong glances one usually reserves for butchers who have a thumb on the scales.

I had to go out to my car, parked right in front of the shop, and they watched me. When I returned to the shop and resumed the conversation, the two young gentlemen walked out, got their bicycles from the wall, and crossed the street right beside my car.

The neatly-furrowed gash that runs from my left front fender all the way to the left rear tire-well, handsomely engraved with a house-key held tightly in a teenaged fist, is charming testimony to the religious fervor *Star Wars* junkies manifest. Fortunately, I drive a very old, very funky car, and the gash doesn't distress me overmuch; but if I ever need crazed True Believers to help me Kill for the Love of Kali, liberate The Holy Grail, or Save Ammurrica from The Red Menace, I will begin my recruiting activities at the Avco Cinema Center on Wilshire.

These three incidents are only grassroots reflections of the blind fanaticism *Star Wars* has generated in such pro- and anti-Establishment journals as *New Times*, *New York*, *New West*, *American Film* and *Time* magazine...good old *Time* magazine that set off the main charge with its six-page, four color, May 30th story and banner-headlined cover (INSIDE: THE YEAR'S BEST MOVIE) (that's what I hate about *Time*: they're so wishy-washy).

Time was so determined to looooove that film, they even told an outright lie. On page 57 of the May 30th article, the following excerpt appears:

> "*Star Wars* is the costume epic of the future," says Ben Bova, editor of *Analog*, one of the leading science fiction magazines. "It's a galactic *Gone with the Wind*. It's perfect summer escapist fare."

Now Ben is one of my closest friends, and I simply could not believe he had bubbled along that way. He's too smart for such an okeydoke. So I called him and asked him if he'd said what *Time* said he's said. After the bellowing ceased, he made it clear that *Time*'s reporters simply were not going to hear anything negative about that flick, no matter what was actually said. Two issues of *Time* later, the following item appeared on page 6, in the Letters column:

> Your quotation of my comments about George Lucas' film *Star Wars* makes it appear that I liked the film. I most emphatically did not. Those of us who work in the science fiction field professionally look for something more than Saturday afternoon shoot-em-ups

133

when we go to a science fiction film. We have been disappointed
many times, but I had expected more of Lucas. Somebody Up There
likes the film, it seems, and no dissenting views are allowed. Too
bad.

Ben Bova, Editor
Analog
New York City

And that's what has been going down with *New Times* with its
June 24th cover story likening the comic-strip characters of *Star
Wars* to such American myth heroes as Charles Lindbergh, Joe
DiMaggio and The Lone Ranger. Hurray for the robots, R2D2
and C3PO! *New Times*'s Jesse Kornbluth sees in the film reassur-
ance that machines are not taking over, that NASA isn't involved
in a sinister conspiracy to keep us from knowing there is intelligent life on Mars, and that The Ole Debbil Technology will not
savage us further. All that terrificness, from a comic strip.

People raves. *Starlog* gushes. Rona Barrett vociferates. The
world loves *Star Wars*! And the studios and the television networks and the fastbuck bluesky independents and the mass
media have once again discovered science fiction. Except they
think it's hip to call it by that hideous neologism "sci-fi" and
nowhere can be heard a discouraging word. All that terrificness,
from a comic strip.

And that is precisely where my cavils with *Star Wars* begin.

As I write this, only the much-damned critic John Simon of
New York magazine has had the courage to say the emperor is
buck naked. While those who seem oblivious to the occasionally
honorable and more-frequently trashy history of fantastic films
that stretch back to Georges Méliès whoop and simper about how
enriching *Star Wars* is, Simon puts his finger dead on the plague-
bearing nature of this film and the way it's being received. In the
June 20th issue of *New York* he said, in part:

> I don't read science fiction, of which this may, for all I know, be a
> prime example; some light years ago I did read *Flash Gordon*, of
> which *Star Wars* is in most respects the equal. But is equaling sci-fi
> and comic strips, or even outstripping them, worthy of the talented
> director of *American Graffiti*, and worth spending all that time and
> money on?
>
> I sincerely hope that science and scientists differ from science
> fiction and its practitioners. Heaven help us if they don't: We may
> be headed for a very boring world indeed. Strip *Star Wars* of its
> often striking images and its high-falutin scientific jargon, and you

get a story, characters, and dialogue of overwhelming banality...
trite characters and paltry verbiage...

Still, *Star Wars* will do very nicely for those lucky enough to be
childish or unlucky enough never to have grown up.

Were it not for Simon's sobriety—for which he must be commended in the face of such overwhelming mass hysteria—I would think I was the only one marching to the beat of that other drummer. Because, when I emerged from the 20th Century–Fox advance screening, as far as I could tell, I was the only turkey evil enough to have ambivalent feelings and a beetled brow. It took me several days to codify my unease.

I pilloried myself. What's the matter with you, Ellison? The damned film is a wonder... filled with sight and sound and flash and filigree. It soars, it sings, it thunders through a wholly-realized universe of Lucas's imagination! Why do you feel as if you've been had? You're always bleating about the lack of magic and simple wonder in contemporary film, the kind of swell dazzlement you knew in Saturday afternoon dream-days of your youth... serials, B westerns, Val Lewton suspense films, great fantasies! Why does this *hommage* to *Flash Gordon* distress you? Have you lost the ability to see as a child sees?

And then I realized that was the problem. When I was a child, I learned from movies. I learned that you never screw a friend, never snooker him or her behind the eight ball; I learned that systems and governments intended to serve human needs frequently spend their time maintaining themselves in power to the anguish of the people; I learned that Hemingway had a workable definition when he said guts was grace under pressure; I learned about what was in store for me when I became an adult. All of these I learned without realizing I was being taught, because even those sappy, illogical schlock flicks of the '40s and '50s had *people* in them.

Star Wars has no people.

Which instantly brought to mind a rule-of-thumb for films of this sort: any motion picture—such as *2001: A Space Odyssey, Demon Seed, Silent Running* or *Forbidden Planet*—or *Star Wars* —in which the most identifiable, likeable characters are robots, is a film without people. And that is a film that's shallow, that cannot uplift or enrich in any genuine sense, because it is a film without soul, without a core. It is merely a diversion, a cheap entertainment, a quick fix with sugar-water, intended to dis-tract, divert and keep an audience from coming to grips with itself.

And in these days of widespread illiteracy, functional illiteracy, future shock, belief in coocoo conspiracies and Bermuda Triangle/UFO/reincarnation/Atlantis/est stupidities, information overload, urban terror and television stereotype, anything that keeps people stupid *is* a felony. "Entertainment is back!" the reviewers trumpeted, as if it had ever vanished. Nabokov is entertainment; Shakespeare is entertainment; Katherine Anne Porter is entertainment. Must "entertainment" be synonymous with "mindless" or "without content"? How foolish of us to have thought Mary Shelley's FRANKENSTEIN was entertaining, or Poe, or Pinter, or Scorsese's *Taxi Driver*. Troubling, yes; forcing us to think, yes; but entertainment nonetheless.

But not *Star Wars*. For all of its length, for all of its astonishing technical expertise, its headlong plunge and its stunning effects, at no time can one discern the passage of a thought. It is all bread and circuses. The human heart is never touched, the lives are unexamined, the characters are comic strip stereotypes.

But that's the point! is the single defense I get when I alienate myself at dinner parties by my negativity. *It's* supposed *to be mindless,* I'm told. And then those professorial types who are safe in loving *Star Wars* where they might be attacked for reading the latest Robert Silverberg or Thomas Disch sf novel, explain to me as carefully and quietly as one would a retarded child, that *Star Wars* is a return to the worship of the Eternal Verities: honor, truth, fighting Evil. All black and white.

Try black and white in a world of credit cards, punk rock, mastectomies, Watergate, the rise of homegrown Nazism, Anita Bryant, and the terrifying fact that more than half of all serious crimes in the United States are committed by people between the ages of ten and seventeen—and that includes rape, murder, robbery, aggravated assault and burglary.

In the Real World, anything that keeps people stupid is hardly a chuckleable item. And for several weeks I resisted putting *Star Wars* in that category. It was fun, I told myself. It was *good* for people to see a simple film in which the Good Guys were extraspecial good and the Bad Guy wore not merely a black hat, but black body-armor and a black death-mask, I told myself. Nor could I bring myself to fault Lucas, who had clearly set out to make an *hommage* to the Saturday afternoon serial and had done it with what Flaubert called "clean hands and composure." Then I heard the comment I mysteriously referred to earlier, from Alan Dean Foster; and I felt no qualms about pinning the butterfly to the board.

Not to keep you in suspense a moment longer. There we were—Alan, myself, Theodore Sturgeon and Frank Catalano—all of us properly or erroneously tagged "science fiction writers"—sitting on a panel at *Space-Con IV*, fielding questions about *Star Wars*. And I began the raving you've witnessed here. And I said the movie keeps people stupid. But I didn't have chapter and verse. All I had was a vague feeling. I said Lucas had done what he wanted to do, and all honor to him for that; he hadn't compromised. But then I remarked that one of the things in the film that was indicative of keeping people stupid was the constant boom one heard when something blew up in outer space throughout the film. And, as everyone *should* know, but most people *don't* know, since there is no air in deep space, since it is for all intents and purposes total vacuum, there can be no transmittal of shock waves, no displacement of molecules of air, and thus...no sound. And I said this was another example of giving people what they want to hear, literally, though it contravenes the laws of the physical universe. And in a time when we're so abysmally uneducated about technology, which rules our lives more each day, that was a criminal act of artistic prostitution.

Then Alan looked thoughtful and seemed reluctant to speak, perhaps because he had just written the sequel to the *Star Wars* novelization that Lucas had sold to Ballantine Books, but in his reserved and gentlemanly fashion he told the audience of a day when he had seen a rough cut of the film and had remarked on just this scientific illiteracy to Lucas. He had even suggested a workable alternative...no, *two* workable alternatives...and Lucas had said words to the effect of (approximate quote), "There's a lot of money tied up in this film and people *expect* to hear a boom when something blows up, so I'll give them the boom."

And at that moment, the cynicism showed through.

If the masses want bread and circuses, we give them bread and circuses. If they want witch-hunts, bear-baitings, kinky sex, Inquisitions, burning crosses, scapegoats, trivia and persiflage —we give it to them. Keep them entertained and they'll never hear the whistle of the executioner's axe.

As a writer who works in the medium of fantasy, both in print and in film, what *Star Wars* and its success portends is frightening to me. Already, Universal Studios is planning a Buck Rogers movie. Already, a major network that has bought one of my stories for a TV film and series, has asked me to alter realistic situations in a future society where absolute realism is the ground, to include "*Star Wars* kind of violence...you know... laser guns and all that."

The dispensers of mass information have once again discovered science fiction. They do it every seven or eight years. The last time was with *2001*. The only trouble is, they've discovered 1939 science fiction. Mindless shoot-em-up and hardware. Paeans of praise to the grommet and spanner. And that means more of the same, just the way it happened in the wake of *2001*. It means that thought-provoking sf, the kind written by Gene Wolfe and Kate Wilhelm and James Tiptree, Jr. and Michael Moorcock, has no value. It means that an entire genre of fiction for our time, material that informs and educates *and entertains*, will be bypassed in favor of more cops&robbers in outer space, more cowboys&indians on Tatooine.

Goodbye science fiction, hello sci-fi.

That's pronounced *skiffy*.

If you like peanuts, you'll *love* skiffy.

In the past month I have received calls from half a dozen film and television producers who are planning "sci-fi" projects. I won't even report on the call I received about a new Disney project-in-discussion called *Star Skirmishes*.

I'll only tell you about the producer who called to ask me if I wanted to do a space war sorta film, and all he could say was, "This is gonna be a winner. We've got really terrific state of the art."

I didn't know what that meant.

So I asked him.

He didn't understand why *I* didn't understand, but he started saying they had Magicam and new miniaturization techniques, and computer graphics, and ChromaKey, and videotape crossovers, and "all the very latest state of the art." I finally got hip. He was talking about special effects, pure and simple. No story, no terrific idea for a film that would illuminate the human condition, not even a plot. He *had* no plot. That's why he was calling me.

To write something stupid around his stupid animation and special effects nonsense.

And nomenclature had struck again. Now they were calling it "state of the art." And I submit that when filmmakers begin thinking that pyrotechnics can replace stories about people, then the ambience of the toilet has set in.

So here we sit. Ben Bova and fantasy film director/animator Jim Danforth and cranky John Simon, and good old me; all alone grumbling about the most wonderful film ever made. Running our main squeeze of sour grapes over the heads of a multimillion person audience that goes back again and again to sit in awe as the Empire dreadnought Death Star roars overhead, making its big boom of passage through airless space. Specters at the Banquet. Loveless, lightless nuisances saying the Emperor has pimples on his bare butt.

And all I can think about, in childlike wonder, is that amazing scene in the 1939 version of *The Thief of Bagdad* where Ahbhu, the little thief, uncorks the bottle and lets out the seventy-foot tall genie. And I ask myself: if *Star Wars* is so goddamn good, howzacome all I can think about is a dumb fantasy made almost forty years ago, that taught me so much about fighting to stay free and individualism and love and the value of friendship and honor...?

And why do I remember that moment of characterization when the evil vizier, Jaffar, as evil as Darth Vader any day, shows how vulnerable his love for the Caliph's daughter has made him? Was that movie less "entertaining" because the evil villain had a touch of identifiable humanity?

Yeah, I sit and think all that; and in my adolescent heart of hearts I know that Luke Skywalker is a nerd, Darth Vader sucks runny eggs, and I'm available for light saber duels any Wednesday between the hours of D2 and 3PO.

STAR TREK—
THE MOTIONLESS PICTURE

And Television begat Roddenberry, and Roddenberry begat *Star Trek*, and *Star Trek* begat Trekkies, and Trekkies begat Clamor, and Clamor begat a *Star Trek* animated cartoon, and the Cartoon begat More Clamor, and More Clamor begat Trek Conventions, and Trek Conventions begat Even More Clamor, and Even More Clamor begat T*H*E M*Y*T*H, and T*H*E M*Y*T*H begat STAR TREK—THE MOTION PICTURE, and the behemoth labored mightily and begat ... a mouse.

Fired by a decade of devoted, dedicated, often fanatical hue and cry, Paramount and producer Gene Roddenberry have given fans of the long-syndicated series precisely and exactly what they have been asking for.

And therein lies an awesome tragedy.

It is not that *Star Trek—The Motion Picture* is a bad film; it isn't. Clearly, it is also not a good film. The saddening reality is simply that it is a dull film: an often boring film, a stultifyingly predictable film, a tragically *average* film. With a two-million-dollar production pricetag one could do no other than applaud it. Bearing a freightload cost of something in excess of forty-four million dollars (not counting how many millions will be spent on prints and sweep advertising) and the unbounded expectations held for it, the timid creation that crawled across premiere movie screens on December 7th, 1979—somehow appropriately on the thirty-eighth anniversary of another great tragedy—deserves little more than regrets and a weary shake of the head.

Nothing more need be said to buttress that view than to point out that *Star Trek—TMP* bears a MPAA censorship code rating of G. General audiences, all ages admitted. The same code can be found on *Mary Poppins*, *Bambi* and *Santa Claus Conquers the Martians*. Our motto: We Take No Chances.

Why should this have come to pass? Certainly no other film in the history of cinema has been looked forward to with such willing suspension of critical reservations. Few films receive the joyous elevation, prerelease, to the status of *event*. No, strike that: to the status of Second Coming. Even those of us who had their reservations about the series were predisposed to *like* this film, to greet it with positive attitude, to review it evenhandedly, faithfully, as allies. So: take risks, be bold!

Yet after the Hollywood press screening I attended last night at the Motion Picture Academy's theater, I saw disappointment that slopped well over into animosity on the part of those who could only benefit from the film doing well. One young person was heard to say, "I waited ten years for *this*?" And on the late newscasts, when those who had seen the film were interviewed coming out of the theaters around Los Angeles, a most woebegone ambience could be perceived. These same sorts of filmgoers who had jumped up and down after *Star Wars*, who were confronted by a television camera on the sidewalk and who raved about Lucas's movie, who bounced off the walls exalting the first major sf flick of the decade, these same sorts of people stood quietly and said, "It's a swell film, very good." They were obviously rationalizing their disappointment. No insane delirium, no wild enthusiasm, just a subdued kind of polite, quiet, let's-not-do-the-movie-any-harm comment. It was obvious this was not the dream they'd expected.

But that's just the point, and cuts directly to the heart of the tragedy. It *is* what they expected! They got no better and no worse than what they deserved. For years the Trekkies have exerted an almost vampiric control over Roddenberry and the spirit of *Star Trek*. The benefits devolved from their support, that kept the idea alive; but the drawbacks now reveal themselves in all their invidious potency; because in Paramount's and Roddenberry's fealty to "maintaining the essence of the television series that fans adored," they have played it too safe.

142

Star Trek—TMP is nothing more than a gussied-up two-hour television segment.

It thereby retains most of the crippling flaws attendant on *all* television episodic series: the shallow, unchanging characterizations; the need to hammer home points already made; the banal dialogue; the illogical and sophomoric "messages"; the posturing of second-rate actors; the slavish subjugation of plot and humanity to special effects.

They were afraid of losing that quality of familiarity generated by the tv series . . . and the tragedy is that they retained in fullest measure that which they should have dispensed with. A major film should be more than a predictable television episode; and *no* amount of special effects can dim that failure. There is simply no growth between the final segment of *Star Trek* and this hyperthyroid motion picture.

The fans have had their way and Paramount may have to pay the terrible price. But one cannot really pillory the fans. It is no crime, however destructive, to *care* deeply. The blame for this film's mediocrity must be heavily laid on the shoulders of Gene Roddenberry and the imitative tiny minds of the Paramount hierarchy. The latter probably more than the former: one cannot condemn Roddenberry too much because this was his chance to revive the dream. But the studio heads, confronted with the opportunity to capitalize—without substantial risk—on the goodwill and affection of a ready audience, to bring forth a production that would have expanded and enriched the original *Star Trek* concept, to go where no studio has gone before, chose to play the game of close-to-the-vest, to mimic *Star Wars* and all its subsequent clone-children.

But audiences have now seen *Close Encounters* and *Buck Rogers* and *Battlestar Ponderosa* and *Alien* and *Starcrash* and even lesser efforts. They are reaching their surface tension with films that offer nothing more than cunningly-cobbled starship models zooming through space. *That* cheap thrill is already a dead issue; and no matter how much they delude themselves that "latest state of the art" will bring in repeat business, audiences have come more and more to hunger for human emotion, involvement and identification with the problems of interesting people, not square-jawed cowboys in stretchpants and plastic booties.

Yes, there is more machinery in this film per inch of footage than one could find in a True-Value hardware commercial, but even the models look cheesy, lacking both the gritty naturalism of *Alien's Nostromo* or the boggling cyclopean presence of *Close* 143

Encounters' mother ship. And when we are confronted by a close shot on the principals, standing near a bulkhead that is intended to be stainless steel, when it is obviously a painted flat, all verisimilitude vanishes for the viewer.

Further, the direction in these scenes of great ships in space is slovenly. The point of view is frequently absent; we are left floating in a cinematic deep that confuses the eye and gives the attentive viewer no sense of correct spatial relationships. One would expect at least professional expertise in such a crucial area when a film has opted for machines over humans.

But Robert Wise, at least in this venture, has seemingly turned a deaf ear to the morphology of filming science fiction. It is bewildering. Wise learned at the knee of Val Lewton, and his credentials prior to this film are unassailable: *Curse of the Cat People*, the 1945 Lugosi *Body Snatcher, The Day the Earth Stood Still, I Want to Live, West Side Story,* the brilliant adaptation of Shirley Jackson's novel in *The Haunting, The Sand Pebbles, The Andromeda Strain*—not to mention that he was an editor on three undeniable classics, *Citizen Kane, The Magnificent Ambersons* and *All That Money Can Buy.*

Perhaps having directed *The Sound of Music* has caught up with him, belatedly. Certainly nothing in the Wise canon but that saccharine perennial casts an ominous shadow that solidifies in his otiose handling of *Star Trek—TMP.*

One has the niggling suspicion that Wise did not take this chore seriously, that he did it with his left hand, that it did not bulk large in his conception of "important" work. Static medium shots, persistent loss of p.o.v., a perplexing disregard for the overacting and mugging of almost everyone among the featured players, and a singular lack of freshness overall in selection of camera angles supports such a supposition.

Even common attention to detail, *de rigueur* for the most amateurish B flicks, is missing here. In one scene, as Shatner moves through the turbolift doors exiting the bridge, the woman sitting to my right (a total stranger) said (audibly enough to generate laughter around us), "Look, his toupee doesn't fit right!" Fortunately the mother of ex–Paramount President Frank Yablans didn't notice it: four seats to my left she had fallen asleep. In another scene, when a plaited headband is placed over the cueball baldness of the highly-touted Ms. Persis Khambatta —about whom more in a moment—a dangling ornament hangs on the left side. Instants later, after a cutaway shot, the ornament is hanging over the *right* side. Editorial matchup, a first-year film-school necessity, was beyond a production crew so multitudinous they could have been deployed as relief team against Xerxes's ravening hordes.

But this fumblefooted, hamhanded amateurishness is not confined to Wise or the editors. It appears throughout, as if the millions chalked off to studio overhead concealed the employment of a squad of gremlins, sent in to wreak havoc on the production.

Even the special effects photography was slipshod. In the opening sequence we see three Klingon battlecruisers skimming through space. The matte lines are jarringly evident. So recurrent is this ineptitude that the editor of a prominent magazine said, "I was so busy looking for the matte fissures, I lost track of the plot. There *was* a plot, wasn't there?"

Well, yes, there was. But I'll deal with that in a while because it contains the burning core of the film's ultimate mediocrity.

But first, as I touched on it above, let me deal with the acting. What little there was.

The first human being who speaks in the film (Klingons not being *homo sapiens*) is a female communications technician in a Starfleet outpost. She speaks her lines so stiltedly, so embarrassingly sophomorically, that I had the uncomfortable feeling I was looking at somebody's daughter, girlfriend or secretary who had been given a bit part. It was common practice on the tv series, but I could not believe that in a major studio production of this magnitude such nepotism could be countenanced. I have since learned that that was precisely the case. The "actress" in question was Michele Billy, production secretary to the scenarist, Harold Livingston.

To have our first exposure to thespic technique in a film this big fall on the clearly nonexistent talent of an amateur is shocking. Further, it is symptomatic of the inbred Old Boys' Network thinking that permeates *Star Trek—TMP*.

Pork-barrel jobs such as filling the rec room scene with fans and associates like Roddenberry's secretary Susan Sackett, novelist David Gerrold, Trekker Denny Arnold and the fannish loon who legally changed his name to James T. Kirk are acceptable, because they were only walk-ons. But putting such lames as Ms. Billy and Jon Rashad Kamal (Lt. Commander Sonak) in positions of even passing prominence speaks to a loss of rationality on the part of Wise and Roddenberry that beggars pejorative description.

Yet these casting gaffes seem minuscule compared to the sins 145 of the principals. With the exceptions of Leonard Nimoy and DeForest Kelley, the cast is (why does this word keep springing to mind!?) embarrassing.

Doohan's Scotty is no different from what we saw in the series, no smarter, no kinkier, no older, no more lovable. It is a standard television performance, competent but instantly forgettable. Barrett, Koenig, Takei and Nichols have such brief moments it is impossible to tell if they have the stuff to transcend their stale material. They are thrown scraps from the table: "Warp five, Captain," "Hailing frequency open, Captain," "Negative, Captain," "We're being scanned, Captain." The kind of verbal make-work larded into the script to keep the series' regulars around as furniture, but wholly insufficient to let them practice the craft they have spent their adult lives developing. Uhura remains a glorified switchboard operator, Chekov is the same button-pusher with a raise in rank, Sulu flies the jalopy and is denied the space to exude even a scintilla of George Takei's enormous personal charm, Doctor Chapel carries bedpans. And if Transporter Chief Grace Lee Whitney had a line during the molecular dissolution sequence, it was drowned out by the embarrassed laughter provoked by Shatner's "Oh, my God!" condolence that stands out in a farrago of moments in which one covers one's face wishing one were elsewhere, as the Mt. Everest of inappropriate, awkward readings.

As said, only Nimoy and Kelley came off interestingly. I've been told that Nimoy wrote most of his own part but that in-depth sessions wound up—along with considerable footage of Koenig, Takei, Barrett and others—on the cutting room floor. But even before that stage of post-production, the *Enterprise* crew found their parts being whittled to nothing. During the course of shooting I had occasion to speak to three or four of the crew regulars who have remained my friends from the old series days. Each of them said, in almost exactly the same words and tone of voice, "Every day when I come in I find my lines a little shorter, my scenes a little more cut."

And to whom were those stolen moments given?

To Shatner, Stephen Collins and Persis Khambatta.

Collins is a drone. His part could have been played by any rock-ribbed, lantern-jawed actor. He is totally unmemorable. I will pillory him no further. He did the best he could, and that's comment sufficiently pathetic for even John Simon.

Persis Khambatta. Oh dear.

After all the prerelease hype, one would have thought the

emergence of a new Ingrid Bergman, or at very least a new Sigourney Weaver, was about to manifest itself.

Such is not the case.

This young woman is quite lovely to look at—but if shaving an esthetically-pleasing head is Makeup's idea of creating a "Vegan" alien then I fear Hal Clement will never work in films—and as for acting ability, well, the poor thing simply has none. I will pillory her no further. She did the best she could, and it is to Wise's credit that he turned her into a machine as quickly as possible, thereby permitting her to function at peak efficiency.

Which leaves us with William Shatner.

He dominates, as usual. Stuffy when he isn't being arch and coy; hamming and mugging when he isn't being lachrymose; playing Kirk as if he actually thinks he *is* Kirk, overbearing and pompous. Yet occasionally appealing, don't ask me why.

Perhaps it is that I remember Shatner from George C. Scott's production of "The Andersonville Trial," in which he was no less than staggeringly brilliant. Perhaps it is that I *wanted* to like the new, resurgent Kirk. Perhaps it is that I am—despite the catalogue of horrors dealt with herein—hopeful that this film will not bury *Star Trek*.

Nonetheless, it is common knowledge that Shatner tried to dominate every segment of the series and that he has permitted his actor's ego to drag him down to the level of actually line-counting scenes in which another actor, even Nimoy, might have the limelight a trifle longer. I have no knowledge that such was the case with the film, though I've been told there were extensive "story-conferences" among Shatner, Wise and the scenarist; yet there is no mistaking Shatner's pushiness in the lead role. He is there, for better or worse, and if the pivotal scenes where emotionalism was necessary do not come off, the responsibility is surely his.

Nimoy remains a marvel, even in the truncated sections where he is permitted to flex his talent. His Spock is a character several degrees more interesting than when last we saw him in the series. Nimoy has aged, and so has Spock. There is compassion and a touching wistfulness just beneath the stoic surface. And in terms of advancement of the original *Star Trek* format, his is the only alteration. At the end of this movie we have seen the two new characters done away with (for sequel purposes) and we're left exactly where we were when the series was canceled. No change, no growth. But Spock has found there is a reason not to be ashamed of his humanity, his feelings; there is a positive note here—attributable to the sensibility of Nimoy, we must assume—that uplifts and enriches.

But for my money, it is DeForest Kelley who sparkles most wondrously. His Dr. McCoy is big, curmudgeonly, interesting and damned fine. Of all the people in this film, McCoy is the only one I'd care to spend an evening with. I will praise him no further. He did better than his previous best and that's praise of a high order in consideration of a film where almost everyone else is ponderously portentous, hammy or overblown, added like raisin afterthoughts to a soggy plot pudding in which the most startling aspect is an almost hysterical series of costume changes more numerous than those to be found in the most overclothed Ross Hunter tearjerker.

Bringing me, at last, and with trembling, to the script.

(This part is difficult. For years there was rancor between Gene Roddenberry and me. Now, for years, there has been amiability. The conclusions I will now draw about the quality of the film deal with Gene's talent as a writer, and with Gene as a human being involved in a project that has dominated nearly twenty years of his life. He cannot love me for these observations; nonetheless I am compelled to be candid and critically honest. I can do no other. Gene knows I'm thus trapped by my love of writing. Enthusiasts of *Star Trek* and of the film may suspect otherwise. I ask those who proceed with the reading of this essay to accept my assurance that I write what follows with difficulty, but with "clean hands and composure." There is no meanness in me.)

The mark of Gene Roddenberry's limits as a creator of stories is heavily, indelibly, inescapably on this production. No matter whose name is on the screenplay, no matter who is credited onscreen for the basic story, this is the work of Gene Roddenberry. Yes, I know that in the years between 1975 and 1979 there was a parade of writers through Paramount's gates whose abilities were sought for a *Star Trek* film. Yes, I know, because twice I was one of them. Yes, I know that runs were made at the screen treatment or script by John D. F. Black, Robert Silverberg, John Povill, Chris Bryant and Allen Scott, by director Phil Kaufman, by Alan Dean Foster, and by Gene himself. Yes, I know that Gene's name was removed from screen credit five times, and finally he was taken to Writers Guild arbitration by Harold Livingston, who wound up with the credit. Yes, I know all of that; nonetheless, this is Gene Roddenberry's story. And he has to be the one pinned to the wall.

This script has all the same dumb flaws that were perpetuated in the series . . . with bigger, prettier pictures.

It is a synthesis of *at least* four segments of the *Star Trek* series: "The Corbomite Maneuver," "The Changeling," "The Immunity Syndrome" and Norman Spinrad's "The Doomsday Machine."

The ending—what one of the *Star Trek* novelists has called "a $44 million f--k"—is a direct ripoff of the ending from the film *The Last Days of Man on Earth*, a strange translation to the screen of Michael Moorcock's THE FINAL PROGRAMME.

The characterizations are monodimensional with the ghastly addition of endless winking, eyebrow-arching, nudging and mugging on the part of almost every player, so that at moments in the film we feel we're watching a parody of the Monty Python routine—"Nudge nudge, wink wink, say no more, say no more."

The basic story, for all its "latest state of the art" and its tricked-up trekkiness, is Gene's standard idea, done so often in the series: we go into space, we find God, and God is (pick one) malevolent, crazy, or a child. Not a bad idea, once or twice. Used it myself from time to time.

But even though Alan Dean Foster is given screen credit for the story, he was handed the basic story outline by Gene. It was a treatment intended as a segment of *Genesis II* back in 1973 when that Roddenberry film-for-tv was being considered as a continuing series. The title of the segment was "Robots' Return."

Thus it is ironic and no doubt painful to Gene that the realized dream is blighted by his name being absent from the writing credits. Because more than as creator, producer or guiding spirit of this project, Gene wanted to be known as the writer. And thus it was that he wrote the novel based on the screenplay. Salvation in print.

Notwithstanding the nobility of Gene's hunger for final recognition as a serious writer, it is clearly his heavy hand on the shoulders of all those who tried to beat this script that crushes any hope of originality. The critical assessment is this: for all his uncommon abilities as producer and developer of science fictional ideas for television, Gene Roddenberry is not a very good writer. And he should have accepted that knowledge, and left the writers alone.

Because *Star Trek—TMP* throws together weary and simplistic concepts that are ultimately boring because they are banal.

The plot is woebegone and predictable. It is also riddled with holes that let one perceive the vacuum lying beyond.

149

I will offer only one example. But not even the most rabid *Star Trek* fan can ignore it.

We are presented with an alien machine intelligence so vast and omniscient and powerful that it can wipe out entire worlds. It is clever enough to build for itself a ship that makes Arthur C. Clarke's Rama look like a TinkerToy. Yet it isn't smart enough to wipe the dirt off a probe from Earth so that it knows the name is VOYAGER, not VGER.

This is the quality of cheat that obtains in television, but cannot be condoned in a forty-four million dollar epic.

The script...

No. I'd rather not go on. This has become too personal, and too painful. I had meant at the outset only to say a film of acceptable mediocrity had been produced. But as the writing emerged I found myself pulled on farther and farther into more damning criticism. I did not want that to happen.

I wanted to end on an upbeat note, to say that one aspect of this film gladdened me. The unswerveable dedication to the concept that the youthful human race is intrinsically noble and capable of living with equanimity in the universe. It is an important thought, and one that is denied in both *Star Wars* and *Close Encounters*. Unlike these previously adored "sci-fi" simplicities, *Star Trek—TMP* does not tell us that we are too base, too dull and too venal to save ourselves and to prevail in an uncaring universe without the help of some kind of bogus Jesus-Saves "Force" or a Pillsbury Doughboy in a galactic chandelier. It says we are the children of Creation and if we are courageous, ethical and steadfast we can achieve our place in the light of many suns.

I take that to be a worthy message.

And that message, in plenty, is here, in this film.

I wanted to say I was delighted that Gene employed the proper authorities who watched the physics and who kept the filmmakers from acceding to studio and dumb audience desires to hear explosions in the vacuum of space. I wanted to say that I was glad the film finally got made.

And I suppose I've said all that. But this, too, must be said: Though the film has reportedly already started doing land-office business, one cannot judge these superspectacular money-eaters from their takeoff, DC-10s do crash. *King Kong* and *Superman* and *Alien* all took off impressively. They have not earned back their costs. While I wish it well, for personal if not artistic reasons, I hope *Star Trek—TMP* succeeds beyond anyone's wildest dreams. But I think the cost of the film makes it a no-win situation. And that means Paramount will have to recoup.

A series would be foolishness. But the final moment of the film, in which we are shown a black frame with the words THE HUMAN ADVENTURE IS JUST BEGINNING, points a direction for Paramount, for Gene Roddenberry, and for all those who truly respect the *idea* of what *Star Trek* might be.

An annual *Star Trek* film, enabling the studio to amortize the cost of the construction of those sets. An annual film almost like the James Bond thrillers (but one hopes with greater intelligence behind them). An annual festival of *Star Trek* that would permit the actors to practice their craft at decent wages, that would dare to do the stories television and the fears attendant on *this* film put beyond consideration, that would finally live up to the vision Gene Roddenberry had at the outset.

In short, and finally, this dollar-guzzling mediocrity should be a first step, and a bitter lesson. And let those who caused this tiresome thing to be born take heed to their own words. If there is a sequel, or many sequels . . . finally and at last . . . let the *human* adventure begin.

HARLAN ELLISON'S WATCHING
[Second Series, 1984–   ]

INSTALLMENT 1:
In Which We Begin Our Journey

It was well-met for Charles Foster Kane, and no less salutary for me; and so I begin this initial installment of these monthly ruminations-on-movies with a *Declaration of Principles*.

I will, first and always, try to entertain. I will judge film both as Art and as Craft. I will never praise a bad film simply because it has spectacular special effects. I will never allow my own film work to impede the honest discussion, favorable or otherwise, of films made by my friends or employers, current or potential. I will not excuse dishonest filmmaking just because it is good sf; I will not excuse good filmmaking if it is bad sf. I will not review sf films as if they were exempt from the highest standards of any art-form . . . to do so would be to apologize for them as if I believed —as many condescending critics do—that they are lame, or trash, and so do not have to measure up to the rigors of High Art. I will use big words from time to time, the meanings of which I may only vaguely perceive, in hopes such cupidity will send you scampering to your dictionary: I will call such behavior "public service."

GREYSTOKE: THE LEGEND OF TARZAN, LORD OF THE APES (Warner Bros.) is, conceptually, not only a disaster, but one of the most shameful examples of directorial *auteurism* since Bertrand

Tavernier gratuitously changed Jim Thompson's Pop. 1280 to Pop. 1278 in *Coup de Torchon* for no better reason than to put his own stamp of squatterdom on a dead novelist's work. It is a film that sells itself as the first authentic rendition of Burroughs's classic high-trash adventure novel of 1914, and is, in truth, as skewed a vision as the horrendous Bo-John Derek version.

What we have been given—and there is a story behind the story that could serve as the classic paradigm for the way the film industry treats its writers—is more *Dr. Jekyll and Mr. Hyde* than the Lord of the Apes. It is *Chimps of Fire* by Hugh Hudson, director of that movie about running on the beach to Vangelis music. It is not the *Greystoke* on which scenarist Robert Towne lavished years and miles of visceral material to shepherd toward production, only to have it taken from his control and given over to another with a Visigoth's respect for the primacy of interest of the creator.

It is Jekyll and Hyde. It is a schizophrenic film. It is half fowl and half foul.

That it has drawn enthusiastic comment from such film critics as Jay Cocks in *Newsweek* and Vincent Canby (who fair wets himself with naïve enthusiasm) in the *New York Times* is more saddening than anomalous. They seem to have swallowed whole the hype that this is the variorum Tarzan text. It is not. When Robert Towne (of whom more in a moment) began transferring his admiration and affection for the book to screenplay form, he understood with a fine writer's clarity of vision that the reason Tarzan has become one of the few universal literary icons is that old Edgar Rice knew precisely what he was doing. Canby seems startled to find resonances of the "wild child" fable as previously best-interpreted in the François Truffaut film of 1970. Of course! It's there; in the book; Burroughs drew on the familiar trope to provide a subtextual archetype. He was—in the best sense of the word—a consummate hack. (It is not by chance that there are only five literary creations known throughout the world. Children in Zaire who have never heard of Hamlet or Jay Gatsby or Emma Bovary or Raskolnikov know these five: Tarzan, Superman, Mickey Mouse, Robin Hood and Sherlock Holmes. They know them because they are free-floating universal images.)

And were parvenus like Canby and Cocks not above familiarizing themselves with the original novel, they would not be trumpeting this hermaphroditic poseur as True Writ.

True Writ was the original screenplay by Robert Towne. He

tried for twelve years to get *Greystoke* produced. Chances were good. Towne is one of the very few scenarists in Hollywood whose storytelling sense is the equal of a good novelist's. And the *only* parts of *Greystoke* that are worth the candle are those that Hudson shot scene-for-scene from the screenplay. How does one know that? Because *Greystoke* was a legend in Hollywood for more than a decade. Copies of the script were available. Many of us read it and marveled. We waited expectantly, hoping someone would have the sense to give Towne the seed money to begin preparations. More about *that* in a moment.

You may not know this story about Robert Towne: the screenplay for *Chinatown* (1974) was based on the historical case of the theft of the Owens Valley water and development of California's San Fernando Valley by machinations so scuzzy that they paralleled for infamous wheeling/dealing the Teapot Dome Scandal. The great Southern California robber barons—after whom streets and highways have been named—Mulholland, May, Doheny, to name a few—fleeced hundreds of thousands of people to effect their scheme. It is rumored that one of the men ruined in this skullduggery was Robert Towne's grandfather. So he wrote *Chinatown* to get even, to make some small gesture toward justice in the name of his family. The film was, of course, taken over by director Roman Polanski, who—like Hugh Hudson—had his own "vision" of what the film should be. And what went up on the screen bore only minimal resemblance to that which Towne had broken his butt to create.

Ten years later: Towne is a gentleman, and continues to resist the temptation to vilify Polanski. He will not speak of the perfidy, but the grinding of his teeth, even today, is like the settling of tectonic plates.

More sinned against than sinning, Towne has had to swallow the bitter vetch of another labor of love being wrenched from his sure hands and given over to an improbable replacement.

The problem for the studios, when they considered his script, was the actualizing of the chimp suits for the jungle sequences. Remember that only in the last ten years have we seen such a quantum leap in technical expertise where such special effects are concerned. The key phrase during those hustling years for Towne was, "The chimps have to age as the child grows up; that means they have to be better costumes than the apes in *2001*." For a long time such a thing was impossible. Finally, Warner Bros. gave Towne five hundred thousand dollars and told him   157 they'd make the film if he could find some SFX guy who could solve the problem.

Towne went to all the best people and eventually everyone said, "The only hope you've got is Rick Baker." Remember: this was before Baker's rise to prominence. Towne gave the script to Baker, who read it and came back to say yes, he could lick the problem, but it would take two years. Towne asked him, if he had unlimited financing, how long would it take? Baker said, "Two years."

So the studio—with the predictable parvenu thinking of bottom-line boobs—went to that season's hot ticket, Carlo Rambaldi, who had just hit it big with his creation of the alien in *E.T. The Extra-Terrestrial*. He read the script and said, "I can do it in eight months; four hundred thousand dollars."

Towne had reservations. He liked what Baker had said; he felt Baker was the answer. But the studio overrode his qualms. They gave Rambaldi the assignment. More than a year and six hundred thousand dollars later: not one suit. And that was the exit for Towne, because the jamook at the studio could not admit it had been *his* miscalculation.

The film was Warner's property at that point, and they decided to repeat their sophomoric mistakes by handing the Towne project to *that* season's hot ticket, Hugh Hudson, whose *Chariots of Fire*, while not actually making much money, had won the Oscar. He was the fairhaired item, and so it didn't matter that they were turning over what is, essentially, for all its English trappings, an American boys' pulp adventure story to a director known for one film of the Old School Tie, King & Country idiom.

And Hudson, surfeited with hubris, has taken the Towne screenplay, a thing of unity and brilliance, and given it to his writer buddy Michael Austin. And they have looked down their snouts at old ERB's magnum opus, and they have said, "Well, yes, there is rawther a crude vigah to this stuff, but mostly it's muck. Let's have done with the messy parts as quickly as we can, and get back to Old Blighty."

If you recall *Dr. Jekyll and Mr. Hyde*, the good doctor Henry Jekyll is something of a bore. A bit more than a bit of a goody-two-shoes, stiff upper-lipped and a model of rectitude. England's answer to the late George Apley. It is not until the appearance of the bestial Hyde that the story comes to life, that the film leaps off the screen, that the excitement begins to crackle. It is our inherent fascination with the Beast. And Stevenson (like Burroughs) knew that about us. So the best parts of ERB and RLS and *Little Caesar* and *Public Enemy* and all the rest are the parts in which the Beast is running loose. Yes, of course, morality almost always insists they get theirs (most notably in the hypocritical ethical code of motion picture and television guidelines which, though loosened these last few years, is still intended to disarm Falwell and his ilk). But what we enjoy most is not the Jekyll goody-goodness, but the Beast.

And that is what is sensational in *Greystoke*: One-third of the film takes place in the jungle as Tarzan is raised by Kala and the chimps. Two-thirds, however, is the Edwardian humdrummery of Henry Jekyll's world: a larger section of scenes we've seen again and again: in *Four Feathers* and *Beau Geste* and every L. P. Hartley yawner in which the tatters of the Empire try to convince the rest of the world that the sun never sets on *dieu et mon droit*.

The story of how Hugh Hudson ruined Rick Baker's Kala costume (oh, did I neglect to mention that the most stunning aspect of that Towne-inspired valid section is the special chimp suits built—in two years—by, er, uh, Rick Baker?) by scheduling as the first scene to be shot the segment in which Tarzan's adoptive mother is riddled by pygmy's arrows—so that Baker had to keep patching it for all the chronologically earlier shootings that came after—is now legend in the industry. (It has been reported that Baker, who had been forbidden by Hudson even to see dailies of the film for which he was in large part responsible, had to be restrained by studio guards from going for Milord Hudson's throat. Up the Colonies!) But Hudson got in all the dull, vapid manor-house clichés his "vision" demanded. And the studio execs, no doubt snowed by Hudson's British accent, nodded and said, swell.

There is very little of the Burroughs novel left. Towne wrote a savage screenplay, in which Tarzan (a name never spoken in the film for some moronic reason) was a savage, sometimes noble, sometimes not. Then Hugh Hudson and his buddy Michael Austin savaged it by removing the savagery. If you are looking for a Tarzan who, as in the novel, is an active entity, you will be disappointed. They have made him constantly and consistently reactive. He is led this way and that way, even by weak English stereotypes. And in the one scene back in England when Jane's suitor James Fox seems about to use a riding crop or somesuch on a mentally-retarded servant, and Lord John Clayton leaps from the parapet to stop him, and we think we will now see the dichotomous savage in reaction to civilization, all he does is pull the riding crop from Fox's hand and look petulant.

Christopher Lambert as the adult Tarzan is splendid. He looks like, and has the same animal charisma, as Belmondo; and no better choice could have been made for the part. Nor could any better choice have been made for the sixth Earl of Greystoke, Tarzan's grandfather, than the late Sir Ralph Richardson, whose warmth and puckishness are memorable.

The only better choice that could have been made, to save this tragic split-personality film, was to have left it in the hands of its creator... and not have given it over to a pompous furriner more attuned to Trollope than Tarzan.

And if, perchance, some passing naîf senses in you a deep well of humanism, and inquires if you can encapsulate the essence of tragedy, you might suggest that s/he note the screenplay credits on *Greystoke*. The scenarists listed are P. H. Vazak and Michael Austin. "P. H. Vazak" is the registered pseudonym used by a fine artist named Robert Towne. And you might quote to your wide-eyed questioner the words of the poet Antonin Artaud, who said: "Very little is needed to destroy a man. He needs only the conviction that his work is useless."

INSTALLMENT 2:
In Which Sublime And Ridiculous Pass Like Ships In The Night

Twenty years ago—it seems like just yesterday it burns for me with such clarity—during the 1964–65 television season, I learned a startling truth about working in the visual mediums of film and video. I was writing for a series you'll all recall titled *The Outer Limits,* and it was the most salutary experience I've ever had as a scenarist. It was the second year for that anthology of sf/fantasy stories; and because ABC-TV had decided they were going to cancel the show; and because it was more fiscally responsible for them to let it go one more season than to lay out large amounts to replace it with something new; and because everyone involved, from production companies to the network itself, was skimming off the top: the budgets were tiny even for those frontier days of black-and-white. So in a very real way, no one was watching what we did. And we were able to write what we wanted to write, because no one really gave a damn.

As long as we stayed within budget.

So that meant what we had available by way of special effects and expensive location shooting was minimal, and we had to substitute imagination.

The plots were more complex than what is usually doled out on network series, and we used misdirection, like "limbo" sets and suspense in place of Anderson opticals. We leaned heavily on characterization and inventiveness. The shows that came out of that wonderful season continue to be rerun in syndication. Not a year goes by that I don't receive tiny residual checks for my *Outer Limits* segments that continue to draw a viewership here and overseas. In England, several years ago, they were a primetime rage.

The startling truth that has become clear to me since I wrote those shows, having afterward worked on multimillion dollar productions, is that vast sums of money budgeted for science fiction films and television specials are more likely to produce an impediment to serious filmmaking than it is to grease the way to the production of films that we remember with pleasure. I'm sure there are exceptions to this rule—*Alien* and *Raiders of the Lost Ark* and *E.T.* and *2001: A Space Odyssey* come immediately to mind—but they are glaring exceptions that seem, to me, only to buttress the rule.

This startling truth intrudes on my perceptions as I view, this month, five films that range from minuscule budgets (by today's acromegalic standards) to bottom lines that would, in times past, have sent dozens of Titanics down the nautical ways.

If *Arthur* (1981) gladdened your heart, and if you squirmed with pleasure in the warmth of that feeling, then I do not think you will regret my recommending SPLASH (Touchstone Films). By the time this review sees print, you may have to hunt beyond the first-run theaters for this marvelous minnow; but if you passed it by on the grounds that the basic premise seemed silly, you'll find a reconsideration and the search eminently worthwhile. Because it is fitting and proper that *Splash* was one of the biggest moneymakers of the summer filmgoing season. It is a dear movie in the sense of that adjective as fondly-considered, honorable, heartfelt and scarce. Scarce, as in reasonably-priced.

It only cost eight million dollars (as opposed to $46 million for the unlovable *Greystoke* reviewed here last month); it was directed by a thirty-year-old actor best known for his tv sitcom role as straight-man to The Fonz, whose most outstanding previous directorial outing was the flawed *Night Shift* (1982) (as opposed to *Greystoke*'s Oscar-winning Hugh Hudson); its leading man comes to the big screen directly from one of the more embarrassing tv series in recent memory (as opposed to *Greystoke*'s internationally-lauded cast); its special effects are so few and so subtle as to seem nonexistent (as opposed to *Greystoke*'s $7 million-plus for Rick Baker's ape makeup alone); and it was distributed—and some say partially financed sub-rosa—as an independent production by Disney's Buena Vista (whose track record for fantasy is notable for *The Black Hole* [1979] and *Tron* [1982]); not to mention a basic plot premise so trivial it might have been rejected for one of the tripartite segments of *Fantasy Island* (as opposed to the alleged canonical presentation of Burroughs's classic novel).

Yet despite all those seeming drawbacks and question marks, *Splash* comes out of nowhere, with a minimum of screamhorn ballyhoo, to endear to us its director, Ron Howard, its leading man, Tom Hanks, its lovely female lead, Daryl Hannah, and the fledgling Touchstone Films, as a gentle, uplifting fantasy that puts most other gargantuan projects in the genre to shame. Most particularly *Greystoke*.

Splash is a love story, the romance between a likeable, average guy who runs a wholesale fruit and vegetable business in New York...and a, uh, er, a mermaid. Now hold it! Don't go running the other way. If you need pith and moment, you can salve your lust for cheap entertainment with a perfectly acceptable rationalization that it's a cunning contemporary reworking of the Orpheus–Eurydice myth. Which it is, truly. Trust me on this one.

There is no need to explicate the storyline further. It is more than strong enough to support the charming, faultless performances of Hanks, Hannah, Howard Morris and those two inspired escapees from *SCTV*, John Candy and Eugene Levy. (Candy, in fact, seems to me to be the worthy inheritor of Belushi's mantle, with a style and charisma that the late comedian never fully developed, for all the mythic revisionism attendant on his death.) Nor need more be said about the plot's twisty turns than to add that it provides a showcase for Ron Howard's abilities as a director: a talent as sure and as correctly self-effacing as that of Sturges or Capra. With this film the lisping Winthrop of *The Music Man* (1962), the freckled Opie of *The Andy Griffith Show*, the straight arrow Steve Bolander of *American Graffiti* (1973) and the incurably naïve Richie Cunningham of *Happy Days* outperforms older and more extolled directors whose finest moments are not the blush on a butterfly's wings to what Howard has done here so, well, endearingly.

One final word before I send you off to see *Splash*, a word about internal logic and the use of restrained, intelligent special effects.

A traditional mark of bad sf films has been the need to   163 "explain" specious reasoning of plots and SFX. Long-winded oratorios that throw around gobbledygook that confuses photons with protons, parsecs with light-years, oxides with oxhides. It is an indication that the makers of the film are ignorant, have perhaps read but not understood an Asimov essay, and hold the audience's intellect in contempt. Too much is said, too much is roundaboutly rationalized, too many flashing lights dominate the screen.

In *Splash*—take note all you parvenu filmmakers—we willingly suspend our disbelief that such a thing as a mermaid can exist, that such a creature could have a tail in the ocean and legs on land (as we never did in *Miranda* [1947] or *Mister Peabody and the Mermaid* [1948] no matter how beguiling Glynis Johns and Ann Blyth were as the sea-nymphs) because the scenarists and the production crew believe it! When you see *Splash* take note of the one brief conversation Eugene Levy has with Howie Morris, in which the rationale is established. It is, they say, because it *is*. Nothing further is needed. But it suffices because in the one special effect scene I can recall, gorgeous Darryl Hannah lies in the bathtub, runs her hand down her thigh...and it begins to pucker as with scales. *C'est ça.*

Both the most and the least a responsible film critic can say is that the third *Star Trek* movie is out, and Trek fans will love it. Like a high mass in Latin or the asking of the four questions at a Passover seder, films continuing the television adventures of the familiar crew of the starship *Enterprise* are formalized ritual. Without all that has gone before—the original NBC series (1966–69), a Saturday morning animated version (1973–75), endless novelizations, a cult following that has spawned its own mini-fandom replete with gossipzines, newszines and even a flourishing underground of soft-core Kirk-*shtups*-Spock pornzines—these films would be non-events. (Though I am told that results of a studio-fostered research sample gathered from an audience last March 17th imparted the confusing statistic that 44% of those queried were "unfamiliar with *Star Trek*." I cannot explain this intelligence.)

But it is all True Writ now, and these movies need not be judged as if they were Film, or Story, or even Art. What it is, bro, is a growth industry.

STAR TREK III: THE SEARCH FOR SPOCK (Paramount) seems less interesting than *ST II: The Wrath of Khan* (1982) but infinitely better than the first feature-length adventure of them as boldly went where no man had gone before, *Star Trek—The Motion Picture* (1979). I'm not sure that's saying much, except to point out that producer-writer Harve Bennett has had the sense to keep creator Gene Roddenberry in a figurehead mode, thus permitting a savvy commercial recycling of time-tested and much-beloved tropes; and by allowing Leonard Nimoy to direct this film, Bennett has kept Spock in the fold: a canny solution by a minister without portfolio of the thorny problem posed by an indispensable star who wanted out.

And with but minor flaws easily credited to, and excused by, this being Nimoy's first major stint behind the camera, he has done a commendable yeoman job. There is, for instance, a pleasing easiness in the performances by the "regulars"; a result (I am told by several of the actors) of Nimoy's sensitivity in directing them as *actors* and not, as in past films directed by Wise and Meyer, as mere button-pushing background, as foils for the "stars" and the SFX whizbang.

There are a few interesting new moments this time: Christopher Lloyd's Klingon villain (strongest in the earlier stages of his appearance onscreen, before he converts from the guttural alien tongue to English); a 6-track Dolby stereo sound system designed to blast you out of the Cineplex box whereat you'll be screening the film; a nice sense of alien landscape on the Genesis Planet, especially the scenes of snow falling on giant cactus; the Klingon "Bird of Prey" battle cruiser.

Contrariwise, there are the usual problems: no one, not even Nimoy-as-Director, seems able to tone down William Shatner's need to mouth embarrassing and spuriously portentous platitudes as if he were readying himself to play the title role in the life story of Charlton Heston; the fine cast of "regulars" is once again denied extended scenes in which their talents can be displayed, in lieu of Shatner's scene-hogging and the expected flaunting of expensive special effects; Robin Curtis, replacing Kirstie Alley as the Vulcan Lt. Saavik, is as memorable as spaetzle; and the plot makes virtually no sense if examined closely.

But neither the positives nor the negatives of such effete critiques matter as much as a dollop of owl sweat. *Star Trek* has become, obviously, a biennial booster shot for Trekkies, Trekkers, Trekists, and fellow-trekolers. And as such, places itself as far beyond relevant analysis as, say, James Bond or Muppets movies.

The most and the least a responsible film critic can say is that   165 the third *Star Trek* movie is out, and Trek fans will love it. For the rest of us, it's better than a poke in the eye with a flaming stick.

THE ICE PIRATES (Metro-Goldwyn-Mayer) is *so* ludicrous it ought to be enshrined in the Academy of Dumb Stuff with such other sterling freaks of nature as the lima bean, poison ivy, the Edsel and the singing of Billy Idol. A space opera that melds (and this is how they're selling it) *Star Wars* (1977) with *Captain Blood* (1935), this poor gooney bird of a movie has all the grace and charm of a heavy object falling downstairs.

If you accept the basic premise that the story takes place in a distant galaxy where the rarest, most valuable commodity is water, and that buccaneer swashbucklers make raids on the incredibly evil Templar Empire to hijack ice cubes from their interstellar refrigerator tankers, then I have some dandy land in the Sargasso Sea for sale that I think you'd like a lot. Furnished.

The acting, keynoted by performances by Robert Urich (late of the tv series *Vega$*) and Mary Crosby (who tried to kill J. R. Ewing on *Dallas*), makes one look back with fondness on the thespic abilities of Jon Hall and Vera Hruba Ralston, Audie Murphy and Jack Webb.

This is the sort of thalidomide offspring of *Battlestar Ponderosa* that ought to be led out of the theater wearing a Hartz Flea Collar.

And yet, may Allah forgive me, there is a devil-may-care quality to this moronic sport that lingers with affection in the memory. There are moments—as when one robot kicks another in the nuts—that plumb such Olympian depths of stupidity that one must credit co-author/director Stewart Raffill with a degree of *chutzpah* unknown since Hitler opined he could conquer Russia in the wintertime.

I cannot in conscience recommend this film, but if you're the sort of entertainment-seeker who ain't embarrassed when the pregnant lady comes out of the audience to do a full striptease on amateur night at The Pink Pussycat, this may be just the grotesquerie for you. If so, don't write to thank me for the tip.

It's not nice, I know, to tempt you with a review of a wonderful film you may never be able to see, but having been privileged to attend a screening of THE QUEST (Okada International), a short film produced and directed by Saul and Elaine Bass, written by Ray Bradbury and based on his 1946 *Planet Stories* allegory,

"Frost and Fire," I must risk your censure in hopes that some convention committee will bust its buns laying on a showing of this remarkable fantasy.

The film (as was so with the novella) operates off a lovely, simple idea: a race of humanoid creatures has a life span of merely eight days. They are born, live and die in the place where they have always dwelled, but a hunger burns in them to know what lies "beyond," out there. Yet by the time an emissary to out-there grows old enough to be trained for the journey, s/he is doomed to death before s/he can reach the goal. The film is the journey finally made by one of these people, set on the path as a child.

Saul Bass, whom cinéastes correctly hold in awe for his innovative maintitles on *The Man with the Golden Arm* (1955), *Around the World in Eighty Days* (1956), *Anatomy of a Murder* (1960), *North By Northwest* (1960), *Psycho* (1961), *Exodus* (1962), *Walk on the Wild Side* (1963), and forty other major films, who directed the shower sequence in *Psycho* and the final battle sequence in *Spartacus* (1961), and whose short films include the unforgettable *Why Man Creates* (1968), has done with live action and animation what studios spending millions have not been able to do: he has conveyed the ephemeral magic of Bradbury's world-view without awkwardness in translation, without stilted dialogue or precious pomposity.

In less than half an hour of the most incredibly affecting visuals since the exundation of computer-generated graphics attendant on *Star Wars* and its horde of imitations, Bass and Bradbury have brought forth a small miracle of cinematic wisdom and beauty. I cannot recommend it too highly.

At present no plans are on line for commercial distribution, but schools, libraries, colleges *and accredited convention committees* can obtain *The Quest* in 16mm or videotape either through Pyramid Films, in Santa Monica, California, or by direct arrangement with Saul Bass/Herb Yager and Associates in Los Angeles. Acquisition is hardly difficult if desire exists.

It is my hope that I've whetted the appetites of those who program films for sf conventions. Before the next imprudent and morally reprehensible scheduling of such *dreck* as John Carpenter's *The Thing* (1982) or one of those detestable *Friday the 13th/Halloween* pukers, let those who pretend to some affection for film, who announce their respect for convention attendees, locate *The Quest* and showcase it. In their lemminglike rush to saturate film programs with dross, scheduling officials would be ennobled by a sober shake of the head and the presentation of an important little film that is *about something more meaningful* than mass slaughter by devious means.

Of the many low blows leveled against Scott Joplin, the great ragtime composer, by a universe that seemed determined to keep him unknown in his lifetime, one of the most unfair was his scandalous treatment by the organizers of the famous "Louisiana Purchase Exposition," the St. Louis Expo of 1904.

Joplin was by far the most popular musician of his day. Yet the nabobs who styled themselves arbiters of taste in those post-Victorian times of Late George Apley anal retention considered his work the merest popular trash, fit only for nautch houses and performances on streetcorners.

After a long and bitter struggle, Joplin's publisher managed to get the Exposition to invite Joplin to perform as one of a number of "American artists." It was a grudging invitation, and they set up the great black innovator in one miserable booth... next door to John Philip Sousa's augmented march band.

Joplin and his exquisite little rags were, perforce, blown away by the brassy riptide of Sousa's martial maelstrom. In the cacophony of "Under the Double Eagle" no one paid pennyfarthing attention to the wonder of "The Cascades."

Preceding as paradigm.

I opened this column with the observation that too often a large budget gets in the way of a good film being made—as witness *Greystoke* at $46 million—while a reasonable financial outlay (for these inflated days) forces the producers to use imagination instead of flash&filigree—as witness *Splash* at $8 million. Concomitant to this theory is the demonstrated truth that films on which so much lucre has been expended get a sales campaign that blasts out of the public consciousness those possibly better films whose budgets don't include a 24-hour-a-day television blitz.

The horrible reality of that low blow trembles in my thoughts as I come to the film I've saved for last: what may be one of the most memorable sf films ever made, a textbook example of *how to* make a motion picture in this genre skillfully, inexpensively, and imaginatively, but a film that may, like the delicate tracery of Scott Joplin's work, be outblasted by the brassy special effects monstrosities being pushed so hard by studios with megabucks invested in inferior product.

I speak of ICEMAN (Universal). And I say it is magnificent.

I suggest that *Iceman* may well be one of those classic films utilizing the furniture of sf to illuminate the human condition that both aficionados and mundanes will overlook, or not even consider sf, as happened to two of the finest movies ever made in our realm: *Seconds* (1966) and *Charly* (1968). Overlooked entirely or, at best, quickly forgotten in the Doppler effect created by the passage of Jedis, Greystokes, firestarters and other assorted treks.

The story: a mining and exploration company, drilling in the Arctic above the 66th parallel, excises a block of ice in which a living Neanderthal has been frozen for 40,000 years. He is revived, he is sequestered in an immense terrarium for study, and communication is established with him.

It is not a new idea. (Richard Ben Sapir does it with greater panache and innovation in his outstanding 1978 novel, THE FAR ARENA, which I commend to your attention.) But within the scope of this uncomplicated plotline, such riches of drama, humanism, compassion and philosophical depth have been thrown up onto the screen that *Iceman* becomes no less than a shining icon of cinematic High Art.

The Australian director of *The Chant of Jimmie Blacksmith* (1978) and *Barbarosa* (1982), Fred Schepisi, has been imported by producer Norman Jewison; and he brings to this film the undeniable brio that seems to mark the work of this entire generation of Aussie directors—Peter Weir, George Miller, Bruce Beresford, Gillian Armstrong—a passion and intelligence against which we in America dare to throw the likes of De Palma, Landis, Ashby, Colin Higgins or Mark Lester. Based on a story by John Drimmer, the screenplay by Chip Proser and Drimmer is a model of clarity and foreshadowing. Engaging performances by Timothy Hutton as the anthropologist who becomes the prehistoric man's teacher and companion, and Lindsay Crouse as the project director, buttress and resonate to the absolutely astonishing acting done by the classically-trained (at the Chin Chiu Academy of the Peking Opera) Eurasian John Lone as "Charlie," the man frozen in time.

It is beyond words to attempt a characterization of the effulgence Lone brings to what might have been no better than a reprise of Victor Mature vaudeville grunting. There is a world of pathos and nobility in Lone's iceman, and if there is a God, Lone will be onstage at the Dorothy Chandler Pavilion next year at Oscar time.

But more than superb acting and intelligent story, *Iceman*   169 reaches toward questions that burn fiercely at the core of the human equation.

And in the final moments, when it seems that an insoluble situation has been constructed from which no satisfying egress exists, the scenarists, director and actors give us a finale that lifts our arms to the skies, that raises our eyes to the heavens, in precisely the bodily position the iceman was first found. As one who despises counterfeit emotion à la *Love Story* (1970), who does not cheer for the Rockys of this world, who winces at the cheap manipulation of much contemporary cinema, I found it difficult to admit that I was sitting with tears at the final freeze-frame of *Iceman*.

This is what filmmaking is all about.

It was made for less than ten million dollars.

If you see it, you will never forget it.

INSTALLMENT 3:
In Which We Scuffle Through The Embers

If tomorrow's early edition of the *New York Times* bore the headline STEPHEN KING NAMED AS DE LOREAN DRUG CONNECTION, it would not by one increment lessen the number of Stephen King books sold this week. Goose the total, more likely.

If Tom Brokaw's lead on the NBC news tonight is, "The King of Chiller Writers, Stephen King, was found late this afternoon in the show window of Saks Fifth Avenue, biting the heads off parochial school children and pouring hot lead down their necks," it would not for an instant slow the rush of film producers to put under option his every published word. Hasten the pace, more likely.

If your cousin Roger from Los Angeles, who works for a food catering service that supplies meals to film companies working on location, called to pass along the latest hot bit of ingroup showbiz gossip, and he confided, "You know Steve King, that weirdo who writes the scary novels? Well, get this: he worked with Errol Flynn as a secret agent for the Nazis during World War II!" it would not drop the latest King tome one notch on the *Publishers Weekly* bestseller listings. Pop it to the top of the chart, more likely.

Stephen King is a phenomenon *sui generis*. I've been told he is fast approaching (if he hasn't already reached it) the point of being the bestselling American author of all time. In a recent survey taken by some outfit or other—and I've looked long and hard for the item but can't find it so you'll have to trust me on this—it was estimated that two out of every five people observed reading a paperback in air terminals or bus stations or suchlike agorae were snout-deep in a King foma.

There has never been anything like King in the genre of the fantastic. Whether you call what he writes "horror stories" or "dark fantasy" or "imaginative thrillers," Stephen King is the undisputed, hands-down, nonpareil, free-form champ, three falls out of three.

This is a Good Thing.

Not only because King is a better writer than the usual gag of bestseller epigones who gorge the highest reaches of the lists —the Judith Krantzes, Sidney Sheldons, Erich Segals and V. C. Andrewses of this functionally illiterate world—or because he is, within the parameters of his incurably puckish nature, a "serious" writer, or because he is truly and in the face of a monumental success that would warp the rest of us, a good guy. It is because he is as honest a popular writer as we've been privileged to experience in many a year. He writes a good stick. He never cheats the buyer of a King book. You may or may not feel he brought off a particular job when you get to page last, but you *never* feel you've been had. He does the one job no writer may ignore at peril of tar and feathers, he *delivers*.

Sometimes what he delivers is as good as a writer can get in his chosen milieu, as in CARRIE and THE SHINING and THE DEAD ZONE and THE DARK TOWER. Sometimes he's just okay, as in CUJO or CHRISTINE. And once in a while, as in the NIGHT SHIFT and DIFFERENT SEASONS collections, he sings way above his range. (And those of us who have been privileged to read the first couple of sections of "The Plant," King's work-in-progress privately printed as annual holiday greeting card, perceive a talent of uncommon dimensions.)

So why is it that films made from Stephen King's stories turn out, for the most part, to be movies that look as if they'd been chiseled out of Silly Putty by escapees from the Home For the Terminally Inept?

This question, surely one of the burning topics of our troubled cosmos, presents itself anew upon viewing FIRESTARTER (Universal), Dino De Laurentiis's latest credential in his struggle to prove to the world that he has all the artistic sensitivity of a
172 piano bench. Based on Steve King's 1980 novel, and a good solid

novel it was, this motion picture is (forgive me) a burnt-out case. We're talking scorched earth. Smokey the Bear would need a sedative. Jesus wept. You get the idea.

The plotline is a minor key-change on the basic fantasy concept King used in CARRIE. Young female with esper abilities as a pyrotic. (Because the people who make these films think human speech is not our natural tongue, they always gussie up simple locutions so their prolixity will sound "scientific." Pyrotic was not good enough for the beanbags who made this film, so they keep referring to the firestarter as "a possessor of pyrokinetic abilities." In the Kingdom of the Beanbags a honey-dipper is a "Defecatory Residue Repository Removal Supervisor for On-Site Effectation.")

The conflict is created by the merciless hunt for the firestarter—eight-year-old Charlene "Charlie" McGee, played by Drew Barrymore of *E.T.* fame—that is carried out by a wholly improbable government agency alternately known as the Department of Scientific Intelligence and "The Shop." Charlie and her daddy, who also has esper abilities, though his seem to shift and alter as the plot demands, are on the run. The Shop has killed Charlie's mommy, for no particularly clear reason, and they want Charlie for their own nefarious purposes, none of which are logically codified; but we can tell from how oily these three-piece-suiters are, that Jack Armstrong would never approve of their program. Charlie and her daddy run, The Shop gnashes its teeth and finally sends George C. Scott as a comic-book hit man after them; and they capture the pair; and they run some special effects tests; and Charlie gets loose; and a lot of people go up in flames; and daddy and the hit man and the head of The Shop all get smoked; and Charlie hitchhikes back to the kindly rustic couple who thought it was cute when she looked at the butter and made it melt.

The screenplay by Stanley Mann, who did not disgrace himself with screen adaptations of THE COLLECTOR and EYE OF THE NEEDLE, here practices a craft that can best be described as creative typing. Or, more in keeping with technology, what he has wrought now explains to me the previously nonsensical phrase "word processing." As practiced by Mr. Mann, this is the processing of words in the Cuisinart School of Homogeneity.

The direction is lugubrious. As windy and psychotic as Mann's scenario may be, it is rendered even more tenebrous by the ponderous, lumbering, pachydermal artlessness of one Mark L. Lester (*not* the kid-grown-up of *Oliver!*). Mr. Lester's fame, the *curriculum vita,* that secured for him this directional sinecure, rests on a quagmire base of *Truck Stop Women, Bobbie Joe and the Outlaw* (starring Lynda Carter and Marjoe Gortner, the most fun couple to come along since Tracy and Hepburn, Gable and Lombard, Cheech and Chong), *Stunts* and the awesome *Roller Boogie.* The breath do catch, don't it!

Like the worst of the television hacks, who tell you everything three times—Look, she's going to open the coffin! / She's opening the coffin now! / Good lord, she opened the coffin!—Lester and Mann reflect their master's contempt for the intelligence of filmgoers by endless sophomoric explanations of things we know, not the least being a tedious rundown on what esp is supposed to be.

The acting is shameful. From the cynical use of "name stars" in cameo roles that they might as well have phoned in, to the weary posturing of the leads, this is a drama coach's nightmare. Louise Fletcher sleepwalks through her scenes like something Papa Doc might have resurrected from a Haitian graveyard; Martin Sheen, whose thinnest performances in the past have been marvels of intelligence and passion, has all the range of a Barry Manilow ballad; David Keith with his constantly bleeding nose is merely ridiculous; and Drew Barrymore, in just two years, has become a puffy, petulant, self-conscious "actor," devoid of the ingenuousness that so endeared her in *E.T.*

And what in the world has happened to George C. Scott's previously flawless intuition about which scripts to do? It was bad enough that he consented to appear as the lead in Paul Schrader's loathsome *Hardcore*; but for him willingly to assay the role of John Rainbird, the ponytailed Amerind government assassin, and to perform the part of what must surely be the most detestable character since Joyboy's mother in *The Loved One*, Divine in *Pink Flamingos* or Jabba the Hut with a verve that borders on teeth-gnashing, is beyond comprehension. It has been a while since I read the novel, but it is not my recollection that the parallel role in the text possessed the McMartin Pre-School child molester mien Scott presents. It is a jangling, counter-productive, unsavory element that is, hideously, difficult to sweep from memory. That it is in some squeamish-making way memorable, is not to Scott's credit. It is the corruption of his talent.

Dino De Laurentiis is the Irwin Allen of his generation: coarse, lacking subtlety, making films of vulgar pretentiousness that personify the most venal attitudes of the industry. He ballyhoos the fact that he had won two Oscars, but hardly anyone realizes they were for Fellini's *La Strada* and *Nights of Cabiria* in 1954 and 1957—and let's not fool ourselves, even if the publicity flaks do: those are *Fellini* films, not De Laurentiis films—long before he became the cottage industry responsible for *Death Wish*, the remakes of *King Kong* and *The Hurricane*, the travesty known as *Flash Gordon, Amityville II* and *Amityville 3-D, Conan the Barbarian* and the embarrassing *King of the Gypsies*.

But Dino De Laurentiis is precisely the sort of intellect most strongly drawn to the works of Stephen King. He is not a lone blade of grass in the desert. He is merely the most visible growth on the King horizon. Stephen King has had nine films made from his words, and there is a formulaic reason why all but one or two of those films have been dross.

Next time I'll try to codify that reason.

Until then, and more about these films later, go see *Repo Man* (if you can find it) and *Indiana Jones and the Temple of Doom*. Avoid with all your might *Streets of Fire*. Don't miss *Ghostbusters*. And prepare yourself to avoid all reviews and blandishments that will suggest you see *Gremlins*, one of the most purely evil films ever visited on the filmgoing public.

I will deal at length with each of these as soon as I blight my friendship with Stephen King.

INSTALLMENT 4:
In Which We Discover Why The Children Don't Look Like Their Parents

Pinter works, though he shouldn't; and I'll be damned if I can discern why; he just does. Bradbury and Hemingway don't; and I think I can figure out why they don't, which is a clue to why Stephen King doesn't, either. Xenogenesis seems to be the question this time around, and if you'll go to your Unabridged and look it up, I'll wait right here for you and tell you all about it when you get back.

Times passes. Leaves flying free from a calendar. The seasons change. The reader returns from the Unabridged.

Now that we understand the meaning of the word Xenogenesis, let us consider why it *is* that King's books—as seemingly hot for metamorphosis as any stuff ever written by anyone—usually wind up as deranged as Idi Amin and as cruel as January in Chicago and as unsatisfying as sex with the pantyhose still on: why it *is* that the children, hideous and crippled offspring, do not resemble their parents.

First, I can just imagine your surprise when I point out that this thing King has been around in the literary consciousness a mere ten years. It was just exactly an eyeblink decade ago that the schoolteacher from Maine wrote:

> Nobody was really surprised when it happened, not really, not at the subconscious level where savage things grow...Showers

turning off one by one, girls stepping out, removing pastel bathing caps, toweling, spraying deodorant, checking the clock over the door. Bras were hooked, underpants stepped into...Calls and cat-calls rebounded with all the snap and flicker of billiard balls after a hard break...Carrie turned off the shower. It died in a drip and a gurgle...It wasn't until she stepped out that they all saw the blood running down her leg.

Second, I'll bet none of you realized what a fluke it was that King took off so abruptly. Well, here's the odd and unpredictable explanation, conveyed because I happened to be there when it happened. (Who else would tell you this stuff, gang?)

Doubleday had purchased CARRIE for a small advance. It was, in the corporate cosmos, just another mid-list title, a spooky story to be marketed without much foofaraw among the first novels, the "learn to love your brown rice and get svelte thighs in 30 minutes" offerings, the books one finds in the knockoff catalogues nine months later at $1.49 plus a free shopping bag. But King's editor read that opening sequence in which the teleki-netic, Carrie White, gets her first menstrual experience before the eyes of a covey of teenage shrikes, and more than the light-bulb in the locker room exploded. Xeroxes of the manuscript were run off; they were disseminated widely in-house; women editors passed them on to female secretaries, who took them home and gave them to their friends. That first scene bit hard. It was the essence of the secret of Stephen King's phenomenal success: the everyday experience raised to the mythic level by the application of fantasy to a potent cultural trope. It was Jungian archetype goosed with ten million volts of emotional power. It was the commonly-shared horrible memory of half the popula-tion, reinterpreted. It was the flash of recognition, the miracle of that rare instant in which readers dulled by years of reading artful lies felt their skin stretched tight by an encounter with artful truth.

Stephen King, in one emblematic image, had taken control of his destiny.

I'm not even sure Steve, for all his self-knowledge, has an unvarnished perception of how close he came to remaining a schoolteacher who writes paperback originals as a hobby and to supplement the family income in his spare time when he's not too fagged out from extracurricular duties at the high school.

But just as Ian Fleming became an "overnight success" when John F. Kennedy idly mentioned that the James Bond books— which had been around for years—were his secret passion; just as DUNE took off in paperback years after its many rejections by publishers and its disappointing sale in hardcover, when Frank Herbert came to be called "the father of Earth Day" and the novel was included in THE WHOLE EARTH CATALOG; just as Joseph Heller, Joseph Heller's agent, Joseph Heller's publisher and the Eastern Literary Establishment that had trashed CATCH-22 when it was first published, began trumpeting Heller's genius when *another* literary agent (not Heller's), named Candida Donadio, ran around New York jamming the book under people's noses, telling them it was a new American classic; in just that inexplicable, unpredictable, magic way, Doubleday's in-house interest spread. To *Publishers Weekly*, to the desk of Bennett Cerf, to the attention of first readers for the film studios on the Coast, to the sales force mandated to sell that season's line, to the bookstore buyers, and into the cocktail-party chatter of the word-of-mouth crowd. The word spread: this CARRIE novel is hot.

And the readers were rewarded. It *was* hot: because King had tapped into the collective unconscious with Carrie White's ordeal. The basic premise was an easy one to swallow, and once down, all that followed was characterization. That is the secret of Stephen King's success in just ten years, and it is the reason why, in my view, movies based on King novels never resemble the perfectly decent novels that inspired them.

In films written by Harold Pinter as screenplay, or in films based on Pinter plays, it is not uncommon for two people to be sitting squarely in the center of a two-shot speaking as follows:

> CORA: (Cockney accent) Would'ja like a nice piece of fried bread for breakfast, Bert?
> BERT: (abstracted grunting) Yup. Fried bread'd be nice.
> CORA: Yes . . . fried bread *is* nice, in't it?
> BERT: Yuh. I like fried bread.
> CORA: Well, then, there 'tis. Nice fried bread.
> BERT: It's nice fried bread.
> CORA: (pleased) Is it nice, then?
> BERT: Yuh. Fried bread's nice.

Unless you have heard me do my absolutely hilarious Pinter parody, or have seen every Pinter play and film out of unconstrained admiration for the man's work—as have I—then the foregoing copy cannot possibly read well; nor should it, by all the laws of dramaturgy, *play* well onscreen. But it does. I cannot decipher the code; but the cadences work like a dray horse, pulling the plot and character development, the ever-tightening

179

tension and emotional conflict, toward the goal of mesmerizing involvement that is Pinter's hallmark.

We have in this use of revivified language a sort of superimposed verbal continuum at once alien to our ear and hypnotically inviting. To say more, is to say less. It *does* work.

But if we use the special written language of Bradbury and Hemingway as examples, we see that such "special speaking" does *not* travel well. It bruises too easily.

Perhaps it is because of the reverence lavished on the material by the scenarists, who are made achingly aware of the fact that they are dealing with *literature*, that blinds them as they build in the flaws we perceive when the film is thrown up on the screen. Perhaps it is because real people in the real world don't usually speak in a kind of poetic scansion. Perhaps it is because we love the primary materials so much that *no* amount of adherence to source can satisfy us. But I don't think any of those hypotheses, singly or as a group, pink the core reason why neither Bradbury's nor Hemingway's arresting fictions ever became memorable films. When Rock Hudson or Rod Steiger or Oskar Werner mouth Bradburyisms such as:

> "Cora. Wouldn't it be nice to take a Sunday walk the way we used to do, with your silk parasol and your long dress swishing along, and sit on those wire-legged chairs at the soda parlor and smell the drugstore the way they used to smell? Why don't drugstores smell that way any more? And order two sarsaparillas for us, Cora, and then ride out in our 1910 Ford to Hannahan's Pier for a box supper and listen to the brass band. How about it?...If you could make a wish and take a ride on those oak-lined country roads like they had before cars started rushing, would you *do* it?"

or Gregory Peck or Ava Gardner carry on this sort of conversation from Hemingway:

> "Where did we stay in Paris?"
> "At the Crillon. You know that."
> "Why do I know that?"
> "That's where we always stayed."
> "No. Not always."
> "There and at the Pavillion Henri-Quatre in St. Germain. You said you loved it there."
> "Love is a dunghill. And I'm the cock that gets on it to crow."
> "If you have to go away, is it absolutely necessary to kill off everything you leave behind? I mean do you have to take away everything? Do you have to kill your horse, and your wife and burn your saddle and your armor?"

what we get is the auditory equivalent of spinach. The actors invariably convey a sense of embarrassment, the dialogue marches from their mouths like Prussian dragoons following Feldmarschall von Blücher's charge at Ligny, and we as audience either wince or giggle at the pomposity of what sounds like posturing.

This "special speaking" is one of the richest elements in Bradbury and Hemingway. It reads as inspired transliteration of the commonplace. But when spoken aloud, by performers whose chief aim is to convey a sense of verisimilitude, it becomes parody. (And that Bradbury and Hemingway have been parodied endlessly, by both high and low talents, only adds to their preeminence. They are *sui generis* for all the gibes.)

The links between King and Bradbury and Hemingway in this respect seem to me to be the explanation why their work does not for good films make. That which links them is this:

Like Harold Pinter and Ernest Hemingway, Ray Bradbury and Stephen King are profoundly allegorical writers.

The four of them *seem* to be mimetic writers, but they aren't! They *seem* to be writing simply, uncomplicatedly, but they aren't! As with the dancing of Fred Astaire—which seems so loose and effortless and easy that even the most lumpfooted of us ought to be able to duplicate the moves—until we try it and fall on our faces—what these writers do is make the creation of High Art seem replicable.

The bare bones of their plots...

A sinister manservant manipulates the life of his employer to the point where their roles are reversed.

An ex-prizefighter is tracked down and killed by hired guns for an offense which is never codified.

A "fireman," whose job it is to burn books because they are seditious, becomes secretly enamored of the joys of reading.

A young girl with the latent telekinetic ability to start fires comes to maturity and lets loose her power vengefully.

...bare bones that have underlain a hundred different stories that differ from these only in the most minimally variant ways. The plots count for little. The stories are not wildly inventive. The sequence of events is not skull-cracking. It is the *style* in which they are written that gives them wing. They are memorable not because of the thin storylines, but because the manner in which they have been written is so compelling that we are drawn into the fictional universe and once there we are bound subjects of the master creator.

181

Each of these examples draws deeply from the well of myth and archetype. The collective unconscious calls to us and we go willingly where Hemingway and Bradbury and Pinter...and King...beckon us to follow.

Stephen King's books work as well as they do, because he is writing more of shadow than of substance. He drills into the flow of cerebro-spinal fluid with the dialectical function of a modern American mythos, dealing with archetypal images from the pre-conscious or conscious that presage crises in our culture even as they become realities.

Like George Lucas, Stephen King has read Campbell's THE MASKS OF GOD, and he knows the power of myth. He knows what makes us tremble. He knows about moonlight reflecting off the fangs. It isn't his plots that press against our chest, it is the impact of his allegory.

But those who bought for film translation 'SALEM'S LOT, CUJO, CHRISTINE, "Children of the Corn" and FIRESTARTER cannot read. For them, the "special speaking" of King's nightmares, the element that sets King's work so far above the general run of chiller fiction, is merely white noise. It is the first thing dropped when work begins on the script, when the scenarist "takes a meeting" to discuss what the producer or the studio wants delivered. What is left is the bare bones plot, the least part of what King has to offer. (Apart from the name *Stephen King*, which is what draws us to the theater.)

And when the script is in work, the scenarist discovers that there isn't enough at hand to make either a coherent or an artful motion picture. So blood is added. Knives are added. Fangs are added. Special effects grotesqueries are added. But the characters have been dumbed-up, the tone has been lost; the mythic undercurrents have been dammed and the dialectical function has been rendered inoperative. What is left for us is bare bones, blood and cliché.

It is difficult to get Steve King to comment on such artsy-fartsy considerations. Like many other extraordinarily successful artists, he is consciously fearful of the spite and envy his preeminence engenders in critics, other writers, a fickle audience that just sits knitting with Mme. Defarge, waiting for the artist to show the tiniest edge of hubris. Suggest, as I did, to Steve King that *Cujo* is a gawdawful lump of indigestible grue, and he will respond, "I like it. It's just a movie that stands there and keeps punching."

How is the critic, angry at the crippling of each new King

novel when it crutches onto the screen, to combat such remarks? By protecting himself in this way—and it is not for the critic to say whether King truly believes these things he says in defense of the butchers who serve up the bloody remnants that were once creditable novels—he unmans all rushes to his defense. Yet without such mounting of the barricades in his support, how can the situation be altered?

Take for instance CHILDREN OF THE CORN (New World Pictures). Here is a minor fable of frightfulness, a mere thirty pages in King's 1978 collection NIGHT SHIFT; a one-punch short story whose weight rests on that most difficult of all themes to handle, little kids in mortal jeopardy. Barely enough there for a short film, much less a feature-length attempt.

How good is this recent adaptation of a King story? *Los Angeles* magazine began its review of *Firestarter* like so: "This latest in a seemingly endless chain of films made from Stephen King novels isn't the worst of the bunch, 'Children of the Corn' wins that title hands down." That's how bad it is.

Within the first 3½ minutes (by stopwatch) we see four people agonizingly die from poison, one man get his throat cut with a butcher knife, one man get his hand taken off with a meat slicer, a death by pruning hook, a death by sickle, a death by tanning knife...at least nine oncamera slaughters, maybe eleven (the intercuts are fastfastfast), and one woman murdered over the telephone, which we don't see, but hear. Stomach go whooops.

Utterly humorless, as ineptly directed as a film school freshman's class project, acted with all the panache of a grope in the backseat of a VW, "Children of the Corn" features the same kind of "dream sequences" proffered as shtick by Landis in *An American Werewolf in London*, De Palma in *Carrie* and *Dressed to Kill*, and by even less talented of the directorial coterie aptly labeled (by Alain Resnais) "the wise guy smart alecks." These and-then-I-woke-up-and-it-had-all-been-a-bad-dream inserts, which in no way advance the plot of the film, are a new dodge by which Fritz Kiersch, *Corn*'s director, and his contemporaries—bloodletters with viewfinders—slip in gratuitous scenes of horror and explicit SFX-enhanced carnage. This has become a trope when adapting King's novels to the screen, a filmic device abhorrent in the extreme not only because it is an abattoir substitute for the artful use of terror, but because it panders to the lowest, vilest tastes of an already debased audience.

It is a bit of cinematic shorthand developed by De Palma

specifically for *Carrie* that now occurs with stultifying regularity in virtually *all* of the later movies made from King's books.

I submit this bogus technique is further evidence that, flensed of characterization and allegory, what the makers of these morbid exploitation films are left with does not suffice to create anything resembling the parent novel, however fudged for visual translation. And so fangs are added, eviscerations are added, sprayed blood is added; subtlety is excised, respect for the audience is excised, all restraint vanishes in an hysterical rush to make the empty and boring seem scintillant.

Children of the Corn is merely the latest validation of the theory; or as *Cinefantastique* said in its September 1984 issue: "King's mass-market fiction has inspired some momentous cinematic dreck, but *Children of the Corn* is a new low even by schlock standards."

Of the nine films that originated with Stephen King's writings, only three (in my view, of course, but now almost uniformly buttressed by audience and media attention) have any resemblance in quality or content—not necessarily both in the same film—to the parent: *Carrie, The Shining* and *The Dead Zone.*

The first, because De Palma had not yet run totally amuck and the allegorical undertones were somewhat preserved by outstanding performances by Sissy Spacek and Piper Laurie.

The second, because it is the vision of Kubrick, always an intriguing way of seeing, even though it is no more King's *The Shining* than Orson Welles's *The Trial* was Kafka's dream.

(The sort of people who call Kubrick's version of King's THE SHINING "self-indulgent" are the same kind of people who think secular humanism is a religion, or that there is some arcane merit in astrology. If I hear "self-indulgent" used once more as a pejorative, violence will follow. Listen very carefully: what else is Art *but* self-indulgence?

(Only the blamming of rivets into Chrysler door panels escapes the denotation "self-indulgent." The Sistine Chapel ceiling is the artistic self-indulgence of Michelangelo; MOBY-DICK was Melville's self-indulgence; sculptor Gutzon Borglum indulged himself by creating Mount Rushmore National Memorial; and bombing Pearl Harbor was the self-indulgence of Japan's prime minister, Hideki Tojo. The former trio of artistic "self-indulgences" brought their creators fame and approbation; the latter "work of art," World War II, got its architect hanged as a war criminal. There is a lesson here.

184   (It seems somehow beyond the intellectual grasp of those who

widely disseminate their opinions on cinema, that King's THE SHINING is not Kubrick's *The Shining*, any more than Kafka's THE TRIAL is Orson Welles's *The Trial*; but all four of these creations of a superior, individual intellect bear the stamp of High Art. Kubrick is one of only seven *real* directors in the world. By that I mean superior beyond comparison. All the rest are craftspersons of greater or lesser merit, but simply not touched by the divine madness suffusing every frame of work by these seven. That to which Kubrick turns his hand becomes, despite your affection for the original, something different, something equally as great as the original. In some cases, greater: Capra's *Lost Horizon* beats out James Hilton's famous novel of the same name by a dozen light-years.

(Apart from Jack Nicholson making a meal of the sets and situation, foaming and frothing to a fare-thee-well, I am nothing less than nuts about Kubrick's film.)

The third, because David Cronenberg as director is the only one of the field hands in this genre who seems artistically motivated; and because Christopher Walken as the protagonist is one of the quirkiest, most fascinating actors working today, and his portrayal of Johnny Smith is, simply put, mesmerizing.

But of *Cujo*'s mindlessness, *Christine*'s cheap tricks, *Firestarter*'s crudeness, *'Salem's Lot*'s television ridiculousness, *Children of the Corn*'s bestial tawdriness and even Steve's own *Creepshow* with its intentional comic book shallowness, nothing much positive can be said. It is the perversion of a solid body of work that serious readers of King, as well as serious movie lovers, must look upon with profound sadness.

We have had come among us in the person of Stephen King a writer of limitless gifts. Perhaps because Stephen himself has taken an attitude of permissiveness toward those who pay him for the right to adopt his offspring, we are left with the choices of enjoying the written work for itself, and the necessity of ignoring everything on film... or of hoping that one day, in a better life, someone with more than a drooling lust for the exploitation dollar attendant on Stephen King's name will perceive the potential cinematic riches passim these special fantasies. There *must* be an honest man or woman out there who understands that King's books are about more than fangs and blood.

All it takes is an awareness of allegory, subtext, the parameters of the human condition... and reasonable family resemblance.

185

INSTALLMENT 5:
In Which The Left Hand Giveth Praise And The Right Hand Sprayeth For Worms Of Evil

I have suffered for your sins, children. I have seen BUCKAROO BANZAI (20th Century–Fox). So you don't have to. An unintelligible farrago of inaudible sound mix, bad whitefolks MTV video acting, blatant but hotly denied ripoff of the *Doc Savage* crew and *ouevre* spiced with swipes from Mike Moorcock's Jerry Cornelius stories, a plot that probably makes sense only in Minkowski Space, six funny lines, four clever sight gags, and billions of dollars' worth of promotional hype such as Big Brother–style rallies at sf conventions—all intended to make this "an instant underground cult classic."

Were you to fail to heed my warning, you might go to see this village idiot of a movie; and you might go back to see it three or four times more in an effort to unravel a storyline in which mindlessness reaches deification and in an effort to decode the garbled soundtrack; all in aid of gleaning some sense from a film you'll be told is "fresh and innovative."

But if you are thus foolhardy, you will find yourself at one with Brother Theodore's monologue about rats, in which he says: "You can train a rat. Yes, if you work for hours and days and months and years, you *can* train a rat. But when you're done, all you'll have is a *trained rat!*"

This has been a homiletic analogy. God knows I've done all I can.

*   *   *

What *Buckaroo Banzai* pretends to be (and with the pretense brings new meaning to the word boredom), REPO MAN (Universal) sure as hell *is*. Cleverly constructed, freshly mounted, engagingly acted, bizarrely inveigling and, in the words of Pliny the Younger, *sui generis*. Ninety-two minutes of enthusiastically nihilistic anarchy.

This is a first feature for writer-director Alex Cox and as a virgin effort indicates arrival on the cinematic scene of a quirky, elitist (in the positive sense) intelligence worthy of our close attention. Through word-of-mouth prior to its initial release, I had been advised there was "something special" going on in *Repo Man*, and I shouldn't miss it. As I had not been as warm to *Quadrophenia* or *Liquid Sky*—two "punk" films about which I'd heard raves—as I'd hoped to be, I didn't expect much from *Repo Man*. In fact, as a "control" element of viewing, I took along both a devotee of the music of Steve Reich (which music makes my headbone throb) and a Jewish American Princess. My thought was that these disparate world-views would provide insights into my own opinion. The overage new-waver burbled with joy, and the Beverly Hills materialist grew more and more bewildered. But when we emerged from the screening, both admitted the film refused to let go of their risibilities.

My Reichfreak contends *Repo Man* is about belief systems. My social butterfly insists it's about people purposely alienating themselves from reality.

I think both of them have too much book-larnin'. This movie is about Otto, a spike-haired layabout who falls in with Bud, a car repossessor; falls in lust with Leila, one of the happyface-wearing numbers of the Smiley cult who live by the tenets of a philosophy to be found in the book DIORETIX: THE NEW SCIENCE OF THE MIND; falls into trouble with the thuglike car thieves, the Rodriguez Brothers, with Agent Rogersz and her cadre of secret service bloodhounds, with his ex-buddies of the pink&purple hair set whose collective social conscience is best expressed by Duke, who says, "Let's go do some crimes," to which Archie responds, "Yeah, let's go order sushi and not pay," and falls into the middle of a situation in which the burned-out nuclear scientist J. Frank Parnell tries to stay ahead of all or some or none of the above who are trying to filch his '64 Chevy Malibu, in the trunk of which reside deadly aliens who can fry you to taco chips with a hellish blast of light.

188   *That's* what it's about.

And get away from me with that strait jacket.

If for no other reason—and don't tell me the plot as outlined above doesn't make you go squishy all over—the acting by the inimitable Harry Dean Stanton as Bud, and Emilio Estevez as Otto makes this a don't-miss flick. Throughout my screening of the film I kept mumbling, "That kid playing Otto is a dead ringer for the young Martin Sheen, even the way he walks, the way he stands, jeez it's uncanny," until my *maven* of minimalist music thumped me and pointed out that Marty Sheen's real name is Estevez, and that Emilio is his kid. Oh.

Dozens of little touches in the movie provide a deranged superimposed reality that draws nothing but admiration: all the food is generic, including blue-striped cans that are simply labeled FOOD; Otto's family is mesmerized by TV evangelist Reverend Larry and his Honor Roll of the Chariots of Fire; no faintest touch of sentimentality is permitted onscreen distraction, as when Otto is about to fly off with the aliens and Leila screams, "But what about our relationship?" and Otto remains true to the tone of the film by replying, "Fuck that!"

Repo Man, when first released, drew such confused reviews that Universal pulled it back quickly. But true madness cannot long be squelched by the mentality of accountants; and now this looney thing has been let loose again. Look around and find it. Unless you are one of those dismal unfortunates who thinks Jerry Lewis is funny, you are guaranteed a filmic experience that can only be compared, in terms of a good time, with watching Richard Nixon sweat on television.

GHOSTBUSTERS (Columbia), as most of you know, was the box-office smash of the summer. Good. It is more wonderful than one would have expected from the directorial paws of Ivan Reitman, source of *Cannibal Girls*, *Animal House*, *National Lampoon's Vacation* and *Heavy Metal*, among other class acts.

But Harold Ramis, Bill Murray, Sigourney Weaver, Rick Moranis, Annie Potts and Dan Aykroyd all running amuck chasing demonic presences in what starts out to be an urbane yet cockeyed slapstick fantasy that smoothly turns into something Lovecraft might have scripted if he'd beaten the Man with the Scythe and lived on into the era of SFX, provide Reitman with such a gobbet of goodies that *Ghostbusters* emerges as one of those films you see again and again for mounting pleasure.

Had I not spent two columns on the Stephen King essay, and had I not been captured by extraterrestrials masquerading as

189

Moonies, who spirited me away to their underground lair beneath Orem, Utah, where they tortured me with Naugahyde and hot fudge sundaes, thereby causing me to miss my deadline last issue (you don't think I was intentionally *late*, do you?)—I'd have had this review of *Ghostbusters* to you in time for you to have made an informed viewing decision, rather than just stumbling across it in the twelve hundred theaters where it was block-booked through the hot months.

And you'd also have gotten my vituperative observations about an evil little item called *Gremlins*. But that will have to wait till next time, when We Who Have Gone Blind From Watching Awful Films On Your Behalf return with the startling conclusion of (wait for it) *Worms of Evil!*

INSTALLMENT 6:
In Which We Learn What Is Worse Than Finding A Worm Of Evil In The Apple

Some of us are better than the rest of you. Oh, yes we are.

One who is better than the rest of you is a guy who lives in Somerville, Massachusetts, name of John G. Maguire. And John G. is better than most of you because not only won't *he* support corrupt films by buying a ticket to something he's been told overandoverandover is The One Not To Miss!!!, but he can smell the puke smell made by the Worms of Evil and he protects his kids from such movies.

Not in the Falwell m.o. that entails the burning of books and the regimenting of thought and the stifling of imagination, but with a sense of responsibility toward the lives he helped bring into the world. That used to be called being a good father.

And that makes John G. better than lots of you who went, like the pod-people you are, right into the burrows of the Worms of Evil.

You were warned, not just twice by me, but by dozens of other film critics all over America, who advised you in clear, precise language that could not be misunderstood: stay away from GREMLINS (Warner Bros.); it is a corrupt thing, vicious at its core; meanspirited and likely to cause harm to your moral sense. Specifically you were warned: keep little kids away from this thing. Don't equate the frights it can cause youthful, plastic

minds with the tolerable terror you cherish from your first viewing of *Snow White and the Seven Dwarfs* when you were an
impressionable tot. This ain't the same *frisson*. But you went,
anyhow, didn't you?

And that makes John G. Maguire leagues better than the rest
of you. Better than those of you I've seen in theaters, late at
night, last show, with a kid half-dozing in the seat beside you,
watching violent movies and teaching your kid to applaud wildly
when some stunt double gets blown apart by a shotgun blast,
when the Trans Am of the bad guy gets bulldozed over a cliff and
tumbles and tumbles and impacts on the hillside and disinte-
grates into a flaming hellflower. I've seen you, and I know Falwell's got you in his pocket, with your viciousness and your
sanctimoniousness. And I dote on the goodness of John G. Maguire.

How do I know about John G. Maguire? I know about him
because he wrote to this magazine between the time of my first
warning in this column (October 1984) and when I sat down to
write this critique; and he said, "I appreciated your warning-off
on *Gremlins*. I haven't seen the movie. I read a promo about it in
Newsweek and decided not to take my kids to it: too vicious. Any
movie that seems too vicious for me is too much for my kids. I'm
old-fashioned like that."

Good for you, John G. No pod-person you.

But as for the rest of you, those of you who have happily
contributed to *Gremlins* doing more than $143,000,000 worth of
box-office in the first fifteen and a half weeks of its theatrical
release...as you sat there watching the ripping and rending...
did it cross your mind that *Gremlins* might be less significant as
a cinematic event than it is as a grotesque breach of trust with
all the kids who hear *Spielberg* and think *E.T.*? And if you can
desist for a moment from the kneejerk animosity this attack on
your bad taste boils up in you, could you give the barest consideration to the concept that one definition of evil is the manipulation of human emotions to support and excuse the excesses of
dishonest art?

Understand: gremlins are a mythic construct toward which I
am particularly well-disposed. Few of you out there will have
heard of a 1943 Walt Disney production, *Victory Through Air
Power*, but that film contained a marvelous episode titled "The
Gremlins" (which, with artwork based on the animation cels,
appeared as a children's book from Random House that year; a
children's book written by a certain Flight Lieutenant Roald

192

Dahl: I still own that book). It was my first exposure to the concept of gremlins, and even at the age of nine, which was what I was in 1943, I resonated to the idea. Dinosaurs, lost lands, the Titanic, gremlins.

Gremlins, like Kilroy, were the creation of a modern world needing modern mythology. I didn't understand (nor had I, in fact, ever heard of) the dialectical function, Joseph Campbell's cosmological symbolism, Jungian archetypal images or the universal psychic structure called The Trickster. But I knowed gremlins was real neat. Me loved they puckish pranks. Not just as Disney fifinellas and widgets, but as a character on a radio program I listened to every Saturday morning: *Smilin' Ed McConnell's Buster Brown Gang*, featuring Froggy the Gremlin.

No one who remembers the famous phrase, "Plunk your magic Twanger, Froggy!" could suspect this reviewer of anything but an overwhelmingly positive attitude as I sat there in the pre-release screening of *Gremlins*.

Further: while I am of a mixed mind about the Spielberg canon, having known him since his days on the Universal TV payroll, I would have to say that I'm solidly in his camp. (For the record—and you'll understand in a moment why I go into such minutiae—I admire the following Spielberg films: *Duel*, *Sugarland Express*, *Jaws*, *Raiders of the Lost Ark*, and *E.T. The Extra-Terrestrial*. I'm not even as great a critic of *1941* as the rest of the world seems to be; it had its whacky moments and I think Steve need not be too bothered that it didn't turn out as he'd intended. My favorite film from the Spielberg factory is, oddly enough, an associational item, as is *Gremlins*: the vastly underrated and strangely unsung *Poltergeist*, which I view as a Tobe Hooper film, influenced by Spielberg. On the other side of the ledger I confess to a dislike of much of *Close Encounters of the Third Kind* and *Twilight Zone—The Movie*.)

Thus, my remarks here about *Gremlins* should not be construed as part of a pattern of denigrating what it is Steven Spielberg turns out. I offer the foregoing as credential in aid of establishing biases.

Thus lighthearted, I jigged a little jog in my seat as the lights dimmed, and with growing horror became as one with the many film critics—from *Time* and *Newsweek* to Gahan Wilson in *The Twilight Zone* magazine—who have perceived *Gremlins* as a film utterly without restraint, exhibiting a streak of malign viciousness that I now suggest has been a part of Spielberg's *oeuvre* from the first... subverted and camouflaged heretofore, but now, with

193

Spielberg's ascendancy to the throne of power and freedom in Hollywood, freed from its Pandora's Box and permitted free rein.

Gremlins suffers from the dreaded Jerry Lewis Syndrome: it vacillates between a disingenuous homeliness and an egomaniacal nastiness. It is by turns so bewilderingly schizoid that one reels from the shifts, cloyingly cut and cuddly—so arch, so coy, so aspartameously endearing that Tonstant Viewer fwowed up— and monstrously evil in such a way that one spike speaks to all crucifixions; embodying in the gremlins the most loathsome traits of human beings without a compensatory balance of positive human values. It is all the specious arguments you've ever heard as to why the human race should be nuked till it glows, rolled into one vile paradigm and served up with an aw-shucks, toe-scuffling, ain't-we-cute anthropomorphism so contemptible one leaves the theater wanting to get one's soul Martinized.

We have been convinced, through hundreds of interviews and analyses of Spielberg's motivations, that he makes the kind of films he wants to see, the kind he liked when he was a kid. Thus we are led to believe that what we're getting, expensively turned out, made with the highest level of cinematic expertise and most *courant* SFX state of the art, are films dreamt by an adult who sees with the eyes of a child. But if this is so, then there is surely a twisted adolescent intelligence at work in this picture. Because, as one of the stars of the film, Hoyt Axton, has said: "*Gremlins* is *E.T.* with teeth."

Fangs is more accurate.

And so, we trust Steven Spielberg. Unlike *Indiana Jones and the Temple of Doom*, released at nearly the same time as *Gremlins* and bearing some sidebar attention (later in this essay) to the thesis at hand, which is obviously a film intended for the mentality of Huck Finn boys, no matter how old they may be, *Gremlins* has been aimed straight at little kids. The same wide-eyed tots who wept when E.T. gasped his last. A trusting, innocent audience that cannot discriminate between Lucas films and Spielberg films—so umbilically linked are these two old chums —and so, when it sees "Steven Spielberg presents *Gremlins*" it thinks *Star Wars*; it thinks *E.T. The Extra-Terrestrial*; it thinks Reese's Pieces (or M&Ms); it thinks Oh boy!

But the mind of Steven Spielberg is not that of a child grown older but not grown-up. It is a mind, from the evidence passim this film, of an adult who has grown to maturity with a subliminal freightload of cynicism and meanspirited animus. Cloaked in the gee-whiz of *hommages* to B sci-fi flicks and simplistic Capra paeans to a small town America that truly existed only in the wish-fulfillment of Hollywood scenarists, *Gremlins* comes to that tot audience with comfy images of lovable aliens, sweetfaced urchins, incompetent parents and stories that come right in the end. All set? Now scare the hell out of those kids! Suck them in, con them with what went before, and then open that corroded Pandora's Box. Let the Worms of Evil eat their fill!

An adult who sees with the eyes of a child? I think not. More probably an adult who retains the meanness of kids in the schoolyard, waiting to strike back for the inequities of getting teased, and being sent to bed without any supper, and having to do as one is told *because.* Let me not venture too deeply into cheap, vest-pocket psychoanalysis. I don't know what is in Steven Spielberg's mind; all I know is what I saw on the screen. And what I saw, apparently what many others also saw, was a grotesque breach of trust with that tot audience.

I heard children scream and cry in *Gremlins.*

I spoke to the manager of a theater in Columbus, Ohio who told me he has never before had so many instances of people demanding their money back. I have my own loathing to reconcile.

One can rend this film on many levels, apart from the ethical. What are we to say about the remarkable similarity between the *mogwai* stage of gremlin development and artist Michael Whelan's conception of Piper's Little Fuzzys? (One tries to be even-handed when crediting the "influences" on Lucas and Spielberg. One credits a lot to *hommage*—until the moment comes with De Palma films, for instance, when one chokes on the phrase "homage to Hitchcock" and simply shouts, "Thief!" One tries to overlook memories of Edd Cartier's hokas when one sees ewoks. Yet one cannot indefinitely put from mind the many, many press items about plagiarism suits directed against this most successful of director-entrepreneurs. One remembers Richard Matheson's short story and *Twilight Zone* teleplay, "Little Girl Lost," and wonders why Matheson never raised a question about *Poltergeist...* until one remembers that Matheson—hardly a member of the Spielberg coterie—was hired to write Spielberg's subsequent production of *Twilight Zone—The Movie.* And one smiles to oneself at the possibility that this gentle, vastly talented writer may have escaped the toils of a decade-long legal imbroglio while yet preserving his integrity. Shadows darken the mythic Spielberg kingdom.)

And what of those endlessly distracting *hommages* that

195

tremble in the corners of every jam-packed frame? (For director Joe Dante has absorbed Spielberg's patented technique of packing every shot as if it were your Granny's bric-a-brac cabinet.) Polly Holliday stalks down the street and the background music, as well as her demeanor, reminds us of Margaret Hamilton in *The Wizard of Oz*; a poster half-seen on a wall is for Agar Pest Control, and we're supposed to chuckle at the reference to John Agar's co-starring role in the 1955 *Tarantula*; at a gadgeteer's convention we see the time machine from the 1960 George Pal adaptation of Wells's classic, we cut away, and when we cut back...it's vanished à la 1979's *Time After Time*; a legend on a door tells us this is the Office of Dr. Moreau; the marquee of a theater, seen fleetingly as the camera pans, announces *Watch the Skies* (the original title intended for *Close Encounters* and the last line of the original version of *The Thing*) and *A Boy's Life* (the working title for *E.T. The Extra-Terrestrial*), and we are not supposed to snort at the filmmaker paying homage to *himself*, fer chrissakes; as Hoyt Axton makes a phone call a man in a hat stands behind him making notes, and the man is the film's composer, Jerry Goldsmith...we cut away...and when we cut back Goldsmith has been replaced by Robby the Robot, wearing Goldsmith's hat, speaking precisely the lines he spake in *Forbidden Planet*. But it goes on and on and on, world without end, amen. This is no longer the mild amusements, the inside jokes of those who love film and its history. It is intrusive. It keeps one's attention partially distracted from the emptiness of soul up there on the screen where the action is hysterical. *Gremlins*, like *Indiana Jones and the Temple of Doom*, and as many other Lucas–Spielberg products as you care to recall, is a showoff's movie.

Spielberg and Lucas and their protégés are scabby-kneed, snotty-nose neighborhood urchins scaring the crap out of their elders by walking a plank across a building excavation. They are so busy letting us know how clever they are, that they counter-productively shatter the best, first rule of film direction: don't make the direction obvious.

As Frank Capra, who is *hommaged* to exhaustion in *Gremlins*, proved: the most artful direction is that which warms the audience into thinking the film was not directed at all, that it's just happening as they watch.

Further, it is possible to savage *Gremlins* on the level of character and motivation. The boy and girl who play the leads are impossible! The boy is supposed to be one of those apple-cheeked virgins Capra used as icons, but he's old enough to work in a bank—though he lives in his parents' attic in a room filled with the toys of a ten-year-old—and his girlfriend is Ms. Phoebe Cates, who has managed to shed her clothes in every film I've seen in which she has a speaking part. (And though I'll be accused of something or other, I suppose we're expected to comment on Ms. Cates's firm flesh, otherwise why are we gifted with such regular peeks at it?) Ms. Cates is also supposed to be an apple-cheeked virgin, yet she is privileged to deliver the speech that is possibly the moment of worst taste in the film, a verbal recounting of that old Gahan Wilson cartoon about daddy dressed as Santa Claus and suffocating in the chimney on Christmas Eve. I submit that this iniquitous moment encapsulates the meanspiritedness of the film: taking the Capra Christmas motif and turning it into a toxic waste dump.

No one seems very surprised at the existence of *mogwai*. Not the father, played by the intelligent Hoyt Axton, not the mother, not the high school science teacher, not the apple-cheeked hero and heroine. It seems to me that not even in the fantasy world of a film such as this should the introduction into everyday life of an impossible thing cause such little startlement.

The instructions given to Axton on the three things one should never never *never* do to a *mogwai* on pain of terrible consequences—shine light in their eyes, let it get wet, and feed it after midnight—are never explored by Axton when he gets the creature. Even a schmuck asks for a book of instructions when he buys a microwave oven. And, of course, because it's an idiot plot, all three caveats are ignored so frivolously, so offhandedly, that we know from the moment we hear them that they have been entered merely to be transgressed.

But since everyone else in the film acts like a bonehead, how naïve of us to pretend to amazement that the plot has been manipulated so crassly. For of fools there is no dearth in this film. Glynn Turman, as the high school science teacher who borrows one of the gremlin offspring to study, has just seen the wire cage containing the creature ripped open, has seen the creature grab a test tube and has heard the sound of the thing eating it, and yet he tracks it around the darkened schoolroom (he had been running a science film for his students and the lights were out) without having the common sense to *turn on the lights*. And though he knows the thing is ravenous enough to eat a *test tube*, fer chrissakes, he nonetheless acts like a fool and extends a candy bar, held in his naked hand, into the shadows under a desk.   197

When we hear him scream, and later when we see him lying dead, just enough in shadow so we cannot tell how far up his body the evil gremlin ate, we are told by apologists for this film's systematic violence that "nothing is shown."

Yet we must remember that film is a simulacrum of life. It is not a "cartoon" (a subject I'll cover next time). A *cartoon* is a cartoon. Live-action is one remove from the real thing. And in this film we see people being smashed by a snowplow that goes right through their house, we see a woman hurled at a prodigious speed through a second-storey window, we see Harry Carey, Jr. stick his hand into a mailbox and hear the sound of gnawing, we see a mother's face bloody with the raking of talons. And we are expected to laugh. We are told this ain't for real, it's a cartoon. But if you chew off someone's arm, they will bleed to death, slowly and horribly. If you run a snowplow through someone's home and smash them, you will grind them to pulp. If you throw someone from a second-storey window at a prodigious speed, her neck will be broken. And no amount of breakdancing and beer-swilling and emulation of human behavior by malevolent fanged creatures can remove the rotten core of violence that poisons this entire film. It is, truly, *The Muppet Chain Saw Massacre.*

Inconsistency: "If these evil gremlins get to water, they'll multiply forever. We have to keep them from water." This film takes place at Christmastime. There is snow everywhere. Last time I checked, snow was mostly made of water.

Rasa, tabula, one each.

Or should we simply point out, and accept wearily, the reality that this film is nothing but a cynical marketing device for Gizmo and Stripe dolls, *Gremlin* lunch buckets, *mogwai* pajamas, premiums, doodads, million-buck marketables?

It has been pointed out to me that I may not, at risk of bearing false witness, lay the onus of moral bankruptcy re *Gremlins* at Steven Spielberg's gate. This, I have been reminded, and scenarist Chris Columbus assured me in a recent telecon that it is so, is a film directed by Joe Dante, that Spielberg was off on location with *Temple of Doom* when *Gremlins* was in production. In all fairness, yes, this is Dante's work and is filled with the kind of violence Dante delivered in *Hollywood Boulevard*, *Piranha*, and *The Howling*. And it emanates from an original screenplay by Columbus (who wrote *Reckless*). But Columbus also told me that he went through several drafts of the script, over a period of months, with Spielberg himself, before he was given Dante as collaborator on another few passes.

All this taken into consideration, true or false, each contributor's part in the action increased or softpedaled for whatever reasons of politics (perhaps in fear of a repeat of the *Poltergeist* fiasco, in which Spielberg was rumored to have done the direction while Tobe Hooper stood around the set with his thumb in his mouth, a rumor that time has proved to be utterly false and destructive to Hooper's reputation), it is Spielberg's bio that leads off the press kit furnished by Warner Bros. It is Spielberg's name above the title in the *TV Guide* two-page advertisement. It is Spielberg's name that sold this film to ten-year-olds and their parents.

And in the same way that the mindless think Walt Disney wrote *Bambi* and *Pinocchio*, never having heard of Felix Salten or Carlo Collodi; in the same way that they think Rod Serling wrote every segment of *The Twilight Zone*; and in the same way that no amount of setting the record straight (with a knowing wink and an elbow nudge) will convince most people that Tobe Hooper, not Spielberg, directed *Poltergeist*; in that same way, and with equal responsibility, this is a Spielberg film bearing the freight of his cinematic vision and execution.

Perhaps I do sin against the innocent when I suggest that this movie fits neatly into the Spielberg canon because it lies under the shadow of his Gray Eminence throughout . . . but it's a belief I cannot, try as I might, shake from my considerations when appraising *Gremlins*.

And I suspect the free ride is over for Spielberg in terms of uncritical adoration. For *Indiana Jones and the Temple of Doom* lets loose the Worms of Evil with its brutalization of children as a device to shock, and that's the first true glimpse of the darker side of the force that motivates the Lucas–Spielberg films— though it's there, subtly, in most of their movies, one way or another—and *Gremlins* fully opens that Pandora's Box: it combines, at last, the softest, most empty-headed, meretricious and dangerous elements of the entire Lucas–Spielberg genre.

And whether you call it Bedford Falls or Kingston Falls, *Gremlins* savages to evil effect a world that need not have been trashed so callously.

Steven Spielberg has more power, more freedom, more top of the mountain access to the best the industry has to offer, than anyone in the history of moviemaking. He has talent coming out of his ears. And I do not think the unquestioning adoration that 199 has been visited on him is repaid by the sort of films he now seems inclined to make. It is presumptuous for me, or anyone, to tell an artist what to create; but it is the responsibility of the audience to alert a force as potent as Spielberg to the possibility that too much isolation, and too many yes-men, and too much money, and too much cynicism can turn the sweetest apple rotten to the core.

We have all taken bites from that apple. And what is worse than finding a Worm of Evil in the apple is finding *half* a Worm.

INSTALLMENT 7:
In Which An Attempt Is Made To Have One's Cake And Eat It, Too

By this time we will have come clean with each other. We will have ceased trying to flummox one another. You will reluctantly admit that these are not actually "reviews" of films, because The Noble Fermans assemble the goods three months before the magazine is published; and that means that even if I review *2010*, *Supergirl*, *The River*, *Dune*, and *Paris, Texas* (all five of which I'll see next week, 12–18 November) immediately, those films will have opened and, in some cases, vanished before you get the dubious benefit of my appraisals. So insofar as being a theater guide to what you should lay out money to see, this column is academic. You'll have guessed well or badly on your own; you'll have been conned by advertising; or you'll have been warned off by word-of-mouth or by Roger Ebert. And for *my* part, I will admit that these are not "reviews" in the way, say, Ayjay's book columns serve you, because the books are still out there three months after pub date; but the films may only be accessible in a second-run house.

By reviewing what is coming out as far in advance of their national premieres as I can, I cut down the time-lag; and in some instances—*Repo Man* and *Gremlins* are the most recent examples—I can abet your own desires by talking up the former, which got a second pass at distribution, or by warning you off the latter, which hung around like a bad case of stomach flu for the entire summer, at least till they'd moved a million of those vile gremlin soft toys off the shelves.

But what is truly being done in these columns is what I like to think of as essays in the realm of film criticism. The discussion of trends, subtexts, effects on the art form and on the commonweal, I suppose in an attempt to broaden your appreciation of film as worthy art. Thus, when I read Gahan Wilson's column in *The Twilight Zone* magazine, and Gahan quite properly wails in pain at the glut of films he has endeavored to see, in order to review, during the summer avalanche, and he professes to going blind and insensitive after seven days of two screenings a day, I sympathize without reservation. And finally, as it must to all men, overload comes to Charles Foster Ellison; and I simply admit that I cannot see everything available in this genre in your behalf; and also admit that it may not be a race worth the candle to *attempt* to see them all, if the best I can do is a mere squib relating basic storyline topped with a smartass one-punch evaluation.

So you get no thoughts from me on *The Last Starfighter, Sheena, Mutant, Red Dawn, Dreamscape, Conan the Destroyer, The Philadelphia Experiment, Night of the Comet* and *The Neverending Story*. By the time those films got to the screening windows, I couldn't see the forest for the trees. (Understand: I am a movie freak, and in order that I don't overload on sf/fantasy films, I see a great many mainstream films, as well. And I must confess that in a world where I can enjoy *Garbo Talks, Amadeus, A Soldier's Story, The River* and *Beverly Hills Cop*, I choose not to pollute my precious bodily fluids with *Sheena* and *Conan* and films notable only by the number of teenage female breasts available for leering at by microcephalic schoolboys.)

Eschewing semiotics and structuralism, techniques better left to the functionaries who rapturously give us shot-by-shot analyses with a meticulous examination of the firing of cinematic codes operative within a given segment, rife in journals such as *Camera Obscura* and *Wide Angle*, I try to look not only at the primary entertainment, storytelling qualities of films, but attempt to consider them as reflections of cultural phenomena.

Movies have always been slow to pick up on new trends and societal predispositions—breakdancing flicks tumbled onto the cineplex screens two years after the fad was hot—but by the time they hit your neighborhood they resonate to attitudes already concretized among the general population. Years after the effects of feminism had manifested themselves in a widespread confusion by men as to how they should now react, publicly and privately, movies reflected their quandary with films of deliberately cultivated sadism and violence toward females. Foreshadowing the unexpected support of Reagan by voters in the heretofore liberal 18-to-35-year-old demographic, such films as the despicable *Risky Business* come late to an observation that this target audience doesn't give much of a damn about the starving children of Ethiopia... they want a sinecure at Dow Chemical, complete with a comprehensive retirement plan. After-the-bomb movies are big right now; and only thirty or so years after the initial fears of nuclear holocaust began to dampen our national spirit.

No film is ever made in a vacuum. It is a murky shadow in the cultural mirror. And thus I am glad we no longer lie to each other that what *you* want is a rating system for what you'll see this weekend, something slight and dopey; that what *I'm* offering here is an exhaustive series of comments on trivial cinematic exploitation exercises.

Yet synchronistically, my concern this outing is in precisely that quarter: the excuse currently proffered by many filmmakers that we should not judge their product too harshly because it *is* trivial. Don't take it seriously, we are told, it's only a movie. Excuse as explanation: they want their cake, and they want to eat it, too.

As the subjects of this month's sermon, I selected STREETS OF FIRE and CLOAK AND DAGGER (Universal) and INDIANA JONES AND THE TEMPLE OF DOOM (Paramount). All share a less-than-salutary press, and all share a common apologia. Which is: "This isn't real-life, folks, it's just a cartoon. So you can't legitimately lynch us for Sins Against Art that serious films may commit."

First example: *Indiana Jones and the Etcetera of Ditto.* There will no doubt be those benighted few who will find fault with this film because it seems to be nothing more than a show-off congeries of tricks, stunts and gags we have learned were, for the most part, left over from *Raiders of the Lost Ark.* These same viewers with disdain will also, no doubt, chastise Steven Spielberg for a certain, how shall we put it delicately, McMartin Pre-School attitude toward children.

They will say that the character of Willie Scott (played by Kate Capshaw), the Shanghai songstress unwillingly dragged into Dr. Jones's latest bloodletting escapade, is demeaning to women because through most of the film she runs around in   203 ever-decreasing circles screaming in terror. They will say that the laws of rationality, not to mention those of gravity and physics, are defied by a three-foot-high Chinese kid dropkicking fanatical, highly-trained, six-foot-four *thuggees*, and by a mine-shaft tram as it leaps its tracks, soars through empty space and lands nicely on rails beyond the abyss. They will say that the depiction of Third World peoples is racist because they spend most of their time quaking in fear or slavering with deranged evil. They will say there is too much gore because people are shot in the forehead, run through with sabers and the occasional kris, ground under rock-pulverizing wheels, burned alive, have their hearts torn still beating from their bodies, are gnawed to shreds by crocodiles, get smashed against rock walls, blow up in car crashes and otherwise meet their demise through means both mundane and innovative, as with one Wily Oriental Gentleman who gets skewered with a rack of shish-kebob.

Those who object on these grounds, well, let's just say their bread ain't completely toasted.

They have lost touch with reality.

Which is not to say that *Indiana Jones and the Thingie of Whatsit* has so much as an elephant's fart to do with reality.

Now I happen to like this film, but then I also like liver and onions and abominate sushi, so what does that say about me? I accept with a childlike willingness the suspension of my disbelief, in order that I may more perfectly resonate in contiguity with the intelligence that conceived this adventure: the mind of a thirteen-year-old boy commando, tipsy with dreams conjured by Sir Walter Scott, H. Rider Haggard, Richard Halliburton, Lester Dent, Walter Gibson, Edmond Hamilton and Frank Buck. Lest you doubt my sincerity in this giving-over of myself to this metempirical state, let me reassure you by asserting that I *do* understand why it is that a piece of buttered bread always falls to the floor buttered-side-down. By the same token, and using the same rudimentary knowledge of gravity, I understand that when Indy, Short Round and Willie fall out of that tri-motor in a rubber life raft, they should by all rights turn upside down. (Which would have added a dimension to the fall that would have made the stunt even *more* exciting, because the raft would have served as a kind of parachute, and they would have been hanging from the life raft's perimeter rope as they dropped toward the Mayapore foothills.) But that's an exercise in logic, the introduction of reality; clearly an inadvisable undertaking, as it would jangle against the impossible view of the received universe that informs such films.)

So I do not sit by the carpfire with those who pick nits. I swallow the adventure whole; and if I find it far less of an exhilarating experience than its predecessor, *Raiders*, it is nonetheless a nifty boy commando imago.

But cake-eating/cake-having disingenuously rears its head when the reviews start coming in. Perhaps it was because of an independent realization on the part of many critics that a certain meanspiritedness was subcutaneously present passim the Spielberg–Lucas *ouevre* and that it was beginning to surface. Released but a few weeks before *Gremlins*, this film drew only foreshadowings of concern that spiraled up into hysterical gardyloos when *Gremlins* made its debut. (The phrase that best synthesizes critical alarm is the one I quoted last time, from David Denby's review of *Gremlins* in the June 18, 1984 issue of *New York* magazine: "I'm tired of being worked over by these people...the master's head-slamming *Indiana Jones and the Temple of Doom*; now this creature bash, which flows with the same black blood as the Thuggee rites in *Indiana Jones*.") But it was a trend, and when groups dedicated to protecting children from Bad Influences began pillorying Spielberg for the child-labor scenes in *Temple*, Spielberg and allied apologists riposted with the disclaimer, "It's all in fun. It's not supposed to be real. It's a cartoon."

Bear that line in mind.

Second example: *Streets of Fire*.

Oft-used phrases no longer available to me: "Director Walter Hill can do no wrong." Remember *Hard Times* (which he also co-wrote) in 1975; *The Driver* (that shamefully undervalued homage to the Parker crime novels of Donald Westlake writing as "Richard Stark") in 1978; the extraordinary production of *The Warriors* in 1979; *Alien*, which he co-produced in the same year; *The Long Riders* in 1980; the absolutely paralyzing terror of *Southern Comfort* in 1981; and *48 Hours* in 1982, providing the perfect debut vehicle for Eddie Murphy; remember those films? Films of originality, incredible movement and power; artistically conceived with a core understanding that they must entertain first and convey philosophical subtext second; filled with fresh insights, and joyously overflowing with images that continue to smolder long after you've left the theater.

Of all the directors I ever wanted to work with, Walter Hill has been for me, as a scenarist, the Impossible Dream.

I'm such a goggle-eyed fan of Walter Hill's work that I had trouble, for at least the first half hour, accepting that *Streets of Fire* is as dreadfully emptyheaded as it appeared to be. But as we say in the world of periodonture, *Streets of Fire* masticates the massive one. My gut aches when I say this, but it is pure crap from start to stop. I simply cannot understand how Walter-*ferchrissakes*Hill! could have done a film this vapid. *The Warriors* was an astonishing exercise in surrealism masquerading as a gang rumble flick; so far ahead of its time that it caused riots when it opened: an augury of urban malignity that made popcorn sociology like *The Blackboard Jungle* and *Rebel Without a Cause* recede into the realm of show biz melodrama where they belong. It was a tough, yet poetic, stylized yet mimetic, fantastic yet naturalistic warping of perceived reality that remains as fresh today as the day it was shot.

And for some goddam dumb reason Walter Hill chose to take his success with the flawed *48 Hours* (ironically, the weakest of his works) and invest it in a production so sophomoric and purely lamebrained that reason founders. He has, in effect, remade *The Warriors* badly. Reportedly given carte blanche by Universal to make any film that piqued his fancy, within twenty-four hours after *48 Hours* broke box-office records, Hill signed the deal for *Streets of Fire*. He is one of the few truly intelligent American directors unhampered by delusions of *auteur*ism. His comments about what he was trying to do with *Streets*, in prerelease interviews (notably in an interview he gave to Kay Anderson in the September 1984 issue of *Cinefantastique*), were astonishing:

"I've always been struck by the morality fables of the Middle Ages, which take place in a framework that looks very real, but in which the events could be outside of reality. Our fantasies, however, tend to be extrapolated into another type of technology, usually futuristic. But if you tell people the film is 'on an interior landscape,' they look at you with question marks. In an unfamiliar setting, people pay attention to the background, trying to orient themselves, instead of just glancing over the familiarity of a here-and-now backdrop."

In those few phrases Hill codifies the esthetic for fantastic film, a series of concepts that the Peter Hyamses and John Carpenters of the world never seem fully to comprehend.

Yet even with his head on straight, and his sensibilities well-ordered, Hill has turned out an expensive exercise in babble. With bubblegum heavymetal new-wave trash music mixed so badly that everything comes up succotash; with cinematography and production design that are the equivalent of purple prose, much of it in a ghastly roast beef red; with mindless violence and a plot that had audiences across the country roaring with unintended laughter; with performances by drone children who must think Stanislavski is a triple-decker sandwich one might order at Nate'n'Al's or the Stage Deli; with nothing going for it save Diane Lane's jailbait sensuality (and on the evidence of her first dozen films, apparently that's where her thespic abilities end) and newcomer Amy Madigan's gritty interpretation of the asskicking reiver McCoy (a part originally written for a guy), *Streets of Fire* was the big Holiday Bomb for Universal. They had the highest expectations, outdid themselves with the kind of hype advertising that should have resulted in queues as long as the Children's Crusade, the videos were omnipresent on MTV, they block-booked it for saturation play...and it went into the dumper so fast it produced a Doppler that could shatter cardboard.

Now we're not talking duds like De Palma or Arthur Hiller (whose batting average is three good films in a thirty-year career, currently onscreen with *Teachers*, which ain't one of the three). This is *Walter Hill* I'm talking about!

Yet even with his keen understanding of what it takes to create that special interior landscape of magic realism, Hill's conception is superficial and spavined.

And the apologia was entered even before the judgment of critics and audience came in. On the jacket of the album of music from the film's soundtrack, Hill has a note dated May, 1984, that reads as follows:

"*Streets of Fire* is, by design, comic book in orientation, mock-epic in structure, movie heroic in acting style, operatic in visual style and cowboy-cliché in dialogue. In short: a rock'n'roll fable where the Leader of the Pack steals the Queen of the Hop and Soldier Boy comes home to do something about it." And he tops off the justification with a quote from Borges: " 'A quite different sort of order rules them, one based not on reason but on association and suggestion—the ancient light of magic.' "

Walter Hill, heretofore a filmmaker on the highest reach of innovation and intellect, has made a film about which the most salient he can say is, "It's a comic book, a parody."

Bear that line in mind.

Third example: *Cloak and Dagger.*   207

Remember what I said earlier about motion pictures—which should be on the cutting edge of cultural phenomena—coming in late as an octogenarian struggling uphill in terms of fad subjects like breakdancing, CB radio talk, punk clothing, etcetera? Well, *Cloak and Dagger* hopped onto the scene all brighteyed and bushytailed with videogames as a major element, as if it were five years ago and we hadn't seen Atari, et al., gasping for survival, with videogame arcades manifesting the business equivalent of cardiac infarction. Fresh concept, very fresh.

A remake of the 1947 suspense film *The Window* starring the late Bobby Driscoll (for which he won an Oscar as best child actor), based originally on a Cornell Woolrich short story, *Cloak and Dagger* is a contemporary updating of the "imaginary playmate" trope. The current Bobby Driscoll, *E.T.*'s Henry Thomas, is one of those mythic whiz kids we see on the cover of *Time* and *Business Week*: imbued with a natural facility for computerstuff that is supposed to shame those of us who still use a manual typewriter into feeling as though we're Cromerian. He is pals with a Bondian father-figure spy named Jack Flack, protagonist of the eponymous fantasy role-playing game Cloak and Dagger. The kid's dream life overlaps the real world on the occasion of his witnessing the murder of an FBI man; and the spies come after him. Jack Flack appears onscreen in the flesh (a dual role for the always interesting Dabney Coleman as the double-ought adventurer and as the kid's father) and advises him how to escape danger.

There isn't much more to it than that, and taken on its own terms it's a frothy confection no better or worse than many another such matinee offering. It's the kind of flick that would have been a cute B feature back in the Forties. Not that a budget in the multimillions should recommend for greater attention a film this slight, but when a movie costs this much, was touted this heavily, and had such solid studio support, and it doesn't draw an audience and is quickly pulled, out come the rationalizations. Which wouldn't hold our interest any longer than alibis usually do, save that once again the apologists countered critical attacks with the now-familiar threnody, "It's not supposed to be realistic; it's just sci-fi fantasy, you know. A cartoon."

And at last, having set this up with examples, we come to the core of the contestation. *Are* these cartoons? Should they be judged on less exacting grounds than "real" movies? Why is it almost always a film of fantasy or sf that gets dismissed in this way? Does the audience swallow such disclaimers?

Let me first establish—on your behalf—feelings of animosity and disgust at the mendacity inherent in this concept of "cartoon." Whenever someone hits you with a conversational shot that is crude or is intended to hurt, and you bristle, the shooter quickly throws up his/her hands and tries to get you to believe, "I was only kidding. It was all in fun. Boy, are you overreacting. You musn't take it seriously, it was just a joke." Well, we *know* it wasn't any such thing. It was a snippet of truth slipping past the cultural safeguards that keep us dealing with one another with civility. It was for real. Similarly, when such films as *Streets of Fire* and *Gremlins* and *Temple of Doom* are made, we are expected to take them seriously enough to plonk down five bucks for a ticket. When they fail to deliver what they've promised in all those tv clips, and we express our anger at having been fleeced, the shooters tell us we're overreacting and we should feel a lot better about losing our five or ten or whatever amount they got out of us, because it was all a gag.

I wonder how well they'd take the gag if we paid for the tickets with counterfeit bills. Or pried open the firedoor at the theater and sneaked in with the entire Duke University Marching Band. "It was all a joke, fellahs; don't take it so *ser*iously; gawd, are you overre*act*ing!"

No, they cannot have that cake and eat it, too. If we are expected to look with solemnity on all the superhype that works as support system for even the least of these films—short films on *The Making of Cloak and Dagger*, or a dozen others; clips on *Entertainment Tonight* that take us behind the scenes; items the pr people have cleverly slipped into the NBC, CBS and ABC nightly news programs with some pseudo-"event" cachet; trailers in movie houses; four color lithography on those double-spreads in every publication from *TV Guide* to *American Film*; all the primetime crashbang commercials; the billboards; the endlessly imaginative *apparat* of publicity that whelms us—then they cannot, dare not, must not, had damned well *better* not, come at us with cop-out cries of "We was only foolin', folks!"

As for the morality of telling us a live-action feature is a "cartoon," I must enter in your behalf even greater disgust and rancorous feelings. A *cartoon* is a cartoon! And a cartoon is a simulacrum of live action. They may not, at risk of tar and feathers, wriggle with that back-formation. They cannot tell us   209 that first came reality, then cinematic reflection of reality, then cartoon interpretation as simulacrum of reflected reality, and then live-action as parody of cartoon interpretation of reflected reality! They are simply lying. It has as much validity as George Wallace nattering on about "state's rights" when what he's really saying is, "Let's keep the niggers in chains."

It is the most repugnant, vilest sort of dissembling; and that so many filmgoers and alleged movie buffs (like Bill Warren and Steve Boyett) go for that okeydoke, is disheartening. For shame, youse guys!

Which leads me to the final consideration of this essay, which is *why* does this "cartoon" cop-out always seem to attach to the sort of films one finds reviewed in a science fiction or fantasy magazine?

I think the answer contains the deepest sort of insult.

Because sf and fantasy have *always* been considered trash by "serious" filmmakers, the sort of stories that a director chooses to film as a lark, not to be taken as seriously as his/her "important" work, it follows that dismissing a failure and the fools who went to see it as a cartoon intended for cartoon-lovers, is logical. No one ever heard the makers of, say, *Gandhi*, suggest to its critics that it wasn't intended as meaningful, that it was just a lark. Not even a Dirty Harry flick gets that kind of write-off. Oh, perhaps, it might extend to the last ten years' James Bond travesties, but I cannot think of too many other candidates for the life-as-cartoon award.

But "sci-fi" and fantasy are clearly marketing fodder; visual aids to sell gremlin soft toys; loss-leaders intended to lure us to the popcorn and candy counter; elegant *merde* shot with state of the art SFX on the new ultrafast Kodak 5293 film. Only that which is conceived as intended for a less discriminating audience would *dare* to be palmed off as unworthy of complaint on the same level as that directed toward "real" movies, "serious" movies, "important" movies.

The excuse that we weren't supposed to be bothered by mean-spiritedness in *Gremlins*, the brutality toward children in *Temple of Doom*, the violence and emptyheadedness blown on a breeze of rock'n'roll in *Streets of Fire*, the plot silliness of *Cloak and Dagger* because they are just "cartoons" intended for a malleable, substandard intelligence audience that will settle for zooming rocketships and flashing light-shows, is a reflection of the deepest-held views of those who run the film industry.

And as long as they can make a buck or five or ten from such a gullible audience, we can stop asking *Why doesn't Hollywood make good sf films?*

For my part, when I want a cartoon, I'll turn on Daffy Duck. Until that time, when I hear the apologia, I will respond as would the Tasmanian Devil.

INSTALLMENT 8:
In Which Some Shrift Is Given Shortly, Some Longly, And The Critic's Laundry Is Reluctantly Aired

Uncle Ayjay (to whom I seem to make reference an inordinate number of times, though reports that we are "an item" are wholly unfounded; we are just friends, despite *USA Today*'s front page revelation on December 13th that he gave me a 20-carat oval sapphire engagement ring) once, a long time ago, when he was trying to teach me how to write, said: "It is not acceptable in trying to create characterization to say, 'He looked exactly like Cary Grant, except the ears were larger.'" By extension, what *Obergruppenfuehrer* Budrys was telling me, is that describing something solely by reference to an existing icon ain't strictly kosher. I mention this as admission of malice aforethought when I write the words that follow:

In 1983 20th Century–Fox released a film titled *Monsignor*, starring Christopher Reeve. In merely one year it has levitated to the top of the list of Worst Movies Ever Made. Worse than *Plan 9 from Outer Space*; worse than *A Countess from Hong Kong*; worse than *The Terror of Tiny Town*; worse than *The Oscar*.

Monsignor is the most astonishingly stupid, cataclysmically wrong-headed, awesomely embarrassing, universally inept stretch of celluloid ever thrown onto a movie screen. One views the film with one's mouth agape in stunned disbelief that so many alleged professionals could so totally have taken leave of their senses as to delude themselves that this cosmic stinker-oonie was worth making; or, having so deluded themselves that, once having screened it, the abomination was worth releasing save for cruel laughter. *Monsignor* is an Olympian exercise in imbecility.

Describing something solely by reference to an existing icon ain't strictly kosher.

SUPERGIRL (Tri-Star Pictures) exists and functions on precisely and exactly the intellectual and artistic level of *Monsignor*. This has been a review.

On the other hand, Tri-Star has given us a genuinely spiffy sf adventure written and directed by Michael Crichton; goes by the name RUNAWAY. And it is what, in my view, a good sf movie ought to be: imaginative, logically consistent, entertaining, unpredictable, exciting and filled with stuff we've never seen. It's not dripping with memorable characterization, but apart from that one scant deficiency which is an acceptable trade-off for the goodies it proffers in abundance (and a last line I can live without), *Runaway* is the filmic equivalent of "a good read."

Tom Selleck is engagingly cast as a police sergeant in charge of the Runaway Squad of a major metropolitan city's law enforcement department in the not-too-distant. Runaways are robots that have gone bonkers and are doing what they oughtn't. The first part of the film swiftly and neatly delineates a society almost identical to today's, with the addition of many kinds of household and industrial machines that perform the kind of scutwork labor white folks abhor and consign to peoples bearing green cards. And though prophesying what our world will be like twenty years hence, with robots to do our cooking and welding, is a mugg's game (and not even sf's vaunted claims of being able "to predict the future" hold up under close historical scrutiny), Crichton has been a model of rectitude injecting those little extrapolative touches we all slaver for. It all seems plausible, which is the most we should ever ask of this kind of woolgathering.

When people start getting killed by otherwise innocuous mechanical helpmates, Selleck finds himself going *mano-a-mano* with the psychopathic high-tech killer, Dr. Luther, played with exquisite malevolence by rock star Gene Simmons, leader of Kiss. (Who walked up to me at the screening to say he was a fan of my work, and scared the shit out of me even *without* his concert makeup. Thank god he didn't stick out his tongue at me.)

Additionally, as if a good original plot, endless action, terrific visuals and heartstopping danger were not enough, *Runaway* showcases the talents and beauty of three women for whom one might gladly burn the topless towers of Ilium: Cynthia Rhodes, Kirstie Alley and Anne-Marie Martin (regularly seen on the *Days of Our Lives* daytime serial). Now ordinarily, making a remark about the pulchritude of the actresses in a film would get both Vonda and Joanna tsk-tsking at me; but since the star of this movie is a sex object for *women*, I take obscene advantage of the opportunity to reprise that blissfully ignorant condition of chauvinism in which I existed for thirty years before Vonda and Joanna put me on the floor with their knees in my chest and pointed out logically where my thinking was screwed.

As for that last line, it's goodness knows a tiny enough nit, but I mention it so Michael doesn't do it again. At the end of the film—and I'm giving nothing away by telling you this, trust me—Selleck and Rhodes have fallen in love. Both are cops, and both have performed athletically and competently throughout the story. But as they kiss, Selleck says to her, "Do you cook?" She answers, "Try me." Apart from the grating cliché of "try me" (which, if the universe is kind, I will never hear from a movie screen again as long as I live or even after, on a level of awful familiarity with someone saying "Just like that?" and reply being "Just like that"), and the recidivist resonance of times past when no matter how competent a woman might be at non-house-wifely occupations, she would only be fulfilled as a "real woman" if she could cook and clean and bear homunculi, the film prominently includes Lois, a cook/babysitter robot in Selleck's home. So Ms. Rhodes should have replied to Sgt. Ramsay's question with a line something like, "I don't have to; Lois can do it. I can fuck; Lois can't do that."

But perhaps I ask too much of the universe.

Then again, when I'm elected god this year…

The ultimate variation of the cinematic convention commonly referred to as "Boy and Girl meet cute" (ref. Dudley Moore and Liza Minnelli in *Arthur*) can be found in a sappy, nay, *goofy*, clinker called STARMAN (Columbia Pictures).

Here in glamorous but Machiavellian Hollywood the Writers Guild has long fought the battle of the possessive credit. You know what I mean: Walt Disney's *Pinocchio* (written by Carlo Collodi); Richard Attenborough's *Gandhi* (written by John Briley); Brian De Palma's *Scarface* (written by Oliver Stone). Directors can continue to flummox the studios and the public only as long as they can continue to cloud our thinking with the *auteur* theory that puts them forward as "the creator" of a film. We are talking about power and money in the possessive credit. They get around it in a thousand ways, this bad feeling they stir in those of us who *actually* create the dream: A Brian De Palma Film / Brian De Palma's Film of / A Film of Brian De Palma...you get the idea. So the Writers Guild goes on fighting this one, against the Producers Guild and the Directors Guild, and not much progress is made, because we're talking about power and money.

However, in the case of JOHN CARPENTER'S STARMAN, I suspect not even bamboo slivers under the fingernails could get scenarists Bruce A. Evans and Raynold Gideon to ask for the possessive credit. It's that dumb.

(On the other hand, which I've been doing a lot in this installment, they *are* the guys who wrote this emgalla, so who's to say how deeply runs their brain damage.) (Emgalla: a South African wart hog.)

Starman's plot is at least thirty-five years old. It is a first contact story that acts as if *The Day the Earth Stood Still* (1951), *The Thing* (1951), *The Man Who Fell to Earth* (1976) and *E.T. The Extra-Terrestrial* (1982) had never been made. Out goes our space probe, it's found by an alien intelligence, the e.t. comes to Earth, the e.t. shape-changes to assume the persona of a woman's dead husband, they fall in love, he runs around a lot trying to evade people trying to capture him, he gives her a baby, and he leaves the planet. No explanation is ever given as to why he was here or why, if he went to the trouble to come here, he runs around madly trying to escape contact with the species he sought to contact in the first place.

Again we have the stupidity of a spaceship whooooooshing noisily past in airless vacuum, again we have the inept and malevolent scientists and military schmucks who seek only to imprison or kill the visitor, again we have sophomoric definitions of "love" and "friendship" as explicated by subliterate characters. What we have here is a 1948 movie made in 1984.

A waste of time.

A contrived, simpleminded, *sappy* film. My patience is fast running out with John Carpenter, who is a talented man, yet who seems hellbent on cranking out one dreary clot after another. And they crucified Michael Cimino for *Heaven's Gate.*

Just wait'll I'm elected.

*   *   *

I'll save *2010* and *Dune* till next time, because it has become necessary to say something about THE TERMINATOR (Orion Pictures).

Yes, folks, I'm more than painfully aware that *The Terminator* resembles my own *Outer Limits* script "Soldier" in ways so obvious and striking that you've been moved to call me, write letters, send me telegrams and pass the gardyloo along by word-of-mouth with my friends. You really must cease waking me in the wee hours to advise me I've been ripped off.

As I write this, attorneys are talking.

Despite the foregoing, permit me to recommend *The Terminator*. It is a superlative piece of work and deserves its success. Director and co-author James Cameron has made an auspicious debut. The film is taut, memorable, and clearly based on brilliant source material. More than that I am not at liberty to say.

If for no other reason, I would celebrate this nifty movie on the grounds that someone has, at last, figured out a way to use Arnold Schwartzenegger effectively. I suppose I'm a bit tired of seeing that *Friday the 13th* horror ending in which the dead monster comes back to life again and again, but in context it plays like a baby doll this time.

Now if you go to see this movie, I want you to put out of your minds all memory of "Soldier" or my other *Outer Limits* script "Demon with a Glass Hand" or my short story "I Have No Mouth, and I Must Scream." Also, do not think of a green cow.

I would be less than responsible if I did not recommend a few non-sf films for your attention.

Beverly Hills Cop with Eddie Murphy is a joy. It was directed by Marty Brest, who needs a hit, so go see it. And do take notice of the actor who plays the role of Taggart, a cop. His name is John Ashton, and he damned near steals the film from Murphy, if you can conceive of such a thing.

Don't miss David Lean's first film in fourteen years, based on the exquisite novel by E. M. Forster, *A Passage to India*. You might even read the book first, couldn't hurt.

The River is the best of the recent spate of country movies in which people lose the farm, and is the only one I've seen that made me give a damn if they did or didn't.

The Cotton Club is Coppola, beyond which nothing need really be said; but for those of you who aren't as much in love with every foot of film Francis Ford has ever turned out, know that *The Cotton Club* is a wonder.

217

Now I know I'm not supposed to be doing this kind of business, urging you to see stuff outside the genre, but my goodness, you'll need *some*thing to wash the taste of *Supergirl* and *Starman* out of your heads.

Think of me as your mother. At least until I'm elected god, on the other hand.

INSTALLMENT 9:
In Which The Fortunate Reader Gets To Peek Inside The Fabled Black Tower

If the Universal Studios Tower didn't exist, it would have to be invented. By some noted fabulist like Borges; or Satie or Arcimboldo; by Gaudi or the Brothers Grimm; more likely by Clifford Irving. (And within days Glen A. Larson—far-famed for his creation of such original television concepts as *Alias Smith and Jones*, *BJ and the Bear* and *Battlestar Galactica*—would have erected, out of cardboard and mucilage, an approximation of the Black Tower just a few miles farther along the Cahuenga Pass.)

At no two consecutive points, one often feels, does what goes on in the Tower touch the rational universe.

The Universal Tower rises from the North Hollywood flats like a Kubrick monolith farted off the Lunar surface. There are rumors Childe Roland is still a prisoner up there on the fifteenth floor. On moonless nights, when the ghosts of Universal executives who thought *A Countess from Hong Kong*, *The Island* and *Streets of Fire* would be smash hits drift silently around the back lot, ectoplasmic hands clapped over ectoplasmic ears in vain endeavor to block out the heavy metal caterwauling from the Universal Amphitheater, if one whizzes past the Tower on the Hollywood Freeway, one can still hear Rapunzel shrieking her guts out for someone to climb up her hair and release her from her starlet's contract.

For five years, commencing on Thursday, September 18th, 1698, the Bertaudiere Tower in the Bastille of Paris held a nameless prisoner whose face was covered by a black velvet cloth that Dumas *père* transformed into "a visor of polished steel soldered to a helmet of the same nature."

For seven weeks, commencing Monday, November 15th, 1971, the northwest corner of the 9th floor of the Universal Tower held a nameless writer whose mind was covered by a black smog ABC-TV transformed into "a lemminglike urge to hurl oneself through the ninth floor window to a messy fadeout."

For seven weeks Dopplering toward, through, and past Christmas 1971, I sold my soul to Universal Studios, then-president Lew Wasserman, a producer named Stan Shpetner, a primetime tv series called *The Sixth Sense*, the American Broadcasting Company, and anybody else who would make a reasonable bid on damaged goods, tacky remnants, floating ethics, and seriously flawed seconds; in short, I departed in a moment of greed and weakness from eleven years as a film and television *writer* to join the enemy on the other side of the desk. Yes, brethren and sistren, I became a story editor. Uck yichh choke!

As the Christ child's natal day celebration neared in that watershed year of 1971, I found myself standing in the stairwell between the eighth and ninth floors of the Black Tower, rattling the walls with Primal Screams that brought secretaries running from all directions to help the poor soul who was obviously being disemboweled. Soon thereafter, mere minutes later, I leaped onto Stan Shpetner's desk, did a deranged adagio, terminated my employment, and fled television for a decade.

(That I have, of late, returned to television is an odd story for yet another day.)

Nor did I, during that decade, have much to do with the Studio of the Black Tower. Once having been touched by the lunacy of that self-contained vertical universe, I tried to live by the wisdom Voltaire demonstrated when, having attended an orgy and having comported himself (we are told) with heroic verve and expertise, refused a second invitation with the classic rejoinder, "Once: a philosopher; twice: a pervert."

Or in the words of Oscar Wilde: "Experience is the name everyone gives to his mistakes."

Recently, however, as the needs of this column have demanded, I have been thrown into assorted liaisons with Universal. I as reviewer, they as hustlers of product they wish reviewed. This is a symbiotic relationship much like that melded from the association of the hippopotamus and the ox-pecker, or tick bird (*Buphaginus Africanus*).

And I must confess I had forgotten how deranged things can get up there at the Black Tower. I select the word *deranged* from among the many words available to me, with great care. (There is a legend—certainly intended to be apocryphal—that in a manner similar to that of the apemen being brought to the Black Monolith in *2001* so they could touch it and have their intelligence raised, so it is that television producers are brought to the monolith of the Black Tower, they lay their hands upon it, and their intelligence is *lowered*.) Yes, I think deranged is the proper adjective; particularly when Universal makes a corporate decision to scramble all its eggs in one basket.

DUNE.

The breath catches when the name is spoken. In the truest sense of the flack-artist's phrase, *Dune* has been one of the most eagerly-awaited sf films of all time. The publicity mill began its abrasive work against the public consciousness in 1969, just four years after the Chilton hardcover was published, combining the two serials John Campbell had first published as "Dune World" (1963–64) and "Prophet of Dune" (1965). Arthur Jacobs, who had produced for 20th Century–Fox the enormously popular *Planet of the Apes* films and the financially-disastrous *Dr. Dolittle*, optioned the book for what would be considered a laughable sum in the light of today's knowledge that the Dune books have sold more than 15 million copies, not to mention that the current option prices even for trash bestsellers are now computed in numbers that could have wiped out the Holy Roman Empire's entire budget deficit. Jacobs died in 1973 and so did the first *Dune* film deal.

Seven years later, surrealist director Alejandro Jodorowsky, Chilean-born, underground famous for *El Topo*—the weirdest "western" ever filmed if you agree that the concept of Jesus as Gunslinger do tend to diddle Jung's archetypal images more than somewhat—secured backing, optioned the book, wrote a script, and began hiring as astonishing an artistic braintrust as *any* filmmaker had ever assembled: British paperback cover artist Chris Foss, whose spaceships were painted as if they'd been sculpted out of Silly Putty; "Moebius," the *Metal Hurlant* comic artist whose distinctive style in such extended works as *L'Homme Est-Il Bon? (Is Man Good?)*, *Cauchemar Blanc* and *Arzach* had influenced an entire generation of Anglo-American illustrators; the Swiss designer H. R. Giger, who would later

221

provide the psycho-sexually arresting look of *Alien*; Salvador Dali; Dan O'Bannon (*Alien, Blue Thunder, Dark Star*) and the nonpareil Ron Cobb. Two million dollars was spent just on salaries for the visionaries. I have seen some of Giger's bizarre, brilliant paintings for Jodorowsky's vision of *Dune*, and if aficionados of the novels have been less than overwhelmed by the eventually-filmed sandworms of Arrakis, I submit that their spines would have been pumped full of Freon had Giger's Arrakeen horror been realized.

But by Christmas of 1975, the volatile combination of Jodorowsky, parvenu backers, erratic artists and banks wary of putting up a completion bond for the film exploded and two years' worth of planning, writing and preproduction went into the dumper. Lights dim; and the myth dozes.

Leaves fly off the calendar. Seasons change. The Proscenium is cleared, flats are taken to storage, the cyclorama is repainted, and in 1978 a new cast of characters enters stage right as Dino De Laurentiis buys into the nightmare the *Dune* dream has become. And he opens the third act of the drama by commissioning Frank Herbert to write a new screenplay.

Digression: in the twenty-two years I've spent working in the visual mediums of film and television, it has been made painfully clear to me that the "rule of thumb," widespread in the industry, that most writers of books and stories simply cannot write screenplays...is correct. Like most old saws, it is a bit of True Writ based solidly in history and personal experience. There is a reason Scott Fitzgerald was yoked with such as Charles Marquis Warren and Budd Schulberg on studio scriptwriting assignments.

When I was working on *Star Trek* in 1966, I went out on the limb half a dozen times by urging Gene Roddenberry and then–story editor John D. F. Black to consider signing well-known sf authors to write segments. Six or eight were, in fact, hired. Of those who had no previous credits as scenarists, only two produced material that was eventually filmed. As for the others, some of the most respected names in the print medium: they just didn't have a clue. What they brought forth—even after extensive meetings and revisions and demonstrations of how a scene could be made to work, and finally even after-hours get-togethers in which scenes were actually rewritten for them—was pathetic.

Even as there are *apparatchiks* of the Eastern Literary Establishment (a state of place and mind we who live here in literary Coventry t'other side of the Rockies are constantly assured by such as Barbara Epstein of *The New York Review of Books* and Mitchel Levitas of *The New York Times Book Review* is only a fevered conjuration of our California-vanilla paranoia) who believe that the presence of too much sunshine and an absence of a dozen police locks on the apartment door prevents us out here from writing Great Art, there are writers who smugly contend that writing for the screens, big and small, is merely a five-finger exercise any Real Writer can perform, a chore fit only for Hacks. I smile far more smugly than they, when I hear such twaddle. Let them try, I say; as you would to one of those culinary *machos* who announces at your favorite Thai or Tex-Mex restaurant that "there ain't a salsa living that's too hot for me!" Let them try, I say. Heh heh heh.

Because for every William Goldman, William Faulkner or Robert Bloch who can swing both ways, book to film and back, there are *thousands* of narrative writers who have fruitlessly thumped their noggins against the enigma of how to write cinematically. It does not detract one iota from their craftsmanship in writing for print, but it ought to humble them summat when next they run a denigration ramadoola about those who *can* hear the song, those who *can* conjure the dream, those who *can* write words to be spoken and action to be actualized.

Which is not to say that Frank Herbert ever manifested such snobbery. Nonetheless, his 175-page screenplay was, by all reports, utterly unworkable. Unshootable because of Frank's inability to prune it, trim it, straightline it, free it of the endless distractions of subplots and minutiae. End of digression.

So Frank Herbert was taken off the project and De Laurentiis decided to go in another direction with the project. He opted for the method of hiring a highly visual director, and letting *him* find the proper scenarist. In 1979 Dino signed Ridley Scott. *Alien* was hot, and the English director seemed right for what was now considered an impossible project that would break the hearts of men or women no matter how tough and talented they might be. Ridley Scott went looking for writers.

On Thursday, September 27th, 1979 Ridley Scott came for a breakfast meeting at my home and offered me the assignment to write *Dune*. He was very nice about it when I told him I would sooner spend my declining years vacationing on Devil's Island. Further, with the wisdom and foresight that has made me a Delphic legend in my own time, with the kind of bold extrapolative thinking personified by Charles H. Duell (who, as Commissioner of the U.S. Office of Patents in 1899, implored President

223

William McKinley to abolish his office because, "Everything that can be invented *has been* invented"), I assured Scott that this was a book so complex and vast in scope that it never *could* be made, for anything under a hundred million dollars. And yet further, I said with sagacity, "Besides, who needs to see *Dune* when David Lean has already made *Lawrence of Arabia*? It's just *King of Kings* with sandworms. No," I said, vibrating with a richness of perspicacity unparalleled since Custer opined that he could kick the crap out of them redskins up there on the hill, "no, this is a fool's enterprise. There isn't a writer living or dead who could beat this project."

Digression: Scott said something remarkable that has stuck in my mind. He said, "The time is ripe for a John Ford of science fiction films. I'm going to be that director." And maybe he hasn't achieved that yet, but sooner the man who helmed *Alien* and *Blade Runner* and *The Duellists* than John Carpenter or George Lucas or Joe Dante. End of digression II.

Though I like to think Ridley's spirit was crushed at not being able to suffer the torments of the damned by having had the bad sense to hire me, he pulled himself together like the special talent he is, and he hired Rudolph Wurlitzer.

Wurlitzer's has been a strange filmwriting career.

In April of 1971—just four months before the magazine would abandon the 10″ × 13″ bedsheet format it had held for 38 years—*Esquire* ran as its hot cover feature a screenplay titled *Two-Lane Blacktop* with the blurb READ IT FIRST! OUR NOMINATION FOR THE MOVIE OF THE YEAR! The screenplay was by Rudolph Wurlitzer and Will Corry.

Well, the film dropped into an abyss and, though it has become something of a cult classic and is an interesting item because of a Warren Oates performance that is a killer, and some offbeat direction by Monte Hellman, not only wasn't it the movie of the year, it vanished without a plop! In the same year Wurlitzer's screenplay for a post-holocaust film called *Glen and Randa* was produced. Another miraculous non-event in cinema history though, again, an interesting piece of writing. Then in 1973 Sam Peckinpah directed Wurlitzer's gawdawful screenplay of *Pat Garrett and Billy the Kid*, starring James Coburn and (wait for it) Kris Kristofferson. That one created its *own* black hole down which it plunged.

And that was it. No other produced credits exist as of this writing for Wurlitzer. But in 1979 Ridley Scott put Rudy Wurlitzer to work. The most memorable aspect of the three drafts

Wurlitzer wrote was his departure from the novel to include a relationship that poor, misguided Frank Herbert had overlooked: a sexual liaison between Paul Atreides and his mother, the Lady Jessica.

Have you ever heard Frank Herbert bellow with rage?

The Sargasso Sea came unblocked. Avalanches on the Siberian Peninsula. Magma solidified. The stars shook.

By 1980 the deal was dead. Scott went on to *Blade Runner*, Wurlitzer went underground, and De Laurentiis went looking for new foot troops to throw into what was becoming the cinematic equivalent of Hitler's Russian campaign.

Dune.

The name had become legend. The bodies that lay in its sandworm track could have populated another whole film industry.

But in 1981 De Laurentiis shocked even those of us who are beyond shock, by signing the director of *Eraserhead* and *The Elephant Man*, and David Lynch stepped up bravely to inhale them bullets.

Four years later *Dune* was a reality, more than forty million dollars had been expended in its production, the world trembled at its imminent release, and in mere moments before it hit the screens of the world, everything hit the fans in that equally-fabled Black Tower where derangement is a way of life.

And in the next issue I'll bring you full circle, as one with the Laocoönian serpent, to complete the bizarre story of Frank Herbert, *Dune*, De Laurentiis father and daughter, untold millions of dollars and lire, and the strange rituals of the priests of the Black Tower.

Don't miss this one, kids. You'll boogie till you puke.

PUBLIC NOTICE: Got a call today from my friend Bill Warren. Bill is a film critic, author of a nifty book on Fifties sf movies, and a cinema researcher who works with the Hollywood Film Archive. When it comes to movies, Bill's middle name is *knowledgeable*. Sometimes, amazingly, our opinions agree on a specific film. For years we have taken mutual pleasure in passionate arguments about the nature of movies. In my installment 7, in the time-honored tradition of gigging my chums, I took Bill's (and Steve Boyett's) name in vain. I said that these "alleged movie buffs" accepted a philosophy expressed by many duplicitous filmmakers that one should not take seriously the evil and gruesome aspects of some films because they were really

225

only live action "cartoons." The word *alleged* was, of course, intended as goodnatured elbow-in-the-ribs hyperbole. That Bill and Steve have expressed to me their concurrence with the "don't take it seriously, it's just a cartoon" disclaimer is true. They've said it to me on a number of occasions, about a number of films. In the case of Bill, most recently in reference to *Gremlins*; Steve said it a short time ago about *Buckaroo Banzai*. But Bill called me in a state of upset today, to say I owe him an apology in the same public forum where I defamed him, in his view. He read my remarks in that column to say that he is a liar. I did not call Bill Warren a liar, nor anything even remotely like it. As far as I know, Bill Warren is not a liar. Nor was I calling Steve Boyett a liar. What I *did* say, is what I said; and it was intended to make my friends smile ruefully. But Bill feels I have done him a mischief. Because he is my friend, and because I respect him, I will apologize here in print, on the off-chance that someone else may have interpreted my remarks in a way I did not intend; but I apologize mostly because Bill is upset, and he is my friend. So one does this sort of thing for friends.

But really, Bill, you shouldn't take it all so seriously: it was just a cartoon.

INSTALLMENT 10:
In Which The Fabled Black Tower Meets Dune With As Much Affection As Godzilla Met Ghidrah

Synopsis of Part One of this thrilling essay:

The critic attempted to establish, as philosophical background for weighty matters to be discussed in Part Two, that an ambience of derangement surrounds the milieu known as Universal Studios. Then, when the reader felt secure that the critic was going to discuss lunacy at the fabled Black Tower of Universal, he jerked them around again, as is his wont, by veering away in a (seemingly) unrelated digression that detailed the fifteen-year frustration of those who have attempted to bring Frank Herbert's DUNE to the big screen. The critic made much of the expectations of the filmgoing audience; their Cheyne–Stokes respiration at the merest mention of the magic name *Dune*; the universal (though as we will see, not Universal) belief that this was one of the most mythic, most exciting, most eagerly-anticipated films of all time. Absolutely. Early on in Part One, the critic made this cryptic remark:

"Yes, I think *deranged* is the proper adjective, particularly when Universal makes a corporate decision to scramble all its eggs in one basket. *Dune.*"

What could this have meant? At what dark secrets was the critic hinting? Did he, in fact, begin to tie together the disparate elements of Part One with this pair'o'paragraphs:

"Four years later *Dune* was a reality; more than forty million dollars had been expended in its production; the world trembled at its imminent release; and in mere moments before it hit the screens of the world, everything hit the fans in that equally fabled Black Tower where derangement is a way of life.

"And in the next issue I'll bring you full circle, as one with the Laocoönian serpent, to complete the bizarre story of Frank Herbert, *Dune*, De Laurentiis father and daughter, untold millions of dollars and lire, and the strange rituals of the priests of the Black Tower."

Now go on, simply all atremble, to the thrilling Part Two!

There will be mass screenings of *Dune*. There will be no mass screenings of *Dune*. There will be several sneak previews of *Dune*, but only on the West Coast. There will be sneak previews of *Dune*, but only in suburban New York and Connecticut. We are running screenings of *Dune* for the press at Universal only for the first two weeks in December, prior to the December 14th nationwide release. All press screenings of *Dune* have been canceled. A screening has been set up, but only those press representatives with specially-accepted credentials will be invited. The special press screening for an elite group has been canceled. Yes on *Dune*. No on *Dune*. *Dune*'s in, *Dune*'s out, surf's up!

Those are notes from my log book of daily appointments. They begin in mid-November of last year, and they go right on through to December 12th when I actually got to see *Dune*.

If the word *deranged* echoes in that paragraph of windy contradictions, well, who're ya gonna call, Ghostbusters?

As I write this in March of 1985, *Dune* has come and gone, and you have very likely seen it. Some of you liked it; some of you didn't like it. Apparently, not one of you was satisfied.

In the time-honored tradition of now-crepuscular fan pundits —so crapulously into their twilight years that their declamations no longer girn from the pages of know-it-all fanzines— every aficionado endowed with mouth has had his/her scream. It was too big. It wasn't enough. It left too much out. It included too much. It was simplistic. It was too convoluted. It was too serious. It wasn't serious enough. *Dune*'s in, *Dune*'s out, surf's up, shut your pie-hole!

Can't anybody see there's something wrong here?

Doesn't anybody else notice that otherwise rational critics have savaged *Dune* way the hell out of proportion to its weaknesses? Even Roger Ebert, former sf fan and good film observer, picked *Dune* as the worst film of the year. Ain't dat the same year that gave us *Children of the Corn, Porky's II, Teachers, Gremlins, Body Double, Conan the Destroyer, Buckaroo Banzai, Streets of Fire, Breakin' 2: Electric Boogaloo, Sheena, Where the Boys Are, Up the Creek, Sahara, Tank, Red Dawn, Rhinestone, Hot Dog . . . The Movie, Angel, Bachelor Party, Bo-lero, Hardbodies,* and *Give My Regards to Broad Street*? Ain't it dat same year?

In such a year of gasp, wheeze, pant, choke, gimme a sec to let my gorge settle, in such a year *Dune* is the worst film!??!

No, gentlefolk, something went wrong. Of a nature that has to do with public and private perceptions. Of a sort that defies logic because, like politics, it is a matter of image. Codification of what happened, of the skewing of expectations, progressed so rapidly and with such economy of action, that if one were given to conspiracy theories one might well take the case of the release of *Dune* to one's bosom for the sheer clarity of its *modus operandi*. But let me, for an instant, give you a f'rinstance. Helpful digression. Explanation by example. A bit of storytelling.

William Friedkin is, in my view, an extraordinary director. There is a subterranean river of dark passion rushing wildly in the subtext of all his films—successful and disastrous—that clearly marks him as an artist almost manic with the need to rearrange the received universe in a personal, newly-folded way. With only two films, *The French Connection* in 1971 and *The Exorcist* in 1973 (neither, in my view, Friedkin's most compelling work), he established himself as the box-office Colossus of Roadshows.

Then he took four years to bring forth an astonishing film called *Sorcerer*. An honorable (and acknowledged) *hommage intense* to Clouzot's 1952 classic *The Wages of Fear*, Friedkin's labors and vision in the jungles of the Dominican Republic—which came close to killing him, so physically near to danger did his pathological involvement force him—produced a motion picture that laid bare the corpus of human compulsion with images that smoldered.

The film died. It was driven into oblivion to such an extent that nowhere in Pauline Kael's five books of criticism is the movie even mentioned. And the core reasons for its universal (and, not surprisingly, Universal) dismissal can be found in *Sorcerer's* listing in HALLIWELL'S FILM GUIDE, the basic reference work on cinema (page 761, 4th edition):

"Why anyone should have wanted to spend twenty million

229

dollars on a remake of *The Wages of Fear*, do it badly, and give it a misleading title is anybody's guess. The result is dire."

Dire? *Dire!?!* Halliwell does not bristle thus at the vile and venal remakes of *Stagecoach*, *King Kong*, *Cat People*, *The Jazz Singer*, *The Thing*, *The Big Sleep* or the 1981 remake of *The Incredible Shrinking Man* (*Woman*) as a vehicle for Lily Tomlin, even while acknowledging their failure. But *Sorcerer* produces uncommon bile in the usually mild-mannered Leslie Halliwell.

And while my theory of movie crib-death may be all blue sky surmise as regards *Dune*, so close to the immolation, we can use Kael and Halliwell as indicators of why Friedkin and *Sorcerer* were summarily dismissed after uncommon savaging, and then extend the premise.

It was expectation and image. *The Wages of Fear* was a classic. Friedkin was considered a Johnny-come-lately, a smartass who had done spectacularly well with "popular" films; but by what right did this upstart manifest the hubris to reshape a film held in worldwide esteem? That he made the movie not only with the blessing of old Clouzot, but with the onscreen dedication to what had inspired him; that he made the film at the highest level of professionalism and expertise, rather than at the level of grave-robbing commercialism that keynotes 99% of all remakes...cut no ice with the critics. They were lying in wait for Billy Friedkin. And they ambushed him. So much for expectations.

Image. The title of the film was *Sorcerer*. For those who paid attention to the film, that was the name of the truck driven by Roy Scheider; and it was the recurring trope treated both visually and mythically throughout the picture. But Bill Friedkin was, unfortunately, the director of *The Exorcist*, and theatergoers went to the movie expecting a hair-raising occult fantasy. Instead, they got a hair-raising action-adventure of doomed men on the run, condemned to a suicidal job. Audiences felt betrayed. The image of the film that had been projected by its title and the resonance with Friedkin's most popular movie, *The Exorcist*, linked with the *a priori* animosity of the critics; and *Sorcerer* had about as much chance of succeeding in the marketplace as Ilse Koch designer lampshades from Buchenwald.

Worth was evaluated not on intrinsic merit, but through skewed expectations and a misleading image.

The studio that dumped *Sorcerer* was Universal. Studio of the Black Tower, where derangement is a way of life.

230   In October of last year I was approached by *USA Today*, the

national newspaper, to write a visiting critic's review of *Dune*. As I was already the film critic of record for *The Magazine of Fantasy & Science Fiction*; as I received press screening notices regularly; as I was on good terms (in this symbiotic relationship) with the pr people at Universal; as I had discussed the upcoming film with Frank Herbert and he had advised the publicity people that I'd be doing a critique; as *USA Today* is a major market for national film publicity and attention by a wide spectrum of potential ticket-buyers; as all of us in the reviewing game had been led to believe *Dune* was going to get a big push from not only De Laurentiis but from Universal as its distributor, I felt sure I'd be able to take my time with the piece. If the movie was scheduled to open on December 14th, then surely I'd see it late in November.

But strange things began happening in the Black Tower.

It was widely rumored in the gossip underground that Frank Price, Chairman of MCA/Universal's Motion Picture Group, and one of the most powerful men in the industry, had screened the film in one or another of its final workups, and had declared—vehemently enough and publicly enough for the words quickly to have seeped under the door of the viewing room and formed a miasma over the entire Universal lot—"This film is a dog. It's gonna drop dead. We're going to take a bath on it. Nobody'll understand it!" (Now those aren't the exact words, because I wasn't there. But the sense is dead accurate. Half a dozen separate verifications from within the MCA organization.)

Now, when God has a bellyache, all the cherubim start dropping Alka-Seltzer.

The word went out fast and wide. Or fastly and widely, depending on your Yuppie level. And the panic set in. Of a sudden *Dune* was a film not to be seen by the laity.

Reviewers couldn't be trusted. Keep it away from them.

Screenings were canceled wholesale. Press releases became circumspect. The usually forthcoming pr people at MCA abruptly developed narcolepsy. Something was very wrong. Any time *Dune* was mentioned, eyes rolled. And the rumors built on an asymptotic curve that had everyone nervous as hell. Then:

A major filmwriter who had been at one of the sneak screenings for exhibitors reported a conversation he had overheard between Dino De Laurentiis and the owner of an important chain of multiplex theaters, after the film had been run.

Dino (he reported) had been effusive. It went like this:

DINO: This is my testament! I can now retire! It is great, it is classic!

EXHIBITOR: Can you save it?

DINO (sadly): Maybe.

Then we all heard that an exhibitors' screening—maybe the one above, maybe another—in New York, when the lights came up, one of the attendees leaped to his feet and screamed at Dino across the theater, "When are you going to stop making shit like this? When are you going to give us a picture we can play that will make some money? Are you trying to kill us?"

And *Dune* was in the toilet. Because the priests of the Black Tower, in their panic and paranoia, did what they *always* do: they prejudged the film and found it dire. Dire. Absolutely. And there would be no screening, not of any kind, not for *anyone*.

Somehow, I knew the film would not be the disaster Universal was compelling the rest of the world to believe it would be. I had spoken to Frank Herbert a number of times in late November. He was living in Manhattan Beach, making himself available for prerelease publicity, and he told me, when I asked him, sans bullshit, "How do you like the film, Frank? Between old friends. The real appraisal": "It begins as DUNE begins, it ends as DUNE ends and I hear my dialogue throughout. How much more could a writer want? Even though I have quibbles—I would've loved to have had David Lynch realize the banquet scene—do I like it? I do. I like it. Very much."

So I wanted to like it, too.

There had been too many intelligent, dedicated people of good faith and enormous talent who had been ground to powder in that sandworm track to dismiss *Dune* merely on the basis of the industry rumor mill's fervor for movie crib-death. (Of *course* the rumor mill wanted *Dune* to founder. If the other studios could cripple one of their big competitors for the Christmas box-office attention, before it ever got out of the starting gate, it would make the chances for *their* holiday blockbusters all the better. Most of the rumors I got came not from Universal, but from other studios. No bad word was left unsaid; no rock was left unturned; and no creepy crawly was prevented from emerging. But why was *Universal* wielding the chainsaw on this unborn artifact?)

Frank called me on the q.t. at the end of November. He told me there was to be a secret screening in projection room #1 at Universal on Friday the 30th, at 2:30 PM. The screening was for the reviewers from *Variety* and *The Hollywood Reporter*. He did not suggest I sneak in; he only reported the event.

On that Friday I visited other friends on the lot, and found my way to projection room #1 at 2:15.

Booker McClay, a decent man, one of the publicists for Universal, was standing by the inner door. He stopped me. We had spoken over the phone, but had never met. I told him who I was, we shook hands. He looked troubled. He knew my credentials as writer, scenarist, critic. He knew of my association with *The Magazine of Fantasy & Science Fiction*. When I told him I was doing the review for *USA Today*, he grew even more troubled. He said I could not go in.

We talked for a few minutes, with me assuring him I was not there to do a hatchet job. He said it was impossible. I showed him my letter from Jerry Shriver, Assistant Entertainment Editor for *USA Today*, confirming my assignment. He said it was impossible that I could have known of this screening, and it was impossible... seeing the film, that is. I cajoled, I chatted, I reasoned. Booker McClay is a good guy, and he said he would call Frank Wright, National Publicity Director for MCA, who was at that moment only a few hundred yards away up in the Black Tower.

Booker went into the screening room, which was empty, as *Variety* and *The Reporter* had not yet arrived. He was extremely upset. It was clear to me that he wanted to let me in to screen *Dune*, but the fear was palpable on the lot. And here was this wild cannon insisting on being given access to The Unviewable!

I followed Booker inside, and stood at a distance from him as he phoned up to the Tower, to Frank Wright. When Booker got Wright, and spoke to him earnestly and softly about the situation, though I was thirty feet from the receiver I heard Frank Wright shout, "What the hell is *he* doing there? How did he find out about this? Get him out of there! No, absolutely not!"

Booker spoke again, hung up the phone, and turned to me. He tried to be ameliorative. It was obvious he'd been put in a shitty position, and didn't want to alienate me. But this was a situation that was to be governed by the laws of the Stalag. I had to leave. He said that Frank Wright had set up this screening only for *Variety* and *The Reporter*, and they had promised to hold the reviews before publishing. He said Frank Wright had said I needed stronger accreditation.

Somehow I managed to get Booker to let *me* call Frank Wright. Seeing his career flashing before his eyes, but too decent a guy simply to come all over authoritarian, Booker let me use the phone in the screening room. I called Wright, and spoke to him, saying *USA Today* was an important medium of pr for the film, and I was inclined to write well of the film as I now thought about it, and I would appreciate it if he'd make an exception in this case. He said if he'd heard from Jack Mathews, the West Coast entertainment editor of *USA Today*, he could have done it. But as he hadn't . . . he had to refuse. He was testy about it, but as polite as he could be, I guess, under the circumstances.

I said, "What if Jack Mathews calls you in the next five minutes and verifies my assignment, and asks you to let me see the film?"

He thought a moment, then said he figured that would be okay. I hung up, called Mathews at the L.A. office of the newspaper, told him what was happening, and he said he'd call Wright on the other line, that I should hold on. Then, as I waited, I heard him call Wright, heard him speak to Wright, and received Mathews's assurance that everything had been fixed.

"Wait there for Wright's call back," he said. I thanked him, hung up, and relayed the chain of command to Booker, who seemed vastly relieved.

Ten minutes later (*Variety* and *The Reporter* had arrived) the phone rang, Booker picked it up, listened, said okay, and hung up. He turned to me, shook his head, and said, "Frank says you can't see the picture."

I left.

But if that was what happened to a reviewer from something as important to Universal as *USA Today*, do you begin to understand how, before the film ever opened, the critical film community was made to feel nervous, negative and nasty about *Dune*?

On Wednesday, December 12th, 1984—just two days before the rest of the world gained access to *Dune* after fifteen tortuous years—I and a carefully-filtered audience of tv pundits, film critics, magazine reviewers and hangers-on were seated in the Alfred Hitchcock Theater on the Universal City Studios lot, and I listened to all the idle chat around me. It's bad. It's dead. It's confusing. It's gonna die. *Dune*'s in, *Dune*'s out.

At 8:30 PM they rolled the film.

When it ended, I took my notes, raced back to my office and wrote the review. The next morning, the 13th, I dictated the entire review via long-distance telephony to one of *USA Today*'s copyeditors. The review ran in conjunction with a critique by Jack Mathews on Friday the 14th, the day *Dune* opened.

Here, reprinted with permission of *USA Today*, is—at long last—what I originally wrote, with everything that was cut for space reinstated. This is what I thought of *Dune*, and this is what I said for "the nation's newspaper" and an audience of 1.3 million readers who would see my words before they rushed toward or away from the nearest theater showing *Dune*.

Only the demon specter of George Lucas looms between *Dune* and millions in box-office profits.

After seven years of having its senses jackhammered by witless space adventures like *Star Wars* and its endless clones, the American filmgoing audience may have lost the ability to appreciate a movie demanding an attention-span greater than that required for a Burt Reynolds car crash. But for those whose brains have not been turned to guava jelly by special effects and cartoon plots, *Dune* is an epic adventure as far ahead in this cinematic genre as *2001: A Space Odyssey* was in 1968.

It is the *Gone with the Wind* and *Birth of a Nation* of science fiction films. Filled with ideas and art-directed with a wonderful baroque look, *Dune* is a complex symphony of mystic grandeur. In its way as compellingly surreal as something Buñuel or Fellini might conjure up, this faithful translation of the enormously popular Frank Herbert novel offers the wonder of secrets within secrets; a congeries of Chinese puzzle boxes opening into visual and intellectual realms the world of cinema has never before revealed.

Simply put, *Dune* is filled with magic! And like an encounter with a wizard, the film stuns normal perceptions, demanding a sense of wonder and close attention.

Scene after scene presents fresh images, cosmic concepts, plot twists and innovations for which standard filmviewing attitudes are wholly inadequate. And therein may lie the essence of the nightmare for director David Lynch, producer Raffaella De Laurentiis, and Universal Studios.

The very strengths of *Dune* contain the seeds of its possible failure in 1984. And it is a casebook study of why most science fiction films of recent memory have been so sophomoric. If one goes to see a western, no explanation is needed to set up the background. See a man in a Stetson with a bandanna over his face, lying in wait with a Winchester, and you know the Wells Fargo stagecoach will be coming down that road in a moment. See a patient being wheeled into a hospital on a gurney, and you know that in mere seconds a noble physician will be performing a tracheotomy. Boy and girl meet cute, and you know love and laughs are on the way.

But science fiction postulates worlds that might be, but have never been. So *everything* has to be explained. And with a de-

235

vious, imaginative story involving four planets, warring Imperial households, alien technology and deeply mystical concepts about our need for messiahs . . . even the smallest details must be explicated. Can an audience corrupted by the soundtrack of an explosion in the airless vacuum of deep space retool its viewing habits to appreciate a film of such complexity?

There are trade-offs that may make it more difficult. In exchange for scope and grandeur, the enormity of vast forces in conflict, the color and fascination of alien places we have never seen, *Dune* sacrifices that which science fiction has too often jettisoned: characters whose hearts we know, humor and wit, insights into the human condition. For all its heroes who are competent and heroic beyond measure, for all its villains so malefic that they make Darth Vader no more ominous than a mugger, *Dune* has no Rocky or *Chariots of Fire* sprinters to root for. Because we did not need to have the Civil War explained to us, *Gone with the Wind* could concentrate on the travails of Scarlett O'Hara and Rhett Butler.

Yet *Dune* proffers unusual, some might say greater, treasures. For a generation of kids who've grown up with word processers and space shuttles and Isaac Asimov on the bestseller lists, an sf film with a brain. For moviegoers treated to the moral and ethical bankruptcy of slasher films and *Porky's*, a film that deals with concepts of home and courage, loyalty and love of family, nationalism and the wonders of the universe.

If the adults who have reviewed this film with confusion are wrong, and more than fifty years of the popularity of serious science fiction has created an audience capable of the joys of the intellectual mind-leap, then *Dune* will reach and uplift its intended viewers. But if the audience has been too far debased with simplistic twaddle, then like *2001*, this film will have to wait for the judgment of time.

The first week *Dune* made $6 million.

Beverly Hills Cop, which premiered December 3rd, in its three day opening pulled in $15,214,805. The five-day total: ever so close to $20 million.

In five weeks, by which time it had nearly vanished from the movie screens of America, *Dune* amassed a total of $27.4 million. In five weeks *Beverly Hills Cop* did more than $122 million in box-office revenues.

As I write this, *Dune* still cost $40–41 million to produce, with (an estimate) of between $7–10 million for prints and advertising. In its first 110 days of release *Beverly Hills Cop* has made one hundred and ninety-one million, eight hundred and sixty-five thousand, six hundred and fifteen dollars. And change.

It is safe to say *Dune* was a disaster.

Because not one of you was satisfied.

And I submit that you were dissatisfied before you ever got to your theater seat, because the priests of the Black Tower, from Frank Price and Frank Wright on down, quaffed deeply from the cup of derangement that is the brew of choice at Universal. They threw the film community into panic, the stock market into flux, the waiting millions who had hungered for *Dune* for a decade-and-a-half into confusion. And they destroyed what I view as a film of considerable worth. Hell, you read my review; I'm on record.

Apparently, only two of the many critics writing for national publications derived sufficient joy from *Dune* to overcome the bad vibes to give the film a positive review. One was David Ansen in *Newsweek*. The other one has just said he's on the record. And nothing could more ironically keynote the symbiotic relationship I described earlier than that Universal, in the person of Frank Wright, after doing everything in his power to scare me off and tilt me toward negativity, exploited my review in major newspaper advertising. With a rueful shake of my head I perceive this to be a demonstration of the kind of chutzpah one associates with embezzlers running for public office.

And Frank Herbert suggests that the phrase "*Dune* was a disaster" be amended by one word. *Dune* was a *created* disaster. Of the five hours of *Dune* committed to film, only two hours and seventeen minutes made it to the screen. Exhibitors like a flick that runs two hours seventeen, rather than five: they can show it more often in a day. They can empty the theater more often, they can pour in a fresh audience more often, they can sell more Coke and popcorn and tooth-rot. Maybe De Laurentiis dad&daughter can cut together a tv mini-series with the outtakes. Maybe they can do a theatrical "special edition" à la *Close Encounters*. But it won't be done for the videocassettes (say, in two versions, such as was effected by Warner Home Video when they recently released both the emasculated theatrical version and the full director's cut of Sergio Leone's wonderful *Once Upon a Time in America*). It won't happen—at least not in the foreseeable future—because they've already announced an early release for *Dune* sometime this summer: two hours seventeen. So Frank Herbert's suggested revision tastes in no way of sour grapes. It *was* a created disaster.

Slash out nearly three-fifths of a film for the convenience of cineplex operators trying to push Mounds Bars, and what you offer to the public is a quadriplegic commanded to dance the gavotte.

Overseas, where Frank Price's writ don't run, *Dune* is breaking box-office records in West Germany, Italy, Austria, South Africa and France. In England, in its third week, *Dune*'s take was up by 39%, the sort of increase in attendance generally credited to word-of-mouth promotion. Opening night in Paris saw queues of more of 40,000 filmgoers.

Dune will no doubt earn out in foreign revenues, cable and cassette sales, and may already have turned a profit just from merchandising. One never knows. But in the logbook of film history, *Dune* is a major disaster. *Heaven's Gate, Cleopatra, Thoroughly Modern Millie, Ryan's Daughter, Dr. Doolittle, Sorcerer...* and *Dune*.

And here is a grace note for you. Something I got from Frank Herbert for use in the review, for which there was no room, so it was put aside. I reveal it here (Frank assures me) for the first time: the precise moment in which Frank Herbert conceived the grand scheme that became DUNE:

"I had long been fascinated by the messianic impulse in human society; our need to follow a charismatic leader, from Jesus to John Kennedy. Men who ought to have a warning sign on their forehead reminding us that they, like us, are subject to human frailties. I wanted to write a meaningful book on the subject, but though I had the theme, I couldn't find just the right setting. Then, early in the 1950s, I was doing a piece on the U.S. Department of Agriculture's project controlling dunes on the Oregon coast, near Florence. I was in a Cessna 150 looking down on that rolling expanse of sand, and suddenly I made the connection between deserts and the rise of Messiahs in such barren lands, and in an instant I had my canvas, the planet Arrakis, called Dune."

Herbert was the god-emperor of Dune, and De Laurentiis was the great sandworm he rode to the big screen. But in that game of gods and businessmen the rules change at the whim of the players; and not even the god-emperor of Dune could triumph over the derangement of the priests of the fabled Black Tower.

This has been a true story.

INSTALLMENT 11:
In Which Nothing Terribly Profound Occurs

Let's see, now. Didn't I promise to say a few words about *2010* (MGM)? That was a while ago. Put on the side-counter warmer till I'd wrung myself dry in re *Dune*, by the way of explanation. Seems somehow moot now. But, as I said I'd say, I'll say so now.

2010 is a great deal smarter and high-minded than the first reviews would have had you believe. For instance, a critic named Michael Ventura appraised the film in the *L.A. Weekly* under the headline: "2010: A Comic Book Is Not a Poem". He didn't consign the movie to hell, but he said it wasn't the lyric icon Kubrick gave us; said he had trouble remembering the sequence of scenes; said it was devoid of that quality we might call "divine." Well, that's true.

And granted that once you get beyond the mystical trappings the plot is considerably thinner than *2001* (with which *2010* has been, and perhaps should be, inevitably compared), and the "philosophy" is homespun, it nonetheless seems to me that the most salient praise one can direct toward *2010* is that the film has a brain. It is *about* something.

In a year redolent with smarm—the clone grotesqueries of the sexually-corrupt *Hardbodies* and *Risky Business*'s ethically bankrupt popularity with filmgoers of all ages—a movie that attempts to say the universe does still contain wonders and intellectual uplift must be treasured. That ain't, as we say in the world of comestibles, chopped liver (a food of my people).

As one who has gone on record at obnoxious length about the inadequacies of director Peter Hyams, I hear the furgle of your eyebrows lifting when I report that if there be substantive inadequacies in *2010*, they cannot be levied against Hyams. He has directed with cool composure and high craft. And as one who has been friend to Arthur Clarke for more than thirty years, again I perceive furgling at my belief that the things-wrong with this film stem directly from Arthur's novel, a book I suggest never should have been written.

Ask Budrys to deal with that aspect of the matter. He's the book evaluator; I'm just the joe who goes blind sitting in dark rooms on your behalf.

For me, a sequel to something as remarkable as *2001* must not only answer the cosmic questions joyously left unanswered in the original, it must take me into equally as extrapolative places. *2010* attempts the former, and I'd rather have been left with my own suppositions. What was proffered as solution to the puzzle seemed rinkytink, commonplace, unmemorable.

Yet feeling the oppression of the sequel's inadequacies is very likely because one has the unrelenting drive to believe that all this massive machinery—$27 million in production and another $24 million for prints and advertising? that's what I think it was—must have been set in motion for some Deep Purpose; and when the payoff comes, the flashing lights and terraforming scintillate not in the glare of the memory of that star child floating toward Earth at the conclusion of *A Space Odyssey*.

There are nice, subtle, futuristic touches that the alert viewer remembers—one player's tie, collar and watch—Arthur feeding the pigeons from a park bench—but one comes away from *2010* with two impressions:

First, that it is peculiarly earthbound film, returning from the wonder and mystery of that ebon slab floating in space to the mundane (by comparison) concerns of loved ones left behind, and terrestrial political squabbles. Literally, a bringdown.

Second, that Peter Hyams pulled off something of a small miracle. Given the book as basis, a story at best mildly innervating; and given the necessity to make the movie based solely on the Everest Principle ("because it's there"); and given that MGM's then–chief operating officer Frank Yablans needed a major vehicle to save his ass at the studio so the film was rushed into production; and given that Hyams at his top-point efficiency isn't Kubrick after a sleepless week; and given that the expectations of those who deify *2001* can never be fulfilled; it is something of a small miracle that *2010* is as intelligent, as inventive, as handsome as it is.

That it makes sense at all, given the above, is much to the director's credit. It earns him respect and a stay on the note of foreclosure that has haunted his previous films.

As of March 10th, *2010* had earned $40,700,000 in domestic box-office, with foreign and ancillary monies yet to come. It was a coup for Hyams. But it didn't save Yablans. Moneyman Kirk Kerkorian was "impatient" with the results and, as of March 13th, Frank Yablans (and later his entire cadre) was fired from MGM/UA Entertainment as President and Chief Operating Officer of MGM Films. And we just might lament that there ain't no justice; but with that slash of the scimitar of retribution heard by the drunk driver who doesn't get nabbed the first fifty times he runs a stop sign and takes a fall on the single occasion he's innocent of wrongdoing, the ever-watchful universe caught up with Frank Yablans for such offenses to the tender sensibilities of filmgoers as *Monsignor*.

Justice: swift and sure.

But *2010* is left to us as merely another movie that didn't quite make it.

ANCILLARY MATTER: Though my mandate in these essays is serviceable only when dealing with motion pictures (though one tv column will soon manifest itself for good and sufficient), I risk your wrath with advisement of an item usually beyond my purview, by use of the specious logic that it is *visual* in nature, and thus can be fudged into this space.

It is the latest book to be illustrated by the man his publisher calls "one of the foremost wood engravers in the United States." This is disingenuousness on the part of The University of California Press, because Barry Moser is to wood engravers as Lenny Bruce was to comedians, as Brother Theodore is to monologists, as Poe was to writers. If you have not seen his Pennyroyal Editions of MOBY-DICK (1981), ALICE'S ADVENTURES IN WONDER-LAND and THROUGH THE LOOKING-GLASS (1982 & 1983) or HUCKLEBERRY FINN (1984), yours is an empty life, devoid of beauty or meaning.

Barry Moser's illustrations are exquisite beyond the telling. He soars at an altitude where only such wondrous birds of passage as Lynd Ward and Rockwell Kent have tasted the wind. The 241 passion, craft and imagination of Moser's work have an impact that leaves the viewer speechless.

Thus, it is a visual event of considerable importance when Barry Moser illustrates Mary Wollstonecraft Shelley's FRANKENSTEIN. Again in a Pennyroyal Edition designed by the artist, this 255 page large-size (8½″ × 12″) interpretation of the 1818 text is the best $29.50 you will spend this year. Fifty-two chilling and unforgettable illustrations in black and white and duotone. A book you must not deny yourself. Such art as this is surely the reason we were given eyes.

INSTALLMENT 12:
In Which Several Things Are Held Up To The Light...
Not A Brain In Sight

I don't know about you, but as a film critic I view the onset of summertime with an almost Kierkegaardian fear and trembling, a sickness unto death. While *you* stretch with yearning toward rubicund visions of two weeks in the Poconos or sipping a Pimm's Cup on the veranda of the Hotel Aswan Oberoi, overlooking Elephantine Island in the middle of the Nile, *I* contemplate being dragged twitching and foaming into screening theaters where I must, perforce, view this year's pukeload of "vacation films." Films, that is, conceived and executed to a warped perception of that demographic wedge of American humanity known as "the teenage audience."

As through a glans dorkly, the demented entrepreneurs who piss down summer plagues of *Porky*s, *Friday the 13th*s and *Stayin' Alive*s, see that wedge of the wad as follows:

From out of the shadows of the parking lot shamble a boy and a girl, mid-teens, savaging gobbets of Bubblicious like brachiosauri masticating palmetto fronds, their hirsute knuckles brushing the tarmac as they shuffle, blank-eyed, toward the lights of the Cineplex. Hanging from the boy's belt is a skinpouch of goodies to be consumed during the film: Jujubes, chicken heads, balls formed of the soft center of slices of Wonder Bread soaked in caramelized sugar and suet, blood sausage and

M&M peanut chocolate candies. The girl's bare left breast bears a tattoo portrait of Tom Cruise in his Jockey shorts. They pause for a moment before entering the theater to drool and smack their paws together at the sight of a ratpack of *vatos locos* stomping and disemboweling a 76-year-old Gold Star mother in a wheelchair, beset while trundling home from the supermarket with her dinner cans of Alpo, purchased in exchange for the entirety of her Social Security check and a quart of plasma. They steal her bedroom slippers as the *pachucos* run off, and they enter the theater. To be enriched intellectually. The film is *Rambo: First Blood Part II.*

No sooner does the bell ring through the halls and classrooms of Charles Manson High School, signaling the disengorgement of post-pubescent fans of John Landis and Joe Dante films, than the film industry unleashes its locust swarm of summertime idiocies. Each film kissed on its flaccid lips by studio shamans, and sent aloft bearing the multimillion-dollar box-office dreams of execs before whose eyes dance the revenue figures of *Beverly Hills Cop.*

But hark!

What is this we see? Only into June (as I write this), the ticket sales for the big summer films are off, way off, terrifyingly off. In the first week of the Summer Push, revenues fell off by 13% from last year's bonanza; second week, the drop was by 27%; and this week the bottom made bye-bye . . . a 35% drop.

What in the world can this mean?

Is it possible that the malformed image of the youth audience heretofore nuzzled by the industry is a chimera? Has it dawned on (what Robert Blake calls) The Suits that there is strong evidence to support the belief that not all kids are slope-browed, prognathic vermin lusting after cheap thrills and rivers of blood? Have we a hope that The Suits noticed huge teen audiences patronizing *Wargames* year before last, and *Amadeus* last year (neither of which, by any stretch, is monkey-movie)? Is this heart-stopping statistic the clarion call of a small revolution? Can The Suits extrapolate the success with kids of these two exemplary and intelligent motion pictures—albeit containing youth-resonant elements—into commercial realms where the movies serve the dual purpose of entertaining *and* uplifting the dear little tots?

One can only hope. Two can only hope. That's you and me, kid. But if either of us expects the barricades to be manned *this* year, color us premature. For, like the brachiosaurus, the industry has its brain located somewhere down at the root of its tail . . . and is slow slow slow to react. Maybe next year.

But *this* year, as summer lazes toward us, I would fain regale you with views of four films created to honor the conceit that the youth audience has a limitless appetite for gore, counterfeit emotion, macho patriotism, repetition of formulaic plots and, on sum, movies best identified as *emptyheaded*.

RAMBO: FIRST BLOOD PART II (Tri-Star) and A VIEW TO A KILL (MGM/UA) may seem peculiar choices for consideration in a critique supposedly dealing with fantasy and science fiction films; at first they may seem so. Nor will I dodge the issue with an imperious wave of my hand and the magisterial utterance that I'll review what I damned well please and if you don't like it you can go squat on a taco. No, I will treat you as equals (though I'd hope you want better for yourselves) by pointing out that both of these films defy even the most minimal judgment of what is "reality" by offering us stories and characters who are *clearly* fantasy constructs. These are films of purest phantasm, no matter *how* they're marketed; and thus become fair game for our scrutiny in the context of this essay.

Or if you'd prefer, "The devil can cite Scripture for his purpose." (*The Merchant of Venice*; Act I, Scene iii.)

Sporting a title as graceful as a hyena with a shattered spine dragging itself to a waterhole, *Rambo: First Blood Part II* proffers despicable manipulation and revisionist history in place of serious consideration of America's reaction (even more than a decade after we got the shit kicked out of us) to the Vietnam War. We are sucked into 92 minutes of nonstop emptyheaded violence through the use of a greased icon known as John Rambo—ex-vet, sullen and *angst*-ridden survivor not only of a war "we didn't really want to win" but of the (real or imagined) disdain of a nation that "refuses to honor those of us who died for you."

As if you didn't know, Sylvester Stallone is Rambo. Or more precisely, Rambo is Rocky. Mike Hodel suggests that this is a film about revenge, and they might as well have staged it as a P.S. to the Napoleonic Wars if they thought Stallone would look good in tights. He's correct, of course. Thematically, it's the *Death Wish* genre, cast in jungle combat. But . . .

It's one hundred and seventy years since the Napoleonic Wars, and only twelve since the Nam. We don't ache in every tendon from the former as we do from the latter. So screw it as regards thematic rationalization. What we have to deal with here is pure fantasy twisted to the service of implanting and/or

245

ripening a hateful, destructive Newspeak. Rambo is as real as Conan; and intellectually, I'd venture to say, the barbarian swordsman could spot Rambo three pawns and a rook, and still whip the vet with the Schoolboy Gambit.

In the previous Rambo film, based on a strong novel by David Morrell, the cranky Viet-vet is arrested for chickenshit reasons in a small town, escapes, lays out half the police department, is hunted through nearby woods and hills, demolishes state troopers, posse comitatus, and National Guardsmen utilizing guerrilla tactics he employed as the most fearsome weapon of Special Forces in Southeast Asia, and finally lays waste to the hamlet itself. Brought to book for his rampage, Rambo (get the suggestion of assonance—*rambo*/*ram*page?)* is talked down from the summit of his destructive fever by his former boss in Special Services, the always-watchable Richard Crenna.

In this second chapter of the Rambo Saga—which now has made so much money that there will *fer shure* be a *Rambo III*—this contemporary Myrmidon is in prison, making little ones out of big ones. He gets sprung by Crenna to tackle a one-man mission the purpose of which is to take photos of a Viet Cong prison camp (from which Rambo escaped during the War) in order to discern if they're holding GI POWs. He is strictly forbidden from attempting rescue of any such personnel, which naturally grinds Rambo's gears, and is offered to us as an allegory for America's alleged refusal to "go all the way" in Vietnam.

Of course, there's a plot twist here—story by Kevin Jarre and screenplay by the omnipresent Stallone in collaboration with James Cameron of *The Terminator* fame—that sends Rambo off on yet another quotidian binge of mayhem during which he wipes out what appears to be half the population of the area. And this is what makes up the bulk of the film: free-fire zone elevated to the status of *chanson de geste*. Yankee pluck winning, in small, what it lost in large.

And in the process Rambo is submitted for our emptyheaded adoration as a fantasy construct. Stallone—photographed by director George P. Cosmatos (whom I encountered many years ago as Georgios Pan Cosmatos) all sweat-slick and pumped up to produce a creature both tumescent and iconic, a thing not-quite-

---

*Silverberg suggests, in a display of lexicological wordplay worthy of Phil Farmer, that this assonance is only marginally likely, while it strikes him as possible that Morrell gave his vengeful fury the name *Rambo* as a homophone for *Rimbaud*, who was also a wild and crazy guy. This way lies madness.

and more-than-human, a poster-ready hunk guaranteed to create masturbatory longings in leather gays and feverish schoolgirls alike—is held center frame virtually every moment, the camera panning in sensual closeup across every last convex surface of deltoid, tricep and trapezius, not to mention the ever-popular latissimus dorsi. Like something fallen off a pedestal in Thrace, Rambo surges, boils, say rather *ejaculates* through this warrior-fantasy, glowing with Vaselined pectorals, as one with The Lone Ranger, Superman or the cinema image of Bruce Lee; the National Rifle Association's own *Übermensch*; the wet dream of every king-cab-riding, deer-hunting, longing-to-be-macho American redneck, slugging away brew after brew at the drive-in, pounding the steering wheel and screaming himself hoarse as Zorro Rambo wipes away his country's shame at having picked a fight it couldn't win, against a tiny adversary, that left names like William Calley to haunt us on Veterans' Day.

A proper fantasy for examination here, Rambo walks through fusillades of machine-gun fire, belts of bullets wrapped around his forearm, impossibly firing something that looks like an M60E1 machine-gun with one hand; and he sustains, if I recall correctly, one minor flesh wound. Never does the weapon track up and to the right, as such ordnance is wont to do, defoliating every rubber tree and banyan in the vicinity. Never does the barrel seize up when overheated by Stallone's visually dramatic but utterly fanciful long bursts. Never do the massed volleys of heavy and light armament fire touch this impossible avenger, not even at point-blank range. But Rambo cleans clocks on every side, blowing the little yellow men into the water and through hooch walls as if they were springloaded.

One wonders—if one wonders at all—if one isn't emptyheaded —how we managed to *lose* a war to these inept gooks or slopes or dinks or whatever the hell we're supposed to call Third World Peoples Arrayed Against Us: they can't hit a bull in the ass with a scoop-shovel, but our Sylvester needn't even aim to take out two or three of them with each round. Sort of the way John Wayne and Gene Autry used to snap off a shot over the shoulder from a galloping horse, and three firewater-crazed Comanches would tumble off their mounts, dragging the horses with them. (One wonders why we never beat the Seminoles. Hell, they didn't even have horses. Used to ride alligators, as I understand it.)

But this is all part of the fantasy.

As unreal as *Starman* or *The Thing* (remake version), and no less a misuse of the fantasy idiom for dubious ends.

Rambo Etc. is making megabucks this summer, and it is an example of emptyheadedness difficult to deny. I admit to being swept up in the breakneck action, no nobler than the drive-in dolt whose camper bears the bumper sticker

MY WIFE YES
MY DOG MAYBE
MY GUN NEVER

and who will certainly go for the twisted "philosophy" that the only thing Rambo wants for himself, after rescuing the POWs and shooting down a latest-model Russian gunship, is that "America love us as much as we love America." I admit to the visceral punch of clever filmmaking, and I warn you that it is all artifice, as manipulative as *Rocky* and as slick as a De Palma knife-kill flick...and as detestable. It is, of course, these smoothyguts versions of otherwise-dismissible genre films, no more important than cartoons, conjured to go through us like *merde* through a merganser, wherein lies the danger. Emptyhead is as emptyhead does. Unthinking, all receptor and no intellect, we sit unprotected before the tsunami of counterfeit emotion, turned into empty vessels waiting to be filled by cheap bravado, bathos and sonic stimuli, becoming mere stipules for the walking vegetation of a vengeance parable.

That it is a man-eating plant never seems to occur to the brew-swillers or the teenage shamblers. But then, isn't that the essence of emptyheadedness?

Nowhere nearly as vile as *Rambo Etc.* but even more emptyheaded is the latest James Bond film, what I wearily perceive to be the eleven hundredth film in the endless series. (When the human race goes to the stars, there will surely be only three things of sufficient obstinacy-of-existence, from all that our species has produced, that will go with us: the little plastic beads that fall out of UPS packages no matter how you struggle to contain them; James Bond films; and Swedish meatballs.)

The menace this time is an uncomfortable-looking Christopher Walken, who should have known better. Oddjob this time is rock singer Grace Jones, who looks incredible (and has always, it seems to me, looked a lot better than she sings), but who ain't even a close second for deadliness to the late Lotte Lenya as SMERSH's liquidator, Rosa Klebb, in *From Russia, with Love.* And as the nubbin from which the film grows is a minor Ian Fleming short story originally published in *Playboy* (under the more grammatical title "From a View to a Kill"), what passes for plot is the now-hoary Bond jiggery-pokery, with gags no more innovative or memorable than those to be found in the last half dozen. This film is pure Grub Street (look up the reference), and the very model of brainless. Running, jumping and standing still, with Roger Moore looking more exhausted and threadbare than ever before. It's a shame, really. Moore seems a right decent chap when he's being interviewed; takes it all with the proper modicum of unselfconscious parody; very little of the Colonel Blimp about him; the sort of elegant gentleman one would like to invite over for an evening of billiards and Mexican coatepec. And if you never saw him in a little adventure film called *ffolkes*, you might continue to believe, incorrectly, that he can't act with any depth of emotion.

But Bond goes on and on, yet another fantasy superman, nattier (god knows) than Rambo, and quarts less oily; but no more a part of the mimetic universe than Tarzan, Conan or Sir Launcelot. Emptyheaded filmmaking long-since canonized and as exquisite an example of how preserved like a fly in amber these things become when they hit the rut of formula.

I go to them on the Everest Principle: "because it's there." But I blush to tell you I fell asleep three times.

And I've saved the remaining pair of emptyheaded summer films with which you'll be tempted for last, because I have some small personal stake in them. And because I don't think they deserve to be savaged as *Rambo Etc.* demanded.

The first is THE BLACK CAULDRON (Walt Disney) and I'm saddened to have to report that it is utterly and completely emptyheaded. The tip-off, I guess, is that nowhere in the credits will one find a listing for an author. More than ten years in the making, at a cost of more than twenty-five million dollars, and described by its producer as "the most ambitious animated production since *Pinocchio*," this is the 25th full-length animated feature from the Disney Studios; and it is a waste of time.

Pre-screening scuttlebutt had it that the animation techniques were the most extraordinary since the heyday of the Nine Old Men who worked with Walt on *Snow White* and *Pinocchio* and *Fantasia*. Scuttlebutt had it that since the leavetaking of Don Bluth and his cohorts, and the deaths or retirements of the remaining Old Men, it had become necessary for the new crew of young turk animators to rediscover the old tricks or invent new ones equally as impressive. That was the scuttlebutt and if, like me, you got wind of such rumors and, like me, you hitched your hopes to that sticking-place, you will be dismayed beyond the containing of such pain. I left the studio screening with a leaden heart. Jessie Horsting and Howard Green suggest I was revved too high. That there was no way my expectations could have been honored.

Well, maybe. Who knows?

All I *do* know is that I enjoyed the Chronicles of Prydain fantasies by Lloyd Alexander on which the film is based . . . but in no way slavishly or with that fan elitism that contends *no* film can top the original material; I was wide open to be dazzled or merely pleasantly entertained, whichever; I am not a recidivist who believes the best work of Disney is past and can never be topped.

And even so, I was bored.

It's not a bad film, it's merely a bore. There is nothing new here. The usual funny sidekick (but Gurgi isn't Dopey or Jiminy Cricket), the usual unisex hero and heroine (but Taran and Eilonwy aren't Prince Phillip or Cinderella), the usual pure-black villain (but the Horned King, for all his death's head and sepulchral wailing could never be, on the most evil day of his life, Queen Grimhelde the Wicked Witch or even Stromboli).

It is a flat film, and I think it is so flat because it was apparently not scripted. Illustrators went from scene to scene and the movie reflects that episodic method. Momentous events turn out to be passing fancies, magical implements are introduced and then are discarded as if all the hue and cry about them had been intended merely to rope you in, characters pop up and never pay off, and the clear intention of the producers to return to some small degree of the genuine fright we felt at the perils passim the first Disney classics is simply not realized.

I nodded off twice.

This seeming recurrence of filmic narcolepsy on my part disturbs me. Yes, I've been working hard, but who the hell falls asleep in either a Disney film or a James Bond adventure? I'll tell you who. Someone who loves movies and wants to be thrilled.

So it is with considerable joylessness that I report *The Black Cauldron* is empty, and the film is emptyheaded.

Which brings me at the final outpost to Stephen King's new film, SILVER BULLET (Paramount). Based on Steve's CYCLE OF THE WEREWOLF, with screenplay by Steve, directed by newcomer Daniel Attias, and produced by a charming and intelligent woman named Martha Schumacher, this is, I fear, one more in the litany of misses made from King product. Not as bad as *Cujo* or *Children of the Corn* or *Christine*, but as emptyheaded as any of the films I've reviewed this time, *Silver Bullet* hasn't much to recommend it save a few nice insights by Steve, two extraordinary performances by a young woman named Megan Follows and a little boy named Corey Haim, who play brother and sister, and a scene in a foggy forest that is cinematically enthralling.

Beyond those minor joys, this is simply another feast of ghast in which heads are ripped from necks, vigilantes get half their faces clawed off, and a young woman is disemboweled. The story is pretty traditional, nothing much innovative after you've seen *The Werewolf of London* or the original Lon Chaney, Jr. classic. The attempts at resonance with *To Kill a Mockingbird* can be credited to Steve, who knows what quality is, but laid into such a stock plot, they are likely to be lost on the sort of audience for which the film is intended.

A word about that audience. I saw this film at a special prerelease screening at Paramount. Steve was in town and was kind enough to invite me to see it with him. As we sat in the back of the theater on the lot, the seats filled by a carefully selected, demographically-perfect crowd of young people—I'd say between seventeen and twenty-five years old—Steve expressed mild surprise that the audience applauded the scenes of strongest violence. I was not surprised. I saw *The Omen* with just such an audience, and I know how they love their blood sports. Steve knows that, too. Maybe sometime soon I'll tell you about an encounter I had with kids at Central Juvenile Hall in L.A. that speaks to this phenomenon. But not right now. It's bad enough that I'm rewarding Steve's and Dino's courtesy with a negative review. Suffice to say, this film will no doubt make money, but it is emptyheaded summer fare, with a soundtrack of the sort that Tara used to call "rats digging their way to China" music.

As for this season's Spielberg offering, well, last year I warned you away from *Gremlins*; and those of you who heeded my gardyloo later thanked me. Some of you who sneered at my vehement contempt shelled out your shekels, laid out your lire, plonked down your pennies, abused your eyeballs, and later wrote me toe-scuffling, red-faced, abnegating appeals for absolution. This year, on the basis of utter emptyheadedness and a soundtrack mix that renders every line of dialogue to spinach, I warn you off *The Goonies*, which I will not mention again. Perhaps you will take a word to the wise this time. If not, well, *caveat*   251 *emptor* and don't come crying to me. (The superlative *E.T. The Extra-Terrestrial* is being re-released, however, and you're better served spending your hard-earned to see that Spielbergian wonder this summer.)

And so that you don't think I'm merely a cranky old fuck who is determined to follow in the footsteps of, say, John Simon, let me urge you to rush out immediately to see *Ladyhawke* and *Cocoon*, both of which are fresh and dear and worth the laying out of pfennig.

Also, ignore all negative reviews of *Return to Oz*, which I *will* review at length. Ignore Siskel and Ebert of ABC's *At the Movies*; ignore Robert Denerstein of the *Rocky Mountain News* in Denver and Robert Osborne of *The Hollywood Reporter* and KTTV; ignore my friends Leonard Maltin of *Entertainment Tonight* and David Sheehan of ABC-TV; ignore Jeffrey Lyons and Neal Gabler of PBS's *Sneak Previews*, and Janet Maslin of *The New York Times*. Shine 'em on, every last one of them. They are wrong, wrong, wrong in their looney denigrations. *Return to Oz* is smashing! For those of us who are familiar with the Oz canon of L. Frank Baum and those who lovingly continued the history of that special wonderland—even though we adore the 1939 MGM classic, watch it again and again, and know a masterpiece when we (and posterity) see one—the Judy Garland musical was hardly the definitive interpretation. And comparing the two films is sheer foolishness. And vilifying *Return to Oz* because it has some genuinely inspired moments of real terror on the grounds that the 1939 film had a purer heart, loses sight of the horrors MGM built into that movie. Or have you forgotten those damned blue, winged monkey monsters *schlepping* Dorothy into the sky as their buddies stomp the crap out of the Scarecrow and the Tin Woodsman? No, my readers, turn a deaf ear to the boos and catcalls of the trendy critics who refuse to judge this absolutely marvelous film on its own merits. Take your kids, let them scream, let your eyes drink in marvels. *Return to Oz* is everything we hoped for.

Also, if *Night of the Comet* comes available on videocassette, catch up on what you missed when it was briefly in theaters, and treat yourself to the same kind of pleasure you derived from *Repo Man*. But these four films come with a warning: they may make you think. And that can be painful for the head what am empty.

INSTALLMENT 13:
In Which Numerous Ends (Loose) Are Tied Up; Some In The Configuration Of A Noose (Hangman's)

As I write this, another film murder is in progress.

I leave for London and Scotland tomorrow (5 July), and this column is my final chore in front of the typewriter. When these words get to your eyes, I'll have returned to Los Angeles; I'll have sat in William Friedkin's back pocket as he directed my teleplay adaptation of Stephen King's "Gramma" for *The Twilight Zone*; I'll have voyaged far to Australia Incognita and will have returned with or without a Hugo for non-fiction; I'll have watched with pleasure the Friday-night-in-September premiere of CBS-TV's revival of *TZ*... and the murder will be merely another footnote in the history of the cinema.

Much will have happened between this writing and your reading of what I'm about to set down.

And were it not that your faithful hawkshaw got the wind up, this killing of a movie—like the crib-death of *Dune*, about which I wrote two columns recently—would be yet another perfect crime. Nor would you be apprised of how willingly you were accomplices.

Much of life will have transpired and in the impression of humanity's footsteps left behind, no one will notice, I fear, that another butterfly has been crushed underfoot. That's poetry.

Last time, I urged you to rush out and see RETURN TO OZ

(Walt Disney Productions). I managed to slip that appeal into the column when the galleys were returned for proofing because I'd gotten the wind up, had begun to smell the *déjà vu* of what had befallen *Dune*, and I didn't want the murder to go unnoticed because of a delay in getting the word to you, resulting from this magazine's monthly publication schedule. I wanted you to catch this film before it vanished from your local theaters.

And it did vanish, didn't it? Quickly.

I have given you the date on which I'm typing these words, because the months between this date and your reading of the words have not yet passed. So what I write is, at this moment, prediction. As you read the words, it's history. If I smelled the charnel house smell, and am not merely a victim of paranoid conspiracy-theory, then you will know what I'm about to say has the ring of truth in it; otherwise how could I have predicted it?

If the events of the intervening months do not back up my assertions, then I'm dyin' cuz I'm lyin'.

I began to smell the odor of filmic crib-death even before *Return to Oz* opened; and I implored you to ignore the witless and intransigent negative reviews that were everywhere to be found; to treat yourselves to an afternoon or evening basking in the marvels of this wondrous fantasy while you could.

Because if my snoot was accurate, if you put off the going to see it, *Return to Oz* would be gone; and who knows how it'll play on videocassette or cable television a year from now?

In the trade, they call it "dumping."

I call it crib-death. Strangling the infant before it gets its legs through word-of-mouth. (In the trade, mixed metaphor works. In the trade, *everything* works, including executives who've been exposed as embezzlers, charlatans, wrong-guessers, idiots and knaves.)

If you followed the reasoning I put forth in the matter of *Dune*'s early demise, you were no doubt left with one nagging question: *why* (if Ellison's correct that Universal sabotaged its own release) did a major film company program the catastrophic failure of a forty million dollar epic that should have made its year-end p&l sheets vibrate with profits?

I had the same question.

It was only recently that an Informed Source gave me the answer. (Informed, but also, necessarily, Unnamed. Bamboo slivers under the fingernails cannot drag the name from me. You'll just have to take my word for it that said Source exists, oh yes said Source do. Everybody in the trade talks, and many there be who will summon up the *cojones* to blow the whistle; but swift and ugly reprisal is a fact of life in the trade, and I see no reason why an act of honesty should result in someone's losing his/her livelihood. Rather would I have you consider what I say with skepticism.)

My Unnamed Source called to tell me that the budget on *Dune* was not, as I and every other American journalist reported, a mere forty million dollars. It was more than $75,000,000!

So unless *Dune* had been a runaway hit on the level of *Beverly Hills Cop* or *Rambo* there was absolutely *no way* Universal was going to come out on the black side of the ledger.

It was very likely going to be a loser, but it need not have been *such* a loser. Sabotage from within, it now seems obvious, was the final nail in *Dune*'s coffin. But why? The answer lies in the power politics and job-hopping of studio executives.

When I expressed disbelief at such a berserk answer, my Informed Source chided me for naïveté. It is not, however, wide-eyed innocence on my part that forces me to express doubts. It is the canker on the rose called libel. In *Synopsis of the Law of Libel and the Right of Privacy*, by Bruce W. Sanford, a pamphlet for journalists published by Scripps–Howard Newspapers, among the words and phrases "red flagged" as containing potentially actionable potency, we find the following: altered records, blackguard, cheats, corruption, coward, crook, fraud, liar, moral delinquency, rascal, scam, sold out, unethical and villain. Also on the list are booze hound, deadbeat, fawning sycophant, groveling office seeker, herpes, Ku Klux Klan and unmarried mother. But those have nothing to do with the topic at hand. Just thought I'd get them in for a little cheap sensationalism.

So what I will report here is carefully written. Facts and some philosophy. The linkages are yours to make.

Success and failure in the film colony are adduced on the basis of one's most recent production. Even an inept booze hound or fawning sycophant affiliated with a hit movie glows with the golden radiance of its success. A set designer or actor who did a splendid job in connection with a flop gets tarred with the same brush as the fools who came a cropper. Take director Martin Brest, as an example. Marty's first film after creating the brilliant *Hot Tomorrows* while still in attendance at the American Film Institute, was *Going in Style* (1979), which did not do well. Marty could not get arrested (as it is warmly phrased in the trade) for three years. That's a long time to go without a job if you're a young director. Then he made *Beverly Hills Cop* in 1984.   255

We all know how big that film hit. (Which was a fluke that Destiny had in its rucksack for Marty, who deserves all good breaks, for he is an enormously talented artist; a fluke in that Stallone was originally set to play the lead, backed out for whatever reasons, and was replaced by Eddie Murphy, who can do no wrong onscreen.)

But now, Martin Brest is the hottest director in Hollywood.

And everyone with the film at Paramount—including then-studio heads Michael Eisner and Barry Diller—got hot with him. So they moved over to Disney. But that gets relevant later in this essay.

The point being that executives hop from studio to studio on the basis of how good they looked when they left. And frequently that has more to do with what happens to a movie than how good or bad the film is intrinsically. So a fact of film industry life that you've never known till now is the truth that an exec wanting to look to his shareholders as one who saved a studio in decline, necessarily tries to make his/her predecessors look bad. The worse they look, the better he/she looks if/when the new exec presents a bountiful p&l sheet at year-end.

I present the preceding as philosophy only.

Here is a fact. In 1982, when Universal picked up *Dune* for distribution from Dino De Laurentiis, the administration of that film mill was under the aegis of President Bob Rehme (now Pres./CEO of New World Pictures). But by 1984 when *Dune* was released, Rehme was gone and Frank Price (who had hopped over from Columbia) was President of Universal.

As I recounted in detail in installments 9 and 10 of this column, what happened to *Dune* bore all the earmarks of a classic "dumping" scenario. That's how it looked to those of us who write about the film industry, and the conclusion is borne out by my Unnamed Source. Change of administration, a disaster credited to Rehme, and the new Priests of the Black Tower can only move upward, appearancewise, even if the next p&l is only adequate.

The same is happening to *Return to Oz* as I write this.

The film is being orphaned by Disney's new management, the Eisner–Diller combine. That's how it looks to me.

The evidence is out there for you to integrate, if you look even casually: no television advertising to speak of; small newsprint ads; few positive quotes; the film yanked from movie houses after a short run. And only now, several weeks after its premiere, are talk-show interviews with principals from the film being booked.

The film came in around $32 million. The studio cut out most of the publicity back in March, three months before *Return to Oz* was scheduled to open; and it had an opening week advertising budget of approximately $4–4.5 million. This is extremely low for a major release. A typical figure for a comparable film would be $7–10 million, aided by heavy saturation on the talk-show circuit. Those are facts; evidence.

But here's what was going on behind the scenes.

The old Disney marketing department was essentially in place from the start of production late in 1983, until early in 1985. Then the new studio management of Eisner and Jeffrey Katzenberg started playing a direct hand.

Barry Glasser, the Vice President of Publicity, was unhappy and left the studio in March for a production development position with a Japanese animation company, TMS.

Frequently, studios hire outside publicity and advertising agencies to work with the in-house marketing department. The new management of Disney hired Young & Rubicam in February or March of 1985. Gordon Weaver, a former head of Paramount's marketing division and head of Y&R Entertainment, was given charge of the *Return to Oz* account. Unlike most agency/studio relationships, the agency started giving the orders to the studio personnel, leaving the marketing department in an unusual and untenable position. Barry Lorie, head of marketing for Disney, was so undercut by these goings-on that he was left with virtually little authority. It is common knowledge that Lorie bided his time, taking what was dished out, until an opportunity to hop presented itself. (It was announced during the last week in June that he would be leaving Disney due to "philosophical differences with the new management of the studio.")

If one were to examine the facts, the evidence, and consider the *modus operandi* of dumping in the trade, one might feel that the situation as regards *Return to Oz* is philosophically consistent with historical precedent. I think that is a safe legal locution.

It is not enough to say, "Well, the critics hated the movie," because audiences seem to love it; and hideous films of virtually no value are hyped in huge measure to get the potential audience's appetite whetted. But nothing much was done for *Oz*, and now the new Disney administration can say, "Well, it isn't reaching the market we thought would welcome it. We have to cut our losses." Orphaned. Dumped. Murdered.

And as producer Gary Kurtz knows, and as he told Disney, it

is important to remember that the 1939 *Wizard of Oz* was a box-office disaster, and remained so until it was purchased for television in the early '60s, from which time it has been regarded by the general public (not just us enthusiasts) as a "classic." But such need not have been the case with *Return to Oz*. It is a remarkable piece of moviemaking, true to the Baum canon, and worthy of being successful.

So we must ask the question, *how* did Eisner know *Return to Oz* wouldn't reach its audience back in February or March, long before it opened? Because that is when the advertising budget was cut and helter-skelter was introduced as the standard operating procedure. Unless he possesses a clairvoyance that ought to be scrutinized by the Committee for the Scientific Investigation of Claims of the Paranormal (3151 Bailey Avenue; Buffalo, New York 14215; publishers of *The Skeptical Inquirer*; an organization and a magazine you should support if you, as I, despise all the obscurantism and illogic from Creationism to Astrology that pollutes our world), one of the few rational explanations is that dumping has occurred.

If there is another rationale that can fit in with the evidence, this column is anxiously waiting to publish such an explanation. From Paramount. From Disney. From anyone who feels compelled to let us know that the world is not what our intellect tells us it is.

Until that time, it saddens me to have to advise those of you who went for the okeydoke that *Return to Oz* was a stinker, that you have been willing accomplices to the murder of a piece of cinematic delight.

And how does it make you feel to be one of those P. T. Barnum was referring to when he said . . . aw, shucks, you know.

INSTALLMENT 14:
In Which We Sail To The Edge Of The World And Confront The Abyss, Having Run Out Of Steam

As fit subject matter for motion pictures, science fiction and fantasy are a pair of dead ducks. We have reached cul-de-sac and the curtain is about to be rung down. There has been a power failure in Metropolis; the Thing has been diced, sliced, riced in a trice and dumped into a pot of goulash; the Forbidden Planet has been subdivided for condos and a mini-mall; things to come has gone and went; and green cards have been denied Kharis, Münchausen, Gort and Lawrence Talbot.

What I'm telling you here is, they're dead, Jim, *dead!*

The trouble with this parrot is that this parrot is dead. I know a dead parrot when I see one, and I'm looking at one right now. It's stone dead. I took the liberty of examining this parrot and I discovered that the only reason it had been sitting on its perch in the first place was that it had been nailed there. And don't tell me that of course it was nailed there because if it hadn't been nailed it would have muscled up to the bars and *voom!* This parrot wouldn't *voom!* if you put four thousand volts through it. It's bleedin' demised. It's not pining for the fjords, it's passed on. This parrot is no more. It has ceased to be. It's expired, and gone to see its Maker. This is a late parrot. It's a stiff! Bereft of life, it rests in peace. If it hadn't been nailed to the perch it would be pushin' up the daisies. It's rung down the curtain and joined the Choir Invisible. This is an *ex*-parrot!

(And no, we haven't any gouda, muenster or red leicester.)

Man and boy, I've been looking at fantasy movies since 1940 when, at age six, I saw the first re-release of Disney's *Snow White and the Seven Dwarfs* at the Utopia Theater in Painesville, Ohio; and I'm here to tell you that in a mere forty-five years the filmic genres of fantasy and science fiction have been wrung dry, have sprouted moss and ugly little white squiggly things, and are no more. Gone. Done. Finis. Kaput. As empty as a line of sappy dialogue emerging from Jennifer Beals's mouth.

This is one of those pronunciamentos one lives to regret at leisure. (My last one, "the mad dogs have kneed us in the groin," has hounded me, er, make that dogged my footsteps, uh, make that blighted my life ... since my teens.) The sort of *I don't know fer sure, Gen'ral Custer, but they look friendly to me* one has thrown up to him ten years later, at the peak of a new golden age of cinema fantasy. Nonetheless, I have been going to the pictures a lot of late, and the scent of mold is in my nostrils. I have witnessed the best the film industry has had to offer from the well of sf/fantasy ideas, and I am here to tell you—despite the risks to my otherwise impeccable reputation—that if this is what passes for the best and brightest, then the end of the road is before us, and sf/fantasy has nothing more to offer.

All in the same month I have seen the latest variations on *Frankenstein*, *Dracula*, and *The Wolf Man*, not to mention a lamebrain time travel picture that seems about to pass *Rambo: First Blood, Part II* as the most popular flick of the summer. I speak of *Back to the Future*, of course. A film that has received almost unanimous salivations of delight from within and without the field. Kids love it, adults love it, sailors on leave off the *Aisukuriimu Maru* love it; intellectuals love it, horny-handed sons of toil love it, Manchester chimney sweeps love it; young women in their teens love it, grizzled pulp magazine sf writers love it, defecating Russian ballerinas love it. So what's *not* to love? I'll *tell* you what's not to love!

(Back to Frankie, Drac and Fangface in a moment, but permit me to savage the sf end of this argument first.)

Understand this:

Time is like a river flowing endlessly through the universe. Circa 500 B.C.: Heraclitus, the early Greek philosopher (there were no *late* Greek philosophers), lying around the agora like all the other unemployed philosophers, just idly thinking deep thoughts and providing a helipad for flies, said it for the first time, as best we know: Time is like a river, flowing endlessly through the universe.

And if you poled your flatboat in that river, you might fight your way against the current and travel upstream into the past. Or go with the flow and rush into the future.

This was in a less cynical time before toxic waste dumping and pollution filled the waterway of Chronus with the detritus of empty hours, wasted minutes, years of repetition and time that has been killed. But I digress.

Of all the pure fantasy plot devices, time travel is the second most prevalent in the genre of speculative fiction—right in there chugging along, trying harder because it's number two, close behind invasion-of-Earth-by-moist-things movies. (And make no mistake, it is *fantasy*, not science fiction. I don't want to argue about this. As that good and dear Isaac has told us: "Science fiction writers have dreamed of finding some device that would make travel along the temporal dimension to be as easily controlled as along any of the three spacial dimensions. First to do so was H. G. Wells in 1895 in his novel THE TIME MACHINE. Many [including myself] have used time machines since, but such a device is not practical and, as far as science now knows, will never be. Time travel, in the sense of moving freely backward and forward at will along the temporal dimension, is impossible.")

But as the ultimate literary device for a story of *what-if?*, time travel abounds in the genre of speculative fiction, notable in such works as Robert Heinlein's classic "By His Bootstraps," in which a man goes through a time portal again and again, meeting himself over and over (a story to be dramatized for the first time this year on the upcoming revival of *The Twilight Zone*); the late Philip K. Dick's THE MAN IN THE HIGH CASTLE, in which Nazi Germany won WWII; PAVANE by Keith Roberts, in which Queen Elizabeth I was assassinated and the Protestant Reformation was crushed, Mary Queen of Scots ascended the throne and the world became wholly Catholicized; and the late Ward Moore's BRING THE JUBILEE, in which the South won the Civil War.

For shrugging off the toils of the here-and-now, for allowing human curiosity to fly unfettered, the *what-if?* theme cannot be bettered.

It is thus little wonder that the motion picture screen has returned to this plot-device with regularity, if not much depth of intellect.

There immediately spring to mind the most obvious films that have employed the time machine: *Somewhere in Time* (1980), based on a marvelous Richard Matheson novel called BID TIME RETURN, in which Christopher Reeve, using something like a Tantric trance, thinks himself into the past so he can woo and win Jane Seymour; *Time After Time* (1979) in which Malcolm McDowell as the young H. G. Wells pursues David Warner as Jack the Ripper from c. 1892 to San Francisco in the present day; the George Pal version of Wells's *The Time Machine* (1960) with Rod Taylor as the temporal traveler, finally linking up with Yvette Mimieux in the far future (as good a reason for going to the far future as one might wish); *Planet of the Apes* (1968) in which a contemporary space probe goes through some kind of timewarp in the outer reaches and returns to a far-future Earth now ruled by simians; *Time Bandits* (1981), in which a little boy abets a group of time-traveling dwarves as they rampage from era to era plundering and screwing up The Natural Order of things; *Slaughterhouse Five* (1972) in which Billy Pilgrim becomes "unstuck in time"; and 1984's *The Terminator* (some say based on writings we will not name here), in which an android assassin from the future is chased back through time to our day by a soldier determined to keep him from slaying a woman whose death would detrimentally affect the world of tomorrow.

But that's only the first calibration on the cinematic chrono-dial. How many filmgoers realized they were seeing a time-travel fantasy when they watched Bing Crosby as *A Connecticut Yankee in King Arthur's Court* (1949)? (Actually, Rhonda Fleming ain't a bad reason to travel back to yore, either.) How about *Brigadoon* (1954) or *Berkeley Square* (1933) with Leslie Howard? *It Happened Tomorrow* (1944) in which the device is the next day's newspaper that falls into Dick Powell's hands; the classic *Portrait of Jenny* (1948) from the famous Robert Nathan novel; and even *A Christmas Carol*, in its many incarnations, has strong time travel elements when Scrooge is taken by the ghosts to see his past and future; all are examples of the ineluctable hold the concept has on the creative intellect and on the curiosity of typical filmgoers.

Why should this be so? Well, consider the following:

If time is like a river that flows endlessly through the universe, then might it not be possible that by going into the past and altering some pivotal moment in history, the river's course could be changed? By damming the past at some seminal nexus, could we not alter our world today?

Say, for instance, you stepped into your time machine today and stepped out in 1963, in the Texas Book Depository, behind Lee Harvey Oswald as he was drawing a bead on JFK, and you yelled, "Hey, you asshole!" might it not startle him for that precious moment during which Kennedy would get out of the target area, and history be forever altered?

What if you were on-site during one of the nexus moments of ancient history; during those months in 218 B.C. in which Hannibal crossed the Italian Alps with his elephants to attack Imperial Rome? And what if you set loose on the mountain a rabbit that dislodged a pebble, that hit a stone, that rolled into a larger stone, that broke loose a rock, that hit a boulder, that started an avalanche, that closed the mountain pass? The flow of Western Civilization would have been utterly diverted.

With such Wells of invention inherent in even the shallowest of time travel stories, with such fecundity of imagination born into the basic concept, it would seem impossible for a filmmaker ladling up riches from that genre to produce a movie anything less than fascinating. Not even forty-five years should run it dry, right? If one thinks so, one has not seen BACK TO THE FUTURE (Universal), a celluloid thing as trivial as a Twinkie and, like much of the recent Steven Spielberg–presented product, equally as saccharine.

Directed by Robert Zemeckis, currently a "hot talent" by dint of having trivialized both romance and high adventure with last year's *Romancing the Stone*, this flapdoodle from Spielberg's Amblin Entertainment uses a plutonium-powered DeLorean to send 17-year-old Michael J. Fox back to 1955 so he can set up the meeting between his mother and father (as high schoolers), thus securing his own future birth. Naturally, his mother gets the hots for him, and the lofty time paradox possibilities are reduced to the imbecile level of sitcom.

With the arrogance of what the great French director Alain Resnais has called "the wise guy *auteurs*," Zemeckis and co-producer Bob Gale have had the effrontery to write a time travel screenplay with seemingly no knowledge of the vast body of such literature. And the story is by turns cheaply theatric, coincidental, obvious and moronic. Not to mention that Robert A. Heinlein and his attorneys are rumored to be murmuring the word *plagiarism* because of the film's freightload of similarities to TIME ENOUGH FOR LOVE, the master's 1973 time travel novel, as well as the famous Heinlein short story " 'All You Zombies——'."

Yet even with such embarrassing trivializations of a concept   263 that seems dolt-proof, if—as Bogdanovich suggests—movies are merely pieces of time*, then surely this idiom as a source for fresh and imaginative films has barely been tapped.

At least one would think so.

Yet here it is, less than sixty years since filmmakers denied the wonders of modern technology, computer graphics, robotics and even the freedom of using models made of plastic or hydrocal, not to mention color or sound, drawing merely from the treasurehouse of imagination, were able to create *Metropolis*; and their artistic descendants can offer us nothing more meaningful or inventive than *Back to the Future*.

If we date the "beginning" of cinematography from Edison's Kinetoscope in 1891—rather than from Roget's Theory of the Persistence of Vision in 1824, or Rudge's 1875 magic lantern projector, or from Muybridge, or from Jules Etienne Marey— then we are talking about a self-proclaimed "art-form" whose age is less than a hundred years. Yet if we are to judge by the trite product that the most advanced crafts and talents offer us—the endless sequels, endless remakes, endless *"hommages"* that are little better than inept plagiarism—this is an "art-form" that has already gone stagnant, if not wholly, then damned certainly insofar as sf/fantasy is concerned.

I think I've reached the core of my thesis.

If we date the age of modern science fiction from Wells, rather than from Verne or Mary Shelley or Lucian of Samosata or the nameless author of the Gilgamesh Epic, we have a second art-form whose age is less than a century. (I'll let adherents of the Verne-versus-Wells school hammer out the rationales for my picking Herbert George over Jules. I don't mean to be either capricious or arbitrary; I merely feel that *modern* sf as we know it, for purposes of this discussion, is better defined as proceeding from Wells's more thoughtful dystopian view of technology's effects on people than from Verne's less-critical utopian fascination with things mechanical.)

Proceeding thus: speculative fiction as a coherent genre is a medium as old as cinema, and the two have been inextricably linked from the outset. Hell, the first movie of them all, according to many experts, was a science fantasy: Georges Méliès's *Le Voyage Dans La Lune*, 1902. But in less than a hundred years, sf in the print medium has come from the naïveté of Verne, the didacticism of Chesney, and the technocracy of Hugo Gernsback

---

264   *Actually a phrase from Jimmy Stewart.

to a sophistication that produces writers as various as Lafferty (our answer to Thurber), Gene Wolfe (as one with Bierce), Kate Wilhelm (Dostoevskian), Benford (Faulknerian), Le Guin (equal to C. S. Lewis), Silverberg (Dickensian), Ballard (Joycean), John Crowley (whose resonances are with Colette) and Moorcock (in the tradition of Fielding)... while filmed sf gives us vapid and grotesque, unnecessary remakes of *Invaders from Mars, The Thing, Cat People* and *King Kong*. Even as the newer writers—Butler, Kim Stanley Robinson, Shepard, Bishop, Connie Willis, Tem, Curval, Bryant and Simmons—assimilate all that was the best of "the New Wave" of the Sixties/Seventies, melding it with elements of traditional sf, to develop ever subtler and more innovative ways of dealing with *what-if*, the cutting edge of sf in film is *Explorers, Cocoon, Baby, Weird Science* and *Back to the Future*.

Even extolling the virtues of *Cocoon* and *Weird Science*, the reality with which we must deal is that sf cinema has come, in a few years (comparatively speaking, as regards the life span of an art-form), to a weary recycling of the same tired themes with mere fillips of variation, cosmetic repaintings of last year's models. In any other art-form, such a manifestation of aridity of invention, such an obvious stasis, would signal the end of development. In just this way did the epic poem give way to the novel form.

A moment's pause. How is that written sf, for all its wrong turns, faddish detours and periodic recidivism, has continued to show constant growth and revitalization, while film—with its mushrooming population growth of new, young talents and astonishing technical expertise—has turned more and more in on itself, cannibalizing the core subject matter and paying false homage to its most trendy newcomers, even as it ignores the experimental work of men and women whose vision opened new paths fifty years ago? Gil Lamont suggests, and I agree, that sf in the print medium continues to show vitality, in defiance of the natural order of such things, precisely because it *is* a ghetto. Since we need not please the masses, the Great Wad, as do television and big-budget films, we continue to produce that which interests *us*. And the *us* that is pleased is one raised on The Word. Not an *us*, like those who come to work in tv and movies, raised on thirty-five years of repetitive sitcoms and episodic series.

Only mass-market sf—"sci-fi"—gives us repackagings of the same old themes: space opera, heroic fantasy, things with fangs, haunted houses. Here in this ghetto, for all its death of soul for writers who aspire to the larger playing fields of general literature, there is a welcoming of the daring and experimental. So the best we have to offer, even thirty years old, is ignored by the motion picture mentality in favor of hackneyed treatments of hoary clichés. *Starman, Ice Pirates, The Last Starfighter* and *Back to the Future* are prime, current examples.

It is clear: those who pass themselves off as creative intellects —Joe Dante, Spielberg, Lucas, Landis, Carpenter, among many whose names fall from the lips unbidden—are truncated things, capable of limited imagination. Oh, their technical flourishes are beyond cavil. They know every new camera lens and stop-action technique. But what they choose to put up on the screen is empty. It is either devoid of intellectual content or so sunk in adolescence that it can appeal to none but the most easily dazzled. Now we get an *hommage, en passant,* in *Mad Max: Beyond Thunderdome* to a line from *Buckaroo Banzai*; *Explorers* tips its dunce cap to *Gremlins*; and Steven Spielberg is on record as having said of *Back to the Future,* "It's the greatest *Leave It to Beaver* episode ever produced."

Isn't that a daring project for the most powerful and artistically unfettered talent in film today!

You'll notice I'm not even attacking these films on their lack of internal logic or extrapolative rationality. This note of the death-knell strikes simply in terms of which stories have been chosen for the telling.

Which brings me to THE BRIDE (Columbia), TEEN WOLF (Atlantic Distributing) and FRIGHT NIGHT (Columbia).

All three have been popular. *Teen Wolf,* a quickie, has a mass appeal based, apparently, solely on the current hot actor status of tv's Michael J. Fox. The other two did well at the box office, it seems, because of subject matter. And what *is* the subject matter? Is it something fresh and new in the canon of fantasy? Is the subject matter sophisticated and newly-slanted as was the case with *Liquid Sky, Repo Man* and *Night of the Comet,* three innovative films that died at the box office, and have become cult favorites precisely because they *are* purely ghetto films that eschew all the Amblin-like appurtenances of moron media hype? Are they even as fresh as, say, 1940s sf films?

No, they are minuscule variations on *Dracula* and *Frankenstein.*

All in the same month, rechewings of the three classic film fantasy archetypes.

Teen Wolf is easy to dismiss. Badly directed, sloppily written, riddled with holes in the storyline logic, all this exploitation hackwork has to recommend it is the kid, Michael J. Fox; and as best I can tell he's got a one-note style of acting developed for NBC's *Family Ties* that is pleasant enough at first encounter, but is already wearing thin in these eyes.

Fright Night is also easy to dispense with. The vampire is charming, the vampire lives next door, the vampire dies in the latest hi-tech manner. That's it. Vivid violence, some sophomoric humor, teenaged protagonists and Roddy McDowell doing his prissy imitation of Vincent Price as a ghoul-show host. That's it. Chris Sarandon—whom you may remember as Al Pacino's gay lover in *Dog Day Afternoon*—plays the bloodsucker in the currently hip Frank Langella/David Bowie/David Niven/George Hamilton charm-the-knickers-off-them manner, intended (one presumes) to set labia lubricating. The specter of Lugosi need have no fears. Sarandon's vampire isn't worthy of whisking the dandruff from Bela's cape. There is more of reminiscence of the young Robert Stack bounding into frame with a grin and a "Tennis, anyone?" than of Carpathian Creepiness.

Tom Holland, who wrote and directed *Fright Night*, is remembered fondly for *Cloak and Dagger, Psycho II* and *The Beast Within*, a trio of humdingers. Stop gnashing your teeth, it's not polite!

The Bride is a little harder to slough off. Principally because it was obviously made with serious intent, considerable intelligence insofar as design is concerned, and a performance by David Rappaport (the leader of the *Time Bandits* dwarves, Randall) that is no less than stunning. The conceit that motivated this film's production was the *what-if?* that follows a created female by Dr. Von Frankenstein that did *not* perish immediately. Not a bad idea. Room for a whole lot of development there. And for the first half hour one is so taken with the look and pace of the film, that it only slowly dawns—through the numbness in your butt—that there isn't much going on up there. At final resolve, the film turns out to be an elegant, handsomely-mounted bore. And Jennifer Beals, essaying the role created by Elsa Lanchester, is simply embarrassing. One expects her to fling free the coils that suspend her in the web of lightning, and flashdance her way into Sting and Quentin Crisp's hearts.

As pretty to look at as *Barry Lyndon* or *Tess*, but no more enriching than *Teen Wolf* or *Back to the Future* or *Fright Night*,

The Bride forms the fourth wall of the box into which cinematic sf/fantasy has chivvied itself.

Once one has seen the original Tod Browning–directed version of *Dracula* (1931) with Lugosi unparalleled for interpretation of the dreaded Count, and once one has seen the 1979 *Love at First Bite* with George Hamilton, Arte Johnson, Susan St. James, Richard Benjamin and Dick Shawn flailing away at every possible hilarious parody variation on the original canon... what is there of significance left to do with the vampire idea?

Once one has seen James Whale's *Frankenstein* (1931) and *The Bride of Frankenstein* (1935), with Karloff unparalleled for interpretation of the Monster, and once one has seen Mel Brooks's 1974 *Young Frankenstein* doing for that classic what *Love at First Bite* did for *Dracula*... why do we need yet another remastication of the original meal?

As for *Teen Wolf* or *An American Werewolf in London* or *The Howling* (not to mention Michael Jackson's *Thriller*), if you can't live up to the tragedy and pathos of Lawrence Talbot being clubbed to death by Claude Rains, if you can't get Madame Maria Ouspenskaya to play the gypsy woman Maleva, and if you can't express the horror of lycanthropy without the special effects folks laying in barrels of gore, then why not think of something new? I mean, hell, John Carpenter thought of a new monster creation for *The Thing* remake: killer Italian food.

These four films, the cutting edge of what is being done *today* in sf/fantasy on the screen, say more about the sere and dusty condition of imaginations brought to bear on the genre. This, sadly, is the best they can do.

It's not that there isn't room for better. Go see KISS OF THE SPIDER WOMAN (Island Alive productions), an astonishing fantasy based on Manuel Puig's extraordinary novel, starring William Hurt, Raul Julia and Sonia Braga. Very likely one of the most important films of the past decade. And see what the *real* talent has to offer these days. Do not go gentle into that good night of movie attendance believing that *Explorers* or *The Goonies* or *Back to the Future* proffer anything more meaningful than background to chew your Jujubes by.

Here are four moneymaking films, top of the rank, best by far, lauded and applauded by the Wad. And they ask for nothing finer, nothing richer. And it's not that the *auteurs* set out to make empty, useless films: *this is the best they can do!*

With greater freedom, superlative technology, exchequer-breaking budgets, neither Spielberg nor Lucas, nor any of the clone-children they have taken under their wings, from Arkush to Zemeckis, can match by one-millionth the achievements of Willis O'Brien, Val Lewton, James Whale or Fritz Lang. They preen and posture and talk about technique in the short takes one sees on the cable movie channels, but in truth they are the whistling pallbearers of the corpse of cinematic fantasy.

The art-form has reached its untimely end. All is ashes and *Porky's* from this time forward.

How tragic that many of you will have attended the wake and never know that the eyes staring back at you are those of the living dead.

INSTALLMENT 14½:
In Which The Unheard-Of Is Heard, Kind Of

In the November 1985 issue of a magazine called *Starlog* there appears the first half of an interview with your humble essayist, given to a very nice young man named Lee Goldberg. Mostly, it concerns my work for the past year on *The Twilight Zone*.

Mr. Goldberg began his introductory notes about me with the following sentence: "No one will ever accuse Harlan Ellison of keeping his mouth shut."

There is a widespread belief that columnists such as myself or Budrys or Erma Bombeck or John Simon or Robert Evans always have a ready opinion on anything that occurs anywhere in the world at any time, past, present or future.

That is because we have deadlines.

We are expected to find a new crusade every time we put pen to paper. We are expected to plumb the depths of every isolated incident, and we are expected to track the path of every emerging trend. And for our sins of regularity in print (or in my case, semi-regularity) we are rewarded with the encomiums Big Mouth, Know-It-All and Vicious Critic.

If one of us raves about a film, say for instance *Dune*, not only is it instantly forgotten that we praised something, but we are pilloried for not following the party line that *Dune* was awful.

(This is much like my situation as regards fiction. Because I once wrote a story in which—for good and sufficient plot reasons—a young woman is killed and eaten by a dog, I am stereotyped by casual readers of my work as one who writes nothing but stories of violence and cannibalism. When I wrote three pages of an X-Men "jam" comic book, proceeds of which went to feed starving children in Ethiopia, a reviewer in *Amazing Heroes* wrote, "Harlan Ellison who, perhaps surprisingly, wrote the most upbeat and positive of the Entity-induced nightmares." Not surprising, perhaps, to those who have read, say, "Jeffty Is Five" or "Paladin of the Lost Hour" or "With Virgil Oddum at the East Pole," or any of the hundreds of other stories I've written in which friendship, courage, kindness and true love are the themes. But you get what I'm trying to say, don't you?)

And if we rationally and painstakingly savage a film we think is ka-ka, like f'rinstance *Back to the Future*, we get letters such as this one from Forrest J. Ackerman:

"Do you suppose you're the only person on Earth who didn't like/love *Back to the Future*? Or can you name me five others? Or don't you give a damn how many cinemicrocephalons there are in the world?"

To which I replied: "Forry, with affection for you personally, I will let Anatole France respond to your question. 'If fifty million people say a foolish thing, it is still a foolish thing.' "

And so the general feeling is that we are Big Mouth, Know-It-All and Vicious Critic. Because we are required to meet the deadlines by which the magazines in which we appear live and die. When you turn to our columns, there we are, opening our big mouths. Because that is what we're being paid to do. And so the Lee Goldbergs of the world say, "No one will ever accuse Harlan Ellison of keeping his mouth shut."

But, in weary truth, there are times when some of us *don't* have anything to say. Times when we haven't seen any films that require analysis. Times when we start an essay on why it is that most sf writers cannot write television scripts, or on why after ten years of publicly denouncing tv I went to work for *The Twilight Zone*, or... well, whatever. But we have those deadlines, so we do it.

And all those who cannot wait to pounce on the latest essay as yet another example of the Big Mouth Know-It-All Vicious Critic shooting off his bazoo nod sagely and say, "Doesn't he ever shut his mouth?"

272   For all of those kindly folks, and for those of you who know

what it is not to have any particular opinion burning in you from time to time, I offer this installment, for which I am asking the editors of this magazine to pay me only one dollar:

I haven't anything to say this time. Maybe next time. Maybe not.

Mr. Goldberg: the millennium is at hand.

INSTALLMENT 15:
In Which A Gourmet Feast Is Prepared Of Words A Mere Two Months Old

I have no idea who "A. Kindsvater" is, but s/he was represented by a quote at the top of a page of a 1982 memo book sent to me four years ago around Christmastime by a roofing repair company I'd engaged to locate a leak under the Robert Silverberg Memorial Cactus and Succulent Roof Garden here at Ellison Wonderland; oh I guess that'd be back around 1979; and they keep sending me these nifty genuine imitation-leather plastic-cover memo & date reminder booklets, little pocket-size jobbies, with birthstones and which-wedding-anniversary-is-the-13th (traditionally lace, but more contemporaneously, textiles and furs are looked on as appropriate), and a place to write in all the appointments you'd have gotten to on time if you'd thought far enough ahead to carry the little genuine imitation-leather plastic-cover memo & date reminder booklet with you, but you didn't think that far ahead and so the booklet lay in a drawer, unused for four years, until a few weeks ago when I tossed it out, along with the reminder booklets from 1983, 1984 and 1985; but not before I went through them and pulled out a few of those obscure quotations that serve as running heads every week. And that's where I discovered this quote by the dreaded "A. Kindsvater" whomever. Which quote was as follows:

"The probability of someone watching you is proportionate to the stupidity of your action."

Kindsvater—about whom I know absolutely nothing, yet whom I choose to capture in my imagination as having devised that truism at the moment s/he was caught by the *Man on the Street*'s minicam as s/he was having perverted sex with a Rocky Mountain oyster in the show window of Bloomingdale's—certainly knew whereof s/he spoke, because no sooner do I write a column in which I explain in detail why there will never again be a worthwhile sf movie, than I see what is not only the greatest sf film ever made but is, in my infallible view, easily one of the ten greatest films of all time.

(This list of 10, which I change in a shamelessly duplicitous fashion to suit the occasion, variously includes *La Strada*, *The Wizard of Oz*, *Casablanca*, *M*, *Viva La Muerte*, *Providence* and *Citizen Kane* and *The Magnificent Ambersons* and *Paths of Glory* and about thirty others; but you get the idea.)

Kindsvater had it absolutely pegged because I know all of you read that column, only two months ago, and have been sharpening your yellow fangs waiting for me to poke my little head up out of the molehill of opinion wherein I reside; waiting with blow-guns to lips for me to register any sort of ameliorative revisionism; waiting to make me eat my words, force-fed through the medium of your ever-vigilant, ever-contentious, ever-maliciously nitpicking letters to the Noble Fermans who edit and publish this magazine.

Well, if I have to masticate my manuscripture, I'll do it in as flamboyantly gourmandising a manner as was my original pronouncement. I herewith eat my words. The belief that sf is dead as a serviceable genre for motion pictures—stated baldly and without equivocation in my January installment—was a precise and correct view of the universe except for one thing; I hadn't seen BRAZIL (20th Century–Fox/Universal). I eat my words, but the *maître d'* is Terry Gilliam. And okay I made an ass of myself in print for the very first time in my life, but I can live with it because, though I may look like a dip, I'm still better off than you, because I've seen what is surely the greatest sf film of all time (and one of the 10 greatest films ever made), and you never will. Nyaah nyaah!

But enough levity. It is enough that your faithful essayist has learned humility through adversity. Let it suffice that unbridled arrogance has been brought to its knees by contradicting evidence so inescapably overwhelming that all that remains to me is the act of contrition in which I drive to this tattoo artist's place

276

I know in Venice (California, not Italy), and have the guy inscribe on my tongue the following, from Montaigne:

"To be cured of ignorance one must first confess it."

Brazil was the talk of London when I was there last summer. The reviews had been strange. Mixed reviews, if truth be told. Reviews that ranged from querulously timid admissions by lesser reviewers that they hadn't understood one frame of this singularly disturbing film, to sheer panegyrics by usually flint-hearted critics in which the word "masterpiece" appeared so often it became suspect.

Moorcock went wild over it. Lisa Tuttle couldn't stop raving about it. One after another English or Scottish fan, upon first meeting, almost before saying, "Glad to meet you," radiated messianic fervor and asked, "Have you seen *Brazil* yet?" Well, no, I hadn't; because it had come and gone so fast in the U.K.

Distributed internationally by 20th (and in the U.S. and Canada by Universal), the film had been shown in England in its original 2-hour 22-minute version, and however well or badly it did at the box office, it left in its wake the kind of awed comment usually reserved for books that turn out to be, fifty years later, contenders for literary immortality.

I was curious, naturally, but took it all the way we usually do when we hear how sensational some upcoming film is supposed to be. Like you, I've been burned too many times in the past few years. So I didn't go too far out of my way to find a suburban theater where *Brazil* might still be viewed.

I knew that *Brazil* was the latest directorial effort of the lone American member of the Monty Python troupe, Terry Gilliam. Having seen Gilliam's three previous films—*Monty Python and the Holy Grail* (1974), *Jabberwocky* (1977), and *Time Bandits* (1981)—I hadn't been wildly impressed with his abilities as regards the first two, but had gone absolutely bugfuck over *Time Bandits*, which remains one of my all-time favorite movies (though not one of the 10 greatest films of all time, like *Lawrence of Arabia*, *The Thief of Bagdad* [1939], *All About Eve*, *Metropolis*, *Throne of Blood*, *Viva Zapata* or *Singin' in the Rain*). I was anxious to see if the talent and inventiveness directorially displayed in *Time Bandits* had progressed to *Brazil* in as startling a quantum leap as it had shown between *Jabberwocky* and *Time Bandits*. And when I learned that Gilliam and Charles McKeown had been joined in the writing of the original screenplay by no

277

less a master of wordplay than dramatist Tom Stoppard, my interest was truly piqued.

The cast sounded wonderful, too. Jonathan Pryce and Robert De Niro and Ian Holm and Bob Hoskins and Michael Palin, among many recognizable American and British names. But of the plot there was little said. No one could really explain to me what *Brazil* was about.

Was it about Brazil?

Well, no, Brazil doesn't enter into it at all.

Then where does the title come from?

Uh, well, you remember that song from the Thirties, "Brazil, where hearts were entertained in June, we stood beneath an amber moon, and softly murmured, 'Some day soon.'" And etcetera. Remember that song?

Yeah, sure, I remember it very well. It was one of my favorites. I remember a terrific version done by Hazel Scott on the organ in some dimly-recalled film or other. So what's that got to do with this movie?

Uh, well, it sort of plays over and under, throughout the film.

Then this is a romance.

Uh. Yes and no.

Well, what the hell *is* it?

It's, well, it's sort of a *1984*-like story, that may make you think of *Blade Runner*, except it isn't anything like either one of them, although it has some resonances with Lindsay Anderson's *O! Lucky Man* and *A Clockwork Orange*, but uh er it isn't very much like either of those, either, and there's elements of a lot of the screwball comedies of the Thirties, with the tough-talking dames in them, and all sorts of non-intrusive *hommages* to films like *Potemkin*, and all this big-screen adventure on a par with *Dune*, but nothing like *Dune* at all, and then there's all this dream sequence stuff and, uh . . . er . . . oh dear . . .

Stop! Stop! What you're trying to tell me is that this film is unclassifiable. It's *sui generis*. It's the kind of film you demean if you try to identify it by saying it's like this or that movie, only more pink. Right?

That is correct.

Brazil is heart-stopping. It is brilliant beyond the meaning of the word. I guarantee you have never seen anything even remotely like this film.

And now here is the bad news.

Universal's Sid Sheinberg wants the film cut. And cut again. And "re-thinked" to give it a happy ending. As "happy" endings were tacked onto the original *Invasion of the Body Snatchers* and *The Magnificent Ambersons*. Or he won't release it in the United States.

Not because he's an evil man, but because he *likes* the film, and he wants to see millions of people go to see it. Sheinberg has said, of this piece of genuine cinematic art, breathtaking in every way, "If we had this other ending and I could show you that it would do 100% more business, you'd be a fool not to agree, wouldn't you?"

Yes, we'd be fools not to agree, if the yardstick were how well a piece of art appealed to the Great Wad, rather than being true to its own creative vision and reaching only those who would weep at its gloriousness. We would be fools were we to suggest that *La Gioconda* might not be a greater work of art if she had a word-balloon coming out of her mouth, and thereby might reach a wider audience.

Terry Gilliam has not been allowed to preview the film here in America. Universal stopped two theater arts department showings at CalArts College and USC in October. Then Terry went on the *Today Show* and talked about it, with De Niro at his side. And all this, after Terry had voluntarily removed eleven minutes from the original version.

(Don't fret. Terry says those eleven minutes don't feel missing. He voices approval of the minus-eleven version.)

And so, all smartass aside, I must tell you that I was stunned by *Brazil* as I have not been stunned by a film in more than twenty years. I saw it by chance, at a very special bootleg screening, in company with half a dozen of the best critics in the country, all of us sworn to secrecy about who and where and how and when.

But it looks as if you, readers, will be cheated out of this extraordinary experience. Sid Sheinberg has always wanted to be a creator. The frustration of his life is that he is merely one of the canniest and most creative businessmen in the world. So he wants to make *Brazil* better in the time-honored tradition of businessmen who run the film industry. He wants to piss in it.

I tell you with cupidity, *Brazil* is one of the greatest motion pictures ever made. All gags aside, it is in the top ten.

I have given you twenty or more titles of what I think are *great* motion pictures, here in this column, because an opinion by a critic means nothing, unless the yardstick is there for you to measure the opinion. If you agree with me that the films I have named in this essay are among the greatest films ever produced, 279 then you may give some small credence to one who eats his words of two months ago, and tells you that *Brazil* is certainly the finest sf movie ever made…and very likely one of the ten greatest films *of any kind* ever made.

And if you feel annoyed that you may never be allowed to judge for yourself, then drop a line to Sid Sheinberg at Universal, and tell him you want him to release Terry Gilliam's 2-hour and 11-minute version of *Brazil*.

And try to keep a civil tongue in your head.

I know how you are.

And Sid's already pissed at me, so you needn't bother to tell him that Harlan sent you. Besides, I've got my mouth full at the moment.

INSTALLMENT 16:
In Which A Forest Is Analyzed Without Recourse To Any Description Of A Tree

There are a few things in this life I have not gotten around to doing. I never did get that date with Sally Field, though I went so far as to script a segment of *The Flying Nun* for just such an opportunity. Never did drop that sugar cube drenched in acid given to me in 1968 by a well-known sf writer, though it lay wrapped in cellophane in the back of my refrigerator until 1980 when it was thrown out with a package of celery that had developed the consistency of Gumby and several Idaho potatoes which had grown such a set of eyes that we had to take the poor things in to have them fitted for contact lenses before they could be dumped. Never got to meet John Gardner, to tell him I admired his work but thought he was a meanspirited man. Still haven't had a homosexual encounter. I've got the shoes, but still haven't gotten around to taking tap dancing lessons.

These are important things I wish I had done, but the chances of getting around to them now seem slim, particularly if I'm going to get around to climbing Mt. Kilimanjaro, which I swear I *will* do, just stop shoving. Similarly, I have never gotten around to reading Barry B. Longyear's novella "Enemy Mine."

I should, I *know* I should; but, well, I put it off, and I put it off, and I put it off, and then it won the triple crown in 1979—Hugo, Locus poll and Nebula awards—and Barry got the Campbell award as Best Writer that same year, and I had to start lying when people talked about the yarn. "Oh, sure," I'd say, "some helluva piece of work. Just brilliant." But then I'd quickly switch the conversation to Céline or W. P. Kinsella's SHOELESS JOE, which I *had* read, god forbid anyone would think I was inadequately prepared for social congress.

But now that I've set myself the chore of discussing ENEMY MINE (20th Century–Fox), I can't use flummery to cover my sin of omission. It is certainly going to enrage my critics that my unceasing dumb luck triumphs once again, because by *not* having read the story it redounds to my (and your) benefit in my capacity as film critic for this august journal. Dump me in cow flop and I'll come up with the Hope Diamond.

I've been wanting for some time to review a film in this genre that is based on a well-known published story, the original version of which I had never read. Purity of vision, is what I was hoping for. A total freedom from the mist and shadow of the original work. Couldn't do that with *Dune* or *Blade Runner* or *2010* or a host of others, because I was already "tainted" by a familiarity with the sourcework. So here it falls right in my lap, this secret shame I've borne since 1979, and (damn that Ellison, doesn't he *ever* fall on his face?!) *badoom!* it's a court-martial that turns into the Distinguished Service Cross.

So I went to my screening of *Enemy Mine*, looking forward to a movie that I'd enjoy—which is the way I go to *all* of them—and I came away thinking it hadn't been such a terrific film at all. Not a thorough stinker, not a *Damnation Alley* or *Outland* or *Gremlins*, but simply a flick that seemed to have had a chance to be 108 minutes and 4 seconds of pretty entertaining adventure. It left me, how shall I put this, unfulfilled. Like a long meal of cotton candy and readings from Kahlil Gibran.

I'll recap the story for you, in the event you've also been lying about having read the published version, and haven't caught the film. Won't take long.

Well, Robinson Crusoe, this human being, crashes on a sort of volcanic island called Fyrine IV, and he finds he's not alone there. This *other* castaway, Friday, also lives there. And at first they don't like each other, and then they do like each other because they've got to work together to survive, making a hut out of palm fronds or creature carapaces or like that. And in the end we understand that it doesn't matter that Friday is a black man with a funny way of talking and Robinson Crusoe is a kind of thick-headed whitey, because under the scales and cranial crests, we're all the same, and we call that brotherhood.

Wait a minute. I think I'm getting my movies mixed. Lemme try again.

Okay. So this white convict named Tony Curtis is handcuffed to this black convict named Sidney Poitier, and they manage to escape from this state work farm, called Fyrine IV, and at first they don't like each other, and then they do like each other because they've got to work together to survive the posse out to find them, and in the end we understand that it doesn't matter that this white guy is actually a Jew named Bernard Schwarz or that this black guy is actually an ex–basketball player named Lew Alcindor, because beneath the spacesuits and overacting we're all handcuffed together in the big prison break of Life, and we call that brotherhood.

Uh. I think I've mixed things up again. Let me go for it just once more.

Okay. So there's this U.S. Marine on a South Pacific island called Fyrine IV where he's forced to work with this alien creature called a nun, which is a female kind of person who dresses all in funny kinda clothes, and who is played by Deborah Kerr, who's really swell at playing this kind of alien creature, and at first they don't like each other, and then they do like each other because they're trying to stay out of the way of the entire Imperial Japanese Navy and because they're both pretty horny, and the Marine, whose name is Mr. Allison, suggests that it doesn't matter that she's this alien kinda creature, they should take off their clothes and their bad habits and sorta have social congress because they're all alone on Fyrine IV and who's to know, and the nun alien tells him, "Heaven knows, Mr. Allison." And from this we understand that it doesn't matter how weird you dress or whether you're a 20-year career man in the Marines, nuns ain't gonna let you screw them unless you're extremely glib, and we call that brotherhood.

Er. Wrong again? Well, then, how about *Hell in the Pacific* (1968) with Lee Marvin and Toshiro Mifune, which was all about this Japanese space pilot and this American space pilot who get stuck on *another* South Pacific island *also* called Fyrine IV (a Melanesian name that means *déjà vu)* and at first they don't like each other, and then they do like each other because they both agree that if Robert *Mitchum*, for crine out loud, can't get laid, then what chance do *we* have, particularly with Deborah Kerr who *should* have been easy, considering how she rolled around in   283 the surf with Burt Lancaster. And we understand that we should call this brotherhood. Or the birth of the blues.

All right, I'll get serious. I wasn't even disappointed in *Enemy Mine*, because for all its overproduced affect—you should see the weapons and ships and the suits and the communications gear: none of it form-follows-function but shiny and futuristic and must have cost a *fortune*—the movie has all the staying power of a Dalkon Shield. But the other day a famous sf film producer stopped by to chat—and I'm purposely *not* dropping his name— and he called *Enemy Mine* "megadumb." Which impressed me, because I hadn't thought it was *that* bad, and I'm curious to know if you readers thought it was "megadumb" also, and if so, why. Which comments I'll boil down and run in a forthcoming install- ment, depending on how vitriolic and original and clever you are with your denigrations. See preceding for format.

But just so you don't go for the obvious missteps the film makes, I thought I'd list a few of the more glaring, thereby throwing you back on native cunning and that dormant sense of filmic discrimination I know lies deep in each of you.

First, they begin the outer space stuff without sound. Nice, I thought. They went the Kubrick route instead of the George Lucas route. Then, of a sudden, they scramble the starfighters and we are treated once again to the *Star Wars* space dogfight à la Industrial Light and Magic, which firm continues to be hired by all and sundry to produce space battles in a vacuum that doesn't seem to hinder spaceships from acting like Spads and Fokkers, and they all go whooooosh and blow up with big bangs slightly smaller than the Big Bang.

Second, though we never see much of Fyrine IV except these fumaroles they shot down in the Canary Islands, and all this petrified wood or whatever, both the human and the alien can breathe without artificial assistance, and I just wonder how that can be on a planet without any greenery to produce oxygen, but I suppose Poul Anderson or Hal Clement could explain how it *might* be possible, which doesn't detract from the quibble be- cause if it *is* possible, they should have given us at least a *small* indication, don't you think? I sure do.

Third, the mood of seriousness that hangs like a gray day over this entire production is gratuitously, and ridiculously, ripped apart by one of the silliest missteps I've ever seen made in a film put together by supposedly professional moviemakers. There is a sequence early on, in which a scuttling creature with a Chelonic carapace is trapped and sucked down into a sand pit by something like an ant lion with nasty complexion and one helluva glandular condition, and it gets sucked down screaming horribly, so we know either the human or the alien will soon be confronting the same problem, and we're scared for a moment until . . . the carapace is flung back up out of the hole and we hear . . . a burp. A low-comedy burp. And everyone laughs. And the mood is broken.

Fourth, that speech near the end where the big bully miner is fighting with the human space pilot, and he does one of those Jimmy Cagney routines about, "I'm gonna kill ya, cuz you killed me brudder Joey." And everyone laughs. And the mood is broken.

Well, that's just a sample. You can't use those when you write in. And don't complain that the human space pilot is carrying a bullet-firing pistol instead of some sort of laser gun, because it's logical that projectile weapons would still be in use as a personal defense a hundred years from now, because the engineering it would take to devise a way of mirror-stacking to make a laser small and portable, is way beyond the abilities of a society as dumb as the one presented in *Enemy Mine*. Also, drop a laser gun, smash one mirror, and you're up the Swanee without a scull. So that one's okay. But only because we were clever enough to figure out why, no thanks to the producers of the film.

So here's your chance to dabble in film criticism. Unleash those Visigoth tendencies! Defame multimillion dollar epics! Voice your paralogical opinions! Savage the great and the near-great! See what fun it is, and you'll understand why I wouldn't trade the writing of this column for anything in the world. Except maybe a date with Sally Field, things being the way they are between Deborah Kerr and me.

ANCILLARY MATTERS: By now you've no doubt learned that Terry Gilliam's wonderful sensational terrific glorious awesome *Brazil* is in release, in its acceptable length. No doubt many of you are taking pleasure in my having said nyaah nyaah I saw it and you never will, and *badoom!* there it is for you to see. So go ahead and have your nasty little laugh. I am content: because of articles such as mine, Universal knuckled under to Art; and I don't mind looking the fool once again. *I* know I'm a saint, so there!

One more thing. While I understand that puns are, for the most part, the highest level of wit available to a lot of sf fans and readers (a singularly humorless lot I often think), nonetheless it behooves me to point out to the reader who wrote in accusing me of stealing the Monty Python dead parrot routine which I integrated into my column several installments ago, because I didn't belabor it by pointing out that it was a Python shtick (which you knew anyway), that this was something known as *parody*. Or parroty. Or something.

And to the reader who accepted at face value my statement that sf was dead as a filmic genre (only to take it back two issues later), this was a literary technique called *engrossment*. Sometimes referred to as *satire*. The art of the *jongleur*.

Some of you act as if you are miraculously free of the ravages of intelligence, and I'm going to tell you kids this just once more, and then to hell with you, you'll just have to wait till your father gets home at which time you're going to get one helluva licking: some of this crap is supposed to be taken with a smile.

You know how to smile, don't you? Just attach fish hooks to each side of your flaccid lips and give a yank straight up!

And that's what we call brotherhood.

INSTALLMENT 17:
In Which We Unflinchingly Look A Gift Horse In The Choppers

One of my pet hates is Christmas cards. No need to go into the convoluted thinking behind my hatred of the damned things; I'm a month or so shy of age fifty-two, and I'm permitted a few eccentricities. Suffice to say that every year, despite many and widely-disseminated appeals to save their money and send what they'd spend on a card to some noble charity, readers and even long-time friends who should know better, fill my already spavined mailbox with gold lamé, embossed, outsized, Oriental silk-screened wishes for a joyous Christmas, Channukah, New Year, Twelfth-night, Hsin Nien, Festival of Tet, Druidmass and End of Days (the last accompanied by a pair of ducats on the 50-yard line for the battle between Gog and Magog).

Most of these are returned to the sender on the same day they are received, with the message I HATE XMAS CARDS AND CATS printed with a large, thick-line green marker, right there on the envelope. I've been doing this for years. But as we know, there are always those who Don't Get The Message. So every year I curse and fume and send back hundreds of Yuletide missives.

You cannot know the enmity this act generates.

Even those faithful who stick with me during my most indefensible, unconscionable periods of social vileness and irrational gaucherie, sprout fangs and fire back letters (in ordinary envelopes, not those square Xmas card wrappings) in which such umbrage, such animosity, such a tone of affront is manifested, that one might think I had used the family budgie for genetic experiments. The thrust of their anger is that I have committed a felony. Let me opine that Heinlein's latest novel isn't up to his best, or that Reagan is so locked into Cold War thinking that he would sacrifice us all to his paranoia, or that *Peanuts* is a dumb comic strip, and they'll all smile protectively and make excuses for me...he's such a sweet man, perhaps he was just having a rotten day.

But let them receive the card they sent, all in good faith and sincerity and camaraderie, scrawled upon in green marker, and they howl for a return of the ducking stool. Defenestration is too good for me, they shriek! Scaphism is too kind a fate, they bellow!

How *dare* I not only turn away this kindly-intended, innocent gesture of goodwill, but let them know I never asked for it in the first place? This is an act of antisocial intercourse guaranteed to sour even the sweetest friendship.

And in what obscure fashion does any of this have to do with YOUNG SHERLOCK HOLMES (Paramount)?

Well, let me put it this way:

It had to've been late in 1942. I was eight years old. I was laid up with the flu. We're talking Painesville, Ohio. And my mother was going downtown to do some shopping, and I was miserably bundled in my bed with more books than I could've read if I'd been down with something serious like rinderpest or beriberi or Dutch Elm blight, and my radio so I could listen to *Jack Armstrong* and *Superman* and *Terry and the Pirates*, and of course my comic books; but I still lacked the one thing short of chicken soup with farfel that could save me from death. And that, simply put, was issue #18 of *Captain Marvel Adventures*, a 10¢ panacea issued every four weeks by the world-famous faith healers, Fawcett Comics.

With great care I explained to my mother that issue #18 had been among the publications received just that very day at the magazine-and-smoke-shop right next to the Utopia Theater (at which venue, I hoped she would notice, I was *not* enjoying the Saturday ritual of seeing Wild Bill Elliott as Red Ryder or Sunset Carson as Sunset Carson mopping up bad guys, to the accompaniment of the crunching of popcorn and the smell of gunsmoke, which personal tragedy surely entitled me to *some* consideration) (if not the Croix de Guerre). I described in detail how the magazines came in all bundled together with wire that had to be snipped by the nice man with the smelly panatella who ran the shop, and that if she had *any* faint shadow of affection for one soon to pass through the veil, she would make sure that the copy of issue #18 of *Captain Marvel Adventures* she selected from the racks was not one that had been scored by the dreaded bundle wire.

I went over the instructions several times. You know how parents can be. And I made absolutely certain she knew it was issue #18, the brand-new one available today for just a few minutes before other, lesser, children (who were not on their deathbeds) savaged the supply. Eighteen, I said again. One eight. I have all the issues up to number eighteen, I said, to her retreating form. Eighteen, I shouted from my bedroom window as she got into the car. Eighteen, I gasped, falling back amid the sodden sheets.

Don't you know I waited *all damned day* for that comic!

Now this part is painful. Not just because of what comes next in the story, but because of my behavior. I have never forgotten what comes next, and if I'd had the courage to say it to her before she died about ten years ago, I'd have told my mother that I spent the next thirty-odd years of my life being ashamed of my behavior. But I was so ashamed that even at age forty-something, I couldn't dredge up that awful moment and ask for absolution.

Because what happened was that my mother came home all laden down with groceries, having spent a difficult day helping my dad in the store and having rushed back to make dinner, and when she answered my endless screams from upstairs, demanding my *Captain Marvel Adventures*, and she handed me the paper bag with the comic in it, the comic she had gone out of her way to buy for me, and I pulled it out of the bag and saw that it was issue number seventeen (#17 for crine out loud, not #18 which I had waited for all day with my tongue hanging out, only the thought of that comic keeping the Man With the Scythe from my person, but sevenbloodyteen!!!), the one with Captain Marvel battling Jap Zeros on the cover, I screamed at my mother and threw the damned comic across the room.

I'm certain that when I really do lie on my deathbed, the look on my mother's face at that moment will sneak back to strangle my spirit. The real crimes we commit cannot, somehow, ever be expunged. We pay and pay, right up to the last moment. There simply isn't enough in the exchequer to settle the debt.

And the terrible part of all this is that I *know* if the same circumstance were set up today, and my mother, or my best friend, or Susan, or Mother Teresa, or God his/her/its self brought me the wrong issue of *Captain Marvel Adventures*, I'd act exactly the same, indefensible, selfish way.

Which brings me to *Young Sherlock Holmes*.

Consider: how many times have good Samaritans "done you a favor" you didn't ask for? How many times have you wished they had kept their kindness to themselves, not put you in a position where you had to smile grimly and say, "That was very thoughtful of you," when what you wanted to do was knock them silly for putting you in a position where you had to clean up the mess engendered by "the thoughtful act of selflessness"?

People are forever doing things for your own good. They are forever giving you gifts *they* want you to have which you don't, frequently, want any part of. They merely want to serve. They want to share. They want you to have a nice, expensive Christmas card with the word Hallmark on the back so you'll know they cared enough to send the very best.

My wretched nature and guilt aside, I suggest this is self-serving on the part of the giver, with no damned concern for the attitude of the recipient.

Everyone gets a fix from "good deeds." I applaud that. I far more trust those who will cop to the truth that they feel terrific when they perform a noble act, than those who try to get us to believe they were solely motivated by a desire to serve the Commonweal. Good Samaritans and philanthropists and those who roll bandages at the local hospital are not much different, at core, it seems to me, than those who attempt to legislate morality, to save us from the devil, or to convince us that we need to believe as they do to preserve the Union. It is a philosophical and ethical membrane that separates us from them.

But I suppose it's part of human nature to give the gift that not coincidentally pushes the giver's viewpoint. Whether as bread-and-butter house gift or as guilt-assuaging invitation to dinner as reciprocation for all the dinners they've given *you*, the seemingly selfless act is, I submit, rooted as deeply in the need of the giver to get his or her fix, as it is to reward the recipient.

The thorn in the paw when one accepts the gift, however, is that seldom are we asked if we want this attention.

When it comes to filmic *hommage*—one of those gifts never sought and usually damaged in transit—the custom of primacy of interest by the creator is more honor'd in the breach than the observance.

Did the Salkinds check with Siegel or Shuster as to their

enthusiasm for having their creation Superman transmogrified into a clown at the hands of David and Leslie Newman? If we listen closely can we hear Edgar Rice Burroughs thrashing in his grave at what befell Tarzan under the tender ministrations of Bo and John Derek, Hugh Hudson, or the blissfully-forgotten hacks who churned out half a dozen Me-Retard-You-Maureen-O'Sullivan idiocies? Was any attempt made by concerned parties, to hire a spiritualist who might pierce the veil and get Val Lewton's reaction to writer-director Paul Schrader's quote in the May-June 1982 issue of *Cinefantastique*, just prior to release of Schrader's remake of the 1942 Lewton-produced *Cat People*, that "Val Lewton's *Cat People* isn't that brilliant. It's a very good B-movie with one or two brilliant sequences. I mean, we're not talking about a real classic"? With how much good grace do you think Ian Fleming would take the jaded, imbecile shenanigans of the James Bond we see in *Octopussy* or *A View to a Kill*?

Even on suicide missions, at least lip service is paid to volunteerism. But Captain Nemo, Sheena, King Kong, Conan and Norman Bates keep getting sent out there to suck up them bullets —a kinder fate than having to suffer the critics' wrath— without any of the "gift-givers" bothering to ask if they mind having their literary personas savaged.

Hommage is usually less a sincere form of flattery than an expensive Xmas card that blows up in your face. In the case of Brian De Palma, of course, *hommage* is merely a license to steal from Hitchcock.

As the unsought gift is tendered, one has the urge to snarl, "Who asked for it, creep?" Nowhere do we find evidence that the recipient has been granted the option of saying, "Thanks but no thanks."

Which brings us, yet again, to *Young Sherlock Holmes*, 109 minutes of just simply awful, lamebrained and inept crapola from the team that brought you *Gremlins*. One hundred and nine minutes of unsolicited *hommage* that utterly corrupts the nobility and artistic value of the original creation; proffered with disingenuous and actively embarrassed apologia front-and-back by young scrivener Chris Columbus and his mentor, an ever-more-millstonelike Steven Spielberg, who managed—one presumes with dangled carrots of fame and pelf and posterity—to suck in yet another excellent filmmaker, director Barry Levinson, whom we heretofore revered for *Diner* and the cinema adaptation of Bernard Malamud's THE NATURAL.

(An aside. No one is more aware of the seemingly incessant   291 flow of aristarchian eloquence I've expended on Spielberg-influenced films, beginning with *Gremlins*, than I. From that first Chris Columbus–scripted abomination, through *Indiana Jones and the Temple of Doom*, to *Goonies*, *Explorers*, and *Back to the Future*, there has been no peace for Spielberg and those who have realized his personal view of movies by the warping of their own vision, from this corner of the critical universe. It has become such a threnody that even I grow weary of the dirge. Yet what is one to do? All I have to work with is what I see on the big screen. And Spielbergian product has so dominated the industry since *E.T.* in 1982—an industry that imitates what it takes to be success to the exclusion of alternate styles of filmmaking—that almost every other trend is as a trickling crick to the Mississippi. As verification of that assertion, if common sense and simple observation fail to convince, consider: taken as a whole, the five films nominated as best of the year for the Oscars earned $220 million in box-office revenues; *Back to the Future*, which was not among those five, earned $200 million. In the face of such success at a strictly commercial level, the level at which the drones and hacks of the industry place value worth emulating, a level of success that is awesome not only because of its height above the mass of financially-remunerative films, but because of the dismaying lack of quality and paucity of content they champion for those whose aspirations are already operating on a subterranean level, how can an observer trying to make sense of it all *not* dwell to almost pathological degree on what Spielberg hath wrought? It is the Spielberg sensibility that informs the writing of scenarists whose work prior to their association with him seems, in my view, stronger and truer and less marred by cutesy trivialism. It is the Spielberg sensibility that poisons the directorial attack of Robert Zemeckis and Kevin Reynolds and Joe Dante and now Barry Levinson. It is the juggernaut that flattens studio considerations of development of projects outside the narrow path of what Spielberg has shown will appeal to the adolescent—or at best sophomoric—demographic wedge that buys tickets. So what is one to do? Either to pretend that *Out of Africa* or *Kiss of the Spider Woman* are more than noble exceptions to a rule of picayune endeavor, or to continue dealing with that which dominates the industry in hopes that someone, somewhere, will take note and break loose from the Accepted Wisdom that the only surefire way to make a buck in movies is to ape the three or four styles of motion pictures that have been raking in the gelt:

knife-kill flicks, *Rambo/Rocky* manipulations, high school epics of tits and food fights, or Spielbergian reductions of life and adventure to the importance of cartoons. I share your exhaustion at these fulminations . . . but what is one to do?)

It is painful to attack a writer as young in years and in time spent working at his craft as Chris Columbus, yet what are we to make of someone whose credits to date include *Reckless, Gremlins, Goonies* and the quisquilian subject under examination here?

Another Spielberg "discovery," Columbus seems sincere, dedicated, and hardworking. I spoke to him via telecon once, soon after *Gremlins*. My natural instinct was to give him the benefit of the doubt on that one; to assume (erroneously, it turns out) that the vileness of *Gremlins* emerged as corruptions of his original intent by Spielberg and/or director Joe Dante.

Turns out that both Dante and Columbus were swayed to the Spielberg view of filmmaking by the amentia of Amblin Entertainment; and we now have a quartet of Columbus screenplays to evaluate; and much as we might like to believe that Columbus is the new Lawrence Kasdan, even his staunchest supporters now admit in private what they will not say in public: Chris Columbus just ain't very good at this thing called screenwriting.

And that wearying aspect of Spielberg-influenced films that masquerades under the encomium *hommage*, that endless truckling to injokes and references to best-forgotten minor films of a generation's childhood, takes center stage with *Young Sherlock Holmes*. Sorrowful headshaking ensues.

There is nothing in this film fresh or innovative or even particularly well-executed beyond the delicious conceit of showing us what Holmes and Watson were like as students. A mindtickler that has intrigued Sherlockians who can never get enough of the adventures of the World's First Consulting Detective contained in the sixty (or, as some savants insist, seventytwo) elements of the canon. Doyle forever possesses our admiration and affection not only because of what he let us know about Sherlock Holmes through the recountings of his escapades via Dr. John H. Watson, but because of what he *didn't* let us know. The tantalizing hints of cases not recorded—yes, lord, let us one day find hidden under a false bottom in that travel-worn and battered tin dispatch box kept safe in the vaults of the bank of Cox and Company, at Charing Cross, the full story of the horrible Giant Rat of Sumatra—and the clues to Holmes's background. We can surmise with some certainty that he was born in Surrey, and we know (because Holmes said it was so) that he was the 293 descendant of country squires, but was Mycroft his only sibling? And why, exactly, had Holmes such suspicion of women?

The gaps in our knowledge are almost as engaging as the vast amount we know, the adventures we read over and over from our first thrilling exposure to the canon till that final rereading of "The Adventure of the Retired Colourman" moments before we go to meet Sir Arthur in person on the other side.

So the pull of *what were Holmes and Watson like as prep school lads?* is a kind of what-if I think no dealer in imagination could resist. I cannot find it in my heart to fault Columbus or Spielberg or Levinson for giving in to the temptation to fiddle with the conceit. It is the shallow and tawdry manner of their dealing with this material that hardens my heart. The word "entertainment" as it has come to be debased—as per Amblin "Entertainment"—falls far short of entertainment as we know it in its highest form, that is, as literature. Which is what the Doyle Sherlockian *oeuvre* has demonstrated itself to be.

Columbus, *et al.*, have treated Holmes as entertainment in this debased context, denying the material's value not only as Literature but, worse, more offensively, as Entertainment in the greater sense. But then, one suspects these people can do no better. Which, if true, is sad enough; yet one might wish that this batch of mediocre ribbon clerks could get past its awesome arrogance, its insular belief in the myth of its own omniscience, to display an uncharacteristic reticence when it comes to laying ham hands on the work of its betters. If the best they can conjure are the screenplay equivalents of fast foods and tv dinners, then swell. In the words of Thomas Carlyle, "Produce! Produce! Were it but the pitifullest infinitesimal fraction of a Product, produce it, in God's name! 'Tis the utmost thou hast in thee: out with it, then. Up, up! Whatsoever thy hand findeth to do, do it with thy whole might." But let them, also in God's name, even if the name be Doyle (but not if the name be Spielberg), have the humility to know that their best is, at best, ephemeral fluff, examples of planned obsolescence, junk that insults the honorable term *junk*, creativity at the level of dispensability where one finds Kleenex and Saran-Wrap. Let them have the common sense to pull back from the posturing foolishness of a Schrader downgrading a Lewton in order to seem less a thief of art. Let them cease trying to fool us that their misappropriations are sincerely motivated *hommage.*

I have more to say on this. It may be that some primal force other than my mere anger has been inflamed through the act of codifying reactions to what is, after all, only a dopey film. It may be that whistle-blowing time has arrived for this gang of pilferers of the literary treasurehouse. Michelangelo said, "Where I steal an idea, I leave my knife." Perhaps we have all been witnesses at the scene of the crime where we have failed to realize how important it was for us to identify the owner of the knife. As Socrates received the unsought gift of hemlock, so Sir Arthur Conan Doyle, he who created Sherlock Holmes and Watson and Moriarty and Colonel Sebastian Moran, receives the unsought gift of *hommage* from Spielberg and Columbus and Company; and in leaping to the defense of one whose work probably needs no defense against the nibbling of minnows, perhaps we defend ourselves.

I'll be back next time to complete the thought.

INSTALLMENT 18:
In Which Youth Goeth Before A Fall

Completing the thoughts begun last time. Subject under scrutiny: *Hommage*, the unsought gift that blights the original creation. In specific: YOUNG SHERLOCK HOLMES (Paramount).

It has been a month since I began this rumination, and the anger that seemed to build in me as I wrote the previous installment has abated somewhat. When I tried to analyze exactly what had sent me up into that spiral of rancor, no rational explanation presented itself. Like each of you, from time to time I find myself furious-beyond-proper-response; but whatever the stimulus—whether something I'd just read, or a snatch of radio news overheard while passing through a room, or a snippet of some television image—when the madness passes and I peel away the layers of emotion, I find that the snatch or snippet was only something that produced a resonance. The home videos of Imelda Marcos and her degenerate guests at Bonbon's birthday party in the Malacanang Palace, punked out and festooned with diamonds while 73% of the Filipino people were subsisting below the poverty level and scrounging for food in garbage heaps; rapists of a nation, cavorting and singing into Mr. Mikes; and the song they were singing was "We Are the World, We Are the Children." An item in the Birmingham, Alabama *News* about a woman clerk in an airport newsstand who had been arrested for selling *Playboy*, and had drawn two years in jail for disseminating pornography. A moment of infuriating disingenuousness during a radio broadcast the day after Tombstone Tex Reagan won one for the Gipper in his shootout with Qaddafi—wrong or right, agree with him or not—that set my teeth on edge: stickily referring to the two F-111 pilots who went down as "heroes of our hearts."

Each produced a level of blinding animosity that spoke to something deeper than the events themselves. For, in truth, unpalatable as it is to admit, the starvation of thousands of little black babies in a faraway place does not affect us as deeply or lastingly or immediately as a stye on our eye, a particularly nasty cold sore on our lip, or our inability to have a good bowel movement. That we can be distracted at all from the petty yet vitally urgent imperatives of our petty yet vitally urgent personal existences is the miracle of the human race. That we can transcend the counterfeit emotions of the nanoseconds in which we lament the travail of those less fortunate than ourselves to feel genuine sorrow for others of our species, that transcendence that produces a Sojourner Truth, a Ralph Nader, or the man who passed the helicopter rescue ring to a drowning woman after the Washington, D.C. airliner crash, that creates Live Aid or the Red Cross, is the miracle that makes us the noblest experiment the universe has ever conjured up. Humbling and shaming as it may be to admit such weakness in ourselves, nonetheless it remains that what sends the burst of adrenaline through us at the snatch or snippet may only be the echo of an entirely personal, entirely human misery.

Shaking my head to clear the fog of anger, I finally located the source of my animosity toward Steven Spielberg and scenarist Chris Columbus and those who made *Young Sherlock Holmes*; the source of my rage at the cavalier rationale called *hommage* that permits, even encourages, less-talented johnny-come-latelies to corrupt the creations of their betters.

I fear another weird digression, by way of explanation, is necessary.

Here, elsewhere, and on many other occasions, I have railed against the indiscriminate acceptance of the loathsome theory of cinematic creation called the *"auteur* theory," wherein all glory and condemnation falls to the director. The writer is merely a hired hand; merely the one who constructs from nothing the "plan" on which the Noble Director builds the edifice of a movie; the creator who dreams the dream, sets it down so the package can be financed by a studio, the one who merely...

But listen to Francis Ford Coppola on this subject:

"I like to think of myself as a writer who directs. When people go to see a movie, 80 percent of the effect it has on them was preconceived and precalculated by the writer. He's the one who imagines opening with a shot of a man walking up the stairs and cutting to another man walking down the stairs. A good script has pre-imagined exactly what the movie is going to do on a story level, on an emotional level, on all these various levels. To me, that's the primary act of creation."

There. Just that and no more. And insert *auteurism* where the passion don't never shine.

Of late, the *auteur* theory has crept into the world of comic books. (I said weird digression, but if you need an excuse not to screw up your face, consider that the comic book is more similar to a film than any other art-form, including the stage play; and thus, if you wanna duke it out, fit grist for this column.)

In some ways it is more a manifestation of the Starfucker Syndrome in commercial circles, but *auteurism* is what it is in bold terms. Whichever comic artist is this week's Big Star, why he or she is the one given carte blanche to rewrite the canon of any pre-existing character. Not even that universal icon, Superman, is safe.

DC Comics hired John Byrne away from Marvel by handing over the fifty-year-old legend of The Man of Steel for Mr. Byrne's tender attentions. With a hubris that would make even Paul Schrader or John Carpenter (but not Michael Cimino) blush, Byrne as *auteur* announced to anyone who would listen that everything that had gone before, from Siegel and Shuster's moment of creation through the decades of writers and artists who worked with the character, till this very instant, was null and void. He demanded, and got, DC to renumber *Superman Comics* —nearing issue #425 as I write this—from #1 with the pronunciamento that his was to be the only, the true, the preferred Superman.

Jim Shooter, at Marvel Comics, wields the *auteur* theory for his personal aggrandizement by creating "a new Marvel universe" containing an entire line of new books featuring characters who will not have to be introduced with the line *Stan Lee Presents*. Now they will say *Jim Shooter Presents*; and since kids only have x number of bucks to spend on items that cost 10¢ when I was a tot, but now cost between 75¢ and $2.50 a pop, that means sales will be diverted from such as Captain America, The Fantastic Four, The Hulk and Thor—creations of Jack Kirby and

299

Stan Lee—that have become staples of the American pop culture idiom, staples whose fame surely must rankle the overweening ego of Mr. Shooter.

Back at DC, simply for bucks because he has confessed in interviews that he never cared a gram about the character, *auteur* Howard Chaykin has taken The Shadow and turned him, in a four-issue mini-series, into a sexist, calloused, clearly psychopathic obscenity. Rather than simply ignoring characters from the Shadow's past, Chaykin has murdered them in full view, blowing off their heads with shotguns through the peephole of apartment doors; strangling and stuffing them into water coolers; recasting them as winos and setting them on fire; impaling them (in defiance of the laws of gravity) through the neck with fireplace pokers and hanging them from balconies; and smashing in their skulls with hospital bedpans. And when Mr. Chaykin was asked why he had this penchant for drawing pictures of thugs jamming 45s into the mouths of terrified women, Mr. Chaykin responded that the only readers who might object to this bastardization of a much-beloved fictional character were "forty-year-old boys." These comics bear the legend FOR MATURE READERS.

For MATURE read DERANGED.

Here is *hommage* run amuck. Here is the delivering into the hands of artistic thugs the dreams and delights of those who were clever enough, and talented enough, to be prime creators. Not enough to suggest that they cobble up their own inventions as sturdy and long-lived as Superman or The Shadow. Not enough to suggest they retain some sense of their place in the creative world. Not enough to suggest they have a scintilla of respect for all the forty-year-old (and in this writer's case, fifty-two-year-old) boys who grew up on these wonders. Not enough.

No, these are the depredations that invoke wrath, that blind us with fury at their temerity, their callous disregard for those who made their employment and elevation to Stardom possible, their dishonest assumption of control of the treasure that ends in debasement of that which succored us in our adolescence.

The digression winds back on itself through funnybookland to the Spielberg-influenced *Young Sherlock Holmes*, written by Columbus, directed by Barry Levinson. And through the wandering, at last the explanation why writing a negative review of what is, at most, an exceedingly dumb movie produced such an unreasoning fulmination. The river runs swiftly, and it runs deep.

Last time I apologized for the seemingly unceasing attacks on Steven Spielberg. Since writing that previous installment I have been apprised that Steven takes no offense at my diatribes, that even when I savage him he finds the locutions so fascinating he cannot get upset. Well, maybe; and I hope that's the case; but it don't beat the bulldog. Spielberg reached the pinnacle of a certain kind of personal filmmaking with *E.T.*, and another summit with *Raiders of the Lost Ark*; pop masterpieces with their own voice and with a reverence for those genres and the best they had produced that endeared him to the cinemagoing world. But his olympian success has brought forth as predictable side-effect a Visigoth horde of lesser-talented imitators who eschew genuine creativity for the despicable *auteurism* they rationalize as *hommage*.

Incapable of creating Superman or The Shadow or Sherlock Holmes, they steal the dream and turn it to their own ends, debasing it in the process.

Young Sherlock Holmes is the prime example.

Holmes, as a prep school boy, is made idiot foil to the extraneous special effects of Industrial Light & Magic truckling to the pinhead sophomorism of today's Cineplex audience needing its bread&circuses of cartoon ghoulies. Nowhere in the film do we see Holmes employ that aspect of his nature that has provided a niche in posterity for the Doyle-created detective—the use of observation, deductive logic, and ratiocination raised to a heroic level. The film is yet another dumb action-adventure featuring racist stereotypes, virgin sacrifices, running and jumping and hooting.

Columbus and his compatriots have swallowed whole the Spielberg idiom and reduced Holmes to a jerk. He dashes about, mostly to ill effect, with a boobish Watson puffing along behind, landing in one imbecile situation after another. The puzzle is finally solved, in defiance of everything in the Holmesian canon, not by logic and deduction, but by brute Ramboism.

Forget the infelicities of plot logic. Forget that one of the basic premises of this puppet-show is that Thuggees could build a gigantic wooden pyramid in the center of London without anyone noticing. Forget that even facts of weather are bent to a moron plot: a major sequence, for instance, demands that we believe the Thames froze over. According to my research, not in recorded memory has the Thames frozen over. Much of the river is, incidentally, tidal; show me such a river that freezes. Forget that everything we found dear in the stories is contravened.

Forget all that. Even forget that the film is mostly boring. But don't forget that *hommage* such as this is simply the muddying of the waters, that it is dirty business.

The fifty-two-year-old boy speaks. Why must the johnny-come-lately destroy the dream? To what end? Is this the act of the responsible artist; is it even the act of one who loves the original?

Does Chaykin care that we derived our understanding of the simplistic but effective ethic that "the weed of crime bears bitter fruit" from a pulp hero who came to us in magazines that flaked apart in our laps, across the ether through cathedral-shaped radios before which we lay with eyes wide?

Does John Byrne consider for a moment between bouts with his own ego that some great section of the world looks on Superman as a paradigm for our own alienation and need to believe there is superness in each of us somewhere?

We chew up and spit out our past.

Honor lasts less long than Warhol's fabled fifteen minutes of notoriety. What remains for the dreamer capable of ushering out a Conan, a Sam Spade, a Tin Woodsman, a Wonder Woman, when any parvenu can misappropriate the vigorous conceit and cripple it by inexactitudes and ineptitude? If this can be done to Mary Shelley's Frankenstein, to Burroughs's Tarzan, to Pyle's Robin Hood or Johnston McCulley's Zorro or Bad Bill's Hamlet . . . what chance do the rest of us have?

Is this too great a stretch of comprehension for you? Have you never slaved and sweated over something—as simple as a brick wall or as complex as a screenplay—and done it with all the grace and talent in you, only to see it taken over by some jamook who puffed himself up with arrogance like a banjo player who had a big breakfast?

We are talking here about the primacy of interest of the creator. We are talking about what it is that steals the souls from filmwriters in Hollywood who are compelled to turn their creations over to effectuators who label themselves *auteurs*.

Here is where the word *hommage* turns to ashes. Once permitted the incursion into the sacred preserve under the terminological rationale *hommage*—as twisty a device as calling revolutionaries "freedom fighters"—anything is permitted. If it succeeds, we say nothing, because art has asserted itself, even if it is derivative art of a secondary importance, of a flesh with pastiche. If it fails, we cluck our tongues and forget it.

This is a dismissal of the artist. It is the corruption in the bone marrow that destroys the purity of the dream. It is the leavening out, the "equality" of the untalented. It is in no way freedom, but a blanding that permits anything, without the nobility of the struggle for originality.

And it seems, these days, to be the pry-bar of the young. That arrogance shrieking at us from billboards and television sets and midget-sized screens of coffin movie theaters—proclaiming (in the words of Ed Begley, senior not junior, in *Wild in the Streets*) that the young conceive of youth as the noblest state to which a human can aspire. Perhaps it is because this fifty-two-year-old boy spent those fifty-two years working toward some small proficiency in life and craft, that such fury is generated. Perhaps it is because movie studios, geared to the viewing tastes of an audience for whom nostalgia is remembering breakfast, refuse to give contracts to writers over the age of thirty. Perhaps it is because more than half the membership of the Writers Guild over the age of fifty is not just unemployed, but *unemployable*. I speak here not of old farts who can't cut it, but writers of both sexes who have won Oscars, who have written the films we call classics, and who merely want to write the best they can, but who have been denied access to the marketplace because every twenty-year-old fresh out of some cornball media communications class in the boonies is pushing another tits&ass coming-of-age flick bearing no greater worth than as *perfect vehicle* for Molly Ringwald or Tom Cruise. Vehicle they calls it; shitwagon, I calls it. Either way, it's spinach, and I don't give a damn.

Spielberg hath wrought a generation of young punks for whom hard work and patience are anathema. And what we have to deal with at the local cinema, what *I* have to deal with in these columns, is transient as snot and only half as uplifting.

Destruction of the past, whether as another De Laurentiis *King Kong* abomination, or as the leveling of an Art Deco building, is an American tradition. We eat yesterday and say it is of value only as sauce for our french fries.

Age, in and of itself, means nothing. But where age has produced craft and invention of a high order, there youth must wait its turn. Trevanian said, in SHIBUMI, "Do not fall into the error of the artisan who boasts of twenty years experience in his craft while in fact he has had only one year of experience—twenty times."

Contrariwise, do not think that brashness and the moment's limelight can supplant years spent making an artist. That is why Picasso remains a giant and Norman Rockwell can never be more than an enormously talented craftsman. Because Picasso could do what Rockwell did, but Rockwell was incapable of doing what Picasso did.

That is to say, Chris Columbus can write from now till doomsday, he can do *hommage* to Charles Foster Kane or Harry Lime till he's blue in the face, but Orson Welles, were he still around, even fat as Iowa, could create him into the ground.

Now that I've gotten *that* off my chest, maybe I can get some sleep.

INSTALLMENT 19:
In Which We Long For The Stillness Of The Lake, The Smooth Swell Of The Lea

At one of those college literary bashes where The Celebrated Visiting Author sits alone on the stage and academics with clipboards pelt him or her with "insightful" questions, I was recently hit with the poser, "What is your definition of maturity?"

I thought about that for a moment before answering.

And in that moment, here is the anecdote that flashed through my head, that I did not impart to the gathered sages:

Most of you know by now that my friend Mike Hodel, host for more than fifteen years of the *Hour 25* radio show on KPFK-FM in Los Angeles, died of brain cancer on Tuesday, May 6th. Because he learned of his terminal state in February, and because the continuation of the program was a matter of concern to him, Mike came to visit and we talked about the darkness soon to come; and Mike asked me to host the show for him when he was gone. Because I loved him, and because his show has been so important to writers and readers of the genre for so long, I agreed to take over *Hour 25*.

But the foreknowledge of Mike's imminent leavetaking, added to the weight of the deaths of so many close friends these last few months, sent me into a tailspin. My thoughts grew wearier and grimmer by the day. Until the anguish and the pressure began to produce a sharp pain behind my left eye.

As I am one of those blessed individuals who almost *never* get headaches, this sharp needlepoint of agony behind my left eye came to obsess me. I knew very well, in my right mind, that I did not share Mike's illness; but every time the pain returned, I tumbled into the abyss of irrationality and thought, "I've got brain cancer. There's a gray pudding on the grow back there behind my eye." It was crazy; and when I saw Woody Allen's *Hannah and Her Sisters* in the middle of March, and Woody went through *exactly* the same hypochondriacal situation, I laughed at myself. But I could not shake the terrible thought, and finally I made an appointment with John Romm, who has been my doctor for decades, and I went to find out if I was more irrational than usual.

John examined me, put the light up to the eye and looked in, and reported back that there didn't seem to be anything in there pressing against the optic nerve. "Shouldn't I get a brain scan?" I said.

"Well, if you're thinking about something like that, there's better state of the art than a CAT scan. It's called an MRI and it costs about a grand."

"MRI?"

"Magnetic Resonance Imaging. About a grand. But if you can't get this lunacy out of your mind, spend the money and put yourself at ease."

"I'll think about it."

So I thought about it. For several weeks. Went to see Mike in Cedars-Sinai Medical Center, couldn't rid myself of the horror, and finally went in for the MRI. The next day, John called to report the findings on the images. "You're fine," he said. "No problems in there at all."

I felt the edge of the desk I had been gripping for the first instant since I'd picked up his call, and realized how mad I'd been driven by Mike's situation. The pain behind my eye vanished instantly.

Then I heard John chuckling. "What's so goddam funny?" I demanded, feeling more the fool than ever.

"Well, it's just something the technician who sent these over said," John replied, trying to keep a straight tone.

"Yeah? And what was that?"

"Uh, well...he asked me, 'Are you *sure* this guy is almost fifty-two years old?' And I said, yes, I was certain; that I'd known you for years and that I knew you'd be fifty-two in May, and he said, 'This is remarkable for a guy his age. The actual brain matter looks like that of a six-year-old boy.' " And John broke up again. When he had it under control he said, "I always suspected you had the brain of a six-year-old."

That was what I thought in the moment before answering the academics. Because it was the anecdote that informed what I've always considered to be a pretty workable definition of maturity. And I said to the questioner, "I take to mean, when you say *maturity*, that you're asking what I think an adult is. And my answer is that being grown-up means having achieved in adult terms what you dreamed of being as a child. In other words, you'd be mature, and an adult grown-up, if—say—when you were a kid you wanted to be a cowboy and now you owned a cattle ranch. Or if you wanted to fly like Superman when you were a kid, if you were now an airline pilot."

And I added this quotation from Rimbaud: "Genius is the recovery of childhood at will."

These thoughts, as random as most with which I open this column every time, tie in with observations about childish and adult visions of what to make as a motion picture in an era when the studios check the growth-rings of writers and directors before they commit to a project.

As rare as it has been in the history of motion picture writing for talent of a high order to emerge—Richard Brooks, James Goldman, Richard L. Breen, Paddy Chayefsky, Herman Mankiewicz, Ring Lardner, Jr. and the Epstein brothers come immediately to mind, though the list is a lot longer than you'd care to have me reproduce here and, sad sad sad, you wouldn't recognize the names of those who dreamed the dreams and put the words into the mouths of Bogart and Lancaster and Bergman and McQueen—as rare as it's been till now, the situation today is fuckin' bloody tragic. We operate in The Age of the Know-Nothing Tots.

Kids raised not on literature, or even on films, but on television reruns, are being hired every minute to write and produce films that have the social import and artistic longevity of zweiback.

(Here are some grim statistics. The current membership of the Writers Guild of America, west is 6181. Of that number only 51% is currently employed. That's 3152 men and women. But of *that* percentage, while 61% of WGAw members under forty years of age are working, only 43% *over* forty have a job. Don't ask what it's like for directors.)

The deals being made at Cannon, at Fox, at Paramount and   307

Universal, are deals for projects brought to executives by second-rate and derivative talents. Deals brought to men and women whose backgrounds are seldom in filmmaking, whose expertise and store of literary precedents is at best meager. (This is a series of generalizations. Of *course* not everyone who sells a script, or more usually a script *idea*, is a superannuated surfer. There are Larry Kasdans and Vickie Patiks and Tom Benedeks who have as much *élan* as Shelagh Delany or Harold Ramis or Horton Foote at the top of their form. But the generalization speaks unquaveringly to the reality of the industry practice today. The young and dumb sell to the only slightly less young and much dumber.)

These deals being made, and the films often made as a result of the deals, are films that cannot be viewed or critiqued by standards that have always obtained for literature, movies or even television segments.

Consider: we learn from the trade papers that filmgoing dropped another 15% last year. We learn that more and more of the audience that used to go out to, say, a movie a week, now stays home and watches videocassettes. The weekly opening of movies convinces us that overwhelmingly the theater-viewing audience is made up of teenagers. In the week that I write this column, here is what dominates the screens of Los Angeles, not much different from the screens where you live:

Molly Ringwald in *Pretty in Pink*; Judd Nelson in *Blue City*; Sean Penn in *At Close Range*; *Band of the Hand*; Nicolas Cage in *The Boy in Blue*; Ally Sheedy in *Short Circuit*; *Dangerously Close*; *Fire with Fire*; *Echo Park*; *Free Ride*; *Girls Just Want to Have Fun*; *Lucas* and *Top Gun* with Tom Cruise.

These are all films either *about* teenagers, or *starring* teenagers (though most of them are now in their twenties . . . the Brat Pack begins to creak and suffer morning arthritis). Most of them belabor the rite of passage, the dawn of sexuality, the pair-bonding of prep school twits, or the confusion of mid-life crisis occurring at age eighteen.

And one realizes, with a shock, that the tradition basics for reviewing films is inapplicable these days. One cannot, at peril of being hincty and irrelevant, evaluate a film on the merits of screenwriting, editing, direction or even design. None of these staples seem to matter to the merchandisers of modern films. Apart from splashy special effects (which is a criterion that has begun to pall for even the most unjudgmental Kallikak), the sole criterion of a movie's worth—looney! lunatic! loopy!—is if the soundtrack can be melded to 2-second snippets of the action sequences to form a music video for MTV, producing, of course, a gold album.

It doesn't matter if the film is a medieval fantasy (*Lady-hawke*), a contemporary aerobatics adventure (*Top Gun*), a western (*Silverado*), an Eddie Murphy–clone cop rampage (*Running Scared*), or retold fairy tales (*Legend, Company of Wolves*). All that counts is that a *sound* is produced that can function in the secondary markets for appeal only to those who cannot listen to music in anything under 200 decibels. That the music doesn't fit, that the music jars, that the music distracts and blunts the mood of scene after scene, seems not to enter into consideration by those responsible for the film's artistic gestalt.

It is adolescent adults playing 3-card monte with the captive kiddie audience, or actual tots saying fuck you to the rest of the world, both younger and older.

This cynical pandering to the sophomoric, unformed and utterly undiscriminating hungers of a juvenile audience disenfranchises the rest of us, both younger and older than the demographic wedge that buys rock music...or worse, that even smaller wedge that doesn't buy but merely derives its calorie-poor musical diet from *watching television!*

Take SHORT CIRCUIT (Tri-Star) and LEGEND (Universal) as specimens under the microscope.

Short Circuit is nothing more than a sappy replay of *E.T.* with a cuddly, anthropomorphized runaway robot replacing a cuddly etcetera etcetera alien. It is last year's *D.A.R.Y.L.* Martinized and reworn. (Only difference is that Barrett Oliver as the robot in *D.A.R.Y.L.* had his gears and cogs and chips camouflaged, while No. 5 in *Short Circuit* has metal in view.) Both films paint authority as not merely inept and evil-with-a-Three-Stooges-silliness, but as implacably stupid and brutish.

Granted, *Short Circuit* posits the philosophical position that violence and killing are not nice things to do, which is a salutary message in this era of *Cobra* and *Rambo*; nonetheless it is a film that panders to the youth audience by giving them two of the three staples of *all* these teen-slanted films.

What are the three?

1) Bare tits. (Absent from this movie, presumably because Ally Sheedy, the omnipresent Ally Sheedy, is such a box-office draw that she doesn't have to bare her bosom.)

2) Disdain for authority.

3) Casual destruction of personal and public property.

309

No. 5 is just a kid, after all. It may be a kid with molybdenum paws, that runs on trunnions instead of sneakers, but it's just a kid. And, like James Dean, it is having a hard time learning who it is. It suffers existential angst in trying to reconcile the creative abilities of humans with the species' need to slaughter. It is the same, tired rebel without a cause yarn. It invests the young with a nobility that is unpossessed, presumably, by anyone over the age of twenty-one.

Short Circuit did big ticket business, but no amount of giving-the-benefit for its anti-killing aspect can disguise the fact that this plate of spinach is a manipulative, sappy truckling to teen hungers and fantasies. And having Steve Guttenberg standing around like something carved from Silly Putty don't help beat the bulldog, if you catch my drift.

Yet *Short Circuit* soared. I suggest this phenomenal turn of events can be linked to the promotion of the film via music videos and its totemization of adolescent rebellion fantasies. It sure as hell couldn't have been on the basis of freshness of material or superlative acting.

It is a kiddie film, made by adults pretending to have the souls of the pure and innocent. Porky, duded up like Peter Pan.

A sidebar thought, probably deeper than we have space here to explore: Is film rendering our impression of the mutable world meaningless?

For more than sixty years we have received a good proportion of our understanding of the world around us from movies. Film was seldom at the cutting edge of the culture in portraying trends, but as soon as a trend became clear, movies were in there, commenting on it, well or badly. *On the Waterfront* may have come to the subject of labor corruption late in the game, but when it came, it made its position known. America took notice. *Saturday Night Fever* may look cornball today, only nine years later, with its stacked-heel disco boots and its Nik-Nik shirts, but it drove America into a spin when the Bee Gees and Travolta made their statement about the social set that lived and foamed in disco palaces. (And it was only about five years into the trend before it got the wind up; pretty good for an essentially conservative industry.)

But is this ability to mirror the world still operating in the mainstream of motion pictures?

I think not. The numbers are skewed, the facts distorted, the picture out of focus. One of those Polaroid shots in which everything comes out roast beef red. Such films as *Short Circuit*—the

310

sf version of a typical teen rebellion flick—send us a view of the world that resembles LORD OF THE FLIES more than it does reality. Kids run everything in these movies. Either kids grown a little older, like Guttenberg and Sheedy and Cage and Estevez and Moore, or kids in their native habitat, like Nelson and Macchio.

It was bad enough when movies beat us about the blades to accept obscurantism and illogic like Amityville as the secret formula to understanding Life, but the current flood of discarded immaturity that pretends to be How It Is *looks* real, no matter how twisted and bent. And this, I submit, is hardly the meal we need to enrich us.

They are films that reject maturity, even in the loose terms I suggested at the outset of this essay.

Films made that play to childish (not childlike) ideas of what the Eternal Verities might be.

Films that sell smash-cut music videos to an audience with only dawning responsibility toward itself and its Times, an audience with too much money burning a hole in its pocket, and the blood-level belief that its youth is the noblest state to which a person can aspire.

Films that sell, with obvious and hidden tropes, in every frame, the bill of goods that anyone not capable of appearing on *Soul Train* is beyond consideration, so what the hell does it matter if we bust up their property and give 'em the finger?

When this pretense of innocence, as in *Short Circuit*, is swallowed whole by presumed adults, we have a situation where filmmakers who should know better gull themselves into selling that hype of Youth Eternal with no understanding of how they corrupt not only their talent, but the very audience they pretend to serve.

Such is the case with *Legend*, which I'll deal with at full length next time. Suffice to say, for now, that this epic brought forth by Ridley Scott and a battalion of equally talented creators, panders as shamefully as *Top Gun* or *Porky's* to teenage fantasies of Good and Evil, Rebellion and Authority, Youth and Age. And does it with the breakneck pace of an MTV potboiler, so loud and so demented in its headlong flight, that we emerge from the screening room gasping for breath, praying for a moment of surcease.

There is no room to breathe in *Legend*, even as there is no room to breathe in *Beverly Hills Cop* or *Top Gun*. We are not permitted a moment's respite to think what all this kiddie fasci-

nation with faeries and unicorns and demons and goblins is all in
aid of.

Do not mistake my meaning. *Legend* is an astonishing film in
many ways. The eyes will behold things they have never seen,
have only conjured in dreams. And that is wonderful, because it's
what movies are *supposed* to do for us.

But *Legend* becomes, in its final American version, a telling
example of studio interference, of Art twisted to serve the ends of
Commerce Unchecked, of a creative intellect operating without
maturity. I'll talk about it next time.

Because *Legend* is something really strange: a fifty-two-year-
old man with the brain of a six-year-old. Something really
strange like that.

312

INSTALLMENT 20:
In Which Manifestations Of Arrested Adolescence Are Shown To Be Symptoms Of A Noncommunicable Dopiness, Thank Goodness

No, no, no, and no! Absolutely not. The threat doesn't exist that could get me to do it. Beg and plead and try to bribe me, it'll never happen: this time I'll get right to it, without one of those convoluted, rambling digressions. Right into it, that's how it's gonna go. Pick up exactly where I left off last time, and complete the thought without maundering on into some cobwebby corner of esoteric philosophy.

Not going to diverge from the main thrust by mentioning that readers familiar with my previous involvement with a writer-director name of James Cameron (*The Terminator, Rambo*) will recall that I am not exactly moved to feelings of kiss-kiss cuddle-cuddle when dealing with films he has had hands and feet in, and thus find it painful but evenhanded to note that his new epic, ALIENS (20th Century–Fox), is a rather good action-adventure with a script by Mr. Cameron that provides the best role for Sigourney Weaver since last she played Warrant Officer Ripley, lone survivor (if you exclude the cat Shithead) of the doomed starship *Nostromo*'s original encounter with the horrendous *Alien* (1979). Not going to be swayed into sidetracks by observing that though Mr. Cameron seems to have only one story to tell—a story that involves one or more Rambo-like protagonists blowing away as many of the opposition as they can manage with exotic armaments that clearly fascinate Mr. Cameron the way lepers are fascinated by their own sores—it is a story that works like crazy in this sequel to what was arguably the most terrifying film made in the last thirty years. Not going to be diverted into gritting my teeth at having to commend Cameron for a job well done, at having to recommend you plonk down your cash for a nifty little film that I'd sorta secretly hoped would bomb out. Not going to do it.

No sidebars, no offshoots, no deviations from completing the arguments begun last time.

Absolutely not going to babble about how much fun BIG TROUBLE IN LITTLE CHINA (20th Century–Fox) turned out to be. Won't register surprise that after the infamous writing-credit imbroglio attendant on the filming of this send-up of the cinematic genre known as "looneytune-fu" (or "kung-kookoo"), that it came up so sweetly nincompoopish that only someone who takes George Bush seriously could find it less than charming. Not going to get into that, because if I did, I'd have to swerve into a discussion of the cupidity and disingenuous obfuscation of director John Carpenter when he blamed the onscreen credit hassle on the Writers Guild of America, west and its punctiliously fair adjudication of just who would get awarded final and sole screenplay credit. To be lured away from the spine of this column's matters-at-hand to explain the fascinating way in which the WGAw sorts out credit controversies, would be to wander even farther from a simple statement that *Big Trouble* is (in the words of gin rummy players) a real no-brainer, intended for one of those nights when you feel lower than Edwin Meese's respect for the First Amendment; a film in which Kurt Russell does an even better imitation of John Wayne than he did of Elvis Presley; a film that combines Indiana Jones–swashbuckle, Oriental goofery, special effects magic, contemporary *hoodlum-kitsch*, pell-mell action to the exclusion of logic but who gives a damn, good old down home Yankee racism, parody, satire, the art of the *jongleur*, and some of the funniest lines spoken by any actor this year to produce a cheerfully blathering live-action cartoon that will give you release from the real pressures of your basically dreary lives. To deal so would be to forget myself and commit another of those long, drawn-out wanderings in the desert of my brain. No way. No way, I say!

Sure, certainly, yes of course, I could get involved with one of those "ancillary matters" I tack onto the end of these essays, in which I scream, "Awright awreddy, get off my case, I admit I was wrong about the Thames not having frozen over in recorded history!" But that would entail me having to credit the dozen or so readers of this column who took gleeful opportunity to let me know, in the words of Cooper McLaughlin of Fresno, that "Ellison has made an a-hole of himself." It would necessitate my acknowledging Arthur Ellis of Parsippany, New Jersey and his documentation that the Thames froze so solid in 1684 that a Frost Fair was set up on the ice, with bull-baiting, horse and coach races, puppet shows and fast-food stands; that it froze again in 1739 and again in 1814. (McLaughlin even sent Xerox copies of etchings, fer crissakes!) I'd love to do one of my famous tap dances about how it was all the fault of my POSSLQ Susan, who assured me such a miracle had never happened, but she's from Manchester, so what the hell does *she* know? But if I were going to roam instead of bearing down on the real topic here, I'd get into all that and admit I was utterly wrong in that one complaint against the interior logic of *Young Sherlock Holmes* but remain unswerving in my belief that it defaces the Holmes canon, and then I'd get into a shouting match with the lot of you, who would start giving me opinions, when you know damned well I'm receptive to no voice but mine own. That's what would happen, so I will avoid the tussle. I will, I swear I will.

So okay, no fooling around here with random diversions, such as pointing out to those of you who know the classic film LOST HORIZON (the 1937 original, not the musical abomination of 1973, which—even if you are dyslexic and reverse the numbers—could not be mistaken one for the other), and those of you who don't *but ought to*, that one of the finest fantasies ever dreamed on celluloid has been restored as a result of thirteen years of intensive research and reconstruction by Robert Gitt (now with the UCLA Film Archives) to its original roadshow release running time of 132 minutes, and is coming to major cities throughout America, and you miss it at your peril. If I had the time here, which I don't, because I have serious matters with which I must deal, I'd tell you that Susan and I went to see it a few weeks ago and it was as breathtaking as ever. I'd tell you that Ronald Colman was never better, that Sam Jaffe as the High Lama remains mystical and touching as ever, that Jane Wyatt and Edward Everett Horton and dear Tommy Mitchell and H. B. Warner and all the rest of the cast capture the heart no less fully than when the film was first released. I'd tell you that next to *Lost Horizon* and its perfectly conjured sense of wonder, the *dreck* we have on view in Cineplex coffins these days pales into utter disposability.

I'd tell you that, and *beg* you to go see this labor of love as reconstructed by men and women who cannot be turned from their love of the medium by the trash wallows that dominate the screen scene in this age of cinematic adolescence.

But I am sworn to a policy of no digressions this time, and you can count on me. Foursquare. As good as my word. You could beat me with I-beams and I wouldn't even *mention* THE GREAT MOUSE DETECTIVE (Walt Disney Productions), the first new Disney animated to recapture the incomparable wonders of *Fantasia*, *Snow White and the Seven Dwarfs*, *Pinocchio* and *The Three Caballeros*. For almost forty years we who experienced terror and amazement when taken to our first movie—and it was *always* a Disney by way of introduction to the aphrodisiacal dark-dwelling that affected our lives so profoundly—we who laughed and cried and shivered through that rite of passage, secure in the hands of Walt and his staff of artists, we have observed with dismay the long, embarrassing slide into mediocrity of the genre known as "the Disney animated feature." And were I not committed to sticking to the main topic, I would trumpet long and loud that Walt's ghost has had enough of the okeydoke, and his ectoplasmic hand guided the brushes on this delicious, imaginative interpretation of the Eve Titus BASIL OF BAKER STREET books about the mouse detective who lives underneath 221B Baker Street. Here is all the old Disney hoopla: the character movements so verisimilitudinously human yet always slightly in defiance of the laws of physics; the precisely selected human voices (with special kudos to Vincent Price's Prof. Ratigan, Candy Candido's Fidget the pegleg bat, and Susanne Pollatschek's winsome Olivia Flaversham); the genuinely fright-producing moments of menace, that fools like the saintly Rev. Wildmon and other "protectors of young minds" have managed to leach out of tv cartoons, on the censorial ground that the kiddies should never be scared (perhaps because they're afraid the kids will turn into foolish adults like themselves...but I doubt it...that much insight is clearly beyond them); the fun and wit and humor that functions as well on the level of adult enrichment as it does on the level of children's enjoyment. If I had the space and inclination to ramble, I would, yes I would, tell you to take the nearest child and go watch Basil and Dr. Dawson save The Mouse Queen of England from the dastardly designs of Ratigan. I would, yes, I would.

316   But, of course, I can't; so I won't.

I can't even indulge myself by thanking readers like Erick Wujcik of Detroit or Dennis Pupello II of Tampa, or the half dozen others, who sent me their attempts at savagery where *Enemy Mine* is concerned. I asked for amateur efforts at scathing film criticism, but I'd be forced to tell all you folks (if I were digressing, which clearly I am not) (and doing it rather rigorously, if I say so myself) that your barbs were velvet-tipped and your brickbats as damaging as cotton candy. Obviously, you need me on a regular basis to show you how to vent your animosity at the low state of American cinema. (And if you need verification from a nobler source, of the things I've been saying here for the last year or so, I would recommend in the strongest possible terms that you obtain a copy of the 21 July issue of *New York* magazine, in which the excellent critic David Denby goes point for point with your humble columnist, and arrives at the same conclusions [albeit with fewer digressions] in a long article titled "Can the Movies Be Saved?")

And it's a good thing I'm pledged to begin this installment right on the money, without hugger-mugger or higgledy-piggledy, because if this were one of the essays in which I start off from left-field and circle around till the seemingly-irrelevant metaphor begins to glow and suddenly shines light on the greater terrain of the real subject—a technique used in Forensic Debating that is known as arguing from the lesser to the greater —I would indulge myself with self-flagellation for having spent two hours, as so many of *you* did, watching a bit of flim-flam called *The Mystery of Al Capone's Vaults* on television back in April. Were I not dedicated this time to plunging straight into it, I'd suggest that the producer of that 2-hour con job, Doug Llewellyn (the guy who interviews the plaintiffs and defendants on *The People's Court*), and the host, the increasingly lacertilian Geraldo Rivera, be forced to defend their hoodwinking of the American tv-viewing audience not before Judge Wapner, but before Judge Roy Bean. With the hemp already knotted.

But because I started some serious discussion of films made by adults with the sensibilities of adolescents; of films that are childish but not childlike; of films that pander to an erroneous conception of what even *kids* want to see; of films that are so commercially slanted for the MTV mentality that they disenfranchise most of the rest of us to the extent that a recent study commissioned by Columbia Pictures tells us that in a nation where for half a century going out to the movies was as formalized a part of the week's activities as saying grace at the dinner

317

table, three out of four Americans now *never* go to a movie; of films that have so cheapened and trivialized what was well on its way to becoming a genuine art-form that the Hollywood movie has become irrelevant, not to mention laughable, in the eyes of the rest of the filmgoing world; because I started that train of thought on its journey last time, I must deny myself the luxury of divertissements. So no time wasted, I will get into a resumption of last time's discussion.

And I trust in the future you'll grant me my little auctorial ways. I really do pay attention to your carping, as you can see from how assiduously I bowed to your wishes this time.

Let us look at two recent films whose similarities of plot and theme and production are far greater than their differences in these areas; whose similarities of quality and intelligence and purpose are almost minuscule and whose end-results up there on the screen could not be more glaringly opposed. The beautiful failure is LEGEND (Universal). The charming success is LABYRINTH (Tri-Star Pictures).

Ridley Scott is, in my estimation, one of the most exciting talents ever to turn his hand to the genres of film fantasy and science fiction. I'm sure that somewhere back in the early days of this column I related the incident in which Mr. Scott came to my home and sounded me out on my interest in doing the screenplay for *Dune*, which at that time he was contracted to direct. It was a marvelous afternoon of conversation, in which his grace and intelligence proclaimed themselves sans the affectations I've come to associate with directors of germinal films...men and women who, for all their pretenses to literacy and omniscience, are buffoons not fit to be mentioned in the same occupation as Fellini or Hawks or Kurosawa. As the afternoon wore on toward dusk, Mr. Scott said something to me that I took to be anything but self-serving. He said: "The time is ripe for a John Ford of science fiction films to emerge. And I'm determined to be that director."

When he said it—and this was after *Alien*—it struck me with the force of unadulterated True Writ. Yes, of course, I thought. Who else fits the bill? Kubrick had had his shot and had made his mark with *2001* and *A Clockwork Orange* (and thereafter with the quirky but laudable *The Shining*), but there was something, for all his undeniable genius, that was distancing, cool and too contemplative; something *so* individual that the films remain almost like views of the human race as seen through the

318

eyes of an alien. No, I thought, as devoutly as I worship the work of Kubrick, he isn't The One. Spielberg, perhaps? *E.T.* remains a great film, as important in its way as *The Wizard Of Oz* or *Lost Horizon*, and whatever his part in the making of *Poltergeist*, his hand can be seen in the final production. But (as I sensed then, and have gone on at length about in these pages for more than a year) there is something sadly hollow at the core in Spielberg's *oeuvre*. Something otiose and ultimately trivial. No, not Spielberg. Then how about George Lucas? Had I been ravished by the wonders others had found in *Star Wars*, I might have considered the man who was, at that moment, the biggest moneymaker in the history of cinema, The One. But even then, as now, I thought *American Graffiti* a far superior film, and more likely to stand the test of time than the space operas. And nothing much since that time has happened to alter my opinion. Perhaps one day soon, but not then, and not now. Beyond those three prominent directors, who was there: Nicholas Roeg? Louis Malle? Brian De Palma? John Boorman? I think not. The concerns are too great for the long haul with each of them.

Yes, I thought at that moment, Ridley Scott is The One. If anyone can bring to the sf/fantasy film the same level of High Art and High Craft that Ford brought to the Western, it is this man. I dreamed of the elegance and respect for original source that Scott had shown with *The Duellists* in 1978. I extrapolated from the sheer virtuosity and Cedric Gibbons–like love of setting and background that had gone so far to making *Alien* a masterpiece of clutching terror. (And if I were not committed to eschewing digressions, I'd suggest a linked viewing of Scott's film and the James Cameron sequel which, as decent a piece of work as it is, cannot even hope to rival the original foray for transcendence of trivial subject matter.)

Since that afternoon that wore on toward evening, I have come to believe that Scott is, indeed, The One. Even *Blade Runner*, which did not collapse me as it did so many of you, has come to look to me, after repeated re-viewings, as a significant achievement, deeper in human values than I'd supposed, far more than a glitzy melodrama of sci-fi machinery and thespic posturing. Over time, my respect and admiration for Scott's vision has grown substantially.

But *Legend*, years in the making and the sort of production nightmare that all but the Michael Ciminos of the world would shun like putting on the feedbag with Falwell, is a tragic enterprise. It is a long, self-conscious Jungian dream filled with awkward symbolism and an adolescent sensibility that I find bewildering in the light of Scott's frequently-manifested maturity and insight. What we received here in America was a chopped-up 89-minute version of the full 129-minute film released in the U.K., so there is no telling if the tale told at greater length worked better.

Legend has a surreal quality, almost Dali-esque; or perhaps reminiscent of the paintings of that school known as the Orientalists—Gérôme and Regnault and Debat-Ponsan. If wonder is the creation of a world in which one would love to live—Oz, Lawrence's Arabia, the streets of *Blade Runner*—then this film conveys wonder. The things that come before one's eyes in this motion picture are quite remarkable. Things we have never before seen. The camera roams as wide-eyed and innocent as Charlie Chaplin through *Modern Times*, and I defy anyone to name another director whose eye for the *outré* is keener.

But after eighty-nine minutes of rushing and flinging and breakneck visuals that leave one gasping, begging, desperate for a moment of peace and leisure—the stillness of the lake, the smooth swell of the lea—all is emptiness. This elaborate fairy tale of Good and Evil, of barechested Tom Cruise playing Bomba the Jungle Boy as if he were Mother Teresa, of unicorns and demons and dryads, is ridiculous. Like Boorman's *Zardoz* and Dante's *Explorers* and Boorman's *Excalibur*, it is the attempt to lift to adult level what is essentially the plaything of children.

As children we found in such fables—Aesop, Howard Pyle, Uncle Wiggily, Grimm and Andersen—touchstones for ethical behavior in the real world. They were tropes, intended to impart broad and simplistic versions of charity and honor, loyalty and gumption. But as adults we learned to our shock and often dismay that the real world was more complex than the fairy tales led us to believe. And we always felt cheated; we always found ourselves thinking, "They lied to us. They didn't tell us life would be this big a pain in the ass!"

Legend is a film made by an astute adult who, when turned loose, when given the power to create any film he desired, fled into a throwaway universe of childish irrelevance. *Legend* is, at final resolve, a husk. A lovely, eye-popping vacuum from which a sad breeze blows. Because it finally gives nothing. It steals our breath, captures our eyes, dazzles and sparkles and, like a 4th of July sparkler, comes to nothing but gray ash at the end.

Unlike *Labyrinth*, which is a film made by adults that renews and revitalizes the perception of the world we held as children, yet operates on many other levels—as does *all* High Art—and invigorates the adult in us. *Labyrinth*, were it the first film to which you'd ever been taken, would be as memorable to you as *Snow White* or *The Wizard of Oz*. And it is as important a film as those; and it is as original as those; and it is as rich in multiple meanings as those.

And I will conclude these thoughts about films made by adults that are childish, and those that are child*like*, next time. Because I seem to have run out of space.

I don't know why that might be.

god knows I've hewn to my stated purpose. I mean, I might have rambled on about all the other films I've seen of late, films I think you might want to know something about, but I didn't. I just hung right in there.

Hoping you are the same . . .

INSTALLMENT 21:
In Which You And A Large Group Of Total Strangers Are Flipped The Finger By The Mad Masters Of Anthropomorphism

If this afternoon you are walking down the street and some geek in a window three storeys above you decides to be cute, and s/he dumps a paper bag full of turds into the abyss, and as you pass beneath you get slimed from head to toe with ka-ka, and you look up and scream at the sonofabitch, and s/he gives you the finger, I'd be willing to make book that you'd register about 9.6 on the Pissed-Off Scale.

If you picked up today's paper and read where Reagan and his cronies had managed to push through a hundred and fifteen million to aid the Contras, but were trying to reduce the aid to retarded children from 9% (which is what it is, though it was supposed to have been 14% and then go as high as 30%, but they never quite got around to doing it) to 7½%, and they tried to con you by telling you we had to do it because of the Domino Effect in Latin America that would permit the Communist Menace to gain a toehold in this hemisphere, I'd put good money on your responding with outrage and a verbal explosion of naughty words.

If you go out to dinner tonight and a car full of no-neck spuds pulls up alongside you at a traffic light, and the feeps inside look across at the one you love, sitting beside you, and yell, "Hey, that is the ugliest piece of crap I've ever seen, I hacked up something prettier than that when I got drunk on Friday, it looks like something I fished outta the sink disposal this morning!" I'd bet my paycheck for this column that your first instinct would be to deck it as you leave the light and centerpunch those dirtballs into a better life.

Yet by the time you read these words many of you (and many of your friends) (and a large group of total strangers all across these great Yewnited States) will have shelled out as much as six bucks a head to sit through FLIGHT OF THE NAVIGATOR (Walt Disney Pictures), and I'll take odds not one of you took sufficient offense at having had your intelligence insulted, at having been flipped the bird by Disney's head of production, Michael Eisner, by director Randal Kleiser (the man who gave you *Grease, The Blue Lagoon, Summer Lovers* and *Grandview, U.S.A.*, four of the dreariest films of the past eight years, despite having made indecent amounts of money, thereby guaranteeing Mr. Kleiser unlimited shots at your insipience threshold), and by a trio of writers named Baker, Burton and MacManus whose first names ought to be Larry, Shemp and Moe, that you rose up in wrath and demanded your money back. Go ahead, tell me that you felt so damned affronted by *Flight of the Navigator* that you nailed the poor theater manager's head to the candy counter. Tell me you felt as used as you did after seeing *The Secret of Al Capone's Vaults*; that you knew to the core of your being that once and for all you weren't going to have the Hollywood Crap Mill stick it to you and break it off inside. Go to it; tell me: I'll believe anything; hell, I'm just a critic, not one of the Great Wad that goes to these abominations and doesn't understand that it's had its pockets picked. And then I'll tell you that pigs can fly, and we'll start even.

What I'm trying to say is that *Flight of the Navigator* is just awful. It has absolutely nothing to recommend it. From a plot that has approximately half as much logic as a Creationist tract to a nauseating passion for anthropomorphizing every machine that they can flog across the screen, this no-brainer is an insult to anything crawling across our planet with the vaguest scintilla of a claim to sentience.

Navigator combines the worst elements of *Explorers, Short Circuit, Goonies* and *The Last Starfighter*, with treacly homages to those early Disney True-Life Adventures in which all manner of flora and fauna were imbued with human characteristics.

No.

I've had it.

I can bear no more. This time I was going to inveigh once again about the juvenilizing of our beloved cinematic art-form, lamenting the horrors visited upon Ridley Scott's *Legend* and comparing it to *Labyrinth* (which, like *Return to Oz*, was never given a fair shake by the press or the critical *apparatchiks*); I was going to conclude with stunning summation the theses advanced in the last two or three columns, using as ghastly examples *The Manhattan Project, Ladyhawke, Sword of the Valiant* (aka *Gawain and the Green Knight*), *SpaceCamp, D.A.R.Y.L.* and all the limping, lurching, broken-backed, blind in one eye, illogicalities I've savaged here these past months, from *Gremlins* to *Young Sherlock Holmes* . . . but I'm simply not up to it. I've been receiving letters from many of you, pleading for respite. Agreeing, with sobs and defeated expressions, that this has been a period of assault on our tolerance for the imperfect unparalleled in moviemaking history; an assault that makes the dreadful indulgences of Pee-Wee Herman (whose voice, you will learn here for the first time, was used as that of Max, the sentient spaceship, in *Navigator*) seem by comparison to be of a stature with the thespic joys of Sirs Gielgud, Olivier and Richardson. Pleading for a brief break from the shrieks of anguish I let out every time one of these spikes is driven into my critic's perception. And at last, finally, I agree. I can say no more for a while. There is apparently no bottoming-out of this trend toward imbecile filmmaking. Every week brings new and more loathsome product; and at last even I am unhorsed.

So I will toss out all my notes on those films.

Happily will I heave a sigh of relief (and do I hear an echo from out there where you lie on your back gasping for surcease?) and let those earwigs, maggots, cockroaches and gnats live their brief lives in your theaters, never again to be available for swatting if you are smart and don't watch them on cable television.

I will go to another insect, with high recommendations. I will tell you that if you missed David Cronenberg's remake of THE FLY (20th Century–Fox), you missed one of the most exciting motion pictures of the year. Unlike *Invaders from Mars*, which began with dreck from its first version in 1953, and was recently remade in an updated, equally as *dreck*oid version, *The Fly* uses lovingly-remembered but nonetheless trivial material—the 1958 "Help me! Help me!" version and two abominable sequels (1959 & 1965)—to form a basis for Cronenberg's latest installment in his celluloid tract on the concept of the New Flesh.

What's that? A new filmic philosophy? Something we can

325

buzz a word at? Oh, ripping, we all say... lay it on us, Oh Observer of Pop Art.

And I will. Next time. I want to discuss Cronenberg at length, because I've been sorta muttering for several years that of all the wise guy directors currently assaulting us, only Cronenberg has the intellectual virility and talent to become *sui generis*. In *Scanners*, *The Brood*, *Videodrome* and now *The Fly*, Cronenberg has leapfrogged his own triumphs and failures to become a director/writer with a voice and a view of the world that could be as important, in its own bizarre way, as that of Hitchcock, Ford, Wilder or Woody Allen.

But I need space for such a discussion, and next time I will allocate that space for myself, The Omnipresent Ferman permitting.

And until then, go to see Coppola's PEGGY SUE GOT MARRIED (Tri-Star), written by Jerry Leichtling and Arlene Sarner, which is what *Back to the Future* wanted to be. It is almost exactly the same story, told from the viewpoint of a woman, rather than that of a simpy, affected, smartass Michael J. Fox; it is time travel and wish-fulfillment treated maturely, rather than simplistically and for yocks; it is adult and sincere and entertaining and everything right that *Back to the Future* did wrong. When I sat in that Hugo awards audience in Atlanta last Labor Day, and saw *Back to the Future* beat out *Brazil* for the statuette, I felt my heart sink. It was a travesty, and in that moment I hated those of you who voted for best film, condemning you in my mind to nothing better than *Back to the Future*. Ever!

But even the most benumbed of you must gleam in the eye of the universe, for you have been given a chance to see the error of your ways. It has been given to you, the possibility of actually comparing what-was with what-might-be. You can go to the theater and see *Peggy Sue Got Married*, waltz up the street to the video shoppe to rent *Back to the Future*, take it home, and compare—while the memory of *Peggy Sue* is still fresh—idiocy and counterfeit emotion and cheap laughs and adolescent bullshit with a mature dream entertainingly spun at proper length.

I cannot recommend *Peggy Sue Got Married* highly enough. I only hope when you make the comparison, that you have not been so hornswoggled that you cannot perceive the quantum leap in excellence and honesty between them.

Having now attempted to do some social work among the artistically impoverished, I go away to regain that sweetness of nature I once possessed, before having been slimed by ka-ka for what seems an eternity.

Hoping you are the same...

INSTALLMENT 22:
In Which The Land Echoes To The Sound Of An Ox Of A Different Color Being Gored

So this toothless, wild-eyed old bag lady comes up to me on the street, and she grabs hold of my sleeve, and she says, "Once upon a time, in a land so far away and so miserably poor that they couldn't even afford a timezone, there lived an authentic Village Wretch whose chief social activities were cadging cantaloupe rinds and vomiting on people's shoes."

This went on for years (she continued, in an auctorial typographic device that relieved me of the burden of having to use quotation marks) until one day an upwardly-mobile wayfaring stranger came to town, and he looked around, and he decided there was room for a second-string, sort of wide-receiver Village Wretch; and *he* began cadging cantaloupe rinds and puking on people's shoes. He wasn't bad at it—something of a comer, everyone said—until one day he beat the original Village Wretch to an especially tasty cantaloupe rind, and then he yorked all over the penny loafers of the original Village Wretch, who made a big Who-Struck-John of it, brought the newcomer up on charges, and had him stoned to death.

She stood there staring at me, did the bag lady, as she concluded this touching tale of cottage industry; and I said, "What is the underlying moral of this *midrash*, O Seer of the Streets?"

And she said, "Give me two dollars and fifty cents or I will breathe Barbasol breath on you." So I gave it to her, and she slumped away, leaving me in an acute state of Anecdotus Interruptus; and I went about my business, deeply troubled in mind unto the Tenth Generation, until a few weeks ago when, at a meeting of the Board of Directors of the Writers Guild of America, west—on which I sit here in Hollywood until September when my term is up and I'll be set free—it came to me in full court press epiphany, what the breathtaking moral to her story had to be:

The person who screams the loudest at having his Bass Weejuns befouled (or his Ox Weejuns gored; whichever comes first), is the clown who's been besmirching yours for as far back as you can remember.

Which leads me to the controversial subject of the colorization of old movies, a topic much in the news these days, a burning topic that has film directors foaming at the mouth. So crazyfying is this new technological gimmick to the fratority of *auteurs* that on November 12th, when Ted Turner's SuperStation, WTBS in Atlanta, premiered the first showing of the "computer colorized" version of *The Maltese Falcon*, the Directors Guild of America (DGA) shlepped out the film's writer-director, John Huston, fitted with nose-breathing apparatus to alleviate his serious emphysema, for a press conference. All across America—and by satellite, one presumes, to the rest of the world—particularly to France where *cinéastes* look on this "advance" with the sort of approbation usually reserved for Quisling, Himmler and the Vichy government—the great John Huston could be seen on news broadcasts, referring to those who had altered his 1941 classic as pimps, thugs and molesters of children. The old man was not happy; and if Ted Turner ever gives a damn about *any* public opinion of his shenanigans, this little brouhaha bids fair to be the one that will give him the greatest pause.

(Let me interject that I am convinced that Turner, one of *Forbes* magazine's 400 wealthiest Americans, the kilowattage of whose hubris could light the entire length of the Autobahn for the rest of the century, a man given to invoking the name of God when he needs moral justification for one of his frequent unfriendly corporate takeover forays, cares as much about negative public opinion as a *yeti* does about a U-2 flyover.)

There sat the old man (himself once the cinematic voice of God), as bucolic-looking as Gregory Peck in *To Kill a Mockingbird* or Jimmy Stewart in *Anatomy of a Murder*, and he told us that Color Systems Technology, one of the two hi-tech film-painting companies responsible for the tinting of such perennials as *Yankee Doodle Dandy, Topper, Way Out West* and *Miracle on 34th Street*, had savaged a great example of film as High Art, a movie designed to be shot in black and white, to be seen in black and white, to be preserved for all time and all film lovers in black and white.

I did not disagree with his outrage, nor with his aesthetic judgments, nor with his passion. And if anyone has a right to an opinion on this matter, it is Huston. He not only directed *The Maltese Falcon*, he also wrote it.

No disagreement with Huston on Hammett's famous novel into film. Anyone who has ever seen it knows just how good American movies can be when they're done by men and women who combine talent and technique with high ethical behavior.

The Maltese Falcon, as ordered up by Turner in response to surveys that told him a generation of *Porky's*-lovers won't stay tv-tuned to films in black and white, has all the filmic design order one finds in a Cobb salad. It looks like shit.

(And here's another nail for the coffin being readied for me by those who say I'm an Elitist. Who gives a damn if Turner's surveys are *right*?!) To hell with anyone loutish enough to need color to keep their minimal attention-span fixed through the commercials. *Casablanca* (which is supposed to be next on the paint-by-numbers hit list) and *Treasure of the Sierra Madre* and *His Girl Friday* and *It Happened One Night* were designed and art-directed for black and white. They have a unified look that is turned to spinach by colorization. Anyone loutish enough not to perceive that ought to be nailed to a movie seat and forced to watch endless reruns of *Top Gun* or *Monsignor*. And to hell with them.

So with agreement this strong, why was it that when Nicholas Meyer, a member of DGA and also one who sits on the Board of Directors of WGAw with me, solicited our vote in aid of condemning the colorization process, I spoke against the motion? Though I finally joined in with my brother and sister writers on the Board, supporting the denunciation with a unanimous vote, why was it that I raged against Nick's request in words and decibel-count usually expended on producers who seek to circumvent the terms of our Minimum Basic Agreement? How is it that one who shudders at a Bogart as Sam Spade with a head that glows pessary pink as if he had spent the night in a cyclotron, can argue against a motion that condemns the atrocious technique? And why is it that when we took a dinner break at that Board meeting, half a dozen other writers thanked me for what I'd said?

Surely it was because for the greater part of my, and their, lives we have been privileged to work at the noblest craft the human race ever devised. The job of writing.

What I said, unleashing an anger that has not abated in almost twenty-five years of working in film and television, is that I found it both ironic and insulting that directors—who have butchered, altered, emasculated, corrupted, revised and once in a while by chance even bettered the work of writers to suit their own egos or artistic visions, to appease and suck up to the even more gargantuan ego of actors, to toady to creatively-tone-deaf producers, to avoid accusations of being politically incorrect, to latch onto trends at the cost of story integrity, to warp the whole in deference to some current special effects technique, and nine times out of ten without asking the creator whether s/he approved of the hatchet job—have the gall, the temerity, the *chutzpah*, to ask writers to support their bleat of pain when *their* vaunted artistic vision has been savaged! Fuck us over for fifty years... and then come smiling the smile of the crocodile, seeking solidarity against the ravening minions of commercial transience. Announce to the world and *Cahiers du Cinéma* that they, the visionaries, the effectuators, the cathexians, are in fact the creators of the cinematic work, the *auteurs*, whole and lambently perfect in their overviewing wisdom; that the script is merely the "floor plan," the "blueprint," the rough materials from which they, in their photomontagic godhood, fashion the dreams that ennoble. Alter, for fifty years, what they wish, without regard to the primacy of interest of the writer who dreamed the dream in the first place; recast the role written for Sidney Greenstreet, to be played by Sammy Davis, Jr. in the more correct view of the God-Director; decide the linchpin speech of the protagonist, in which his entire character is limned, is unnecessary, is more "cinematic" encapsulated in a zoom shot into the narrowing eyes; put on the possessive credit before the title even if it was an original screenplay; go on *Entertainment Tonight* and describe how s/he and the lead players worked out the real story, rewriting all that awful dialogue on the set as they went along; exclude the writer from the rehearsals and make him/her chilly unwelcome on the set; do all that and more... and then come like Hansel or Gretel seeking bread crumbs to aid them in their trek through the nasty forest. Does this come down to a matter of personal pique? You'd damned well better believe it. Personal pique filtered through me by fifty and more years of honest writers and wage hacks, mad geniuses and simple craftspersons, great novelists taking a fling in films and kids who grew up with television wanting only to write movies. Pique channeled through me for all the uncountable hours of personal abuse, degradation, threats, arbitrary alterations, canceled contracts, lawsuits and lies told to the press and producers that it was because the *writer* did such a shitty job that the film was a dog, and that it was only because of heroic efforts of the flawless director that *anything* was salvaged! I speak here, and I spoke at that WGAw Board of Directors meeting for every writer who cried and tore hair and raged in the privacy of his or her home when s/he was taken off a film because s/he wouldn't knuckle under to the moronic demands of businessmen, conveyed through the director-posing-as-creator!

(Let me digress for a second. Not really a digression, but a statement about Nick Meyer.

(Nicholas Meyer is a writer of considerable distinction. A novelist and a scenarist whose body of work thus far commends him to the attention of anyone who thinks film is a serious art-form. As a director of such films as *The Day After, Time After Time, The Seven Percent Solution* and the second Star Trek movie, Nick has demonstrated both a wide eye and a keen sense in presenting material with rich subtexts. If I have differences with him on several of these films, they are based on glitches that are wholly my own, and which need not concern him, or you, ever.

(I'm not a friend of Nick Meyer's, and I'm definitely not an enemy of Nick Meyer. We are friendly acquaintances who have shared attendance at one dinner party, a number of evenings of WGAw Board meetings, some casual encounters at public functions, and similar political positions. From what I can tell, he's a good guy, and an honest man. I've already said I consider him a talented man. That I spoke against Nick's appeal at that meeting, had nothing to do with him. He was only the messenger and, I fear, he was only the guy who happened to be standing in the tunnel when the shrapnel hit.

(I wish to make this distinction clear, for him, and for my readers. As one who holds dual union credentials, in the DGA and the WGAw, it was absolutely appropriate for Nick Meyer to be the one to carry the appeal to us. Let no reader make the mistake of thinking that my anger and passion were intended as a manifestation of pique at Nick.)

No one who loves movies, no one who believes this is a legitimate art-form, no one who honors the work of the known and unknown thousands who have labored on films good and bad and merely mediocre, can approve of the colorization practice. I *had* to make that WGAw vote unanimous. It was not only the right thing to do, it was the *only* thing to do.

When the computerized coloring concept was first announced, some years ago, I thought it was at least intriguing. When the first film to be so treated was released, a pastelized rendering of one of my all-time favorites, *Topper*, I bought it and viewed it. It was so-so. Nothing very good there—I knew damned well that George and Marion Kerby's Hispano-Suiza (or whatever it is) was creamy white, not the bilious yellow someone had decided it ought to be—but nothing much terribly bad, either. It looked amateurish; it looked hastily processed; it looked like a diversion, in much the way one looks on 3-D: mildly amusing, but not worth taking seriously.

When they colored *Yankee Doodle Dandy*, even with Jimmy Cagney's glowing pink head like a balloon about to detach itself from his body, I couldn't get too worked up: I'd always seen the black and white film in color in my head, anyway. And I sorta supposed that if they'd considered it at the time it was being made, they might well have opted to do it in Technicolor. Certainly, if there was ever a b&w film that cried for color it was *Yankee Doodle Dandy*.

But when Turner came away from his brief ownership of MGM with a film library of great memories, that he then culled for one hundred films to be laid in the line of the moving Crayola, I became distressed. And now we see *The Maltese Falcon*, and now we understand that there were films intended for the chiaroscuro of magisterial design unity; and we realize that what Turner and his techno-thugs are doing is the rape of an American art treasure.

Apart from the sinister and deeply disturbing copyright questions even now being considered by the general counsel of the Copyright Office, even apart from all the aesthetic revulsion we feel, there is the problem of the marketplace. With colored versions of these films being played on free tv and wending their way to cable or pay-tv, the audience for these films in their pristine state will dwindle. Kids simply have no sense of history, and as they have been steadily brainwashed to accept nothing but roast beef red and car crashes, what will be the inducement for them to pay out money to go to the few art revival houses left in this country, to see a black and white version of, say, *Casablanca*, which they get for free on the little box and which they *know* oughtta be in color?

When I tell people that I still use a manual typewriter, not even an electric, much less a word-processor, they look at me as if I'm the king of the Luddites. Yet, it seems only sane and rational to me, that one adopts the level of technology that most conveniently permits one to produce the work at the highest level of craft, and eschews anything beyond that as merely playing with a new toy. I suppose that's the core of my objection to colorization. We don't really need it. The universe doesn't really *need* an aquatint rendering of those stark vistas and black and white emotions we know by heart from *Treasure of the Sierra Madre*. We do continue to need the arrangement of shadows out of which Bogart steps in *The Maltese Falcon*.

It's like going to see a club act in which a whistling dog performs "The Stars and Stripes Forever." Once, it's interesting; more than once it's merely a curiosity. That has very little, if anything, to do with art. And pandering to the corrupted tastes of a generation of kids for whom movies are nothing more than a prelude to getting laid, is loathsome in every way.

None of the foregoing withstanding, when Nick Meyer came to the Board and said, rally 'round the flag, boys and girls, even feeling as I do about this matter, my instant reaction was: big fuckin' deal! *Now* you're unhappy. *Now* you know how it feels. Too damned bad, directors. You are the ones who've done it to us with impunity forever, and now you squeal like pigs that they're doing it to you!

The Philistines have invaded your holy environs and you don't like it. But that won't stop you from continuing to do it to us. Because with the power to change, comes the power to demand more money, and artistic control, and devil take the hindmost... which has traditionally been the writers.

Whether the directors win this one, or lose this one, they've made the Writers Guild their bedfellow; but if there is even one writer out there who thinks that s/he can see the hideous parallel, who thinks that this will bring forth a wellspring of compassion for those of us who labor at the words before they ever see the project, then I submit that the writer ain't living in the same arena the rest of us know.

The directors are having their ox gored by a man even more ruthless, even crasser than they. And dem widdle folkses doesn't wuv it even a widdle. To which reaction I fear I can display very little compassion. Good, I say! Good, you fat-assed bunch of self-anointed Michelangelos. Suffer, mudderfuggers! Get just a tiny taste of the bile we have to swallow every day, on every job, in Hollywood.

You got us to go along with you this time, because it is a terrible thing. For directors, for writers, for film lovers of all times and all places.

But do try to remember why you felt so badly, and how it felt, during this first, brief moment of your inconvenience. Because it is what lies at the heart of why so many of us hate so many of you.

Color you blue right now. Color us crimson always.

INSTALLMENT 23:
In Which Premonitions Of The Future Lie In Wait To Swallow Shadows Of The Past

I'm at 30,000 feet aboard United flight 104, on my way to speak at a seminar on the creation of the universe (about which, you may be certain, I know even less than you) in company with Sir Fred Hoyle and Robert Jastrow at the University of Rochester; and as fear of making a total buffoon of myself has rendered me *tabula rasa* on the subject, precluding preparation of salient remarks, my mind is ratlike scurrying toward anything *but* the creation of the universe, so whatthehell, why don't I write this overdue column instead; and most of all I'm thinking, mostly, about my friend Walter Koenig who is not speaking to me at the moment.

My friend Walter is a writer of screenplays, a fine teacher of acting, a collector of Big Little Books, and an actor who, for twenty years, has assayed the role of Ensign (now Lt.-Commander) Chekov on a television series, and in a quartet of motion pictures, generically known as *Star Trek*. A series and films with which many of you may be familiar. (I say *may be familiar* because, of late, things have gotten even worse than I'd imagined them to be, cultural memorywise. I mentioned all-chocolate Necco Wafers to a bunch of people in their early twenties the other day, and they looked at me blankly. That, added to the fact that on my *Hour 25* radio show, during an interview with the talented artist Phil Foglio, he admitted he'd *heard* the phrase "civil rights" but didn't really know what the Civil Rights Act of 1964 alluded to, has given me pause. Thus have the Sixties and their history been flensed from the world in the minds of those under forty. So I take *nothing* for granted any more.)

Now Walter being pissed at me may not, at first blush, seem to be fit fodder for philippic, but the *reason* he's pissed at me, the shadowy philosophical subtext of our minor contretemps, ties in with a few random thoughts about the new film STAR TREK IV: *The Voyage Home* (Paramount), which Walter arranged for me to see a few weeks ago, as I fly overhead writing this.

A momentary pause. A short while ago I promised you a long column analyzing and praising the films that David Cronenberg has directed. I'm working on it. Mr. Cronenberg has made available to me cassettes of his earliest, most-difficult-to-locate films (*Stereo*, made when he was 26 years old; *Crimes of the Future* from 1970; *The Parasite Murders*—which you may know either as *Shivers* or *They Came from Within*—and the uncut version of *The Brood*), and I am going at this essay with care and measured reason. It will be along shortly. Last time I ventured some thoughts on the coloring of films. Since that column—which has caused some small stir in the film community, including a spirited essay of response even *before* my column saw print, from screenwriter/director Nicholas Meyer, in the L.A. *Times*—I have learned of even more horrifying technology about to be brought to bear on classic films now in the clutches of Ted Turner, and I am amassing data on same with director Joe Dante, in preparation for a follow-up column. That one should blow your socks off, and I expect if all goes well it will be my next installment. I haven't lost my place, as you might have suspicioned: I am simply trying to develop a sense of punctiliousness in my declining years. I tell you this to forestall *kvetching*.

So Walter isn't speaking to me.

That isn't unusual. Since the evening in 1963 when I met Walter on the Universal Studios backlot "New York street" where the *Alfred Hitchcock Hour* was filming my "Memo from Purgatory" teleplay, he has sent me to Coventry many times, occasionally even for just cause. I am not permitted to get angry with Walter, that isn't in the contract; so I am not pissed at Walter; but since I don't deserve his animus this time, I have decided to wait until he apologizes for being such a poop. Nonetheless, the circumstances by which this crankiness developed, and the subtext which is more than slightly intriguing, prove germane to a theory about *Star Trek* that I've worked out exhaustively since I first thought of it way back, oh an hour ago, will this flight *never* end?!?

Presumably because I asked for $500,000 to write the screenplay of *Star Trek IV* when I met with Leonard Nimoy and Harve Bennett on Friday, January 25th, 1985—on the grounds that if I had to write for Shatner, if I had to write in a part for Eddie Murphy, if I would have to face the imbroglio of others wanting to share screen credit with me, if I was going to have to put up with the *tsuriss* I knew would be attendant on *any* involvement with Paramount and its peculiar attitude toward the *Star Trek* films, I would have to be compensated in heavy balance—a demand that was greeted first with disbelief, then consternation, then with disdain, and finally with utter rejection (as sane a decision as ever Paramount made), I was never invited to a prerelease screening of the movie.

I mentioned having been "overlooked" during a conversation with Walter, and he thereafter broke his hump getting me comped into the Cinerama Dome. Not an easy thing to do.

A day or so later, when I called Walter to thank him for his efforts, I made some casual remarks about my reaction to the film —which were positive—not foamingly laudatory, but positive, about which more in a moment—but the main reason I'd called was to urge him to get into the queue for script assignments on the newly-proposed return of *Star Trek* as a television series for syndication, with an all-new cast. We talked about that for a few minutes and then, with an edge in his voice, Walter said, "Okay, so what did you think of my performance?"

For an instant I was thrown off-balance. The subject had been changed without warning. And I answered quickly, with what I consider honesty and candor, "It was fine. I said I thought it was the best ensemble work from the regulars that I'd seen in any of the four films, remember? They didn't give you quite as much to do in this one as they did in *Star Trek II*, but it was a lot more onscreen time than you got in the first or third films. And what you did, I liked. You know. You did Chekov, and you did him just fine."

Walter's anger was instant. "Don't break your back straining yourself!" I fumfuh'd, not understanding why he was so hot, and only made matters worse (apparently) by saying, "Come on, Walter, I'm not bullshitting you. It was fine. I mean, they don't really give you Gielgud or Olivier material to play...what you were given you did very well, indeed." Which only raised his ire the more. And he snapped my head off that he was through discussing it, and I said we can talk about it more later, if you like, and Walter snarled, "Yeah, sure," or bit-off words to that effect, and he hung up on me; and we haven't talked since, which is a while ago; and I don't like having Walter pissed at me, but there's not much I can do about it this time till he cools down and chooses to honor my honestly-delivered remarks.

Which would be, taken at face value, merely the recounting of an unfortunate misunderstanding between long-time chums, were it not that (upon reflection born of gloom) what I said to Walter emerges from a response to the totality of the *Star Trek* phenomenon. Which is, at last, the proper fodder for this column.

It is no secret that for many years I was not exactly the biggest booster of *ST*. Having been in at the beginning *before* the beginning of the series, having been one of the first writers hired to write the show, I was wildly enthusiastic about the series as Gene Roddenberry had initially conceived it. (In fact, at the very first Nebula Awards banquet of the Science Fiction Writers of America, which I set up at the Tail O' The Cock here in Los Angeles, I arranged for a predebut screening of the pilot segment.) The show debuted on September 8th, 1966 and by December it was in trouble with NBC. The Nielsens were very low, and Gene asked me if there was anything I could do to get the popularity the show was experiencing in science fiction circles conveyed to the network. I set up "The Committee" and using the facilities of Desilu Studios, I sent out five thousand letters of appeal to fandom, urging the viewers to inundate NBC with demands that the show be kept on the air. (The original of that letter, seen here for the first time in print, is reproduced as a sidebar courtesy of The Noble Ferman Editors.)————————→

And so it was with heavy heart that I fell away, as it were. I had my thorny problems with Gene over "The City on the Edge of Forever," about which I've written elsewhere; and after my segment aired I divorced myself from *ST* with a passion that frequently slopped over into meanspiritedness. When the first film came out in 1979, I wrote a long and bruising review that resulted in fannish animus up to and well past the egging of my home. This, despite the fact that by now everyone agrees *Star Trek—The Motion Picture* was a dismal piece of business.

I was not much more impressed with *ST* as the subject for full-length features when *ST-II* was released in 1982, chiefly because Paramount thought it could amortize some of the sets

THE COMMITTEE

Poul Anderson • Robert Bloch • Lester del Rey • Harlan Ellison
Philip José Farmer • Frank Herbert • Richard Matheson • Theodore Sturgeon
A. E. Van Vogt

Dear _____,

It's finally happened. You've been in the know for a long time, you've known the worth of mature science fiction, and you've squirmed at the adolescent manner with which it has generally been presented on television. Now, finally, we've lucked-out, we've gotten a show on prime time that is attempting to do the missionary job for the field of speculative fiction. The show is STAR TREK, of course, and its aims have been lofty. STAR TREK has been carrying the good word out to the boondocks. Those who have seen the show know it is frequently written by authentic science fiction writers, it is made with enormous difficulty and with considerable pride. If you were at the World Science Fiction Convention in Cleveland you know it received standing ovations and was awarded a special citation by the Convention. STAR TREK has finally showed the mass audience that science fiction need not be situation comedy in space suits. The reason for this letter -- and frankly, its appeal for help -- is that we've learned this show, despite its healthy growth, could face trouble soon. The Nielsen Roulette game is being played. They say, "If mature science fiction is so hot, howzacome that kiddie space show on the other network is doing so much better?" There is no sense explaining it's the second year for the competition and the first year for STAR TREK; all they understand are the decimal places. And the sound of voices raised. Which is where you come in.

STAR TREK's cancellation or a change to a less adult format would be tragic, seeming to demonstrate that real science fiction cannot attract a mass audience.

We need letters! Yours and ours, plus every science fiction fan and TV viewer we can reach through our publications and personal contacts. Important: Not form letters, not using our phrases here; They should be the fan's own words and honest attitudes. They should go to: (a) local television stations which carry STAR TREK; (b) to sponsors who advertise on STAR TREK; (c) local and syndicated television columnists; and (d) TV GUIDE and other television magazines.

The situation is critical; it has to happen now or it will be too late. We're giving it all our efforts; we hope we can count on yours.

Sincerely,

Harlan Ellison
for The Committee

December 1, 1966

341

and recoup their losses on the first flick. Or if not losses, at least make a few bucks on the residue.

The Search for Spock in 1984 seemed to me a decent piece of work, and I said so in print. But by that time *ST* had already been an animated cartoon series, and the original shows were a vast moneymaking machine for Paramount in syndication. Not to mention videocassettes, which sold steadily and well.

Now comes the fourth feature-length outing of the crew of the NCC 1701, and it is far and away the best of the bunch, a film that capitalizes on what the series did best when it was at the peak of its limited form. It is a film about the crew, who have become family for millions of people around the world, and it is filled with humanity, with caring, and with simple, uncomplicated elements of decency and responsibility. It eschews almost all of the jiggery-pokery of abstruse theology, gimcrack hardware, imbecile space battles and embarrassingly sophomoric "message" philosophy to present an uncomplicated story of the clock ticking down to doom while decent people struggle to find a timely and humane solution.

While I have my Writers Guild of America member reservations about the propriety of a solo credit that reads A LEONARD NIMOY FILM for the man's second directorial outing, and while I still see the hideous thumbprint of Bill Shatner's demand for more and more domination of scene after scene, I recommend this film to those few of you who may have missed it. It is a *good* movie, and the best presentation yet of all of the regular cast members—except for Nichelle and George, who caught the short end of the script this time—and is, at last, a *ST* venture at full length that no one who loves movies can carp about.

But as the film does well in theaters, and as the new series is prepared for nationwide syndication, as the fast-food joints market their *ST* glasses and the K-Marts hawk their *ST* lunch boxes, we must recognize that a miracle has been passed.

Star Trek has, at last, become more than an underground fetish; it has surpassed the mingy goal of networks and studios for a five-season run; it has gone beyond an addiction that needs a filmic fix every two or three years; it is larger than just a tv/movie staple, like the boring James Bond things that come to us as regularly as summer colds. It has absorbed its own legend and hewn a niche in posterity against all odds.

The series had serious flaws, taken as a whole. The studio and the network were never comfortable with it, and did little to preserve it. The first two films were, at best, cannon fodder. Its greatest strength, the seven or eight fine actors who comprise the crew of the *Enterprise*—with the exceptions, of course, of Shatner and Nimoy—have been used badly and treated on too many occasions as spear-carriers for name guest actors or special effects trickery. The pandering to trekkies, trekists, trekkers and trekoids has been shameless, to the detriment of chance-taking and plots that ventured farther afield.

Despite all that, *Star Trek* has held on. It has clawed its way out of the genre category to become a universal part of the American cultural scene. And *Star Trek IV* (about whose plot I need say nothing, for you have either seen it and know it, or haven't seen it and don't need to spoil it) is the first light on *ST*'s road into the future. *Star Trek* is now a given. It has swallowed the inadequacies of its past, and now can do no wrong. The new series, and however many full-length films there may be, are now assured of an unstinting affection usually reserved for Lindberghs or Rutans&Yeagers. It is a seamless whole, a household word, the speaking of whose title conjures memories and an all-encompassing warmth for several generations who have grown up with these space adventurers. Like Tarzan and Robin Hood and Sherlock Holmes, like Mickey Mouse and Superman and Hamlet, they are forever. Or as close to forever as a nation rushing toward total illiteracy can proffer.

Thus, when Walter asked me how he had performed in this latest icon of the legend, my response was as *de facto* as that of the ballerina in *The Red Shoes* who, when asked by the impresario, "Why must you dance?" replied almost without thinking, "Why must you breathe?"

I am guilty of forgetting that Walter is, among his many other personas, an actor. And actors need to hear if they did the acting well or badly. I am guilty of thinking (for the first time, and without recognizing the shift in my own perceptions) of Chekov as part of a gestalt, and a gestalt that worked so wonderfully well for me, for the first time, that I overlooked Walter's need as a human being to be singled out.

I am guilty of consigning Walter Koenig to the seamless oneness of the *Star Trek* mythos. If a brick had asked me how well it had performed as a brick, I would have said, "Your wall holds up the roof splendidly." That is at once ennobling him and demeaning him. But until I said it, and until I worried the repercussions of having said it, I did not understand that the miracle had been passed, and that *Star Trek* had become something

343

about which ordinary criticism could not be ventured, at risk of being beside-the-point or redundant.

Like the politician whose nobility in high office blots out all the picayune malfeasances on the way to investiture as icon, *ST* has eaten its past and has lit its way into the annals of Art that is beyond Entertainment.

That I find myself saying all this, after more than twenty years, surprises me as much as you.

Now if Koenig will just lighten up, perhaps I can concentrate on the creation of the universe, and other less knotty problems, such as *when the hell will this damned jet land!?!*

INSTALLMENT 24:
In Which Flora And Fauna Come To A Last Minute Rescue, Thereby Preventing The Forlorn From Handing It All Over To The Cockroaches

I was talking to Woody Allen the other afternoon, as we sat together in a bathyscaphe at the bottom of the Cayman Trench, trying to decide if marshmallow toppings on our hot fudge sundaes was Us or Non-Us, and he looked at me out of the middle of a conversation about something else entirely, and he asked me, "How come they've never given me a Hugo award? Whaddaya think, anti-Semitism?"

Startled? Well, just you bet I was. It took me a while to recover, and while so doing I kinda fumfuh'd and assured him, "It's not because you're a Jew. They're *forever* giving Hugos to Jews. They gave one just a while ago to Orson Scott Card, and *he's* a Jew. They even gave me one last year, and I'm *sure* they know I'm Jewish. Of course, they keep nominating Silverberg and then give the award to anybody else in the category, so maybe it has something to do with *sounding* as if you're Jewish. We could get Sam Moskowitz to do a paper on it."

Then I shrugged and said, "What the hell do you expect from such schmucks? They gave a Hugo to that piece of drippy dreck, *Back to the Future*, and ignored *Brazil*. They didn't even put *The Purple Rose of Cairo* on the final ballot. Go figure."

Woody looked forlorn. I was getting a tot forlorn myself. "But I've done so *much* fantasy and science fiction," he said. There was a lamentable *Weltschmerz* suffusing his words, a gray threnody undertoning his precise phraseology. "*Sleeper* was pure sf. So was *Zelig*. And what about that flying saucer at the end of *Stardust Memories*? Or the fantasy subtext of *A Midsummer Night's Sex Comedy*; or the sperm fantasy segment in *Everything You Always Wanted to Know About Sex (But Etcetera)*? I bet if L. Ron Hubbard had written *Purple Rose of Cairo* they'd have given it a Hugo...I mean, it *is* sort of a hip, updated version of TYPEWRITER IN THE SKY. Pass the marshmallow topping."

Well, after we surfaced—a bit too rapidly and Woody got the bends and had to be admitted to Flower & Fifth Avenue Hospital —I decided to put some megawattage of thought into this apparent unfairness, prompted by Woody's last words to me as he was schlepped away on the gurney: "Do you think they'll even notice that my new film, RADIO DAYS (Orion Pictures), is a loving tribute to the sense of wonder?"

So I thunk about it some heavy. One doesn't like to think s/he is wasting his/her time on a species that watches wrestling on television—staged bogus "feuds" everyone *knows* are lousy choreography neither The Supremes nor The Temptations would tolerate, among grown men who, if they dressed that way in the city streets, would not only make Mr. Blackwell's Worst-Dressed List every year, but might be netted and taken in for psychiatric evaluation—voluntarily buys Barry Manilow, Prince and Beastie Boys albums; bans forty-five textbooks in Alabama because they contain humanistic values, on the bonkers theory that "humanism" is a religion; complains because it isn't permitted to fuck up other people's lungs with cigarette smoke on the Me-First grounds that their civil rights are being infringed; and gives Hugos to dopey flicks like *Back to the Future* while ignoring *Brazil* and *The Purple Rose of Cairo*.

I mean, if you don't mind slapstick burping from alien critters, then I suppose *Enemy Mine* is a great film; but by the same judgment, so is *Porky's*.

And I was ready to pack it in, throw up my hands as well as my lunch, and just say to hell with it, give the whole inhabited parking lot to the cockroaches!

But suddenly I remembered this great quote from John Simon, a critic most of you can't stand because he's smarter than you and I and George Bush, *en masse, en grande tenue, en casserole*; and just because he had the honesty once to point out that Liza Minnelli has about as much talent as a rug-beater and looks a whole lot like a plucked chicken, you all get down on his case and think him a meanie. Well, I'm here to tell you he's no meaner than I. And so . . . he said this thing that gave me pause:

"The ultimate evil is the weakness, cowardice, that is one of the constituents of so much human nature. When, rarely, unalloyed nobility does occur, its chances of prevailing are slim. Yet it exists, and its mere existence is reason enough for not wiping the name of mankind off the slate."

The thought of nobility, as manifested in the art and craft of Woody Allen, came to the rescue. In a week during which I sat through the entertaining but outstandingly mindless *Lethal Weapon*; *Heat*, the latest Burt Reynolds gawdawfuller, made even more unpalatable by having been lugubriously scripted by William Goldman from his dreary novel (a situation that distresses me more than I can say, for one of my all-time favorite writers has been Bill Goldman, whose fiction—with intermittent echoes of the books of grandeur—THE TEMPLE OF GOLD, THE THING OF IT IS, NO WAY TO TREAT A LADY, SOLDIER IN THE RAIN, THE SILENT GONDOLIERS and MARATHON MAN—for the past eleven years has seemed to me more and more slapdash, more and more written as way-station incarnation on the way to becoming screenplays); and *Mannequin*, a sophomoric "youth-oriented" ripoff of *One Touch of Venus*, *Pygmalion* and John Collier's "Evening Primrose," well, in such a week the thought of Woody Allen somehow keeps me from taking the gas pipe, saves the world from being consigned to the *cucarachas*.

But I think of Woody lying there in the hospital, losing all fight to live as he becomes more forlorn in the contemplation that the fans who vote the Hugo awards will not understand that *Radio Days* is a wondrous paean to the joys of imagination. Is the cockroach creator equivalent of Woody waiting to be born out there in some damp sewer? Will the insects have more love for *their* special visionaries? On some day a mere dozen million years from now, will the Academy of Orthopterous Arts & Sciences convey to that splendid *Periplaneta americana*, all six legs' worth of him, the entomological equivalent of an Oscar, while insect fandom bestows the Jiminy on *Larva Trek IV*?

My mind whirls.

Can I be the only reader of fantastic literature to perceive that Woody Allen has been, and continues to be, one of our best filmic interpreters of that *je ne sais quoi* we call "the sense of wonder"? Surely not. Surely some other observer of the flickering screen image has stumbled on this obvious truth!

But I search in vain through all the treatises on Woody, and I find no support for my theory. Nowhere outside the specialist semiotics of cinema lucubration (do I speak their langwidge or don't I!?) analyzing *The Terminator* till one could retch; nowhere in the totality of non-fantasy incunabula. They talk of his ambivalence between roots as a Brooklyn Jew and foliage as an adult who wants to make it with *goyishe* cheerleaders. They prate of his influences; from Wittgenstein to Ingmar Bergman. They totemize him as the germinal influence in raising the nerd to hunk status. But nowhere does anyone simply say, "This guy has a for-real science-fictional-fantasy outlook."

So in the spirit of unalloyed nobility, I bring to the wandering attention of the genre audience that has poured millions into the pockets of Spielberg and Lucas, the advisement that *Radio Days* is a miraculous fantasy of imagination, drenched in the sense of wonder. A film about those of us who learned the universe is filled with magic through the medium of voices drifting to us in the night. The days of radio listening, the days before television turned us into wombats who will tolerate the cacophony of John Madden's voice, the empty Barbie-ism of Vanna White, the sleaze of telemogrified Judith Krantz potboilers; the days of adventure and suspense and drama that we conjured in our own minds, without recourse to the production budgets of businessmen in charge of an art-form; the days of The Green Hornet and Jack Armstrong and Buck Rogers and Sam Spade; the days when listening to the radio was an integral part of one's education, rather than an induced zombieism, an interruption of life, sitting goggle-eyed before that box that permits of no imaginative participation from the drowsing dreamer.

Radio Days, a kind of cockeyed and utterly dear variation on the multiple-plot-thread structure Buñuel pioneered in *The Phantom of Liberty* (what Leonard Maltin calls "a dreamlike comedy of irony, composed of surreal, randomly connected anecdotes"); it is narrated by Woody, word-painting a portrait of life in America in the early Forties, when one's imagination could encompass a wealthy playboy whose alter ego could cloud men's minds so they could not see him, a temple of vampires through which a Jack, Doc and Reggie would wander in constant jeopardy, and a "Masked Avenger" whom we did not need to see in the flesh of Wallace Shawn to understand the nature of Good and Evil. In *Radio Days*—absolutely dripping with scenes that could make a paving stone roar with laughter—Woody Allen has created a fantasy structure of affection and memory that no one over the age of forty dare miss at peril of forgetting how wonder-

348

ful was that time of youth, a film that no one *under* the age of forty dare miss at peril of being misled into accepting the squalor of television as the best of all possible mediums.

I have told you nothing much of the plot. That's not my job. I wouldn't steal an instant of *Radio Days* from your joy of discovery. But in the name of unalloyed nobility I beg you to do yourself a favor...go see it. Don't wait for the cassette...go see it. See it today, this very evening, and then go see it next week, to prove to yourself that the rush you got was not an aberration.

And send a get-well card to Woody. Tell him Harlan sent you.

Woody, that brave little beast (as Moorcock once called your humble columnist), was the fauna (or is it faun*um*?) (what the hell *is* the singular of fauna?) (who the hell am I?) (it only hurts when I screw the electrodes too tightly, doctor) who saved all of us from the cockroaches, but to buttress my new faith in the human race you also have to thank the flora called Audrey. A bloodsucking, flesh-nibbling, badass-talking, monomaniacal plant that dominates the spectacularly enjoyable LITTLE SHOP OF HORRORS (Warner Brothers).

I, like you, enjoyed the old Roger Corman film of 1960; I, like you, applauded the 1982 off-Broadway musical version; but neither predisposition to be charmed provided one one-millionth of the pleasure I derived from this film. Ellen Greene, Rick Moranis, Vincent Gardenia and a Greek Chorus of (Supremes-) *manqués* simply wow the spats off you. And one may now add to the W. C. Fields list of those with whom a smart actor should never work—dogs and children—talking plants. Because as sublimely cavorting as the people are, Audrey damned near steals the film. Howard Ashman's screenplay adds an almost believable sf rationale to the absolutely believable fantasy of it all, and gives Audrey a *raison d'être* for flytrap behavior that was absent in the Corman original; a conceit that enhances the story immeasurably.

Flora and fauna. Came they hence to save y'all from paying property taxes to the termites, tithes to the cockroaches, dues to the potato bugs. And I'm feeling so *up* about a human race that includes Woody Allen and Howard Ashman, if the bugs try to claim dominion I'm prepared to introduce them to Audrey.

ANCILLARY MATTERS: The follow-up essay on new technology of the Dr. Frankenstein style is in the works. Joe Dante is busy editing his new film, so we haven't had a chance yet to go do the Sam Spadework. Be patient. But until that time, let us stop referring to the depredations visited on *The Maltese Falcon*, et al., as "colorization." Colorization is the trademarked process and the name of the company that does the butchery. What it is, folks, is simply *coloring*. Apart from resisting the academese of what R. Mitchell calls "the educationists," we must not permit the coloring thugs to get us thinking their way at all. If we begin by using their heavy-breathing circumlocutions (like calling rebel insurgents "freedom fighters" and the napalming of villages as "Operation Sunshine"), then too soon we will not perceive that when Reagan's current mouthpiece says, "Yesterday's statements are inoperative," it is simply doublespeak for, "What he told you yesterday was a lie," and then, finally, they may be able to convince us that "colorization" is something nobler than parvenus with computer Crayolas. So eschew "colorization," good readers. Call it what it is, call it coloring. Call it *merde*.

Also in work is the long study of David Cronenberg's films. I've been busy writing a pilot film for NBC and Roger Corman, completing THE LAST DANGEROUS VISIONS, putting together a volume of film essays that include these columns, handing in THE HARLAN ELLISON HORNBOOK to Jack Chalker, who's been waiting more than ten years for it, and in general trying to clear away all my debts to people like Stuart Schiff, who has been patient to the point of beatification. So please don't *nuhdz* me; when it gets written, it'll get written.

And finally, I must bring to your attention volume two of a work already noted in these columns.

Bill Warren, who knows more than any person in his or her right mind ought to know about American science fiction films of the fifties, gave us volume one of KEEP WATCHING THE SKIES! in 1982. He has now lost complete control of the beast, and volume two, at 839 pages with a price tag of $39.95, has escaped to terrorize a placid world and . . . *it's alive!*

If you missed volume one—a mere piddly 467 pages covering hundreds of films released between 1950 and 1957—a staggering compendium of wise, witty, weird essays on everything from *Abbott and Costello Go to Mars* to *Zontar the Thing from Venus*, then fer pete's sake don't let volume two slip past you.

Yes, these books are pricey. (Of course, if you buy them separately they're $39.95 each, but if you buy the duo, it's only $65.00.) But, on my oath as a methane-breathing entity, this is a buck well spent. Warren doesn't merely give you the plot synopsis and the cast and the rest of the creative team, he doesn't merely put the film into historical and cinematic context, he doesn't merely describe the advertising and promotion and effect the film had on America as a whole or the sf world in part, he also lavishes each essay with bits of minutiae, arcane knowledge, bizarre connections and berserk influences, sidebar comments about the personal lives of the stars and writers and directors and producers. But on the plus side he does it with an absolutely charming affection for even the worst dog, the most inept pig, the lamest dromedary of a stinkeroo. Bill Warren really and truly *loves* this stuff, and his honest obsession cannot be resisted.

Volume two covers 1958 through 1962, with appendixes that list full cast and credits, order of release of the films, announced (but not produced) titles, a bibliography, an addendum and an index to the more hundreds of movies that Bill has sat through from beginning to end so we don't have to.

These are the sort of books one keeps to hand in the bathroom. As those of you who read understand, that is high compliment indeed. The potty is the last private place for a reader in the world. No one bothers you. Unless you live in large Italian family, which is another sociological can of worms entirely. But you can't be in there *too* long, or someone will think you're enjoying yourself in ways you're not supposed to, so you have to have reading material that can be enjoyed in medium-short bursts. *Time* is okay, and a book of Fredric Brown's short stories; comic books work well, and *The National Review* (because *no* one can read it for very long without throwing it across the toilet into the tub). Which is to say, KEEP WATCHING THE SKIES! is made up of delicious morsels that can be enjoyed over a long period of time. At peace, and with pleasure.

If your bookstore has trouble ordering them, suggest they contact McFarland & Company, Inc., Publishers; Box 611; Jefferson, North Carolina 28640. Pony up the sixty-five bucks for the pair. I do not think you will hate me too much for this recommendation.

And tell 'em Woody sent you.

INSTALLMENT 25:

In Which The Specter At The Banquet Takes A Healthy Swig From The Flagon With The Dragon, Or Maybe The Chalice From The Palace

Let us speak of guilty pleasures, and of *outré* nights at the cinema. Of windows nailed shut in the soul, and of dreadful dreams we would pay never to have again. Of winds that blow out of our skulls, carrying with them the sounds of sparrows singing in the eaves of madhouses. Of chocolate decadence, sleek limbs, cheap adventure novels, people we ought not to have anything to do with, and the reflection off the blade.

When I rise at six every morning, and pad into the kitchen naked and still warm from the bed where my wife lies till a decent hour, to begin building my first great mug of Mexican Coatapec or Guatemala Antigua, the first thing I do is turn on the radio to KNX, L.A.'s CBS outlet. And as I spoon in the nutmeg and cardamon, the mortar-and-pestle-ground chocolate from El Popular in East Chicago, Indiana . . . I listen to the doings of my species. I listen to tales from the night before: a fourteen-year-old boy gunned down by *vatos locos* as he walked home from a basketball game; another dead black woman found in a dumpster, possibly the latest victim of the uncatchable South Side Killer; a disgruntled electrician who had been fired by a computer company, who returned with a pump shotgun and blew three night shift workers into pieces; a bomb thrown into a crowded bus station in Colombo, Sri Lanka, by Tamil separatists one week after a hundred men, women and children were machinegunned to death on a rural bus: another 156 dead; another fourteen-year-old boy shoots a truck driver on a bet by a playmate; in Soweto township, South Africa, a grenade thrown into a group of police trainees on a parade ground, shredding the face of a young black man.

These are not guilty pleasures of which we speak here.

These are the manifestations of the amateur sporting events my species has enjoyed for at least the last million years. There is nothing secret about these pleasures. They are as openly trumpeted as home run statistics. They are the cold wind that blows from windows in the soul, whose nails have been prised loose, the sash thrown open wide.

The guilty pleasure of violence that intrigues us. Draughts from the flagon with the dragon, filled with the opiate of the human race. The brew that is true.

One is told that if one wishes to survive a rattlesnake's bite, one should imbibe incrementally larger doses of rattler venom, proceeding from *soupçon* to spoonfuls, to build up a tolerance that results in immunity when the snake strikes. If that is so, then why do we not grow inured to violence? Why must we always have more, and more imaginative, cinematic depictions of slaughter? Do I hear a demur from Canton, Illinois? From teenager John D. Payne, who wrote the editor of this magazine urging him to drop my little essays because I'm always bumrapping "his age-group (those between thirteen and nineteen)" which slavers after rip&rend flicks like turkey vultures after carrion? (That's the species that forks out the eyeballs of the carcass first.) I presume I'm getting these psychometric readings from Johnny D. because everyone in "his age-group" in Canton, Illinois puts in a minimum of forty hours a week doing community service, belongs to the 4-H Club, eschews Bud Light and Maui Wowie, and the police force in Canton, Illinois had to be reduced to one septuagenarian on a Schwinn because of lack of youthful indiscretions. Do I hear another wail of pain for a savaged segment of the species? Or is it possible that the age-group that includes Johnny D., the group for whom knife-kill flicks and Spring Break movies are made because that is the group that spends its newspaper route and chore money to *see* such films, is an age-group that does not consider films of excessive mad violence a guilty pleasure, but an openly-stated staple of its intellectual (?) diet?

354   There *is* a critique of an important new film somewhere in

this essay; but let me run one of my little digressions on you . . . as lead-in to that critique. By way of offering Johnny D. and all of his clean-scrubbed, god-fearing Skippy age-group in Canton, Illinois some data that may persuade them their Frank Capra–like town must be a singular, an anomalous Valhalla, free of the horrors that afflict the rest of the nation. And the digression is this:

On Wednesday, March 27, 1985, at about four in the afternoon, I drove off the CBS Studio Center lot where we'd been filming *The Twilight Zone*—one sort of world in which I live from time to time—and entered the *real* twilight zone. I had been asked (as it turned out, I'd been conned) to speak to the inmates of Central Juvenile Hall. Anybody under eighteen who had committed a crime in Los Angeles serious enough to have drawn time inside, was to be my audience. About seven hundred boys, I'd been told by the "recreation director," name of Ford. It seemed weird to me . . . to be asked to come and lecture kids that age . . . for the most part hardcases convicted of everything from shoplifting to aggravated assault to manslaughter. It had been years since I'd worked with juvenile delinquents, and though I'd spoken at joints where the population had been adults pulling hard time, this was a situation that somehow didn't parse.

Central Juvie, as they call it, is located at the ass-end of nowhere on Eastlake Avenue down in the center of the old city. It is like every other grand slam I've ever entered—big, square, squat and ominous—as much iron and concrete as you'd ever want to be inside—and though Ford was pleasant enough, I soon realized I'd been jobbed by one of the kids working as trusty for him. This kid, unlike all the others I encountered that evening, had been remanded for boosting thousands of dollars' worth of computer equipment; a kid from an upper-class family in the posh Pacific Palisades section of L.A. He was a con man of the first order, and he had been reading my books, and had decided that meeting me would be a nice break in his otherwise boring routine. So he'd lied when he'd called me, telling me that he was an assistant recreation director; he'd lied when he'd told me that the staff had asked him to contact me as part of their "recreation" program; he'd lied when he'd told me the kids were big fans of my work and were anxious to hear what I might have to say about this'n'that.

But I was in it before I figured out that I'd been hustled. (Remember: your brain never outgrows its need to have games run on it.)

I had imagined it would be one session of talking to the few inmates who gave a damn that a live human being had come in to take up the slack of their empty hours, but I soon found out that it would be *three* separate encounters. The older kids were assembled at one time, the younger at another, and a third off-the-cuff presentation after I'd had dinner with them. Jail food is no better now than it was years ago when I'd been compelled to eat it.

All went fairly well through the first two meetings. There were mostly trusties at the dinner thing. And the younger kids in the second get-together responded well enough to anecdotes about old gang days in Brooklyn and running away from home and staying smart enough to avoid people who'd skin you...the kind of bullshit a fifty-year-old man hopes won't bore a ten-year-old kid serving time for bludgeoning an eighty-year-old woman for her social security money and food stamps. I don't fool myself that I was of any value beyond distraction of the same sort that could be provided by watching a mouse work on a slice of Wonder Bread. All I wanted to accomplish—after I got hip to what was *really* happening—was to recount enough anecdotes not to bore the ass off them. It went fairly well.

Then came the session for the older boys who had been fed on the second shift, who had been given the head 'em up, move 'em out treatment through the showers, and who had been *ordered* to attend the evening's festivities. Under the direction of guards with billy clubs—evident but not used—seventy or so teenaged boys were herded into a large day room with chairs set up around the perimeter. My chair was in the center of the ring.

They looked at me as if I'd come from Mars. Or Beverly Hills. The latter no more alien than the former to street kids from Watts and the *barrio*. I confess to trepidation: only twice, in all the times I have been inside the joint as a visitor, have I felt fear. Once, on a journey to Death Row at San Quentin (about which I've written elsewhere)...and at Central Juvie that evening, surrounded by kids as cold and mean as any I've ever been around. These were children who had killed, raped, set fires that incinerated whole families; who had been in *pachuco* street gangs since they could walk, who had been heavy dopers since they could swallow, who had discovered just how crummy the world can be for those the city pretends don't exist. (Not knee-jerk Liberalism, only pragmatic observation.) Few of them could read anything beyond the level of comic books, all of them came with a freightload of anger and distrust that could be physically felt. They sat there, under the gaze of the guards, waiting and watching this Martian from Beverly Hills.

I'd sent on ahead, earlier that week, a carton of paperbacks. Fifty mint copies of MEMOS FROM PURGATORY, a book I'd written about gangs, and about being in jail. So now, seeing the veil that hung between me and my "audience," I asked one of the guards if the books had been given to the kids. (Hoping, I suppose, that the reality of holding a book in one's hands would lend some credibility to the person sitting in front of them.)

All the boys looked at one of the guards, a man who seemed to be in charge. He looked chagrined for a moment, then muttered that the box had been kept in the office. I got the immediate message that those books had been picked over by the staff, and if the occasion presented itself to reward one of the inmates, a paperback book might be liberated from the cache.

I said, "Well, I'll tell you what: let's haul that box out and we'll pass around some books so these guys know I'm at least what I say I am."

There was a moment's hesitation. The guard was clearly not overjoyed with my suggestion. But there wasn't much he could do about it. Not in front of seventy pairs of eyes watching to see where the control was going to come to rest.

He nodded to the guard nearest the door, and he left. In a few minutes the box had been *shlepped* in, and set at my feet. It had been opened. Ten or fifteen copies were gone. I asked the boy nearest me to assist, and we handed out as many of the books as remained. I gave them a few minutes to examine the artifacts, and then the weirdness that prompts this digression began.

"Hey, man," one of the kids said, turning the book over and over in his hands, "what is that?"

I thought he was kidding. "It's a book. I wrote it."

"No it ain't," he said.

"Like hell," I said. "It's my book . . . I wrote it."

"How do I know that?"

"Because it's got my name on the front cover, bigger than the title."

"The what?"

"The title. The name of the book."

"Where's that?"

I realized at that point that he wasn't hosing me. He had no idea what a title was, and maybe couldn't even read it—or my name—if he *did* understand which was which.

I got up and walked across the big circle to him. The others

357

watched, still holding their copies as if they were plates of something wet and slippery they'd been ordered to eat. I leaned over the kid and pointed to my name. "See that. 'Harlan Ellison.' That's me."

"How come?"

"Because I wrote it."

"What'cha mean, you wrote it? You wrote this?" And his finger pointed to the letters that made up my name above the title. It took me a moment to understand that he thought I'd been saying I'd written *those two words*. "No," I said, very carefully, riffling the pages of the book he held, "I wrote all of this. Every word in here."

"Get outta town!" he said, and I could see other boys in their chairs also riffling the pages, as if they'd never examined a book this close up in their lives. He didn't believe me.

"I'm not kidding." I said. "This's what I do for a living. I write books and movies and tv."

He looked at me with the look that says *you got to open the sack before I'll believe there's a cat in there.* "How do I know that's you?"

I turned the book over. My picture was on the back cover. That should do it. "That's me," I said.

He looked closely at me, hovering over him, then he looked at the photo again. "No, it ain't."

Kafka had programmed the evening. "Sure it is," I said, "look at it . . . that's me . . . can't you see it?"

"No it ain't," he said. "This guy ain't wearin' no glasses."

Miguel De Unamuno once wrote: "In order to attain the impossible one must attempt the absurd."

I took off my glasses. "They took that picture of me about five years ago," I said. "It's me. Look close." He looked, and looked back, and looked at the photo again; and reluctantly he decided I wasn't lying to make myself a big man. Then he riffled the pages again. "You wrote all this in here?"

I nodded. "Can you read it?"

He got cold and angry. "Yeah. I can, if I want to."

I didn't push it.

But when I returned to my chair, with most of them still holding the books as if they didn't know what to do with such alien objects, one of them yelled across the room, "You write movies?"

"Yeah. And the stuff you see on teevee," I said, thankful for *any* point of entry.

And here's where the digression ties in.

Another kid yelled, "You write that *Friday the Thirteen, Part Two?*"

"No," I said, smiling, not knowing what was about to transpire, "I don't like movies where people get stuck with icepicks. I don't even *go* to that kind of—"

(What an asshole, Ellison! Don't just put in the time and make the best of a bum deal, don't just try to keep them distracted for an hour, be a hotshot: give 'em a moral! Jeezus, what a nitwit, Ellison! Go get your brain lubed.)

I may still have been speaking, but they didn't hear it. They were now yelling back and forth to one another. They were, for the first time, animated, interested, excited. And here's what they were saying:

"Oh, yeah, man, didju see that part where the woman gets the axe in her back?"

"Yeah, that was cool. She wuz crawlin' 'cross the floor, an' the guy was cuttin' on her!"

"That was okay, but you see that one where the guy stuck that bitch through the mouth with the power drill an' the guy who's comin' to save her sees the drill come down through the ceiling upstairs?!!!"

"Oooh, *yeah!* That was cool ... but didju see ..."

How, I wondered insanely, could he remember which part movie of the *Friday the 13th* series it had been?

I tried shouting into that maelstrom of voices. Almost every kid in the room was enthusiastically recounting his favorite slaughter scene to some kid sitting in the circle. And their voices rose and rose in the cage, and they got into it, warmed it in their mouths, relishing every nuance, recounting every cinematic trick that had been used to hook them—squirting eyeballs, faces ripped away in bloody strips, limbs torn off but still quivering, the stroke of the muscled arm as the razor came away festooned. And on, and on, and on ...

When I left Central Juvie, the recreation director Ford, having had an evening of recreation, took pleasure in my stunned condition. The nice white boy from showbiz looked as if he'd been gutted. He thanked me prettily for donating my valuable oh so valuable time to these deserving unfortunates; and he smiled straight and hard and with obvious amusement into my look of horror; and I stumbled out into the lightless, empty parking lot, got into my car, dropped my keys, fumbled in the darkness for them, and got out of there as if the demons of hell were after me.

Not for the first time did I cast back in memory to the time
Bob Heinlein described to me the horror he had felt when he'd
learned that Charlie Manson adored STRANGER IN A STRANGE
LAND, thought of it as his bible, and had named his child Valentine Michael Smith. But for the first time I *knew* how Bob had
felt. For the first time, in all the times I had had that intellectual
discussion with myself and others about the responsibility of
what a writer writes, was I frozen at the point of knowledge that
yes, maybe, yes, what we write has a demonstrable effect on
them.

Don't ask me, please, to identify "them." I mean the *them* who
go to see larger-than-life-size mayhem on the silver screen and
think of those fantasies of gore as templates for reality.

These films that teenagers go to see so avidly. These films
that make box-office millions from ticket sales to teenagers.
These films that John D. Payne of Canton, Illinois tells me "his
age-group" does not condone, if I read the psychometric messages correctly.

These secret icons. These guilty pleasures.

No, I'm not talking about *those* guilty pleasures. At least, I
don't think I am. What I'm talking about, is secretly loving the
films of Ken Russell, the way you secretly love Baby Ruth bars
and *Gilligan's Island* reruns, and won't cop to such love in open
court. I think what I'm talking about is admiring and secretly
loving the violence and ruthlessness in Ken Russell films,
brought to these pages now on the release of Russell's latest film,
GOTHIC (Virgin Vision and Vestron Pictures).

Ken Russell. Where do I begin . . .

Once I wrote that, in my view, there were only seven genius-level directors currently working in film. Just seven. That is,
Directors. Unmistakable talents of the highest order of Art. I
named them: Altman, Coppola, Fellini, Kurosawa, Resnais,
Kubrick and (then alive) Buñuel. I hastened to add that this list
was not intended to denigrate the work of other directors, merely
that I saw all the others as *craftspersons*. As creative intellects of
greater or lesser ability—from, say, Woody Allen and David
Cronenberg and Ron Howard above, to Brian De Palma and
Frank Perry post-1974 and Alan Rudolph (always) below. (Not to
mention Richard Land, Mark L. Lester and Joe Zito, from whom
all is dross and chaff.)

I fudged the list. I was reluctant to endanger the credibility of
that list of seven by including Ken Russell. But if my definition
of *directorial genius* is the one by which my opinions stand or fall,

then Russell makes that short-list, despite his lunacy and colossal pratfalls, his mind-boggling gaffes and infantile obsessions.

(Definition: the genius director is one whose work bears little or no resonance of any predecessor; whose work is so determinedly *his* that even if you walk in during the middle of the film, you can look up and say, "Fellini" or "Kurosawa"; whose work is never safe, never calm, never predictable; whose work never elicits the phrase, as one leaves the theater, "That was a nice film." Examples: *Providence*; *Paths of Glory*; *Dersu Uzala*; *The Godfather, Part Two*; *La Strada*; *McCabe and Mrs. Miller*; *Los Olvidados*.)

There is no other Fellini, no other Kubrick, no other Kurosawa. Try to think of one. Try to fit any others into all the points of that compass. Some come close. Some may yet reach that Apennine headiness of individuality. Most will, at best, only get as staggeringly superlative as Capra or Ford or Von Stroheim or Wilder at their breathtaking best. That is not, as you can see, chopped liver.

But there is a craziness, a disregard for approbation, a dismissal of posterity, a dangerous recklessness in those seven and in Ken Russell (and in Orson Welles), that sets them above and apart. In my view.

Notwithstanding all of the preceding, no one will hit me with a brick if I name the seven and say they can't be touched; but let me add that guilty pleasure Ken Russell, and all of my well-ordered theorizing crumbles. Laughter begins. People will point their fingers and then make circular motions with that finger alongside their ear. They will stare and wonder how anyone who admires Kurosawa can even *tolerate* the blatancy, the gagging bad taste, the ri*dic*ulousness of Ken Russell! I mean, fer pete's sake, do you remember that idiotic scene in *The Music Lovers* where Russell accompanied the cannons in the "1812 Overture" with the heads being blown off mannequins bearing the visages of characters from Tchaikovsky's life? Come *on*! That was sophomoric . . . no, hell, it was downright dopey!

Hold the brick.

Yes, that was downright dopey. And in *every* Ken Russell film there is dopiness; pure Howdy Doody time. And there is excess. And there is bad taste. And there is imaginary gone bugfuck. And there are performances by actors who seem to have dined *alfresco* on jimson weed.

But in that same film, *The Music Lovers*, Ken Russell put on celluloid the single most frightening cinematic image I can remember in nearly fifty years of moviegoing. (Because the morbidly curious will demand I specify, I will recount it here for you. If you are easily shocked, or even if you are hard to shock, I urge you to skip to the paragraph below beginning with the big bullet: ● I am not being facetious. There is no coy duplicity in my warning. I am not trying to titillate you with a "guilty pleasure." What I will describe rocked me even when I saw it; the theater audience with whom I shared the raw experience was moved in large numbers to depart the screening. You have been alerted. Read on if you wish, but don't send one of those outraged letters to the Noble Ferman Editors; if you remained, it was free choice.)

In *The Music Lovers*, a bizarre film biography of Pëtr Ilich Tchaikovsky that distorts historical fact and the flow of the composer's real life to Russell's nefarious ends, we are presented with an encounter in the open yard of a madhouse between Tchaikovsky's nymphomaniac wife, Antonina Milyukova, and her mother. Nina (who actually only lived with Tchaikovsky for a few weeks) has been consigned to bedlam by the mother who, in the film, is portrayed as a monster who has pimped her daughter to well-heeled gentlemen in Moscow. Nina is so far gone into lunacy that the mother presents these callers (who have been told they can fuck "Tchaikovsky's wife" for a few rubles) as "Rimsky-Korsakov," "Mussorgsky," "Borodin." Nina has already slipped so far into suicidal psychosis that she accepts the duplicitous fantasy, and becomes a merchandised sex object for her mother's gain. She contracts syphilis, goes completely out of her head, and is sent to the institution. (In fact, this happened three years after Tchaikovsky's death, but Russell uses it to his own purposes as having happened while Tchaikovsky was still a youngish man.)

The mother, decked out in rare plumage, silks and a haughty manner, comes to see her daughter. Nina, played by Glenda Jackson, joins her in the exercise yard. All around we see barred windows and grates set into the ground, and from these cell openings we see hands and scabrous arms reaching, reaching, imploring. Jammed into every cell in this awful place are those the nineteenth century chose to lock away rather than attempt to understand and cure. The screams. The wails of the damned. It is as flamboyant and sickeningly sensual as Russell has ever been. Nina is covered with running sores, her eyes red-rimmed and lit with the fire of lunacy. She wears a gray rough-cloth shift that billows around her feet.

They have a conversation that only faintly touches on reality. And at the end of the chat, Nina wanders coquettishly toward one of those grates in the cobblestones, from which hands reach, from which fingers writhe like fat white worms, against which faces of demented men are pressed, their rheumy eyes shining out like those of rats in a sewer.

And with the grace of a royal courtesan, Nina begins to lower herself onto the grating, thighs wide, bending at the knees, settling down like an ashy flower, shift spread wide around her to cover the grate. She settles down till she is pressed to the grate, naked beneath her garment; and as the mother (and we) watch in disbelief, we hear the slurping, sucking sounds of those diseased madmen working at the secret places of Tchaikovsky's mad wife.

● To those rejoining us, relax: you're safe now. For those who traveled through the preceding four paragraphs with me, I cannot apologize for having demonstrated my eloquent *gueule*—which translates from the French, roughly, as "bad mouth." As George Orwell once pointed out, "There are some situations from which one can only escape by acting like a devil or a madman." Real Art has the capacity to make us nervous. In my view, that scene is Real Art. Twisted, depraved, wildly disturbing Art, but Real Art nonetheless. It is the essence of Russell's raw power to capture something infinitely darker in the human psyche than Lovecraft at his most beguiling. I cannot apologize for exposing you to Art, no matter how deeply it distresses either of us. It is important, if you are to understand why I perceive Russell as a Great Director, that specifics be tendered.

For all of his shenanigans and his belly-whoppers, Ken Russell uses film to look at things we not only don't care to see, but to look at things we don't even imagine exist!

Does that not lie near to the burning center of what we seek in fantasy literature? The unknowable. The inexplicable. The monstrous that abides in sweet humanity. Is it not what we see corrupted and ineptly proffered by the slasher-film directors? Does it not tear at our perceptions in ways that treacly abominations like *Short Circuit* and *Gremlins* cannot?

So here we have Russell's vision of that single night—June 16, 1816—in the Villa Diodati near Geneva, Switzerland; a night on the shores of Lac Leman in which the opium addicted poet Percy Bysshe Shelley, in the company of his lover, Mary Godwin, her

363

wild half-sister Claire, Dr. Polidori, and their cruelly jesting host Lord Byron, experience the debauchery and reckless mind-games that will one day produce Polidori's THE VAMPYRE (from which, authorities argue, DRACULA and the genre of horror fiction as we know it, proceeds) and Mary Shelley's FRANKENSTEIN.

In fact, the session went on among these five for an entire summer; but Russell gives us a night of storm and drugs and sex and terror and frenetic submission to the moist and gagging secret fears that encapsulates for dramatic effect, all that transpired during that legendary encounter.

The film has the surrealistic feel of such classics as Arrabal's 1970 *Viva la Muerte (Hurrah for Death)*, Buñuel and Dali's 1928 *Un Chien Andalou* and Jean Cocteau's 1950 *Orphée*. Mark my caution: this is nowhere near being in a class with such great films, but it has the same *sensibility*. Images flash and burn and flee almost before we have had the moment to set them correctly into the jigsaw. An attack by a suit of armor culminates in the helmet's visor being thrown up to reveal a face of raw meat writhing with leeches. A painting on a wall, representative of the work of Henry Fuseli, showing a troggish demon astride the naked body of an houri, comes to life and Mary sees herself as the violated victim. It is an Odilon Redon nightmare come to the tender membrane of sanity and clawing its way into the real world. It is redolent with symbolism.

Much of that symbolism is ludicrous: Miriam Cyr as Claire, in a laudanum-induced vision as perceived by Shelley, bares her breasts, and in place of nipples there are staring eyes... which blink at him. The audience roars with laughter. Russell had overindulged his adolescent fantasies.

And this excess, ultimately, undermines the film. What was there to be discovered, is revealed at last to be the silliness and self-indulgence of people we find foolish and vain and empty. As Mary Godwin and Lord Byron and Polidori and Shelley were not. Like a child trying too hard to get the attention of adults, finally pissing on the living room carpet, Russell's conceit shreds itself with its strumpet-painted nails. It is too diffuse, too bizarre, too distorted to be taken seriously.

By presenting the accumulated phantasms of a summer in one night's grisly carrying-on, Russell has reduced the premier idea of a horror film to the level of Bogdanovich's *What's Up, Doc?*—a running, jumping and standing still charade; the shipboard stateroom scene from the Marx Bros.' *A Night at the Opera*. Distorted closeups like parodies of shots from Sergio Leone westerns. Icons of slime, rats, ichor, cobwebs, dirt, meat, blood, water. Gothic? No, more precisely, rococo; grotesquerie piled on grotesquerie without pause, without release, without a moment for reflection. Formless, over the top, obsessively goofy...such screaming and running around and eye-rolling that we perceive the film as one cacophonous shriek. While at the same time it takes itself so seriously we feel we must laugh behind our hand. And all of this played out to Thomas Dolby's molar-grinding electronic score. Whatever happened to real symphony orchestras, playing scores by Waxman and Newman and Rosza, as background for "big" pictures such as this?

No one in his or her right mind could truly be said to "like" this film, for in this film no one is in his or her right mind; and so we have no place to moor our sympathy.

At final consideration, *Gothic* is loopy and fatally flawed and an aberration.

Yet I treasure this film. So may you. If you, as am I, are out of your head...you will cleave to this tortured bit of cinematic epilepsy because it is *alive*. It is yet another crime of passion committed by Ken Russell, and his sort of berserk creativity has fallen on such hard times in this age of Reagan and yuppie sensibility, that simply to be exposed to the ravings of an inspired madman is cathartic.

I came away from *Gothic* with my soul on fire.

It drove me to this essay, all 5000 + words of it.

Back to the Future had no such effect on me. Nor have any of the hundred or so films I've seen in the last six months had anything remotely like that effect. We live in a time of "safe" art that is noway art, but merely artifice. *Gothic* frightens, after the fact, because it is dangerously conceived, impudently mounted, uncaring of its footing, determined to crawl the wall or tumble into the abyss, all in the name of disgorging the absurd demon in the thought.

I cannot in conscience recommend *Gothic* to anyone. You would no doubt lynch me. But I tell you this: for every teenager in Canton, Illinois who would have us believe his "age-group" is free of potential slashers, there are a hundred slashers-in-waiting within the bedlam cells of our natures to populate a Lovecraftian duchy; for every insipid film that rakes in millions by offering 1980s visions of floating ethics and looking out for #1, there are greedyguts viewers who see such films as a license to indulge moral turpitude; and for every nut-case like your faithful columnist, who tells you to embrace a wonky failure like *Gothic* be-

365

cause a pulse beats in it, a pulse that signifies life means more than what one finds confined to the screen of a tv set, there will be legions who tell you disorder is chaos, riot is recklessness, art is quantifiable.

The final assertion of critical judgment on *Gothic* is not whether or not it is good, or whether one likes it or not. The undeniable truth of *Gothic*, as in all the work of Ken Russell (an artist who is either so mad or so foolhardy as not to care if he wins or loses), is that it is palpably *alive*. It is riot and ruin and pandemonium. But it will have you by the nerve-ends.

And isn't that what Real Art is supposed to do? Even in Canton, Illinois?

INSTALLMENT 26:
In Which A Good Time Was Had By All And An Irrelevant Name-Dropping Of Fritz Leiber Occurs For No Better Reason Than To Remind Him How Much We Love And Admire Him

Though her name be not Calliope, Euterpe, Thalia or any of the other six, a Muse of my East Coast acquaintance also happens to be on a first-name basis with John Updike, and she happened to mention a month or two ago that Updike had said the new Warner Bros. film adaptation of his 1984 fantasy THE WITCHES OF EASTWICK only superficially resembled the novel, but it sure as hell captured the feeling of the book.

Now, this was not Updike's first picnic in the enchanted forest of our mythic genre. Back in 1963, he did a sorta kinda symbolic fantasy called THE CENTAUR. It is my least favorite of all the fifteen or sixteen Updike books I've read. No, let me be more specific: surgeons have it easier; they are blessed and cursed with the ability to bury their mistakes; novelists have to live with the walking dead of their failed efforts. THE CENTAUR made my hide itch. I ground away valuable layers of tooth enamel during the reading.

So it was with considerable pleasure that I found Updike's second sojourn down our way considerably more successful. (Like all of us who have access to the range and spiced variety of fantasy literature that includes writers *The New York Review of Books* has never even heard of, I often find myself subscribing to the Accepted Wisdom that visitors from The Mainstream more often than not make asses of themselves when they decide to try their hand at what we do. I am ashamed when I catch myself thinking that way; and for every Doris Lessing, Herman Wouk, Jacqueline Susann, Taylor Caldwell or Andrew Greeley who makes us rend our flesh and spit up our breakfast, there is an appositely wonderful Peter Straub, Naomi Mitchison, John Hersey, Peter Carey or Russell Hoban who teaches us old dogs some new tricks. So it is surely unfair to me, of us, to go to our graves bearing that ignoble misconception. So I was *happy* that Updike pulled it off, rather than wallowing in smug pleasure at his earlier misstep.)

While it is impossible to read *any* novel in which suburban witches appear in a contemporary setting without taking out the prayer rug and intoning the hallowed names of Fritz Leiber and CONJURE WIFE, Updike's literary conceit is a good read, an honest reexamination of the basic fantasy construct, and is filled with some of his liveliest writing.

What would be made of the book by the Tony and Pulitzer Prize-winning playwright Michael Cristofer, the brilliant *Mad Max* director George Miller, and the "hot" but frequently tasteless producers Peter Guber and Jon Peters (we're talking here *Flashdance, A Star Is Born, The Deep* and *The Color Purple*, among others), was anybody's guess. But the odds weren't terribly terrific. Updike ain't that easy to translate onto celluloid, and the stats of previous attempts look like readouts on the value of the Mexican *peso*.

But I am here to tell you that *The Witches of Eastwick* is great fun. Get it out of your head that it's Updike's book, scene for scene, or line for line, or even character for character. But no matter how you saw Darryl Van Horne (they've dropped one of the "r"s from his first name in the film), Alexandra, Jane and Sukie in the novel, you would have to possess the soul of a pigeon-kicker to object to the interpretations of those characters by Jack Nicholson, Cher, Susan Sarandon and Michelle Pfeiffer. Veronica Cartwright and Richard Jenkins are also not too dusty as Felicia and Clyde Alden.

Updike's Eastwick, Rhode Island (found and filmed in Cohasset, Massachusetts) is the safe, settled Late George Apleyesque cubbyhole of life in which Alex, Jane and Sukie mark off the days of their lives as victims of "the dreaded three D's": death, desertion and divorce. Alex's husband is dead, Jane's husband has divorced, and Sukie's old man has deserted, leaving her with six daughters.

The women possess "the source," the secret power of witch-craft that *all* men—naïvely or cynically—believe lies in the female. (Van Horne delivers a brief but impassioned codification of this cliché near the beginning of the film and, near the end, does it again with the kid gloves off, inquiring whether God has made women as a mistake or as some sort of ghastly punishment for men. I take no side in this matter. I merely report what is on the screen.) This power manifests itself fully only with the arrival in Eastwick—perhaps by wish-fulfillment of the women's group fantasy—of "a prince traveling under a dark curse... very handsome... with a cock neither too large nor too small, but right in the middle": Daryl (one "r") Van Horne.

Well, Jack Nicholson may be many things, but "handsome" ain't one of them. There is too much pasta in that face. Yet in a few minutes, like the exquisite three women, we are conned into accepting Nicholson and Van Horne as just such a "dark prince." And he proceeds, without too much butter, to seduce all three of them. To tell you more would steal from you that which you deserve: the pleasure of getting coshed over the noggin by a satanically charming romp courtesy of all concerned.

And even if Fritz Leiber did most of this to perfection in 1943, preceded only by René Clair, Fredric March, Veronica Lake, Cecil Kellaway and Robert Benchley (from a screenplay by Robert Pirosh and Marc Connelly) in 1942's *I Married A Witch*, you would have to be the kind of person who enjoys pissing on the snowy egret to carp about this delicious film.

As Stan Lee would put it, 'nuff said!

But:

Unceasing in my efforts to broaden your filmgoing experience (and by way of thanking all of you for saving Woody Allen's life by retroactively awarding him a Hugo for *Sleeper* in 1974, which fannish largesse was imparted to him on the operating table, thereby giving him the will to live), I have preserved my notes from the Warner Bros. screening, and I offer them here in brief, to give you things to watch for.

• The Writers Guild fought long and hard for proper credit onscreen for the scenarist(s). But notice, when you go to see *The Witches of Eastwick*, how cunningly the Directors Guild has circumvented the rules. All but two of the opening credits are committed, concluding with the writer, before there is an intrusion of a complete scene. Then, after that space, we return to more bucolic camerawork (by the inspired Vilmos Zsigmond, who could make rice pudding as breathtaking as Walden Pond) and in

369

the artistic respite that follows, the downtime, as it were, they flash the producers' and director's credits. It isn't *exactly* a degrading-to-writers cheat, but in terms of cinematic vocabulary, of what the eye sees and registers, it is a now-commonplace dodge that establishes who is below the salt and who ain't. Watch for it. Notice it.

• The editing by Richard Francis-Bruce is marvelous. Very suspenseful. Particularly in the ways in which it is integrated with what may be the best film score by John Williams in a decade. The aural package melded to the visual freight, is as good as anything you'll currently find on the big screen. It *looks* like a movie, not just another of those slambang tv eye-rippers tossed into the microwave and toughened up for theater release.

• Note the intelligence of everyone in the film. People may act weirdly, but consistently. There are no dopes in this story. Which is a tribute to Cristofer and the canny players, because Updike gave us a fantasy trope, and the scenarist and actors have rendered it mimetically, sequentially, logically.

• Catch the flies. Every time Nicholson comes onscreen, we get a not-obtrusive LORD OF THE FLIES echo. More would have been to pull a Spielberg ("Hey, looka me! See how well I know my subtext! See how cute I am!") and less would have been lost in the rush of the story.

• Consider if it isn't time to send a letter to your regional movie *maven*, to suggest we may indeed have had enough vomiting scenes in films. *The Exorcist* did it as well as any of us cared to have it done, and if *quality* of puke were not sufficient, Terry Gilliam gave us Mr. Creosote in *Monty Python's The Meaning of Life* for sheer *quantity*. Beyond those seminal upchuck icons, all else is, well, simply parking the tiger. Calico carpet comment. What I mean, mate, you seen one spring-loaded tsunami of york, you've seen it all, in't it?

• The tennis scene. See and delight. Then catch the resonance from the ultimate sequence in Antonioni's *Blow-Up* (1966). Upper crust athletic activity as mystical ritual.

• If costume designer Aggie Guerard Rodgers doesn't get an Oscar for Jack Nicholson's wardrobe (provided by Cerruti 1881 Paris), then we ought to call in Lt. Col. Oliver North to start collecting funds for the overthrow of Hollywood's Academy.

• Rob Bottin's special makeup effects. Are you, as am I, getting weary of that same Bottin monster look? Would you kindly pay some attention to it in this film and ask your kids or the nearest SFX freak if it doesn't look boringly as if Bottin uses the same damned slavering, hunching critter every time, with a bit more or a bit less hair. Tell his mother. Bottin's, not the critter's.

In conclusion: I'm not sure John Updike would like one of his serious novels thought of as simply great fun, but that's the way this film has turned out. And unless I'm off my feed, I think you'll look at this drollery and recognize it as a germinal piece of American cinema. One of those films people will use as reference for years to come. A very *American* movie, beautifully directed by an Australian, co-produced by a talented ex-hairdresser (we'll never let you get above your station, Jon), persuasively acted by three of the most seductive women in film today, and written with brio by a man who should be kept working at his craft by whips, if necessary.

Even Fritz Leiber will enjoy this one.

INSTALLMENT 27:
In Which The Fur Is Picked Clean of Nits, Gnats, Nuts, Naggers And Nuhdzes

Because it might get nasty, I've been putting off having this little chat with you. But when I walked in this evening, your mother told me you'd been absolutely *impossible* all day —"just wait till your father gets home!"—so just ignore the fact that I've removed my belt and have it lying here waiting for you to cop an attitude; and let us discuss this stuff as calmly as possible.

First, let's get this understood: unless I lose my mind entirely and make the error of savaging someone so scurrilously that it falls beyond the First Amendment's protection of opinion and criticism—which is simply not gonna happen as I have recently won a bogus, six-year-long slander suit brought against me and a magazine to which I gave an interview, and I am up to *here* in casebook law smarts about what berserk lengths one would have to go, to write something truly actionable—there is no way your cranky letters will convince The Editors Ferman to drop this column. That righteously ain't gonna happen, so save your breath.

Let me tell you *why* that ain't gonna happen...

Oh, wait a minute. Just so you don't think this entire column will be housekeeping, cleaning up ancillary hokey-pokey, here is a review for you.

ROBOCOP (Orion), despite its popularity, is as vicious a piece of wetwork* as anything I've encountered in recent memory. Devoid of even the faintest scintilla of compassion or common-sense, it is as low as the foreheads of those members of the screening audience who cheered and laughed at each escalated scene of violence. It is a film about, and intended for, no less than brutes. It is a film that struck me as being made by, and for, savages and ghouls. Written by Edward Neumeier and Michael Miner, and directed by the Dutchman Paul Verhoeven, this is a template for everything rabid and drooling in our culture. That it has been touted—after the fact—as being a "satirical" film, a "funny" film, is either ass-covering or a genuine representation of the filmmaker's ethically myopic view of what they've spawned. If the former, it's despicable hypocrisy; if the latter, that's just flat scary.

It is also, clearly and shockingly, a ripoff of the *Judge Dredd* comic strip from the U.K. And if the creators and owners of that character fail to initiate a copyright infringement action against producer Jon Davison, Orion and the scenarists, they are missing what is, in my opinion, an opportunity to get rich by bringing what appear to be literary graverobbers to justice. Stay away from this one at all costs.

Now, where were we? Right.

Why it isn't in the cards that your outraged letters will convince the management of this publication that I am a blot on their table of contents.

These essays are exceedingly popular.

Despite the half dozen or so letters that have been passed on to me, complaining about . . . well, I'll tell you what they've been complaining about in a moment . . . there have been hundreds of letters commending the work. And even when one of you stomps his/her widdle foot and demands his/her subscription be terminated forthwith, it isn't even a piddle matched against the occasional readers who have subscribed just so they *can* be assured of getting the material. (It's also bone stupid, and severs nose from noggin just to spite itself, because this is a *wonderful* magazine, filled every month with the best writing being done in the genre, and maybe some of the best being done in America in *any* form; with Budrys and Asimov working at the peak of their form in

---

*"Wetwork": the "intelligence community's" currently fashionable doublespeak for the dirtiest of dirty deeds, the act of assassination, termination with extreme unction, or whatever.

their specialties; and just ripping out or flipping past that which offends thee, is far more rational.)

Now we come to the bottom line, which is purely that ten times the number of you who fret over my essays tell the Fermans and me that the first thing they turn to is *Watching*. And that is just the letters received. Most readers are decent folks who either like what they're getting, or flip past/rip out what they're getting that they *don't* like. So unless a groundswell of vituperation is raised, and an economically-potent segment of the readership says it's had enough, we're going to be locked in this literary embrace for some time to come.

I must make a clear distinction here, about the types of letters we get. There are times when I make mistakes, either out of ignorance or slipped memory, and those of you who bring me to task for such errors are dear and valuable to me. At such times, I make every effort to retrace my steps in a later column, to clean up the picnic grounds, as it were:

(F'rinstance. Two issues ago, in reviewing *Gothic*, I opined that director Ken Russell was indulging his adolescent fantasies when he presented us with a scene in which the poet Shelley has a vision of Claire Clairmont's breasts with eyes that blink in place of nipples. Three or four readers—most notably Margaret L. Carter, Ph.D. and Teresa Nielsen Hayden—hurriedly [but politely, informedly] advised me that "every well-read devotee of Gothic horror knows that Shelley actually experienced such a vision... It's in writing... Shelley was inspired by a cryptic passage from Coleridge's 'Christabel,' describing the vampire-witch Geraldine: 'Behold! her bosom and half her side—a sight to dream of, not to tell!' "

(I freely cop to not being as encyclopedic in my familiarity with Gothic literature as many of you, but, in fact, I *was* aware of the referent. Nor is there anything in what I actually *wrote* that indicates otherwise. Here is what I wrote:

> It is redolent with symbolism.
> Much of that symbolism is ludicrous: Miriam Cyr as Claire, in a laudanum-induced vision as perceived by Shelley, bares her breasts, and in place of nipples there are staring eyes... which blink at him. The audience roars with laughter. Russell had over-indulged his adolescent fantasies.

(What I was saying—and I think clearly—was that Russell had made an *artistic choice* in showing breast-eyes that blink. I then described the reaction of an audience *to that choice*. The

375

question raised by readers familiar with the actual historic background, is moot. Whether the image as presented by Russell sprang from the director's imagination, or from Shelley's, is beside the point.

(Frequently, in writers' workshops I've taught, someone will hand in a story in which something happens that is of great importance to the writer, but which does not work on the page. And when it is brought to the writer's attention that it isn't believable, the unvarying response is, "But this *really* happened to my cousin Ernie and his wife. I was there, I saw it happen." To which, the proper reply is precisely the same I offer to Dr. Carter and Teresa: it doesn't *matter* if it's true; it matters if we *believe* it's true. The question, thus, devolves not on authenticity, but verisimilitude. This is a lesson difficult to impart to novice writers, for whom craft and expertise come only with time and trial.

(What I said in that snippet of the essay, was that Ken Russell, as the guiding intelligence behind the film, had *chosen* to show breasts with eyes . . . and then to make them blink. Now it is possible that merely the sight of the eyes would not have sent the audience into paroxysms of hilarity; but topping the grotesquerie by having those nipple-orbs *blink* was pure vaudeville; and the audience responded appropriately, thereby breaking the mood of bizarre fascination Russell was striving for. I was writing about a *film*, friends, not trying to demonstrate how arcane my wisdom might be.

(The interesting thing here, it seems to me, is that not one of the persons who called me on this "omission," had seen the movie. I was being chided for *apparently* not knowing something, even though the knowing or not-knowing didn't mean a whistle in context. For the purpose of the critique, I gave every bit of information that was needed.

(And as Einstein once observed, "Everything should be made as simple as possible. But not simpler."

(Get what I'm saying here? *Gothic* was not a film in which Shelley's fantasies, adolescent or otherwise, were being presented; it was a film in which Ken Russell's *interpretation* of those fantasies was being presented. The choice was not Shelley's, it was Russell's. And in my view—shared with a large audience—it was a ludicrous artistic choice.

(And isn't that what film, or book, or dance, or art criticism is about? The correctness of choices. The coherent and effective vision that coalesces from a congeries of artistic selections.)

376   With such letters, I have no problem. The careful reader has

caught what may or may not be a slip in the critic's mantle of authority. As we have nothing to go on with a critic but our agreement to trust him/her and his/her viewpoint based on past performance, it is absolutely proper—and appreciated—for the careful reader to suggest, "You seemed not to know such&such, and this puts your infallibility in shadow. Please comment."

But there is another sort of letter. It is the splenic rodomontade that is intended to dismay the editors and pique my animosity. These are written by people who need attention. As one who needs attention, and who works out that need in a constructive manner by pursuing a career in which I write what I want to be noticed, I am on to these twits from line one, in which they say things almost always like this:

"You think you're pretty cute, don't you, Mr. Allison. Well, my name is George S- - - - - - - , and you've never heard of me, but I just wanted to tell you that you're rude and stupid and not nearly as sharp as you think you are . . ." (But then, George, who among us *is*?)

These letters almost always go via the editors, and lament the leavetaking of the former film observer from these pages, suggesting that said person should be sought out with sled-dogs and sonar, and be brought back to that previous state of critical beatitude. On pain of having George's subscription canceled, should the suggested program not be adopted.

Well, forget that, too. It ain't gonna happen.

So if it isn't legitimate attempts to have errors corrected, to what complaints *do* I object?

There are three, basically.

1) Ellison doesn't do reviews. He does these long, weird essays that once in a while *mention* a movie.

2) The first rule of being a columnist is that s/he will appear in each and every issue of the publication. Ellison keeps appearing irregularly. He'll do three or four in a row, then miss a month.

3) Ellison usually talks about movies that have come and gone from the theaters. He doesn't give us reviews that we can use as a guide to what to see.

There is also a lesser 4) which speaks to my not "reviewing everything," which usually means I've missed telling you about the latest autopsy movie in which a doorway to Hell opens in the basement of a boutique in a shopping mall built over an ancient graveyard that has been defiled by rutting yuppies, and a succubus takes possession of the mind and body of the busty jazzercise instructor, who slinks out whenever there's a Conelrad test on the Top 40 station, and eviscerates people in Ban-Lon pull-overs by slovenly use of a cheese grater or apple corer.

Let me respond once and only, for the record, to these cavils. Here's where it may get nasty.

1) You're correct. I *don't* do reviews. I'm not much interested in doing reviews. There is a plethora of such reviewing already being done. In magazines published weekly, in newspapers published daily, on telecasts aired hourly; in specialty magazines used to huckster forthcoming films, that are endowed by the film companies themselves, available at every video shoppe and theater lobby in America; on the radio, in *American Film* and *Starlog* and *Cinefantastique* and *Prevue*. We are hip-deep in reviewers, ranging from Pauline Kael and Molly Haskell, who know what they're talking about, to Gary Franklin and David Sheehan, who have the intellectual insight of a speed bump. I won't even comment on the Siamese-critics whose syndicated review shows demonstrate even greater snippiness and discordancy than *I* visit on you.

What I am interested in (and the vast majority of those who have commented on these columns seem to share that interest) is the concept of film as potential Art. Books are reviewed in these pages by Mr. Budrys in essay form, speaking to the intentions of the creators, the effectiveness of their vision, the value of the writing in the greater context of establishing artistic criteria by which we can make informed judgments as to what is, and what ain't, worth our valuable reading time. Why should films not be treated equally as seriously?

These are *essays on film*. Not academic, stodgy *Cahiers du Cinéma* wearinesses, intended to demonstrate the *cinéaste*'s erudition, or his Trivial Pursuit noodling of the least line from an obscure offering by Arnold Fanck (German director, 1889–1974, known for his mountaineering films), but an attempt by one who both loves and works in film, to illuminate technique, intentions, historical context, ethical values...*choices*...

The better to widen the aperture of a filmgoer's perceptions. The better to suggest a subtext for what may appear to be only momentary entertainment. The better, some might say, to educate and broaden horizons and afford more pleasure; as well as to suggest bases on which critical judgments can be made.

If the essays seem inconsistent, well, I rush to the words of Bernard Berenson: "Consistency requires you to be as ignorant today as you were a year ago."

378   As for the *way* in which I write these essays, well, I write to

please myself first. If they also please *you*, then that's swell. If they don't, sorry about that, kiddo. But if I were to write for a supposed audience, I would wind up as bland and shallow as most of the reviewers you channel-hop to avoid. I write what interests me, and that pretty well takes care of complaint 4) because I am utterly disinterested in most of the hack films slambanged at you in saturation tv advertisements. I have no axes to grind, I am on the secret payroll of no studio or filmmaker, and if you think I'm going to sit through *Evil Dead 2* or *The Barbarians* just so your avaricious little heart doesn't feel it's missed something, then you'd better get out pad and pencil and dash off one of those letters to the Fermans, threatening them with loss of readership if they don't recall the previous tenant; because that is not what I'm about, and stop eyeing the belt, I haven't threatened you once, have I?

2) is easily handled. I do the best I can. I appear as frequently as my often-otherwise-occupied schedule permits. I do have to make a living writing other things. And though suchlike as Charles Platt and Christopher Priest bend themselves into hyperbolic pretzels proving I'll never complete THE LAST DANGEROUS VISIONS, that and other matters of import command most of my attention most of the time. I *enjoy* writing these essays. I do them because they are things I *want* to write, not because I have a deadline that *demands* I write them. It is my naïve belief that you would rather read something the author was compelled to write, rather than just space-filler because a presumed readership expected to see something in this space. Don't fret about it: when I'm not here, there'll be a nifty story in this space that has put food on the table of a deserving writer.

And sometimes—though I know you'll find this difficult to believe—even though I once did a column saying *just* this—every once in a while I have *nothing* to say. It may have been a dry period for films worth detailing, it may have been that my brain wasn't all that fresh with concepts, it may have been that even films worth noting had been covered *in kind* in a previous column.

So. Sometimes I'm busy. Sometimes I miss my deadlines. Sometimes the well is dry. That's life, kids. It's also Art. You can have it good, but you may not have it Thursday.

But I've never seen stone tablets with the "rules for columnists" (as one jerk suggested) on which it is chiseled that a columnist *has* to appear regularly. I do the best I can, and I trust that when I can, it serves. If not, turn the dial or get out that pencil and pad.

On the third count, 3) that is, many of you do not seem to understand that this is a *monthly* publication, assembled at least three months before you get it. I'm writing this column on September 17th, having missed two issues because I was earning my living writing a 2-hour sf film for Roger Corman and NBC. Check the date on which you're reading this. *That's* what the lead-time is, every issue.

Now, because I live and work in the center of the film industry, I get to screen a great many films long before they are released, so I can cut down the lead-time in certain cases. And you reap that benefit, for whatever it's worth. I mean, how many of you will *actually* avoid seeing *Robocop* on the basis of my warning? You do have, after all, Free Will, despite what John Paul II tells you.

But even if I were to see any film I wanted to discuss in rough cut (and finding producers who'll let you see a film in that state of pre-final edit, no matter how knowledgeable you may be, is like trying to find a viable concept of ethics in Fawn Hall's tousled head), we'd still get that critique to you after the film had vanished from your Six-Plex.

So I discuss films I consider of merit or demerit, with my hope that you will seek them out or not, when they hit the nabes, as they say. Apparently I don't do all that badly, because I get letters from you telling me that you took my comments on, say, *The Witches of Eastwick* to heart and looked for the little things I pointed out. And you told me it made the evening's entertainment richer, and that you made a lot of points with your crowd discussing all that obscure shit.

So. This isn't a Maltin Guide to what to see at this moment. It is a column of essays on film. That's what it's supposed to be, what it's supposed to do, and what I *want* to do. For those of you eyeing the belt, I know you'll advise the Fermans of your thwarted desires. For the rest of you, if you have a moment, you might drop a postcard to the editors.

They do so feel besieged from time to time. It's not easy having a resident feral child on the premises.

ANCILLARY MATTERS: While it is not, strictly speaking, the province of these columns to deal with books (heaven knows this magazine already boasts a small cadre of the best reviewers and critics in the game), every now and again I fudge the rules in a way I find ethically supportable—complementary in the mode used to make statistics gibber and dance so they unarguably prove contradictory theses—and I attempt to enrich your souls with special titles that have, at least, a thematic link to the fantastic in films. To that end, I draw your attention to a trio of slim trade paperbacks from Copper Canyon Press: three cycles of poetry by Pablo Neruda.

Having been lately disabused of the frivolous conceit that there are some things in the world that everyone *must* be aware of (a casual remark to a human being in its mid-thirties, the other day, on the long-overdue death of Rudolf Hess in Spandau, brought me a querulous stare and the response *Who?*), I hasten to repeat the name Neruda for those few of you who are unfamiliar with the exquisite writings of the late Chilean poet. (That anyone could reach his/her majority not having read and marveled at Neruda's *The Heights of Maccu Picchu*, is a concept I grapple with, with difficulty.)

Neruda, then.

THE SEPARATE ROSE (*La Rosa Separada*) is the first English translation (by William O'Daly, who has splendidly recast all three of these important works) of a poem sequence proceeding from Neruda's visit to Easter Island in 1971. Don Pablo was dying of cancer, and knew it (he passed away in September of 1973). The great poet had grown steadily disenchanted with much of the human race. As O'Daly puts it in his introduction, "By the late 1960s, Neruda had come to consider himself one member of a global civilization gone awry. He felt that the entire world was caught up in the trend of escalating national defense budgets at the expense of the human stomach and spirit." And so, perhaps to reestablish contact with an innocence of Nature that would succor him in those days dwindling to darkness, he journeyed to that last island in the Polynesian chain to be settled, called Rapanui by its inhabitants (who also identify themselves by that name), to touch, at final moments, the fantastic; the mysterious; the primal.

The sequence alternates sections called *The Men* and *The Island*. Here is one of the latter:

When the giants multiplied
and walked tall and straight
till they covered the island with stone noses
and, so very alive, ordained their descendants: the children
of wind and lava, the grandchildren

of air and ash, they would stride
on gigantic feet across their island:
the breeze worked harder than ever
with her hands,
the typhoon with her crime,
that persistence of Oceania.

There is a moral plangency in every line of *La Rosa Separada* that cries Neruda had paid the price for sharing, perhaps at too severe a measure, all decent people's concern for the condition of the human condition. There is, as O'Daly notes, "the guilty pathos of our time" passim the work, a quality at once sobering and ineffably human, that reminds us how much of singing wind and stinging self-examination we derive from the Nerudas among us, who weep that we are no better than we think we are . . . rather than how much better we wish we were.

STILL ANOTHER DAY (*Aún*) is special even as part of a special canon. In these 433 verses written in two days of July, 1969, the Nobel laureate—knowing he was soon to die—bid farewell to his beloved Chilean people. He said this:

Pardon me, if when I want
to tell the story of my life
it's the land I talk about.
This is the land.
It grows in your blood
and you grow.
If it dies in your blood
you die out.

Therein, resonating to the words of another poet, W. S. Merwin, that "the story of each stone leads back to a mountain," lies my rationale for including book reviews in what is usually an essay on film. In these days of the "harmonic convergence" we perceive that the places of power on this planet draw our noblest attention. Neruda's soul and artistry were similarly drawn; and throughout his *oeuvre* we encounter the Mystic Venue as both trope and supernatural icon. It is this specific element of Neruda's sensibility that provides me the interstice through which to wriggle his wonderfulness before you. Please do not upbraid me too severely for this jiggery-pokery; as your mother or the head matron at the Home used to say when she forced you to swallow such yuchhh as lima beans or castor oil, "It's for your own good." The difference being, Neruda goes down sweetly and easily, producing smile rather than stricture.

And finally, WINTER GARDEN (*Jardín de Invierno*), in O'Daly's lyrical, authorized translation, is one of the eight unpublished manuscripts found on Neruda's desk on the day of his death. In its twenty verses, this tidy offering sums up Neruda's life and work, expresses his understanding of his imminent death, speaks of solitude and duty as necessary for the proper life, but returns once again to Nature as the wellspring of regeneration.

Taken in sum (and available from Copper Canyon Press, PO Box 271, Port Townsend, Washington 98368—$8.00 each for the first and third titles noted here, $7.00 for *Aún*) these books are a legacy of buoyancy for the spirit; words that not only enrich and uplift, but ennoble; important art for a world too often compelled to contemplate mud and shoetops. For those of you who know not of Neruda, whose reading time is spent with paperback novels whose exteriors feature die-cut and embossing and whose interiors feature disembowelment and ennui, set yourselves the delirious, the heady task of soaring with one of the great souls this century has produced. Forego just one film and treat yourself to Neruda. It's for your own good.

And next time—now that the June-to-September hell in which I lived while writing *Cutter's World* for Corman and NBC has reached an end—get your fangs set for an essay I've been dying to write for several years. I only needed a hook. The hook is Mel Brooks's *Spaceballs*, and the subject is my belief that *most* (not all, note that I said not *all*) sf fans and/or readers have no sense of humor, and that which they do have is fit only for films such as *Spaceballs*.

The subject next time will be wit. Not a sense of humor, but *wit*.

And just so you don't feel cheated because I didn't "review" anything else, here's another: HARRY AND THE HENDERSONS (Universal/Amblin Entertainment) is a delight. It's manipulative as a *Rocky* flick, but the manipulation is in service of making us feel good, and hey, I'll invest in that any day.

See how good I am to you? Now stop crying, and go downstairs and apologize to your mother, and wash up for dinner while I put my belt back on and burn these imbecile letters George and the others sent.

INSTALLMENT 28:
In Which, With Wiles And Winces,
We Waft Words Warranting,
To Wit, Wonderful Wit

In the words of Joseph L. Mankiewicz, placed by that superlative scenarist in the mouth of Bette Davis, in the 1950 film *All About Eve*, "Fasten your seat belts, it's going to be a bumpy night."

But first, as is my wont, anecdotes (one short, one medium long, both absolutely true) in aid of setting the tone and laying the groundwork. With assistance from the editors of THE RANDOM HOUSE DICTIONARY OF THE ENGLISH LANGUAGE, *Unabridged Edition*.

Anecdote the first.

A friend of mine, a woman who heads up "development" of projects in the area of television specials for one of the three major networks, called me from her office, oh, roughly, about a year ago, and she said, "Sit down. You're going to *love* this one. Are you sitting?" I told her I was, and she proceeded to tell me that thirty seconds earlier a man had left her office. This man—who, like my confidante, shall remain nameless for obvious reasons—is a major supplier of endless hundreds of hours of prime-time product. He is a Big Name in the world of films and teevee; we're talking on a level with Chuck Fries or Aaron Spelling; a man whose assorted production companies have multimillion-dollar contracts with the networks. And he said to my friend, a woman empowered to say yes or no for the go-ahead or turn-down of his big-ticket projects, "I've got the most sensational idea for a Special that you've ever heard! This is fantastic, it'll get you the numbers like nothing else you've ever done!" And my friend, blown back against her chair by the intensity and passion of this man's enthusiasm, replied, "Well, *tell me!* What *is* this incredible concept for a Special that will blow America out of the water?"

And the man said: "Let's do *The Wiz . . .*

"*. . . white!*"

As she paused for my reaction that day, oh, roughly, about a year ago, so I now pause for *your* reaction.

Depending on whether your stomach aches from laughing as you now read this sentence, or you have a blank look on your face and the phrase *Why is that funny?* in your head, you will find yourself in one of two categories: those who need this essay desperately but won't perceive themselves as being the subject of the discussion . . . or those who already understand what I'm going to be getting at here, and know themselves not to be lacking. For those with the blank look, those in the first category, relate that anecdote to a friend you consider to possess a finely-tuned sense of humor, and check his/her response. Though like seeks like, you may have lucked-out and your friend can help you along with the rest of this confabulation. Not to mention the rest of your life.

(This has been, as stated, an absolutely *true* story. The man was dead serious. If this gives you pause as to the level of acuity demonstrated by those who cobble up what you watch on the tube, well, what took you so long to get The Word?)

Anecdote the second.

A number of years ago, while under the spell of Providence, Rhode Island, once the haunt of H. P. Lovecraft and Edgar Allan Poe, I began writing a short story titled "On the Slab" as an *hommage* to HPL. While only passingly echoic of the great fantasist's style, it was my admiring nod to the best of what he had written that had impressed me as a tyro.

One thing and another, I set the first few pages of the story aside after Providence, and was unable to return to the piece for several years. But when I did, I completed the yarn and sold it to *Omni*. "On the Slab" was a contemporary retelling of the Prometheus legend, told a bit more in the dark fantasy mode than is my usual approach with such efforts. I liked that story a lot.

And so it chanced that after the sale to *Omni*, but before it

was published, I was engaged to deliver a lecture at New York

University and, as is my wont, I read my latest (usually unpublished) story as part of the presentation. On that night in April of 1981, the story was "On the Slab."

When I finished the reading, I was rewarded with considerable applause from the large audience, thanked them prettily, and asked if there were any questions.

Rising from the shoals of attendees was a young man in his middle twenties, a largish young man whose somatotype and manner stirred instant recognition in me: *This is a stone science fiction fan,* I thought.

(Pause. The more contumelious among you, of whom I wrote at length last time, will no doubt snarl that I had no way of affirming such a snap judgment. That I was pre-judging the largish young man and saw him as stereotype. Maybe. But if you think those of us who deal with fans and readers constantly can't spot the fans in a crowd of ten thousand ordinary humans, I suggest you ask your nearest sf writer. It is an amalgam of clues informed by an understanding of body language, cultural taxonomy, deductive logic, the eye of the artist and the sad-but-true repetition of fan behavior as witnessed firsthand for more than three decades. Anyone who has ever read the Sherlock Holmes canon can do the same. And as we shall see in a moment, as the anecdote proceeds, whether an actual card-carrying, registered with N3F or FAPA fan, or merely one who is obsessed by the genre in the fannish manner, though unallied... this was a stone fan.)

So he stood, and I asked, "Do you have a question about the story?"

He said, "Have you ever heard of the Prometheus legend?"

The snickering in the audience kept me from answering for a moment. He looked around in confusion. My instant reaction was to be gentle. "Yes, I have," I replied.

"Well, your story is a ripoff of that, it seems to me." Now the audience was chuckling at him. And though I wasn't exactly toe-tappingly delighted at being accused of plagiarism by a total stranger, I tried to maintain a humane demeanor.

"You mean the way Alfred Bester's THE STARS MY DESTINATION was a ripoff of Dumas's THE COUNT OF MONTE CRISTO?" He just looked at me; hadn't the scarcest what I was talking about.

"But you made a lot of mistakes," he said, oblivious to the whispering of the audience throughout Eisner and Lubin Auditorium as those who knew what was happening explained to those who did not. He was determined to press on, and there

387

wasn't a lot I could do to keep him from making a fool of himself. Had I tried to cut him off, I'd have been pilloried for savaging this naîf.

"Oh?" I said, as pockets of laughter around the hall gave him a warning he refused to hear.

"Yes, you made a lot of mistakes. You see, in the Prometheus legend it was his *liver* that was eaten out every day, not his heart, the way you wrote it. And it was an eagle that ate his liver every day, not a vulture like you wrote in your story."

"Carrion crow," I said.

"What?"

"I called it a vulture, and also a carrion crow."

"Yes. You got it all wrong. Why did you do that?"

The laughter was now ubiquitous. The largish young man kept turning and looking. He was beginning to understand that whatever it was he'd said wrong, it was apparent to everyone else in the audience...but him. In anger, he turned back to me and demanded, "*So why did you do that?!*"

At which point I'd had about enough, and I said, as flatly and GeorgeS.Pattonly as I could, "Because I damn well *felt* like it."

My tone made it quite clear to those ridiculing the young man, that the game was over. Now came the lesson. "Sir," I said, "everyone is laughing at you because it is obvious from the story that I am familiar with the Prometheus legend and have, in fact, written a pastiche on that myth, a retelling, an updating, a variant version, if you wish. When one writes a variant on a well-established legend, one reinterprets it to contemporize it, or to focus on aspects the original either saw one way or ignored entirely. I used the heart, rather than the liver, because in the days when the Prometheus legend was new, it was commonly thought that the liver was the residence of the soul...which is why the victors often ate the livers of those they'd vanquished, to absorb the fallen enemy's bravery and wisdom. Did you ever hear this expression, 'Bring me his liver and lights'? That meant his soul and his eyes. But today we think of the heart as the organ of choice. As for the crow, or vulture, rather than the eagle...well, I wanted a darker image. We think of the eagle as our national symbol, as a creature of honor and fortitude, soaring and pure. I wanted a bird that feasted on carrion. So I changed it. He isn't chained to a rock, either. These are what we call 'artistic license' and if used within the consistent framework of logic in a story, they are considered quite artful and legitimate."

388   I thought that would do it, and would get him off the hook. I

thought anyone of even passing intelligence would understand and be content. I thought I was dealing with a rational human being. What I was dealing with, sadly, was a stone science fiction fan.

"Well, I still think you shouldn't have written it wrong," he said, and sat down heavily, to a tsunami of hisses and catcalls. Realizing I could do no better, I threw up my hands and went on with the evening's presentation.

Perhaps medium long was inaccurate, because all of the foregoing is merely backstory for the punchline of the anecdote.

I thought no more about that interchange, returned to Los Angeles, and was startled a week later when I received a *most* troubled phone call from the then–fiction editor of *Omni*. (I hasten to advise that the fiction editor at that time was, and remains, a superlative writer, as well as a friend of many years. It was not the current fiction editor, Ellen Datlow, who has been at her post with distinction for quite a few years. The editor of whom I speak knows I bear him illimitable affection, and we have laughed over this anecdote many times. It is not told to embarrass him, or to make him seem less worthy an editor than he proved himself. It just happens to be one of those dopey things we all do every once in a while, and I need it to make my point, so don't go looking for anything malicious, because it ain't there.)

Anyhow. He called, and he said, "Listen, we got a letter in the office the other day, from a guy who heard you read 'On the Slab' at NYU, and he's pointed out a lot of errors in the story, and we'd like you to rewrite them to take care of it."

I couldn't believe what I was hearing. "You're putting me on!" I cried. "You mean to tell me that humorless dweeb *wrote you a letter*?!?!"

"Uh-huh."

"And you actually are taking it seriously, about a story that hasn't even been *published* yet, and you're asking me to honor the imbecile nitpicking of some yotz with a flat affect who may, for all I know, believe Bacon wrote Shakespeare's stuff, who may, for all I know, think Stephen Crane had no right to do a Civil War novel because he wasn't in the fight, who may, for all I know, interpret everything so literally that he wonders if the light goes out in the refrigerator when he closes the door? *Is that what you're telling me?!*"

My friend the editor fumfuh'd for a moment, and then said in a smaller voice, "Well, he said in the letter that it would embarrass us at *Omni* if readers thought we didn't know it was Prometheus's liver, and not his heart, that was eaten..."

"Send back the story," I howled. "I'll return your fucking check! This is unconscionable! It's deranged! I'm going to kill you!"

Well, it worked out just fine. I calmed down after the fourth phone call—yes, we discussed this hot and cold and tepid for more than a week—because he refused to send back the story (demonstrating a lot more good sense than previously), and at one point I said something like, "Look, kiddo, myth and legend are plastic, they're fluid, they're malleable. They belong to whatever culture takes them up. And we, as Artists, are *required* to examine and retool not only myths and legends, but all variations of those myths, and all commentaries on those myths and legends and variations! It is our bloody *job*, fer crissakes!" And along about the fifth or sixth phone call he came on the line and said, with awe in his voice, "How did you manage to do that?"

"Do what?"

"Get that into the book."

"What the hell are you talking about?"

"You telling me you haven't seen William Irwin Thompson's book, THE TIME FALLING BODIES TAKE TO LIGHT? Mythology, sexuality, and the origins of culture? Everybody's reading it; it's knocking people on their asses; it's the cutting edge of new thinking about mythology."

I had not, at that moment, even *heard* about the Thompson book though now, six years later, I must have given away at least a dozen copies to other writers. And if you haven't found it yet, run don't crawl.

"So what's all this about me being in the book, or whatever?"

"No, you geek," he said, happy to turn it all back to me, "it's what you *said* that's in the book."

"And what wisdom is *that*, may I ask?"

I heard him riffling pages. "Listen to this: it's from the prologue." And this is what he read to me:

> The structural anthropologist urges us to ignore the orthodox who labor so patiently trying to eliminate the apocryphal variants from the one true text. The priests of the temple of Solomon worked to construct the canon of Biblical literature, and in this work the dubious folktales of the peasantry were dismissed, but for us a legend or *midrash* (a folktale variation on Biblical stories) may be a greater opening to the archetypal world than the overly refined reactions of the urban priestly intelligentsia.

(He stopped there, but the very next paragraph—page 11 of the St. Martin's Press hardcover edition—was even better:)

> Once we are freed from the quest for the one true version of a myth, we are also freed from the concern for determining the exact provenance of the variant. How can one tell where a myth comes from? A *midrash* from the Middle Ages may go back as an oral tradition into the darkness of time. Where do children's rhymes come from? What ancient motif is simply reclothed in a modern story or a children's skip-rope song? Can one really claim that the date of the singing is the date of the song?...Libraries have been burnt and whole religious movements wiped out because their belief and myths have been considered to be of dubious origin by the upholders of orthodoxy; yet it is sometimes precisely the heretical myth that opens a doorway into the archetypal world. ...But there are other reasons why all the version of a myth must be considered...

...and he goes on brilliantly for another two hundred and sixty pages—including feetnotes but excluding index—to codify them reasons for my not having to rewrite "On the Slab" to satisfy the witless pecksniffery of a stone science fiction fan. But had I not worked my magicks and caused William Irwin Thompson to write that book overnight so that St. Martin's Press could print it the next day and get it into the editor's paws by the following afternoon, I'd have had to return a check I'd long-since cashed and turned into groceries.

End of anecdote the second.

I approach the subject of this dissertation which is, in truth, a film review, as well as a discussion of one of the truly Forbidden Topics one does not broach with those who read magazines such as this one.

I won't keep you in suspense any longer. The thread that links my opening anecdotes is an obvious one: the prime mover in each is a person demonstrating boorishness posturing as wit. Narrowness of vision coupled with a literal-mindedness that is insensitive to a jocular interpretation. Both are so concretized in egocentrism that they have been walled off from recognition of the truth that insufficient knowledge has turned them into a parodic absurdity. They come to this unfortunate state, I submit, because they are devoid of true wit. And that, I further submit, as the core of my argument, is a widespread condition among science fiction readers and fans.

(Before I go on, let me state for the record that this is not a *universal* flaw in sf readers and fans. I speak here not of *all*, but

391

of *most*.) If you take instant umbrage at this essay, consider for a moment that those who do *not* credit this absence in their own makeup will not be bothered. They will chuckle and murmur, "How true, how true." But those who twitch may well perceive a node of familiarity, and will rush to accuse the messenger of garbling the communique; for them, the self-examination may founder on guilt (however mild) and the potential revelation of this Forbidden Topic will be obscured by subconscious self-serving. For every Sidney Coleman and Mike Glyer, every Lee Hoffman and Mick Glicksohn, there are a hundred Marley E. Bechtels and Jacopo Madaros, two hundred Gerald B. Storrows and George Sokols.

The former group are well-known and unarguably funny men and a woman who also happen to be sf readers and fans; the latter group are sf readers who are, in my view, at one with the largish young man from the NYU audience. It is not important for our purposes here that you know the former group, or what it is they have said and written over the years that marks them as witty. They are offered as palliatives for those who will forget that I carefully said *most*, not *all*.

But the latter group are paradigms I need to press my premise that *most* readers of science fiction, and *most* fans, are devoid of true wit. So here is the litany of unbreathing metal that passes for sensibility in these (otherwise probably wonderful) stone science fiction fans.

● In a clearly antic short story I wrote that appeared in *Asimov's* in December 1986, a fantasy titled "Laugh Track," the protagonist, a man given to first person recollections presented much in the manner of Damon Runyon, muses about his employment with a despicable tv producer named Bill Tidy. I wrote:

> Each of us has one dark eminence in his or her life who somehow has the hoodoo sign on us. Persons so cosmically loathsome that we continually spend our time when in their company silently asking ourselves *What the hell, what the bloody hell, what the everlasting Technicolor hell am I doing here with this ambulatory piece of offal? This is the worst person who ever got born, and someone ought to wash out his life with a bar of Fels-Naptha.*
> But there you sit, and the next time you blink, there you sit again. It was probably the way Catherine the Great felt on her dates with Rasputin.
> Bill Tidy had that hold over me.

In the September 1987 issue of *Asimov's*, Marley E. Bechtel of

Kenmore, NY had a letter published. The salient sections for our interest here are these:

"Dear Dr. Asimov:
"In the mid-December issue, there seem to be at least a couple of mistakes that should have been caught in the editing. First, in 'Neptune's Reach,' we are told ..."
[And Bechtel goes on at some length to fault the story's author on what may well have been a valid technical point. Bechtel then gets to the second dire "mistake":]
"In Harlan Ellison's 'Laugh Track,' he comments that 'It was probably the way Catherine the Great felt on her dates with Rasputin.' How could they have dated, as she died in 1796 and he was not born until around 1871?"

To which one should properly respond, in the original Prometheus legend the line read "It was probably the way Fay Wray felt on her dates with King Kong."

Literalmindedness, pecksniffery, sententiousness; the egocentrism of needing to demonstrate a humorless familiarity with data that contravenes the purpose of an attempt at wit. The mark of the cloven hoof of the stone sf fan.

● In a recent installment of this column, I eased into a seminal discussion of Woody Allen as a consummate director of fantasy—an obviousness that seemed to me to have escaped the notice of most critics—with a completely hoked-up bit of tomfoolery that had me and Allen in a bathyscaphe at the bottom of the Cayman Trench, eating hot fudge sundaes. As almost everyone was aware, Woody had received both the Hugo and Nebula awards for Best Dramatic Presentation in 1974 for *Sleeper*, but in my thesis that sf *aficionados* had overlooked much more significant fantasywork by Allen, I employed the literary contrivances known as absurdity, engrossment, farce and sarcasm, which included Allen's inquiring if he had never been awarded a Hugo (clearly untrue) because he was Jewish. I then cited as refutation the fact that I, as a Jew, had been so honored, as well as Silverberg and Asimov and others, and included in the list of prominent Jews who owned Hugos the well-known Mormon, Orson Scott Card. If *those* lunacies had not tipped off any but the dullest intellects that this was a bit of vaudeville, surely having Woody Allen get the bends as we surfaced in our bathyscaphe should have.

Yet the editors of this magazine (and I personally) received about a dozen letters protesting the content of that essay, all of them reading that crazy stuff as *absolutely true*!

393

A Gerald B. Storrow wrote, in part: "... are we to gather that Ellison considers it a worthwhile use of your pages to seriously ask [sic] ourselves if there is truly anti-Semitism in Hollywood?" Apart from splitting the infinitive, Mr. Storrow went on at some length seriously accusing me of "name-dropping" because I used Woody Allen's name. (How he expected me to talk about Allen without using his name is a manifestation of paralogia that amazes even one as jaded in these matters as I.)

When I made the error of responding to Mr. Storrow's letter, I wrote: "I have long said that readers and fans of science fiction are as devoid of wit as cardboard; and sadly, sadly, my theory keeps reproving itself.

"A sense of humor isn't what counts. *Every*one has some sort of rudimentary sense of humor. Hell, lizards, puppies and potato bugs have a sense of humor. It is *wit* that is in such short supply. And nowhere more tragically than among those who preen and strut with false pride that they are Slans, drenched in the ability to 'understand' science fiction."

I then pointed out all the glaring tip-offs that the essay had been written in an antic manner, suggesting that he might not really be as perceptive as his insulting letter contended. And I concluded as follows: "Yet this condition of yours does trouble me. While I'm not licensed to practice medicine, I would suggest a double-dose daily of James Thurber, Peter De Vries, Will Cuppy, Max Shulman, S. J. Perelman, Dave Barry and Daniel Manus Pinkwater. Stay away from fried foods and Henry James."

(Courtesy with the humorless, however, is a mugg's game, and it became obvious when this attempt to uncloud Mr. Storrow's mind produced further egregiously crabby letters, that the gentleman merely craved attention. This will be the last of *that*, you may be sure.)

• George Sokol of Montreal sent a letter alternately praising and vilifying me, to what end I'm not sure even after rereading the letter several times. But the gist of it (though he obviously understood the bathyscaphe/bends business was a put-on) was this: "Why... why would you want to include that ghastly bit about Mr. Allen getting the bends (oh, Godly ghosts, that awful desease [sic] dreaded by all bathyscaphers!)?

"The very purpose of the bathyscaphe was so that the need for gradual decompression could be eliminated, thus eliminating the risk of getting the bends. The bathyscaphe is a pressurized, navigable underwater ship, or vehicle! Please, I would think you would know that whenever a writer is being cute while writing, he should try and be as sincere and real as possible, and not just pile on the 'style' for style's sake."

Well, Mr. Sokol is certainly being sincere and real, and in his sincerity and realoidness he reaffirms the thesis of this discussion. And *he's* one of the *good* guys who seems to be enjoying the columns! So I hope he'll believe I'm sincere and real when I tell him though I'm bewildered by the s&r of his letter, and consider him a nice fella for not being mean to me in his communique, I will raise this matter of liver versus bends, and eagle versus bathyscaphe on my next date with either Fay Wray or Catherine the Great, whoever comes first.

● And finally, we come to Jacopo M. Madaro of East Boston who took the following offhand drollery from my July column as matter for umbrage...I wrote:

> The potty is the last private place for a reader in the world. No one bothers you. Unless you live in a large Italian family, which is another sociological can of worms entirely.

Jacopo responded to my larking as follows: "It just happens that I am both Italian (a bona fide alien) and a sociologist. I am not aware of any sociological taxonomy based upon national or ethnic 'cans of worms.' Therefore, I have to conclude that your statement is well worthy its excretory context. Cordially yours, worms notwithstanding, Jacopo M. Madaro."

You think *you* get weird mail!?!

(Pause. I had not, in fact, planned for the preamble to my thesis and review to go on at this length. Honest. But once I got into it, the floodgates opened. And during the days through which I have been writing this, I have had occasion to read the preceding sections to a fairly large number of professionals in the sf field. Just to make sure that what I was saying here was not merely a product of my meanspirited nature. Was I bumrapping fans without cause? Does anyone else feel as I do about this subject, that fans in the main are a humorless bunch who could drive you crazy if you try to write funnystuff? So I called F- - - -, and I called M - - -, and I called W - - - - -, and I called A - - - - long distance, and a couple of others, and every one of them whooped and laughed and said, "True! How true! Oh, yeah, ain't that *true!*" And then they told me *their* proofs of the thesis, and then they egged me on to sic'm, to write it all, and then they made me promise I wouldn't use their names because if anyone was going to get killed for this, as much as they loved me, they'd

395

rather it was I, not them. So okay, B & N & D & D, I won't used your names, you buncha pork scraps, you! And I make this pause, and tell you all this, because each of the above initials said I *had* to include my reply to Dr. Jacopo M. Madaro, which I hadn't intended to do because it was what *he* wrote that counts, not what I replied. But since they all made such a who-struck-John about it, I've decided to include the response here; but I feel I am trying your patience with these many side-channels to the main stream, and I want to spare those of you who grow weary. So. My letter of response to Dr. Madaro follows. It will be set in smaller type so you can identify where it starts and ends. If you wish to skip it, feel free. If not, read on.)

Dear Dr. Madaro:
Sorry it took me from May till now to respond to your charming note. I've been busy.

Apart from the usual umbrage taken by those who puff up their chests in letters because they think they are safe from actual, slap-in-the-face retribution for unsolicited rudeness, your rush to the defense of all Italians everywhere, since the dawn of time till the final tick of eternity (one presumes), is touching. Imbecile, but touching.

Nonetheless, I will reply to your snitty remarks as if they made sense. I do this in the spirit of kindness toward the afflicted; something like social work among the intellectually impacted.

I had not realized that merely by claiming ownership of the appellation "sociologist" one was accorded the right to issue *obiter dicta* on all human behavior. But as you not only manifest a need to make such pronouncements, but apparently are unfamiliar with a commonplace in large Italian families that *I* and a number of my Italian-American friends have experienced firsthand, let me poke a pinhole in the darkness and permit the light of new data to illuminate your store of taxonomical minutiae:

In large Italian families (and to very nearly the same degree in Jewish families of *any* size), unless they are extremely wealthy and have a plethora of bathrooms, members of the household bang on the door to the toilet and demand immediate access, at any hour of the day or night, even if you sneak in at 4am to read Thomas Hardy or *Playboy*.

There is a bewildering manifestation of some sort of specialized telepathy in this matter. Even if dead asleep or outside in the yard, members of large Italian families (and to lesser degree in Jewish families of *any* size) rise as if under the voodoo command, and rush to the potty to bang on the door and demand immediate access. Silent as the grave, as one may keep, they *know* you are in there, and the banging commences.

This is a fact of life. Sorry you never caught up with it in your pursuit of the title "sociologist." Sometime maybe I'll explain to you why women put a roll of toilet paper on the roller one way, and men do it the other way. But enough education is enough. We mustn't strain, don't you agree?

And in conclusion: as a Jew who was raised in and around many Italian families, I assure you my offhand comment was made on the basis of experience in the field. It was not offered as a veiled slur against Italians. I know what a tough time you have keeping Italian names off the gangster characters in tv shows, and I don't want you to think I was trying to add to your burden. Yet I confess to a sinister subliminal resentment of Italians, based no doubt on my having discovered that Columbus was a Jew, and his discovery of America was likely his way of finding a place for his people safe from the Inquisition, and the resultant animus I harbor deep within myself at Italian Catholics copping the credit for yet another superlative act by the lowly Semite.

Is that what you were fishing for? Yours in unbridled bigotry, with the hope that the next time you try for "cultured prose" you scribble a note deserving of something better than a C–.

For those of you who seek the core of the argument, your reward is at hand.

There is far less humor written in the genre of sf than in almost any other category of fiction I can think of, with the possible exceptions of the western, the heavy-breathing bodice-rippers (unless you interpret them not at face-value but as hilarious put-ons from word one), and the Dostoevskian *angst-klatsch*. I submit that's because those who write this stuff understand *a priori* that the audience is *muy* serioso, and the giggles won't go down smoothly. If one tries to name the writers of sf who have made a mark with humor, the list is not a long one. De Camp, Reynolds, Fred Brown, Geo. Alec Effinger, Harvey Jacobs, Bob Sheckley, sometimes Dick Lupoff, and perhaps a few more whose names escape me at the moment, with absolutely no intent to ignore those equally as proficient but simply absent from recall as I write this.

(I have to write apologia like that. You do send mail.)

And though you'll get no argument from me that humor is a specialized way of thinking and writing, nonetheless it is self-evident from existing evidence of sixty-one years of material published as scientifiction, sf, sci-fi, or science fiction, that this is not a canon overbrimming with yocks.

As I wrote earlier in this essay, possibly *years* earlier in this essay, a "sense of humor" is not the problem. It is the Gobi aridity of what *does* pass for a sense of humor among fans and readers. It is the absence of True Wit. And so we will understand, in the General Semantics sense, what is meant by "humor" and what is

397

meant by "wit," which are no more the same thing than "morality" is the same as "ethics," I adjure you to pay heed to my lexicological chums from the unabridged RANDOM HOUSE DICTIONARY OF THE ENGLISH LANGUAGE.

hu·mor (hyōō′mər *or, often,* yōō′-), *n.* **1.** a comic quality causing amusement: *the humor of a situation.* **2.** the faculty of perceiving what is amusing or comical: *His humor buoyed him up through many depressing situations.* **3.** the faculty of expressing the amusing or comical: *The author's humor came across better in the book than in the movie.* **4.** comical writing or talk in general; comical books, skits, plays, etc. **5. humors,** amusing or comical features: *humors of the occasion.* **6.** mental disposition or temperament. **7.** a temporary mood or frame of mind: *He's in a bad humor today.* **8.** a capricious or freakish inclination; whim or caprice; odd trait. **9.** *Old Physiol.* one of the four elemental fluids of the body, blood, phlegm, black bile, and yellow bile, regarded as determining, by their relative proportions, a person's physical and mental constitution. **10.** *Biol.* any animal or plant fluid, whether natural or morbid, such as the blood or lymph. **11. out of humor,** displeased; dissatisfied; cross: *The chef is feeling out of humor again and will have to be pampered.* —*v.t.* **12.** to comply with the humor or mood of in order to soothe or make content or more agreeable: *to humor a child.* **13.** to adapt or accommodate oneself to. Also, *esp. Brit.,* **humour.** [ME *(h)umour* < AF < L *(h)ūmōr-* (s. of *(h)ūmor*) moisture, fluid (medical L: body fluid), equiv. to *ūm(ēre)* to wet + *-or* -OR¹] –**hu′mor·ful,** *adj.* –**hu′mor·less,** *adj.* –**hu′mor·less·ness,** *n.* —**Syn. 3.** HUMOR, WIT are contrasting terms that agree in referring to an ability to perceive and express a sense of the clever or amusing. HUMOR consists principally in the recognition and expression of incongruities or peculiarities present in a situation or character. It is frequently used to illustrate some fundamental absurdity in human nature or conduct, and is generally thought of as more kindly than wit: *a genial and mellow type of humor; his biting wit.* WIT is a purely intellectual manifestation of cleverness and quickness of apprehension in discovering analogies between things really unlike, and expressing them in brief, diverting, and often sharp observations or remarks. **8.** fancy, vagary. **12.** HUMOR, GRATIFY, INDULGE imply attempting to satisfy the wishes or whims of (oneself or others). TO HUMOR is to comply with the mood, fancy, or caprice of another, as in order to satisfy, soothe, or manage: *to humor an invalid, a child.* TO GRATIFY is to please by satisfying the likings or desires: *to gratify someone by praising him.* INDULGE suggests a yielding to wishes by way of favor or complaisance, and may imply a habitual or excessive yielding to whims: *to indulge an unreasonable demand; to indulge an irresponsible son.* —**Ant. 12.** discipline, restrain.

wit¹ (wit), *n.* **1.** the keen perception and cleverly apt expression of those connections between ideas which awaken amusement and pleasure. **2.** speech or writing showing such perception and ex-

pression. **3.** a person having or noted for such perception and expression. **4.** understanding, intelligence, or sagacity: *He doesn't have wit enough to come in out of the rain.* **5.** Usually, **wits. a.** mental abilities or powers of intelligent observation, keen perception, ingenious contrivance, etc.: *using one's wits to get ahead.* **b.** mental faculties; senses: *to lose one's wits.* **6. at one's wit's end.** See **end**[1] (def. 23). **7. keep or have one's wits about one,** to remain alert and observant; be prepared for or equal to anything: *It pays to keep your wits about you if you plan to drive at night.* **8. live by one's wits,** to provide for oneself by employing ingenuity or cunning; live precariously: *He traveled around the world, living by his wits.* [ME, OE; c. G *Witz,* leel *vit;* akin to WIT[2]]
—**Syn. 1.** drollery, facetiousness, waggishness, repartee. See **humor. 4.** wisdom, sense, mind.

Now if you have paid close attention to the section in the definition of *humor* noted as Syn. 3, you and I will both share an understanding of why "sense of humor" isn't the problem, but "true wit" is. Because most of what passes for humor in this genre is a sorry adumbration of that which we find howlingly funny in other literary forms.

In the vast archives of sf we find an inadequate portion of caricature and burlesque; absurdity and buffoonery (at least of the intentional sort); ridicule and farce; satire and high comedy; burlesque and black humor; overstatement and engrossment; travesty, sarcasm, slapstick and drollery. There *are* some exceptions, of course. There are and have been writers who could not keep a straight face as they wrote some of this longwinded, far-flung, heroically self-important fustian . . . and they have palliated the pomposity of it all. But even those who have done it well, done it well enough so that we actually smiled once in a while as we read, and even more rarely laughed out loud at the printed page—laughing *with* the author's invention, rather than *at* it—have done it as five-finger exercise. No decent living can be made from humor in this field, not even by a Sheckley or a Goulart or a Harrison.

Try to recall the last full-length comic novel you read that could be counted as science fiction. Sheckley and Goulart come immediately to mind and then pffft! Spinrad, who reads a lot of this stuff, when I called him to jog my memory in case some prominent practitioner had slipped through the interstices, came up with the same list I'd already assembled, and stressed Effinger. So I called Effinger to see how well *he'd* done with humor, and he said, "Are you kidding? They *hate* my funny stuff. They send me letters asking me why such-and-such is supposed to be funny. I write it to amuse *myself*. It's hard enough making a paycheck with the serious stuff, but why get myself creamed on purpose trying to make fans laugh? Most of them don't get the point, anyhow."

But fans *do* enjoy one form of humor. And that is the saddest part of it all.

The form of humor that fans dote on, that they slaver over, that they indulge in among themselves, that they slather across fanzine pages, that they interlineate and cross-quote, that they revere and unmercifully visit on the rest of us is...

The pun.

That most witless thalidomide bastard of True Wit. That intellectually-debased sediment found at the lowest level of humor. That coarse-surfaced imposition on our good offices that *never* produces a titter, a giggle, a chuckle or a laugh, but which takes as a measure of its effectiveness...a groan of pain. The pun is what sf fans and readers hoist banners in aid of.

But (as film historian and sf reader Bill Warren pointed out, when I called to read him the preceding pages) fans don't even do real *puns*. They change one letter of a word and think "sci-fri" is hilarious. Kindergarten word-play.

There are some things in this life that one definitely *does not do*.

You don't make jokes about air piracy as you go through the metal detector of O'Hare Airport. You don't drive down to East L.A. and scream *Puto pendejo!* at a Chicano street gang. You don't eat unidentifiable mushrooms while on a forest stroll. You don't tug on Superman's cape, you don't spit into the wind, you don't pull the mask off that old Lone Ranger, and you don't mess around with Jim.

While in Paris, during a sober interview on French television, because I was pissed at Parisian rudeness, I vouchsafed the opinion that the one thing the French know nothing about is love. You can tell the French that their cooking sucks, that their army is comprised of cowards, or that their admiration for Jerry Lewis proves they have no taste, but you do *not* tell them they don't understand love. There remains a warrant for my arrest, still valid in France.

Similarly, one does not tell fans they have no sense of humor. That fans are clever beyond belief is Accepted Wisdom with which one does not tamper. To write an essay of this length, pointing out what nearly *every* sf professional knows but will never say aloud, is tantamount to suicide.

400

But because that is so, in my view, it explains why sf fans and readers have championed one of the worst films in recent memory, SPACEBALLS (Brooksfilms/MGM) co-written, produced and directed by Mel Brooks.

See how it all ties together, however long it took me?

Spaceballs rivals *L'Avventura* as the single most obstinately boring film of all time. An invincibly tasteless farrago of lame jokes, obvious parodies, telegraphed punchlines, wretched acting and idiot plot so sad that its funniest bit is a rip-off of Chuck Jones's "One Froggy Evening."

Mel Brooks. Since *The Producers* we have watched a Brobdingnagian wit shrink in on itself as if suffering from some hideous malaise, with only one period of remission—*Blazing Saddles* and *Young Frankenstein* (1973–74)—until it has become dwarfish. And if "dwarfish," the sensibility that has given us *Spaceballs* goes by the name Dopey. And its confreres are certainly Sleazy, Farty, Mockie, Shallow, Sleepy and Tyro. Farty makes all the scatological and potty-training remarks; Tyro is in charge of the "home movies" look and sound of the film; Shallow selects the subjects to be satirized; Sleepy is in charge of keeping the boredom quotient high; Sleazy makes all the sophomoric sex comments and the sexist asides as if he had just discovered his wee-wee; and Mockie makes sure there is an abundance of self-hating Jewish references. But Dopey is the governing intelligence, selected by secret ballot on which None of the Above is the lone candidate.

An incredibly self-conscious movie. One grows weary of the *Moonlighting* shtick (totemized as "breaking the fourth wall between players and audience") in which characters turn and speak to the camera: "Nice dissolve." And when the head and arm of the Statue of Liberty come spiraling down out of space to the planet, only those who batten on puns can fail to perceive that they are about to see an *hommage* to *Planet of the Apes*, and only they laugh when the icons hit the sand and two people in monkey masks ride up. (When I saw this film in the company of a selected fan audience, and they did indeed react as described, it gave me a firm conviction that Brooks had reached precisely the audience he wanted: adolescents, and those who suffer from arrested adolescence.)

What sort of dribblebrain chooses to parody the *Star Wars* films (themselves parodies of the first of the trilogy and the totality a parody of the parodic form called "space opera") ten years too late? *Hardware Wars*, a twelve-minute live-action short

401

written, produced and directed by Ernie Fosselius in 1978 did it all funnier, faster, and with infinitely greater panache.

The writing is so much succotash that one has to have one's leash jerked to remember that this howling, blithering runa-muck was actually directed by something approximating a human intelligence, not just slopped together in a tureen in some biochemistry lab, plugged into a Voss electrostatic genera-tor and shot up with ten million volts of idiocy, at which point it leaped through a casement window and ran off shrieking into the countryside, with a deranged Mel Brooks tearing his hair, rending his flesh, ripping his raiment, and shouting, "It's *alive!* It's *alive!*"

Brooks's direction is an infirm, broken-backed, whimpering creature, shot through the brain and the heart, and left to thrash out its tormented death in the bush. Direction that does not even have the sense to be passively bad, but is Brooks's usual bombas-tic, farting, *geshry*ingly aggressive one-man Grand Guignol... written, directed and acted by Brooks with the same maturity and insight one encounters at lunchtime in a grade school, when one of your playmates turns his eyelids inside-out just as you're biting into your peanutbutter&jelly sandwich.

Brooks continues to be more interested in—perhaps obsessed with—his own obnoxious comic persona than anything else, to the sacrifice of pacing, content, idea development or even honest humor above the level of the *tuchis* or bellybutton. He is a greedy talent, unwilling to give up a single ort from the groaning board of his films to other performers, sequential storytelling, or the ultimate primacy of loyalty to the work as a whole. It is a stark demonstration of disrespect for the audience, a loathing that says, "Open your mouth, I wanna pee in it again." He will cut the throat of logic, put out the eyes of artistic ambition, and disem-bowel integration of gag with story for the sake of one more booger or fart.

The moral of this film is: don't trust the coming attractions. (Your physician would refer to them technically as "trailers.") The trailers for *Spaceballs* were hilarious. Kids, don't try this at home.

And though *Spaceballs* made $28 million after 26 days, it is considered a critical and financial basket case. But it has been halloo'ed and praised by flotillas of sf fans and readers. (It is only interesting, I suppose, that Ebert—an ex–fanzine publisher and one-time fan—loved it while Siskel—with whom I seem to agree only when a two-headed calf is born—found it a dreary effort about as momentarily filling as a toxic waste burrito, my words not his.)

It is a film fans seem to love, following my thesis, because True Wit is wasted on them. They respond to the pun, to the trumpeting bleat of dumb humor...like the call of the wild as like seeks like.

There have been witty films. *The Princess Bride* is an exemplar. *Splash. Dr. Strangelove.* And outside the genre, a plethora, most evident at the moment being *In the Mood.*

But *Spaceballs* is a fan's movie.

It is one sustained pun groan from opening credits to fadeout. One throws up one's hands in sorrow and frustration, and wonders why we bother.

Why the liver and not the heart.

Why the carrion calf and not the eagle.

Why Catherine the Great never had a date with King Kong.

And why it should be that the literature we love should be dominated by readers and fans who are capable of laughing at this film...the same sort of people who laugh at paraplegics and old men falling downstairs.

The great French director Alain Resnais (and I've quoted this before) calls Brooks and his ilk, "The smart-aleck directors." Those who crave such inordinate portions of self-attention that they abandon all hope or desire for anything like Art or even a good story. And fandom clasps *Spaceballs* to its Kiss-A-Wookiee T-shirt. Lepetomane lives! The pun rides triumphant!

Now don't be angry because I revealed the Forbidden Truth. Maybe I'm wrong. Maybe you folks *are* as clever as you think you are. Maybe I'm not as clever as I think *I* am. Maybe pigs'll fly.

Just remember: who loves ya, baby?

INSTALLMENT 29:
In Which Li'l White Lies Are Revealed to Be At Least Tattletale Gray

Among the many readers' letters to the Noble Fermans who edit this magazine, responding to my column before last, in which I asked those who enjoyed these outings to drop a note vouchsafing same as palliative to the incessant bitching of those who *don't* like the cut of my jib (to reassure my employers that *Watching* isn't Ferman's Folly), was a lovely note from a woman in Hilton, Pennsylvania, containing a question no one had asked me before. A question that I had to think about for several days before I understood how important it is in setting the cut of my jib. I've waited to answer her here, because I wanted the thoughts and response to be absolutely fresh, since I'm setting down this personal revelation for the first time.

She asked: "You always seem so angry. Perhaps it is your bellicose manner that puts off the readers who write such nasty letters. How is it that you can get so upset about what is, after all, only a movie? Sometimes you seem so filled with rage that I feel the heat through the paper. Wouldn't your comments be just as effective with a little less of the flamethrower?"

Hmmm. And several days more of hmmm. Till I'd thought it out, working diligently to strip my response of self-serving rationalizations. And after much self-examination, this is what I get:

I am no different from any of you in this major attitude: I don't like being lied to.

Like you, I get crazy when someone tells me untruths that serve their ends and in the bargain warp the perception of reality. It is why I despise Edwin Meese, our soon-to-be-dumped Attorney General. He lies about the way we, as a nation, look at erotic material, the family unit, personal ethics, and the role of the government in handling lawlessness. It's why I can abide Billy Graham and lust for an Uzi to silence Falwell and Swaggart and Robertson. The former has a deep and abiding faith in something I may consider arrant superstition, but he seems genuine in his belief and willing to let others carry on their lives without ramming his book down their throats. The latter are self-serving demagogues; tyranny and elitism of the worst sort in their hearts; playing on the fears and prejudices of the gullible who seek succor in a world seemingly deteriorating around them. They lie endlessly, in aid of nothing nobler than divisiveness, with a Salem witch trial methodology that only serves to send their constituency into a tighter downward spiral of hatred, alienation and dependency on the irrational. They lie about the way the world works, and their obfuscations serve not the commonweal, but the demagogues' need for power, and their exchequers.

When we are lied to by a used car dealer or respond to tv advertising and buy a product that is not as represented, the least rancorous of us flails against the walls within our head, and cries for redress. We are lied to by governments, by our elected officials with secret agendas set down by lobbyists, by relatives and friends who think they are doing it "for our own good," but who are, in fact, trying to keep the lake calm for their own journey, and by a business community that deals in floating ethics for the benefit of the bottom line.

We are lied to constantly, in a thousand small ways every day; and the less actively we call them on it, the greater and more easily institutionalized are the lies that follow.

Lying, as a matter of policy, has always been one of the staples of the hype attendant on promotion of films. Some of it is fairly harmless, and even amusing: the bogus biographies of stars, cobbled up in the pr departments of the studios back to the '20s; William Castle's publicity tricks and hyperbole that assured the filmgoer s/he would have a heart attack if s/he sat through the latest Castle offering, and so a nurse and pulmotor squad was in attendance at every screening; the hokey-pokey about 10 YEARS IN THE MAKING! that served to legitimatize ghastly extravaganzas, failing to mention that it had taken ten years to unleash the dog because the financing kept falling through.

But other movies have been sold to us, have been judged of note, on the basis of outright whoppers intended to add a patina of social value to otherwise tawdry efforts. These are not the little white lies that we wink at, because they're silly and do no harm—the belief that a western actor actually punched cattle, when in truth the closest he had ever come to beeves was in their T-bone persona, slathered with ketchup—but the actively dishonest representations that coerce us into plonking down our money to see something special because of its origins.

Take, for instance, *The Emerald Forest*, a 1985 film written by Rospo Pallenberg and directed by John Boorman. This was a movie trumpeted in advance of its release as "based on a true story." Its advertising and most of the reviews about the film stressed the following claim:

"He was seven years old when he disappeared from the Amazon damsite where his father... was at work... For ten years, the father spent every spare moment searching for his son. But when they met again, the boy knew only one father, the chief of the primitive Indian tribe called the 'Invisible People'..."

In the film, the father is played by Powers Boothe and the son is portrayed by Boorman's curly-blond-headed son Charley. They are Americans. In the postscript to the excellent Robert Holdstock novelization of the film (New York Zoetrope, 1985), we are told that the father was actually "a Peruvian whose son, Ezequiel, was kidnapped by Indians who attacked the family campsite along Peru's Javari Mirim River." Already we begin to see a fudging of "the true story." And, reluctant to dismiss this sensational story, we accept the dishonesty by saying, "Well, the producers did it because they needed a box-office name for the general audience, and using a great Peruvian actor might be more authentic, but we wouldn't enjoy the movie as much as if we can identify with an American, Powers Boothe or whomever."

But, as it turns out, converting the protagonists from Peruvian to Yanks is nowhere near the core of duplicity used to con us into validating this film as "based on a true story."

SCAN (which stands for Southern California Answer Network) is a reference program network set up to field inquiries from area librarians unable to locate answers to reference questions through the usual sources. They publish a splendid newsletter, filled with the responses to arcane queries initiated by librarians and other seekers after enlightenment.

In their Sept/Oct 1985 bulletin, Judy Herman, identified as "SCAN Humanities Subject Specialist," pulled the plug on Embassy Pictures and Mr. Boorman. I quote, in part, from her findings:

"Interviews with director John Boorman reported that he had read the story in 'the Times' in 1972, but library systems were unable to find such an account through indexes to the Los Angeles, New York and London *Times*.

"SCAN called the agent for screenwriter Rospo Pallenberg, and asked for the citation to the story Boorman read in 'the Times.' He said, 'Let me make it clear: Rospo saw the story, not Boorman.' " (And so, another step away from the Given Truth.)

"The agent said he would check with Rospo and get back to us. He didn't, so we called again. He said, 'Let me make it clear: there was no one story the film was based on; it was a conglomeration of several stories. On the advice of our attorneys I cannot say more. If you need more information call Embassy Pictures.'

"Surprisingly, Embassy gave the citation: *Los Angeles Times*, October 8, 1972, sec. F, p. 10.

"The L.A. *Times* story is datelined Brazil but all the places mentioned in it are in Peru. It does not name the father, but says he was a Peruvian working as a lumberman 'along the Javari Mirim River, a tributary of the Javari, which lies in Peru.'

"On the radio program 'All Things Considered,' Boorman said that he did not try to contact the father again because the story had been changed so much in the film he didn't feel it *really pertained to this father and son any more* [italics Ellison's], but he had talked to an anthropologist who had visited the tribe recently and the son was still living with them, now aged about 35." The tribe was called (in the *Times* piece) the Mayorunas.

The SCAN piece concludes with this politely querulous note: "This is rather strange, because an article in *American Indigena* (abril/junio 1975, pp. 329–347) reports on the Mayorunas, with a detailed census by age and sex, and does not mention that one of them was an adopted outsider." Much less a blond-curlyheaded son of either a Peruvian *or* an American.

Thus, a rational consideration of all the tumult re: "based on a true story" leads any but the most gullible to the conclusion that a writer of fiction, Rospo Pallenberg, was sparked into creating an interesting fiction by an idea proceeding from a news snippet. So far, okay. It was then bought or appropriated by

Boorman, who sold it to the Embassy honchos as "based on a true story" *he* had read. From that point on, it was never really questioned, and was set on its journey to your wallet by studio flacks who embellished and aggrandized and pumped hot air. And at the terminus, you and I went to that film, amazed at the bizarre and heartrending circumstances transmogrified from Real Life onto the Silver Screen.

We were lied to, and we bought it.

Not that knowing it was principally fabrication, as opposed to slightly-altered-for-dramatic-effect made the film any less a pompous, strutting bore. But the being lied to... produces in me and possibly in you, now that you know you bit on it, a genuine anger. Like you, I don't like being made to play the fool.

Or consider such pure fantasies as *Hangar 18* (1980), a Sunn Classic Picture that was sold with the cross-my-heart-and-hope-to-plotz assurance of the producers that this was a movie that revealed the U.S. Air Force had captured a UFO, and that the spacecraft was concealed in Hangar 18... or *Flying Saucer* (1950) that received enormous amounts of publicity as containing actual footage of an Alaskan UFO sighting... or *Frankenstein: The True Story* (1973), from a screenplay by Christopher Isherwood, which was no closer to Mary Shelley's novel than most of the other versions of the Modern Prometheus... or *Sharks' Treasure* (1975), a Cornel Wilde potboiler that made back its nut by advertising that swore you would see live sharks gnawing on happy natives, but which actually used *dead* sharks, pushed by hand from offcamera ... or *Ladyhawke* (1985) that swore up'n'down that it was based on a genuine Medieval folktale, and was in fact simply a fictional construct cobbled up in the brain of the modern-day screenwriter... or *The Philadelphia Experiment* (1984), that was promoted as being the true story of a World War II battleship that slipped through a hole in time and wound up in the Eighties.

These are lies of a flagrant sort. They treat the audience as if it were populated by morons. At the very least they are films that consciously lie to promote themselves at the cost of spreading more obscurantism and looney beliefs in crap like channeling, "communion" with aliens, crystals, creationism, and a vast array of newly-reborn scams that only serve to alienate an already-befuddled populace from the Real World and the directing of their lives at their own responsibility. At worst, they actively convince the gullible that they are powerless in the grip of "cosmic forces" that are responsible for their bad luck, lack of a job, fucked-up relationships, and imminent demise from nuclear holocaust or angels with fiery swords.

Thus do I attempt to codify for the kind lady in Hilton, Pennsylvania why "just a movie" can send me into paroxysms of gibbering, thereby producing the flamethrower heat she finds overreactive. I wish I had a more rational answer to that anger— which I try to ennoble by the word "passionate"—but the simple truth as I've been able to perceive it, is that for the time I spend in the grip of a movie, I willingly surrender my disbelief; I am a child again, attending *Snow White and the Seven Dwarfs* for the first time, and all I ask is: do it to me!

When the film lies, when it loses my trust by any one of a hundred different ineptitudes or flummeries, I respond like a betrayed lover. I fume at *Lethal Weapon* because I know damned well that Mel Gibson would never be able to make that idiotic run down Hollywood Boulevard in his bare feet, because the street is *never* as empty as the film showed it, and the overpass at which he caught up with the fleeing Gary Busey is *miles* away from Hollywood Boulevard, and not even Paavo Nurmi with JATO Adidas could overtake a felon in a speeding car. I rage at *Someone to Watch Over Me* and *Suspect* because cops and lawyers are just flat-out not stupid enough to engage in such behavior that will get them stripped of their badges or disbarred. And if it is *absolutely* necessary for them to act in ways that are so anti-survival, then I can only suspend my disbelief if the scenarist displays a level of artfulness that blows away my perceptions of the Real World and explains it all so I can accept the rationalization. What we're talking about is Art, as opposed to artifice. And when *no* attempt is made to reconcile the unbelievable fictive construct with my commonsense view of reality, then I get angry. Because I've been lied to.

Does that explain it?

Perhaps not. But I swear it's the best I can do.

All of which leads me to the "review" of THE RUNNING MAN (Taft Entertainment Pictures/Keith Barish Productions/Tri-Star), a film both Erick Wujcik of Detroit and Brian Siano of Philadelphia have asked me to discuss in detail. I had actually planned to deal with this latest vehicle for filmdom's leading mesomorph, Arnold Schwarzenegger, rather summarily. But the subject of lying has spread its petals so appealingly, that I think I'll put it over to next time, using this installment as a sort of preamble. So keep this screed in mind, and we'll meet back here next month for *Li'l White Lies*, part two. And we'll try to discover if *The Running Man* is actually a ripoff of Robert Sheckley's "The Prize of Peril" and if *The Hidden* is really a ripoff of Hal Clement's NEEDLE or just a misappropriation of a 1982 script by Gerald Gaiser called *Alien Cop*.

And I'll try to keep my temper.

ANCILLARY MATTERS: There are a handful of mythic icons that fantasists and their fans never tire of using or seeing used in stories. Hitler, the Titanic, King Kong, King Arthur, Marilyn Monroe, Jack the Ripper...you get the idea. Very likely topping that small list is dinosaurs. You show me a kid or an adult who doesn't get a smile and the shivers when you mention dinosaurs, and I'll show you a kid or an adult who would happily eat lima beans or vote for Pat Robertson. Well, it's not often that we are dazzled by some new variation on the presentation of the saurians, but Celestial Arts (PO Box 7327, Berkeley, CA 94707) has released a set of four dinosaur posters in their Dinosauria Graphics Series that will absolutely steal your breath away. They're big—24 × 32 inches each—and they come in four flavors: Stegosaurus, Brachiosaurus, Triceratops and Tyrannosaurus. The artwork is by Earl C. Bateman III, each one has a background grid with a metric scale to provide a sense of size, and each one has—are you ready for this—an overprinted skeleton that *glows in the dark*! Each one comes with a nifty little 16-page illustrated booklet that contains the latest skinny on what we know about the saurians, and I've got to tell you that these are knockout posters. And you will love me for turning your attention to the set of four. Even if your spouse or roomie is a lima bean eater, you can pretend you're buying these for some kid's room, and make nocturnal visits to enjoy the glow-in-the-dark skeletons. These are visuals that will make you feel ten years old again.

In my February essay I used the old expression "liver and lights" and explained that it referred to "the soul and eyes." Well, y'know how you go through years and years mispronouncing some word you've only read, and never actually heard spoken, and you get it wrong till one day you hear someone say it correctly and you thank your stars that no one ever caught you making a fool of yourself, and thereafter you pronounce it properly? (With me it was the word *minutiae*, but that's another story for another time.) I'd been using "liver and lights" for years and always thought it meant the soul and the eyes. I was wrong. As (among others) Jim Bennett of Newport, RI and Brad Strickland of Oakwood, GA politely pointed out. *Liver and lights*, as the first pirate or barbarian warlord who used the phrase intended it, meant the liver and *lungs*, the entrails, the 'umbles. Of which said pirate or warlord might make an " 'umble pie," or of use to feed his dogs. Jim advised me "lights" is hunters' jargon for "lungs." I hate being wrong, but I love it when I'm set straight. We are all in this together, it seems.

A NOTE ON SEQUENTIALITY

There is nothing wrong with your neocortex. We control the vertical, we control the horizontal. These columns are in precisely the order I wish them to be: Installment 29, followed by Installment 30½, followed by 30 and 31. You can see from the publication dates that these are the sequence in which they appeared in print. If you ask why, I tell you it was because my attention was diverted. If you say that is irresponsible, I tell you that it's my party, and I'll cry if I want to. Yours truly, The White Rabbit.

INSTALLMENT 30½:
In Which 3 Cinematic Variations On "The Whimper of Whipped Dogs" Are Presented

On September 9th, 1977, I left for Paris to begin work with director William Friedkin on a theatrical feature based on my short story, "The Whimper of Whipped Dogs." The story, winner of a Mystery Writers of America Edgar Allan Poe award as best short story of 1974, was to have starred Jeanne Moreau. Because of film industry problems pursuant to the trade unions' contract raises, due early in 1978, it was contractually imperative that I have the script completed by the end of October. I was not able to meet that deadline.

The short story from which the screenplay was to have been expanded, was a fantasy based on the real-life murder of a woman named Catherine Genovese, in the section of Queens called Kew Gardens, in 1964.

At the time, the killing made worldwide headlines chiefly because it had been witnessed by thirty-eight neighbors of Kitty Genovese, not one of whom made the slightest effort to save her, to scream at the killer, or even to call the police. (One man, in fact, viewing the murder from his third-floor apartment window, stated later that he rushed to turn up his radio so he wouldn't hear the woman's screams.) The excuse offered by almost every one of those wretched thirty-eight witnesses, was that "I didn't want to get involved." It became an emblematic incident of an alienated society, and entire books have been written on the phenomenon.

(And for those who have sought to dismiss the incident as an isolated aberration of its time, here are excerpts from the opening paragraphs of a *New York Times* article dated Friday, December 28th, 1974: "While at least one neighbor heard her dying screams and did nothing, a 25-year-old model was beaten to death early Christmas morning in her Kew Gardens, Queens, apartment, which virtually overlooks the scene of the murder of Catherine Genovese 10 years ago.... The 10-story red brick building where the latest murder occurred was the residence of many of the 38 witnesses who heard or saw the knife-slaying of Miss Genovese on the street below in the early morning hours of March 13, 1964, and neither called the police nor took any other action.... The latest victim, Sandra Zahler of 82-67 Austin Street, was apparently slain about 3:20 A.M. Wednesday, when a woman in the next-door apartment on the fifth floor said she heard screams and the sounds of a fierce struggle.... Madeline Hartmann, who lives in the apartment next to the victim's and who recalled having heard the screams of Miss Genovese 10 years ago, told in an interview of having heard Miss Zahler scream and of other sounds of an apparent struggle.... While most of those who witnessed the murder of Miss Genovese have moved away from Kew Gardens, some because of negative publicity about their inaction, some still remain in the neighborhood and a few still live in the building where Miss Zahler died.") In an eerie way, the fantasy-horror explanation I presented in my story for the behavior of those 38 people, was validated by the murder of the Zahler woman ten years later. In fact, Sandra Zahler might easily have been the real-life model for the heroine of "The Whimper of Whipped Dogs," and the fate that befell her might as easily have come straight out of my fiction. (For those unfamiliar with the story, it can be found in my collections DEATHBIRD STORIES and last year's THE ESSENTIAL ELLISON, as well as in a number of anthologies including BEST DETECTIVE STORIES OF THE YEAR: 1974 and THE YEAR'S BEST HORROR STORIES, Series III and the recent David Hartwell–edited anthology, THE DARK DESCENT.)

Neither in the nine years between the murder of Kitty Genovese and the writing of "The Whimper of Whipped Dogs," nor in the fifteen years since its publication, did it ever occur to me that I would someday have to explain *who* Kitty Genovese was, why her death was (and remains) a modern, urban horror of the most paralyzing sort, or what it was about that slaying that so obsessed me that I would be driven to write a story that to this day frightens me no less than at the moment I completed it; a story that I think is the most chilling thing I've ever written.

I would have instantly dismissed such a silly thought. To forget Kitty Genovese and the cultural icon she became, would be as impossible as forgetting the mythic origins of Jack the Ripper, Dr. Crippen, Gilles de Rais, Sawney Beane, Charles Manson, Lee Harvey Oswald or John Dillinger. Nothing less than unthinkable!

But a terrible cultural amnesia assails us, and young people today seem to learn no history in their schools; and that which they learn they forget immediately after their spot quizzes. The Korean War is as misty in the public mind as the Wars of the Roses.

The National Endowment for the Humanities recently released a report mandated by Congress entitled *American Memory*, which indicates that while our students may be great at analyzing, contemplating, reasoning, in short, "thinking," their education has not given them very much to think *about*. Method, in our public schools and universities, has been emphasized over content. Teachers, themselves, are rewarded for "process" more than knowledge of anything in particular.

A survey of more than eight thousand 17-year-old Americans last Spring revealed that 68% had no idea in what half-century the American Civil War had taken place. 69% didn't know what the Magna Carta was. Hardly any of them knew who Chaucer, Cervantes, Dante or Dostoevsky were. Many were dimly aware that Columbus is alleged to have discovered America first, but they didn't have a clue in what year. History as a required subject has virtually vanished from school curricula, lumped in haphazardly as "Social Studies"; geography hasn't been taught in many of our schools in years; English courses are transformed into something called "Language Arts"; and don't even think about what vast gaps in historical and scientific knowledge are caused by the ever-present specter of the Fundamentalists.

According to Lynn Chaney, Chairman of the National Endowment for the Humanities, most elementary reading texts contain little literature, and instead of learning about George Washington, Joan of Arc or King Arthur, children are subjected to dry, contemporary prose aimed at teaching such skills as how to make out grocery lists, how to give change, and how to use a telephone book.

415

And even though I know all of the preceding to be tragically true, and probably woefully understated as to the *real* severity of the problem of widespread ignorance, it never occurred to me that I would have to explain who Kitty Genovese was.

But in the past six months I've received two or three letters from readers frightened and mesmerized by "The Whimper of Whipped Dogs," asking me how I'd thought up such a scarifying idea. There was even a reader who wrote in to the *Comic Buyer's Guide*, who had read the story, and had come across a variation on the Genovese slaying in some comic book or other, and wanted to know who had ripped off whom. (Fortunately, the editors of *CBG*, Don and Maggie Thompson, knew the referent, and they attempted to provide a background for that hapless product of the American Educational System.) And so, it is with heavy heart that I have prefaced the snippets of screenplay that follow with snippets of history not that old...bits of tragic real-life I never thought would grow dim in the minds of people who swore Kitty Genovese had not been murdered in vain. (And how many of you subscribe to *The Underground Grammarian* of R. Mitchell? Which may seem to be a *non sequitur*, but if you go to your nearest library and check it out, you'll see I'm only being purposefully obtuse in your best interests.)

But in 1977, when Billy Friedkin brought me to Paris to turn "The Whimper of Whipped Dogs" into a film of terror that spoke to the violence of cities, the omen that Kitty Genovese had become, an omen of slasher films we take for granted only a decade later, was as bright as the blood on a knife blade.

It's a shame time constraints killed the project...

The production entity that had bankrolled Friedkin's deal, put me in breach; standard operating procedure. The film, therefore, would not be made. No one's fault but mine...and time. With which I've had problems before. But...

While in Paris, I wrote three visual openings for the screenplay. They are sequences intended to set the tone for the film, this ugly, mean horror-fantasy about evil in big cities. If you look up the short story, then the subliminal thrust of these openings will link for you.

They are three very different openings, yet each one goes to the thematic core of the story. I have arranged them in order of preference, from least desirable to most appealing. They are offered as examples of the way in which a writer of books and stories can adapt him- or herself to writing for motion pictures.

416 It's a matter of thinking visually.

Offered as addenda to these essays, in which I extoll the art and craft of screenwriting, for those few of you who may never have had the chance to enjoy the visual magic endemic to that special form of fantastic literature.

Offered as a sorta kinda bonus column, so you won't feel cheated out of your chosen portion of *Watching*. And I would be less than forthright with you were I not to add this:

Quite a few years ago I rancorously resigned from membership in Science Fiction Writers of America, an organization that I helped to found and which, in the capacity of its first Vice-President, I served. I resigned because the membership at large decided, in its wisdom, to drop the Nebula category of Best Dramatic Presentation.

I'll not go into the affront to SFWA's members who work in *both* film and books that this action proffered. Nor will I dwell on the horrors that resulted from SFWA having previously given Nebulas not to the author(s) of notable screenplays, but to the finished, collaborative films—and being pissed-off when Woody Allen didn't come to the Banquet to accept the award—rather than understanding that what scenarists do is different from what novelists do, and that the best screenplay category should have been judged not by a large membership to whom the scripts were unavailable, but by a blue ribbon panel changed from year to year, a panel that would scrutinize the *written words*. That's *really* ancient history. So I won't go into all that.

But this year, my screenplay based on Isaac Asimov's I, ROBOT cycle of stories (an unproduced film that exists *only* as the written word) has garnered a number of recommendations for the Nebula in the category of Best Novel. (Well, the form of it may be different from the standard novel, but it *is* about 100,000 novel-length words; and it appeared as a serial in a competitor to this journal you now read; and the Nebula Awards Committee judged it eligible.) So for the first time, a work written to be filmed, rather than published between covers, has a chance to demonstrate to a frequently-irrational stick-in-the-mud constituency that—out of ignorance, I presume—their out of hand and off the wall dismissal of filmwriting has been a tunnel-visioned kind of snobbery as outdated and jejune as that of the land warfare experts who *knew* the Maginot Line was unbreachable, or the cavalry supporters who sneered at the possibility that air power would forever alter the forms of waging war. This effete dismissal of screenwriting by a cadre of writers concretized in their thinking, serves two non-productive ends:

First, it perpetuates an almost hayseed attitude, provincial and purblind; rooted in a fearfully uneducated perception of the film industry as *Terra Incognita*: a land of savages and arrivistes lying in wait for the unwary sf writer; slavering Philistines who debased and crushed the souls of Scott Fitzgerald and Nathanael West and William Faulkner and Dashiell Hammett and Dorothy Parker, and wasted their talent; a place of goofy non-writing in which no self-respecting "sci-fi guy" would deign to soil his/her pristine perfection. (A pristine perfection that is apparently unsullied by the penning of paperback adaptations of hack, commercial movies; cheap horror novels chiefly distinguished and distinguishable one from another by embossed foil covers featuring fangs dripping blood and demon children brandishing meat cleavers; Tolkien and Malory ripoffs awash with elfin creatures and swordspersons with unpronounceable names forever on the road in search of mystic jewels, coronets of kingship or keys to alternate universes; and endless one-note ideas meretriciously bloated for the tawdriest commercial reasons into trilogy, quartet, sextet, octology, nonology and dekalogy. It escapes me how working in film could be any more witless or talent-bashing than what these literary elitists do for low advances and specious career motives.)

But this reiteration of yokel mythology about Cloud Cuckoo Land spreads a miasma of trepidation and booga-booga boogey-men that deters good writers in our genre from attempting to work in the screenplay form. In this way, they are relegated to writing only in the printed media, and they are cut off not only from a salutary expansion of their talents—writing for film hones the visual sense better than any other exercise I've ever come across, in the way photography sharpens the eye of the painter—but from the vast sums of money and the pleasures of filming attendant on such projects.

As for Hollywood crushing the sensitive blossom of a writer's abilities, "Pep" West wrote what was unarguably his finest novel, THE DAY OF THE LOCUST, during the five years in which he flourished as a successful studio scenarist, and would no doubt have continued his brilliant auctorial career had he not stupidly snuffed out his life (and that of his wife, Eileen McKinney) in a senseless car accident resulting from a penchant for speeding, which had caused rollovers and warnings from friends previously; Scott Fitzgerald's "Pat Hobby" stories, written while he sank lower and lower in Hollywood due to alcoholism and the deteriorating mental condition of Zelda, may not be the apex of

418

his writing (though they remain charmingly antic and mordant despite the pecksniffian cavils of quite another set of literary elitists), but it *was* writing done in Hollywood while he worked at the studios (ineptly, it turns out), and don't forget he put together almost all of THE LAST TYCOON, which many scholars contend would have been his most mature work, while being "destroyed" by Tinseltown; Faulkner's studio work supported his wife, his family, his lover and himself while he turned out brilliant novels that were critically acclaimed, but were not bookstall runaways, and in that way his screen writing was like a day job, freeing him financially to indulge his muse as sybaritically as he wished in books.

As Saul Bellow has pointed out: "Writers are not necessarily corrupted by money. They are distracted—diverted to other avenues."

As living testimony to this, may I point out that whatever you, dear reader, think of my writing—pro or con—almost *all* of what I have done that is of worth has been done right here in Hollywood, where I have lived happily for 26 years. There is no deep secret to it, not for me, not for Fitzgerald, not for Michael Crichton or George R. R. Martin or for Richard Matheson. It is commonsense. If one retains a sense of one's literary worth, and writes for film with the same punctiliousness brought to the books and stories, one can live decently and have all the time one wishes to write books that challenge and explore the limits of one's talent...rather than signing on to do yet another furry-footed fantasy for a paperback publisher whose already overloaded schedule guarantees that the book it took you six months or a year to write will get a mingy six days of display and then be stripped and returned for credit, effectively putting a year of hard work out-of-print almost before it's been published.

But because of the widespread Accepted Wisdom of writers who, in their imperial fiat, deigned to kill the Best Dramatic Presentation Nebula, many sf/fantasy writers who could move comfortably and profitably between film and books look toward the West Coast as if it were the Bermuda Triangle.

Which brings me to the second non-productive aspect of the matter. Because the people who *could* and *should* be doing films of the fantastic are frightened away from the medium, the jobs fall into the clutches of hacks and parvenus who think an alien invasion is a fresh idea. And we all suffer. Because they write shitty films.

The producers don't know any better. They aren't conversant

with the fecundity of imagination regularly demonstrated in the genre, so they can't be blamed for thinking the dusty old stuff they're getting is fresh and innovative. Nor can they really be blamed for buying plagiaristic, watered-down ideas stolen from the best of our people (see column #30). They know no better.

By eschewing jobs in feature films, sf/fantasy writers abandon the field of creative battle to the hypesters and ex–talent agency mailroom boys who become "writers." And what results I review here regularly, with hysteria and disgust.

The days in which there were only Beaumont, Bloch, Matheson, Ellison, Gerrold, Crais and a few others writing films, are gone. John Varley works here. So does George R. R. Martin. And Steven Barnes and John Shirley and Norman Spinrad and Thomas Disch (to greater or lesser degree of involvement), to name just a few.

With I, ROBOT a possibility for inclusion on the Nebula final ballot, the time is right to raise the question again: *Why is screenwriting not treated with equal dignity by SFWA?*

Chances of its winning are infinitesimal, but I am, at this moment, inordinately proud to have a work in the scenario form even vying for a slot as Best Novel. It heartens my brother and sister writers in this genre who move between the two mediums. It seems there will always be those so limited in their perception of what is "appropriate" that the screenplay will be pooh-pooh'd —of the many letters received by the sf magazine that published I, ROBOT recently, there were the expected few that came from readers who said, "What *is* this? I don't know how to read it," or "Why did you waste space on a script...it was good, but it just ain't like what you usually publish," and one can feel little more than sadness at readers who wear blinders—but movies are *the* popular medium in which outstanding work can be done (don't get me onto tv, please!), and it's twenty-five years past time that SFWA should be rewarding that excellence of craft seen by many more millions all over the world than ever read one of our short stories.

Which is not to say that working in Hollywood is free of angst or heartbreak or time-waste or horror. Probably no less of any of that than one finds in any industry. And heaven knows I've written about those horrors and inequities at tedious length in a hundred different forums. And may again, here in these pages. But I am not suggesting that every good writer of a page of prose chuck it all in New Jersey and rush to knock on doors at Universal. I *am* suggesting that careful, imaginative, worthy work is being done by many of SFWA's writer-members in this dazzlingly inventive form, and it's time those who sneer at film writing because of their own fears and limited abilities be countered by an equally vocal segment of the writing community raised in a later time that acknowledges the importance and seriousness of motion pictures as Art.

So, because I'm nuts about these snippets intended for "The Whimper of Whipped Dogs," a film that was never made, and to get the dialogue going, I offer examples of *script*.

I talk a great deal about the script in these columns. I quote from Ring Lardner, Jr., who said: "No good film was ever made from a poor script." And I try to convince those of you who "can't read this script stuff" and those of you who, like me, love movies, that without first the *word*, the directors and actors would stand there with their fingers up their noses. This, as palliative to the endless interviews with arrogant thespians who tell the Rex Reeds and Mary Harts of the world how they "rewrote the dialogue" right there on the set, the day they began to roll the cameras.

I have digressed wildly, for purpose, but at last, in three quick scenes, I offer you some direct evidence of where the vision comes from that results finally in a motion picture. It comes from the writer. And the better the writers available to know-nothing producers, the better will be the films we see, the movies I review here. In these three snippets the eye of the writer becomes the vision of the scenarist. They're easy to read. Just let the inner eye *see* what the words tell you to see. Read and close your eyes and roll the cameras in your head. This isn't work, it's a paid vacation.

And no matter what those men and women who yell *Action!* try to con you into believing, they are afoot in the desert without the art and craft of the writer.

THE WHIMPER OF WHIPPED DOGS: *Variation 1*

FADE IN:

1   NEW YORK STREET—NIGHT

Chill and damp. The pavements look as though they're coated with fever-sweat. Fog and mist silently swirl and hang like torn lace in the air. An upper West Side sort of street with ancient light stanchions that cast dull illumination, fog-shrouded light, just enough to see vaguely, with halations around them.

421

CAMERA MOVES STEADILY down the street at waist height.
Past withering brownstones, battered garbage cans that are
chained by their lids to iron fences, flaking stone stoops, steps
leading down to basement apartments, huge plastic bags of refuse
at the curbs, cars parked almost one atop another. And all of it
swathed in obscuring fog. CAMERA PANS LEFT as it CON-
TINUES MOVE IN and we see down a short throw of steps into a
sub-street cul-de-sac entrance to an apartment. A man in shape-
less clothes lies unmoving with his feet and legs aimed toward us.
His head and shoulders below. Upside-down. One arm outflung.
Head twisted at an unnatural angle. As though he fell backward
down the stairs. Clearly dead, though we cannot see his face.

CAMERA SWINGS BACK and CONTINUES MOVING down the
street with a smooth, casual movement. A woman lies dead in the
gutter, face toward the curb so we cannot see her features, one arm
bent up and lying on the sidewalk above her. CAMERA does not
linger.

As CAMERA MOVES DOWN STREET toward the park and the
river, seen vaguely through the trembling mist, we find ourselves
looking for more bodies, but we cannot be certain if those two
huddled shapes in the VW at the curb are dead; they are slumped
forward on the dash but they might be just sleeping; that pile of
rags at the mouth of the alley might be an old man with a battered
hat jammed down on his dead face, but it could be just trash; and as
we enter the small park abutting the drop to the Hudson River we
see what could be a woman's naked arm protruding from under a
bush, but it might be only a dead branch. It might be.

But we know for certain that the man sitting on the bench is dead.
His head hangs back as only a head with its throat cut can hang. At
that awkward angle, arms out to the sides, legs spread, body braced
against the bench. CAMERA SWINGS PAST and PASSES ON to
HOLD the silent river, fog rising and tumbling. Then, out on the
River, lonely and desperate, we HEAR the SOUND of a tug heading
for the Narrows. Once, twice, distantly. Then silence again. The
city is silent.

FADE TO BLACK

and

FADE OUT.

       *   *   *

THE WHIMPER OF WHIPPED DOGS: *Variation 2*

FADE IN:

1   RED FRAME—IN MAGMA POOL

Around the CAMERA molten lava bubbles and seethes. No sound.
High contrast. CAMERA BEGINS TO RISE up through the mael-

strom. It does not tilt, but RISES VERTICALLY. It reaches the surface of the magma pool, breaks the tension and we see across the leaping, spitting surface. CAMERA CONTINUES RISING through steam in the chamber above the lava. To the dendritic stone of the cavern ceiling. CAMERA PASSES THROUGH, STILL RISING

DISSOLVE THRU:

2   CAMERA RISING THRU ROCK—EFFECT

Varying levels of light and dark, indicating stratification of rock. Through iron, mica schist, diatomaceous earth, layers of roiling oil, feldspar, marble, sparkling levels of gold, diamonds, phosphates, solid granite, up and up.

DISSOLVE THRU TO:

3   CAMERA IN SOIL—EFFECT

RISING SMOOTHLY as we view it in the manner of someone in an elevator sees floor after floor dropping past. Up through rock and soil to empty spaces, through and up to hard-packed sub-soil, concrete slabbing, coils and snakes of cable, electrical conduit, pipes. Up past them through metal sheathing, into flowing water —a sewer system. CAMERA RISES to feature a metal ladder used by maintenance crews. Up to the ladder to a grating above as we

DISSOLVE THRU:

4   STREET—NIGHT

CAMERA RISES up out of the sewer grating to HOLD for a beat the silent night street of New York. SHOOT THE LENGTH of the street in fog and rain. CAMERA CONTINUES to RISE after beat; TILT CAMERA UP to feature the huge and silent monoliths of incredibly tall buildings that close in overhead.

HOLD the ominous leaning structures as the clouds tear apart for a moment and the single white eye of the Moon is seen. In the b.g. DISTANCE we HEAR the SOUND of dogs crying, as though they are being beaten. Not loud. We may not hear it at all. Then the clouds close over again, the Moon is gone, and the fog swirls in to FILL FRAME.

FRAME TO BLACK.

*   *   *

THE WHIMPER OF WHIPPED DOGS: *Variation 3*

FADE IN:

1   SHOT ACROSS WATER—NIGHT

Dark, slick water. Oily. CAMERA MOVES IN just above the softly undulating surface. An occasional silvered flash across a gentle

423

swell, as of moonlight skimming into darkness. Fog rolls across the lens. CAMERA IN STEADILY toward a massive throw of land that rises up in b.g. We can make out nothing but the gray shape coming toward us.

SLOW STEADY MOVE IN across the water till we perceive we are beaching on an island. Fog rolls up the naked beach. CAMERA IN to climb the beach and MOVES IN through darkness across low dunes. Now something rises up through the darkness. Tall. CAMERA KEEPS MOVING in on the shape. It is an Easter Island menhir. One of the great stone faces of antiquity. Silence.

CAMERA ANGLES SMOOTHLY AROUND the statue and goes past. Across the dead island to another head. And past to another. And another. To the largest of them. CAMERA TILTS DOWN and MOVES IN for EXTREME CLOSEUP through the roiling fog of the ashy ground.

HOLD EXTREME CLOSEUP of a bright, clean very modern knife lying in the sandy ash at the foot of the menhir. Again, a brief flash of silver light, this time across the blade—as if the moon had hurled one single beam through the clouds and the fog.

Then a drop of water strikes the knife blade. Then a drop of water dimples the sand beside it. Then another. Then it begins to rain steadily. The knife sinks slowly into the rain-soaked absorbent ash and sand, and as its haft goes under, the fog closes down, swirls and FILLS FRAME.

CAMERA HOLDS on fog as we HEAR in the b.g. DISTANCE the SOUND of a ululating siren: an ambulance, a police car perhaps, a truck carrying people to ovens; we cannot quite place it. It recedes and SILENCE resumes.

FRAME TO BLACK.

INSTALLMENT 30:
In Which The Li'l White Lies Thesis (Part Two) Takes Us By The Snout And Drags Us Unwillingly Toward A Door We Fear To Open

We were talking about being lied to, and how it unhinges us. How it makes us feel used and foolish, that we were so damned *anxious* to believe the hype. How irrationally *angry* it makes us to know that no matter how wise and experienced we have become as we grew older, that adroit liars can still manipulate us by plumbing our ever-regenerating gullibility, our *need* to believe. (In this way, I suspect, no amount of revelation of corruption on the part of televangelists will ever free their supporters. They discover one awfulness after another about the Falwells, Swaggarts, Popoffs, Robertsons and Bakkers, and yet they fling themselves again and again into the wash of hossanahs that keeps them asea in ignorance.)

As Michel de Montaigne, the French moralist, wrote: "Nothing is so firmly believed as that which we least know."

We were talking about the false lures thrown out by the makers of movies to convince us that trash has sidebar merit, value apart from the work itself. And I mentioned that we had been lied to as regards, among other films, the 1985 fantasy *Ladyhawke*. And one of you wrote insisting that I was wrong, that the film *was* based on some obscure medieval legends. And Faithful Reader upbraided me for mischievously shattering beliefs.

Well, I never went into detail on that matter, because I'm trying (in what now appears to be a series of three columns) to codify a thesis of gullibility and duplicity that *seems* to have some credibility; and I simply didn't have the time to linger. But perhaps you do need a bit more convincing.

In the September/October 1987 issue of *Scannings*, an information search and retrieval newsletter for librarians, we find the following Q&A exchange:

Q: On what legends was the movie "Ladyhawke" based? The story concerns lovers who are cursed. He is a wolf at night, she a hawk during the day. They assume their human forms only at opposite times.

A: The Academy of Motion Picture Arts and Sciences Library had a press release from Warner Bros. stating, "legend dates back to the 13th century from paintings on the walls of the Mauseturm Castle in the Rhine Valley to the Loup Garou legend of France's Auvergne Forest to Rodriguez de la Fuente in Spain."

When we went to gather these legends... we found the Mauseturm story did not match, the loup-garou, or werewolf, story was too vague, and the only Rodriguez de la Fuente we found was a 20th century Spanish naturalist.

We wrote to scriptwriter Edward Khmara for an explanation. Here is his reply:

The story of two lovers kept apart by taking human form only at opposite times of the day was an inspiration that occurred to me while jogging on the roof of the Hollywood YMCA.

The studio contention that "Ladyhawke" is based on an old legend is, in fact, a violation of Writers Guild rules, since it denies me full rights of authorship. The Guild undertook an action against Warner Bros. on this account... and a small amount of money was paid as compensation... Warner Bros., or its publicity department, continues to circulate material restating the old legend story.

The inspiration for the character of Phillipe the Mouse was Francois Villon. His "Testament" recounts his imprisonment and mistreatment by Bishop Thibault d'Aussigny, in the dungeons of Meung. When the Dauphin, soon to be Louis XI of France, passed through Meung on the way to his coronation, he freed the prisoners, including Villon. This incident was actually used in the original story of "Ladyhawke."

So I may have been wrong about the meaning of "liver and lights," but I definitely knew what I was talking about when I used *Ladyhawke* as an example of how we are lied to.

Lied to, that is, in the specific sense of misrepresentation. And here, as I promised in Installment 29, we'll move on to another kind of lying, another species of misrepresentation:

plagiarism.

If one elects to pursue a plagiarism suit in a court of law, one must *never* solicit "expert testimony" from a Renaissance or Medieval scholar, because stealing the work, ideas, manner of others, in those times, was considered nothing unusual. In fact, quite acceptable.

The modern concept of plagiarism, paradoxically, is both specific and nebulous. What is theft, and what is "coincidental simultaneous generation" of idea or ambience? What is the rapacity of producers, network development executives, main chance hustlers and all those who denigrate writers but don't know how to construct a plot themselves... and what is acceptable, even flattering, literary crossover, feedback, input, stimulation?

In the world of publishing, plagiarism is so rare that its occurrence startles everyone, and it makes the news section of *Publishers Weekly*.

(Oddly enough—given the almost encyclopedic memories of so many readers and writers and fans, guaranteeing near-instantaneous unmasking—there *have* been a few notable instances of book/story plagiarism in the sf/fantasy genre in recent memory. There was a guy who took Gardner F. Fox's 1964 Paperback Library novel, ESCAPE ACROSS THE COSMOS, changed the names of the characters, and sold it to another paperback house some years later. There is considerable mythology surrounding that most flagrant case, and while I'm certain some readers will know the specifics, the best I can do is present *all* the data I can dredge up from imperfect memories, both actual and emblematic. Trying to get the anecdote accurately, I savaged the recollections of Charlie Brown of *Locus*, Silverberg, Joe Haldeman and several others, but understandably enough none of these rational gentlemen cared to depart from their creative labors to spend several hours rummaging through ancient issues of the SFWA *Forum* or other sources to get me the data. *You've got to be kidding* and *Piss off, kid* were the politest responses. Can't say I blame 'em; so you'll have to do with this jumble of truths and fancies intended to make the point, not to reflect what actually happened. Anyhow, one story has it that a customer came into a specialty bookshop bearing a copy of a paperback bought the day before, screaming scorched earth at the bookseller for having sold the outraged reader a novel that was *exactly* like one the customer had read. When the bookseller compared the new title with the Fox book, it was discovered that the theft was line-for-line. The author had copied the entire novel, merely changing

427

the names of the characters. When the bookseller advised the publisher—some say it was Belmont, a well-known schlock operation, thus making this a classic case of poetic justice—the publisher sought out the writer and discovered he was hard at work doing the same job on an old Robert Moore Williams Ace double. When confronted with his crime, the guy is alleged to have been utterly bewildered. "I didn't do anything wrong," he's reported to have said. "Isn't this the way all books are written?" If *that* part isn't whole cloth, then it was a case of doltish behavior raised to the *n*th power. But other versions of the yarn have it that the guy also sold the Fox novel a second time, to the hardcover publisher Thomas Nelson, having changed the names again. And when they went looking for the clown, he'd cashed the check and split. Either way, it doesn't speak well to the familiarity-with-genre of the editors involved. Usually, this kind of thing is the result of uncomplicated amateurism, a lack of commonsense, naïveté almost impossible to conceive if one has even a passing familiarity with writing and publishing. Impossible for *us* to believe, yet far more common than one might suspect. But once in a while the plagiarism comes from a professional who *does* know better, who does the deed fully cognizant of what s/he is pulling off. In 1974 a well-known fantasy author—whose identity, though known to me, has never been publicly revealed, nor will I do so now—masquerading as "Terry Dixon," supposedly a young black male writer, copped the famous Anatole France short story, "The Procurator of Judæa," rewrote it as "The Prophet of Zorayne," and passed it off for sale to Roger Elwood for a Trident Press/Pocket Books anthology. A private detective named Sam Bluth was hired to track down the culprit, and the writer—neither young nor black—was brought to book. A rare, bizarre case.)

But if the foregoing produce hilo because of their rarity, not even a hiccup is produced by the *daily* thefts in the worlds of television and motion pictures. It is *so* common, this thuggish misappropriation of other's stories—both produced and in raw manuscript form—that when Ben Bova and I won our plagiarism suit against ABC-TV and Paramount in 1980, both the media and industry were astonished that someone had actually pursued such a pilferage beyond the *pro forma* out-of-court, keep-your-mouth-shut, take-the-money-and-scamper cash settlement (*Sci-fi writers win $337,000 in plagiarism suit!* said the front page of the Los Angeles *Herald-Examiner* with a word-choice that made my toenails ache).

428

It is no less than institutionalized behavior; no more needful of exculpation, in the larcenous souls of these dandiprats, than is the gnawing of long pig off a femur in the view of a cannibal. How to explain it...in terms a rational, ethical human being can comprehend...this singularly irrational and unethical behavior...how to explain it...

Perhaps this:

I have written the anecdote elsewhere, but I cannot remember just where. Don't stop me if you've heard this one before, I'm on a roll.

Two hundred thousand years ago, when I was youngish in the movie business, I was called in to the offices of a producer who had been on the Paramount lot forever. He made B films. Still does. Saw him on *Entertainment Tonight* just a few weeks ago. Must be older than Angkor Wat. You'd recognize the name. Anyway. He sat me down, and he ran the *de rigueur* chat, and then he puffed up and spread his petals like the *Rafflesia microbilorum** and he told me he had the most sensational idea for a science fiction monster movie since Santa Claus conquered the Martians, and he wanted widdle ole me to write it. There was one of these at the end of his pitch: !

"Delight me," I said, all aglow at the prospect of hearing a basic concept so effulgent in its fecundity that it would knock me ass over teakettle. And he grinned hugely, and he said:

"Ta hell with all the giant ant movies, and the giant spider movies, and the giant leech movies! I already have the studio backing to produce the first giant *locust* movie!"

We then began, in those pre-Maddie&David days, to do *Moonlighting* stichomythia:

"No," I said.

"No?" he said.

"No."

"What, no?"

"No, not possible."

---

*A stemless, leafless, parasitic plant of the genus *Rafflesia*, named after Sir T. Stamford Raffles, British East Indian administrator and founder (1819) of Singapore, who was largely responsible for the creation of Britain's Far Eastern empire; in honor of his discovery of this plant order during the period of his governorship of Java. The *microbilorum* is the largest-known rafflesiaceous plant of the genus, weighing 37 lbs. and a yard wide. Indigenous to the Malay Peninsula, it was first identified in central Sumatra by naturalist Arnold Newman, who reports that it takes the bud three years to develop, then it springs open in an instant with the hiss of a striking cobra. Open, it smells like rotten meat.

"What, not possible?"

"Me writing such a dumb."

"It's dumb?"

"It is cataclysmically dumb."

"Why, dumb?"

"Look," I said, speaking slowly and making sure he was watching my lips, "there is this absolutely ironclad, irrevocable, no way to get around, under, over or through it rule in physics. It is called . . ." and I cut in the echo chamber effect to make sure he knew this was Big Stuff, " . . . THE SQUARE CUBE LAWahwah-wahwah . . ."

"Square Cube Law." He repeated it. Then again.

"That's right. The Square Cube Law. And you know what the Square Cube Law of physics, that is *the law of the universe*, says?"

"What does it say?"

"It says that if you increase the size by squaring it, you *cube* the weight. Now. Do you know what that means in practical terms?"

"No, I don't know what that means."

"It means that if, say, you take the largest ant known, which is maybe a quarter of an inch long, and you blow it up a thousand times, which would make it something over twenty feet high . . . would that be a big enough ant for you . . . ?"

"Locust."

"Okay! Locust, fer chrissakes! Pretend the goddam *locust* is a quarter inch long and you make it a thousand times bigger. Is that a big enough *locust* for you?"

"Could it be *sixty* feet?"

"*Please!* Settle for twenty, just for the sake of discussion."

"Okay, for this talk, twenty. But if we're gonna have a special effect that looks terrific on the screen, it really should be at *least* sixt—" He could see my eyes were rolling, and little bits of foam were flecking the corners of my mouth, so he hastily placated me. "Twenty is okay. Twenty is good."

"Right. So now we have a twenty foot high locust. We have increased the size by a thousand times. But the Square Cube Law says the *weight* isn't merely squared, it's cubed . . . that means three times three times three . . . okay?"

"If you say so."

"I say so. The fuckin' *Law* says so! Which means the weight has been increased not a thousand times, but a *million* times. And since the ant or the locust or the katydid or whateverthehell it is, is only made out of balsa wood and crepe paper and held together by flour-and-water paste or maybe the bug world equivalent of Elmer's Glue, the whole damned thing won't be able to support its own weight, and it will come crashing down like the second week's receipts on a Jerry Lewis movie. Got it?"

"Uh."

"Okay. Let me quote to you from a great scientist, scholar, philosopher and very wealthy man (I threw in that last to get his attention) named L. Sprague de Camp. He said, simply, 'Every time you double the insect's dimensions, you increase its strength and the area of its breathing passages by four, but you multiply its mass by eight, so you can't enlarge him much before he can no longer move or breathe.'"

"Oooooh."

"Yeah. Oh. So you see, it's a dumb idea that won't work, even though a lot of dumb movies have been made that way, which was okay when people were stupid and believed the Earth was flat and you could sail over the edge, but not today when every kid wants to be an astronaut."

So he thought about that for a few minutes, in silence. And then he brightened. He said, "So okay, I take your point. That's why I called *you* in. You're smart about this kind of stuff." (Little did he know I had to call Silverberg to get him to explain the damned Square Cube Law to me.) "So if you don't like *that* idea, take any one of those up there..." And he pointed to a chifforobe in the corner, atop which sat, mildewing under a patina of dust and silverfish droppings, a stack of old Ziff-Davis pulp magazines. *Amazing Stories, Fantastic Adventures, Giant Insect Tales.* "Go through 'em. Take any idea you like. We'll make that one!"

"Are you crazy?"

"What, crazy?"

"That's *stealing*! It's plagiarism!"

"Who'll know?"

"*I'll* know, you asshole!"

"I don't have to listen to that kinda talk!"

"You're right," I said, rising. "You don't." And I left.

To this day, he doesn't realize he was suggesting something disreputable beyond the telling.

And *that* is the attitude that prevails in Hollywood. *Now* do you understand?

There is, in these people, the imbrication of arrogance and stupidity that is as impenetrable to ethic as an armadillo's hide. If they chance upon a concept that manages to penetrate, and they can identify it with some film already made that did big

431

box-office, and if it is not *so* different that when they pitch it, the similarity to the successful former film escapes the studio boss or the network honcho, they will offer it as their own. That it came from some other creative source does not enter into their thinking. *We'll change it, it'll work,* they say. And those to whom they are pitching are equally as ignorant of sources, so they enter unwittingly into the conspiracy to steal.

Which may or may not be what happened with *The Running Man* and *The Hidden.* But though we've drawn nearer to that door behind which lies a horror unspeakable, we will all have to wait till installment 31 for the conclusion of the thesis of Li'l White Lies. Which may not be a goddam LAW OF THE UNIVERSE but if it ain't, it oughtta be!

INSTALLMENT 31:
In Which the Li'l White Lies Thesis (Part Three) Approaches A Nascent State, Approaches The Dreadful Door, And En Route Questions Meat Idolatry

Being lied to. Selling inferior goods by duping us with assertions that said grubby goods have "phantom values" apart from what we see on the screen: *The Emerald Forest* supposedly based on a true story; *Ladyhawke* a retelling of medieval legends; *Hangar 18* revealing suppressed Air Force knowledge of UFOs; lies, every one of them. Lures, cynically dangled.

Being lied to. Promoting films of rape, violence, ethical debasement, moral turpitude, inhuman behavior, sexism with prolonged graphic representations in adoring closeup, and then justifying it by wide-eyed explanation that "we show you this woman having an icepick driven into her eye to show you how much we *dis*approve of it." Exploitation, pandering to the debased nature of the contemporary audience, feeding the sickness. Rationalizing and justifying and excusing . . . with lies.

Being lied to. Using the ignorance of the audience against itself. Telling us that by coloring stylish black-and-white films like *Casablanca* and *The Maltese Falcon*, they offer them to a generation of young viewers who won't go to a movie if it isn't in color. Denying to that generation the experience of seeing such *objets d'art* as they were intended to be seen. Producing by such corruption of the audience a self-fulfilling prophecy in which the ignorant are *kept* ignorant, in the sense of uneducated.

Being lied to. As we examined such misrepresentation last time, through the nothous practice of plagiarism. Parvenus and no-talents, rampant in the film industry, incapable of creating the work themselves, hungering for sinecures as directors and producers while condemning writers to the beanfield labor of actually doing the screenplay and then having it wrested from them so they can "reinterpret." Unabashedly stealing ideas and concepts and entire screenplays, recasting them in their own cliché-riddled manner, and sending them out to market, to an audience with either short memories or no memories. If you have seen the Clint Eastwood film *Pale Rider* and are not deeply infuriated at it...then you are the ignorant of whom I speak. And if you look bewildered at that remark, and your attitude turns rancid against he who points out that you are cerebrose in this matter, then I suggest you go and rent videocassettes of that film and *Shane*. And if you do not perceive very quickly that *Pale Rider* is a shameless, awful ripoff of the A.B. Guthrie–Jack Sher adaptation of Jack Schaefer's exquisite novel (combined with a ripoff of the "ghost" element from the 1972 Eastwood vehicle *High Plains Drifter*, written by Ernest Tidyman), then you are dumber than I think. And you deserve no better than rudeness, because your ignorance only permits this evil to flourish.

So let us consider two recent films that may or may not be ripoffs of famous science fiction stories. Two films that did extremely well at the box office, and have been lauded as fresh and original ideas by critics utterly unaware of the vast body of sf material that has been fueling the engines of film thieves for fifty years. Two films that take the basic ideas already existent in sf stories, simplify them, render them in much cruder form, and deny to the original authors the ability ever to have *their* work translated to the screen.

The first is THE RUNNING MAN (Taft Entertainment/Keith Barish Productions) and the second is THE HIDDEN (New Line Cinema).

In the Los Angeles *Daily News* of 13 November 87, a gentleman named Michael Healy, who is identified as "Daily News Film Critic," says this of *The Running Man*:

"Schwarzenegger stumbles and falls flat in this futuristic satire on TV game shows with a plot lifted from Richard Connell's story 'The Most Dangerous Game.' Stephen King did the lifting under the name Richard Bachman, and Steven de Souza turned it all into a screenplay about as original as a speech by Joe Biden."

Close. Very close. And one must admire Mr. Healy for not only getting full writing credits into the first three paragraphs of his review—as opposed to most "film critics" who find it less of a strain on their limited intelligence to use the odious crushword "sci-fi" than to describe an individual film as what it *is*, without recourse to a demeaning neologism... and who ease that strain on their gray tapioca matter even more by pretending the director wrote the film, with never a scenarist credit to be found passim the review, much less a reference to the original source material—but Healy draws our applause for additionally noting the historical precedent for the plot. A film critic who not only *reads* (New Miracles! New Miracles!) but who has a sense of literary ebb and flow. And he's close, very close.

Yes, the famous 1924 Connell short story (oft-refilmed) is certainly the master template for *The Running Man*, but it isn't the *specific* work pilfered. We come to Steven de Souza's ankyloglossial screenplay by way of the 1982 NAL paperback novel pseudonymously penned by Stephen King. And we come to Bachman's THE RUNNING MAN by way of Robert Sheckley's famous short story "The Prize of Peril" (*The Magazine of Fantasy & Science Fiction*, May 1958). If you don't remember the yarn, go find it in Sheck's collections STORE OF INFINITY, THE WONDERFUL WORLD OF ROBERT SHECKLEY, or any one of several dozen anthologies in which it has been reprinted. It's about this guy who becomes an unwilling contestant on a nationally-obsessive tv program where you run and run and people try to kill you.

It was the story that sparked the campus fad some years back, for hunter/victim games in which students stalked each other and "killed" each other with paint-squibs from toy guns. Which fad, in turn, sparked a dreadful movie titled *Gotcha!*

When the Bachman book first appeared, it drew almost no attention, because no one knew it was Stephen behind the nom-de-plume. But when it came out, and prices for those four NAL throwaway adventure novels by "Bachman" went through the roof in antiquarian bookdealer catalogues that provide Colombian Gold–level fixes for King addicts, and NAL reissued the books in an omnibus volume, I received a call from Sheckley.

"Have you read THE RUNNING MAN?" he asked me.

"Yes," I said.

"Listen: I may be crazy," Sheck said, with considerable nervousness and more than a scintilla of reluctance to rush to judgment, "but do you see a lot of my story 'The Prize of Peril' in that book?"

I said, "Yes, I see it as being damned nearly the same plot, done at length."

A silence passed between us. A long silence, in which each of us tried to find a way to speak the unspeakable, to approach that dreadful door behind which lay the necessity to think the unthinkable. Finally, Bob said:

"Well, what do you think?"

And I said, very carefully, "I know Steve, and I know damned well he wouldn't steal. It's that simple. But Stephen has often said that he's been inspired by films and stories he's read years before, that slipped down into the back of his head. This might be one of those cases."

Again a silence. And at last Sheckley asked, very hesitantly, "Do you think I should do something about this?"

"I think you ought to talk to Stephen."

What lay in the subtext of our conversation was the dire possibility that *something would have to be done.* As one who has been compelled to pursue legal means to redress the sins of plagiarism committed against me by film companies and tv networks, I was careful not to put Sheckley in a state of paranoia about *The Running Man.* But talking to Stephen King seemed the correct way to go about it. Sheckley asked me if I'd call Steve and give him Bob's number, and ask if he'd call.

I said I would; I called Steve and we talked; and he said he remembered reading "The Prize of Peril" years and years before; and he assured me he'd call Sheckley to work it out.

That call transpired, and Sheckley later told me he was satisfied with King's open remarks. The sense I got from what Sheck said, was that Steve may well have dredged out of the mire of memory the basic plotline of "Prize of Peril," never remembering it as an actual reading experience but transforming it, as all writers do, into the self-generated conceit that was published as THE RUNNING MAN.

The aphorist Olin Miller has said, "Of all liars, the smoothest and most convincing is memory."

For those who have read Stephen King's THE TOMMY-KNOCKERS and continue to endure the *frisson* of *déjà vu*, I suggest you rent the videocassette of *Five Million Years to Earth* (1968). And when you compare them, understand that I do not in even the tiniest way suggest that Stephen King cops the work of other writers. Let me say that again, even stronger, so no one of even the most diminished capacity can read into my words the ugly intimation: *Stephen King does not steal.* He's too good to *have* to

436

steal. But in the realm of sf/fantasy there are ideas that we rework and re-rework, recast and refashion, expand and transmogrify, that become common coin. James Blish was not the first writer to use the "enclosed universe" concept, but who would deny his reinterpretation of Bob Heinlein's "Universe" as the extraordinary "Surface Tension"? And if Heinlein was sparked to write THE PUPPET MASTERS after being enthralled by Wells's WAR OF THE WORLDS, is there anyone idiot enough to suggest it was plagiarism?

No, literary crossover happens. And we are all enriched by it.

But "The Prize of Peril" is a richer way of telling the story at hand than THE RUNNING MAN, especially as debased by Steven de Souza and Schwarzenegger. The lie we are fed, is the lie that *The Running Man* is a fresh, bold, new idea.

And if we look at *The Hidden*, from a screenplay by Robert Hunt, we can see the basic plot core of Hal Clement's famous novel of interplanetary cops-and-robbers, NEEDLE. And we can see *The Hidden* ripped off for television as NBC's *Something Is Out There*, the pilot of which aired recently, with the promise that if there *is* a Fall Season, we'll be getting Hal Clement's NEEDLE as a series written and produced by people who think *Something Is Out There* is only first-generation theft, when it all proceeds from Clement... who won't see a cent of the millions these arrivistes will rake in.

The lie we are told is that these watered-down, scientifically illiterate, mook-level ripoffs are the Real Thing. And that is why, in installment 30½ of this column, I urged the Science Fiction Writers of America to reinstate the Dramatic Writing category in the Nebula awards. If sf writers don't move to quash the lie, then who will? And if the readers and writers in the genre don't come to their senses and stop accepting this institutionalized theft, on which the lie floats blissfully, then those of you who praise *dreck* like *The Running Man* deserve no better than you get. Behind that dreadful door through which you, as innocent moviegoers, pass to nullify your reason with special effects and the idolatry of Schwarzeneggers and Stallones and Michael J. Foxes, lies the awful truth that the treasurehouse of ideas sf has filled since (at least) 1926, is being systematically looted by people who sneer at the concept of primacy of ownership of the creators.

As coda to this essay, and to satisfy Brian Siano of Philadelphia, and the others who requested it, let me make my feelings known about Arnold Schwarzenegger, *et al.*

Somewhere in the commercially ongoing practice of (how shall I put this delicately) "Idolizing Meat" there is a nubbin of rationale that has always escaped me.

Idolizing Meat may have been started in 1917 when the silent film actor Otto Elmo Linkenhelter was retitled Elmo Lincoln, and cast as the first incarnation of Burroughs's lord of the jungle in *Tarzan of the Apes*...but there are very likely a dozen even earlier isometric idols that cine-historians can point out.

But thereafter, fer shoor, the film industry mentality has gifted us with one musclebound matinee idol after another, from Victor Mature and Steve Reeves to the current batch of melon-smugglers—a curl of Cro-Magnons, perhaps?—whose thespic abilities seem to me best subsumed in the quote from Dorothy Parker, or Alexander Wollcott, or somebody swell like that, who commented that a certain actress had flung her talent the full range from A to B.

I speak now of the cinematic lineal descendants of Johnny Weismuller, Buster Crabbe, and Gordon Scott: the vacuous Miles O'Keeffe, the anthracitelike Dolph Lundgren, the spectacularly untalented Sam J. Jones, to whom human speech does not appear to be a natural tongue, and those *rara avae*, Sylvester Stallone and Arnold Schwarzenegger (were there ever two more perfect names for such as these?), who have transcended species, perhaps even phylum.

If one cannot fathom the mythic pull of the tongue-tied, lumbering beefcake as exemplified by Mature or Lundgren (and dontcha just know that in their heart of hearts they all want to assay the role of Hamlet), there is at least an inkling of what it is that draws us to the last of this parade of Idolized Meat.

Stallone first captured our respect and affection by turning his life into an American success story worthy of Horatio Alger, and then gave us a genuine sternum punch of an object-lesson in our own schizoid national character by JekyllHydeing into a Rocky/Rambo gaucherie of arrogance, insolence, brutality, and crippled expectations.

Schwarzenegger departs from the enigma of beefcake through the exeunt left of having demonstrated a cynical sense of humor about himself, about "the business," and about the archetypes he is supposed to represent. The superman, the unstoppable engine, the noble savage. Any man who can make a joke on himself about how much more gracefully the stop-motion robot in *Terminator* moves than *he* does, is a man whose career as an actor might well outdistance mere testosterone.

438

But as Michael Healy points out in the review I quoted earlier, the sneaky pleasure we derived from watching Schwarzenegger in *Pumping Iron* and *Terminator* is absent from humorless, jaundiced slaughterfests like *Commando, Raw Deal, Predator* and, most particularly, *The Running Man.*

This film is the latest in a demonstration of how paucive intelligences will loot the treasurehouse. It knows nothing of the logic of science fiction. Nothing of the internal tensions that make sf work on the screen, à la *Blade Runner.* Nothing of extrapolation along sensible lines. This is one of those utterly unworkable "future societies" that makes no sense, save in the rathole rationalizations of know-nothings and studio heads. There is no characterization—which in a film that stars Schwarzenegger is a knife through the gut—not even for an actor as compelling as Yaphet Kotto. They are set-ups, to be gunned down for the predilection of thug audiences for whom the judgment scale of quality is measured in liters of blood and spilled entrails.

And so Schwarzenegger's Ben Richards becomes, in the clubby hands of Steven E. de Souza and director Paul Michael Glaser (who I can never remember which he was, Starsky or Hutch), nothing but a chunk of Idolized Meat with bad puns grafted on.

If this film has *any* claim to posterity, it will be due to the spectacular performance of Richard Dawson as Damon Killian, the tv game show host. It is a performance so dazzling that one can assume Dickie Dawson wasn't this year's Oscar winner for Best Male Supporting because of the redolent nature of the film itself.

And the crusher that denied Dawson his moment of international acclaim is the same crusher that flattens us, as aficionados of the literature of imagination. The crusher is the Little White Lie that steals from the treasurehouse and dulls the patina of the artifact, and substitutes Idolized Meat for the rapture of the sense of wonder. And gets you to pay for, and then praise indiscriminately, the devalued product.

Can it be that you have been reduced to the lowest idiot expectancy because of the untutored nature of the Illiterate Audience?

Well, let me leave you with the words of Stephen King, who has often said the best a writer can hope for, from Hollywood is when "they buy the rights, pay you half a million dollars, for some reason never make the movie—but you get to keep the half million without the embarrassment of some awful film coming out."

Which is a whole helluva lot sweeter than no one knowing Sheckley or Clement were there first, and ain't gonna see a kopeck for the error of cleverness and early arrival.

INSTALLMENT 32:
In Which The Switch Is Thrown

It often seems laughable to me how I, and other film critics, ceaselessly belabor the lack of verisimilitude in films. As a practitioner of fiction—

the pure cobbling-up of lies that have the *semblance* of truth but which are, at splashdown, merely inventions abutting Reality only where necessary to sucker in the reader

—it does frequently seem to me to be a hypocritical carp that operates off a double standard, serving the critic in a not entirely respectable fashion.

Like demanding a greater nobility from oppressed peoples than that demonstrated by those who oppress them. South Africa, for instance. Botha's government can repress, brutalize, maim, lock-out, censor, incarcerate, and kill—and that's "maintaining order." But let a Homelands black pick up a rock and shag it at an Afrikander with a water cannon, and it's "terrorist activity."

Yet when we reach the target area of criticism, it is just such an unsettling absence of verisimilitude that looms largest in our judgments of a film's worth. Our trust can be lost in an instant. Just one flip we don't believe, and we're off the menu. Go figure.

I'm not talking about technical or factual errors that don't impede the flow of story. (The kind that apologists for films, as well as arrogant producers and studio flacks, sneer at, and say, "Who the hell will know the difference?" Thus allowing, even condoning, the perpetuation of intentional or just dumbheaded corruptions of fact for "story value.") I'm not talking about re-leasing a film titled *Krakatoa: East of Java*, when that volcanic island actually lies in the Sunda Strait, *west* of Java. I'm not talking about having the sun set in the east in the recent film *Sunset*, or having the sun rising in the west in *The Green Berets*. I'm not talking about having Metropolis (which is New York City) and the Great Wall of China simultaneously in daylight in *Superman IV*, though they're on opposite sides of the planet, Daily or otherwise. I'm not talking about ex-slaves in the crowd scenes of *Spartacus* wearing wristwatches.

That sort of thing is pooh-pooh'd by the same phylum of semi-literate plant life that excuses the soundtrack explosions in deep space and the whoooosh of spaceships as they dart around in imbecile imitation of Spads and Fokkers (a convention now so institutionalized that I've thrown up my hands and swear never to mention it again). No, I'm not talking about such thousand natural shocks to which the flesh is heir.

I'm talking about the visual *shticks* that make us groan. The moments we are expected to accept, in action films usually, that wrench from an audience the involuntary cry of, "Oh fer chris-sakes, gimme a *break!*"

I suppose, for want of proper ThinkTank stats on this, that something like a Common Sense Switch cuts in, when we're asked to believe the foma of filmmakers. We seem to have no trouble accepting, say, the convention of Wile E. Coyote standing in midair, just beyond the lip of the cliff, looking around for the Road Runner, scratching his head, perfectly safe in defiance of the laws of the physical universe, just buoyed up by nothing, till he glances down and sees the abyss beneath his feet. We gladly accept that he has time to register a forlorn double-take, still standing in midair, until the epiphany of imminent gravity sinks in... and *then* he falls. But let the same sort of thing happen in live-action, and we deliver a raspberry at the screen that is as sincere as it is succulent. What I'm talking about is:

• James Bond hop-skipping across the backs of the alligators in *Live and Let Die*.

• Schwarzenegger in *Commando*, falling 350 feet from an L10-11, into a swamp, getting up without even shaking his head, and trotting blithely away at peak efficiency to do battle.

• "Bones" McCoy being such an inept physician that he injects *himself* by mistake in the rewritten version of "City on the Edge of Forever."

• The rubber life raft containing Indy, Short Round and Willie not flipping upside-down like buttered bread when it's dropped, as they go over the cliff in *Indiana Jones and the Temple of Doom*; or the four-foot-tall Short Round karate-kicking into unconsciousness all those six-feet-tall trained *thuggee* assassins.

• "The best hired killers in the galaxy" using heat-seeking laser rifles that lock onto a target automatically, regularly missing their first shots, so they alert Sean Connery to each bushwhack in *Outland*.

• The hi-tech choppers in *Blue Thunder* strafing each other in the center of downtown high-rise Los Angeles, blowing up buildings that rain glass and concrete on crowds, and harming not one pedestrian, save when they are pelted by fried chickens.

• *Robocop* firing through the skirt of a woman hostage, missing her pudenda, and searing off the balls of the thug holding her up in front of him as a shield.

• Stallone, in *Rambo: First Blood II* apparently doing what cannot be done by a human being, when he literally *flies* up from a lake to the port of a chopper hovering twenty-five feet above the water. Apparently kicking off from the lake bottom and defying water pressure to break all world's championship high jumping records.

• And my all-time favorite: the assassins of *Rame Tep*, by the hundreds, come-and-go to-and-from a gigantic wooden pyramid built smack in the middle of Victoria's London, in *Young Sherlock Holmes*, and no one has ever noticed the tons of building materials schlepped into the area, nor heard the sound of sawing and hammering, nor paid any attention to the skinheaded hordes frequenting the vicinity.

What I'm talking about here is, "Oh, fer chrissakes, gimme a *break!*"

In that instant, the Common Sense Switch is thrown, and they've lost us. From that instant forward, they have to work very hard, very diligently, and with absolute purity of intent to win back our willing suspension of disbelief. (For all of us, that is, save those undiscriminating filmgoers who perceive of their lot in life as being one with the doorknob: to be turned and shoved and left covered with smudgy handprints. Those who *expect* to be lied to, and don't think they can do anything about it. Those who cannot summon up sufficient feelings of self-worth to

443

believe they are *due* something truer and more inventive. Those who believe in *boom!* and *whoooosh!*)

It is the single cinematic common denominator that brooks no defense, that unites even navel-lint examiners like me with F/X-dulled adolescents like a very few of you. Such importunate demands on audience credibility can be *seen*, and the groans are pandemic; whether interpreted by a critic as "the film suffers from a herky-jerky rhythm" or by the casual filmgoer as "I didn't believe it ... it was dumb." Dumb, as in dull-witted, stupid; not as in speechless.

That having been said, I submit (without the faintest ort of anger or outrage, truly more in sorrow than glee) that the instant throwing of the Common Sense Switch by whole theaters-full of movie nuts is the reason WILLOW (MGM/Lucasfilm) died a quick and awful death at the box office, while WHO FRAMED ROGER RABBIT (Touchstone) has made more than one hundred and fifty million dollars to the date I write this. And both deserve what they got: though the former is live-action, meticulously rendered with as much state of the art cleverness as a $35 million budget can buy in terms of the most accomplished technicians in the world; and the latter is utterly wacky, combining jaw-popping animation and live-action players pantomiming and reacting against *toons* that were not there when they spoke their lines. The former, for all its heavy-breathing and sweaty struggles to make fantasy realms mimetic, is not for a moment believable. The latter, despite its clearly deranged juxtaposition of animated cartoons and live knockabout comedy, captures our trust from the first frames.

Apart from the awesome risk-taking of *Roger Rabbit*, from original conception to final cut, there is a surefootedness, an imperial arrogance at its brave beastliness, a confidence in its ability to cajole even Scrooge into adoration, that one cannot find in parallel unless one goes back to *Alien, Fantasia, Pinocchio* or the 1939 *Thief of Bagdad*.

(The film becomes a yardstick. You show me someone who has seen *Roger Rabbit*, whose face doesn't break into an idiot grin, who doesn't fall over him/herself to recollect a shot, a shtick, a boffo line that brought convulsions, who prefaces any remarks with "Well, I have problems with it ..." and I'll show you a Grinch unfit to live with decent people. You show me someone who didn't like, who didn't *love* that film, and I'll show you someone whose opinion on *any*thing should not be trusted. In a world ass-deep in cupidity, ineptitude, meanspiritedness, fanaticism, random vio-

444

lence and anguish, how often are we given a treasure like *Roger Rabbit*, a dear soft fuzzy thing that asks only that we be happy and roll around in it like a puppy in a goose-down comforter? You show me a damfool who carps about *anything* in *Roger Rabbit*, and I'll show you...someone who likes eating lima beans.)

Deponent sayeth this: the fault lies not in its stars, but in its basic conception. *Willow*, that is. I'll get to the conception of *Roger Rabbit* anon. Because of its excellence, it requires less attention. We learn more from failures than from successes, because if a success is based on originality, then by deconstructing it, by trying to analyze it and codify it, we only find the replicable elements. And that's of value primarily if we're trying to emulate the success in an imitation. By the very nature of its originality, it ran risks that could not be gauged beforehand. It's akin to dissecting a butterfly to learn why it flies as it does, and in so doing, we destroy the beauty that was its essence. And since this column is foursquare against cheap imitations, we need not shred *Roger Rabbit* merely to discover that it was the first of its kind to go as far as it did. We know that. And we know *that's* why it wows. But *Willow* falls far and falls fast and falls flat: from which height we can learn the angle and severity of the trajectory of failure.

Deponent sayeth: the fault lies in George Lucas. No one else had a hand in it. Not the hundreds of technicians, not the actors, not the unfortunate writer Bob Dolman, who was called in to complete the script, not even one of the names or companies we see on the extended credits. It was George Lucas who (as prerelease publicity told us) "studied myths from around the world before defining *Willow* to his satisfaction." It is the film Lucas wanted to make, based on the story Lucas dreamed up, execproduced by Lucas, and directed in Lucas-fashion by his handpicked choice, Ron Howard.

And what are we presented with?

The "saga" of Willow Ufgood is a ramekin of congealed porridge and curdled cream. There is far more of farina than fantasy in this wearisome, woebegone farrago of stolen set-pieces and New Age muddleheadedness. George Lucas has either taken utter leave of his senses, or the world of today has taken utter leave of George Lucas. For this is the kind of sloppy, inarticulate, inconsistent, unbelievable, fuzzyheaded crap that flower children read to one another in crash pads in Iowa. After half a century of C. S. Lewis, Mervyn Peake, Clifford Simak, Daniel Manus Pinkwater, *Time Bandits*, Madeleine L'Engle, Fritz

Leiber and—though most prominently, scarcely my fave—
J. R. R. Tolkien, for a rational adult even remotely *au courant* to
believe this pile of unwashed hand-me-downs has any freshness,
is a delusion at least on a par with those held by Ponce de Leon,
Mary Baker Eddy, and Bishop James Ussher.

Instead of Moses in the bullrushes, we have a cynical nod to
NOW and a silly male's idea of feminism with the foundling
converted to baby girl. Instead of *Snow White*'s Queen Grimhilde,
we have Queen Bavmorda, rasping, clenching, *geshry*ing, and
seeking the death of this child bearing "the sign" that a seer has
vouchsafed marks the one who will overthrow the evil ruler.
Instead of Han Solo, we have Val Kilmer as the cocky freebooter
Madmartigan: liar, deceiver, cutpurse, self-server, but with a
whore's heart of iron pyrite. Instead of Munchkins, we have
Nelwyns. At least they don't have fuzzy feet. Instead of—

But you catch my drift.

Hand-me-downs. Flotsam and jetsam from a thousand ripoff
Middle-Earth, Middle-Ages, Middle-Class fantasies. Cobbled together into one of those interminable "journey" templates where
an unruly assortment of bizarre traveling companions dashes
about like Michael Jackson fans in search of scalper's tickets.
Weird beasties, much senseless swordplay, magic without logic
introduced helterskelter when the "plot" begins to falter, noise
and fireworks...and none of it able to pluck the heart-strings,
much less appeal to the rational.

All of it, despite its pomposity and bench-press sweatiness
intended to convince us it's possible, nothing but impetus for the
throwing of the Common Sense Switch. We watch it, we leave,
and we forget it. Having wasted our time and our ticket money.

George Lucas has wasted years, however.

Following, as it does, on the heels of Lucas's last bold plunge
into idiocy, *Howard the Duck*, we can only stare in utter confusion at such a suicidal effort. Has Lucas taken leave of his
senses? Did he truly think there was anything in this mush to
compel our love?

Deponent suggests the Blight of Shirley MacLaine has
caught up with the Executive Producer.

In an upcoming essay it is my intention to go at considerable
length to an examination of the Illiterate Audience. Not now. But
part of the thesis is prefaced in the artifact called *Willow*. That
element of the total theory dealing with the rampant spread of
obscurantism that manifests itself in the foolish antics of
446 pseudo-Christians at *The Last Temptation of Christ*, the resur-

gence of acceptance of spiritualism, now called "channeling," the goofy vogue for crystals, traveling to "focus locations" for Harmonic Convergences, the seeming lack of outrage that the Reagan Oligarchy regularly consulted and paid heed to a court astrologer (the last major world leader to have such a soothsayer on the payroll was Hitler, if you recall), and all the other sophomoric diddles the average citizen now considers part of the Rational Universe. Geraldo Rivera and Oprah and Morton Dunderhead, Jr. present . . .

Road signs on the journey back into ignorance.

And *Willow*, product of this New Age nonsense, tells a story that not even the shriven can tolerate. Dulled, confused, awash in their own inability to cope with a world filled with tax forms and interfacing and accessing and Star Wars Defense Systems, a world in which mediocre men seek to be President and giant corporations truly rule, a world in which blame can only be supported if it can be laid at the feet of Chance or God, even in such a world the faithful cannot accept such arrant nonsense.

And the Common Sense Switch is thrown.

We can only be thankful that we have been given *Roger Rabbit*. A film as mad as anything we've ever seen; a story as unlikely as any we've ever known; a dream and a delight that for all its unbelievable elements, is a more down-to-earth and sensible than the "realistic" films we're told reflect Our Times.

Deponent suggests we ponder for an instant, without anger and without raising our voices, in what a lowly state we exist, that the most rational icon given to us to adore, is an adaptation of Gary Wolf's bugfuck novel, in a cinematic ordering of what used to be considered absolute fantasy. Is something odd here, or did I wake up this morning in an alternate universe?

Further, deponent sayeth not.

INSTALLMENT 33:
In Which The Canine Of Vacuity Is Wagged By The Far More Interesting Tale Of O'Bannon

Quite a bit more than a few, but less than many, years ago, I attended the premiere of a major motion picture I had written. Well, yes, I'd written it, but it had been *re*written by both the director and the producer. Not very much to its benefit, as it turned out. Which is not to say that I, as a first-time scenarist, had written a screenplay that would have given Richard Brooks or Richard Breen even twinges of envy...but it had some sprightly moments, this screenplay as I'd written it; and it has a few lines that I can still hear without wincing (when, in moments of masochism, I pull out the videocassette for a crawl down Memory Slough). Every once in a while, no doubt fully aware of my anhedonia as regards this film, no doubt aware of my embarrassment at how badly the film turned out—though it made millions for the studio and production company—no doubt aware that it will cause me pain, some reincarnated dung-beetle now reborn as a fan, complete with rancid breath and overinflated opinion of his/her skills with the *bon mot*, oozes up to me in a public place and (usually loud enough to include total strangers) demands to know how I could have written such an awful film.

Well, there are all sorts of explanations for a film having gone wrong, but in this case it was probably at least one-third my fault. It was terribly directed, extravagantly and expensively produced but with an impoverishment of taste or imagination; it was miscast hideously; and rewritten till every vestige of fun or originality had been removed from my original screenplay based on a not-very-good popular novel of the time. Which is not, I say again, to let me off the hook. It was my first film, and I thought I could do no wrong, and if I were to go back and re-read that scenario I'd certainly wince at the sophomorisms.

(Which has nothing to do with the rudeness of the human chancre who throws it up in my face in much the same way, I'm sure, that smartasses prod Roger Ebert with his having worked on the raunchy 1970 *Beyond the Valley of the Dolls*, directed and co-scripted with Ebert by Russ Meyer. I've seen pod-brothers of the ambulatory phlegm who gig me for [the intentionally un-named] cinematic abomination I wrote when I was in my early thirties, more than two decades ago, who have smarmily leered at Roger and oh-so-innocently inquired how such an erudite film critic and excellent journalist could have been part of "a project like that." And I've seen that tight, brave little smile Roger substitutes for the more appropriate, but less gentlemanly, left cross to the moron's jaw, and I identify with it, because I've used it myself. And I know just how Roger feels. I can recall with agonizing clarity the night I attended the world premiere of my filmic *mea culpa*, at a great old movie palace on Hollywood Boulevard, with searchlight beams cutting wedges out of the sky above the City of the Angels, with live tv coverage and crowds being held back behind velvet ropes, and entering the theater having been kept from seeing even one frame of the produced film *a priori* by producers and studio fearful I'd piss on their parade by way of prerelease denunciation in *Variety*. As the film was run, and the audience roared ever more often and ever more derisively at what was *not* intended as a comedy, I shrank within my rented tuxedo and slipped lower and lower in my seat till I could barely see the screen. I withered, understanding that before my eyes I was witnessing the ritual slaughter of my budding career as a writer of theatrical motion pictures. I was dead on, of course. There is a moment near the outset of one's career in Hollywood, when the Big Break manifests itself. Taken at the flood, that moment can stretch and carry one into a word-of-mouth security that can withstand an occasional flop. But if the moment goes sour, for whatever reasons, one can continue working, making a decent living, but there is a taint that thereafter attaches to all who are identified with the plague-bearing item. And that stigma became the word-of-

450

mouth that lobbied against my getting other big-budget, serious writing assignments for the large screen. It's been a long time since it all happened, and though I suffer a *frisson* of sadness for What Might Have Been, like Roger Ebert I've put it behind me, and work as skillfully as I can on the projects that do come my way. But I remember. And I suppose it is logged in my life as one of the few episodes on the list of If I Could Do It Over...)

So I know, to the core I know, how my friend Rockne O'Bannon feels when he tells me he has not seen, and will not accompany me and Susan to see, a screening of his first feature film, ALIEN NATION (20th Century–Fox). I know how he feels, and I hear him explain how the producer, Gale Anne Hurd, she who was allied with, married to, separated from, director James Cameron, altered his vision. I hear him, and I sympathize, because the litany is not only one I've shrilled endlessly, but which bears within itself the echoes of artistic pain from thousands of screenwriters who came before us. He cannot bear to sit watching what became of his work, as I was forced to sit that long-ago night on Hollywood Boulevard, writhing before the projected images of corrupted invention.

Let me tell you a little about Rock O'Bannon. Not only because he is a pal of mine, or because we worked together on the 1985–86 revival of *The Twilight Zone* television series for CBS (though that is a secret agenda I would be less than forthright to conceal), but because I tell you what I truly and deeply believe: Rock O'Bannon is a writer of uncommon talent, vast promise, and urgently in need of a kick in the ass from one he knows likes and admires him. But more important, he is emblematic of the kind of men and women who are, more and more overwhelmingly, coming to be the model of young people writing films these days in a medium schizophrenic to the point of hysteria.

Here is what the studio press packet on *Alien Nation* says of Rock:

Born in Los Angeles, Rockne S. O'Bannon was raised in the film industry; his father was a gaffer and his mother a contract dancer at MGM. While most ten-year-olds were reading "The Hardy Boys" and comic books, he was reading screenplays smuggled home by his father. He learned the business by working in the mailroom and leading guided tours at a major studio. He went on to work as a production assistant on Lorimar's television productions *The Waltons* and *Apple's Way*.

From age eight O'Bannon knew he wanted to be a writer. His first stab at screenwriting was developing a script for what he

451

thought was a natural spin-off of his then favorite television series *The Man from U.N.C.L.E.* entitled "Boy from U.N.C.L.E." O'Bannon continued writing screenplays through high school and upon graduation took six months off to concentrate seriously on his writing. That's when he moved from mailroom to production assistant at Lorimar.

After leaving Lorimar, he returned to college to continue his English studies, but in a short time dropped out when he got a job at MGM. He stayed there several years working in the publicity department and the story department, simultaneously writing the studio's company newspaper.

Having an office to himself afforded O'Bannon the means to continue writing scripts while working at his job. After he had written several scripts on spec, his agent submitted a script for the recently revived *Twilight Zone* television series. The producers were so impressed with his "Wordplay" episode that they hired him to write more scripts and to serve as the story editor for the first season. He went on to work as a consultant during the second season. During the hiatus, he wrote the "Life on Death Row" episode of Steven Spielberg's anthology series, *Amazing Stories*.

It was during this period that O'Bannon met *Alien Nation*'s co-producer, Richard Kobritz, and told him of his story idea for the film, formerly titled *Outer Heat*. They have since formed a partnership and are developing a project which O'Bannon plans to direct with Kobritz serving as the producer.

When the producers of *The Twilight Zone* were trying to inveigle me into returning to television after ten years of voluntary abstinence from that most beguiling and lucrative of addictions, they sent me a small stack of scripts that had been accepted by CBS as correct for the re-thunk, contemporary version of that classic series. Several of them were knockouts, several of them were acceptable, several of them were stinkers, and one of them blew me into orbit.

It was Rock's eighteen-page, airtime-seventeen-minute story, "Wordplay." It was a marvel. Nothing less than a marvel.

If you missed it, you missed one of the classic moments of fantasy on television, and a tale of imagination that is, in my view, on a par with the very best that has ever been done in the genre of the fantastic:

A perfectly average guy wakes one odd day to find that everyone is speaking a different language. Well, not exactly. It's still

English, but the words have different meanings, different uses. A brash, young guy who works in the protagonist's company approaches him for advice. He says: "Hey, Mr. Thompson. You know that new girl in accounting? Barbie? I've been asking her out and finally, today, she says okay—but she's gonna be here in five minutes and I can't think of anyplace to take her for dinosaur. I mean, I thought of the Capitol Inn, but then that might look like I'm trying too hard. What d'you think?"

Thompson looks at him and laughs. He replies, "You're planning to take this young woman out for *dinosaur*, huh?"

And when the kid repeats it, confused at Thompson's wry response, Thompson thinks he's putting him on. The kid gets huffy. "Look, Mr. Thompson, if you don't want to, uh, or can't think of anyplace, I'll just ask somebody else."

It gets worse and worse. More and more words gibber and dance out of Thompson's reach. Dinosaur, for lunch. Peaches, for rain. Segregate, for clear. On and on, till people are calling him Hinge instead of Bill, and his wife, trying to tell him that their child is dying and they must get him to a hospital, shrieks, "Dark outer! Kettle rod that thought collins around! Moon tight! Moon tight!"

In seventeen minutes, Rock O'Bannon creates, complicates and solves an apocryphal human dilemma that, in terms of modern fable, encapsulates the terror and helplessness of modern man's inability to orient himself in a bewildering technocratic society.

It is, in my view, simply brilliant, by every standard of fine writing we accept as necessary for the creation of true literature, true Art. He was twenty-eight years old when he wrote it.

I took the job on *TZ*, in large part, because the producers had been smart enough to snap up that script from the slush pile. If they could spot top-level writing like that, then there was hope for the series, and I might yet find myself working among artists, not sausage-merchants.

Working with Rock O'Bannon was a delight. I never thought of him as a tyro, as a youngster breaking in. He was a peer. And so he remains today.

But *Alien Nation*, his debut as a feature film writer, is a woeful, empty thing. He was thirty-two when he wrote it, last year. I'll get back to Rock, and that kick in the ass, in a moment; but first, let me review *Alien Nation* for you, so you won't waste your money seeing it.

Los Angeles. Near future. Three hundred thousand aliens, 453 bred to be workers, slaves, beanfield hands from outer space, arrive on Earth. They look a lot like us, but are grotty enough to be considered the new "niggers." They are shunted into a ghetto, and because they have been bred to adapt almost totally to whatever environment becomes their lot, they are soon just like all of us—shopkeepers, cops, hookers, fast-food clerks, mechanics, street thugs. Suddenly, there is a murder of a human by a "slag" (the epithet for "newcomer"). Unthinkable. So a human cop, played by James Caan, is linked with the first "newcomer" to make the grade of detective on the LAPD, Mandy Patinkin as Sam Francisco. Together they set out to solve the baffling murder, mysteriously linked to the slaying of two "newcomers."

Baffling, as in *Oh, did I nod off, dear? Did I miss anything?*

Mysterious, as in *I've got to take a leak; tell me what I missed. Want me to pick up some popcorn while I'm out there?*

And for the next 94 minutes of running time, we have the cinematic equivalent of Gerald Ford's presidency. Nothing of consequence happens.

Here is a sixteen–seventeen million dollar film that functions as a perfect soporific. It isn't even bad enough to be a howler, bad enough to spark vituperation, bad enough to become a cult favorite for those who dote on turkeys. It is just lugubrious. Somnolent. Derivative. Empty. Yes, that's just what it is: empty calories. Not even interesting junk food. No spice, no jump, not even stupid enough to provide uncooked meat for the disputatious critic to amuse his basest instincts. It is, in the vernacular of my people, a lox. It doth but lie there and rot from the head down.

With the arrogance of the *arriviste*, above the credits we are told this is A GRAHAM BAKER FILM. Now, if that fails to bring you to your feet with an admixture of awe and gladness, it is because you probably never heard of Graham Baker. His previous credits are the classic draughts from the Waters of Lethe titled *The Final Conflict* and *Impulse*. If we are to judge Mr. Baker's potential from this trio of bow-wows, I suggest that the degree of directorial scintillance contained in the batch prepares Mr. Baker for a world-class dive into oblivion.

Or a return to directing television commercials in England.

As for the acting, both Terence Stamp and Mandy Patinkin are wasted, performing like shamble-ons excised from a rough cut of *Night of the Living Dead*; James Caan looks old, tired, puffy and lackadaisical, employing the same thespic shrugs and tics we've seen him substitute for character insight before and since his outstanding performances in *The Gambler* (1974) and *Thief* (1981); and everyone else appears to be as one with Jay McInerney's "brigades of tiny Bolivian soldiers" waiting for the Bolivian Marching Powder of cocaine to galvanize them into frenetic action.

Not only is the film slow as the erosion of mountains, but it is slovenly in its basic logic and in its tiniest details: the latter exemplified by Caan returning to his home, trying to find something to eat, eyeing the detritus of a dozen fast food banquets littering the kitchen, living room, bedroom, a vast terrain of garbage...and not one cockroach in sight. Trust me on this one, folks. I live in Los Angeles, and while we aren't the cockroach paradise of, say, New Orleans or New York City, it is impossible to leave that much crap lying about in the heat without sounding an orthopterous klaxon that would draw *Blattidae* from as far away as Pomona. But pristine is Caan's pad, nary an ant—black, red or white—as far as the camera eye can see.

The former is exemplified by the simplistic treatment of three hundred thousand *aliens from outer space* being plopped into the middle of Los Angeles. There is virtually *no* social or physical alteration in the makeup of the city as we know it today. Everyone dresses the same, talks the same, acts the same, and for a budget of 16–17 million, the minutiae of a major new immigrant population is nil. The only one that sticks in my memory is the repellent concept of fast food burger joints serving "raw beaver" (with the fur still on it) alongside the fishwich and fries.

Consider, if you will, the changes in Miami with the arrival of far fewer Cuban refugees. The changes in Los Angeles, San Diego and Orange County with the arrival of Laotians, Cambodians, Koreans and Vietnamese. The changes in New York that altered even that endlessly mutable melting pot at each new wave of Irish, Middle Europeans, Jews, Puerto Ricans. If you have no sense of history to point out the ludicrousness of what *Alien Nation* substitutes for solid sociological ideation, just compare what I've described here with the society portrayed in *Blade Runner*.

And the worst part of this imbecile determination to discount even the least venturous attempt at extrapolation, is that for 94 minutes we have *nothing original to look at*.

Coupled with that boring, overexposed, overfamiliar Los Angeles setting we've wearily endured through ten thousand flicks, is a sound mix of intrusive rock so excruciating that we cannot

455

decipher the dialogue, which may be, on further consideration, a blessing in disguise. Ah, yes, disguise.

Which brings us to disguise.

This is nothing more than the same old buddy-movie formula with dopey latex masks. Mask disguises for a good ole boys liaison.

And here is where I draw back my Lou Groza toe to dropkick Rock O'Bannon's ass.

The great scenarist Ring Lardner, Jr.—*The Cross of Lorraine*, *M*A*S*H*, *Woman of the Year*, and *Tomorrow, The World* just to name a few—once opined: "No good film was ever made from a poor script." So, though I have made it clear that affection and respect inform my opinions of Rockne S. O'Bannon, even as I accept about one-third of the blame for that long-ago awfulness I wrote when a newcomer to the screenplay, Rock must accept the initial blame for *Alien Nation*. It's a commercially cynical idea. Rock sat there one day (I was a fly on the wall...this is how it happened...trust me) and suddenly he said aloud, "Hey, what a great obvious idea for a thriller! A cop-buddy movie with a human being and an alien! Hell, we can cast Patrick Swayze as the human and put John Candy in a funny suit for the alien! Hot shit, this'll make me a fortune!"

And he took it to market; and because he is dealing with the sort of people I noted a few columns ago, the sort who wanted to make a tv special: "Let's do *The Wiz*...white!" he had no trouble selling the project. Before Gale Anne Hurd picked up on it at 20th in April of 1987, Warners and Paramount wanted it. It was a "hot" idea. Like Pete Hyams standing in front of Alan Ladd, Jr. and getting a deal to make *Outland* when he suggested, "Let's do *High Noon* in outer space." Rock O'Bannon is a cagey guy, a canny assayer of the lowered expectations, petty pretensions, and cultural illiteracy of the New Executives who run this industry. Rock is (with one important difference) the very model of the kind of writer who is hitting it big in Hollywood these days. He has his eye not on the sparrow, but on the box office. He spots, early on, the trend for the season; and he boils it down to basics; and he pushes a simplistic version of that trendy idea couched in derivative terms that make the New Execs comfortable. He understands, as do his brethren who write films like *The Hidden* and *Robocop* and the *Nightmare on Elm Street* features, that he is dealing with men and women who are not only ignorant, but who are arrogant about their lack of knowledge. He understands that for such people, the daring offbeat original ideas are anathema.

He knows on a primal level the truth of Ellison's First Law of Movie Marketing:

PHILISTINISM MAKES LUCID COPY FOR DOLTS.

The important difference between Rock O'Bannon and the larger measure of his brethren, is that Rock has it in him to reach an artistic level most writers can only shade their eyes and aspire to from far below. Up there in the sun, where the air is crisp and the mind seeks to unravel the secrets of the human condition and the universe, few of us are given to exist. For the Steven de Souzas of the world, the Chris Columbuses, even the Steve Cannells, it is a summit unreachable and forever intimidating. They do the best they can, but it is the difference between Alfred Hitchcock and Brian De Palma. King Kong and Mighty Joe Young. Jefferson and Dukakis/Bush.

The kick in the ass is necessary, because Rock O'Bannon is *better*. He wrote "Wordplay." He can go there again. For him to get his foot in the feature film door with *Alien Nation* was cynical and self-destructive. Like the film, it was a calculated act of empty calories, artistic vacuum. For the soul, no surge of enrichment; there were only money and "clout" to be garnered.

For those who now ask, "Well, what's wrong with that?" I suggest you find another film columnist to read: surely we are dealing with concepts of self-respect and responsibility forever beyond your ken. For those of you who remain, let me digress only slightly to explain why this film was doomed from the starting blocks . . . and please bear in mind that quotation from Ring Lardner, Jr.: "No good film was ever made from a poor script."

Only god and Bill Warren know where the idea of the buddy-movie began. It has to be somewhen subsequent to the Edison Kinetoscope filmstrip *The Kiss* (1896), but prior to the most recent Pee-wee Herman extravaganza. After Cain and Abel, but prior to Sly and Brigitte. After the creation of the Heaven and the Earth, but prior to Burke and Hare. If you get my drift: this is an *old* formula we're looking at.

Even before the spate of flying buddies movies—exemplified by Cagney and Pat O'Brien in 1935's *Devil Dogs of the Air*—the genre was in full swing, but the chum flick as a separate form was most obvious in the aeronautic alliances. Perhaps the lineal descent is from the first attempt to put Sherlock Holmes and Dr. Watson on film (about which more in a moment), though the

457

Quirt and Flagg buddydom of the 1926 *What Price Glory?* certainly sticks out as a watershed event.

For those who contend the buddy-movie reached its highest point of originality and vigor with the 1939 *Gunga Din*, in which Cary Grant, Victor McLaglen and Doug Fairbanks, Jr. stood off Eduardo Ciannelli and his ravening hordes howling "Kill for the low of Kali," I'd like to point out that Ben Hecht and Charles MacArthur, who cobbled up that cockeyed adventure plot, were only rewriting their 1931 hit *The Front Page*, as perfect an example of the buddy-movie as has ever been remade more times than we can count.

But by the '40s it was a staple commodity, requiring not much more thought for inclusion on a production schedule than an offhand "Who'll we buddy-up with whom?" Or is that *who*?

A staple commodity, having manifested itself in dozens of Republic and Monogram westerns of the "Three Mesquiteers" type (and does anyone else remember that ventriloquist Max Terhune and Crash Corrigan were but two-thirds of that rootin' tootin' shootin' trio completed by John Wayne?), reprised to the point of fugue state boredom in all the Dennis Morgan–Jack Carson "Two Guys From—" comedies, the Crosby–Hope roaders, and even proffered in the Batman&Robin mode with Wild Bill Elliott as Red Ryder, Bobby Blake as Little Beaver.

Through all such flotsam and jetsam (another terrific buddy pairing), the huffingpuffing exhausted idiom dragged itself into the modern era with Duncan Renaldo as The Cisco Kid and Leo Carillo as Pancho.

("Oh Seesko!" "Oh Pancho!" "Ha ha ha ha ha!" Which is the way all Saturday morning cartoons and most tv sitcoms from Lucy to Cosby end.)

This discounts all the Mr. and Mrs. North or Nick and Nora Charles *Thin Man* flicks, which really don't fit the mold, and I discount them openly just to remind you that I'm being nothing but fair in my selections as the form burgeoned in feature films when *The Defiant Ones* (1958) proved that if you made the buddy-buddy connection a bizarre one, you might triumph at the box office using a template already hoary and creaky, because critics would tend to overlook the paucity of invention at a plot level, and focus on the acting of the principals, their "relationship": just manacle a tough-but-heart-of-gold black convict (Sidney Poitier) to a bigoted white convict (Tony Curtis), let them escape from the chain gang, and send them on the run. This was the great icon of the buddies-with-animus-toward-each-other subgenre, most recently reprised with Secret Service bodyguard Charles Bronson "manacled and on the run" to his real-life wife, Jill Ireland, as the First Lady in *Assassination*...and bounty hunter Robert De Niro "manacled and on the run" with bail-jumping Federal witness Charles Grodin in *Midnight Run*.

Seriatim, the gang-buddy idea overinflated two years later with the success of *The Magnificent Seven* (from Kurosawa's *Seven Samurai*), followed by *The Professionals* in 1966, *The Dirty Dozen* in 1967, *The Devil's Brigade* in 1968, and Peckinpah's 1969 gang-buddy classic, *The Wild Bunch*, ending the decade that year with the buddy-movie that sent the entire film industry scrambling to flood the screen with chums, pals, mates...*Butch Cassidy and the Sundance Kid*. And the sluicegates were opened.

By 1971 you could spot the variations sans recourse to dowsing rod: *They Might Be Giants*, like the aforementioned *Assassination* a male-female buddy-up, recasting George C. Scott as Holmes with Joanne Woodward as Dr. Watson. (This is such an obvious duo for the perpetuation of the genre, that hardly a year goes by without a new note being sounded as coda to Conan Doyle's original duet, echoic currently with Michael Caine as a dunderhead Sherlock and Ben Kingsley as a brains-of-the-act Watson in *Without a Clue*, which I recommend unreservedly.) Other boy-girl buddy-ups: *The Late Show* (1977) with Art Carney and Lily Tomlin, *Foul Play* (1978) with Chevy Chase and Goldie Hawn, *Hanky Panky* (1982), *Runaway* with Tom Selleck and Cynthia Rhodes and *Romancing the Stone* (both 1984), and *Stone's* sequel, *Jewel of the Nile* and *Into the Night* with Jeff Goldblum and Michelle Pfeiffer (both 1985). And that's just iceberg-tip of boy-girl buddy-movies.

To demonstrate how interchangeable these phony-friendship-flicks are, *Hanky Panky* was originally intended as a followup to the successful buddy-movies of Gene Wilder and Richard Pryor —*Silver Streak* (1976) and *Stir Crazy* (1980)—but for reasons I'm too weary to recount, Pryor's role in *Hanky Panky* was revised for Gilda Radner, and no one noticed any dichotomy.

But what, there's more!

Scarecrow with Hackman and Pacino; *City Heat* with Eastwood and Reynolds; *Partners* with John Hurt and Ryan O'Neal; *The Sting* with Redford and Newman; *Wise Guys* with Piscopo and De Vito; *Ishtar* with Beatty and Hoffman; *Planes, Trains and Automobiles* with John Candy and Steve Martin; *Lethal Weapon* with Mel Gibson and Danny Glover, and *Running Scared* with Billy Crystal and Gregory Hines (as we return to black and white pairings à la *The Defiant Ones*); *Buddy Buddy*, the Billy Wilder– I. A. L. Diamond remake of the French *A Pain in the A—*, recast with Lemmon and Matthau; *Red Heat* with Schwarzenegger and Jim Belushi; another girl-boy linking that substitutes Debra Winger for Paul Newman in *Legal Eagles* with Redford; *The In-Laws* with Falk and Alan Arkin; *Mikey and Nicky* with Falk and Cassavetes; *¡Three Amigos!* with Chevy Chase, Martin Short and Steve Martin; *48 Hrs.* with Nolte and Eddie Murphy; *Tough Guys* with Lancaster and Douglas; *Dragnet* with Aykroyd and Tom Hanks; *Stakeout* with Dreyfuss and Emilio Estevez; *Real Men* with Belushi and John Ritter; *Number One with a Bullet* with Billy Dee Williams and Robert Carradine; and *Nighthawks* with Billy Dee Williams and Stallone.

Not to mention all the girl-girl buddy-ups—"biddy-movies"? —like *Outrageous Fortune* with Bette Midler and Shelley Long or *Big Business* with a pair of Bette Midlers and a pair of Lily Tomlins, which makes it the first buddy-buddy-buddy-buddy movie . . .

Or such offbeat pairings as those found in films like, uh, er, *A Boy and His Dog* with Vic and Blood played by Don Johnson and Tiger . . .

Or even precursors of the human-alien tieup in *Alien Nation* (which makes it an even *less* original conception) like *The Hidden* with Michael Nouri and Kyle MacLachlan or *Enemy Mine* with Dennis Quaid and Lou Gossett, Jr. And all of them foreshadowed in print by Isaac Asimov with his human-robot pairing of R. Daneel Olivaw and Lije Baley in CAVES OF STEEL, *et al.*

Which list, rendered here as exhausting (though hardly exhaus*tive*) evidence that the buddy-buddy idea was worn to the nub long before Rock O'Bannon came to it, should indicate just how hackneyed and cynical is the core of *Alien Nation*.

We would expect no better from a producer like Gale Anne Hurd, whose contract with 20th Century–Fox was not picked up this summer in large part because of the disposability of *Alien Nation*; but we are *required* to expect more from Rockne O'Bannon.

Now here's the good news.

O'Bannon won't be killed by this film. Unlike my situation, which parallels Rock's, it will do him no harm. *Alien Nation* is *so* empty of calories, *so* forgettable, that it will not cast a pall over his name. With the sharp eyes and Me Decade smarts of his scriptwriting brethren, Rock understood that to get what he wanted in this business, he had to toss out a commercial film like this one. *It got made.* And that is the lowest factor of survival in film work. It got made, and because it got made at a major studio, with major stars, and had a big budget, he has sold another. And next year he gets to direct it.

Perhaps the means justify the end in a business where Art is anathema. Perhaps.

But the free ride is ended. Rock O'Bannon is a rare and original writer when he struggles against the rigors of the marketplace. He wrote "Wordplay." And if we choose to give him a pass on *Alien Nation*, if we choose to let that one go through our memory like shit through a tin trumpet, let him understand this: the free ride is over.

The next time—and we're all going to be watching—he had damned well better do battle with the gods. And even if he doesn't win, we'd damned well better see some sweat.

This has been a public service announcement.

INSTALLMENT 34:
In Which We Praise Those Whose Pants're On Fire, Noses Long As A Telephone Wire

Right around World Series time last Fall, readers of these columns in California, Oregon, Nevada and Washington, also Hawaii, suffered mild cognitive dissonance when they turned on their television sets and saw Your Obedient Servant as on-camera spokesman in a series of Chevrolet commercials, extolling the virtues of a line of Japanese-designed, American-built cars called the Geo Imports. In these sixty- and thirty-second mini-encounters, as I walk through an elegant museum setting, the super that flashes across my body says *Harlan Ellison*, and under the name appear the words *Noted Futurist*.

This designation—however marginally appropriate—however startling to, say, Isaac Asimov or Alvin Toffler or Roberto Vacca, who are commonly held to be both futurists and noted as such—was the appellation of choice of Chevrolet, its West Coast advertising agency, and the director, Mr. Terry Galanoy.

Friends, acquaintances and casual thugs (who suggest I was selected for these commercials not on the basis of charisma or ability, but because I make the cars look larger), have expressed some startlement at my having been labeled *Noted Futurist*. "What the hell does that mean?" they codify their confusion, further asking, "Why did they call you that?"

To which I respond: "It seemed to Chevrolet that it was a more trustable identification than *Paid Liar*."

As a creator of fictions, I have frequently referred to myself as a *Paid Liar*; that is, a storyteller; one who receives monies from publishers and moviemakers for cobbling up what Vonnegut called *foma*, "harmless untruths." Thus, a paid liar in the context of dreaming fantastic dreams...not (he said very sternly, looking them straight in the eye) in any way suggesting that what I say about the Geo Imports is less than the absolute truth, spoken with conviction and sincerity. (It is not my intention to get into discussion of these commercials, why I did them, or the astonishing effect their airing has had on Susan's and my life, save to assure you that I would not present myself as spokesman for a product in which I did not believe. The cars are excellent, I drive them myself, they are remarkably responsible environmentally-speaking at 53 mph in the city and 58 in the country, and I add this aside *only* to avoid the gibes of those who would purposely misinterpret the term *Paid Liar* in conjunction with the commercials.)

Pushkin said: "Better the illusions that exalt us than ten thousand truths."

The great liars of narrative literature remain, from century to century, some of our most treasured teachers. The truly great ones come along all too infrequently, and if we manage to get one every other generation we feel that our lot is salutary. Mary Shelley, Poe, Borges, Kafka, Bierce, James Branch Cabell, Lovecraft, Shirley Jackson, John Collier, Roald Dahl, Fritz Leiber... these are the transcendentally untruthful, the paid liars who, like Mark Twain and Jules Verne, shine a revelatory light— through the power-source of invention—on our woebegone and duplicitous world. Through noble mendacity, enlightenment!

As Isaac Bashevis Singer has said, "When I was a little boy, they called me a liar, but now that I'm grown up, they call me a writer."

In the late 1700s, the hands-down titleholder of the belt for prevarication, flyweight, middle- and welterweight, cruiser-, bruiser- and heavyweight, was Karl Friedrich Hieronymus, the Baron von Munchausen. Recounting his no-less-than-eyeopening exploits as a cavalry officer in the service of Frederick the Great against the ravaging, pillaging, bestial Ottoman Empire, Munchausen (1720–1797) erected towers of tales so tall they dwarfed Babel or Trump. Behind his back, his drinking companions rolled their eyes and called him *Luegenbaron*, the lying Baron; but one of them, Rudolf Erich Raspe, hied himself to England where, in 1785, he wrote and caused to have published

BARON MUNCHAUSEN'S NARRATIVE OF HIS MARVELLOUS TRAVELS AND CAMPAIGNS IN RUSSIA, a book instantly a bestseller.

The tales contained in that volume can be counted among the biggest lies ever wafted on hot air across our planet. Or so we must believe. Who would impart even a scintilla of truth to the anecdotes of a man who swore he had been blown by hurricane to the Moon, had enjoyed carnal knowledge of the goddess Venus while visiting in the bowels of Mt. Etna, had been swallowed by a Monstro-the-whale–like sea beast and had escaped by dint of Balkan snuff, and asserted, "On another occasion I wished to jump across a lake. When I was in the middle of the jump, I found it was much larger than I had imagined at first. So I at once turned back in the middle of my leap, and returned to the bank I had just left, to take a stronger spring." Add a large question mark to the end of that last sentence.

Filmmakers took the Baron to their bosom from the start. His adventures have been chronicled on celluloid more than a dozen times, from 1909 (as far as we know) to the classic Méliès version in 1911 to the legendary two-reelers of the 1930s, to the charming and sweethearted 1961 Czech fantasy filled with loopy special effects, as conceived, co-scripted and directed by Karel Zeman.

But only Méliès, one of the great Paid Liars of all time, could claim a breadth of imagination capable of lying up to the level of the Baron. The others were mere fibbers. Talented, but hardly in that ballpark of audacity. Dilettantes. Pishers.

It is our happy lot to be blessed in these days of inept lying (as exemplified by the recently ended Presidential campaign) with one of the great, consummately eloquent diegesists, a falsifier of such singular abilities that he rivals the Baron in ability to make the jaw drop; and like Méliès, his medium is movies. He is, of course, ex-Python Terry Gilliam. And just around Eastertime, Columbia Pictures will release his most magnificent lie to date, THE ADVENTURES OF BARON MUNCHAUSEN.

And if ever there was one destined to assume the mantle of the Baron, it is Gilliam. He has become a shoo-in for the Whopper Teller's Hall of Fame. He is a world-class liar whose potential value to us as a teller of truth through tommyrot ranks with that credited to Scheherazade, Don Marquis, and the nameless whiffle-merchants who cobbled up Paul Bunyan, the Loch Ness Monster and the Bible.

Gilliam's new film, the final third of the trilogy begun with *Time Bandits* (1981) and *Brazil* (1985), is a two hour and seven minute string of shameless lies—edited by Gilliam from its initial 2:41 length—that will make you roar with laughter, disbelieve what you're seeing, and have you clapping your hands in childlike delight. It is:

A carnival! A wonderland! A weekend with nine Friday nights! Terry Gilliam's lavish dreams are beyond those of mere mortals. *Munchausen* is everything you secretly hope a movie will be. What most movies turn out not to be: adequate or exceeding your expectations.

In this column, three years ago, I urged you not to miss *Brazil*, one of the exceptional fantasies of all time. Compound that enthusiasm by an order of ten and you may begin to approach my delight in alerting you to *Munchausen*. Every frame is filled to trembling surface tension with visual astonishments so rich, so lush, so audacious, that you will beg for mercy. As with *Brazil*, a film that despised moderation and was thus mildly disparaged by stiffnecked critics incapable of the proper sybaritic gluttony for sensory overload, *Munchausen* simply will not quit. Like Cool Hand Luke or Joe Namath at the end of the '76 season, it won't stay down for the count. It keeps coming at you, image after image, ferocious in its fecundity of imagination, wonder after wonder, relentless in its desire to knock your block off!

It is a great and original artist's latest masterwork of joy, and despite reports that it has opened in Europe to tepid box-office, it is a film that lives up to everything the Baron tried to put over on us. It is—without tipping one delight you deserve to savor fresh and on your own—one of the most wonderful films I've ever seen. And I ain't lying.

ANCILLARY MATTERS: (The following taken *in toto* from an item by Steven Smith in the *Los Angeles Times* of 8 January.)

Remember back in 1985, when director Terry Gilliam battled MCA-Universal prez Sid Sheinberg over the final cut of Gilliam's Orwellian comedy, *Brazil* . . . and won? Well, maybe he didn't.

Universal released Gilliam's 131-minute version to numberous raves and a best picture award from the L.A. Film Critics Assn., albeit to lackluster box-office.

But last week, a 93-minute version of *Brazil* aired on KTLA Channel 5 as part of a Universal syndicated tv package—promoting it with raves actually written about the original.

But scenes have been recut and rescored, using new takes and dialogue dubbed by sound-alike actors. The story—about a clerk who escapes a repressive society through fantasy, but is finally lobotomized—was changed and simplified, with a new, happy ending assembled from unused footage. Elaborate dream sequences now total 47 seconds.

Who's responsible?

Sheinberg hadn't returned calls by press time. But the new *Brazil* closely follows the "radical rethink" devised three years ago by Sheinberg, as described since by two film editors hired to make the changes.

Gilliam, reached in London and apprised of the altered state of his movie, told us: "It's wonderful, because it gives Sid a chance to break into tv. The only sad thing is, the world doesn't get to appreciate that Sid made this film."

Late last year, Gilliam said, Universal asked for his "input" on the latest edit (he declined)—and that the studio wouldn't let him remove his name.

Now, he added, "They're selling it as *Brazil*, the film that won best picture, and that's nonsense."

There is a special sea of boiling hyena vomit in the deepest and darkest level of Hell, tenanted thus far only by those who burned the Great Library of Alexandria, by the dolt who bowdlerized LADY CHATTERLEY'S LOVER, and by those who have torn down elegant art deco buildings to erect mini-malls. It is my certain belief that Sid Sheinberg will sizzle there throughout eternity. Standing on Ted Turner's shoulders.

Harlan Ellison's film criticism appears on a more-or-less monthly basis in the pages of *The Magazine of Fantasy and Science Fiction*, edited by Edward and Audrey Ferman, available by subscription (Box 56, Cornwall, Connecticut 06753) or at your local, well-stocked newsstand. Ellison continues *Watching*.

APPENDIX A
Twentieth Century–Fox Film Has Science Fiction Theme

Hollywood, awakening to the fact that the public is tired of trite westerns and mysteries, has tried something new.

Fantasies and science fiction films, until now, have been attempted with a "tongue-in-cheek" attitude.

But Twentieth Century–Fox has now taken the lead in presenting a truly adult science fiction thriller. At a preview in the Hippodrome Theatre, Tuesday, September 11, THE DAY THE EARTH STOOD STILL, starring Patricia Neal, Hugh Marlowe and a promising newcomer, Michael Rennie, was unveiled.

Taken from a story by Harry Bates, the plot concerns the repercussions resulting from the landing of a flying saucer on the Mall in Washington, D.C.

Moving rapidly from scene to scene, the film boasts such unusual occurrences as the melting of a General Sherman tank by a robot, the stopping of all electricity in the world and the restoration to life of a man who was dead.

Besides having a fascinating plot, the acting in the picture was excellent. Mr. Rennie, as the man from space, is so convincingly real, that one immediately believes he is an actual alien.

Patricia Neal, as a widowed mother, gives a lifelike and convincing portrayal.

But, undoubtedly, the real star of the picture is a large fellow named Gort. Gort is a metal robot with the ability to fire a beam of energy from his eyes which are really photoelectric cells.

Unlike other fantastic movies, *The Day*... has no fake props but portrays the futuristic "saucer" in an adult manner.

In the picture there are no bug-eyed monsters killing innocent people or Buck Rogers heroics, but there is a story that is fast-paced, different and thoroughly enjoyable.

For an entertaining evening, and for one that will keep you continually in a state of wonder, don't miss *The Day the Earth Stood Still*.

APPENDIX B
Nightmare Nights
At The Daisy

As referenced on page xxxvii
of the Introduction.

In the hell-images of Hieronymous Bosch, one sees the tormented, writhing in anguishes of their own making: a garden of earthly delights predicated on the suffering of themselves and others, a playpen of sado-masochism. Beheaded corpses lying chill and white in shrouds of their own wound hair; serpentlike creatures with knives thrust through their throats, breathing fire on pickled humans peering beatifically from barrels of toadridden brine; sex-circuses in which the participants are so intertwined that none know which are their own extremities or those of another; bare men strung like crucified offerings on the wires of giant harps while oily, ebony salamanders slither over their naked flesh; burning buildings casting a fire of the pit against the sky; carnivorous fish and stalking plants; halfhumans composed of all arms and legs; the stench of sensory pleasure carried to a visual level that can only be described in terms of the sense of smell:

The scent of rotting gardenias, vomitously sweet and cloying.

Bosch would have loved to spend an evening on the town in Los Angeles. He would have felt at home in The Daisy. The scene just described, adding the names of television producers, hungry starlets, clean-shaven hero actors, the children of Beverly Hills merchants, expensively coiffed hookers, lean-hipped models, fading sports stars and assorted kept types, would be a 20th century *doppelganger* of Bosch's 15th century madhouse.

Once again the scent of the rotting gardenias fills the night. Cloying and sweet, and called by its contemporary appellation, it is the stench of paranoia. On far Rodeo Drive has Jack Hanson a stately pleasure dome decreed, and it is called The Daisy.

Were it not a reality, composed half of myth and half of urgency, necessity would compel its invention. Did it not in fact exist, hysteria would conjure it up from the dark ingredients specified in the Hollywood grimoire:

Eye of a lecher, toe of a Terpsichore, sweat of a hustler, blood of starlet, the faded memories of a slipping star, glory dreams of a social-climbing toy manufacturer, intimations of class by a street urchin newly *nouveau-riche*, insults, gossip, infidelities, violence, and moneymoneymoney.

Bosch would have capered and gibbered with joy. He would have identified with them instantly. The lineal descendants of his Bedlam dwellers, cloaked in silks and essences, cavorting and swilling in an upholstered, red velvet ghetto of their own fears and insecurities, clinging to one another with bonds of venality and hatred and common use.

Hi-ho and away we go! For an evening at The Daisy.

Be sure to bring your switchblade and your smile.

You come by car. If you are Sal Mineo you come in a Rolls. If you are Peter Bren you come in a Ferrari. If you are Phyllis Diller you come in an Excalibur S•S with your boyfriend, dressed like an Eskimo. If you are Herbert Hutner your Rolls has a right-hand drive. If you are Eddie Fisher you come in a Bentley convertible. If you are me, you come in a 1953 Healey and park it yourself.

If you don't know where to look for it, you can pass The Daisy a hundred times a day and be blinded by the sterling silver in the windows of David Orgell, or by the jewelry, furs and Tiffany lamps in the shop windows on the other side, and never notice the unobtrusive brick-front building with its huge wooden daisy high up in the darkness of the unlighted façade. For those who need specifics, modern America's number one pleasure dome is located at 326 North Rodeo Drive, Beverly Hills, on the east side of the street, between Little Santa Monica and Wilshire.

You enter by a tiny alcove, at the rear of which is a stout wooden door with a knocker. One can imagine this door as the setting for a thousand mid-Victorian poppas pointing into the blizzard where their daughters and their illegitimate offspring must go. Or if you're unfamiliar with the cartoon reference, consider it any large, carved, wooden door you've ever had slammed in your face.

If you don't happen to be Soupy Sales or Bill Wyman of the Rolling Stones or Lynda Bird Johnson or Princess Margaret or Governor Pat Brown or Cary Grant, that door will more than likely slam on *your* face.

(*Vignette The First:* A ten-thirty night, a stout woman in a pink dress has her foot in the door. "I'm Mrs. Stockmeier. Would you tell Mr. Hanson I'm out here, I've got several guests with me from out of —"

("Mr. Hanson isn't here this evening," the doorman says, looking uncomfortable; the populace is demonstrating. Cut off in mid-sentence, Mrs. Stockmeier grins helplessly at her several guests, in from out of.

(Two mid-thirties teenagers slide out the door, past Mrs. Stockmeier's foot. The doorman tries to get it closed but she agilely re-inserts it. "But we met Mr. and Mrs. Hanson in—"

(Mrs. Stockmeier removes her foot as three cuddly types in poorboys and Jax slacks, all lean meat and dark eyes, slip like oil through the door. This time the doorman gets it closed. The little speakeasy window is open. Mrs. Stockmeier is yelling through it at the disembodied head of the doorman. Her voice is strident. "We were supposed to mention his name, we have guests in from out of—"

(The window closes. Mrs. Stockmeier will return to The Beverly Hills Hotel in her husband's rented Cadillac, making weak excuses to her guests in from out of. They will smile understanding. It may be too much for her. She may take an overdose that night. Maybe not.)

But if the door doesn't slam, you've walked right up, unafraid, to the brass knocker and the brass letters MEMBERS ONLY on the wall, and you've banged in your special staccato and the door has opened wide for you, ring-a-ding right down the rabbit-hole to wonderland.

In the foyer there is a white marble statue. It is a statue of something or other. Not one out of a hundred can tell you what it is a statue of, for the view through the inner door to the poolroom arrests the attention immediately. It is usually a view of something like Jocelyn Laine or Samantha Eggar or a Jax girl, sling-hippedly walking through into the chandelier room. There used to be a huge papier-mâché daisy in a flowerpot on the pedestal, but it isn't there any longer. Someone boosted it.

In the tiny foyer there is a table. On this table there are printed forms that you will sign if you are a card-carrying Daisy member, in the event you are bringing in more than the one guest allotted to you freebie. Each additional guest will cost you two dollars.

Up the short flight of stairs into the first of the seven rooms of the establishment, you find yourself in the poolroom. An old but venerable pool table dominates the room. Framed covers from Hanson's *Cinema* magazine line one wall. Photos of Hanson's Daisy softball team with television producer Aaron Spelling pitching...a portrait of Jill St. John...a portrait of Nancy Sinatra...the cover of a French magazine featuring Natalie Wood...a huge and grotesque collage in the shape of a bull's-eye, composed of fashion photos and oddments from slick magazines.

On the green baize of that table some of the best, and some of the worst, pool players in Hollywood restore their virility.

Of an evening, one may see aging matinee idols in the company of sleek, well-fed women, doffing their suit jackets and sighting down the shanks of pool cues like Minnesota Fats, preparatory to demonstrating to their paramours and the gathering-at-large that they are as good as they ever were.

But when the duffs and the spastics cease showing off, some of the most bravura stickwork in the L.A. area may be seen executed on that sloping, rutted, butt-burned table by the likes of Peter Falk, Omar Sharif, Richard Conte, Telly Savalas and Leo Durocher, who is so adept he can let you win, out of general all-around kindness.

(*Vignette The Second:* Paul Newman is playing eight ball. He shoots and stands silently waiting his next turn. He loses. He loses handily. He goes into the bar and sits down to have a drink. A young man, watching the game with wide eyes and closed mouth, follows him.

("Mr. Newman," the boy says politely, at the elbow of the star of *The Hustler*. Newman half turns and looks. It is the same pale-blue-eyed polar ice chill stare Newman gave Minnesota Fats, just before the pool marathon known to millions of people around the world as the penultimate moment of truth contest. "Mr. Newman," the boy says again, with difficulty, looking as though someone had dumped it on him, "you're the greatest disappointment in my life."

(He walks away. Newman stares into his drink.)

The chandelier room, the barroom, with its antique mirrors and antique ceiling fixtures, leads off from the poolroom, past the private party room and the phone booth where the legend SUZANNE SIDNEY WAS HERE AND DON'T YOU FORGET IT! remained unerased for several months on the blackboard beside the telephone. An interesting—and possibly apocryphal—sidelight is that the private party room, which was originally conceived for any large name guest who might want to have an *intime* gathering without the bother of the general clientele looking over his shoulder, has seldom been used. It would seem no one wants to miss out on the action in the big room.

The chandelier room, containing the bar, is 25' wide by 75' long. It is filled with tables that clog the center of the room and line the wall.

And directly ahead, is the main room, the dance floor room, where the major activity takes place. And it is from here that one receives the first totally overwhelming assault of sensory impressions. A dark, kaleidoscopic and somehow vegetable movement of bodies in motion, a noise level of voices that runs subcurrent to the aural slam of rock music blared through a P.A. system at full gain.

Martha and the Vandellas are singing "Jimmy Mack" on the Gordy label.

Waiters ply back and forth at top-point efficiency through aisles clogged with dancers and talkers and gawkers and a surfeit of the beautiful people. Tables that were built for four or six are jammed with eighteen and twenty. One clique here, another there, laughter skirling up from the center like smoke in the Abner Dean cartoon of the few close friends left after the party, their arms umbilically joined, the fire burning in their center and their statement "Ain't we great!"

A lush redhead elbows past on her way to the little ladies' sandbox. Her step is wavery, but the movement is pure MGM circa 1935. And you realize all at once that there are more beautiful women gathered here than you have ever seen before. Not just in one place, at one time, but in your whole life, all counted, from the moment you hit puberty. Tall, short, blonde *au naturel* and blonde by bottle, dark-eyed or smoldering, these women are the true artifacts of our culture. They spend most of their days and nights keeping their bodies in fine tune, like a birdcage Maserati. There is no dust on them, no slightest hint of chrome rust, no vaguest sign of tackiness or impoverishment or loss or stricture. Only platinum and alabaster and lapis-lazuli.

When our culture has gone ten million years into the slag-heaps of eternity, and the aphids that will inherit the planet do their archeological restorations, surely these...these slim-limbed creatures of exquisite emptiness...these will be rebuilt molecule by molecule and put on display in the plasteel showcases, as the finest, highest achievement of a society dedicated to gorgeousness.

The Turtles are singing "Happy Together" on the White Whale label.

You sit down at a table in the back, near the tiny room where the disc jockey puts his sides on the turntable. You stare through the steel mesh curtains at the empty patio outside, where it is much cooler, where the press of bodies is so much less, which you wouldn't *think* of patronizing, for fear of missing something here in Valhalla.

The maître d', George Samama—who started out working steamships and prior to coming to The Daisy did ten years at La Scala Restaurant—has led you to your table. He smiles and asks if this table is all right. If it isn't, he will change it. Unless it happens that you want one of the tables with the phoney setups on it, the tables reserved for the cliques that have declared them private turf.

You look around and receive the distinct impression that you are in the eye of a hurricane. There is movement from every corner. Not merely the movement of dancers doing the watusi, the jerk, the stroll, the shotgun, the fish, the Philly dog, the monkey, the backbone slip, the slop, the hitchhiker, the James Brown walk, the long tall Sally, the bomp, the Hully-Gully, the swim, walkin' the dog, the Slauson and that poor old arteriosclerotic septuagenarian over there with the chick in the floral-patterned, bell-bottom hip-huggers and Courreges boots, who is pathetically doing a Cro-Magnon twist with softly vanishing hopes of having enough left to hustle that fine young body jerking and shimmying in front of him.

But the movement is a deeper, more oiled, roiling presence. The sway and pulse of bodies leaning into and away from the essences of the room. The sound of voices raised in anger pulls everyone southwesterly, leaning into it, sniffing the aroma of frenzy, harkening to the possibility of actual, authentic *reality* in the raw, as fist meets jaw. The tinkle of uncontrolled laughter pulls the crowd northeasterly, as they struggle with eardrums stretched taut to catch the bit of gossip or newest joke in from the Via Veneto. And there is the movement of history in the room.

476

The history that was this room when it belonged to Prince Mike Romanoff during its heyday in the shadows of World War II. The history of the ten years it was The Friars Club before Jack and Sally Hanson spent a quarter of a million dollars to buy the property. History in the ghostly sighs of the vanished—Bogart, Cooper, Lombard, Power, Gable, Don "Red" Berry, Monty Woolley, S. Z. Sakall, and even all the bright, pretty, ankle-strap wedgie'd starlets who found a moment within these walls when the dream-dust settled on their shapely shoulders. All gone now, replaced by the new generation, the new fastback breed of Hollywood famous, all moving, moving around you as you drink your drink and drink in the sight of grandeur.

The Lovin' Spoonful is singing "Darlin' Be Home Soon" on the Kama Sutra label.

Upstairs there is a ping-pong room. It is very hot up there, no air-conditioning. Only one of the glossy and indolent children of the Beverly Hills wealthy, conditioned to retain their cool through Armageddon if need be, can play a game there and not come downstairs totally unstarched.

In back there is a huge kitchen, It is unused. Jack Hanson does not believe the beautiful people wish to watch other beautiful people eating, so no food is served at The Daisy. Beautiful people are not beautiful when eating. This is a corner of the Hanson/Daisy philosophy, of which more later. Bear it in mind.

There are thirty-eight tables in The Daisy. The legal room capacity is three hundred people, all breathing at once. Yet on a weekend night it will seem that *all* of the 350–400 customers are jammed on that 30′ × 75′ dance floor all at once, and wondrously, no one perspires. They certainly don't sweat. Perhaps one of the less classy ladies will "glow" a bit, but the house rules prohibit anything that smacks even faintly of crassness.

Bodily functions, not to mention reality, are suspended during a night at The Daisy as

The Seekers sing "Georgy Girl" on the Capitol label.

Despite Hanson's aversion to people stuffing their faces with food, empty stomachs receive a passing nod by the serving of pies, cheesecake or a fruit plate featuring apples and cheese. There are no bowls of peanuts and popcorn, by which absence we discover a laudable and significant keynote to the Hanson conception of what The Daisy means in terms of monetary return:

On many occasions, not the least of which was this author's interview with The Hansons, they have said again and again that the primary motive for opening The Daisy was not to make 477 money. When one considers the incredible payoff the place has made, this remark seems suspect. But when laid against something as bone-marrow basic as the lack of salty incentives to drinking more and spending more money, the remark *must* be believed.

For every liquor distributor who deals with The Daisy has urged Hanson to add these loss-leaders; people who jam peanuts and other thirst quickeners into their mouths through the course of a long evening, in a bar without food, invariably up the bar take by twenty percent. But Hanson has passed this traditional trick of the trade. It would seem he is sincerely *not* in the business of mulcting his customers.

Then what, precisely, motivated a successful clothing merchant and his attractive wife to embark on a financial venture that costs them three hundred dollars every time they open the door? (Computed conservatively—on the basis of salaries paid to maître d', three bartenders, a doorman, a record jockey, between five and nine waiters, a gardener, a maid and janitor, and a bookkeeper.)

Now we plunge head first into The Hanson Philosophy.

It provides an answer, of sorts.

The Rolling Stones are singing "Ruby Tuesday" on the London label.

"Sally and I feel this: The time when an individual in our culture can be sustained merely by communication between himself and his mate is past. We find ourselves living in a time when religion, social contacts, the family unit, all of them have undergone a metamorphosis. Inhabitants of almost every social strata have places to go where they can meet with people of similar backgrounds and tastes, to express themselves, to release their tensions and feel they belong. We looked around and were surprised to see that many of the people we considered valuable and interesting had no such place. So we conceived The Daisy. We never thought for a moment it wouldn't succeed, but making money was the smallest part of the original conception."

(*Vignette The Third:* The Daisy will be two years old on October 15th. When the first invitations went out, to anyone the Hansons thought would fit into their world view of The Beautiful People, the cost was $200 plus $40 Federal tax, merely for membership plus $10 per month dues plus $2 Federal tax plus the bar bill per visit. Drinks are $1.50 each. For the first two months after mailing, they had only one member—and he lived in New York. Jack Hanson, dressed in tennis sweater, white ducks and sneakers, walks up Beverly Drive, on his way to lunch at La Scala Boutique. A multimillionaire contractor leans out of his Imperial's window, paused at the stoplight on the corner of Santa Monica. "Hey, Jack!" he yells. "How's it going with the Daisy?" Hanson grins his infectious, ageless grin "Terrific!" he yells back. "We're going to have to close off membership in about two weeks, we've got almost four hundred now." He waves and jogs on toward lunch. The contractor in the Imperial sits at the light, lips pursed. The cars behind him honk angrily. He takes off in a hurry. That night he returns his membership blank, with a check.)

Even knowing that Hollywood folk are legendary for not wanting to be associated with a flop (as in the expression "flop house"), Hanson had invested another hundred thousand dollars to remodel the old Romanoff's. Black and rust walls, fireplace in the main room, heavy liquor stock, because he was also aware that these same tippy-toe types from the Land of Trepidation are petrified *not* to be associated with success.

While he only had four members, he was announcing he had four hundred. And soon, myth became reality. Open from nine to two, seven nights a week, even at prices only the leisure class would consider reasonable, The Daisy's membership is now relatively sealed up. It now costs $500 to join, though the Federal taxes have been removed. Uh, sealed up, that is, unless you happen to be Julie Andrews, who recently became a member. Says Hanson, "There are some people you have to let join, even if you're booked solid. The other members like to be around them, to be where the famous hang out." And if you happen to be a Mrs. Stockmeier the polite reply is, "We have over three hundred people waiting to join." Polite, but firm.

The Beatles are singing "Penny Lane" on the Capitol label. Harper's Bizarre is singing "Feelin' Groovy" on the Warner Bros. label. Billie Holiday is singing "Night and Day" on the Vocalion label. (Who??)

But when one talks at greater length with the Hansons, one realizes that what they are postulating is not merely a village cracker barrel scene for the very rich, but a totality—an empire of many-dimensioned sensuality; a pleasure dome that reaches The Beautiful People on many levels. They sell the special Jax clothes to a certain kind of women, with the accent on the legs and backside. And those Beautiful Women wear those Jax clothes to The Daisy where they build their social scene and talk about Daisy-oriented topics. And they read *Cinema* magazine (a recent Hanson acquisition, a Hanson "hobby") where they find

479

the Daisy-oriented things to talk about. And they play softball on Sunday at Barrington Plaza Park with Hanson, where they can look at the women who wear Jax clothes sitting in the bleachers, and think about getting invited to the Hansons' after-hours sessions at the big house in Beverly Hills where they'll play "sardines" and "kick the can."

The Daisy is the future of the leisure class in microcosm, as the Hansons see it. "Everybody lovely, everybody rich."

The Electric Prunes are singing "I Had Too Much to Dream Last Night" on the Warner Bros. label.

(*Vignette The Fourth:* Two of the Beautiful People, Peter O'Toole and Jason Robards, Jr. come staggering into The Daisy after 2 A.M. when the fountains stop flowing. They demand liquor. They are refused. They get ugly. They are bounced. They are excluded from The Daisy. "Creative people are often hostile," says Jack Hanson, "and The Daisy is filled with, and caters to, creative people.")

A nightmare night at The Daisy. All the self-conscious cliques finding their strength in numbers, sitting in their corners, looking beautiful. It's jammed. Bodies pressed on bodies. A studio head, deep in his cups, does the watusi on the toes of a man beside him. He is asked to stop it. He gets surly, tells the other man to pack his bags, he'll never work in Hollywood again. A business executive of a smaller television studio comes through the door with his mistress. The night before he was in attendance with his wife. His ego needs the boost so much, he doesn't really care if word gets back through the jungle telegraph to his wife. He plays pool as though his life depended on it; his mistress watches, bemused. Hoagy Carmichael orders another Highland Queen Scotch mist. Donovan sings "Mellow Yellow" on the Epic label.

A conversation is overheard: "We saw Britt Ekland in the new Peter Sellers film." "How did she look?" "Gorgeous." "We saw her on several magazine covers in London, she was on *Vogue.*" "How old is she?" "Twenty-one." "Not quite over the hill yet." The favorite customers of The Daisy move in and out, around and about...the Peter Brens; Frank Sinatra and Dean Martin and their children; Ronnie Buck who owns the 9000 Building on Sunset and now wants to be known as a film producer; Jack Haley, Jr.; Tom Mankiewicz; Alan Ladd, Jr.; Richard Pryor, the comic; Mike Brown, sitting quietly at the bar, then asking the bartender, Rich, how many boys are working that night, and when told, leaving a heavy sugar tip to be split among them.

And the women. All the long-legged, pale women with their hungry eyes. The movement of the highest-priced pelvises in the world, the swirl of long flat blonde hair, the arch of eyebrows, the salivation of men tied to wives who know they cheat. "Anyone who doesn't have a strong marriage shouldn't come into The Daisy," Jack Hanson says, and he says it soberly. A man could go mad here. The sheer, overwhelming bulk of beauty is gagging. A starving child turned loose in a candy store. The famous, the elegant, the sinewy, they all parade naked to the eyes. Doug McClure dances in the very center of the floor with a small girl wearing a white leather Beatle cap. He is the very epitome of a high school girl's image of what a "hero" should be. He is absolutely perfect, formed and molded out of all the perfection dreams of a society that worships beauty. And finally magic becomes reality...

(*Vignette The Last:* Dancing together, there amidst the flotsam and jetsam of Hollywood's glory, is the perfect jewel of meaning that explains what The Daisy is all about.

(A couple. A boy and a girl. Elegant. Poised. They dance in each other's arms. They are Betty Anderson from the little New England village called Peyton Place, and her escort, Batman.

(Barbara Parkins and Adam West are dancing. There in the dimness of a building that was, is, and will always be the very apotheosis of the magic dreams the Beautiful People need to sustain them in a world where tragedy can be as simple as a crows-foot alongside a dimming eye.)

It becomes clear to all but those hip-deep in the scene that the constitution needed to sustain a life like this, is a rare and remarkable one indeed. Jack Hanson thus assumes the proportions of a man imbued with great kindness, deep perceptivity. He is the keeper of the madhouse. He manages to contain in a red velvet ghetto all the electric insecurities and hostilities of an entire social strata that might otherwise be loosed unsuspecting on the common folk in their dreary streets.

Movement continues in The Daisy as the nights grow inexorably toward their tomorrows. All the tomorrows in which careers will crumble like castles of spiderwebs and the owners of those careers—which are, in fact, their lives—will hesitate to come into The Daisy, for fear they will not be in the coterie, laughing and scratching in the proper corner.

And Petula Clark sings "I Couldn't Live Without Your Love"   481 on the Warner Bros. label making you suddenly aware that of all the words used about The Daisy and its customers, not once has anyone but the amplified singer mentioned the word love.

Who, then, are the real Mrs. Stockmeiers?

INDEX

The Introduction and the Appendices have not been included in this Index.

483

485

488

489

493

494

"Lord of the Earthquake" (Brackett), 117
LORD OF THE FLIES (Golding), 311, 370
"Lorelei of the Red Mist" (Brackett & Bradbury), 117
Loren, Sophia, 88
Lorie, Barry, 257
Lorimar Productions, 451, 452
Los Angeles, CA, 74, 82, 106, 142, 167, 171, 234, 251, 253, 305, 340, 353, 355, 389, 443, 451, 453, 455
Los Angeles magazine, 183
Los Angeles Convention Center, 131
Los Angeles County Museum of Art, 105, 107
Los Angeles *Daily News* newspaper, 434
Los Angeles Film Critics Association, 466
Los Angeles *Herald-Examiner* newspaper, 428
Los Angeles Times newspaper, 338, 408, 466
Losey, Joseph, 36
Los Olvidados (1950), 361
LOST HORIZON (Hilton), 185
Lost Horizon (1937), 185, 315–316, 319
Lost Horizon (1973), 315
Louis XI, 426
Louis XVI, 70
"Louisiana Purchase Exposition" (1904), 168
Love at First Bite (1979), 268
Lovecraft, H. P., 189, 363, 386, 464
Loved One, The (1965), 174
Love Story (1970), 90, 170
Lovin' Spoonful, The, 42
Lucan (tv), 127
Lucas (1986), 308
Lucas, George, 129, 133, 134, 135, 137, 142, 182, 194, 196, 199, 205, 224, 235, 266, 268, 284, 319, 348, 445, 446
Lucasfilm *see* MGM/Lucasfilm
Luce, Henry, 47
Lucian of Samosata, 264
Lugosi, Bela, 144, 267, 268
Luna/Lunar *see* the Moon
Lundgren, Dolph, 438
Lupoff, Richard, 397
Lux Presents Hollywood (radio), 3
Lynch, David, 225, 232, 235
Lyons, Jeffrey, 252
"Lysistrata" (Aristophanes), 58
M (1931), 94, 276
MacArthur, Charles, 458
Macbeth (1971), 114
Macchio, Ralph, 311
MacDonald, John D., 116

Macdonald, Ross, 116
MacGraw, Ali, 89–90
Machiavellian/Niccolò Machiavelli, 49, 215
MacLachlan, Kyle, 460
MacLaine, Shirley, 446
Madaro, Jacopo H., 392, 395, 396–397
Madden, John, 348
Madigan, Amy, 207
Mad Max (1979), 368
Mad Max Beyond Thunderdome (1985), 266
Madrid, Spain, 65
Mafia, 94
Magazine of Fantasy and Science Fiction, The magazine, 231, 233, 435
Magicam, 138
Magna Carta, 415
Magnificent Ambersons, The (1942), 144, 276, 278
Magnificent Seven, The (1960), 15, 64, 459
Maguire, John G., 191, 192
Magus, The (1968), 93
Maine, 177
Malamud, Bernard, 291
　THE NATURAL, 291
Malle, Louis, 319
Malory, Sir Thomas, 418
Maltese Falcon, The (1941), 330, 331, 335, 350, 433
Maltin, Leonard, 252, 348, 380
Man from U.N.C.L.E., The (tv), 452
Manchester, England, 315
Mancini, Henry, 110
M&Ms candy, 194, 244
Manet, Édouard, 10
Man for All Seasons, A (1966), 114
Man from Atlantis, The (tv), 127
Manhattan (New York, NY), 23, 41, 50, 74, 89, 94
Manhattan Beach, CA, 232
Manhattan Project, The (1986), 325
Manilow, Barry, 174, 346
MAN IN THE HIGH CASTLE, THE (Dick), 261
Mankiewicz, Herman, 307
Mankiewicz, Joseph L., 91, 385
Mann, Stanley, 173, 174
Mannequin (1987), 347
Man of La Mancha (1972), 88
Manson, Charles, 244, 360, 415
MAN WHO FELL TO EARTH, THE (Tevis), 127
Man Who Fell to Earth, The (1976), 125, 216

501

507

509

511

513